LOVE AND LABOUR

RED-BUTTON YEARS: VOLUME 1

Love and Labour

Ken Fuller

By Ken Fuller

Non-Fiction

Radical Aristocrats: London Busworkers from the 1880s to the 1980s (1985)

Forcing the Pace: The Partido Komunista ng Pilipinas, from Foundation to Armed Struggle (2007)

A Movement Divided: Philippine Communism, 1957-1986 (2011)

The Long Crisis: Gloria Macapagal Arroyo and Philippine Underdevelopment (2013)

The Lost Vision: The Philippine Left, 1986-2010 (2015)

Hardboiled Activist: The Work and Politics of Dashiell Hammett (2017)

Fiction

Foreigners (2019)

Love and Labour (2019)

CONTENTS

Part One: 1913   1

Part Two: 1914   113

Part Three: 1915   213

Part Four: 1916   357

Part Five: 1917   443

Author's Note   549

About the Author   553

PART ONE

1913

1

It was a fine summer morning in 1913 when the sun touched Mickey Rice's face as he stepped from the tram in Broad Street. He waved to the motorman who, grinning madly, shook a finger at him and shouted something he could not quite hear, although he could guess the words: "You behave yourself up there in London, Mickey!"

We'll have to see about that, thought Mickey. He was twenty-four, something over average height, with a firm body and even features, and the possibility that he would *not* behave himself brought an extra charge of exuberance to his step. He caught sight of his reflection in a shop window and thought that dressed in his best— soft green hacking jacket, sharply-creased grey trousers and straw boater—he didn't look so bad. A smile on his face, he swung his bag in his right hand while he turned left into Queen Victoria Street, crossed Friar Street and made his way to the station. Turning to the statue of Edward VII, these three years dead, he touched the brim of his boater. Ta-ta, playboy prince. Hopefully you'll be gone by the time I get back.

Glancing at Reading General Station's clock tower, he saw that there was still twenty-five minutes before his train. He purchased a single ticket to Paddington at the booking office and made his way to the eastbound platform. With fifteen minutes still to go, he took a seat on one of the green benches and, reaching into his bag, drew out a small blue-covered Mills & Boon book and began to read.

> I received a letter the other day. It was from a man in Arizona. It began, "Dear Comrade." It ended, "Yours for the Revolution." I replied to the letter, and my letter began "Dear Comrade." It ended "Yours for the Revolution." In the United States there are 400,000 men, of men and women nearly 1,000,000, who begin their letters "Dear Comrade," and end them "Yours for the Revolution."

As always when he read the opening lines of Jack London's "Revolution"—and he had read them many times—he was at once reassured that socialist ideas were held by so many and filled with the desire to share this knowledge.

He looked about the platform as if in the hope of spotting a possible convert or kindred spirit. There were a number of men in lounge suits and waistcoats, probably businessmen on their way to late-morning meetings. Most of the women, some with small children, wore skirts which narrowed to the hem, stopping a foot short of the ankle, while a few wore matching skirts and jackets with raised waists; a variety of hats, some feathered, were on display and some of the women twirled parasols. All at once, his own wardrobe seemed less impressive. There was, however, a small knot of mature worker-types, with collarless shirts, jackets bearing signs of hard wear and baggy, unpressed trousers, puffing their pipes as they engaged in casual conversation. But this was small consolation, as they stood apart from the other passengers, seemingly conscious of, and by their distancing complicit in, their social inferiority; Mickey could clearly see that, while they might at times be ferocious with each other, they would never dream of even raising their voices to any of the others—apart from him—on the platform. There was not one who looked as if he might begin a letter with "Dear Comrade."

And that really was one of the problems with Reading, only fifty miles from the largest city in the world and yet so provincial. Travel to the southwest of the town and pedal down the Burghfield Road and you were in the country, where ideas had not changed for a century or more. Life could be lonely for a budding socialist in Reading, and that was one of the reasons why he was on his way— for the first time ever—to London.

He placed his book in his jacket pocket as the train, green engine and coaches in the chocolate and cream livery of the Great Western Railway, drew alongside the platform, the engine exhaling steam as it came to a halt, seeming to sigh with relief after a recent sprint.

Several of the well-dressed men and women climbed into First Class carriages at the front end of the train, while Mickey occupied a window seat in Third Class opposite a woman of around thirty in a long black skirt and frilly white blouse; as a porter closed the door, she removed her straw boater and used it to fan her face. Placing his own boater on his knee, Mickey leaned his head against the window and watched the east end of Reading pass. Soon, the town was gone, replaced by Berkshire fields in which, with the harvest still weeks away, there was little activity. On a narrow road between two fields, a black car and a horse and cart faced each other, the cart driver, in shirt sleeves and a flat cap, standing up from his seat and pointing the way the car had come, as if indicating that a short distance back there might be a point where they could pass each other; the driver of the car seemed to have the same idea, and it was the cart that gave way.

"Excuse me, sir."

Mickey looked from the small drama outside to the woman opposite, who was flushed and fanning herself furiously with her boater.

"It's such a warm day. I wonder if you would mind opening the window for me." From her accent, he would have thought her more at home in First Class, although he could detect no note of assumed superiority.

"Of course, madam, no trouble." Mickey stood and confronted the door, wondering whether he had spoken too hastily. But no, it seemed simple enough: a leather belt held the window shut, its first hole threaded onto a brass nipple. He eased the belt off the nipple and allowed the window to descend until it was half-open. Having glanced over his shoulder at the woman and received her nod, he lodged the nipple onto the nearest hole and resumed his seat.

The woman sighed. "Ah, that's much better. Thank you so much."

She gave him a gentle smile and he now saw that she was very attractive, her short dark hair framing an oval face, her flawless skin a light olive in hue, and large brown eyes. He glanced briefly at her hands and could see no rings. She had no luggage, but the long strap of a handbag in soft brown leather lay on her left shoulder.

He debated whether to engage her in conversation—whether, indeed, it was socially acceptable for two strangers of the opposite sex to go beyond the brief exchange they had already had; but his attention was diverted by a murmured discussion between two men in their mid-forties seated opposite each other on the other side of the compartment. "Well," said one, "he seems well-behaved. Not like some of them." With regard to attire, they fell between the businessmen and the workmen he had seen on the platform, and their moustaches were not particularly neat. He thought they might be greengrocers, off to see their wholesaler. "Oh, I know," replied the other. "I was travelling on this line last week and I caught one of them with his *boots* on the seat. The very idea of it!" Mickey turned in their direction, certain that, although their voices were lowered, they could be under no illusion that he was unable to hear them. It was if they found him insufficiently important to make a serious attempt to avoid bruising his feelings. He was aware that his face was hot and that he had clenched his fists. At this moment, the woman opposite cleared her throat and, as he glanced at her, gave him a tight grin and shook her head secretively. As he looked into her eyes, a feeling very like relief swept through him and he found himself laughing.

"Thank you," he said, with a nod. "You're right."

Her grin broadened into a smile. Oh Christ, she was beautiful. "I usually am."

He wondered whether she might begin her letters with "Dear Comrade." If anyone had suggested that she would soon become his lover, however, he would have laughed at the notion.

As the train came into Twyford, the two men got to their feet and made to disembark. "Two greengrocers off to see their wholesaler," Mickey remarked to the woman, making no effort to lower his voice. Sensing one of them pause, Mickey turned to look at him. The man's eyes narrowed, his colour rising, but he must have seen something in Mickey's face to give him pause, for he tore his eyes away, opened his door and stepped onto the platform.

"That was very naughty of you," the woman said.

Mickey grinned and shrugged. "Sorry. Couldn't help it."

Emboldened as he was, he still lacked the courage to strike up a conversation, but he was given his opportunity a few minutes later, when, a cinder having entered the window as the train gathered speed, his anonymous travelling companion began desperately brushing the front of her blouse, her mouth open in alarm. Mickey hoped that his expression conveyed concern and sympathy but, of course, given the location of the accident there was nothing he could do to assist. The emergency was over soon enough, but left in its wake a sizeable black streak down the front of the blouse. She looked downcast, although there was no sign of tears.

"I suggest," said Mickey, "that we move to the other side of the compartment. Unless you would like the window closed, of course."

She shook her head and did as he suggested. He moved with her.

"Don't look so worried," he comforted her. "It could have been a lot worse."

She smiled gamely. "Hardly, in the circumstances."

"The circumstances?"

"I'm on my way to an interview for a job. Looking like this, I'll not stand much of a chance, will I?"

"Oh, I don't know. They're not going to interview your blouse, are they?"

She laughed. "But even so..." She waved her right hand in the direction of the damage.

"Listen, before we go any further…" He extended his hand. "My name's Michael Rice, known as Mickey."

She smiled and shook his hand. "Emily Richardson."

"So what job are you going for?"

"An office job at the London General."

"The bus company?" Mickey fell back in his seat, his mouth open in amazement.

*

As they disembarked at Paddington, Mickey walked alongside Emily, his eyes sweeping the platform for a sight of Eric. Glancing across at platform five, he saw crowds of men in top hats and tails and women in white flowing dresses all making their way to the front of a train, presumably to the First Class carriages.

And there he was, thinner and taller than Mickey and six years older, arms folded across the jacket of a tight, single-breasted suit as he stood at the barrier and shook his head in disbelief as Mickey approached.

"Miss Richardson, this is my brother Eric."

Eric smiled from one to the other. "Didn't tell me you were bringing the wife, Mickey."

"As we only just met on the train, that would be rushing things, mate. Eric, this is Emily Richardson. Off for an interview at the London General, but she's got a problem. Show him, Miss Richardson."

Emily, who had been carrying her boater over her bosom, now raised it in a gesture rather like that of a magician pulling a rabbit out of a hat.

"At London General, you say?" It was almost as if Eric had not seen the damaged blouse.

"Yes," confirmed Emily. "Why are you two so fascinated by this company? Do you both work there?"

"Not exactly," said Eric in his gravelly voice, an amused smile beneath his sandy moustache. "What time's your interview?"

"Three o'clock."

Eric glanced at the station clock. "Plenty of time. We'll go and wet our whistles and see if we can do something about that blouse."

"But then I have to get to the company."

"We'll see to that as well, so don't you worry."

They were now in Praed Street, and the giant Great Western Hotel stood before them, a tower at either end of the building crowning its five stories. Meanwhile, more top hats and white dresses were passing them or alighting from taxis. Both men and women seemed completely indifferent to their surroundings, interested only in themselves and each other. Mickey watched them carefully, noting their...confidence, and it brought home to him the size of the task which lay before people who started their letters with "Dear Comrade."

"What's all this about, Eric?" asked Mickey, whose Reading accent now became apparent as he pronounced "about" as "abeht."

"Platform five, Michael. Special train to the Windsor Royal Garden Party, so you mind your manners if one of these fine gentlemen should push past you."

"Well," said Mickey, causing Emily to laugh, "I hope for their sake that they don't travel with the windows open." Despite his jocularity, it was a sobering moment, and he fell silent.

"What's up, Mickey?"

"I was just thinking that these are the people who hold the power of the country in their hands. I was wondering how"—haiew—"that made me feel."

Eric laughed. "Don't you believe it, mate. These are just the lieutenants." He leaned close to Mickey and lowered his voice. "Do you think our real rulers will travel to Windsor in a fucking train? No, mate, they'll be chauffeur-driven in Rolls-Royces."

"Anyway, where are you taking us? Not here, surely?" He nodded at the Great Western.

"Why not? Their beer's as good as anyone else's, and they do a nice sandwich."

"But a bit dear, I'll bet."

"A bit. A steak dinner will set you back four or five bob. But as you won't be paying you don't have to worry." He looked at Emily and chuckled. "You're quite a pair of worriers, aren't you? Are you sure you're not married?"

They entered the Great Western and found the bar as the last of the top hats made their way towards platform five. A middle-aged man stood alone at the bar, a bowler hat at his elbow, a cigarette between his fingers. As they approached the bar, the barman held up a restraining hand. "Sorry, gents, no ladies at the bar."

The customer looked to his right and gave Emily a moment's scrutiny. "That's alright, Tom, she's with me. But we'll take a table anyway. Ask Pete to come over and take our order." He turned to the others and pointed to a corner table that a waiter was just clearing, then, picking up his bowler, led the way.

Eric started to do the introductions when they were seated.

"Mickey Rice, Emily Richardson, this is..."

"George Sanders," said Emily, causing some dismay on the part of Eric and Mickey.

Sanders smiled. "We're old friends—and comrades," he explained. Sanders was a fit 42, losing some hair at the front, with a handsome, sun-browned face and a dark brown moustache curling over the corners of his wide mouth. The skin around his eyes bore the effect of long hours and the first two fingers of his right hand, which lay on top of his left on the table, were stained with nicotine. He took a card from his top pocket and handed it to Emily. "Should you need to," he said, "you can contact me there."

"'George Sanders, Organiser,'" she read aloud from the card. "'London and Provincial Union of Licensed Vehicle Workers.' No longer the Cabdrivers' Union, then." Not only was she beautiful, thought Mickey, but her voice, while decidedly posh, was musical and flowing.

"No, we're busy organising the busworkers, and so we're now the LPU."

Eric felt in his jacket pocket and pulled out some badges, passing one to Emily and another to Mickey. "Otherwise known as the red-button union."

"Well, I hope that refers to more than the colour of the badge, Brother Sanders," Emily joked, and it was obvious from this that they were well enough acquainted to poke fun at each other.

"You can rest assured that it does, Sister Richardson," he responded, "especially when compared to our rival, the Amalgamated Association of Tramway and Vehicle Workers."

"Otherwise known as the *blue*-button union," Eric chipped in.

"And I see you've graduated to a bowler hat," Emily continued her friendly assault.

Sanders laughed. "Yes, Tom Mann says it makes me look like an engineer."

"It's been two years since I've seen Tom..."

Sanders narrowed his eyes, and the gaze he gave her had in it a significance that only she could decipher. He swallowed and turned to Mickey. "And you're Eric's brother, up here to lend a hand."

"I'll do what I can," Mickey offered, saying no more because he found Sanders, while apparently friendly enough, a little intimidating, full of a confidence which spoke of broad experience and even broader knowledge.

"And you're a tram driver?"

"Yes, Mr Sanders..."

"Brother will do, Mickey," Sanders smiled and shrugged. "Or just

George."

"Yes, with Reading Corporation. It was private until 1901 and then…"

Sanders nodded. "We're aware of the history. No motor buses yet?"

"Not yet," Mickey replied, although he suspected that Sanders was fully aware of this.

"Did you hand in your notice?"

"No, I just took five days unpaid leave to investigate the situation here in London."

"That's wise." Sanders reached into his jacket pocket and drew out a yellow packet of Gold Flake cigarettes and a box of matches. He selected a cigarette and lighted it, and during this operation of several seconds seemed to be brooding on Mickey's position. "Well," he said eventually, expelling a plume of smoke, "there are three possibilities. First, we could employ you, at least for the time being, on organising work. My own position is that of organiser, but that's an elected position. There are four of us at the moment, Eric, Ben Smith and a man called Larry Russell being the other three. Russell is actually the organising secretary. Most of the real organising activity is done by lay members on a volunteer basis, so it would almost certainly lead to some ill-feeling if we paid you to do it; and you being Eric's brother wouldn't help matters. Then again, I probably wouldn't be able to get the general secretary or the Executive Council to authorise the expenditure, given our tight budget."

"But wouldn't the job pay for itself, George," Eric interjected, "given the fact that Mickey would be recruiting members every day?"

Sanders smiled at Mickey before turning his attention to Eric. "Well, hopefully he would. But I don't think Harry Bywater or the Executive would be prepared to gamble on that. Don't let's forget that we've just been through a big cabdrivers' strike." He switched to Mickey. "On 1 January, the London cab proprietors increased their petrol charges. The whole of the trade stopped work, and that's the way it stayed until 21 March, when the owners withdrew the increase. Yes, the drivers received financial support from their comrades in several northern cities and help also came from other trade unions. Even Paris cabdrivers held collections for our members—a magnificent gesture!" He shook his head and continued in a more sober tone. "But you don't have to be a genius to understand that a strike of almost three months' duration must have been a drain on our resources."

"Some in our union," said Eric, "think that the answer to the financial problem lies in us merging with the other vehicle workers' unions, but George here pointed out that the London busmen were unorganised."

Sanders nodded. "We need to be much bigger before we think of amalgamation. We certainly don't want to be outnumbered by a right-wing union like the AAT." He paused and regathered his thoughts. "Anyway, I think we have to rule out paid organising work for you, Mickey. The other two possibilities are organising from within, by taking a job on either the buses or the trams, and helping to build up our membership there."

Eric took a watch from his fob pocket and flipped it open, casting a glance at Emily. "I think you should know, George," he said, "that Miss Richardson here has a job interview at the London General at three o'clock."

Sanders turned his chair and uttered a long sigh as he regarded Emily. "Well, the day is just full of surprises," he said. "At Electric Railway House?"

Emily nodded.

"Broadway, above St. James's Park station."

"That's where I have to be, George," she said. She gestured to her blouse. "But first I have to do something about this."

"You don't have a spare blouse?"

"Nor money to buy another. Like Mickey, I wisely decided not to burn my bridges, and came here on a return ticket."

Sanders held up a hand and beckoned the waiter over. "Okay, let me order us all a sandwich and a drink. While that's coming, Emily, I'll lend you some money so that you can step out to the ladies' outfitters just down Praed Street here. After we've had our sandwiches, I'll drive you to your appointment."

"How do you know," she asked with a smile, "that you'll get your money back?"

"Because I know you, Emily."

*

"So how do you know Emily?" Mickey asked.

Sanders took out another cigarette and tapped it on the packet to firm up the tobacco. "From political meetings. Originally, she was with the Social Democratic Federation, as were a number of us, but the SDF tended to ignore the trade unions. Two years ago, however, it merged with the left wing of the Independent Labour Party and a few other groups to form the British Socialist Party. Both Emily and

I became BSP members. Over the past few years we saw each other at meetings and conferences, usually where there were loud arguments about the direction the movement should take. By and large, we found ourselves on the same side." He laughed. "And maybe that's just as well, because I've seen what can happen when a man finds himself in her sights! In 1911, during the big transport strike, she was in Liverpool for that huge demonstration when the police attacked the crowd—men women and children. Jesus, what a terrible thing that was! You should hear Tom Mann talk about it! Anyway, one stupid copper decided to take on Emily. Came at her with his truncheon raised, leaving his more delicate parts unprotected. Thing is, she didn't leave it at that." Pausing, he looked first at Eric, then at Mickey. "Took out her hatpin. The problem with that was that it was on camera." He regarded the glowing tip of his cigarette and shook his head, grinning wryly. "So I suppose she's been lying low ever since. Certainly I've neither seen nor heard of her since then."

"So," murmured Mickey, "she probably *does* begin her letters with 'Dear Comrade.'"

"Hey, you been reading that Jack London book I left you?" said Eric.

Mickey drew the small blue volume from his pocket and grinned at his brother.

"A good enough man," said Sanders, "but an awful drunkard."

"You've met him?" asked Mickey, only now beginning to fully comprehend the esteemed company in which he found himself.

"He was here in 1902 to study social conditions in the East End. Wrote a book about it called *The People of the Abyss*. We bumped into each other a couple of times." He smiled warmly at Mickey and patted his arm. "Don't be over-impressed by so-called great men, Mickey. Despite whatever greatness might be in them, they all have their flaws."

"Will we be going with you when you drop off Miss Richardson at Electric Railway House?" Eric asked. "Be nice for Mickey to take in a few of the sights."

"Glad you asked, Eric." Sanders stubbed out his cigarette in the ashtray. "No, I'd rather you didn't, because I'd like a quiet word or two with Miss Richardson. So you hang around here—you can sit in the lobby after you finish your drink—and I'll come back for you and we'll show Mickey the office. In the meantime, you can brief him on the possibilities on the buses and trams."

*

"Don't we need to pay?" asked Mickey, gesturing at the empty plates and glasses on their table; Emily, due to her pending interview, had taken lemonade, half of which remained in the glass.

"George settled it before he left with Emily."

"Seems the union's not all *that* short of cash, then."

Eric smiled and waved a finger at his brother. "You heard what George said about great men, Mickey. Well, I think George Sanders might be a great man, and I know he has his flaws—but drinking the members' money ain't one of 'em. Whatever he spent here came out of his own pocket."

Chastened, Mickey raised his glass, toasted "To George," and drained the remaining inch of bitter.

"To George," followed Eric.

They found a quiet corner in the lobby and, while Mickey spent the first few moments casting his eye over the plush carpeting, the gleaming furniture, and the magnificent staircase to the left of the reception area, Eric quietly scrutinised his brother.

"So," said Eric finally, "how are things at home?" Although he had almost lost his Reading accent, "at home" came out as "a-tome."

Mickey grinned. "Pretty much the same. Nothing you'd want to hurry back to, mate."

"The old man still the same?"

"No changes there."

"He still use the belt on you?"

"Last time he tried that was a couple of years ago."

"And how did that turn out?"

"He had to take the next day off work."

This brought a smile to Eric's lips. "Fucking good for you, Mickey. Good for you!"

Mickey shrugged. "Other than that, it's all the same. He's still on the piss."

"Did you leave your stuff at home? The bugger's likely to sell it."

Mickey tapped the side of his nose. "Carted it around to a mate's place last night, what there is of it."

A mischievous grin tugged at the corner of Eric's mouth. He nodded in the direction of his brother's attire. "Thought you might have left that stuff there, mate. From the look of the jacket, anyone would think you were off for a day with the local hunt, but from the boater I'd say you were out for the afternoon at Henley Regatta."

This dealt Mickey's pride in his wardrobe the final blow. Nevertheless, he rallied. "Well, the members of the local hunt seem to be on their way to Windsor, don't they?" He tugged at the lapels of his hacking jacket. "Anyway, I thought this was pretty smart. Picked it up for a song from the Sally Army."

"Nah, don't pay any attention to me, Mickey. I'm just having a laugh with you. The jacket's nice. Looks very comfortable." The grin reappeared. "You *have* brought a change of clothes, though, haven't you?"

"Fuck off. When you've finished taking the piss, maybe you can tell me about my future."

Eric leaned back in his chair and laced his fingers over his stomach. "Ah, yes. Your future." He gazed up at the chandelier and released a sigh. "Well, it's a choice between buses and trams. Trams wouldn't be a problem, as you're already a motorman."

Mickey leaned forward, elbows on his knees, and lowered his voice. "To be honest, mate, it's driving me crazy. Round and round the same old route, day after day, six days a week. You start to feel dizzy halfway through a duty—or earlier if you're on the Whitley route, and the wind is blowing north from the Manor Farm sewage works."

"Ah, the Whitley whiff! So what are you saying about a job on the trams?"

"I daresay it would be different up here: longer routes and, let's face it, more interesting places."

"Well, yeah, maybe." Eric scratched his chin. "There are a number of smaller tram companies, like the London United in West London; we organise almost half the tramworkers employed by the London County Council, but most of our members are south of the river."

"And in the north?"

"The AAT—or nothing at all, in some cases."

"And the buses?"

"Apart from Thomas Tilling, it's pretty much a one-man show, although British Automobile Traction operate a few. The LGOC— London General Omnibus Company—is almost a monopoly. We've got around a third of the men in membership at the moment, and we reckon we'll have 'em all by the end of the year." He sighed and passed a hand over his face. "And if George and I are looking a bit tired, that's why."

"Long hours, eh?"

"All hours, mate. One of the best ways to put the union case to the men is at midnight meetings, and believe me we've had a few."

"Sounds exciting."

"Oh, it can be, it can be." He grinned. "And I can see from the expression on your face that you're interested. But there's a problem."

"What's that?"

"You can't drive a bus, mate."

"Maybe not—yet. But I can count."

Eric's brow wrinkled. "Eh?"

"I could become a conductor."

"Fuck me that never occurred to me, you being a tram driver."

"Any drawbacks?"

"Oh, yeah, mainly in the pay packet. You'll earn about a bob a day less than a driver."

"How much a week?"

"Around thirty bob without overtime, but while you're on the spare list the minimum's a bit less than that."

"But apart from that conductors have the same conditions as drivers?"

Eric nodded. "Pretty much."

"Paid leave?"

"No."

"Free uniform?"

Eric shook his head.

"Free travel?"

"Nope."

"Minimum meal relief?"

"Nah."

"A limit on split shifts?"

"Forget it. We call 'em spreadovers, by the way."

"Maximum time on duty?"

"There ain't one." Eric, a look of determination on his face, leaned forward and looked his brother in the eye. "This is the kind of thing," he growled, "that we're going to change, Mickey, have no fucking doubt about it."

Mickey winked at him. "I think I may take a crack at it."

*

Sanders, bowler set at a rakish angle, led Emily, now clad in a smart green blouse, to the station taxi rank. As he opened the passenger door of his bottle-green Unic cab to let Emily in, a policeman stepped across from the station.

"I'm sure you know it's an offence to leave your cab unattended

15

on the rank, sir. It's been here for over an hour."

Sanders smiled and pointed to the gold-painted sign on the door. "Been here on business, constable."

"London Cabdrivers' Union," the frowning policeman read aloud. He looked up at the well-dressed middle-aged man. "Not in for another strike, are we?"

"No, constable." Sanders shook his head and smiled before adding, "Not in the cab trade, anyway."

The policeman, perhaps deciding that this was a topic best not pursued, coughed and waved towards the street. "Very well, sir, off you go."

Sanders leaned in and lowered a window behind the driver's seat. "We had the speaking tube taken out and this window put in," he explained to his passenger, "so if you sit on this side we should be able to hear each other." He nodded to the policeman, putting a finger to the brim of his bowler, climbed into the driver's seat and started the engine. "We need to get that sign painted over," he said over his shoulder to Emily, "but no rush. As you've just seen, it has its uses."

"Yes, driver," said Emily, mimicking the part of the passenger, "now take me to Electric Railway House."

"Yes, madam. Praed Street, forward Spring Street, right Sussex Gardens, left Bayswater Road to Hyde Park Corner, right Duke of Wellington Place, left Grosvenor Place, left Victoria Street, and there you are, madam, within walking distance of the notorious Traffic Combine."

She clapped her hands in delight. "That's wonderful, George! You realise that this is the first time I've seen you in your professional capacity."

"I've not been a cabdriver for some years now..." He paused, passing his tongue over his lower lip. "And this is the first time I've seen you as Emily Richardson. What happened to Dorothy Bridgeman?"

"Ah, so now we're getting down to business."

"Seems like a good idea. Don't you agree?"

She nodded. "Well, outside St. George's Hall, Liverpool two years ago, Dorothy was captured on a cinematograph picture as she got the better of a brutal policeman. The Strike Committee had arranged for two cameras to record the event which, as you know, turned into a bloody battle. The cameras should have been a good thing, as they recorded the whole melee, providing evidence of the shocking police behaviour. But, as Tom Mann discovered the following day when he and the other strike leaders viewed the film at a local picture palace, the police had confiscated the reels, only releasing them after ordering the excision of all material that might prove embarrassing to them, which they took away with them. The record of my heroic battle against a man twice my size was part of that material. So shortly thereafter Dorothy disappeared from view."

He caught her eyes in the rear-view mirror and nodded. "That's pretty much what I heard. But surely the police would have simply destroyed those parts of the film in their possession."

"That was my view at first. But when I returned to London a few days later, my landlady told me that a plainclothes policeman had been asking for me."

"Oh, fair enough."

"So do you think I'll pass?"

"In what way?"

"The shorter hair, somewhat darker. Is there any danger of this modest, almost retiring person being mistaken for the dangerous Dorothy Bridgeman?"

"Those who were close to you will have no problem identifying you. But the police? No, I think you're probably safe." He sighed. "As long as you exercise a degree of prudence, that is."

"As long as I keep my opinions to myself, you mean?"

"To be honest, yes. Will that be a problem for you?"

"To be honest, yes."

They both laughed, exchanging glances in the mirror.

"So what have you been doing these two years?"

She shrugged. "This and that. To begin with, I even did a bit of nannying, and discovered that I liked children. Can you believe that?"

Sanders found the question uncomfortable. Dorothy—or must he now think of her as Emily?—was around 30 and unmarried. "If you say so. And after nannying?"

She regarded his eyes in the rear-view mirror, smiling as she enjoyed his discomfort. "After nannying I taught myself to type and take shorthand, and so did some office work in Swindon."

"In Swindon?"

"Yes, that's where I've been living." She sighed. "And that was something of a problem for me. It's not London, is it?"

"So you missed London?"

"Oh, not just the city itself, but everything that goes with it: the cultural life, having friends with whom one can discuss more than the prices in the butcher's shop or the greengrocer's, and the, the..."

"The politics," he supplied for her. "The excitement."

"Well, yes, of course, but don't be so dismissive, George. What would *you* do if you were exiled to Swindon?"

"Organise the men at the railway works."

"Of course you would, George. But if you were a woman, and the police were looking for you?"

"I don't know what I'd do in those circumstances, Dorothy, but I'd think twice about coming back to London for politics and excitement."

"I did think twice. And here I am."

He sighed. "And here you are. Why the LGOC?"

She shrugged. "There was an advertisement in the newspaper for a secretary. It's a job I think I can do, and it's in London."

"And the fact that we're organising this company has nothing to do with it?"

"I didn't even know about that, George. The last I heard of you or your union was during the cabdrivers' strike. I've been completely out of touch. But now I know you're organising the busworkers, it seems to me that I could be of assistance to you."

Sanders nodded. "Yes, you could. Certainly on the information front." He looked at her in the mirror, his face hard and uncompromising. "But that would only work with the utmost discretion, Dorothy. That must be understood. *If* you get the job."

She smiled. "That's understood, George. Now tell me: you referred earlier to the Traffic Combine…"

They were at Hyde Park Corner, thinly populated with private traffic at this time of day, but with several LGOC buses in their cream and red livery, the company name in gold, every available space carrying advertisements for such consumer essentials as Lux Soap, Vaseline, the Daily Mail, and the latest hit at the Apollo Theatre. There were a few X-types, rather more of the newer B-types, the passengers on the open top decks, some of them probably tourists, enjoying the fine day. Turning into Grosvenor Place, he calculated that he would have just enough time to brief her on the company. He didn't want there to be time for anything else, because he was remembering now that Dorothy Bridgeman had been reputed to be a difficult—yes, even a dangerous—woman. He had only known her from meetings, but some who had known her in industrial circumstances had spoken of her tendencies to an extremism that was sometimes counterproductive.

"A man called Charles Tyson Yerkes established the London Underground Electric Railways Company of London—or UERL—in 1902. Yerkes was American, and had built a transport empire in Chicago. His business methods were not particularly honest, and he spent some time in prison for larceny." He glanced in the mirror. "Do you read Theodore Dreiser, Dorothy?"

She looked mystified. "*Sister Carrie*, of course. Why do you ask?"

"Have you seen his latest, *The Financier*?"

"Not yet."

"Well, he calls the corrupt central character Frank Cowperwood. But Cowperwood is based on Yerkes."

"Goodness. I had no idea."

"Corrupt as he was, Yerkes was a formidable operator. For example, when J. P. Morgan tried to enter the underground railway business here, it was Yerkes who kept him out. Yerkes died in 1905. A couple of years later, Albert Stanley joined the Underground company; three years ago, he became managing director."

"A name I know, at last! Isn't he another Yank?"

"Almost, but not quite. He was born in this country, but his parents emigrated to Detroit when he was a kid. When he left school, he went to work for the Detroit Street Railways Company and rose to a top position. After that he took a top job in the New Jersey transport system and rose even higher. Then in 1907 he was offered the post of general manager of the UERL, so he moved to London. Now he's the managing director."

"You've obviously done your homework, George. But why? What has this to do with the LGOC?"

"Because last year the UERL took over the London General. That's why your interview is at Electric Railway House."

"And hence the Traffic Combine."

"Exactly, and that could prove to be a mixed blessing. The London General pays a dividend of almost 20 percent. That tells me that there's plenty of financial leeway to make major improvements to wages and conditions. The Underground operations, on the other hand, are far less profitable, so the danger is that Stanley will take money which should be going to our members and bung it to his Underground shareholders."

"Not sure I'll rise sufficiently high to be able to prevent that, George."

"Information, Dorothy," Sanders repeated, his expression tense. "That's all I ask."

"I'm joking, George."

"Glad to hear it. Do you know which department, you'll be in?"

"The advertisement merely called for someone with the ability to type and take shorthand—both at the requisite speeds, of course—in the managing director's office."

"Ohhh." Impressed, Sanders inclined his head. "Now isn't that convenient! But I doubt that you'll be in his private office, as his personal secretary. Someone with a bit of seniority will occupy that position. It's more likely that you'll be one of several in an outer office, called upon to take on tasks as they arise."

"Oh, it also mentioned filing..."

"Yes, that's more like it."

"...And taking minutes."

Sanders hit the steering wheel with the palm of his right hand. "That's even *more* like it, Dorothy. What kind of meetings require to be minuted? Meetings of top management. Meetings with government officials. And...meetings with the trade union, once we're recognised! Jackpot!"

"*If* I get the job, George."

"Dorothy, I know you well enough to appreciate that you're not the kind of person who travels up from Wiltshire to apply for a job she's not going to get. And, milady, here we are.

"I'll let you out a bit further down the road," he said as he drove down Victoria Street. "It wouldn't do either of us any good if you were seen getting out of this vehicle. You've got fifteen minutes to spare. Just walk up Broadway and you'll see the station in front of you; the entrance to the offices is just around the corner in Petty France."

As the vehicle came to a halt, Sanders turned and saw Dorothy leaning forward, her face at the open communication window, and he found himself wishing that she were not so beautiful.

"Wish me luck, George."

"All the best, Dorothy."

Appearing a little disappointed, she drew back and extended her hand, which he duly took in his own, shaking it chastely. "I'll let you know what happens."

"You have my card, Dorothy."

He remained at the kerb for a minute or two, watching through the wing mirror as she walked towards Electric Railway House. He was, he knew, about to be placed in a situation which would need to be handled with the greatest of care. He took out his cigarettes.

2

Having collected Eric and Mickey, Sanders drove to Soho and parked outside the LPU office at 39, Gerrard Street.

"Here we are, Mickey," joked Eric. "You're about to enter London's citadel of militant trade unionism."

"But don't confuse 'citadel' with 'palace'," Sanders cracked with a smile, "because you'll find no luxury behind these doors." He turned at the entrance and leaned close to Eric. "We'll park ourselves in the meeting room for a chat, but if Russell or Harry decide to join us, watch what you say—and not a word about young Emily until we're on our own."

Sanders led the way, and as they entered the meeting room on the ground floor Mickey could see that he had been right: all was functional, with not even a potted plant to break the monotony of the dull furnishings. A faint odour of polish struggled unsuccessfully to overcome the smell of stale tobacco smoke. A large, bare table with seating for twelve or fifteen stood just inside the door, while the rear of the room was occupied by three rows of wooden chairs, around which a man in his middle fifties was pushing a broom.

"Hey, Frankie," called Eric, "come and shake hands with my little brother. Frank's our caretaker, Mickey."

"Afternoon, Frank," greeted Sanders. "Any chance of a pot of tea and three mugs, mate?"

Having exchanged greetings with Mickey, Frank limped upstairs on his errand, while the other three seated themselves at the table.

"Frank was a stout man in his day," Sanders told Mickey. "A good soldier in the Cabdrivers' Union until a road accident robbed him of his licence."

"Trouble now," added Eric in a low voice, "is that because he works in the headquarters he sometimes thinks he's the general secretary. You should hear him with some of the members who come here for meetings!"

"Hah!" Sanders, wreathed in smiles, threw back his head. "I recall the time, a couple of years ago, when Tich Smith, our president, was off sick. We had to reshuffle the pack to cover his absence, but that left us with the need for someone to step in on a temporary basis to keep us up to strength." He turned to Mickey. "What we call a stand-down officer, someone taken off the cab and paid by the union for the duration. Well, I had in mind a likely lad called Gerry Norman, but I didn't know whether he'd agree to it. So after seeing Tich at the hospital one evening, I called in and Frank answered the phone. 'Is Gerry still there for the committee meeting?' I asked. 'Well,' said Frank, 'he was five minutes ago.' 'Okay, Frank, tell him I need to talk to him.' A couple of minutes later, someone picked up the receiver. 'Hello?' So I explain the circumstances, most of which Gerry would have been aware of anyway, and ask him whether he would agree to act in a stand-down capacity for six or eight weeks. There was a bit of a pause, then this voice says, 'Well, George, that's a very flattering offer, but I think me age would tell against me. And I've got this gammy leg.' It was Frank! 'I thought I told you to get Gerry for me,' I said. 'I tried, George, but turns out the meeting broke up early and he's gorn 'ome.' But the bugger let me rabbit on for about three minutes!"

Minutes later, a foot hit the door, and Eric stood to open it, revealing the man himself, laden with a tray bearing a large pot of tea, sugar bowl, an open bottle of milk and several enamel mugs.

"Were your ears burning Frankie?" Sanders asked. "I was just telling Mickey about the time I made a job proposal to you, thinking you were Gerry Norman. Why didn't you stop me?

Frank placed the tray on the end of the table and looked at Sanders in mock amazement. "Have you ever known me to interrupt a paid officer?" he asked, provoking laughter from the others.

Eric made a show of counting the mugs on the tray. "Why five, Frank?"

Frank gave him a look. "And there was me, thinking you was intelligent, Brother Rice."

As Frank was about to leave, two men appeared at the door, supplying Eric with the answer to his question. The caretaker bowed low and threw out an arm to wave them in. Harry Bywater was a short man still in his late thirties, with fair hair turning grey, in a dark three-piece suit; a short cigar burned between his fingers and he had the flushed appearance of a man partial to a drink. The man who followed him, Larry Russell, was a full six feet, lean and sallow and in need of a haircut.

Russell nodded to the caretaker. His long, thin face gave the impression that a smile might be an infrequent visitor, a likelihood strengthened by the morose expression it currently wore. "I'm sure there's a spot for you at the Victoria Palace, Frank."

Sanders did the introductions. "Mickey, this is Harry Bywater, general secretary, and Larry Russell, organising secretary and editor of our journal, the *Licensed Vehicle Trades Record*. Brothers, say hello to Mickey Rice, sibling to our esteemed colleague Eric."

"In fact," said Russell as he shook Mickey's hand, "it's *Lawrence*," and Mickey noticed a look pass between Sanders and Eric.

"I've been wondering," said Mickey, "about the rows of chairs over there. Are they for conferences?"

"Not really," replied Sanders. "This room couldn't hold a conference. On those occasions we have to hire a theatre or a public hall. No, they're mainly used during Executive Council meetings, which are open to the members—or as many as can fit in here."

"It's called democracy," said Eric.

"Not always a very comfortable experience," said Bywater with a wry smile, revealing beneath his ragged moustache a set of uneven teeth in a wide, thin-lipped mouth, "for those of us sat around this table during the meetings. The ordinary members are supposed to observe rather than participate, but I've come to realise that busworkers can be just as unruly as cabdrivers. Hey, lads: tea's getting cold." He began to help himself and the others followed suit.

"Any excitement here today, Harry?" asked Sanders as they sipped their tea.

"Pretty quiet. No disputes, anyway," he laughed. "Ben Smith came in earlier with a big bundle of application forms, so I think we're well on course to meet our target by the end of the year. How did you get on?"

"Spent the morning in South London, talking to the Tilling's boys and recruiting those who are ready." He glanced at Russell. "Dropped the forms in earlier, before I went to Paddington." He pursed his lips and turned to Bywater. "I think there might be trouble brewing there, Harry. A couple of the lads told me that the local management have been trying to stop them wearing the red button on their uniforms."

Russell, in waistcoat and shirtsleeves, having left his jacket in his office, shook his head. "I suggest you tell them to leave the button at home, George, at least until we've got our feet under the table."

"The company would be on stronger ground," said Eric, "if they provided the uniform free. As far as I'm concerned, if a lad has paid for his uniform, he can put on it whatever he fucking pleases."

Bywater held up a palm. "Do watch your language, Eric, at least in the office here. I can see that you have to talk that way when you meet the lads at the terminuses, but don't do it here, boy." He turned to Sanders. "Just keep an eye on the situation, George, and see how it develops—*if* it develops."

"So how many buses do Tilling's operate?" asked Mickey.

"They've been around for a long time," said Bywater. "but they've come up against the mighty LGOC. After the London General had bought up the rest of the competition, it agreed to let Tilling's alone, but on condition that it would operate only 150 buses. So the company will need to look to the provinces if it's interested in expansion—which I'm sure it is."

"Why hasn't the A...?" Mickey began, but faltered on the acronym.

"AAT," Eric helped him out. "Amalgamated Association of Tramway and Vehicle Workers. Or, like I told you earlier, the blue-button union."

"Yes, the AAT. Why hasn't it had more success organising busworkers."

"A number of reasons," said Eric. "They're seen as mainly tram-oriented, which doesn't help them. Then again, they're based in Manchester, and the lads here want a London union."

"Yes," Bywater laughed, "if London busworkers must have a general secretary, they want him where they can get their hands on him."

"But the main reason is they're too bloody soft. And there's little consistency in their agreements. They're not called the blue-button union for nothing, Mickey. They have one good organiser, a man called Archie Henderson, but I don't see him sticking with 'em for much longer."

"And they're not as democratic as us," Sanders added. "Very top-down."

"Okay," Mickey nodded, "but it still strikes me as strange that it's only now that the busworkers are being organised." He looked from Sanders to Bywater. "Why has it taken so long?"

Bywater pointed to Sanders. "That's a question for George."

Sanders grinned and took his cigarettes and matches from his pocket. "I'll need a smoke for this one, Mickey."

Russell patted his waistcoat. "Left me panatelas upstairs."

"Want one of these, Larry?" Sanders held up his packet of Gold Flake.

"No, that's okay, George. I'll have to shoot back in a minute anyway. Still a bit to do on the *Record*."

Sanders expelled a column of smoke and looked at the ceiling, noting as he did so the yellow pallor left by years of tobacco smoke. He then launched into a history lesson, telling of the earlier attempts to organise London busworkers: the union formed by the barrister Thomas Sutherst in 1889, which never managed to secure more than three thousand members, and which petered out after a partially successful strike in 1891; the London Bus, Tram and Motor Workers' Union in the early years of the present century, which failed because the upsurge of militancy and organisation which had begun with the victories of the London dockworkers and gasworkers in 1889 had not been sustained.

"There were arguments in the socialist societies, with some of the leaders looking forward to the day when they could purchase their first top hat. Some of 'em, like Hyndman in the Social Democratic Federation, didn't bother with industrial organisation, thinking it would be enough to gain political power and introduce socialism through parliamentary means. That wasn't going to assist in mobilising the workers to defend their interests. And, of course, the employers didn't take the upsurge in trade unionism lying down, and pretty soon were doing what they could to smash the unions."

"So how is it different now?" asked Mickey.

"The water in which we swim has got a bit warmer," said Sanders with a smile.

In 1906, 29 Labour MPs had been elected, up from four in 1901. Problems still existed in the Labour Representation Committee, or Labour Party as it came to be called, but people could now see that victory—of a kind—was possible. The Independent Labour Party and the SDF both established numerous new branches. Then in 1911 several socialist groups had come together to form the British Socialist Party. By this time, socialist pamphlets and newspapers were more widely available, distributed not just to middle-class sympathisers but to working-class activists and trade unionists. Workers' education groups and study circles either sprang up or came back to life all over the country.

"Industrially, you don't need me to tell you the last two or three years has seen a wave of strike action and militancy. There never was such a time as this, Mickey!"

Sanders spread his hands and looked at each of the other four, seemingly forgetting that there was only one neophyte among them. "So you can see that the circumstances in which we are working are completely different from previously, and that partly explains our success."

Russell heaved a sigh, seemingly glad that Sanders had brought the lesson to a close, and made a move to rise.

"But that's only part of the story," Sanders continued, causing Russell to slump back into his chair, to the amusement of the others. "We also need to consider the changes that have taken place in the trade, and the character of the men. Ten years ago, if you knew how to drive a horse and cart you could probably get a job as a bus driver. No shortage of applicants, so little pressure on the companies to raise wages. This also meant that the drivers didn't have too much pride in the job.

"Now you have to know how to drive a motor vehicle, or have the company train you. There's only about a thousand LGOC men that have been in the job for more than three years. It's an almost completely new workforce." He paused and held up a finger. "Bear in mind, though, that Tilling's still have quite a few horse-buses on the road.

"The higher standards demanded by the employers mean fewer applicants, and those who are accepted develop a sense of professional pride and self-esteem. That doesn't mean that the companies don't try to work the men to death, because they do. But the bus driver of today isn't prepared to take this for too long. That's why we're finding it fairly easy to organise them.

"And the busworker of today is open to new political ideas. You know, speaking of the workers organised in that wave of new unionism in 1889, Engels said..."

This proved too much for Russell, who now looked at his pocket watch and got to his feet. "Have to finish some work on the paper, George."

Sanders grinned and waved him farewell. "Engels said that their minds were 'virgin soil, entirely free from the inherited respectable bourgeois prejudices which hampered the brains of the better situated "old" unionists.' That also seems to be true of many of the new busworkers." He looked at Eric and Mickey and winked. "Lucky for us, eh?"

"Sounds like I should get some reading done," said Mickey, directing the remark to Bywater.

"Well," replied Bywater, taking out his watch, "once again Brother Sanders is your man. If the union ever needs to advertise for a theoretician, I reckon he'll get it, hands down." He looked at his watch. "Think I'll wander off."

"Fair enough, Harry. We'll go upstairs and see if we can find some reading material for the lad."

*

The caretaker, dust-pan and brush in hand, was just leaving Sanders' office as they reached the first floor. "Couldn't do much with it, George," he complained. "When you gonna shift all that paper from your desk?"

"We've been through this, Frank. I know exactly where everything is, so don't touch anything. All you need to do it empty the ash trays."

Frank held the dustpan out at arm's length, displaying a large number of cigarette-ends. "Job done, then."

As they entered the small office, Mickey immediately saw the cause of the caretaker's complaint: a large wooden desk completely covered with piles of paper, some of them eighteen inches high, except for a small space before Sander's chair, which held a blotter, an inkstand and a jar containing several pens and pencils.

Sanders spread his arms and shrugged. "Well, this is it. Warned you about the luxury, didn't I?

Down the corridor, someone was ponderously hitting the keys of a typewriter. "Is that Larry?" asked Mickey, cocking an ear.

"Most probably," said Sanders, striding over to a small bookcase which stood against the far wall.

"Unless it's *Lawrence*," said Eric, causing Sanders to snort with laughter.

"Here, Mickey," Sanders said, holding out two slim pamphlets. "*Socialism*, by Tom Mann, was written while he was in Australia. Marx's *Wage Labour and Capital* was written in 1847, but this pamphlet was published in 1891. Will they be alright?"

"I'll have to ask me dad."

Sanders turned to Eric. "Are they all jokers in your family?

"All except our dad," replied Eric with a straight face, causing a round of laughter.

Sanders handed Mickey the pamphlets. "Take care of 'em, because they're a bit fragile."

Mickey took the pamphlets while running his eye along the shelves of the book case, wondering why he had not been given a more substantial volume.

Sanders smiled with understanding. "You can come back for more when you're ready," he said, "but if you're going to be working in the trade and doing some organising when the opportunity arises, you'll find you won't have too much time for reading. Talking of which, have you decided on a job?"

"I'm thinking bus conductor, George, and maybe train for driver a bit later."

Sanders nodded thoughtfully. "What do you think, Eric?

"We'll see if we can get him into Middle Row, just a stone's throw from my flat. In fact, we'll walk up to Oxford Street and ride home on a number 7. Give him a feel for it."

"What's the membership at Middle Row?"

"Around 40 percent."

Sanders smiled at Mickey. "Not for long, eh?"

Eric walked to the door, closed it and returned to Sanders. "So what about Emily?" he asked in little above a whisper.

"Seems as if she might be of use, Eric. The job she's applied for is in Stanley's office. Nothing too elevated, but one of the requirements is minute-taking." He winked.

"Now that *could* be useful—if she's with them during the adjournments, anyway."

Sanders nodded. "Exactly. But she can be somewhat impulsive, so we need to handle her very carefully, Eric. There can be no question of inviting her to meetings, even restricted ones, at the moment. I'll be her contact."

"Seems like you've lost your missus, Mickey," Eric joked.

"I told you," protested his somewhat embarrassed brother, "we only just met on the train. Besides, she's too old for me."

"Very pretty, though," said Eric, and Sanders looked away.

*

Oxford Street was thronged with home-going office workers and last-minute shoppers, but luckily a westbound number 7 arrived just as another had departed fully laden, and Eric pushed Mickey towards the staircase. On the top deck, they went to the front of the bus and sat opposite each other, as the seats ran lengthwise, against the sides of the vehicle.

"You'll see a bit of London from this position," said Eric. "Just as well it's been a fine day, though."

As the vehicle puttered towards Oxford Circus, Mickey lifted his face to the balmy air of the early summer evening, a feeling of great freedom descending upon him. London!

"This is the X-type," Eric advised him, assuming the tutorial role previously performed by Sanders. "Built by the LGOC itself at its works in Walthamstow. Stopped making them a few years back, though. Now they're turning out the B-type. Much better bus. Last year, when the Underground took over the General, they turned the bus works into a separate company called AEC."

"But it's still part of the Combine?"

"Oh, yeah."

"Do they have B-types on this route as well?"

"Afraid not, mate. For some reason, they decided that route 7 should be all X-types."

They crossed Oxford Circus, and Mickey looked behind him, glimpsing the Liberty department store in Regent Street, and the confusion of traffic—private cars, taxis and bus after bus after bus—clogging the famous thoroughfare. London!

The top deck was soon filled to capacity, and the conductor, a short man in his late twenties, made his appearance, utilising the delay caused by the traffic to move rapidly down the two lines of passengers, dropping coins in his leather bag and issuing tickets from his bell punch machine, before he was required downstairs to supervise boarding and alighting passengers.

"Well, well, Mr Rice," he chirped in a Lancashire accent when he reached the front of the bus, "to what do we owe this enormous pleasure?"

"I'm having an early night, Steve, so the pleasure's all mine. But meet my brother Mickey; he may be joining you at Middle Row soon." Eric held out his coins. "Two to Ladbroke Grove."

The conductor winked and shook his head, but Eric pushed the money on him. "Don't take chances, Steve. We need you around for a while."

"Right you are, sir, two to Ladbroke Grove!" The bell punch rang and he handed the tickets to Mickey, pointing to the red button on his blue summer jacket as he did so. "Make sure you wear one of these if you're coming on the buses, Mickey."

3

"Rice!" It was three in the afternoon when the bellow came from a small office in the building known as "the Bungalow," adjacent to the old site of the Metropolitan Police headquarters in Whitehall Place, where officers of the Public Carriage Office interviewed aspiring drivers and conductors, even though they had passed their respective tests, before granting their licences.

Mickey walked through the door and saw two police officers, both stout and in not particularly smart civilian clothes, behind a desk upon which sat three piles of papers.

"Stand there!" The officer with the flushed face and beard, somewhere in his fifties, pointed to a spot on the floor about three feet from the desk.

The younger, clean-shaven officer coughed. "So you're..."

"Wait!" The older man seemed unable to employ a reasonable tone. He glared up at Mickey. "These papers," he said, slapping one of the larger piles, "are applications approved. But *these*"—a harder slap descended on the smaller pile—"are applications rejected." He lifted his hand and pointed a fat red finger at the applicant. "So don't stand there thinking that this is all cut and dried and that you've got a job for life." He turned to his colleague. "Proceed, constable."

"So you're up from Reading," the younger man observed in a well-modulated voice as he scanned the sheet of paper before him. He pointed at a line on the page. "It says here that..."

Mickey took an involuntary strep forward.

"Did we ask you to move forward?" bellowed the older man.

"Stand where I told you!"

"It says here that you were a tram driver in Reading. And now you want to be a bus conductor. Isn't that a somewhat unusual career development, Mr Rice?"

"It might be, if I'd stayed in Reading, sir. But I'm moving from Reading to London, from Reading Corporation to the London General..."

"You hope!" This was, of course, the older man.

"...and plan in future to train as a driver."

"In which case," said the younger man with a smile, "you'll have to go through this all over again. Can't be looking forward to that, can you?" More polite than his colleague and obviously the more intelligent of the two, he seemed to be inviting Mickey to share his humour.

But Mickey, fearing a trap, kept a straight face. "I'm sure that interview will be just as fair and impartial as this one, sir."

"I see you have no criminal record, observed the younger man swiftly, forestalling another intervention by his colleague. "Are you sure there's nothing you're holding back?"

"Absolutely sure, sir."

"As I'm sure you realise, we have asked our colleagues in Reading if you're known to them."

Mickey finally allowed himself a smile. "I have nothing to fear, sir."

The constable nodded. "Good. Sergeant?"

The older man's red finger came up once more. "You'll be employed by the London General Omnibus Company, young man, and they have high standards. But even more important than that, you'll be licensed by the Commissioner of Police to conduct a bus. If you so much as put one foot outside of the law, we'll take that licence from you and you'll be on your way back to Reading, if you're not in clink. Is that clear?"

"Very clear, sir."

"Alright, off you go."

"Thank you, sir." Mickey turned and made for the door.

"Oh, Mr Rice!" It was the sergeant's bellow, but at least he was now addressed as "Mister."

Mickey turned and saw the sergeant waving him back into the office. He stepped back in, halting eighteen inches from the desk. The sergeant noted this position but did not remark upon it. Instead, he asked a question to which, Mickey felt sure, he already knew the answer.

"Are you by any chance related to Eric Rice?"

"He's my brother."

"In more ways than one, I daresay. As far as I know, your brother still has a cabdriver's licence." He smiled, suddenly avuncular. "Wise of him to hang onto it, because the job he's doing now probably won't last long. Anyway, give him my regards." The finger again. "And you keep your nose clean."

Mickey passed the line of applicants, most, having overheard Mickey's interview, wearing apprehensive expressions, and made his way down to the lobby, where he found Eric shaking hands with a short man in a flat cap. The man thanked Eric and walked towards the rear exit.

"Was that the accused?"

Eric nodded. "Violation of section 61 of the Town Police Clauses Act of 1847, to wit, 'that by wanton or furious driving he did injure or endanger any person in his life, limbs or property.' Seems the copper who pulled him had it in for him, because I was able to show that at the time in question, on that particular day, it would have been difficult to get above five miles an hour on that stretch of Edgware Road. Result: I have a friend for life in Fred Twomey, the driver, and a sworn enemy in PC Venables. Let's get the droshky."

"A friend of yours sends his regards," Mickey said as they passed out of the rear door into the car park.

"Oh?"

"The fat sergeant on the interview panel."

"Hah! Bascomb."

"That his name? I could have throttled the bastard."

"Keep your voice down; we're still in enemy territory. So how did it go?"

"Piece of cake, really. All I had to do was swallow my pride and dignity and keep calling them sir."

"That's the ticket. Bascomb's bark is worse than his bite. A lot of that is just play-acting."

"I still didn't like it."

"No one does, Mickey. Anyway, what did he say about me?"

"He said it was just as well that you'd hung onto your cabdriver's licence, because the job you're doing won't last."

Eric laughed. "That's his usual line. But I'm still here."

*

Eric rapped on the door of Sanders' office, opened it and peered in. "I'm back."

Sanders, sat at his desk with his jacket on the chair behind him,

31

looked up. "So I see. How did the boy get on?"

"No problem. Bascomb gave him the usual bullshit, but he seemed to sail through it."

"Where is he now?" Sanders stubbed out his cigarette in an overflowing ashtray.

"I dropped him back to Middle Row." Eric coughed. "You working this evening?"

"Got an appointment locally at 5.30, then I thought I'd go across the river and have a chat with some of the Tilling's boys. The cab outside?"

"Right at the door. You taking it?"

"I can walk to the first appointment, but I'll nip back and take it, so make sure no one else grabs it."

"Okay." Eric turned to leave. "Thanks for asking about my case, by the way."

"Didn't think I needed to. You won it, didn't you?"

"Of course I won it."

"There you are then."

"Is your first appointment important, George?"

"So-so. Why?"

"Because you'll be late for it unless you get a move on."

Sanders whipped out his pocket watch. "Bugger! Okay, see you tomorrow."

*

Sanders hurried to the end of Gerrard Street, turned left and strode down to Coventry Street. Glancing at his pocket watch, he saw that he was only a few minutes late and so slowed his pace as he walked to the junction with Rupert Street. There, he looked up at the "Lyons Corner House" sign and entered, finding himself confronted with a whirl of waitresses, their black skirts contrasting with the white of their starched caps, collars and aprons. The place was packed, mostly with middle-class women in large hats, and he thought at first that he would never find her, but having ascended two flights of stairs he found that the second floor was less populated, and there she was, seated at a corner table, wearing the same white blouse he had seen her in at Paddington, the blemish from the Great Western Railway's cinder now removed.

"I've ordered the tea," she said as he sat opposite her. "And I hope you like Swiss Roll."

"There's nothing I like better with a cup of tea," he smilingly assured her, "than a nice slice of Lyons' Swiss Roll."

"You've visited the Corner Houses before?" She was inspecting him closely, as if suspecting that his reply to this innocent enquiry might be significant. The hint of a smile touched her lips.

"Ah..." He hesitated, regarding her evenly, although trying not to look at her lips. "No, but I've had their Swiss Roll. Eric sometimes buys one and brings it to the office."

"How...quaint." She laughed lightly. "One never thinks of a union office as a nest of domesticity."

"It's hardly that, Dorothy, but we're surprisingly human."

She brought a hand to her chin, elbow on the table, and tilted her head. "Have you never been married, George?"

Sanders caught a movement out of the corner of his eye and smiled "Ah, our tea!"

The young waitress, puffing and blowing quite needlessly, presumably as a protest at Dorothy's choice of table at the far end of the room, quite removed from the other customers, placed her tray on an adjacent table and began to transfer its contents to their own. She placed the teapot rather carelessly on its wooden stand and a tear of brown liquid landed on the white tablecloth.

"Oh, I *am* sorry, mum."

Now it was Sanders' turn to regard Dorothy, interested to see how she would handle this.

She passed with flying colours. "Don't worry, dear," she said, smiling kindly at the girl. "It's quite alright."

"And so," said Sanders, indicating with his right hand that Dorothy should pour first, "here we are."

But Dorothy would not let herself be deflected so easily. "So I take it you've never been married."

Sanders gave this some thought, finally deciding that he should leave Dorothy in no doubt regarding his intentions or availability. He leaned forward slightly, dropping his voice. "Dorothy, you are one of the loveliest women I've ever known, and we have a fair amount in common. If I were free you'd have to fight me off." He paused and took a breath. "But I *am* married. I'm married to this movement of ours and I've time for nothing else. Believe me, Dorothy, it's the truth."

She sighed, neither visibly deterred nor upset, and he realised immediately that this was the answer she had been expecting. "Oh, I quite realise that. But I wasn't proposing marriage, George."

He knew better than to allow her to pursue this line of argument. He cleared his throat. "So, are you settling in?"

"I think so," she said as she raised the teapot. "To be honest, Mr

Stanley seems nice enough."

"On a personal level, I'm sure many capitalists are, but we shouldn't confuse that with the role they play in the system."

"No, of course not," she said, replacing the teapot on its stand.

Sanders poured milk into his cup before the tea. "And the job itself? Pretty mundane, is it?"

"For much of the time, yes, but there is the occasional interesting task. For example, on the third or fourth day I was asked to take the minutes at a meeting with the police."

"*Really?*" He inclined his head as he speared a slice of Swiss Roll with his fork and transferred it to his plate. "What was all that about?"

"Nothing very exciting, to be honest," she said, looking across her cup at him. "It was what they call a TLM. Traffic Liaison Meeting— held, would you believe, every two months."

"But surely Stanley doesn't involve himself in that kind of thing?"

"Not really. It seems he feels it important to put in an appearance, but last week he left after ten minutes, leaving it to one of his managers."

"How many police at these meetings?"

"Last week, there were two. A Chief Inspector Griffiths"—she gave Sanders an inquiring look, thinking he might know of him, but he shook his head—"and a sergeant who took notes for their side." She took a mouthful of tea and replaced her cup on its saucer, then placed both hands on the table and leaned forward. "The informal chat that Mr Stanley had with the Chief Inspector *before* the meeting was *very* interesting, George."

He was hooked. "Go on."

"The Chief Inspector mentioned that, 'according to our information,' substantial numbers of busworkers were joining the red-button union."

"And what did Stanley say to that?"

"He just nodded, as if it was something he had no power to prevent." She paused, allowing that to sink in. "When the Chief Inspector asked if he thought it was just a matter of time before the union officials would be sitting across the negotiating table from him, he said, 'I fear so.' He said that in other circumstances this might be prevented, but with the current level of unrest in the country it would be foolish to try. 'The most we can hope,' he said, 'is that their leaders turn out to be reasonable men.' He said that he had permitted one leader to meet him for a discussion in confidence, and he thought that if that man remained at the helm, things might work out."

"At the helm? Did he give a name?

"No." Dorothy grinned mischievously. "But he described him as being quite moderate and not very bright."

The crockery rattled and danced as Sanders brought his palm down onto the table. "Bloody Harry Bywater!"

*

Sanders' mind was racing as he drove down to Trafalgar Square. Bywater! What was the man thinking of? Bywater owed his position in the union due to his base in the Owner-Drivers' branch of the Cab Section, and it had always been clear that his petty-proprietary outlook made it difficult for him to accept the collective discipline required in a trade union, and this was even more apparent now, when the organisation's numbers were being swelled by a rapid influx of busmen. Was that all there was to it? What concerned Sanders most was not that Bywater had met Albert Stanley, but that he had done so without telling anyone. One possibility, of course, was that he was out to line his own pockets, but this was difficult to believe, much as Sanders might distrust him. Then, of course, Bywater was, like his pal Larry Russell, a member of the Independent Labour Party, the official line of which favoured parliamentary action as against class struggle. Was that what this was about? Well, time would tell.

He had not expected his arrangement with Dorothy to pay dividends quite so soon, and he was grateful for her information, but her revelation had created a dilemma for him. Was he to confront Bywater immediately, or bide his time; and if the latter, should he share his knowledge with one or two of his close comrades? Who among them would be able to hang onto the potentially explosive information while continuing to deal with Bywater as if nothing had happened? Eric? No, young Rice was more likely to knock Bywater onto the seat of his pants. Despite himself, Sanders smiled at the image. So who? Ben Smith. Yes, he would discuss the matter with Ben.

Having negotiated Trafalgar Square, Sanders drove down to the Victoria Embankment, and turning left was immediately bathed in the gold of early evening, the rays of the declining sun dappling the waters of the Thames and burnishing the edges of the leaves of the trees which stood evenly spaced on the opposite side of the road. In leaving the shade of Northumberland Avenue, he had also left the workaday world and entered a realm of leisure, for across the street couples and families strolled by the riverside, some of the women with summer-bright dresses, laughing gaily with their menfolk and friends. For a while, Sanders' heart lifted, and he was glad to be part of such a time and place; all too soon, though, he was sobered by darker thoughts, for how much longer would such a carefree world continue to exist?

4

Fearful of waking the whole house, Mickey Rice eased the front door closed and stepped lightly down the narrow side street, heading towards the Harrow Road. For the time being, until he could afford a room or flat of his own, he was living with Eric, his wife Elsie and their young son, who occupied the upstairs flat in the small house; for this, Eric asked five shillings a week rent and another three for food.

At 5.40 on this July morning, the Harrow Road was almost empty, the only sound the clop-clop of a horse as a milkman—to judge from the full crates on the float—began his round. Mickey strode swiftly across the street, relishing the relative cool of the morning. He continued down Harrow Road, sniffing breakfast smells here and there, until he reached the footbridge, where he crossed the Grand Union Canal and entered Kensal Road.

He reached Middle Row garage at 5.53, two minutes before his sign-on time. Buses had been leaving the garage for some time, and by the time Mickey walked through the open double doors the place was full of blue smoke and a quarter empty. He turned left into the output office, where you signed on at the start of a duty and, if you were a conductor, paid in at the end of it. This was full of another kind of smoke, from pipes and hand-rolled cigarettes. He nodded to the drivers and conductors who stood about, awaiting the arrival of their mates, walked to the window and pulled the sign-on sheets towards him, inserting his name and pay number against duty 7/3. The third duty on route 7 was a spreadover—a split shift—which would require him to work from 0555 to 1217—this was how the times appeared on the schedules displayed outside the output office—when he and his driver would be have an unpaid break of over three hours, resuming work at 1529 until 1945, thereby covering both rush hours; thus a spreadover of 13 hours, 50 minutes, of which they would be paid only the time on duty of 10 hours, 38 minutes, minus the "stand-time" at the termini. Glancing at the name next to his, he saw that he would be working with Driver Mortlake.

The garage official pushed his box, containing tickets and bell-punch machine, through the window. As Mickey took the box, the official, squinting, demanded, "What's that?"

"What's what?"

"On your lapel." The official wore glasses and had a liverish complexion.

"That's my union badge."

"Your *union* badge. Well, didn't take *you* long, did it?" He squinted again. "I think you'd better see the garage superintendent when you make your part pay-in."

"You mean during the three hours and twelve minutes when I'm not being paid?"

"That's what I mean, conductor."

"So I'll be paid overtime for that."

"Don't be silly, conductor. Just do what you're told."

"Well, what I was told during my training last week is that it's up to the conductor whether he makes a part pay-in halfway through his duty. So I think I'll give it a miss today."

Mickey turned away and saw that he had an audience. Ted Middleton, a short, middle-aged driver, his grey hair parted in the middle, was shaking his head, obviously doubting the wisdom of the new boy's attitude, but the other, mostly younger, occupants of the output were smiling and one, wearing a red button himself, raised his thumb.

He hurriedly checked his tickets and waybill, then turned to face the other men. "Driver Mortlake?"

The man who had raised his thumb, tall, thin and around thirty years of age, winked. "Okay, let's go. Bus is ready."

Mortlake drove the short distance to Ladbroke Grove and then, just short of the station, turned right towards Wormwood Scrubs. He put his foot down, stopping to pick up only two passengers, and by the time they reached the Scrubs they had ten minutes to spare before their scheduled departure time.

Mortlake climbed out of the cab and crossed the road to a tea truck which had just opened, beckoning Mickey to follow.

"Dick." Mortlake held out his hand as Mickey joined him.

"Mickey."

"One of the problems with Middle Row is that there's no canteen. Only three years old, and no canteen!"

"Hardly big enough for one, I would have thought."

"Yes, I suppose that's the reason." Dick Mortlake was a well-spoken young man, hardly the average bus-driver. "Of course, the mobile canteen turns up for several hours a day. Anyway, how are you finding life on the spare list?" Drivers and conductors on the spare list covered for casual vacancies, and so were unlikely to work the same duty—or even the same route—from one day to the next.

"First day, Dick."

Dick grimaced. "Poor man. I don't envy you. But I must say you made a bloody good showing with Butcher this morning."

"Is that his name?"

"Taking a bit of a chance, though, being on probation."

"Will anything come of it?"

Dick Mortlake shrugged. "He'll almost certainly complain to Shilling, the garage superintendent, and he'll probably drag you into his office—as soon as you give him the opportunity, that is—to give you a bollocking." He paused. "But you need to be a bit careful while you're still on probation."

"Hopefully, before long we'll be in a position to prevent them from picking on someone just because he's a union man. Talking of which"—he gestured to Dick's lapel—"how long have you been with the red-button union?"

Dick grinned. "A few weeks. In fact, I was almost disappointed when I saw you were wearing the button this morning. I like working with the new men because it gives me the opportunity to recruit them."

"Do you know a conductor called Steve? Lancashire man?"

He nodded. "Steve Urmshaw. Yes, he's active as well."

"Then let's have a meeting and make some plans."

*

On that first journey to Liverpool Street, Mickey Rice's career as a bus conductor began.

Dick took the bus to the other side of the road, swung it around the little island which served as a turning circle, and headed east. The first passengers were half a dozen prison officers coming off the night shift at the Scrubs. Mickey stayed on the platform as they passed the prison; he had assumed that it would be hidden from public view but there, down a short access road, was the huge, studded door, plain as the day. The guards clumped upstairs so that they could smoke, and Mickey followed with a sigh, knowing that this was the first of many times he would climb these stairs during his working day.

The bus was a third full by the time they reached Ladbroke Grove station, but here most passengers disembarked, switching to the Underground, while a new set boarded. There were several women office cleaners and a few manual workers, but few office workers at this time of the morning. Between Ladbroke Grove and Paddington Station they picked up passengers in threes and fours, but frequently enough to fill the bus by the time they reached Praed Street, and here there was another exchange, as most disembarked, to be replaced by passengers recently disgorged by the Great Western Railway. So the pattern was repeated several times as they travelled to Marble Arch, Oxford Street, Holborn, Newgate Street, and Bank until they reached Liverpool Street. Throughout the journey, Mickey found that he had little time to relax on the platform, constantly having to squeeze past standing passengers to collect the fares on the lower deck and then dash upstairs to do the same on the upper deck. During training, he had been advised to make sure he had plenty of copper and small silver in order to make change, but he soon discovered that a too strict observance of this resulted in a growing strain on his neck and right shoulder as the weight of his leather cash-bag increased, and so he began to get rid of the small stuff as the opportunity arose.

If he thought that their arrival at Liverpool Street would afford him some relief, he was disappointed. It was now 7.30, and their departure was already two minutes overdue as the bus began to fill with arrivals from East Anglia and East London, and so he dashed upstairs and began to issue tickets while the lower deck was still filling. Returning downstairs, he politely asked two standing passengers to alight, the maximum number having been exceeded, then gave Dick the double bell signalling departure before turning his attention to the lower deck. By the time they arrived at Bank, the job had been completed and Mickey felt a sense of achievement. This did not last, as passengers now began to disembark, to be replaced by others, many of them cleaners bound for the Oxford Street shops. By now, however, traffic was beginning to build, slowing the bus sufficiently for him to collect the fares with relative ease.

They were running seven minutes late by the time they arrived back at the Scrubs, and if they stuck to the schedule would have needed to leave immediately, but there were two buses in front of them, also running late due to traffic, still on the stand.

As Mickey stepped down, an inspector approached the bus. He looked at his book of arrivals and departures, his tongue appearing in the corner of his mouth as he made an adjustment with his pencil.

"Okay, lads, the one in front is leaving now, the second will depart in five, and I want you to kick off in ten. OK?"

Mickey and Dick shrugged. They were ready for another tea anyway.

"Plenty of milk, George," Dick instructed the proprietor of the tea van, "because we haven't got long." He turned to grin at Mickey. "Bearing up?"

"Just about," Mickey nodded, "but the fucking novelty has well and truly worn off, I can tell you that!"

It was the man behind the counter, thin and in need of a shave, who laughed. "Yeah, it don't last long, does it? Used to be on the job meself before I amassed enough capital to invest in this thrivin' business."

"Although it wasn't exactly all his own money," added the inspector, who had crossed the road to join them.

George, who apparently took no offence at this, winked at Mickey. "'Ad me 'and in the bag, didn't I?" He chuckled. "This your first day? Well, you just wait until tomorrah morning.'"

"What did he mean by that?" Mickey asked as they recrossed the road.

"You may find you have a few aches and pains," Dick replied with a wry smile. He looked at his pocket watch and sighed. "Even if we don't lose any more time, it looks as if we'll be coming off fifteen minutes late."

"And no overtime pay."

"Correct. This bloody payment-by-mileage system is one of our biggest grievances. It's one of the first things that'll have to go."

*

In fact, they finished their first spell of duty twenty minutes late and, due to the weight around his neck, Mickey changed his mind about the part pay-in. He bagged up most of the copper and stacked the silver on a tray, entering the amounts on his waybill, then pushed the tray through the window where a garage official waited to receive it. As he finished checking the amounts, the official called over his shoulder. "Your friend is here, Mr Butcher!"

Butcher came to the window. "Ah, Mr Rice!" he exclaimed, his face breaking into a smile at this unexpected opportunity. He levelled a finger at Mickey. "Stay there."

Mickey turned to Dick, who had entered the output to wait for him. "This is a bit like being back at the Public Carriage Office."

Butcher, in the meantime, had crossed to the other side of the allocation office, where he rapped on a door and, opening it, called in a loud voice, "Mr Rice is at your disposal, Mr Shilling. Says he can fit you into his busy schedule."

He returned to the window, once again pointing at Mickey. "Garage superintendent's office now," he instructed. "You know where it is? If not, I'm sure that Mr Mortlake, who is a frequent visitor, will show you the way."

Outside the output, Mickey spent some time studying the spare rota and the schedules, seeing that the following day he was allocated a middle shift, 1005 to 1910, on route 31—Chelsea to Swiss Cottage. He turned to grin at Dick. "That's not bad. Gives me a bit of a lie-in."

"Believe me, you'll need it, Mickey." He pointed to the door of the garage superintendent's office and lowered his voice. "Now remember what I said about probation."

James Shilling was a short, slender man of around fifty with wavy red hair and piercing blue eyes. He wore a grey lounge suit and a green tie. He waved at the chair in front of his desk, inviting Mickey to sit; then, placing his arms on the desk and lacing his fingers, he considered his newest employee.

"It seems you upset Mr Butcher this morning." He spoke with a soft West Country burr.

Mickey considered this statement for a moment. "Well, yes, I could see that Mr Butcher was upset, Mr Shilling. But to be honest, he brought it on himself."

"And how did he do that, Mr Rice?" There was in Shilling's eyes the suggestion of amusement.

"By making unreasonable demands, Mr Shilling."

"Which were?"

"That I see you because I was wearing a union badge"—he gestured to his red button—"and that I do so in my own time."

"Your own time, Mr Rice?"

Mickey nodded, holding his gaze. "Yes. Time not paid by the company."

Shilling cocked his head to one side. "Well, that's the way things are done in the company, Mr Rice." He smiled. "Just something you'll have to get used to."

"I accept that, Mr Shilling—until it's changed."

"That's very good of you, Mr Rice." He inspected his fingernails and then looked up at Mickey. "Do you think it *will* be changed?"

"Very possibly, although it would hardly be a priority."

"A priority? A priority for whom?"

41

"For the men in general. For the union, when it comes in."

"And do you think the union *will* come in?"

"Oh, that day will come, Mr Shilling, that day will come."

"And what do you think its priorities will be?"

"Ohhh, the abolition of the mileage system, so that, for example, my driver and I would be paid for the twenty minutes overtime we've just done. And the payment of stand-time. That kind of thing."

"Well, that's very interesting, Mr Rice." Shilling pulled a lined pad towards him and dashed off a few notes. He looked up and smiled. "You realise that we know who you are?"

"Well, I would hope so, Mr Shilling, after all the forms I filled out since I applied for the job."

The smile did not leave his face. "Very amusing, son. But you know what I mean. Did they direct you to work here?"

"They?"

Shilling threw out a hand, betraying the first signs of irritation. "The union. The British Socialist Party. Whichever organisation is in a position to direct you."

Mickey threw back his head and laughed.

"You find this amusing, Mr Rice?"

"I do, Mr Shilling." He paused, licked his lips. "From your accent, I would guess that you come from farther west than I do. I would imagine that you came to the big city because it offered opportunities that were not available in your home town." He spread his hands. "Why would anyone think that it was any different for me?"

They sat looking at each other until finally Shilling nodded. "Yes, I can see how that might be the case. But I didn't come to London to stir up union trouble."

Mickey shook his head. "Mr Shilling, how many men in this garage do you see wearing the red button? How many men in the General as a whole are wearing it? How much unrest do you read about in your morning newspaper—not just on the buses but in trade after trade?"

"Your point being?"

"Why pick on the boy who's just come up from Reading?"

"Ah." Shilling smiled. "Perhaps because his brother is a union leader, Mr Rice. We're very well informed, you know."

Mickey nodded. "So you had a call from Sergeant Bascomb."

Shilling's smile was not quite so sure of itself now.

"But maybe we can return to the reason I'm here, Mr Shilling. I am wearing the red button." He shrugged. "As far as I know, the General has no rule against this."

Shilling regained his composure. "I accept that, Mr Rice—until it's changed," he said, throwing Mickey's words back at him.

"It seems to me, Mr Shilling, that by his unreasonable behaviour this morning Mr Butcher has done you a disservice."

Shilling frowned. "You've lost me there, Mr Rice."

"You have just hinted that a ban on the wearing of the red button might be under consideration. Indeed, it's entirely possible that you're waiting to see if other companies—the LPU also has members in the provinces, you know, and at Tilling's—will take action on this matter. In that case, Mr Butcher has let the cat out of the bag, hasn't he?"

Shilling held up his palms. "Oh, I couldn't possibly give you an answer on that, Mr Rice." He consulted his pocket watch.

"Call it fifteen minutes, Mr Shilling."

"Fifteen minutes?"

"Yes. We're now agreed that Mr Butcher instructed me to come to your office, even though I had breached no rule. Now, I have accepted that interviews in this office for legitimate reasons are unpaid—until it's agreed otherwise. I ask you to accept that in the current circumstances, due to Mr Butcher' unfortunate mistake, payment of fifteen minutes' overtime is justified."

Shilling threw back his head and laughed. "Oh, Mr Rice, you are a sharp young man."

Mickey rose from his chair, ready to leave.

"Wait!" Shilling raised a hand, gesturing that Mickey should remain seated. He leaned back in his chair, and eased open the inner office door. "Mr Butcher!"

Butcher appeared at the door, clearly pleased to have been invited to witness Rice's downfall.

"Mr Butcher, pay Mr Rice fifteen minutes' overtime!" Shilling ordered, voice and face stern.

Butcher' face darkened to a thunderous hue. "You *what*?"

"Make it thirty minutes!"

*

In the second spell of duty on that first day, there were two noteworthy events.

Just before five o'clock, they were at Liverpool Street station when Mickey called Dick's attention to the driver of a number 11 in the bay next to theirs.

"Hey, Dick, there's a black bloke in the cab of that bus." With three minutes before departure time, they were standing at the head of their bus, waiting for the passengers to board.

Dick glanced across at the number 11 and nodded. "That's Joe Clough, works out of Shepherd's Bush. He's from Jamaica, London's first black bus driver, been on the job two or three years."

Mickey shook his head in amazement. "Well, who would have thought it?"

"To be honest," said Dick with a chuckle, "not too many, at the time. But they're all used to him now. A popular fellow, by all accounts."

The second incident was, to Mickey, even more amazing, its effect longer-lasting. At around 7.30, he was collecting fares on the top deck as they were stalled in the Oxford Street traffic, when he looked across the street and there, on the top deck of a B-type going in the opposite direction, was Emily. On impulse, he raised his cap to attract her attention—he later wondered if she thought he was saluting her—and called her name. Just as her bus began to slowly move away, she turned and saw him, standing and clutching the rail with one hand while waving at him with the other, the white smile on her lovely olive face communicating her delight at this chance encounter. She remained standing and waving, as did he, until they passed from each other's sight.

Feeling as if the breath had been taken from him, he sat down next to a somewhat startled male passenger and passed a hand over his face, and it suddenly came to him that his life had been changed forever.

*

Ben Smith was a broad-chested man of medium height, still only 34 despite years of activity in the Cabdrivers' Union, and clean-shaven apart from dark sideboards. The Gerrard Street office was quiet and, with the exception of the light in Smith's room, dark. He took out his pocket-watch. Almost nine o'clock, and George had promised to be here by eight-thirty. He sat at an open window, blowing the smoke from his pipe into the street as he looked through the latest issue of the *Record*. A few minutes later, he heard a rattle of keys down on the street and knew that Sanders had arrived. Then the corridor light came on.

"Sorry, mate," Sanders apologised as he stood at Smith's door. He removed his bowler and hung it on a peg before taking out his cigarettes and seating himself across the desk from Smith. "Got held up by the Tilling's lads. Seems there's a dispute brewing there over the wearing of the badge."

"Company's asking for trouble, then," Smith grunted. He closed the *Record* and tossed it on the desk. "So what's up?"

Sanders struck a match and brought the flame to his cigarette. "Better close the window, Ben."

The sash lowered, Smith turned back to face his colleague. He stretched across the desk and began knocking the contents of his pipe into a large metal ashtray. He cocked an eye at Sanders. "All ears, George."

"It seems that Albert Stanley is taking precautions, Ben."

"Precautions?"

"Ben," Sanders said urgently, "what I'm about to say has to remain between the two of us, at least for the time being."

A nod from Smith.

"The good news is that Stanley is of the view that recognition of the union is inevitable. That being the case he has, as I said, been taking certain precautions." He placed a hand on the desk and leaned forward. "He's had a meeting with Harry, Ben."

"He's fucking what?"

Sanders nodded. "Had a meeting with Harry. And Harry, of course, has kept this to himself." He paused as a thought occurred to him. "Well, he certainly hasn't discussed it with me. He mention anything to you?"

"Not a dickie-bird, George. What the..." Smith turned his head from side to side as he sought an explanation for the behaviour of their general secretary. "Ah, but hang on! When *was* this meeting? If it was recent, maybe he's just not had the opportunity..."

Sanders, a little disappointed at Smith's search for excuses, moved swiftly to quash all doubt. "It was several weeks ago, Ben, and he's had ample opportunity to discuss it with us—and, come to that, with the Executive Council. The proper course of action, of course, would have been to discuss it with the Executive, or at least with us and our leading lay members at the General, *before* the meeting."

Smith considered this for a moment before nodding. "Of course it would, of course it would. Yes, you're right, George." He frowned. "But how did you come by this?"

Sanders held up his palms. "I'm sworn to secrecy, Ben. But the source is absolutely reliable, have no doubt about that."

Smith leaned back in his chair. "Well I'll be fucked."

"It's our members who'll be fucked, Ben, if we're not careful."

"Do you know what was said at the meeting?"

"No, but I imagine Stanley gave Harry assurances regarding

recognition and negotiating rights on condition that the union behaves reasonably. You know, no outrageous wage demands, no strike action, that kind of thing. What else could they have discussed?"

"Yes, I suppose it must have gone something like that. But our members won't stand for that."

Sanders shrugged. "Presumably Albert Stanley thinks Harry Bywater runs the LPU the way he runs the LGOC."

Smith chuckled. "Then he's got a surprise coming."

"The question is, what do we do now?"

"Will your source continue to provide you with information of this kind?"

"Oh, yes."

"Then I suggest we do nothing for the time being, and use it when it'll do the most good."

Sanders smiled. "That's what I've been thinking too, Ben. But we also have to make sure that when the time comes for our team to sit down at Electric Railway House, we get there on our terms and not on Stanley's—or Harry's." He smoothed down his moustache and gazed up at the ceiling. "If the situation at Tilling's flares up the way I think it will, maybe we can use it to kill two birds with one stone."

5

Mickey Rice soon learned that one of the few perks of being on the spare list was that when there was nothing else on which he could be employed he might be utilised as a messenger, conveying correspondence between Middle Row and 9, Grosvenor Road, the former LGOC headquarters which was now used to house the schedules compilers, the revenue section and the lower levels of management, or, indeed, Electric Railway House.

Two days after he had spotted Emily Richardson on Oxford Street, he was assigned a stand-by duty, reporting at 7 a.m. Having scrawled his signature and payroll number on the sign-on sheet, he looked up at Mr Phillips, a far more civil garage official than Butcher, expecting to be told to cover a duty fallen vacant due to the absence or lateness of a colleague, but the official merely shook his head and pointed his pencil into the output. So Mickey took a stool and waited. And waited. While his boredom was initially relieved by the arrival of crews reporting for duty, providing the opportunity for a series of brief chats before they took their vehicles onto the road, as the morning wore on these diversions became less frequent, and he regretted that he had not slipped a book or pamphlet into his pocket before leaving home.

At 8.30, he heard the mobile canteen pull into the garage, now largely free of buses. A voice came from the allocation office. "Mr Rice!"

Mickey walked to the window and peered into the office. "Mr Phillips."

The official nodded in the direction of the garage. "Get yourself a cuppa, Mr Rice."

"Will I have time for a sandwich?"

"Should do. Off you go now. We might have something for you when you get back."

He didn't need to be told a second time. In the garage, the mobile canteen, its arrival timed to meet the first crews coming off the first half of their spreadovers, was open and the kettle was on the boil. Mickey ordered a cup of tea and a sausage sandwich.

When, fifteen minutes later, he re-entered the output, the official was waiting for him at the window. "Do you know your way to Electric Railway House, Mr Rice?"

His heart leapt. "I think I can find it, Mr Phillips."

"You're to go there and pick up a large envelope addressed to Mr Shilling."

"Who do I ask for?"

"Just say you're there to pick up the envelope from the managing director's office."

Mickey's heart looped the loop.

"How do I find that?"

"You don't have to. Just tell reception and he'll ring up; they'll send the envelope down to you." His arm came through the window. "And here's your travel pass. Make sure you hand it in when you arrive back."

Mickey rode as a passenger on the next 31 to leave the garage, travelling as far as Kensington High Street, where he hopped off at the corner of Church Street and waited at the next stop for a Victoria-bound vehicle; from there, it was a short walk to St James's Park station. In other circumstances, he would have been exulting in his unexpected freedom, taking in the sights—Kensington Palace Gardens, the Albert Hall, Hyde Park Corner—but he was unable to free his mind of Emily. Just as, two evenings ago, he had known that his life had changed, he was, against all logic, confident that she felt the same way, and he was equally sure that he would now be seeing her at Electric Railway House.

He therefore should not have been surprised when, four minutes after he had stated his mission to the man on reception duty, Emily, having descended the stairs, stepped into the lobby, but he felt the breath leave his body and his cheeks redden as, wearing a high-waisted grey skirt and black blouse, she walked straight to him, head held aloft and offering up a large buff-covered envelope.

"Mickey," she said quietly, smiling as she passed him the envelope. "It was so nice to see you the other evening,"

And suddenly, the embarrassment was gone. "Yes, it was. I've been thinking about you ever since."

This, he could tell by the softening of her features, pleased her. He glanced down at the envelope, noticing that the front was divided into a number of rectangles, in each of which an address had been written over the past days or weeks; all had been crossed out, with the exception of the current one. He placed the envelope under his arm.

Emily grinned. "They like to economise on envelopes." She glanced over his shoulder towards the reception desk before passing him a small square of paper. "This is my address. I've taken a small flat across the river in Clapham."

"And this is your telephone number?"

"No, a neighbour's. She lives two doors along. Can we see each other this evening?"

"I don't know what time I'll finish, Emily."

"If you can't make it, please try to telephone. Ask for me and my friend will come and get me."

He lifted the piece of paper and frowned. "But how did you know I would be the one to collect the envelope?"

She smiled her wonderful white smile. "I just knew."

*

At 11.30, when he arrived back at Middle Row, there was a lone driver in the output, sucking on a pipe as he read a newspaper. This was a bad sign. Even worse, Butcher had taken over from Phillips and he now thrust his palm through the window as Mickey approached and demanded, "Travel pass!"

Mickey slapped the pass on the counter and pushed it through the window. He waved the buff envelope. "Thought you might like this as well. Or shall I deliver it to Mr Shilling personally?"

"Give it here," Butcher growled. "Your postman's duties are over for today, Mr Rice. The rest of duty 17 on route 31 awaits you." He reached behind him. "Here's your box."

Mickey turned to the driver who, folding his newspaper and placing it in his pocket, shrugged and gave him an apologetic smile.

"Not your fault, mate," Mickey told him. "What time's it finish?

"2015 on the road."

Fuck it. This meant he would have to walk down to the garage from Westbourne Park, so it would be at least 8.45 before he finished paying in: too late to travel to Clapham. Having made up his waybill, he followed the driver into the garage, stopping to check the rota. Tomorrow, he had been allocated duty 5 on route 7, finishing at 1630. Perfect.

*

They had both known that this—or something very like it—was going to happen, so neither was shy. As she opened the door of her small flat to him, their eyes locked and he knew it was going to be alright. He stepped smartly inside, pushing the door closed behind him as she came into his arms. When they kissed, he was suddenly aware of his omission. No chocolates, no flowers.

"I'm sorry," he said.

She looked up at him questioningly. "Whatever for?"

"I didn't bring you anything."

"I wouldn't say that," she said, pressing her body to his.

In her small bedroom, she helped him unbutton the back of her blouse and less than ten minutes after he had come through the door her breasts—slightly lighter in shade than her face, not small, with pointed, dark brown nipples—were before him.

"They're lovely," he said, knowing that he could say anything to her, and that she, without giving it a thought, would be equally frank with him.

"Kiss them, Michael," she said, immediately establishing that his lovemaking name would be forever Michael.

"Bite my nipples, my love."

The endearment excited him even more than the instruction, and now he began to struggle out of his clothes, watching as her skirt fell to the floor.

Later, as she rode him, she asked casually, "Have you done much of this sort of thing, Michael?"

It did not even occur to him to lie. "Not so very much." If she had asked, he would have told her about the hurried gropes behind the ovens in the large Reading bakery where he had worked before going

49

on the trams, or the two uncomfortable couplings in Prospect Park. "And you?"

"This is my first time in two years, my sweet."

He grinned up at her. "You do seem...hungry."

"That is probably something of an understatement, Michael," she said, causing him to laugh.

"Why did you ask about me? Do I seem cack-handed?"

"Not at all. In fact, I've known since we waved to each other across Oxford Street that together we would make the most expert lovers. It's strange, because when we met on the train I didn't feel this way about you at all. But in Oxford Street I suddenly knew."

He reached up to squeeze her breasts. "So did I, although I didn't imagine anything quite like this. It's just that now it's happening it seems as if it was meant to, and that I should have known it would."

"It's alright, you can pull my nipples."

Later, when he was on top, it became obvious to her that a climax was approaching. "Just withdraw," she advised him.

"But it will..."

"Just do it, Michael."

And so it continued, this leisurely, utterly relaxed lovemaking, with each eager to satisfy the curiosity of the other.

The only time he came close to striking a jarring note was when, as they lay in each other's arms after the first round, he asked her whether her approach to sex was a part of her rebellion. She gave this serious consideration before replying.

"I regret to say, Michael," she said eventually, "that that is a profoundly silly question."

He propped himself on an elbow, a worried expression on his face, as if fearing that he had ruined it all. But she calmed his fears by smiling and laying a finger on his lips.

"I am not a bohemian. Bohemian? You know, those middle-class people who try to dress like workers and live loose lives in the mistaken belief that they are challenging the status quo. Writers and painters, many of them, although some of their kind are attracted to the socialist movement. But of course the status quo—despite what its moral guardians might say publicly—doesn't care a hoot if they choose to drown themselves in alcohol and fornicate until their brains rattle. They are no threat whatsoever to the bourgeois order—unless, that is, they also embrace class struggle.

"If I rebel, as you put it, it is in part because I believe that we should be able to do this whenever we choose, regardless of the fact that we are not married, or that I am a few years older than you." She cocked an eyebrow at him. "Don't you think that what we are doing is wonderful, beautiful?"

"You know I do. It's the most wonderful thing I've ever done."

"Do you think we would still be doing this if the social conventions took a more adult view of it?"

"Of course we would. Wouldn't we?

She nodded with mock gravity. "We would. Hence, rather than being an integral part of my rebellion, it is simply something I quite desperately want to do."

He laughed joyously and pulled her to him.

"Now tell me, Michael," she enquired a few minutes later. "Have you ever had the opportunity to inspect a vagina?"

"Not really."

"Would you care to inspect mine?"

"Should I?"

"Yes, I think you should. I suggest this because in my experience—which, by the way, is nothing like as extensive as you might imagine—men find the vagina a complete mystery, and are a little afraid of it. One can tell this by the fumbling way in which they sometimes insert themselves into it." She sighed and parted her legs. "So...feel free."

Feeling both free and privileged, he bent to the task, tracing the whorls and lips of the pudendum with the tip of his finger. "Quim," he murmured, savouring the word.

"Pardon?"

"Quim. It's what we call it in Reading."

"Really." She gave this some thought. "Quim. Quimquimquim. Yes, it's actually quite appropriate, isn't it? That 'im' coming after the 'qu' sound seems to suggest the shape of it." More thought. "Mind you, 'quiver' would probably do just as well. Then you would place your arrow in my quiver, for example. Don't you think that sounds nice? Seriously now, Michael, place your finger a little deeper and *I* will quiver."

He did, gently. "And this little bugger here..."

"Is the little-known and even-less-talked-about clitoris. Rub him for a while and you'll see a *real* quiver. Ah. That's it."

This went on for a while.

"Enough!" she cried finally, pushing him off. "Before I die of pleasure."

They lay quietly for a while, studying each other. She brushed his cheek with the back of her hand. "You must be hungry, my sweet."

"I hadn't thought of it."

She swung her legs over the side of the bed. "Well, I *did* think of it, and actually prepared a meal before you arrived. Then, due to certain occurrences, I forgot all about it. It must be cold by now. And probably dried up." She slapped his leg. "Come."

She watched as he moved to pick his trousers off the floor. "What *are* you doing, Michael? It's not as if anyone can see us. Follow me."

Emily made that command sound as if they had a whole labyrinth to negotiate, but of course two steps took them into her living room, against one wall of which was a small oven with two gas burners, a sink and a cabinet containing a small amount of crockery. She opened the oven door and removed two plates, each containing a pork chop, two halves of roasted potato and a modest amount of green beans. She touched one of the chops with a finger.

"Not a complete disaster, maybe. A little on the cool side, but I think our repast may be rescued if I reheat the contents of the gravy boat. Knives and forks in the drawer, sweet one."

And so they sat, naked, at her small table in the dining/living room of her small flat, and ate.

"You should realise," she said as she dissected her chop, "that I have not slipped into the role of the little wife here, and that if I had been the one to visit you, I would have expected you to prepare the meal."

"I think I do realise that, Emily," he nodded. "By the way, did you know the woman who threw herself in front of the King's horse at Epsom a few weeks ago?"

"Another Emily. Davison. No, I didn't know her." She was with the Women's Social and Political Union of Emmeline Pankhurst, an organisation with little support in socialist circles."

"Really? That surprises me."

"You'll see why." She extended a forefinger. "Mrs Pankhurst runs the WSPU as if she owns it. Their conference five or six years ago was to consider a constitution, but Mrs Pankhurst, her daughter Christabel and the Pethick Lawrences, who provided much of the funds for the WSPU, decided there would be no conference, let alone a constitution. Why? In the previous months there had been indications of resistance to the Pankhursts' authoritarianism, so they decided to deny the dissidents any opportunity of airing their grievances. That evening at the Essex Hall, the London delegates were told that there would be no constitution, no voting members. No democracy, in fact."

"And they took it lying down?"

"Not all of them: one group, led by Mrs Despard, broke away and called themselves the Women's Freedom League." She paused, extending a second finger. "Then there is the question of what Mrs Pankhurst's suffragettes are calling for." She frowned. "Not votes for all women, but 'votes for women on the same basis as for men.'" Emily laughed scornfully. "In other words, votes for those meeting the property qualification, and no votes for working-class women. Mrs Pankhurst and her suffragettes are bourgeois reformers, Michael."

"I don't have a vote," said Mickey.

Emily looked at him in mild surprise, as if this was something that had not occurred to her.

"Well, no, I don't suppose you do."

"Anyway, how did her conference take it when she tore up the constitution?"

"Many of the delegates walked out and formed the Women's Freedom League. The WFL calls for universal suffrage and goes much farther than the WSPU, demanding equal opportunities, equal pay, equality before the law. So unlike the WSPU it's really a feminist organisation. It also involves itself in industrial struggles—much like the East London group, in which, ironically, Sylia Pankhurst, another daughter of Emmeline, is involved. In fact, most of the members of the East London group are working-class women."

"How about you, Emily?"

She grinned. "I've been out of circulation for a while, but I joined the British Socialist Party when it was formed just before my...I had a little adventure in Liverpool, Mickey." Now that they were discussing politics, he was "Mickey" once more.

"I know. George mentioned it."

"*Did* he, now? Did he mention anything else?"

"Only that you had probably been lying low."

"Did he tell you that my name is not really Emily Richardson?"

He looked stunned. "No, he didn't tell us that."

"Us?"

"This was in the Great Western Hotel, while you went looking for a blouse. He told Eric and me."

"Ah, I see. Well, that wasn't so *very* indiscreet, I suppose." She sighed. "Well, it's Dorothy Bridgeman. My name."

"So what would you like me call you?"

"I'd *like* you to call me Dorothy, but I suppose for safety's sake it had better be Emily for now."

"Shall we wash the plates?"

"What time do you start work tomorrow?"

"Nine-thirty. A middle shift."

"And the next day, Sunday?"

"That's my rest day."

Oh, that white smile. "That's nice. We can spend the day

together—as long as you've nothing else arranged."

He was impressed that she would consider that he might have other plans; she was treating him as an equal, although he strongly suspected that socially he was not. "We could do that," he said, "if that's what you would like."

She grinned. "If you think I'd rather do anything else, it's perfectly clear that I have failed to impress upon you just how much I like you."

"You know, Emily," he said, choosing this moment to clear the air, "when we were at Paddington I got the impression that you liked George."

"Of course I like George. Everybody likes George—apart from the employers, that is."

"You know what I mean, Emily."

She nodded and met his eye, and it later occurred to him that she too was keen to clarify this matter. "I do." This was followed by one of her thoughtful pauses. "I suppose I have always looked upon George…fondly. He is, after all, an attractive man. To me, of course, he's also attractive politically. I now realise, however, that while he meets all the requirements of a dear friend and comrade, George would probably be a disaster as a lover. No, that's unfair. As *my* lover."

"How can you know that?"

"Well, he actually told me that his marriage is to the movement and that he has no time for any other kind. Now, to a certain extent one can take that with a pinch of salt, because there have been plenty of rumours concerning lovers he's had in the past. But the other thing is, I think that George is terrified of me."

Mickey laughed. "Why would that be?"

"In part his terror is political in nature. I know that I can be quite…*shrill* at times, and sometimes in the past I've acted impulsively. For that reason alone, George wants to keep me at arm's length. But there is also a part of his fear that is sexual. Now, a week ago—maybe even a day ago—I would have been unable to explain this, but I simply cannot imagine George and Dorothy doing what Michael and Emily have been doing this evening." She looked at him and spread her hands. "As simple as that. Now, I don't mean to suggest that with someone else George would be unable to be as…liberated as you are with me, but I certainly cannot envisage him being so with me. There does not exist between us that *frisson*, that charge of electricity that leaps between you and me and back again." She shrugged. "So I suppose you've cured me of George Sanders, Michael."

"Do you know what I think?"

"Probably."

"I think Michael and Emily should go back to the bedroom."

"You see, I was right!"

"Shall we wash the plates first?

"No."

6

They were at the breakfast table when he arrived back home at just after eight the next morning: Eric bent over his plate, two-year-old Jacko in his high chair, and Elsie turning from the gas ring, just about to sit down with her own plate.

"Well I'll be buggered," said Eric, looking up as the door opened to reveal a Mickey apparently clean, sober and wide awake.

Elsie slapped her husband's arm. "You will be if you talk like that in front of the boy." She looked to Mickey. "Come in and sit down, Mickey. You have this one and I'll do meself another."

"Don't go to any trouble, Elsie. Sorry to just barge in like this." He might be clean, sober and awake, but he was also looking a touch sheepish.

"Don't be soft," Elsie told him. "Sit yourself down." She was blond, in her late twenties, pretty and stockily built.

"You be in time for work?" Eric asked as he took a chair.

"Yeah, I'm on a middle. Plenty of time." He sliced the rasher of bacon in front of him and brought his fork to his mouth.

"You need to wash and brush up before you go in?"

"All done, mate." He concentrated on his breakfast, not looking at his brother, knowing that he would be unable to avoid asking about his whereabouts the previous night for much longer.

Eric reached for his mug of tea, brought it to his lips but set it down again without drinking, regarding Mickey in silence while he built up to his question.

Mickey nodded at Eric's tea. "Too hot for you?"

Elsie sat down with her new plate, looking with amusement from one brother to the other. Jacko sat with a spoonful of food in his fist, staring intently at Mickey as if trying to place him.

"You must have been up early, then," Eric ventured. He now took a swallow of tea.

"Pretty early. Caught a bus at ha' past six."

"Get away." Eric sniffed and risked a glance at Elsie, who good-naturedly gave him the slightest shake of her head. "You must've come quite a way, then."

"A fair distance, I suppose." He placed his knife and fork on the plate and looked across at his nephew. "Jacko! Good morning, Jacko! You were so quiet, I didn't notice you there."

Jacko, apparently finally recognising Mickey, laughed happily and placed the spoon in his mouth.

"This side of the river, or south?"

Elsie now flicked Eric with the tea cloth she had brought from the stove. "Do stop pestering him, Eric. 'Ask no questions, you'll be told no lies,' is what my mother always used to say."

Mickey grinned. "Ours too, didn't she Eric?" He had noticed over the past week or so how Elsie sometimes playfully scolded Eric, and he wondered now whether he saw in her, if only in part, a replacement for their mother.

"She did," Eric nodded, "that's true."

"What have you got on this morning, then?"

"Executive Council meeting at ten. Nothing exciting, I wouldn't think." He chewed his lip, somewhat disappointed that Mickey had succeeded in changing the subject. "Anyway, I haven't really had a chance to talk to you lately. Bit like ships in the night, us two. How have you found the first few days?"

Mickey laughed. "I was full of aches and pains after the first day on the 7s..."

"That'll be the stairs and that bag across your shoulder."

"That's right. But I'm getting used to it now."

"And the other men. How are you getting along with them?"

"Pretty well, I think. I've met a few likely lads, and I reckon that if we give it a bit of a push we could have a hundred percent membership in a few weeks' time."

"I heard how you dealt with that garage official, Mickey." Eric laughed, obviously proud of his younger brother. "And then you got half an hour's overtime out of the superintendent!"

"Who told you that?"

"Just about every conductor I meet when I ride on route 7. It must be all around the garage. You're making a name for yourself, Mickey."

Mickey nodded. "Okay..."

"Here, let me get out of your way," said Elsie. "This baby needs changing, I think."

Eric waited until she had picked up Jacko and left the kitchen and then leaned across the table, grinning at Mickey and growling, "So, no more beating about the bush: where were you?"

Mickey met his eye. "Clapham."

"But you don't know anyone in Clapham!"

"I do now."

Eric cocked his head to one side. "Someone you met on the bus?"

"No. Well, yes, sort of. She was on a bus across the street."

"But how..."

"Because we'd already met."

Eric's mouth dropped open as realisation began to dawn. "You don't mean..."

"I do. Yes, Emily."

"But you said she was too old for you."

"I've grown up in the past few days."

Eric chuckled. "Yeah, I daresay you have." For a moment, he was at a loss. "Listen, lad," he said finally, "I know she's a lovely woman, but if anything I would have thought that she's too... posh for you."

Now it was Mickey's turn to search for words, and the depth of his involvement became obvious. "That way she talks, Eric? It just sends shivers down my spine. Well, it does when she's speaking that way to me, anyway." He looked squarely at his brother. "Eric, I have never known anyone like her in my whole life."

Despite himself, Eric grunted. "In all the twenty-four years of it."

Mickey laughed happily. "She's knocked me sideways, Eric, and I don't know whether I'm coming or going."

"So you're obviously seeing her again."

"Tonight. And tomorrow's my rest day, so I'll be spending the day with her."

"In Clapham."

He shrugged. "Wherever."

"Does this mean that you'll be easing up on the union work?"

"No, I told her that after this weekend we might not be able to see each other quite so often because I've got a garage to organise. She said that she wouldn't've expected anything else."

Eric smiled across the table at his brother. He reached across and clapped a hand over his. "Well, Mickey, I wish you the best of luck," he said in his growl. "I sincerely hope it works out for you. And if you find that the union work is getting in the way of your personal happiness, just make sure you've lined up people to take some of the burden from you."

"Eric, this is Emily I'm talking about. From what you've seen of her, do you honestly think she'd let me ease up on the class struggle?"

*

Before long, they had a small organising committee, although nobody thought to call it that. Starting with Mickey, Dick Mortlake and Steve Urmshaw, they pulled in another three drivers—Charlie Adams, Andy Dixon and Frank Chambers—and two conductors—Malcolm Lewis and Billy Franklin—, taking care to ensure that they had every route in the garage covered. The original idea was Mickey's, and because none of the others had taken such an initiative they all deferred to him, even though they outranked him in seniority in both the company and the union.

To plan their strategy, they met at Dick Mortlake's flat, and this proved to be something of a revelation. Dick, it turned out, was posh. He occupied a ground-floor flat in Alexander Street, in one of those large houses which until fairly recently had contained single families, with servants' quarters in the basements. The flat's furnishings, although far from new, bordered on the luxurious: deep armchairs, a carpet that almost swallowed your feet. The only sign of Dick's personality was to be found in the bookcase, which contained the first two volumes of Marx's *Capital*, a hoard of socialist pamphlets, and a few American novels by Upton Sinclair and Jack London.

As soon as the budding organisers walked into the living room, they were reduced to silence, behaving as if Dick Mortlake had been suddenly revealed to be suffering from a horrible disease; they seemed embarrassed for him. It was left to Mickey to break the ice.

"How the fucking hell," he asked as his gaze swept the room, "can you afford this place, Dick? You must spend all your wages on rent."

Mortlake took it in his stride. "Don't pay rent, Mickey," he replied, ushering his colleagues towards a large dining table at the far end of the room. "I own it."

"Bloody 'ell," said Malcolm Lewis, a rotund Welshman. "So what are you doin' on the buses?" Malcolm's attitude was sympathetic, for it now seemed that Dick, rather than having an exotic ailment, was languishing in hospital when he could have walked out of the door at any time.

Dick shrugged. "Earning a living. My mother left me this place, but there was nothing else. I'm not really rich, you know."

"But you sound like an educated man," said big Frank Chambers. "What did you do before the buses?"

58

"Promise you won't laugh." This was directed at all of them.

"We won't laugh," vowed Charlie Adams, a tall, lean man with spectacles.

"I was a classical flautist."

"Oh." Young Billy Franklin frowned while he absorbed this information. "So you play the flaut?"

It was Dick's turn to look embarrassed. Was Billy really unaware that a flautist played the flute? Would he be insulting Billy if he corrected him? Dick's face registered indecision.

Billy rescued him. "Kidding, Dick."

Now they laughed, including Dick.

"What, in big concerts? Like at the Albert Hall?" asked an awestruck Steve Urmshaw.

Dick nodded.

"But that must be a well-paying job, Dick!" Malcolm persisted.

"Look," said Dick, "just because you see us in ties and tails in the concert hall, don't run away with the idea that we can afford to dress like that all the time. How often do you think we get work? And you'd be shocked if I told you how little I earned for a performance." He sighed, indicating that as far as he was concerned this subject was now exhausted. "Anyway, I also thought that it was about time I did something useful. So here I am."

"Oh, there's no doubt that driving a bus is *useful*..." conceded Malcolm.

Mickey winked at Dick, knowing that it was not bus-driving that he considered useful, but the trade union activity in which he was now becoming involved; but he said nothing.

While the others now sat around the large table, Andy Dixon held back, inspecting the furniture. "Well, you've got some lovely pieces here, Dick, I must say." He ran his hand over a small cabinet. "This little chiffonier is a real beauty. Mahogany, if I'm not mistaken."

"Dick, don't take your eyes off that geezer," advised Billy Franklin. "If you're not careful, you'll wake up one morning and find your furniture missing. Probably turn up on Golborne Road."

Andy, whose father ran a second-hand shop on Golborne Road, smilingly held up two fingers and joined the others at the table.

*

For the next hour, they drew up a calendar of activity, allocating recruitment activity to each man. This would be conducted at the terminal points of each route, in canteen facilities where they existed, and wherever they came across non-members on the road.

"Some days, of course," said Dick Mortlake when this phase of the meeting was drawing to a close, "I don't see a single non-member on route 7. Just the luck of the draw, I suppose."

"Well, let's not ignore existing members," counselled Mickey. "They've joined because they want to see some changes made, so we need to hammer it home to them that the sooner we get fully organised, the sooner they'll see those changes. So if you think they're keen enough, give 'em a few applications and ask 'em to do some recruitment of their own, and get the completed forms back to you."

"That's a bloody good idea," said Malcolm Lewis.

"Many hands make light work," agreed Andy Dixon.

Amid a rumble of affirmation, Mickey first passed piles of applications around the table, followed by handfuls of red buttons. "We need to try to see that every member wears the button. That will do two things: first, it will show the management that we're strong and getting stronger; second, it'll convince some of the faint-hearted among us to join up. Safety in numbers."

"Okay." Charlie Adams lifted his pile of forms and tapped them on the table, bringing them into alignment as he looked at Mickey over the top of his glasses. "Is that it?"

"Not quite. I think we need to compile a list of minor grievances for each route."

"Why minor ones?" Andy Dixon wanted to know.

"Because there's nothing we can do about the major ones, like the length of duties, until we get recognition. But there might be smaller stuff we can tackle now, even before recognition. That'll show the men what organisation can do. Don't make a big show of it, though, as if we're going solve a lot of problems before dinner time tomorrow. Just keep your ears to the ground and make a note of the little grievances as they come up and report back at the next meeting."

"Which will be...?" asked Charlie.

"Week from today? A fortnight? What do you think, lads?"

"I would say a fortnight," said Steve Urmshaw. "Same time, same place. That'll give us plenty of time to get changeovers if any of us are given late turns that day."

"Okay," Mickey brought the meeting to a conclusion. "A fortnight today, and we'll review progress, take a look at the grievances, and see if we're ready for our first branch meeting."

*

During these weeks, the generally fine weather was occasionally broken by a shower, and Mickey became acquainted with a major drawback of the X- and B-type buses. With no roof, life for the conductor was sometimes a trial, with only his cap to protect him. Usually, on these occasions, members of the public unable to find seats on the lower deck either waited for the next bus or opened their umbrellas; the company provided waterproof knee covers, but these ensured the formation of puddles on the floor, providing another hazard for the conductor. And this was not, Mickey had learned during his training, an example of company stupidity, but a result of the Metropolitan Police's refusal to countenance closed tops on the double-deckers, for fear that this would render the vehicles top-heavy and likely to topple over.

The recruitment activity was not hard, but it could become repetitive. True, it was often the case that a man would snatch a form and hurriedly complete it, telling Mickey that the only reason he hadn't done it before was because he had never been asked. But sometimes a reticent recruit would ask a question that several of his colleagues had posed before, and then Mickey would find that his reply sounded formulaic, as he had delivered it countless times before.

"What's the point of me joining before you get recognition? I'll just be wasting me money." This was the most common objection.

"We won't *get* recognition unless men like you join. Besides, there's other things the union can do for you, apart from negotiating with the company. Do you want to represent yourself if you get in trouble with the Public Carriage Office, or do you want a union officer at your side?"

Sometimes, it would take real effort to answer an objection, as when a young conductor recalled that his father had worked for the company a decade or so earlier, when an attempt to build a union had come to nothing. "How do I know that this won't end up the same way?"

"Because times have changed," Mickey replied, thankful now for that discussion with George Sanders on his first day in London. "The General has got rid of all its horse-buses, and the men we work with now are a new breed, proud of their skill and determined to improve their conditions." He threw out an arm. "And take a look about you: workers everywhere are standing up for their rights, and the

61

employers are on the retreat!"

He only met with one adamant refusal. "I don't see that you're going to make any difference," said a driver called Lenny Hawkins. "This company will do whatever it wants with us. Look what happened to me: worked five days on a Monday to Friday job with only seven and a half hours off between duties. Then, on the fifth day, when I can hardly keep my eyes open, I have an accident, and they give me a final written warning. Next time, I'll be out the door. You do something about that and I might change me mind."

Mickey could see that it would be futile to expect Hawkins to sign up now. "Okay, what duty are you talking about? Is this recent? Been no new schedules since your accident?"

"Duty number 21 on route 7—a real sod." Now that it looked as if Mickey was at least going to investigate the issue, Hawkins became less hostile. "It's not as if the company pays for its own repairs. You know we all have to pay into the so-called Accident Club?"

Mickey nodded. "Yes, sixpence a week for conductors and a bob a week for drivers. But that's something that'll have to wait until we get recognition," Mickey told him with a smile. "But duty 21 on the 7s? Let me take a look at it."

There came a point when the recruitment suddenly became easier, and this, Mickey guessed, was because the hold-outs, seeing that the majority of their colleagues were wearing the red button, sensed that this union was on the road to success.

There were one or two pleasant surprises. Ted Middleton actually asked for a form. Ted was the man who had silently disapproved of Mickey's behaviour towards Butcher that first day. But he was, Mickey had learned, more than that for, probably in an attempt to delay the arrival of trade unionism, the company had encouraged the men to elect garage representatives, and Ted was the rep at Middle Row. He was able to discuss minor problems at garage level, but according to Dick Mortlake he had met with little success. Dick didn't trust him, but Mickey saw his request for a form as an indication that even he realised that big changes were afoot.

Then, one day, he was weaving through the tables in the canteen at Liverpool Street, looking for Middle Row crews. Blue everywhere: blue busmen's jackets, blue busmen's caps, blue tobacco smoke. Feeling a hand on his arm, he looked down and saw the black driver from Shepherds Bush.

"I'll teck one of those, if yuh have one to spare," he told Mickey.

Mickey slid into the chair opposite him. "You're Joe Clough," he said, holding out his hand.

"How do you know that?" asked the black man with a smile,

shaking his hand.

"Everybody knows your name, Brother Clough."

He nodded with a smile. "And you're Mickey Rice."

"Oh?"

Joe Clough smiled again and leaned forward. "We both famous," he said. "Me because I'm black, and you because you're red." He took an application from Mickey's hand and made to stand up.

Mickey held up a hand to delay him, put a hand in his pocket and took out a red button, carefully placing it on the table before Joe Clough.

Clough picked up the badge and spent some moments scrutinising it, although this could hardly have been the first one he had seen. He looked up at Mickey and nodded. "Thank you, bredda," he said softly. He held out his palm. "Give me some more forms." He stood up and waved the forms in farewell. "You teck care, Mickey Rice."

*

At its next meeting, the organising committee found that eighty percent of Middle Row operating staff were now LPU members; on this basis, they agreed that an inaugural branch meeting should take place on Tuesday, 4 August, the day after the Summer Bank Holiday, at the Eagle public house on Ladbroke Grove. The only matter of debate concerned the timing of the meeting.

"A lot of the garages are having midnight meetings for important matters," Mickey suggested.

This met with little enthusiasm.

Charlie Adams: "There may come a time when we have to do that, but I don't think the members would thank you for it just now. Can you imagine finishing the meeting at two in the morning, tramping home to get some kip and then turning out for an early turn starting at five or six? I don't think the landlord of the Eagle would be too keen to have a couple of hundred busmen clumping up and down his stairs at that time, either."

Malcolm Lewis: "Fair point, but what's the alternative?"

Dick Mortlake: "Two meetings. One late morning and the other early evening. That should ensure that most members have the chance to get there."

Andy Dixon: "But what about us? Ain't we supposed to be there throughout, so we can make our reports?"

Mickey Rice: "If we need to, we can ask for rest-day exchanges, so we'll be available all day."

Frank Chambers: "Can you see them agreeing to that?"

Mickey Rice: "Leave it to me. I'll have a word with the superintendent. If I have a problem, I'll let you know."

Steve Urmshaw: "But how's the union gonna feel about two room-bookings instead of one?"

Mickey Rice: "I'll discuss it with Eric. Again, any problems, I'll get back to you."

Dick Mortlake: "And, of course, we'll need Eric at the meeting. He can give a report on the London-wide situation, and supervise the nominations."

Mickey Rice: "I wouldn't be happy about that, seeing as he's my brother. I'll ask him to get one of the other organisers to cover it."

Charlie Adams. "Anything else?"

Mickey Rice: "Only the grievances. I've picked up one, and I've done a bit of homework on it. Only thing is, it's really a drivers' problem, so maybe one of you should take it up with Mr Shilling."

Dick Mortlake/Charlie Adams/Andy Dixon/Frank Chambers: "Well, since you've done some work on it...As you're seeing him anyway, Mickey...We're all members, Mickey...Nah, you get on with it, mate, and if it goes wrong we'll pick up the pieces."

7

Emily Richardson sat at her desk, typing up correspondence from her shorthand as she awaited the call from Albert Stanley, who had told her that he wanted her to take the notes of a small meeting to be held later in the morning.

As so often on these slow days, she found her thoughts wandering to Mickey—and, sometimes, when she permitted them, even to Michael. After their first night together, she had expected to see him again on the Sunday, instead of which he had rapped on her door mid-evening on the Saturday. When she opened the door, there he was, a bunch of flowers in one hand and a small leather bag—containing, she assumed, a change of clothes— hanging from a strap on his shoulder. She laughed at the sight of him, not in surprise, because she had known that only he would be knocking on her door, but in delight and sheer happiness. She thought back to that moment now, and found herself smiling. She was, she realised, perilously close to being in love.

That night was much like the first, apart from the fact that

Michael, still recovering from the exertions of that debut performance and the full day's work following it, was unable to keep his eyes open beyond 1 a.m. She woke at 6.30 on the Sunday morning and, leaning on an elbow at his side, spent twenty minutes studying this young man who had made such a dramatic entry into her life. His body was compact and well-muscled. She loved to touch him, but did not, for fear that he would open his eyes before she had completed her examination. He had a full head of short, light brown hair, from which descended a steep brow and straight slender nose, on either side of which sat a large, luxuriously—almost femininely—lashed eye. When open, those eyes could startle with their brightness, although when he looked at her they appeared softer and darker, not penetrating but gentle, almost as if they were caressing her. And then his wide mouth, the lips not too full, which could cause her heart to jump with its smile. A strong, assertive chin. It was, she was forced to admit, a huge relief that, unlike some workers, he was clean, and obviously took care of himself. When he awoke, she knew that he would insist on brushing his teeth. She suspected that he had little idea how physically attractive he was. And yet this alone would have been insufficient to attract her. He was also someone who looked at the world and knew that it was wrong—indeed, how could it have been otherwise, given what she suspected of his background and upbringing?—and was gaining the ability to describe what he saw. They could talk to each other. They were comrades.

She touched his cheek and he came awake, smiling when he saw her face above him.

"A good morning kiss?" she suggested.

"I must brush my teeth." This made her kick her legs and squeal with delight.

In the afternoon, they walked to Clapham Common, anonymous among the Sunday promenaders, Mickey admiring the fine residences overlooking the green space, while Emily seemed unimpressed. They walked hand in hand, noting the incongruity of the grazing sheep and allotments on the wilder north side of the common and the trams which could be glimpsed on the distant south side, rattling down Clapham High Street. They made their way to the bandstand in the centre of the park, where a military band played for families picnicking on the grass. The lovers stayed for Holst's suite in E flat, followed by the first movement of Percy Fletcher's tone poem, "Labour and Love," the title of which they found appropriate, given their circumstances.

"You should know, however," said Emily, "that the theme is most reactionary. It concerns a man who rebels against the bestial nature of his working life, slaving away for no purpose of his own. Enter dear wifey, who pleads with him to see that his seemingly pointless toil is essential for the upkeep of her and the darling kiddies. The man is converted, and thereafter commits himself to serving his employer's interests to the best of his ability."

"In that case," said Mickey, squeezing Emily's hand, "I suggest that we take our love and labour elsewhere."

Finding an isolated tree in a quieter part of the common, they rested against its trunk and talked of their past lives. Mickey had not much to tell: left school at thirteen, worked at a succession of menial jobs until he entered a bakery at the age of seventeen, then gained employment on the trams three years later. His mother, who had worked at the giant Huntley & Palmer's biscuit factory on the King's Road in Reading, died when he was fifteen, leaving him and his brother Eric alone with their drunkard father, who worked in the cask-washing shed at, fittingly enough, Simonds Brewery. When Mickey had started at the bakery, Eric, feeling that his brother could now look after himself, moved to London, where he studied the Knowledge and became a cabdriver for a taxi firm in Finsbury Park; having become active in the Cabdrivers Union, he was elected an organiser in 1911. After Eric left home, Mickey became little more than a lodger at the small house in Tidmarsh Street where he had been born, having as little as possible to do with his father.

"Will I ever meet your father?" Emily asked, resting her head against Mickey's shoulder.

"Not if I have anything to do with it, sweetheart," he replied, and it was obvious to her that he was horrified at the very thought of such an encounter.

She straightened up and turned to face him, placing her slim right hand on his forearm. "Would you like to meet *my* father, Mickey?" she asked.

He looked at her calmly, as if wondering what she was seeking to discover about him by asking such a question. "I honestly don't know, Emily," he replied eventually. He shrugged. "Probably not."

The suggestion of a smile touched her lips. "Why do you say that?"

"Because if he were the kind of man I would like to meet, you would probably be still sharing his roof."

She nodded. "Mm. Maybe." She touched his lips with a forefinger. "Do you want me to tell you about my privileged upbringing?"

"Emily, please don't do that, because if you get me excited we'll end up getting arrested." He grinned. "Then your father will come and take you away from me."

She laughed. "Well, he could try, but I very much doubt that he would succeed, Michael."

"I can't be Michael here, Emily. And please don't look at me that way."

"Never?"

"*Always*. Just not here."

Her teasing over, she patted his hand. "So do you want me to tell you?"

"Of course I do."

"Very well." She sighed. "I was born in Bristol. My father owns— or is a major shareholder in—a shipping company. A rather big one. Freight. Plying between Bristol and, more recently London, and the colonies. He brings in colonial produce—rubber, mahogany, oil and other minerals—and carries British manufactured goods on the return journey. My mother is Portuguese."

"Ah."

"What?"

"Your complexion, your eyes."

"Yes. She comes from a business family—somewhat in decline— in Lisbon, although I think she has some colonial blood. My parents met when my father was on a business trip to Portugal."

"Was their marriage a..."

"Commercial arrangement? Not at all, at least not as far as they were concerned. My father is deeply in love with my mother, and I think she feels the same way. Good for them. Not quite so good for little Dorothy, however. I was brought up to believe that I would end up being married to someone rather like my father, following which my job would be to produce children—sons by preference—for him. By studying my parents' friends, I could see that such marriages were little more than commercial contracts, and almost always loveless." She smiled. "Engels quotes Fourier at one stage, saying that, just as two negatives make an affirmative in grammar, so in the morality surrounding the bourgeois marriage two prostitutions are presented as virtue.

"Anyway, the education I received was tailored to this end. In other words, it was not much of an education at all. I have an older brother, and I simply could not believe that the education Edwin received was being denied to me simply on the grounds of gender. So in my late teens I simply put my foot down. No education, no marriage. Eventually, my parents agreed. I came to London, initially to stay with an aunt, my mother's sister, and enrolled in Bedford College. You know it?"

He shook his head.

"The first college for women, founded in 1849. By the time I got there, it was located in Regent's Park. A few years before, it had become part of the University of London." She screwed her eyes shut and shook her head. "You have no *idea* how difficult it was! Men, you see, are prepared for university, as they receive an adequate education at the previous levels. But women? Most of us were floundering at the outset, and so had to study things that we should have mastered—mistressed?—much earlier."

"What subject were you studying?"

"Biology."

"Ah."

She grinned. "Yes, I understand what you mean by that, but you're mistaken. You see, I'd read Darwin's *The Origin of Species*, and it simply changed my whole outlook. The subject fascinated me. Of course, that led to a few arguments at the college, as many members of the administration and the faculty still wore religious blinkers. Anyway, one thing, as it very often does, led to another. A fellow student pointed me in the direction of Engels' *The Origin of the Family, Private Property and the State*, and I managed to get a copy of the American edition—it still hasn't been published in this country—from the Social Democratic Federation. That, in turn, whetted my appetite for more Engels and, of course, Marx, and it wasn't long before the bourgeois caterpillar was turning into the socialist butterfly you see before you. Hah! I was free!"

"How did your family take all this?"

"Well, they didn't know. At first anyway. But events over the past few years changed all that. My father is a member of the International Shipping Federation, which until a couple of years ago refused to employ union members. On my infrequent visits home, the talk at the dinner table inevitably turned to industrial matters." She turned to Mickey, seeking his understanding. "Well, I did *try* to hold my peace, but it was just impossible. So the truth came out."

"When did you finish at the college?"

"I didn't. On the one hand, I was being drawn into political activity, and on the other life at the college—I was a residential student—was just too claustrophobic. So in 1903 I left. I told my parents that I was working as a freelance journalist—not a total lie, as I wrote for several socialist journals, although the payments I received weren't enough to live on. From time to time my father would send me money, so I survived. But it wasn't until a couple of years ago that the whole truth came out. My mother was at a complete loss to understand what had happened to me, and may have considered having me put away."

"Put away?"

"In an asylum." She grasped Mickey's hand. "Perhaps surprisingly, my father was rather more understanding. He knew he would be unable to change me. You know, although he's very much on the other side of the barricades, I think he's been closely enough involved in the industrial turmoil of the past few years to have developed an understanding of people like me. Did I tell you that he met Tom Mann? Yes, it was at the height of the seamen's strike, and he seemed surprised to find that, leaving aside his ideas, Tom was such a decent man." She shrugged. "Anyway, perhaps in the hope that I would undergo a dramatic reconversion, he's as much as told me that I'm basically free to go my own way, the unspoken condition being that I bring no dishonour on the family name." She chuckled. "In which case, he would approve of the fact that I'm now Emily Richardson. He still sends me money, but I place it in an account that I never touch, although if the movement is ever desperate for funds I may be persuaded to break into it."

That evening, before leaving for home, Mickey searched through her collection of books and asked if he could borrow *The Origin of the Family* and the Darwin.

In the weeks since then, she saw Mickey whenever he was available. Initially, he had thought that he would have to use the occasional rest day in order to pursue his organising activity, but as it turned out he and his comrades were able to make sufficient progress without any of them making this sacrifice. This, however, did not mean that her access to him was very greatly improved, as it was only infrequently that his rest day fell on a weekend, and so apart from these welcome occasions, their time together was limited to those evenings when he finished sufficiently early for him to get to Clapham at a reasonable hour, and when his duty the following day started late enough for him to be able to travel home in time for a hurried breakfast before dashing to the garage to sign on. And then she found that there were sometimes evenings when, even though his shift would allow it, he was unavailable due to the fact that he had decided to join a BSP study group at the home of a lawyer in Gloucester Terrace.

"Well, that's very commendable, Mickey," she said, hiding her disappointment. "How did you come to meet this lawyer?"

"Through a driver at the garage: Dick Mortlake. He's a Marxist, too."

"The flautist?"

"You know him?"

"I came across him once or twice before I had to disappear. The

69

last I heard, he was with a little group in the East End. Tell me, are there any other budding Marxists at Middle Row?"

"Not in our organising group, anyway."

"Why do your sound so sure?"

"We meet at Dick's flat. Apart from me, no one bothers to look at the bookcase."

Ah, Mickey! Michael! What a find!

*

"Whenever you're ready, Miss Richardson."

Albert Stanley stood at the door of his inner office. Just under forty, he was a tall, slim man whose greying hair was receding; always smartly dressed, he wore a dark suit, a wing-tipped white shirt and a dark floral tie with a diamond stickpin.

"Yes, Mr Stanley." Emerging from her reverie, Emily shuffled the pile of correspondence she had typed, placed it in the drawer of her desk, picked up her shorthand pad and two sharp pencils, and walked to Stanley's inner office. Ever the gentleman, he waved her in before re-entering himself and closing the door.

"Where would you like me to sit, Mr Stanley?"

"That, Miss Richardson, is a very good question." His eyes roamed the office. Clearly, he would have preferred to station himself behind his large walnut desk, but where then would his note-taker have sat? And there was another consideration. "This meeting, you see, is not very formal, and the last thing I wish is to have the two men I shall be seeing struck dumb by the magnificence of my station. I want them to speak freely."

Stanley could be such a humorous man, and Emily could not help liking him. "Might I then suggest the small meeting room down the corridor, sir?"

He clapped his hands. "Excellent, Miss Richardson! Have my two guests arrived in the outer office? I must confess that I didn't notice when I called you. No? In which case, tell the girls to send them down to us as soon as they arrive. In the meantime, you and I will make ourselves comfortable in the small meeting room."

The meeting room was indeed small. Stanley frowned as he entered. The plain, ash-blond table at its centre could seat six; the chairs were straight-backed and equally plain. He moved one chair from each side and placed them against the wall, then so arranged the remainder that he would be sitting opposite the two guests, who would be close together, while Emily would sit on the same side as he, but at the opposite end of the table.

"You know," he said, leaning back in his chair, hands on his stomach as he examined the ceiling, "I don't think I've ever been in this room before."

"Or will be again, sir?" she ventured a small joke.

He laughed. "Well, these chairs are not particularly comfortable, so let's hope this meeting is a short one." He turned his chair to the left and regarded Emily silently for a few moments. "If I may say so, Miss Richardson," he purred, his tone accented by a slight American burr, "you appear happy."

Albert Stanley was not only humorous but, when he wanted to be, charming. Emily reminded herself that he was married to a lady from New York and had two young daughters. But what could he mean? "Well," she advanced tentatively, "I find my duties here very agreeable, and..."

He shook his head. "Well, it's nice that you do, of course, but that's not what I meant." He narrowed his eyes, tilting his head to one side. "When I called you from the outer office, you were smiling."

Taken by surprise, she could do nothing else but laugh. "Oh, I may have been. A little day-dreaming, I suppose."

"Possibly." He smiled pleasantly. "Are you able to day-dream without making mistakes in your work?"

"I won't know that until I check the work, Mr Stanley. I'm sorry."

"What? Never apologise for being happy, Miss Richardson! And I'm sure your work will prove to be flawless. Anyway,"—he tapped the table-top with his fingers—"I hope he deserves you, whoever he is."

She now surprised herself and her employer. "That's possibly why I was smiling, Mr Stanley."

He laughed aloud at this, but was brought up short by the entry of Miss McKewan, his personal secretary.

"Mr Shilling and Mr Butcher, sir," she announced, ushering the two men into the room.

Albert Stanley was immediately transformed, his light mood replaced by a more serious, although not yet stern, manner. "Mr Shilling," he announced for Emily's sake, gesturing to the better-dressed of the two, "is our garage superintendent at Middle Row, and Mr Butcher is one of his garage officials. Miss Richardson will be taking a note of our discussion, gentlemen."

Middle Row! Emily swallowed hard, but succeeded in maintaining an outward calm, her expression scrupulously neutral.

Stanley folded his hands on the desk and sat with a straight back as he regarded his two employees. "Let me say at the outset, gentlemen, that this is something which would normally be dealt with in the first instance by Mr Watts at Grosvenor Road. However, Mr Watts sought my advice and I, finding that the matter touched upon a question of...policy, asked that he allow me to speak to you both. And this explains the delay in resolving the case, for which I seek your understanding, as of late there have been so many demands on my time." He looked at the sallow Butcher who, although not smart, had probably taken more than usual care over his appearance. "If, though, I find at the end of our discussion that disciplinary action is required, I will indeed refer it back to Mr Watts for his attention. Is this acceptable to you both?"

Both men nodded, Butcher murmuring a "Sir."

"Very well. Now, Mr Butcher, you have filed a complaint against Mr Shilling, and so maybe I should start by asking you to state your case."

A nervous cough from Butcher. "When I forwarded the complaint to Mr Watts, I gave a full written report..."

"Yes, I know you did, and if this were a disciplinary hearing that's undoubtedly what we would be relying on. But here we are, three chaps together, so let's just hear it in your own words."

A clearing of the throat. "Well, sir, I had occasion to speak to a young conductor about the badge he was wearing—a union badge."

"Was this the dreaded red button about which we have been hearing so much?"

Having detected no irony in Stanley's words, and feeling now that he had a sympathetic audience, Butcher relaxed somewhat. "It wasn't *just* that the boy was wearing the badge, sir. Oh, no. This was his first day on the *job*. He'd only been cleared by the PCO the afternoon before. Believe me, sir, I've been behind the counter for a few years now, and I think I know trouble when I see it. This boy was *trouble*. Since then, of course, he's been actively recruiting for the union."

"Well, Mr Butcher, as deplorable as that may be, I think we have to confine ourselves to the events of that morning, the events that gave rise to your complaint."

"Yes, sir. But you'll never guess who his brother turns out to be! None other than Eric Rice, the union organiser!"

"Were you aware of that at the time, Mr Butcher?" Stanley maintained a level tone, seemingly deeply interested in Butcher's version of events.

"Well, no, sir. No, I take your point, Mr Stanley."

Stanley inclined his head. "Might I ask how you came by that knowledge?"

"Well, sir, as a matter of fact it was Mr Shilling what told me."

"*Really?* So Mr Shilling was already aware of this at the time."

In his excitement, Butcher's grammar went to pieces. "He musta bin, sir, 'cos it was later that morning when he told me!" He briefly turned to Shilling in a "Got you now!" gesture.

"This was after he had met the conductor—whose name, presumably is also Rice?"

Emily broke the point of her pencil, placed it on the table and picked up the other.

"That's right, sir."

"Very well. Now can you tell me how that meeting came about? It was at your instigation?"

"Yes, sir, I told Rice to see the garage superintendent when he made his part pay-in later that morning. I didn't think he would at first, but he musta changed his mind." He sighed. "And this really was the worst part of the whole thing, because it turned out that Rice demanded an overtime payment for attending the meeting! No, the worst thing was that Mr Shilling here"—a sideways jerk of the thumb—"*agreed*. He then called me in and told me to make sure it was paid."

"And how did you feel about that, Mr Butcher?"

"Well, I was livid, wasn't I? Mr Shilling and me is supposed to be on the same side. You know, on the management side of the fence. And here he was, coming down on me in front of a conductor still wet behind the ears. What authority do I have over Rice after that?"

"Yes, I see your point, Mr Butcher, and maybe I'll say something about that a little later. Now, can you tell me if other members of staff display the red button on their uniforms?"

"Yes, they do. At the time, it was only a minority, but since this business, and since Rice has been recruiting for the union, most of 'em do."

"Have you ever asked any other member of staff to see Mr Shilling for wearing the red button?"

"Well...no, sir. But I could tell from this one's attitude..."

Stanley held up a palm. "Alright, that's enough. Now, Mr Shilling, thank you for your patience. It seems to me that the nub of Mr Butcher' complaint is that you first of all took no action against Conductor Rice, and that you compounded this by agreeing to his demand for an overtime payment and then—and this is a far greater sin in the eyes of Mr Butcher—you humiliated him in *front* of Conductor Rice. What do you say to all of this?"

James Shilling had been sitting throughout this interview as if he had little to fear, unmoved even by Butcher's occasional display of truculence in front of the managing director. "Thank you, Mr Stanley," he said now in his soft West Country tones. "Why did I take no action against Conductor Rice for wearing the red button? For the same reason that I have taken no action against others who wear it."

Butcher, having completely misinterpreted the direction in which the discussion was going, could not control himself. "Because you're too soft!" he exploded.

Holding up a hand to stay Shilling, Stanley held Butcher in his gaze for a full five seconds. "There will be no more of that, Mr Butcher. Do you hear me?" Although his voice was still level, there was now steel in it. He turned to Shilling. "Please continue, Mr Shilling."

"I took no such action because the company has issued no instruction on this matter. That, on the policy level, was my reason."

"Was there another?"

"Indeed." Shilling sighed and placed his hands on the table. "It is perfectly obvious that the LPU is making a very determined attempt to organise the operating staff in this company. In the past few months, its membership must have doubled. This being the case, it seems to me that we're sitting on a powder keg. It has been my concern—and still is—that the flame that touches off that keg should not be lit at Middle Row, and an unthinking attempt to ban the red button might lead to such an explosion."

"And the overtime payment?"

"Mr Butcher has told only part of the story. Conductor Rice and I had a fairly lengthy discussion, during which he readily conceded that had he been called to my office for a legitimate reason there would be no question of an overtime payment—until, at least, the union had been granted negotiating rights and such payments were agreed. In this case, however, he considered that Mr Butcher's instruction had been illegitimate, as there was no company ban on the red button, and thus his demand for an overtime payment was reasonable."

"This sounds like a clever lad you've got on your hands, Mr Shilling." Stanley's eyes danced with amusement.

"Ohhh, *very*," Shilling replied.

Emily could not stop herself gulping, but continued her rapid script.

"And so you granted the payment. But was it necessary to humiliate Mr Butcher?"

"Again, Mr Butcher has told only part of the story, neglecting to mention that after I issued the instruction, he began to disagree with me. Now, Mr Butcher cannot have it both ways: if we're both on the management side, he should not seek to challenge my authority in front of a conductor. So I doubled the payment to thirty minutes, sir."

"But—and I know this doesn't form part of Mr Butcher's complaint—why did you take no action against this conductor when you knew that his brother was employed full-time by the union?"

"And cause the explosion I'm anxious to avoid?"

"Alright, I think I've heard enough." Stanley turned to Butcher, hands clasped before him. "You've heard Mr Shilling say, Mr Butcher, that the company has issued no policy prohibiting the wearing of the red button. Can it be that he is wrong? Have *you* seen any such instruction?"

"No, sir," replied a dull Butcher, "but I know people at Tilling's, and they..."

Now Stanley was on fire. "Yes," he roared, "I *know*"—banging the table, causing Emily to jump—"what they're doing in that company, and I think we'll all live to see the day when they learn the error of their ways. Are you employed by Thomas Tilling, Mr Butcher? Are you?"

"No, sir."

"Would you *like* to be?" Glancing up, Emily noticed the right corner of Shilling's mouth twitch as he suppressed a smile.

"No, sir."

"Then you should pay less attention to their employment practices and more to those of the General. I, Mr Butcher, am a member of the Conservative and Unionist Party. *Look* at me when I'm talking to you! Do you think I welcome the prospect of inviting the London and Provincial Union of Licensed Vehicle Workers to sit across the table with me and seek to change the way this company is run? *Do* you?" He sighed as the storm passed and gestured at Shilling. "But your garage superintendent is right: it is going to happen. Moreover, his way of dealing with this situation is to my mind eminently sensible. We want no explosions, Mr Butcher, and we want no actions by garage officials which will inflame the situation and encourage the more extreme element. Do I make myself clear?"

It was a crestfallen Butcher, barely understanding what had just happened, who silently nodded.

"It will not surprise you, then, to learn that your complaint will not be referred back to Grosvenor Road. It is dead, finished. And I trust, Mr Butcher, that you will learn from this discussion and will adopt a more thoughtful approach in your dealings with the staff, if you truly want to gain their respect. When in doubt, consult your garage superintendent, as he at least appears to understand what is required. Thank you for your attendance, gentlemen. I bid you good morning."

Butcher got to his feet and turned towards the door, anxious to escape, but Shilling remained where he was.

"Is there something else, Mr Shilling?"

"There is," replied Shilling, "a matter on which I would appreciate your advice." He smiled. "It's not a million miles away from what we've been discussing."

*

"I take it you're a West Country man, Mr Shilling," Stanley remarked.

"I am, sir, but I've been up here twenty years."

"When I first returned to this country, some people mistook my accent for West Country." He smiled. "Had to tell them that I picked it up in a place a little farther west." He tapped the table. "Look, before we go any further, I'd like to thank you for speaking so plainly just now. I think your approach to the trade-union question is eminently sensible." He grinned. "I think thirty minutes' overtime was a little extravagant, though."

"Quite possibly, sir," Shilling replied, knowing that he was not being admonished.

"Alright, how can I help you now?"

"Are you sure, Mr Stanley, that you want me to remain?" Emily asked.

"I don't see why not, Miss Richardson. Any objections, Mr Shilling? No? Good." Suddenly, he turned to look at Emily. "Oh, how thoughtless of me. Am I trespassing on your lunch break?"

"No, that's quite alright, Mr Stanley."

"Good girl." He looked across the table. "So, Mr Shilling, please proceed."

"A few days ago, I had another visit from Conductor Rice."

"Did you, indeed?" Stanley's elbows were on the table as he leaned forward, indicating that Shilling had returned to a subject in which he was keenly interested.

"I did. It seems that he had been approached by a driver to whom I administered a final warning a few months ago following an accident."

Stanley's expression changed, his brow clouding. "Ah, now, Mr Shilling, that is another kettle of fish entirely. I do *not* want these union people interfering in the company's disciplinary system."

"But he was seeking to interfere—if, indeed, that is the word—in rather more than that. It was his case that this particular accident was caused, at least in part, by the fact that the driver, Hawkins by name, was fatigued by the onerous duty on which he had been working all week."

"And was it onerous?"

Shilling shook his head in disbelief rather than implying an answer in the negative. "It is, sir, if you'll forgive me"—he paused, glancing at Emily, and then silently mouthed— "a bastard."

Stanley laughed aloud at this and turned to Emily. "Mr Shilling considers this duty to be a bastard, Miss Richardson." He looked back at Shilling. "I'm sure Miss Richardson must have come across the word, Mr Shilling."

"I have overheard it on occasion, Mr Stanley," Emily confirmed, thereby pleasing Stanley and putting Shilling at his ease.

Stanley turned up his palms. "You see? Very well, but tell me precisely in what sense this duty might be considered illegitimate."

Shilling smiled broadly, enjoying this discussion with his managing director. "It is a very long spreadover on route 7, our busiest road..."

"How long?"

"Sixteen hours and thirty minutes."

"Good grief. So only seven hours and thirty minutes off between duties. Why do our people schedule such things?"

"I took the liberty of putting this question to the schedules compiler, sir, and the reply I received was that unless the mileage was to be reduced, any shortening of this particular duty would result in the requirement for an additional duty."

Stanley touched his chin with the fingers of his right hand. "Ah, well, that must always be a consideration, I suppose." He paused for thought. "But tell me, how many days had this driver been working this duty?"

"This was his fifth and final day, sir, a Friday."

"And at what point during the day did the accident occur?"

"During the second spell, sir, quite close to Hawkins' completion of the duty."

"Are you able to recall the circumstances of the accident?"

"Yes, sir. Moderate to heavy traffic on Oxford Street. A private car stopped suddenly in front of Hawkins' bus. He swung the wheel to avoid a collision, but clipped the offside corner or the car, resulting in damage to the tune of ten pounds."

"To the car?"

"Yes; the bus also suffered a buckled mudguard which had to be replaced."

"I see." Stanley shook his head, as if to clear it. "But I fail to see where this is taking us, Mr Shilling. This is surely something which could have been discussed at Grosvenor Road."

"Ah, but there's more, sir, leading us onto what you referred to earlier as a question of policy. You see, young Rice not only thinks that the penalty received by Hawkins should be reduced, but has suggested that we jointly conduct a survey of all accidents occurring in the past year, with the object of determining whether the nature of the duties worked at the time of the accidents could have had a bearing on the accidents themselves."

"Well, of all the..." Stanley's face had reddened.

"Allow me to say, sir, that I have found that it is sometimes a mistake to dismiss Rice's arguments out of hand. For example, I decided to test his theory, so I investigated just half a dozen accidents."

"Oh?" Stanley's interest was rekindled.

Shilling nodded. "And if these six cases are representative, I would concede that Rice has a case. Three of the six concerned inexperienced drivers, one really fitted no category, but the other two occurred on what we might call onerous duties."

"Mm. Now tell me, how does Rice propose that an investigation be conducted?"

"His proposal is that he and I sit down with a list of accident dates, copies of the rotas and schedules, and jointly go through the exercise."

"Well, look, Shilling, I would not be at all happy allowing the union to encroach on what we might call our territory in this manner. Surely it's our people who should be conducting such an exercise."

"That is precisely what I said to him, Mr Stanley."

"And how did he respond to that?"

"He said, 'In that case, Mr Shilling, why haven't they done it already?'"

"And surely it should be conducted at Grosvenor Road."

Shilling nodded, a small smile on his lips. "Yes, sir, I also made that point."

Stanley sighed and placed a hand over his eyes, spacing his fingers so that he could see his garage superintendent. "Come on, tell me what he said to that."

"He said that our people at the Grosvenor Road office would have an interest in minimising the connection between accidents and arduous duties. Hence the need for the involvement of a union representative."

"Do you think he has a point?" The expression on Stanley's face indicated a suspicion that he might not like the answer to this question.

"I do, sir, and so, I think, do you."

Stanley was quiet for a moment, a hand clasped over his mouth as, deep in thought, he regarded the table top in front of him. Then he let his hand fall as a laugh escaped him. "You know, I'm beginning to see how a relationship with the union might not be *entirely* to the detriment of the company. Conductor Rice is right: our own people should have been thinking along these lines long ago. So maybe the presence of the union will provide the jolt they need. Now don't get me wrong: I'm sure that in the months and years ahead, we will have to face many unreasonable demands, but if our schedule compilers are forced to be more creative, if our managers are forced to actually *manage*, that will surely be to our advantage."

"Indeed, sir."

"However, let's not run away with the idea that all union people at local level are going to be as bright as Rice." He paused and leaned forward, eyes narrowed. "I don't suppose there is any possibility that he could be persuaded to work for us, is there?"

"He does work for us, sir."

"No, I mean in the sense of representing the company rather than the union."

"No, sir. On the one hand, I feel that his commitment to the union is in large part ideological, and in that sense Mr Butcher may have something of a point. On the other hand, if his activity is occasionally going to benefit the company, it will be far cheaper to leave him where he is, on a conductor's wages."

"Ha! Mr Shilling, I think you may be just as clever as Conductor Rice!"

"High praise indeed, Mr Stanley."

Stanley drew himself up, prepared to draw proceedings to a close. "Alright. Look, I don't want to make major concessions even before we've signed an agreement with the union, so tell him that Grosvenor Road will undertake this investigation into accidents at Middle Row. There will be no union involvement. I will ensure that the investigation is conducted speedily and fairly and one of my managers here will be checking the results. You can tell Mr Rice that, if it will prove cost-effective, that onerous duty on route 7 will be replaced with something more civilised. Does that sound alright to you?"

"It does, sir, thank you. There is, however, one last thing."

"Go on."

"Rice and his colleagues are preparing to hold a couple of meetings regarding the formation of their own branch of the union. He has some kind of ad hoc committee and wants to ensure that its members—eight, including himself—are available to attend both meetings, which will be held on the same day. He has requested that where necessary the men be granted rest-day exchanges to facilitate this."

Stanley held up his hands. "Is this so novel a request? Don't men routinely ask to change their rest day?"

"Yes, sir, but this is for union business."

"Ah, I see. But that should not concern us, Mr Shilling. So do it, if it's possible." A mischievous grin appeared on his face. "In fact, you might ask Butcher to make the arrangements." His eyes narrowed once more. "As a matter of interest, do you have anyone who reports to you on the activities of Mr Rice and his committee?"

Shilling smiled. "I do, sir."

"Good man. You might also ensure that he attends both of those meetings. Oh, and by the way…"

"Sir?"

"This Hawkins. A good man?"

"Not a bad one, sir. There are a couple of other entries on his record, otherwise I wouldn't have given him a final warning. Come to think of it, I think those previous entries arose following altercations with Mr Butcher."

Stanley smiled. "In which case, you might consider reducing Hawkins' final warning to a first warning."

When Shilling had left, Stanley turned to Emily. "Now, Miss Richardson, you go off and get some lunch. Be in no rush to type up the notes. My intention was what they should act as an *aide memoire*, but to be honest I think it will be quite some time before I forget this meeting. I just hope it wasn't too boring for you."

Emily stood and held her shorthand pad at her breast. "Not at all," she replied with a smile. "I found it quite fascinating, Mr Stanley, quite fascinating."

8

By 11.15, the meeting room on the first floor of the Eagle was almost full—of smoke and noise as well as men. Ben Smith sat at the small table at the head of the room and watched as the men filed in, entering their names in the attendance book that Dick Mortlake had placed on a table just inside the door. Those attending the first meeting fell into three categories: some had just finished the first spell of a spreadover duty, others would be signing on during the afternoon, and a few were sacrificing a few hours of their rest-days to attend this important meeting. The evening meeting would be attended by crews who had worked early or middle turns that day or were on their rest-days. At Ben's suggestion, Mickey, Dick Mortlake and the rest of the organising committee occupied chairs in the front row, ready to make their own brief speeches or respond to points raised from the floor.

Ben now rose from his chair and rapped his knuckles on the table. He stood before them, broad chested and erect, and waited for the noise to subside. Inevitably, as all eyes were directed to him, he overheard some murmurs of "Who's this geezer?" and "Ain't seen 'im before."

"Well, brothers," he said with a broad smile, "let's begin by clearing up that mystery. My name's Ben Smith, and I'm a full-time organiser for your union, the London and Provincial Union of Licensed Vehicle Workers. Ordinarily, Eric Rice—who is probably less of a stranger to you than I am—would be standing here instead of me, but his brother is one of your members. He's still a bit of a new boy, so it's possible that you don't all know Mickey Rice..."

A chorus of cheers told him that he was mistaken.

"But anyway, Mickey suggested that it wouldn't be right for this meeting to be presided over by his own brother, and Eric agreed. So here I am."

"You know anything about buses?" someone called out.

"Probably not as much as you, brother," Ben responded with good humour, "so it's just as well that I'm not here to *talk* about buses. My job today is to ascertain whether you want to form a branch of the LPU and, if you do, to explain what officers you'll need to elect and what their jobs will be. After we've done that, you can talk about whatever you like, including buses, because my job will be done."

"Then let's get on with it, Brother Smith," suggested a man at the back, "because some of us want to put our feet up for an hour before we go back for our second half!"

"Suits me fine, brother. First on the order of business is to get ourselves a minute secretary. Every meeting of the branch must be minuted, and the reading and approval of those minutes will be the first item of business at your next meeting. Normally, the minutes would be taken by your Branch Secretary, but we won't have one until the conclusion of tonight's meeting. So who do you want to jot down the minutes of this meeting? It doesn't *have* to be the same person who minutes tonight's meeting, although that would be convenient, if he's available. So come, on, brothers, give me a name."

Mickey threw up his hand. "I nominate Dick Mortlake."

"That bloke could write a book," commented an anonymous joker, "let alone the minutes."

"Are you seconding the nomination, brother?"

"Seconded."

"Bring your chair up here, Brother Mortlake, and..." Ben dipped into the briefcase at his feet, drawing out a marbled ledger, "cop hold of this."

Dick first went to the door and recovered the attendance book before joining Ben Smith at the top table, where he ran his eye down the columns of names.

"The first major question, brothers: do you wish to form your own branch of the London and Provincial Union of Licenced Vehicle Workers?"

This was greeted by a roar of affirmation.

"Alright, but we must do it properly: mover and seconder!"

"Moved!"

"Seconded!"

"All those in favour, please show."

The same roar, accompanied by a forest of arms.

"Brothers, we need tellers to count the vote, so that it can be properly recorded. Don't forget that there's a second meeting this evening."

"But that's going to vote the same way as this one!" protested the man who had questioned Ben Smith's knowledge of buses.

"Maybe so, but the votes still have to be counted."

"There's surely an easier way to do this," Dick Mortlake suggested mildly. "Why don't you ask if there are any votes against or abstentions, Brother Smith?"

"All those against?"

None.

"Abstentions?"

None.

"In which case," said Dick, "The vote is 62 for and none against."

"Might a mere mortal like me," asked Ben with a wide grin, "ask how you know that?"

Dick held up the attendance book. "I counted the names," he said, provoking a chorus of cheers and laughter.

"I know that I'm supposed to be strictly impartial," Ben told his audience, "but I have one piece of advice to impart: whatever you do, brothers"—he clapped Dick on the shoulder—"don't let this one go!"

*

For the most part, the meeting proceeded smoothly. The members of the ad hoc organising committee made brief reports, following which Malcolm Lewis was nominated for the post of Branch Chairman, Dick Mortlake secured the sole nomination, to no one's surprise, for the position of Branch Secretary, and it was suggested that the six remaining members of the ad hoc committee be adopted en bloc as the Branch Committee. This went through, following which Mickey suggested that if there were any volunteers, they would be welcome to join the committee if they were nominated, seconded and duly voted in. When the meeting agreed to this, Lenny Hawkins, who had been one of the most reluctant recruits, stood up. "If the men are prepared to put up with me," he said, "I'm willing to give it a go." Another vote of 62-0.

"Anybody else?" Ben asked, looking around the room.

Ben's attention was drawn to a short, stocky man who, sitting in the middle of the room, was glancing from side to side and biting his lip, obviously in two minds as to whether he should offer himself. This was Ted Middleton. Ben gave him a few more seconds and then declared branch committee nominations closed.

"Well, brothers," he announced, "I think that brings our deliberations to a conclusion. Any other business?"

Lenny Hawkins stood up again. "Yes, Mister Chairman," he said. "As we're here anyway, why don't you take nominations for a shop steward?"

"Yes, we could do that," Ben replied, "but it's maybe a bit premature to elect a shop steward or garage representative before the union's recognised by the company."

"Why wait?" said Hawkins. "Recognition can't be far off. Are you saying we have to wait until the agreement's signed, then hold another meeting just to elect our representative?"

"No, once we're recognised and the company's cooperating with us, you can put up a notice calling for nominations, and if there's more than one you can hold a ballot."

"I agree with Lenny," said Steve Urmshaw. "Let's do it now, so that we can send Mick...so that we can send the successful candidate into Mr Shilling's office the day after recognition is agreed."

All but one in the meeting seemed to agree with this proposal. That one was Ted Middleton, who now stood up and walked to the front of the hall, crying "Point of order, Mr Chairman, point of order." He then began to address the meeting. "This vote is not proper..."

"Brother," Ben Smith cut him short, "if you're raising a point of order, you should address your remarks to the chairman, not to the meeting. Now, what's your point of order?"

"You can't hold an election for a garage representative," said Middleton, speaking in a West Country accent, "because we've already got one." He jabbed a thumb at his own chest. "Me! Okay, once the company recognises the union, we'll have to have an election, but until then I'm still the rep!"

"What have you ever done for us?" demanded Lenny Hawkins.

Middleton's lower lip was trembling. "What *could* I do for you, with no backup? If you vote me back in after we get recognition, you'll see the difference! If Mr Shilling knows that he'll have to justify himself at Grosvenor Road if he's unreasonable with me, you'll soon see a change in him!"

Ben Smith, although knowing that the debate was straying beyond the bounds of a simple point of order, seemed content to let it continue for a while.

"If you knew you couldn't do anything for us, why did you take the job on?" asked Charlie Adams.

"And why, in that case, do you spend so much time in the office, drinking tea with Shilling while some poor bugger on the spare list has to cover your duty?" demanded Frank Chambers.

Ben Smith now held up his hands. "Brothers, brothers, brothers," he entreated, "I have to call you to order. If you're going to pull each other to pieces, the only victor will be the employer. Let's return to that point of order. We've been told that there is a garage representative, recognised by the company, who has the right to raise problems with the local management on your behalf. Is that correct?"

A grumbling, moaning sound rolled off the meeting.

"Very well, but the proposal put forward is that you now take nominations for a *union* representative who will take office once recognition of the union is secured." He turned to Middleton. "That means, brother, that you can continue in your role until that time. Furthermore, if you're nominated, there's nothing to stop you standing for the post of *union* representative. The point of order is therefore denied and I now call for nominations for the *union's* garage representative."

"Mickey Rice! Mickey Rice! Mickey Rice!" The name must have been called thirty or forty times.

"All we need, brothers, is one nomination and one seconder."

"Moved!"

"Seconded!"

Middleton now lost control. "And you have the nerve to tell me I've done nothing for you!" he protested, his eyes glassy with tears. He threw an arm in Mickey's direction. "Tell me what *he's* done for you! He hasn't been on the job ten minutes! And he's not even a driver!"

Throughout all this, Mickey had sat with his head bowed, gazing at the floor between his feet. His head now came up, his eyes blazing with anger as he got to his feet.

"Hey, Mickey! Sit down and let me deal with this!" Once again, it was Lenny Hawkins, the reluctant recruit transformed into a zealot. He strode to the front of the hall and stood opposite Middleton, the top table between them. Ben Smith, rather than ruling Middleton's rhetorical points out of order, allowed the drama to run its course.

"What has Mickey Rice done for us?" Lenny repeated Middleton's question. "I'll tell you, brothers. You remember that accident I had a few months back, that got me a final warning? Mr Shilling tells me that that has been reduced to a first warning! Why? Did Ted Middleton burst into his office, demanding justice for Lenny Hawkins?" He looked at his audience and chuckled. "No, it was Mickey Rice who got my penalty reduced. And do you know what caused my accident? Duty fucking 21..."

"Language, brother, language!" objected Ben Smith.

"Duty 21 on route 7. Anybody familiar with it?"

A chorus of groans came in reply.

"Well, brothers, Mr Shilling also told me that we'll be getting new schedules soon, and that particular duty will be a damn sight shorter than it is now. And not only that! Mickey Rice has convinced Mr Shilling that several accidents have been caused by these irksome duties, and so Grosvenor Road been told—by none other than the high and mighty Mr Albert Stanley himself!—to do everything they can to bring in a few changes. So does the fact that he's a conductor prevent him from representing us drivers? What's Mickey Rice done for *us*?" He clapped a palm to his forehead, provoking cheers and laughter from the men.

"Oh," he continued, "he hasn't been on the job ten minutes, and he's *young*! Let me tell you, brothers, I used to go to some of the meetings Ted Middleton called. And what I noticed was that whenever a young feller would make a suggestion, no matter how sensible it was, one of the grey-heads—this was *experience* speaking—would take a puff on his pipe and tell us that the idea was impractical, that the company would never wear it." He jabbed the air with his finger. "Those. Days. Are. Over. If Mickey Rice can do what he's done after less than two months on the job, just using his brain and, I daresay, the gift of the gab..."—he grinned toward Mickey, but he had returned to his contemplation of the floor—"...he's got my vote, because I want to see what he can win for us when we *do* have the support of the union behind us! Mickey Rice, brothers, Mickey Rice!"

As Hawkins returned to his seat to great applause, Dick Mortlake looked up from his minute book and smiled. "And before we forget, brothers," he said, "has anyone had a problem with Mr Butcher lately?"

As laughter convulsed the room, Ben Smith banged the table. "Any other nominations?"

There were none.

*

"You know," said Ben Smith when the members had vacated the room, "I *wondered* why that fellow Middleton was hesitating to put himself forward for the committee. He obviously had his eye on the main prize. Daft, really, because I daresay the members would have accepted him onto the committee readily enough."

"Not necessarily, Ben," said Dick Mortlake. "I was checking the rest-day exchanges for today and saw that Middleton had one as well as us. And his accent? Comes from the same part of the country as our garage superintendent. So if he had been nominated for the committee, I would have had to say something. I think he was here as the guvnor's spy. I would hazard a guess that he's now scurrying back to the garage to report to Mr Shilling."

The evening meeting went the same way as the first, the only difference being that Ted Middleton did not bother to attend.

9

One morning in mid-September, George Sanders, flanked by a driver and conductor, both active trade unionists within the company, entered Winchester House, Peckham, the head office of Thomas Tilling, Ltd.

"Can I help you gentlemen?" This from a portly man at the reception desk.

"We're here to see Mr Richard Tilling," replied a polite Sanders. After the death of the patriarch, the business had passed to his sons Richard and Edward, and his son-in-law Walter Wolsey.

"And you are?"

"A delegation from the London & Provincial Union of Licenced Vehicle Workers. My name is Sanders."

"Might I ask the purpose of your visit, Mr Sanders?"

"We're here to discuss the recent suspensions with Mr Tilling."

"Is Mr Tilling expecting you?"

Sanders' patience was stretched. "I suspect that he is. But if you're asking whether we have an appointment, we do not."

The portly gent reached for the black upright telephone on the counter, removed the earpiece and dialled a one-digit internal number. He cleared his throat. "Yes, reception here. We have a delegation from the London and...from a trade union here to see Mr Richard. Yes, I'll wait." He looked up and gave Sanders an insincere grin. "I see," he said into the mouthpiece, following a pause of some twenty seconds. "Yes, I'll tell them." His gaze returned to Sanders. "Mr Richard Tilling is unavailable, I'm afraid."

"Then we will see Mr *Edward* Tilling."

The portly man, having transmitted this request, looked at Sanders and shook his head.

"Mr Walter Wolsey?"

No director was available. "Perhaps you'd like to leave a message," suggested the man, who still held the earpiece in his right hand.

"I would," said Sanders, speaking loud enough for the person at the other end of the line to hear. "Twelve of my members were suspended from their jobs yesterday for the high crime on wearing a union badge on their uniforms. You can tell your directors that unless the men are put back to work, there will not be a single Tilling bus on a London road, and it may be they—or their local managers— who are seeking alternative employment. Here is my card. I can be reached at that number. Good day to you!"

A day later, the LPU's Executive Council met at Gerrard Street.

"How does the situation stand now?" asked Larry Russell who, in the absence of President Alfred "Tich" Smith on sick leave, occupied the chair.

"Four further suspensions this morning. All conductors. And guess what," replied Sanders with a smirk. "It just so happens that they have a surplus of conductors. Even so, some of the men continue to wear the red button..."

"How many?"

Sanders shrugged. "Not too many, according to my information," he conceded, "but it would be a mistake to read too much into that. The men are ready to strike in order to establish their *right* to wear it." He snorted. "*Ready* to strike? No, they're *demanding* a strike!"

Russell turned to Harry Bywater and raised an eyebrow, seeking confirmation for this claim.

Bywater nodded, albeit with an intimation of regret in his expression. "The telephone hasn't stopped ringing all day, and we've had petitions hand-delivered from Walworth, Catford, Peckham, Camberwell and Lewisham. But I disagree with George when he says the men want to establish the right to wear the badge. I think they're more about coming to the defence of their comrades."

"What do the petitions demand?" asked Russell.

Sanders lifted a sheet from a pile placed in the centre of the table and read. "'We, being drivers, conductors and mechanics at Lewisham garage, urge our union to declare a strike without delay with the demands that our suspended colleagues be immediately reinstated and no future action be taken against men who choose to wear the red button.'"

"Seems you're both right, then." Russell brushed a lock of overlong hair away from his forehead. "Well, some in this room may remember that weeks ago I advised against making this an issue. Far better, I said, if the men left their badges off and waited until we got recognition. It's a great pity it's come to this." He shook his head. "And isn't it funny that the wording on all the petitions is exactly the same? This has been organised."

Executive member Barney Macauley, a bald, burly man of fifty, turned to quietly regard Russell. He had never been happy with Russell's election as organising secretary, added to which he had discovered a personal dislike for the man. "I believe you're right," he said at last. "It's as plain as a pikestaff that these petitions have been organised." He leaned towards Russell, placing an arm on the table. "But that's what trade unions do, Larry. We *organise*."

A ripple of laughter went around the table, more from the lay members, several of whom were cabdrivers, than from the paid officers.

"But it seems to me," said Harry Bywater, addressing himself to Macauley, "that Larry was implying that the petitions were organised by George, which would be another thing entirely."

Macauley touched his chin with the fingers of his left hand, looking at Sanders from beneath a lowered brow. "George?" There was a sudden stillness in the room.

Sanders instantly dispelled the tension by commencing his reply with a laugh. "If anyone thinks that this is my work, I'm deeply disappointed. Why? In my view, the wording doesn't go far enough. If I had organised the petitions, I would have added a further demand." He looked around the table, knowing that this was his opportunity to decisively influence the outcome of the meeting, and keen to ensure that everyone present understood his point. "Let's take the suggestion that Larry made back in June: leave the badges off until we get recognition. That begs the question of how we *get* that recognition. We could simply go to the company and say, 'Well, Mr Tilling, we've got an awful lot of members, so we think you should allow us to negotiate terms and conditions.' I could be wrong, but I've a feeling that his response would be the same as it was yesterday.

"In any case, would we be telling the truth if we claimed that we had a huge amount of members in his company?" Once more, he looked around the table, but no one responded. "At the moment, we have a bare majority. Not enough to impress the likes of the Tilling brothers. How do we turn that bare majority into an overwhelming one?" He stabbed the surface of the table with his forefinger. "By showing the men that their employer has bitten off a damn sight more than he can chew! And it's in *these* circumstances that we're more likely to achieve recognition, brothers. So if I'd written these petitions I would have added one more demand, so that it would read"—he picked up the top petition sheet once more to remind himself of the wording—"that we 'urge our union to declare a strike without delay with the demands that our suspended colleagues be reinstated forthwith, that the company immediately recognise the LPU for the purpose of negotiating terms and conditions, and that no future action be taken against men who choose to wear the red button.'" He sat back in his chair.

"It seems to me, Brother Russell," said a West London busman called Frank Mead, "that Brother Sanders has just given us the wording for the motion that I now move."

"Which is?" asked Russell, hoping to trip him up.

Mead, who had been taking notes throughout the discussion, did not hesitate. "That this Executive Council calls upon our members employed by Thomas Tilling Limited to take strike action, commencing from the first bus on 18 September, until such time as the suspended men are reinstated, the company recognises the LPU for the purposes of negotiating terms and conditions, and an undertaking is given that no future action will be taken against men who choose to wear the red button.'"

Russell nodded. "I'm impressed. Is there a seconder for the motion?"

"Seconded!" snapped a short man called Charley Shiers, another busman.

"Does either the mover or the seconder wish to speak in support of the motion?

Both shook their heads.

"George has made the case," said Macauley.

"Does anyone wish to discuss the motion before I put it to the vote?"

Morris Frankenberg, a dapper cabman with a pencil-line moustache, raised a hand. "It seems to me," he ventured cautiously, "that we could do with an amendment. After all, we've been organising busmen throughout this year, and the company in our sights has always been the General..."

Sanders watched carefully as Harry Bywater began to register signs of alarm.

But Frankenberg's tentative approach allowed Macauley to come in. "That's not an amendment we would like to see defeated, so I would suggest that Brother Frankenberg leave it for another day, Brother Russell. We'll deal with the General when the time is right."

With a shrug, Frankenberg conceded.

Russell looked around the table. "Any further discussion? No? In which case, all those in favour of the motion please show."

Each of the thirteen lay members, the only ones entitled to vote, raised a hand.

"Carried unanimously!" Russell announced. He turned to Sanders. "Now, how do we propose to convey the news to our members at Tilling's?"

Sanders smiled. "Our esteemed caretaker is currently entertaining representatives from each of the garages in our kitchen. Come tomorrow, the company will be locked down solid."

*

And it was.

That the strike was successful first became clear the next morning when, having driven the Unic down Lewisham Way, Sanders turned right into the High Street and immediately spotted the crowd outside the bus garage. He drove onto the garage forecourt, waving to the men.

"How are they bearing up, Dave?" he asked, walking up to his leading activist.

Dave Marston, a handsome young man with a spade-shaped beard, raised a thumb and grinned. "They've got the bit between their teeth now, George, so there'll be no stopping 'em. Early on, a few of 'em were grumbling that it seemed a bit extreme to go on strike over a badge, but they soon changed their tune."

"Oh?" said Sanders, keenly interested. "How did you bring 'em around?"

"Told 'em it was about a damn sight more than the red button, and that if they didn't believe me they should read the resolution the EC passed."

Sanders laughed, sure now that his inspiration the previous day had been vindicated. "Good man, Dave."

"Oh, and the company has announced that it's prepared to reinstate the men and allow us all to wear the badge as long as it doesn't interfere with any equipment."

"What do the lads say to that?"

"They say fuck 'em, George."

The picket line slowly assumed the shape of a horseshoe, surrounding Sanders and Marston, the men, most of whom displayed the red button, pressing forward. Still, thought Sanders, they looked no more threatening than a crowd of pedestrians drawn by curiosity to a pavement magician.

"It's not badges that have whipped them into this mood," said Marston, "but long spreadovers and short wages."

This served to develop the mood of the men. If Marston had been speaking in Parliament, his words would have elicited cries of "Hear, hear!" On the forecourt of Lewisham bus garage, however, they drew forth variations of "Fucking right, Dave!" Some of the pickets now began to curse the company and offer words of encouragement to Marston and Sanders.

"Talking of badges, though," said Marston, "we've run out. Had a

91

bit of a run on 'em this morning. Funny, that."

"Not a problem, Dave. Send one of your members to bring that box from the passenger seat of the car."

"Harold, can you do that?" Marston asked a tall, thin man at his elbow.

"Will do. Which one is yours, Mr Sanders?"

"You see that dark green Unic? What does it say on the panel?"

Harold peered at the Unic, one of three vehicles parked near the forecourt. "'London & Provincial Union of Licensed Vehicle Workers,'" he read aloud.

Sanders smiled. The old name had been painted over a month earlier. "Correct. That means it's your car, not mine, Harold."

The men cheered.

"And my name's George, or Brother Sanders. Definitely not *Mister* Sanders."

The men cheered again.

When Harold passed the box to Sanders, he ripped it open and pulled back the flaps. "Here, Dave, take as many as you need, only try to leave me enough for the other garages. Speaking of which, I'd better get going."

Marston leaned close, murmuring, "Say a few words to the men before you go, George."

Sanders removed his bowler, stepped back a few paces and threw back his head. "Brothers! You have taken an important step today, one that will be—must be!—followed by all London busmen. Today, you have become trade unionists, standing up for what is right. But over the next few days and weeks, you will also become different men. Bigger men. Better men. After you have won your demands and you resume work, and your employers show themselves, you will see that they have changed as well. You will see that they are now *smaller* men, less *powerful* men, and that they will look at you with a new respect—perhaps even fear. And you will realise that they were never as big and powerful as you thought they were. Hah! As *they* thought they were."

This was greeted by considerable celebration and some merriment, and Sanders saw that they were now no casual onlookers but a determined group, united. He held up his hands and, lowering his voice a notch, advised: "But, brothers, never underestimate them. The way this system is run means that they will forever be attempting to claw back whatever gains you make, forever trying to maximise their profits at your expense." He paused, regarding the men soberly, seeing that the enormity of the step they had taken was beginning to sink in. "And they—not just *your* employers, but all of them—are not alone. The police will attack *you* to protect *them*, never the other way about. The government passes laws to protect their exploitation of you rather than freeing you of the shackles that seek to prevent you from fighting *against* that exploitation. That's the way this system works. And they will keep coming at you, brothers, until the working class of this country decides that enough is enough, and that the time has come to bring down this system built on exploitation and build a better one in its place, one in which businesses like this one will be owned collectively and run by you, the people who have created its wealth."

Some in his audience, probably not strangers to socialist argument, found this an exciting prospect, and gave vent to their enthusiasm. Others, however, had but a hazy understanding of his final point, and Sanders now acted to reassure them. "One step at a time, though, brothers!" he laughed. "First let's win the current dispute. Step two will be to see what we can do about those spreadovers and your wages. The leadership of the red-button union is fully behind you. And if its support ever slackens, I advise you to give it the same kind of hell that you're giving the employer today." He waved his bowler in the air. "Good luck, and let's work together to win!"

As the men cheered, Dave Marston accompanied Sanders to the Unic. "Fuck me, George," he said, with no possibility of being overheard, "I was expecting that you'd just give 'em a bit of a boost. For the life of me, I can't remember any mention of social revolution in that resolution."

"Well spotted, Dave," Sanders laughed. "We'll see if we can rectify that next time!"

*

The other Tilling's garages were just as solid as Lewisham. Sanders drove down to Catford, the southernmost outpost, and then worked his way back towards town, stopping at Peckham, Camberwell and Walworth. In some of these garages, horse-buses were still in use, and Walworth employed both horse- and motor-buses. At each one, Sanders stopped at the picket line to boost morale, although he now omitted any mention of the never-ending class struggle and the eventual need for a socialist society. He provided the leading activists with a supply of red buttons, and was cheered to hear that application forms were also in demand. Though initially surprised to see that the horse-bus crews were as firm as their motorised comrades, he then realised that they had little to lose, for they—the drivers, at least—must have known that they were doomed to extinction.

It was mid-afternoon when he arrived back in Central London.

He stepped through the front door of the Gerrard Street office and approached the receptionist. "Hello, Rose, who's in?"

Rose, a middle-aged woman with red hair and an emerald green blouse, looked up from her magazine and smiled. "Full house, George, apart from you."

"Have Eric and Ben been out for lunch?"

"Don't believe so, George."

"In that case, Rose, do me a favour and ask them to meet me in the café down the street. If either of the other two ask about me, you haven't seen me. Alright?"

After seating himself in the inexpensive Italian café, he had only a few minutes to wait until he was joined by Ben and Eric. He had asked them to wait until his return and, as he had arrived later than planned, knew they would be as hungry as he.

"Bloody hell, George," complained Ben Smith, "half an hour more and I'd've passed out. You have problems?"

"How'd you think I feel? Problems? Not a bit of it, Ben." He smiled at Ben and gave Eric a wink. "Detained by the militant enthusiasm of the Tilling's membership. Just as I predicted, the company doesn't have a bus on the road."

The Italian waitress, the wife of the owner, passed around menus. They each ordered a chicken salad sandwich and tea, and she returned to the counter.

"So, how has the telephone been behaving?" Sanders asked.

"Busier than yesterday," Smith nodded. "Apart from the General members demanding strike action, the Lord Mayor has been in touch with Harry, asking to meet him and Tilling's tomorrow at 4 p.m. at Mansion House."

"Well, that sounds promising, but I doubt if anything will come of it."

"And the LGOC company reps are on their way here," added Eric. "They've just met the company at Electric Railway House and now want to meet the EC. A lot of 'em want to join the strike."

"In support of the Tilling's membership?"

"In part," said Ben Smith. "But they've also heard the news that recognition is included in the demands for the Tilling's membership, and they don't want to be left behind."

Sanders smiled. "I suppose we'd better let 'em off the leash, then, hadn't we?"

"Harry won't like it," said Ben Smith.

"Then he'll have to lump it, won't he?" This from Eric.

Ben Smith was wearing a frown. "But I understand that at the EC meeting yesterday Frankenberg was about to move an amendment to include the General members in the dispute but he couldn't get any support."

"That's right. Because there was a danger that Harry would have talked them out of it, especially if he had persuaded Russell that it was a wrong move. This way, Harry and Russell will be facing an avalanche. The General lads have to suffer long spreadovers and low wages just as much as the Tilling's members, and they've been itching to come out. Now they've got their opportunity."

"But," said Eric, "won't we have a problem with Harry if sees that we're encouraging the General members to strike?"

Sanders winked at Ben Smith. "Not really, Eric. But listen, let's be sensible about it. If a number of garages stay off the road tomorrow morning, we can then argue that it was inevitable that a sizeable proportion of the General membership were going to join the strike and that this is now an opportunity not to be missed. And never forget: these are the members who elect us."

"Well, most of these garage reps are already in the union, so I'll try and have a word with those from my district as they leave the meeting," said Eric. He scratched his chin and gazed at the ceiling. "I wonder how the lad'll do at Middle Row," he mused, "because it would be a mistake to trust that Middleton bugger."

*

By the time the three officials returned to the union headquarters, the meeting room was filled with the LGOC reps—those men elected, one from each garage, in the company's attempt to keep out the union. The meeting was brief, although the resolution they passed was lengthy enough:

> That this meeting of garage representatives employed by the T.O.T (Trains, Omnibuses and Trams) Combine hereby resolves that the LGOC and all companies having working agreements with them are requested to receive a deputation of our elected representatives, namely, our Trade Union officials, with a view to complete recognition, and further pledge themselves to advise our fellow drivers and conductors to support their society to the last ditch: that

in the opinion of garage representatives the time has now arrived for the abolition of the system of garage representation, as we consider this system is not in the best interests of the men and we further consider that we should be represented by the properly elected representatives of our Trade Union.

"What we're seeing here," said Ben Smith to George Sanders as the hands went up, "is the end of an era."

"And the beginning of a new one," said Sanders.

*

As luck would have it, Eric had charge of the Unic that evening. Having arrived home fairly early, intending to tell Mickey the news as soon as he got in, he discovered that this was a study circle night, and so he returned to the vehicle and drove to Gloucester Terrace.

"Sorry, comrade," he said to Sidney Landles as the lawyer let him into his book-lined flat, "but I think you're going to lose a couple of the members of your group for the rest of the evening. A pressing industrial matter."

Entering the living room, he saw Mickey and Dick Mortlake sitting with half a dozen others, three of them women. He inclined his head towards the hallway, and they got to their feet.

"Lads," he said, when they were out of earshot of the others, "the garage reps have decided that the old system is finished and that we should go for recognition. It looks as though a number of garages will be out tomorrow. Will you be joining them?"

"Who have you got so far?" asked Mickey.

"Dollis Hill, Willesden, Holloway, Chelverton Road and the Bush in my allocation."

"Well, we'll have to get the committee together," Mickey responded. "Have you got the droshky outside?" He had quickly picked up this Russian term, meaning public carriage, from his brother, who in turn had leaned it from a Jewish cabdriver.

"Yeah. Do you want me to rustle 'em up for you?"

"Look, no need to go to that trouble," Dick broke in. "I'll send them all a telegram telling them to be outside the garage at five in the morning. They're almost certain to agree to join the strike, so it'll be a five-minute discussion, following which we'll be the picket line."

"You have their addresses on you?"

"Of course, in my case." Since becoming Branch Secretary, Dick had acquired a pigskin briefcase.

"Dick," Mickey protested, "the branch won't go to the expense of telegrams, and we can't claim it from head office because it's unofficial action."

"Don't worry," said Dick, closing his eyes, as if the financial worries of the proletariat were still a novelty to him, "I'll cover it."

Eric looked at him in amazement. "Bloody 'ell," he said.

*

The next morning, the committee members, with the exception of Billy Franklin, arrived at the garage on time, to be greeted by Mickey, who had been there since 4.50.

"So we're on strike?" asked Frank Chambers.

"Only if you all say so," Mickey replied.

"Shouldn't we wait for Billy?" asked Steve Urmshaw.

"Shall we give him fifteen minutes?" suggested Dick Mortlake.

"How can we wait?" Charlie Adams pointed out. "The first duty's about to sign on. We have to decide now."

"So what are the issues?" asked Malcolm Lewis.

"There's really only one," Mickey replied. "We're going for recognition, the same as the Tilling's boys."

Frank Chambers rubbed his hands together. "That'll do me! Come on, Malc, put it to the vote."

"All those in favour..." called Malcolm, stepping into his role as Branch Chairman.

Six hands went up.

"That's that, then," said Frank. "You know, I fucking *knew* you were bringing us here to call a strike, Dick."

"How did you know that, Frank?"

"Because instead of asking us to meet *at* the garage, that telegram of yours said *outside* the garage."

Soon, the first crews began to arrive, to be told by the committee that they were on strike. Most accepted it without question, and a few were exultant. Two members questioned the purpose of the action, suspecting that it had been called to win the right to wear the red button for their Tilling's comrades, but on being told that the push was on for recognition, they gladly came into line, one asking for a badge. Although some members cheerfully returned home to bed, most stayed outside the garage for a while, and as time passed, the crowd came to block the narrow street, stretching around the corner into Conlan Street.

Billy Franklin arrived at 6.15, looking stressed and weary, greeted by the cheers and jeers of the other committee members.

"What happened to you, Billy-boy?" Frank Chambers asked him.

"Any time I have to get to the garage early," he explained, shoulders raised and palms held upwards, "I rely on the first bus out of the Bush, don't I? But the Bush is on fucking strike!"

The whole street rocked with laughter.

At 6.50, the crowd began to part and Mickey saw that they were allowing a grim-faced Butcher to approach the garage on a bicycle.

"Bit late, this morning, Mr Butcher!" Mickey greeted him as he dismounted.

"No bloody buses in this part of town, are there?" the garage official replied gruffly. "Had to go back home and get the bike."

This was the occasion for a further tumult of laughter from the strikers. "Not to worry, Mr Butcher," cried Andy Dixon. "There's no work for you, anyway!"

Just before eight, standing on the kerb and peering over the heads of the strikers, Mickey saw a taxi turn into Middle Row from Kensal Road. It halted just short of Conlan Street and out stepped James Shilling, calm and dignified. He walked easily through the crowd, greeted by murmurs of "Morning, Mr Shilling," which he acknowledged with good grace. As he drew level with Mickey, he paused and turned to him, nodding. "Well, Mr Rice," he said, merely stating a fact, "it seems that the day has arrived at last."

"It would seem so," replied, Mickey. "Good morning, Mr Shilling."

"Do you know," Dick Mortlake said later, as he and Mickey stood together on the kerb, regarding the strikers, "I feel something that I've never felt before."

Mickey turned to him and smiled. "Me too," he said. "The day has arrived at last."

10

"Thank you, Miss Richardson," Albert Stanley nodded to her across his desk and smiled familiarly. "Time for your lunch, I think."

Stanley's sole visitor, a short man with an untidy greying moustache, smiled politely as she gathered her materials and prepared to leave the office. He remained seated, although his ordeal appeared to be over.

In the outer office, Emily asked Miss McKewan if she knew the whereabouts of the nearest Post Office, as it was necessary that she post a letter.

"It has been known," replied Miss McKewan in hushed tones, "for staff in this office to send their personal letters down to the post room along with our outgoing correspondence. No one minds very much as long as it doesn't become a habit."

Emily managed to look shocked. "Oh, I wouldn't dream of it, Miss McKewan."

Miss McKewan smiled half-heartedly. "In which case, dear, I think you'll find a Post Office in Victoria."

Emily collected her jacket, a lightweight grey while the weather still held, and made her way to the stairs. Outside, she walked briskly to Victoria Street and turned right. Office workers, the men in sober grey suits and the more numerous women in ankle-length dresses, were leaving their workplaces in search of lunch or to perform some minor shopping errand while they had the opportunity. The only real colour was provided by the occasional bus. In Victoria, the crowds were denser, and Emily hoped that not too many of their members were heading for the Post Office. Entering the building, she was relieved to note that although there were queues waiting to have their envelopes stamped, there were few at the telegram window. She took a form from the holder on the counter and swiftly composed her message.

*

"Why do you think I've brought you here?"

Harry Bywater directed his question at George Sanders, Ben Smith and Eric Rice. These latter three sat around the table in the Gerrard Street meeting room. Of the three, Sanders appeared the most relaxed, his legs stretched under the table, his bowler on the table, a cigarette between his fingers; Ben sat calmly enough, hands clasped before him on the table; only Eric appeared a little uncomfortable, his eyes following Bywater as, agitated and red-faced, he walked to and fro at the head of the table, hands behind his back.

The door creaked open and the caretaker peered into the room. "Do you want me to bring some...?"

"No!" shouted Bywater. "And make sure we're not disturbed!" He continued his pacing, then whirled on the three organisers, snapping, "Well?"

Sanders let out a column of smoke in a long sigh. "I would imagine," he said, stubbing out his cigarette in a nearby ashtray, "that you want to discuss the current dispute. But for Christ's sake sit down, Harry; you're making Eric nervous." He turned to grin at Eric.

Bywater stepped past his chair and leaned forward, his fists balled on the table top. "Don't you tell me what to do, Brother Sanders! And yes, I *do* want to discuss the dispute. But which dispute do you have in mind? The dispute with Tilling's? Or the one with the General, the one we don't officially have? Do you really think this is the way to build a relationship with an employer?"

"Correct me if I'm wrong, Harry, but we don't have a relationship with the General. Or *do* we?"

Bywater threw out an arm in the direction of the window. "Do you realise that there are now 600 General buses off the road? *Do* you?"

"Ah, now, that's another question entirely. But the men have the bit between their teeth, Harry. You can instruct them to return to work until you're blue in the face, but they won't do it until we've won recognition."

He banged the table with a fist. "Now you listen to me," he said, straightening up and pointing a finger at Sanders. "Once this is over, you three are going to find yourselves in the disciplinary procedure. You hear me?"

Sanders took another cigarette from his Gold Flake packet and lighted it, squinting through the smoke at Bywater. "Harry, if you're threatening us with discipline, I would suggest that we ask Eric to leave the room for a few minutes."

"Why?"

"Because there's something of which only Ben and I have knowledge that we wish to discuss with you. Believe me, it's in your own interest."

A nonplussed Bywater frowned at Sanders, his lower jaw ajar while the various possibilities passed rapidly through his mind. Eventually, he nodded. "Ok, Eric, go up to your office. I'll call you when I need you."

Ben spoke up a few seconds after Eric had closed the door. "You say there are 600 General buses off the road, Harry," he said, scratching his right sideboard. "As a matter of interest, how do you come by that number?"

Bywater was flustered, his face slowly draining of colour. "Damned if I know. Oh, wait, I think it was one of the newspapers. Yes, that's it: the *Evening News* rang up wanting to know why 600 General buses were off the road. Probably got the number from the company."

"So *you* didn't get the number from the company, Harry?" This from Sanders.

"No, I *didn't* get it from the company. What are you suggesting?"

"I'm not suggesting, Harry. I *know* that you were in Albert Stanley's office back in June. Seems Stanley mentioned your visit to a copper in the Traffic Division. He must have talked about it back at the Yard, because it was told to me by a young constable of my acquaintance."

Bywater tried to put a brave face on it. "Oh, yes, and when was this?"

"I told you: back in June."

"I mean when did you hear of it?"

"Shortly after it happened."

Ben nodded. "That's right. It was around that time that George told me about it."

"And why is it only now, three months later, that you're raising the matter with me?"

Sanders nodded to Bywater's chair. "Sit down, Harry." A man who is sitting, he calculated, was less likely to bolt through the door when the going got rough.

Bywater sat, swallowing hard, knowing he was caught.

Because," Sanders said, his voice low but menacing as he leaned forward, "it suits me to raise it now." He used his forefinger to tap off the points against Bywater on the table top. "You take it into your head to meet the managing director of London's largest bus company. Without telling a soul. With no consultation with us. Or the leading activists in the company. Not to mention the Executive Council. Either before or after the event. And now you have the gall to threaten *us* with the disciplinary procedure." His heat rising, his voice became a growl. "Let me tell you, Harry, if you so much as mention the disciplinary procedure again with regard to this dispute, it will be you who'll be facing charges, not us."

"And George is right, Harry," Ben Smith came in. "The General membership is now out for recognition, and they're not going to stop until they get it."

"But I've received an offer," said Bywater.

It was the turn of the other two to look nonplussed.

"Oh, yes." Bywater's confidence returned, and with it his colour. Suddenly, he looked pleased with himself.

"Are you saying you've been in negotiations, Harry?" asked Ben Smith. "On your own?"

"Well, I wouldn't say that exactly..." He now saw that this would not be quite as simple as he had supposed, and he began to falter.

"So what *would* you say?" Sanders demanded. "Exactly? And who does the offer come from? Tilling's?"

"From Albert Stanley. But he's confident that he can get the Tilling brothers to go along with it."

Sanders passed a hand over his face before looking across at Bywater. "And the offer is?"

"Arbitration by the Chief Industrial Commissioner's department."

"Arbitration," repeated Ben Smith. "But the issue is recognition, and there are only two possible answers: yes or no. How is arbitration going to help with that?"

"And the men suspended at Tilling's?" Sanders asked before Bywater had a chance to respond to Ben Smith's question.

"That will also be subject to the arbitration proceedings."

"Will it now?" said Sanders. "Sounds to me, Harry, as if this is all sewn up."

Bywater sat back in his chair and folded his arms, looking as if he were about to assert his authority. "I've agreed to the proposal, George, and that's an end of it. My concern is that our members don't go on losing money."

"Well, I hope that's your only concern, Harry." He paused to allow Bywater time to question his meaning, and knew from the latter's silence that his suspicions regarding the general secretary were fully justified. "Tell me, how was this offer conveyed to you? Did you pay another visit to Electric Railway House?"

Bywater reddened, but held his temper. "I received a telephone call from Mr Stanley."

"I see. Negotiation by telephone. With no consultation. Wonders will never cease, will they, Ben?"

Ben Smith grimaced. "And who will represent the men at the arbitration proceedings?"

"Me as general secretary, Tich as president—if he's back from sick leave—and Larry Russell as organising secretary."

"And the Executive Council," insisted Ben Smith.

"We can't have the whole executive at the meeting, for God's sake."

"Why not?" Sanders objected. "The Board of Trade has plenty of space."

"Alright, I'll put it to him," Bywater reluctantly conceded.

"Him?"

"Stanley."

"You'd better get him to agree a sight more than that, Harry," Sanders insisted. "We need the arbitration proposal in writing, spelling out quite clearly the matters to be discussed. That letter must be then presented to the EC."

"But I've told him..."

"Told him what, Harry?"

Bywater cast about for assistance and, finding none, decided merely to alter the wording of his reply. "He wants his buses back on the road by tomorrow morning."

Ben Smith snorted. "Well, he can't have 'em, can he?" He shook his head in disbelief. "A return to work before we know the result of the arbitration? I never heard the like! On top of which, the Tilling's dispute was declared official by the EC, so *only* the EC can terminate it."

"Listen," suggested Sanders, "it's Friday. Call a meeting of the EC here for tomorrow morning. Tell Stanley to proceed on the basis that the arbitration will go ahead, so today he can ask the Board of Trade to make arrangements for Monday. Tell him he'll have confirmation—or otherwise—sometime tomorrow. And make sure he knows that our Executive Council will be at that meeting on Monday."

"But that means our members will be losing money for another three days!" Bywater objected, almost in desperation.

"Yes, and the companies will have to lose their profits for another three days as well!" responded Sanders, slapping the table. "For once, Harry, use your head! If Albert Stanley can see that he can lay down the law to the general secretary of this union and have his buses back on the road immediately, what sort of agreement do you think you'll get when you meet him at the Board of Trade?"

"One not worth having!" Ben Smith supplied the answer for Bywater.

"So," Sanders continued, without giving Bywater the opportunity to respond, "Mr Albert Stanley has to learn one or two things. First of all, he has to learn that if he wants any kind of agreement with this union, he has to strike it with the lay leadership, not the general secretary..."

"And that," added Ben Smith, "is a lesson you have to learn as well, Harry."

"And he'll hopefully learn by Monday morning that unless he's prepared to concede full recognition, he won't have any buses on Tuesday either!"

Defeated, Bywater could only sigh and shake his head. "But think of the cost to the union," he nevertheless persisted. "The Tilling's dispute is official, and so we'll be paying strike pay. Then there'll be the loss of earnings and travel expenses we'll need to pay the EC tomorrow..."

Sanders laughed. "Do you know how many new members we've

made since this dispute began a few days ago? Seven hundred and fifty, Harry. And I'll guarantee you that number will be doubled once the men know we're meeting the companies at the Board of Trade, and tripled if you come out of there with a decent agreement!"

"Well," Bywater sighed, slowly rising from his chair and looking a decade older than his age, "I suppose I'd better make some telephone calls." He glanced at the clock on the wall. "And then get to the Mansion House."

*

"George," said Ben Smith when they were alone, "I almost felt sorry for the bugger. Even so, it looks as if we'll come out of this dispute alright. But for the life of me I don't know how we'll be able to trust him after this."

"It's even worse than you think, Ben," Sanders said. He took a small brown envelope from the inside pocket of his jacket and passed it to Smith. "As before, this is strictly between the two of us. When I arrived here this afternoon, Rose handed me this telegram."

Ben Smith removed the telegram from its envelope and read aloud: "HB with AS at ERH this morning. Stop. Arbitration agreed. Stop. DB."

*

Harry Bywater, Larry Russell and EC member Dennis Davies arrived at Gerrard Street the following morning with nothing to show for their visit to the Mansion House: Sir David Burnett, the Lord Mayor, had listened to their fairly simple demands and then transmitted these to the Tilling's team in another room. Tilling's being adamantly opposed to recognition of the union, the LPU men thanked His Worship for his hospitality and made for home.

The EC meeting that Saturday morning went fairly smoothly—if sometimes noisily, due to the presence of a sizeable contingent of lay members in the "gallery" seats. There was a debate about whether the proposal of arbitration should be accepted, particularly in view of the fact that even the Lord Mayor had been unable to sway the directors of Tilling's. Bywater was able to point out, however, that Sir David Burnett had been equipped with none of the powers of an arbitrator, and those who supported the continuation of the strike until the companies had capitulated were further hampered by the fact that their general secretary had presented them with a *fait accompli*; the motion to reject arbitration and continue the strike was therefore withdrawn. Just as Bywater was heaving a sigh of relief, however, Barney Macauley, who had moved that motion, now introduced another, instructing the general secretary and all paid officials to involve the appropriate lay leaders in all negotiations with employers and to seek the endorsement of the membership before concluding any agreement. This evoked lusty support from the gallery and, watched closely by Ben Smith and George Sanders, Bywater offered no defence, as a result of which the motion was carried unanimously.

Macauley then questioned the representation at the arbitration proceedings, moving that the organisers, who by their hard work had contributed so much to what promised to be a stunning victory, should be present at the negotiations. But Sanders declined, smiling at Barney Macauley and declaring, "Brother Macauley, as you and so many other staunch comrades will be present on Monday, I feel my presence is not required."

But Macauley had one more proposal. "Brother Russell, the situation has been transformed since a few evenings ago this committee declared the Tilling's dispute official. That we are now on the brink of victory is due in large part to the fact that so many of our London General members have joined the dispute not only in support of their comrades at Tilling's, but also to demand recognition from their own company, and this too is now within reach. This being the case, it is surely only just that we also declare the London General dispute official. I so move."

There followed pandemonium from the gallery and acclamation by the other members of the committee as Bywater muttered objections about the expense involved, to which no one paid attention. Russell immediately called a vote and declared the motion carried unanimously. In such an atmosphere, no one dared move an immediate return to work.

*

The proceedings at the Board of Trade in Old Palace Yard on Monday, 22 September were, although somewhat more prolonged, largely due to the frequency with which the employers demanded adjournments, almost as smooth.

The conference convened at 11 a.m., and at 2.30 p.m., Sanders,

Ben Smith, Eric Rice and a number of lay members, including Mickey, sat in the lobby and watched as the delegations came down for a late lunch break. For the union, Bywater, a now fit Tich Smith, Larry Russell and thirteen members of the Executive Council. Some EC members were quite shabbily dressed, but the Board of Trade staff seemed quite relaxed about this, and Sanders reasoned that they would be no strangers to the working class, as arbitration hearings had recently been conducted for the baking and other industries. As he passed Sanders, Tich Smith looked across and grimaced, indicating the absence of progress. Then came the employers, represented by Albert Stanley and W. J. Iden for the London General, and Richard Tilling and Walter Wolsey for Tilling's. An hour later, the distinguished figure of Sir George Askwith, Chief Industrial Commissioner, with his handlebar moustache and dressed in a grey morning suit, was visible near the lift as he welcomed each delegation upon their return from lunch. And then they were gone.

At 8 p.m., the lift disgorged most of the union's delegation, led by a beaming Tich Smith, who waved a small bundle of papers. As his nickname implied, Smith was small—even smaller than Harry Bywater—in stature; a former cabdriver, he was smartly dressed in a well-pressed three-piece suit; a full beard covered his broad face. "Sweet as a nut!" he proclaimed as he passed out copies of the agreement.

Sanders swiftly scanned the eight points.

1. In view of the representations now made that the majority of the drivers and conductors in the employment of the London General Omnibus Company Limited and Messrs. Tilling (Limited) have become members of the London and Provincial Union of Licensed Vehicle Workers, and in view of the representations made by the executive officers of this union, that the drivers and conductors desire to abolish the present   system of garage representatives, and to have any matters which may be in dispute between the companies and their drivers and conductors dealt with by the union officials, the companies do not desire to raise objection to the recognition of the trade union.

2. Matters in dispute first to be dealt with directly between employees and their representative officers at the garage, but, failing agreement, the matter to be referred to the general engineer, or his nominee, and the officers of the union.

3. The companies are not to be affected by disputes with companies with whom they have no direct concern.

4. Questions of discipline and management are not to be interfered with, such questions not to prevent officers of the union conferring with the management on matters of wages or working conditions.

5. No objection to be taken to a union button, the button to be worn so as not to interfere with the official equipment.

6. All men now out at Messrs. Tilling's to resume work in their former positions.

7. No employee to be intimidated or interfered with in the discharge of his duties by any member of the union.

8. Any question of interpretation of this agreement to be referred to the Chief Industrial Commissioner.

"As you say, Tich," said Sanders. "Sweet as a nut. Not happy about clause 3, but that was to be expected, and I'm not sure what they mean about interfering in questions of discipline in clause 4. But it'll do. Well done, brother!"

Eric sought out Mickey. "Back to the Harrow Road before the Kilburn meeting, mate?" The results of the arbitration conference were to be reported at midnight meetings arranged at a number of centres, many of them picture palaces, throughout London.

"Can't do it." He glanced at the clock over the reception desk. "Have to be in Duke Street in ten minutes."

Eric's eyebrows went up, and he shrugged at Sanders, who was standing nearby. "Duke Street?"

"Yeah. I'm going to the theatre with Emily. But I'll be in Kilburn for the meeting."

"The new Shaw play?" enquired Sanders, who had overheard their exchange. His face was unreadable.

"Yes, at the St. James's. *Androcles and the Lion.*"

"With Emily Richardson."

"That's right."

Sanders frowned at Eric. "And you said nothing?"

"Was I supposed to, George?"

"Well, considering the nature of her employment..." He turned to

Mickey and forced a grin. "You'd better get a move on, son. Enjoy the play. But be careful of that Shaw: he's a Fabian, you know."

*

Ten days later, Sanders brooded as he waited for Emily at the Lyons Corner House at the junction of Rupert and Coventry Streets. He should have been in high spirits: the dispute with Tilling's and the London General, and the recognition agreements it achieved, had led to 2,700 new members for the union, so that it now represented 90 percent of all London busworkers. And yet he felt low. How could that possibly be?

True, he might be suffering the effects of overwork, but in truth his workload since the victory of 22 September had reduced. There were a couple of niggling concerns, but not the sort of thing he was usually unable to handle. Within the union, things were not as rosy as they might be. Of course, Harry Bywater was fast becoming a liability, but it was possible to contain him, although this would have been easier if the president was less likely to side with him on occasion. There had been a recent incident in which, presented with new schedules which they found unacceptable, members at several garages had threatened strike action. Instead of letting the men off the leash—if only for a short while, to demonstrate their strength of feeling to the company—Tich had not only instructed them to remain at work but, in the pages of the *Record*, had issued what amounted to a permanent prohibition of such action. Sanders found himself intensely irritated as he called the words to mind:

> If the company issues an order or regulation that, in the opinion and judgment of the drivers and conductors is of an unsatisfactory nature, their duty as trade unionists is   very clear: they must obey it and at the same time report the matter at once to us...if you are going to take steps such as were suggested at some of the garages last week, you not only do an injury to yourselves, but make the position for us much more difficult to handle.

Sanders would have thought that his recent experience at the Board of Trade would have convinced Tich Smith that a little industrial action by the members in fact made "the position" much *easier* to handle. Of course, it was telling that the statement had been issued by Tich instead, as normally would have been the case, by Harry. Possibly Tich had felt that such an edict by Harry would have been ignored.

Of course, Sanders was quite aware that his impatience and irritation was largely the mark of the man who, having played the role of agitator and mobiliser, suddenly finds that, with recognition, he is expected to act "responsibly." However, although the time for statesmanship might well come in due course, that time surely was not now, when the whole working-class movement was in a ferment which had lasted for almost three years and showed no signs of subsiding. Unless the enthusiasm of the membership met with support and encouragement by the leadership, the result could only be demoralisation, and it was then that the employers would mount their counter-attack.

And yet such problems could not explain his mood because George Sanders was nothing if not combative; and, indeed, he could feel his pulse race now, as he considered what was as yet no more than a possibility.

He was therefore brought face to face with the fact that the sombre note underlying all else was caused by the knowledge that Emily Richardson had a lover. He was now forced to admit to himself that he had long been sexually attracted to her, and that when, as Dorothy Bridgeman, she had been close to him at meetings and in discussions, he had often yearned just to reach out and touch her face, to feel its softness beneath his fingers. Often, though, she had been a firebrand, excoriating her opponents with such biting sarcasm that in those moments he found it difficult to picture her as a lover, or even imagine that she might wish to *be* a lover—anybody's lover, let alone his. But there had also been quieter times, times when she looked at him with a frankness he found a little frightening, and when he held himself aloof for fear that if he made advances to her she might embrace him so completely that he would never—would never want to—escape, and that all his work would, while it might continue, be subordinated to his hopeless enslavement to her.

And now it was too late. Dorothy/Emily was no longer available. And she *had* been available. Why, the first time they had met at this corner house she had explicitly told him that she was not proposing marriage, practically advising him that she would welcome an affair. After he had learned the truth in the lobby at the Board of Trade, he had returned home as depressed as he had ever felt. But what could have been at the back of his mind all this time? That, should there come a time when he felt the overwhelming desire for a deep relationship, she would be there for him? Did he think that she had allowed the second half of her twenties to go by without marriage because she was marking time until George Sanders woke up to the fact that she had almost always been in his mind? Was he that arrogant? Had he really thought her that bedazzled by him? What a fool he had been!

"Well, George," he heard a voice say, "I'm not at all sure that I want to sit down. You look *awfully* angry."

He looked up and there she was, standing at his table and smiling down at him. He stumbled to his feet. "I...I'm sorry, Dorothy. I was miles away, thinking about Tich Smith." He raised a hand, signalling the waitress to bring the tea that he had ordered.

She feigned irritation, hissing "For God's sake sit down, George. Stop being so bloody bourgeois." Having seated herself, she smiled across the table, adding, "And you shouldn't be so angry with Brother Smith, if I were you. According to my employer, it was he who—along with a couple of the executive members—supplied Harry Bywater with what passes for his backbone during the arbitration hearing."

Sanders laughed in surprise. "Well, that's encouraging to hear, Dorothy. And before we go any further, I must thank you for your telegram."

"You're most welcome. Did you have occasion to use it?"

"Only in that I showed it to Ben Smith. He and I will doubtless clobber Bywater with it at some stage in the future."

There was a pause in their conversation while the waitress served the tea. After her departure, Sanders hesitated, seeking an elegant way to introduce the next topic. Failing, he proceeded clumsily. "How was your evening with Shaw?"

"*Androcles*?" She gave him a guarded look. "It was very pleasant. I do so enjoy Shaw's wit. For example, there's a delicious line in this play in which he says something about revolutionary movements attracting those who are not good enough for the status quo as well as those who are too good for it."

Despite himself, Sanders smiled. "I'll try to remember that one. Never know when it might come in useful on the platform."

"Quite." She drew in her lips and gave him a more serious look. "Would I be mistaken if I suggested that you really want to ask about my evening with Mickey?"

Well, there it was: Dorothy, as direct as ever. "Not so much your evening at the theatre. But I must admit that your relationship with him took me by surprise."

She shrugged. "You're beginning to sound like my father."

"Isn't he a little green, Dorothy?"

"Mickey? Not at all. He's six years younger than me, it's true, but that is entirely unimportant."

"I see." He smoothed the tablecloth with his fingers. "Well, it's really none of my business, Dorothy."

"Yes and no, George, yes and no." She sighed. "Look, I know I made eyes at you in the past, but the last time we sat at this table you made it abundantly clear that there could be nothing between us. And maybe you did us both a favour, George."

"You'll need to explain that, Dorothy."

"I will, but I would ask that you give serious thought to what I'm going to say." She sighed again. "What do you think would have happened if you had succumbed to my feminine wiles?"

"I suspect you're going to tell me."

"I am. We would have had a very intense physical relationship lasting a month or two, during which you would have been less than assiduous with your work. Then you would have begun to resent me. Resenting me, you would have begun to loosen the ties between us. I, on the other hand, would have resisted this. It would have ended acrimoniously, George, so acrimoniously that we could never have been friends afterwards. Think about it, comrade, and you'll see that I'm right."

To her surprise, there was the promise of a smile on his lips. "Do you know, Dorothy, that comes very close to what I was thinking when you arrived. Now you've said it, it seems perfectly obvious." He nodded. "Once before in my life, I was in a relationship that was going something like that, but just in time we both realised that we were meant to be friends rather than lovers."

She smiled pleasantly. "George, I had momentarily forgotten what a mature man you are. I think we would have been making that same mistake. And the last thing I would want would be to lose you as a friend."

He smiled and regarded her through narrowed, discerning eyes. "I think I can learn to live with that, Dorothy."

She reached across the table and placed a hand on his. "Thank goodness for that."

He cleared his throat and became suddenly business-like. "However, we do need to discuss how we handle young Mickey. It's important that your position in Stanley's office is not compromised, for example. Then again, how much will you be telling him before you report to me?"

She was somewhat taken aback by this and it was only with a struggle that she maintained a calm exterior. "George, we need to get a few things straight. First, I am *not* your subordinate. I am doing what I'm doing as a service to the movement. Second, I have passed you information on two occasions. Do I discuss these matters with Mickey? Yes, of *course* I do. I have also passed him information of direct interest to him, as a result of a discussion between Albert Stanley and his garage superintendent. And for the future? Well, I will continue to pass information to you, if that is convenient. If it is *more* convenient to let Mickey have it, so that *he* can pass it to you, I will do that."

Sanders took this without flinching. "So you have absolute trust in Mickey Rice?"

This time, she was unable to suppress a defiant glare. "Yes, I do."

He raised both hands, fingers outstretched. "Fine. Now, if I recall, Dorothy, it was you who suggested this meeting. Do you have something to tell me?"

"Ah, yes." It was almost as if she had forgotten the purpose of her request, or as if it had suddenly assumed less importance. She leaned forward. "I've been working for the London General for just over three months, George. Now, I won't say it's not interesting, because it is. But it's not enough."

Sanders became wary.

"What are you saying, Dorothy?"

"I need to get back into political activity, George."

PART TWO

1914

11

On this mild but wet Sunday evening in February, the Hackney Empire was just over half-full. Tonight there would be no music hall performances, no Charlie Chaplin, no Marie Lloyd, for the theatre had been hired by the British Socialist Party, as the drums of war began to beat more incessantly in both Europe and Whitehall, to further promote its opposition to armed conflicts serving the interests of the ruling class.

Perhaps conscious of the neglect of the trade union movement by its predecessor organisation, the Social Democratic Foundation, the party had asked George Sanders to chair this meeting. Upon hearing that Henry Hyndman, leader of the pro-armament faction, although now deposed from the leadership, would be a speaker, he had at first declined, but relented as he reasoned that he would at least have the opportunity to ensure that the discussion did not stray too far from party policy.

Mickey Rice sat with Emily, veiled because she could not afford to divulge either of her identities, in the front row of the balcony. Scanning the stalls below, Mickey spotted several union members: Barney Macauley, Dick Mortlake, Morris Frankenberg and a number of local busmen.

"Internationally," Sanders began, having welcomed the audience and introduced himself, "the position of the socialist movement on the war question has within the last few years been stated very clearly. In 1907, the Stuttgart conference of the Second International resolved, thanks to amendments by Rosa Luxemburg and the delegates of the Russian Social-Democratic and Labour Party, that we should do more than try to prevent war from breaking out or, when it did, seek its conclusion." He raised his voice and thumped the table with his fist. "More than that, comrades, the conference said that we should use the crisis created by war *to hasten the overthrow of the bourgeoisie*—those in whose interests the war will be waged!" He paused to allow the applause to die. "Five years later, with war having broken out in the Balkans, the Basel conference confirmed that decision, saying that the economic and political crisis caused by war should be used to hasten the downfall of the rule of capital.

"That seems clear enough to me, comrades. I fail to see how it could be misunderstood by anyone."

This caused a ripple of laughter from those who realised that he was referring to Hyndman.

"Nevertheless, within our own British Socialist Party there has sometimes been a degree of misunderstanding. For example, Comrade Hyndman, who was in fact a delegate to the Stuttgart conference, has argued the need for this country to build up its armaments in preparation for a possible war with Germany. It might be said, however, that the position of the party was clarified when, at its second conference in May of last year, opposition to war carried the day and the composition of the executive was changed."

A further ripple of laughter, from the same people, who realised that Sanders was referring to Hyndman's loss of his position on the executive; but this was joined now by a roll of moans from those who thought this uncharitable of Sanders.

"However, our party is nothing if not democratic, and it has decided that Comrade Hyndman should be given the opportunity to restate his views. Our first speaker, therefore, is Henry Hyndman, founder of the Social Democratic Federation and former executive member of the British Socialist Party."

Hyndman, 72, his greying beard reaching to his chest, took the rostrum. He spent a moment surveying his audience, moistening his lips with his tongue, before commencing.

"There are certain socialists," he began, with a sideways glance at the speakers' table, where Theodore Rothstein sat next to Sanders, "who imagine that because we are all working for international unity, and admit fully there is no real cause for enmity among the peoples, that, therefore, there is no probability of any further war, and that all armaments should at once be suspended, regardless of what may be going on all over the world.

"Unfortunately, Socialists have no direct control in any country: they have, in fact, at present little influence on the policy of those particular countries which are arming with the greatest assiduity. Nobody can deny, for instance, that our party in Germany is by far the strongest socialist party in the world. Yet, even in Germany, the Social-Democrats are as yet quite powerless to arrest the enormous expenditure by land and by sea used to back up the traditional Prussian policy of aggression, which, in my opinion, is at the present moment a serious menace to Europe."

Emily began to bristle. "That, surely," she whispered to Mickey, "is the whole *point* of the Stuttgart and Basel decisions: that those who *do* have the power and influence should be overthrown in the event of war!"

"What I cannot understand," Hyndman continued, "is how

radicals, who very properly object to schemes of aggression on the part of Great Britain, of Russia, of France, of America, of Japan, are absolutely indifferent to the dangerous action of Germany in Europe and elsewhere. They seem to have forgotten the history of Prussia altogether. They pay no attention to the fact that the Poles in Prussian Poland are worse off than they were under Russian rule; they are indifferent to the treatment of the inhabitants of Schleswig-Holstein; they care not at all about the suppression of popular rights in Alsace-Lorraine, and make no comment on the farce of a 'constitution' which is being thrust contemptuously upon those two provinces; they deliberately maintain a conspiracy of silence about the threatening attitude of Germany towards Holland; they are equally indifferent to the highhanded proceedings of that country in China; and if anybody dares to hint that the enormous increase of the German navy, built up by borrowed money in a time of profound peace, is directed against this country in order to obtain for Prussian policy a free hand in working towards the dominance of Europe by direct menace in the North Sea, that man is denounced as a chauvinist and a fire-eater!"

He paused to gaze around the theatre, as if in an attempt to identify enemies or locate friends. "I myself have been most bitterly attacked on this issue, and if I were to collect all the imputations and epithets piled up upon me by people whom I supposed to be my friends I think they themselves would be a little astonished at the sort of language they have permitted themselves to use about me."

This called forth a wave of feigned sympathy, a prolonged "Aaaaahhh…" from one section of the audience.

Hyndman shrugged this off, and emphasised his point: "Germany is the modern Macedon, and though Kaiser Wilhelm is neither a Philip nor an Alexander, he is at bottom a man of peace of about the same kidney as those two insatiable expansionists. What Germany can gain by peace she will acquire pacifically; what she cannot obtain by persuasion she will, when quite ready, take by main force."

He continued with a review of the situation in a Europe where, he maintained, Germany was seen to be asserting its will in virtually every corner.

Finally, he placed both hands on the rostrum and leaned towards his audience. "*If*," he thundered, "the socialists of Great Britain come to the conclusion that this island is not worth defending, and that they have no duties towards other nations which they are called upon to perform, then let them sell out their fleet, suppress their futile army, and go forth as Quakers with empty hands before the world."

This drew some catcalls.

"*If*, on the other hand, it is recognised that naval armaments and military forces are necessary under the conditions of to-day, then let our own policy towards foreign nations be discussed without prejudice or bitterness, and let us take full account of the course we should follow in view of the threatening aspect of affairs. The persistent bleating of 'Peace, Peace' where there is no peace has landed us in war before to-day, and not so very long ago either. But that war is fatal to socialist progress we are all agreed."

That final sentence did, as he doubtless had intended it to, bring him some applause, but this was almost drowned by the calls of "Peace, Peace" which he had inadvertently suggested to his opponents. Emily sat so stonily silent that Mickey was dissuaded from offering even polite applause. He placed his hand on hers and turned towards her, but she was unresponsive, her hand cold and the face behind the veil seemingly impassive.

Theodore Rothstein, a Lithuanian émigré resident in Britain for twenty years, was, at almost 43, a vigorous-looking man with a short beard and full moustache. A journalist, within British social democracy he was a recognised leader of the anti-war faction. His umbrella lay at his feet beneath the speakers' table, indicating that he had probably walked to the meeting from his house in Clapton Square where, when the Russian socialist leader was in London, he played host to Lenin. He walked to the rostrum, upon which he placed his notes, adjusting his glasses on his nose before smiling up at the audience.

"I propose," he began, speaking casually, "to deal with some of the aspects of this question, which has frequently been discussed by Comrade Hyndman and others, and has given rise to considerable controversy in our party. I propose to do it in the spirit which Hyndman has recommended—that is, without prejudice or bitterness. My object will be to convince you that Comrade Hyndman is wrong in the attitude he has assumed on this important subject— wrong both as to his premises and conclusions.

"You know, I think that a Marxist ought to be the last person in the world to introduce in an explanation of a grave political crisis, such as the present almost warlike tension between this country and Germany, factors of a personal or purely moral nature. It is, to my mind, highly unscientific to represent a modern monarch, however powerful and self-willed he may be, as the cause of a crisis which may, and indeed must, according to many, lead to a war. Even Napoleon was but an instrument of a class, and only carried out a piece of historical necessity.

"The present Kaiser is not even a Napoleon, and those who are acquainted with the course of German history during the last twenty years will know that he is but the tool of a court clique, and, in a larger and more historical sense, of the class of Junkers and of large capitalists. Though he has a mind and a will of his own, the power which he possesses to translate his mind and will into action is strictly limited by the mind and will of the classes of which he is the unconscious mouthpiece. A Marxist, if nobody else, ought to understand this, and to dismiss the introduction of the personal factor of the Kaiser as utterly irrelevant."

Rothstein now pointed out that the build-up of the German navy had been planned and announced a full decade-and-a-half earlier, and yet at that time Britain had been silent, having apparently no objection to this development.

"Wonderful, is it not? Here was the German naval programme not only proclaimed from all house tops, but actually in the course of construction, and yet England continued to entertain towards her terrible rival the friendliest sentiments! It may be added that the so called Pan-Germans had been active already for several years, that the worst phases of Prussian brutality towards the Poles—the flogging of Polish children for refusing to abandon their mother tongue, and the famous comparison by Chancellor von Bülow of the Polish population with rabbits—fell within this period of 1900-1902, and that it was in 1902 that Professor Halle published the sensational book suggesting the annexation of Holland. Yet the British Government saw no reason for coming forward as the champion of downtrodden nationalities, and arming itself against Germany.

"How is such blindness to be explained? Quite simply—those 'sinister' designs were only discovered at a later period when it suited the purposes of certain politicians to do so. What lay at the bottom of the German government's decision to construct a big navy was the very simple factor that Germany had become a big capitalist state, strong not only in industry, but also in export-seeking financial capital, and that, as every state that arrives at such a stage, she wanted to acquire colonies, spheres of influence, and all those pretty little things which form the object of modern colonial and imperialist policy.

"Was Germany going to be left behind in the international race for what was called by the Kaiser 'places in the sun?' 'The proposed increase of the Navy,' declared Foreign Secretary—as he was then— von Bülow in the autumn of 1899 'has become necessary owing to the change in the international position. We do not want to interfere with any other country, but we do not wish that any other country should interfere with us, should violate our rights or push us aside either in political or commercial questions. Germany cannot stand aside while other nations divide the world among them. We must be strong enough to be secure against surprises not only on land, but also at sea. We must build a fleet strong enough to exclude all possibility of attack being made on us.'

"These declarations make the objects with which the creation of a big navy was conceived perfectly clear—to acquire commercial and financial markets, while the world was not yet entirely shared out. It was a pre-eminently capitalist conception, which every German Social-Democrat combatted tooth and nail. But there was no point against England except this: If England should at any moment conceive the idea of barring Germany's way to financial and colonial expansion, she would be fought as Italy or France or the United States would, in similar circumstances, be fought."

Rothstein then followed the example of Hyndman, conducting an exhaustive survey of recent events on the world scene.

"I have now," he rounded off this section of his long speech, "surveyed the chief events of international politics of the last few years, and if I have succeeded in establishing anything at all it is this fact: that whatever quarrel there has been between England and Germany was due not to the latter's aggression against this or any other country, but solely to England's jealousy of a powerful rival in commerce and the world's finance. It is for this reason that the cry has been raised about the balance of power; the peace of the world; the sanctity of international treaties; and the freedom of small nationalities.

"For forty years Germany, notwithstanding her enormous strength and the megalomania of her Kaiser, has not disturbed the world's peace. During this period England has carried on incessant wars all over the world; has stolen Egypt; has annexed two independent republics; has driven France from the Sudan; has robbed Portugal of her vast colonial possessions in South Africa—I allude to Matabeleland and Mashonaland—; has permitted and encouraged France to establish herself in Morocco; and has almost effected the partition of Persia. Yet it is Germany which is supposed to entertain sinister designs upon the territories and colonial possessions of other states and to threaten the peace of the world! Has anyone heard of such exquisite hypocrisy? What is true is that Germany is disturbing the peace of the British capitalist's soul!

"That is the source and fountain of all the allegations concerning the objects of the German navy and German foreign policy, and this is whence England derives her sudden love for smaller nationalities and her great respect for the sacredness of international treaties!"

Rothstein now placed both arms on the rostrum, seemingly resting from his labours. After a moment, he straightened, removed his glasses and, taking a handkerchief from his trouser pocket, started to polish them. Finished with his notes, he stepped aside from the rostrum and walked to the edge of the stage.

"But, comrades," he said slowly, "the hour is late. What are we do if, despite our most valiant efforts, war should come? I hope I have convinced you, or those who were not convinced already, that this war, should it come, will not be *our* war." He was forced to pause here, waving off a roar from his supporters in the audience. "It will, instead, be a war of British imperialists on the one side and German imperialists on the other, with the former seeking to retain its empire and possibly even expand it at the expense of the smaller empire of its foe, while the latter will have its eye on the British colonies. If social democrats have an ally in such a war, it is surely the peoples of those colonies rather than the ruling class of either of the belligerents!" This was greeted by another wave of enthusiasm from his supporters, for which he paused, before he stood erect, raised his voice and, waving his fist, concluded: "Certainly, British and German workers have no reason to slaughter each other in the interests of their masters. Should war come, then, our duty, surely, *is to translate into action the decisions of the Stuttgart and Basel conferences of the Second International and bring to an end the rule of capital!*"

At times during his long speech, especially when speaking of incidents with which only the most astute students of world politics were familiar, Rothstein had run the risk of losing his audience, but with his concluding remarks he had won them, and they, with the exception of the Hyndman partisans, now responded by giving him a rousing burst of applause, some of them standing and cheering.

Mickey applauded enthusiastically but did not stand, for it was clear to him that Emily had no such intention, although she did applaud. Conscious that she was trembling slightly, and fearing that she had caught a cold, he leaned towards her, placing a hand on her arm. "Emily, are you feeling alright? You're trembling, sweetheart."

"Yes, I'm perfectly alright, Mickey. But I'm *very* angry!"

"Angry?" He was at a loss to understand what could have brought about such a mood.

"Yes, *angry*! He calls himself a Marxist and yet he..." She paused, aware that the applause was dying and that she ran the risk of being overheard. "Oh, I'll explain later." She even sounded angry at Mickey for failing to understand.

He assumed that her anger was caused by the performance of Hyndman, and his un-Marxist concentration on the roles played by Kaiser Wilhelm and the Prussian character in the present crisis, and so he relaxed back into his seat as Sanders called for questions and discussion contributions from the audience.

"I wonder," speculated Emily, "whether I should make my point in public." She hesitated, half raising her arm, before standing and, grasping Mickey's hand, commanding: "Come! We'll go backstage and I'll tell him to his face."

*

Mickey's heart was hammering as they descended the staircase and, entering the stalls, marched down the aisle. He remembered now that day in Paddington when Sanders had pitied any man who found himself in Emily's sights. He thought he might have been able to cope with that, but here she was apparently intent upon bearding Henry Hyndman—who, regardless of his mistakes and reputedly high-handed attitude, was a figure of some significance. Sanders, at least, was warned as, his attention attracted to their progress down the aisle, he recognised Mickey and nodded; although he would be unable to identify the veiled Emily, he must have realised that it was she.

They mounted the few steps at the left side of the stage, to be confronted by a large man bursting from a suit that may have fitted him several years earlier. "You can't come 'ere," he protested. "No one's allowed backstage."

"We're friends of George Sanders," Emily announced, "and it is imperative that I see one of the speakers once the curtain comes down."

"What's your name?"

"Dorothy Bridgeman."

"Well, you stand 'ere while I get word to Mr Sanders." He turned to walk onto the stage, but paused and turned back, raising a finger. "Don't you move."

They remained in the wings while the security man darted onstage and whispered in Sanders' ear. When he returned, he nodded and pointed several times at the spot where they were standing, murmuring, "About ten minutes."

During that interval, Mickey took Emily's hand and again

enquired whether she was feeling unwell. She taught him the error of this by tearing her hand away and telling him, in a voice louder than strictly necessary, that she was perfectly fine. She was, he noticed, still trembling.

It was, in fact, fifteen minutes before the final discussion point had been answered by both speakers and Sanders was able to bring the meeting to a close. As the curtain came down, the security man stood aside and Emily/Dorothy swept past him. Sanders was standing with Hyndman and Rothstein, engaged in casual—and, apparently, perfectly friendly—conversation as she and Mickey advanced on them. Rothstein looked in their direction and smiled, at which point a youth in his mid-teens skipped past Emily and Mickey.

"This is my son Andrew," said Rothstein. "Andrew, I'd like you to meet George Sanders, one of our leading trade union figures, and Mr Henry Hyndman, the founder of our movement."

Emily stopped at the side of Hyndman, who was at that point closest to her, and threw back her veil. "Why," gasped Hyndman in surprise, "I do believe it's Comrade Bridgeman. How nice to see…"

"Harry," Dorothy/Emily nodded brusquely, stepping past him.

"Well," muttered Harry Hyndman in what sounded like relief as he looked around the small group, "it's approaching this old man's bedtime, so I'll leave you to it, if it's all the same to you." With that, he exited stage right, a tiny smile on his face.

"Comrade Rothstein…" began Dorothy/Emily, her voice shaking with what appeared to be rage rather than nervousness.

"Ah, Theo," Sanders intervened, banishing his alarmed expression and stepping forward, "please meet Mickey Rice. He is a young busman who's already making his mark. He will, I am sure, make a major contribution to our movement in years to come."

Rothstein offered Mickey, upon whom awful realisation had now dawned, his hand, apparently unperturbed by the very evident anger of Mickey's companion.

"And," continued the gallant Sanders, "you know Dorothy Bridgeman…"

"Of course." Rothstein smiled and extended his hand. "It's been a few years, I believe since…"

"Comrade Rothstein," Dorothy/Emily, entirely unmollified by these interventions, began once more, "I simply must comment upon your speech. George, kindly step out of the way! It's not as if I'm going to hit him!"

Rothstein nodded gently. "Yes, George, I think I'm quite safe." He turned to his son. "Andrew, why don't you and George wait for me in the stalls? I won't be long." Andrew, more amused than fearful of his father's safety, nodded at Dorothy/Emily and Mickey and exited stage left with Sanders. "Now, Comrade, my speech."

"At one point, Comrade Rothstein, half of the audience was convinced that you were nothing more than a German apologist!" Her anger was still present, but now it was a cold anger, and her face was drained of colour.

"But surely his point was..." Mickey attempted, bravely but vainly.

"Keep out of this, Mickey! While you quite correctly made the point that British imperialism is aggressive, and has done little for the peace of the world, you seemed to take the view that German imperialism is and will always be pacific and benign." She was looking full at Rothstein, like a teacher confronting a pupil who has delivered less than his best. "We know that is not the case. *You* know that is not the case. But you didn't *say* it!"

"So you have moved to Harry's position?" Rothstein asked, tilting his head to one side. "You now think that Britain is right to arm against the German menace?"

This inflamed her all the more, the colour returning to her face. "No I do *not*"—she stamped her foot—"take Harry's position! Both imperialisms are to be combatted rather than siding with one against the other. But this is something that you did not say until the very end of your speech. In fact, your speech appeared to be cobbled together from the articles you wrote for *Justice* in 1911. You should have realised that the tonight's audience would be different to, would perhaps be less knowledgeable than, the readership of the SDF journal. You should have simplified the issue.

"Quite correctly, you took Harry to task for his un-Marxist approach in bringing in the role of the Kaiser. A Marxist, you said, should know better than to do that. Of course! But what does a *real* Marxist say about war? What did Lenin, criticising one of the participants, say on the occasion of the Stuttgart conference? War, he said, is the 'necessary product of capitalism.' And yet where in your speech was this point made, Comrade Rothstein? Where? *No*where!" Her arms were straight at her sides, her hands balled into fists, while the sinews of her neck were prominent as she forced her face closer to Rothstein, and it occurred to Mickey that he did not know this person. This was not Emily.

"And you call yourself a Marxist, Comrade Rothstein! Tell me, how are we to utilise the crisis brought about by war to bring down the capitalist system if our leading thinkers neglect to tell their audiences that war is the inevitable *product* of that system! Oh, your speech was *such* a disappointment!"

Rothstein stood there and took it, perhaps mindful of the possibility that any attempt to defend himself would lead Dorothy/Emily to further heights of fury. Now he nodded sagely. "There is, Comrade Bridgeman, something in what you say. I will do better next time."

"I should hope *so!*" she replied, turning on her heel and exiting stage left.

A forlorn Mickey looked at Rothstein, desperately wanting to apologise for his lover's behaviour but not knowing how to, not even knowing whether he should. Rothstein gave him a grin and shook his head, implying that he should not make the attempt. "Dorothy and I have known each other for several years," he said. "And she *does* have a point." He shrugged. "Let's join George and Andrew."

These two were waiting halfway down the aisle. "Did you hear your father being admonished?" laughed Rothstein.

"Every word," replied Andrew. "It was most unfair."

Sanders, grinning wryly, wagged an I-told-you-so finger at Mickey.

"Oh, not really so unfair," said Rothstein, placing a hand on his son's shoulder. "True, our comrade could have delivered her rebuke in a different manner, but if you heard every word you know that I conceded that she had a point. And she did!" He sighed and rubbed his hands together. "Now, why don't we all go to my house for something that will warm us on a wet Sunday evening?"

"Oh, I'm sorry," said Mickey, pointing to the exit. "I have to..."

"Ah, I see," Rothstein nodded as he fully realised the relationship between Mickey and Dorothy/Emily. "Yes, you must. Go now." He extended a hand. "Let's hope that we will have time to talk the next time we meet, Comrade Mickey."

*

She was waiting for him by the darkened box office.

"What took you so long?" she snapped. "I hope you've not been apologising for me!" She was still not Emily.

"No," he said, the sound almost a groan as he felt a wave of fatigue pass over him, "but not because I didn't want to."

Without a word, she left him there and, grasping a large brass door-handle, threw open the heavy door and walked onto the street. He ran after her, detaining her by placing a hand on her arm. "But Emily, what is *wrong?* Why are you behaving like this?" he asked earnestly, at a complete loss to know how to act in this situation.

She whirled on him, and he could see that she was almost as furious with him as she had been with Rothstein. "Are you telling me you really don't know? How *should* I behave after you've practically betrayed me?"

"*Betrayed* you?" His face was stamped with incredulity. "How have I betrayed you?"

"You've just told me that you wanted to apologise on my behalf. She prodded his chest with a finger. "Don't you *ever* apologise for me! *Ever!* Don't you remember that on the train to Paddington I told you that I am usually right? Do you remember that? *You* apologise for *me*?"

The social gulf separating them, previously hidden behind a cloak of genuine affection and sometimes ferocious carnality, was now revealed for the first time. But the distance between them was increased by something else, some demon deep inside Dorothy/Emily that had been released this evening. Mickey had no sympathy for this person, and he now wished to resist her the way he would resist an overbearing employer. "Who do you..." he began.

"Don't interrupt me! And then, even before I had said more than a dozen words to Rothstein, you began to defend him. *That*, Mr Rice, was the first betrayal. Don't you realise what this movement means to me? I desperately *care* about it, and if someone acts in a way that might harm it or do it less than justice, I *must* speak up. Why can't you understand that?" There were tears in her eyes now, but they betokened not regret but frustration that she was unable to convince him and trepidation as she sensed that the rebellion mounting within him would give rise to a line of argument that she was less able to combat. And it did.

"Listen to me, Miss Stuck-up Richardson or Bridgeman or whatever you want to call yourself," he growled, leaning over her, "do you think that the way you've behaved this evening doesn't harm the movement? *Do* you? If you do, you don't live in the same world as the rest of us! It wasn't what you said to Rothstein. In fact, you heard him say that you had a point. But the way you said it, Emily, was just fucking disgraceful! Rothstein could handle it because he's far more intelligent than most of us—including you!—and he has all the social skills. But try talking that way to others in the movement—to *workers*—and you'll lose them forever. How does that help the movement! Eh? And I haven't even mentioned the way you treated me. You drag me down the aisle without even attempting to explain what you're about to do. And we're comrades? You didn't treat me like a comrade this evening, Emily. You treated me like a fucking servant, leading me onstage without it even occurring to you to introduce me. And let me tell you, Emily: I didn't. Fucking. Like it!" He straightened up and sighed. "You tell me you didn't get the education you deserved? Bloody right, because it seems that nobody took the trouble to teach you good manners. So maybe you should think this over. I'm going home now."

He turned and walked away from her, not looking back, for a moment not caring whether she made her way home. He walked briskly for five minutes, unmindful of the rain as, the anger churning within him, he replayed the events of the evening in his mind. In the succeeding minutes, however, other pictures, unbidden, presented themselves to him, and his pace slowed. He suddenly realised that if he kept walking he would lose not only the Dorothy Bridgeman revealed to him this evening, but also the soft, beautiful, loving Emily who might be now lost in Hackney, alone in the rain, prey to thieves and rapists. Something clutched his heart. He turned and walked back the way he had come, soon breaking into a trot, panic welling within him. As he approached the Empire, a taxicab approached, slowing and finally pulling into the kerb. Emily opened the passenger door and beckoned to him.

Sliding in beside her, he reached for her and could have wept with relief as she came into his arms. He covered her face with desperate kisses, which she, equally desperate, reciprocated.

"Come back to me, Emily, please come back to me," he whispered.

She placed a hand on either side of his face and smiled that smile. Emily was back.

"What time are you working tomorrow, my love?" she asked.

"Late."

"Then you must come home with me, Michael."

"But my clothes are wet."

"I'll light the gas fire."

As the cab executed a U-turn and drove south, a small car which had been idling at the side of the road turned and followed.

*

Once inside the Clapham flat, they found that their desperation was undiminished. Mickey pulled her to him, kissing her mouth, one arm about her slim waist, pressing her to him, wanting her to know, to feel, the level of his excitement, while she, having discarded her jacket, reached behind her to unbutton her blouse.

Seeing her blouse fall, he reached for her breasts. "I don't want to lose you, Emily," he whispered urgently. "Please don't go away from me again. I want this to last forever. I love you, Emily."

As he unhooked her brassiere, she unbuckled his belt and opened his fly. "You haven't lost me, Michael, and I don't want to go away from you." She swallowed, experiencing a shortness of breath as she told him: "Tell me what you want—which part of me." She gulped, as she always did when they were like this, more so when they spoke frankly of their act and their body parts, which excited her in a way she had never before known.

"All of you, my sweetheart."

"But first?"

"Your breasts, of course."

"Then give them their proper name, my Michael."

"Your tits."

"Make love to my tits, Michael." She threw back her head, exposing her long neck, exulting, "Tits. How I love to hear you say it! Now, please tell me what you love about my tits, my sweet."

Up against the wall of the passageway, he bent to kiss her breasts, licking her nipples, biting them, as she reached between his legs and clutched the tent in his underpants.

"I love the soft, silky feel of them, Em..."

"Em! Yes, call me Em!"

"And I love their size, colour and shape, the way they curve up to the nipples."

She moaned and tightened her grip on his penis.

"And is that what you want, my lovely Emily?"

"Of course, Michael. I want this cock of yours. Cock! Take off those trousers, so that we can let him out. "

"And your skirt, Em."

"Why, is there something under there that you want, Michael?"

"Your quim, Em, I want your quimquimquim!"

Trembling uncontrollably as she felt her juices descend, she let her skirt fall to the floor and wriggled out of her drawers, then gasped as he fell to his knees and buried his face between her legs. "It's wet, my darling, I'm so sorry, it's wet. You mustn't! Oohhh, yes, do it! Lick me, Michael, lick my quim." She parted her legs further and sank onto his face, clasping her own breasts, pulling the nipples as she leaned back against the wall, trembling anew and glorying in this act of abandonment and the knowledge that it was something they both wanted and loved. As her juices stirred once more, she released her breasts and clutched his head, holding him to her as, to her delight, she felt him withdraw his tongue from her vagina and find her clitoris, nipping it, sucking it, flicking it with his tongue. She bucked and rolled as she released her juices, shuddering as she removed her hands from his head, returning them to her breasts. Seeing as he got to his feet that his lips and chin shone with her juice, one hand now left its breast and reached for his hair, pulling his face to hers so that she might fasten her mouth on his and put her tongue in his mouth. Feeling his hand pull at her vacant breast, she sobbed with pleasure and love for him, covering his face with kisses, as she reached for his hard penis, running her thumb over its head.

"You're wet too, my love," she panted.

He smiled and uttered a long sigh. "Nobody has ever felt like this, Em." He took a breath, reached behind her to grip her buttocks, and lifted her off the floor. "Put your legs around me, Em."

"Yes!"

"Em, are you going to leave your hat on?"

She laughed, and bent to kiss his mouth. "Let's try it. In fact, we could make it even more interesting if I..." She reached up and let the veil fall over her face.

"Oh Jesus." The sight seemed to electrify him, and he manoeuvred her onto his penis as her legs closed about his hips.

"We need a change of plan, darling. You can't really fuck me in this position, so I'll fuck you. Just swing around, sweetheart, so your back is against the wall."

With Mickey's back to the wall and her legs wrapped around him, she clasped his neck with both hands and lowered herself onto him to the fullest extent, feeling him inside her and flexing her muscles as she remained there for a few moments, before lifting her buttocks until his penis was barely in her vagina, then moving back and forth, just an inch, titillating both of them. And then she forced herself onto him, causing them both to cry out in wonder. The veiled lady moved back and forth with increasing speed and aggression, her breasts swinging in time with her thrusts, until she began to feel her biggest orgasm yet begin to break.

"Oh, Christ, what's that, Em? Have I come?"

"No. That. Was. *Me!*"

"Don't let me come inside you, my love, please."

"Don't. Worry. I. Have. Something. In. *Mind!*"

At this, feeling his penis grow warm, she released him, dropped to her knees, flicked aside her veil and, for the first time, took him in her mouth.

"You were different tonight, Em."

It was an hour later, and they had both dozed. She had known that this conversation would come. She didn't want it, but knew she must endure it, somehow get through it, and tell as much of the truth as possible.

"You mean when we made love?"

"No." He laughed: a good sign. "Or rather yes, very much so. But I meant earlier, Em, at the Empire."

She sighed. "Yes, I know what you mean, Mickey."

"Do you want to try to...explain? Only if you want to, Em."

She smiled. "That's very considerate of you, my love." A pause as her gaze wandered over the ceiling. "I really must do something about these cobwebs."

He gave her a comradely nudge.

"Alright. Well, I believe I told you that sometimes I get...shrill."

"Yes, you *were* quite shrill. I'm just wondering why, Em."

She pushed herself into a sitting position and leaned her back against the headboard of the bed, picking up her hat from the bedside table and placing it on her head; she let the veil fall over her face.

"Are you hiding from me, Em?"

She shook her head. "No, Mickey, I'm not hiding from you."

"That's good."

Another sigh. "Well, I suppose it has something to do with my childhood—or, rather my youth. Those years were dominated by my father and my brother, two older males, and I was so often made to feel that my opinions, my thoughts—me as a person—were not considered important, when they were considered at all. So I sometimes felt that I had to...*assert* myself. For example, on the question of education, which I told you about."

"What about your mother?"

"Ohhh, Mama was in the same position as me, more or less, but she tended, superficially anyway, to accept it as her role. Her Catholic upbringing and her social background had a lot to do with that, of course, and she'd had no exposure to what we might call advanced thinking. Whenever we had family discussions—which sometimes developed into arguments—she tended to restrict herself to agreeing with Papa and Edwin."

"But didn't you tell me that it was your mother who had suggested that you...?"

"Be put away? Yes, that was her contribution to the discussion.

As you can imagine, I've given that considerable thought over the years, and I just wonder whether, at some level, there was an element of jealousy there."

"You think she was jealous of you?"

"Maybe. Although jealousy might not be the word. Fear, perhaps. Fear that, in breaking away from the suffocating confines of bourgeois family life—although she would not have put it in these terms, of course—I would in some way reveal to her that her own life had been essentially empty, meaningless. That's what I mean when I say that her acceptance of her role might be merely superficial. If I were put away, that danger would no longer exist."

"But you said that your parents were very much in love."

"Yes, they were, and are, I suppose. But imagine if the roles were reversed, and my mother was the breadwinner. Would my father be satisfied with a life solely centred on his love for his wife and children? I think not. So why should she be?"

"But Em, sweetheart, that possibility just sounds so...*cruel*. That she would even consider..."

She was silent for a moment. Behind the veil, her eyes closed as she gazed into the emotional chasm which lay beneath this possible truth. She blinked, and the first tear rolled down her cheek. She sniffed.

"Yes, and since I first considered this possibility I find that I have become even more determined to assert myself—not only to ensure that I am taken seriously in a male world, but also to ensure that I *never* become like my mother.

"But that's only *one* possible explanation. Another is that her suggestion that I be put away was one of *her* rare attempts to assert *her*self, to contribute something original. If so, of course, it was entirely inappropriate, and neither my father nor Edwin gave it a moment's thought. And this is something I share with her: my attempts at self-assertion are sometimes, while not necessarily inappropriate themselves, sometimes made in inappropriate circumstances, or in an inappropriate manner, and that, I fear, is what you saw in Hackney."

From behind the veil, she watched as he nodded, looked up and grinned at her. "So now I know you. It's alright, Em. Really."

"Yes," she agreed, as something caught in her throat. "Now you know me."

"So you can remove the veil, sweetheart."

"Not yet, Mickey. I don't want you to see me like this."

"Like what, Em?" he asked softly, wonderingly.

"Vulnerable."

131

He thought about this, then nodded. "Alright. So tell me, then: when you were letting fly at poor old Rothstein, you seemed a different person, someone I'd never seen before, but when you picked me up in the taxi, you'd changed back to my Emily." He shook his head in puzzlement. "What happened to cause that?"

Now, at last, she felt a smile lift her lips. "Just think back, my love, to what had happened in the meantime?"

"We...had an argument in the street..."

"You gave me a good telling off, Michael. *That's* what happened. Nobody had ever done that before, and it was just what I needed. You showed me not just what I had done to Theo, but also how I had treated you."

He laughed. "Well, I'm giving you another one now: it doesn't matter if I see you while you're feeling vulnerable, because I love you, Em. So take off that bloody veil, you silly girl."

She removed hat and veil, presenting her swollen eyes and tear-streaked face to him.

"There she is: my Emily."

"Michael."

12

Superintendent Patrick Quinn, head of Special Branch, stood at the securely sealed window of his office in New Scotland Yard, watching the street traffic on the Victoria Embankment below and, beyond that, the movement of the ferries and cargo vessels on the Thames. Now sixty years of age, Quinn had left his County Mayo home at the age of nineteen to become a London police officer, and ten years later had been selected to join the new Special Irish Branch of the Metropolitan Police. As the bombing campaign of the Irish Republican Brotherhood had receded, the department had dropped the "Irish" from its name and had broadened its remit to include the investigation of all activities which might be termed "subversive" and to provide protection for high officials, whether British or, if they were visiting this country, foreign.

Of late, the Branch had focused its attention on the excesses of Mrs Pankhurst's suffragette movement, with Quinn taking a direct supervisory role. In truth, the activities of this movement were sufficient to keep the whole department busy. Last year, for example, a bomb had caused considerable damage to a Surrey cottage being built for Chancellor of the Exchequer David Lloyd

George, and there had been several attempts to invade Downing Street. With the seemingly inexorable increase in industrial unrest, however, it was also necessary to keep an eye on the syndicalists and other socialists, but resources were stretched dangerously thin: the establishment figure for the Branch was, at 114, low enough, but there were in fact only 86 officers on books.

Hearing a knock at the door of the office, Quinn called "Come!" and young Ralph Kitchener presented himself. As Quinn turned from the window, this is the figure Kitchener would have seen: a tall, unsmiling man with thick, dark eyebrows and a grey goatee, a hard veteran of military bearing; Quinn was a man who often made seemingly impossible demands of his officers, and Kitchener was never comfortable in his presence.

"Here to report a success, Kitchener?"

"I believe so, sir. You'll recall that you asked me to take a look at the BSP meeting at the Hackney Empire..."

"Of course, of course. But, my, you must have had a long day yesterday!"

"I did, sir. But, as you know, we're overstretched and..."

"Yes, I *do* know that, Detective Constable, and I have made the appropriate representations to the Commissioner. So, the trip to Hackney was fruitful?"

"That's possibly for you to say, sir." He drew a thick notebook from his jacket pocket and flipped it open. "The main speaker, Rothman, was most unpatriotic..."

"Roth*stein*. How long have you been with us, Kitchener?"

"I joined the Branch in 1910, sir."

"Then you may not know that Rothstein is Russian. Not only that, he is known to be a friend of Vladimir Ilyich Ulyanov, known to his comrades as Lenin. Indeed, so close are they that Lenin has stayed at Rothstein's house on several occasions while in London."

Kitchener managed to look impressed. "Oh well, sir, that does put a somewhat different complexion on the matter. The point is, Superintendent, he often seemed to be making excuses for Germany, suggesting that if there's a danger of war it's our fault rather than the Kaiser's..."

"Look, Kitchener, it sounds to me as if he made the kind of speech we might have expected. We've kept track of his writings and we know what his line is—although it's maybe not quite as simple as you suggest."

A somewhat crestfallen Kitchener now flipped over several pages of his notebook. "I see, sir. Well, as you know, socialism is not my speciality, and maybe if we were not so stretched..."

"Yes, yes, Kitchener: if someone else had been available...Is that all?"

Kitchener raised his head. "Not by a long chalk, sir. I was seated right up in the circle, in one of the back rows, and that's where I remained after the meeting had been closed. There was a lady who walked onto the stage—apparently known to the speaker and to Sanders, who chaired the meeting..."

"George Sanders? They're giving trade union leaders prominence now?" He nodded. "Well, yes, that *is* interesting, Kitchener."

"We have an interest in the lady who joined them onstage, sir."

Quinn narrowed his eyes at the young detective constable. "We do?"

"Yes, sir. Dorothy Bridgeman."

Momentarily, Quinn was at a loss, but then his eyes opened wide as he located the memory. "Liverpool, 1911! Stabbed a bobby with her hatpin! Well, you certainly have a memory on you, Detective Constable!"

Kitchener smiled self-deprecatingly. "Not really, sir: when we received the request from Liverpool, I was the officer assigned to trace her whereabouts. She had not been to her last-known address for several days. We kept it under surveillance for some time, but she did not show up there—or anywhere else, that we could ascertain."

"All the same, Kitchener, good work." He thought for a moment, and then frowned. "But you say you were right at the back of the circle, and presumably the curtain was down at this point. Are you sure...?"

"Despite the distance, I could hear every word, or most of them, at least. The Empire is not a large theatre." He smiled. "And, I have to say, Miss Bridgeman's voice was very loud."

"So where do we find her, Kitchener?"

"She was with a young man, sir, a busman called Mickey Rice. Although he said hardly anything, Sanders spoke highly of him to Rothstein. She stormed out of the theatre and Rice followed. In the meantime, I made my way to an emergency exit and joined Detective Constable Rees, who was waiting in a car a short distance down Mare Street. Bridgeman and Rice appeared to be having a heated argument, and at one point Rice turned and walked away. Bridgeman walked to and fro outside the theatre, seemingly muttering to herself and gesticulating."

"Were you able to hear any of this?"

"Regrettably not, sir. We were too far away and, besides, it was raining. After some minutes, Bridgeman hailed a passing cab and we followed. Very shortly, the cab stopped to pick up Rice, who apparently had been walking back to Bridgeman. From what we could see, from several vehicle-lengths behind them, there was a warm reconciliation between the two before the cab did a U-turn. We followed it to an address in Clapham, which they both entered. We stayed there for just under an hour and, as there was no sign of either of them emerging, called it a night."

"Had you stayed until morning, you might have learned a great deal more!" Quinn blustered.

Without allowing this outburst to perturb him, Kitchener, knowing that he still had to impart his most valuable intelligence, proceeded with a confident smile. "We returned at 0700 hours this morning, sir."

This gave Quinn something of a jolt. He smiled apologetically, murmuring, "You have my full attention, Detective Constable. Have no fear of further interruption by me."

"Rice emerged at 0800. As he was on foot and one of us had to stay with the vehicle, we let him go. Bridgeman came out fifteen minutes later and I followed her. She boarded a bus, with me behind her. She alighted at Vauxhall Bridge Road and took a tram to Victoria, from where she made her way to St James's Park station, and this worried me, because if she took the Underground I knew I would become separated from Rees, who had been following our progress. But instead of entering the station she went to the entrance to Electric Railway House in Petty France. As she seemed to be entirely oblivious of my presence, I closed the distance between us, and as I entered the building saw her exchange greetings with the man at the reception desk as she made her way to the stairs. Slowing my pace until she had disappeared from view, I asked the reception man whether that was Miss Bridgeman who had just come in. 'Oh no, sir,' he said. 'That was our Miss Richardson.' He expressed surprise that Miss Richardson, who is extremely attractive, could possibly have been mistaken for anyone else. I made my excuses and left, joining Rees outside."

Quinn regarded Kitchener with new eyes. "You are, Detective Constable," he said, "to be congratulated on your initiative. And sit down, for God's sake! You look like a schoolboy in the headmaster's office!"

"Thank you, sir."

There were two upright telephones on Quinn's desk, black for external calls and dark green for internal. Pulling the green one towards him, he lifted the earpiece and dialled. "Detective Sergeant Delaney? Will you do me the great kindness of bringing me the file on Miss Dorothy Bridgeman." His usual harsh tone had given way to a soft Irish lilt, and as he glanced across at Kitchener there was a sparkle in his eye. Superintendent Quinn was enjoying himself.

Delaney, one of several Irishmen recruited to the Branch in its early years, had been largely deskbound since a bullet had disabled him in the Sidney Street siege in January 1911. After the most perfunctory of knocks, he entered the office and limped to Quinn's desk, dropping on it a thin buff folder and uttering a single word: "Chief."

"I'm obliged, Kevin." Quinn, it seemed, often took a softer approach towards those on the brink of retirement, particularly if they were injured, and even more so if they came from the old country. He picked up the folder and weighed it, grimacing at Kitchener. "Not much here, I fancy."

Kitchener watched as Quinn first riffled through the pages of the thin file and then took them out and placed them on his desk until they made an incomplete rectangle of seven sheets. Starting at the top left-hand side, he rapidly scanned them until he reached the bottom right-hand sheet. Looking up at Kitchener, he pronounced, "No, not so very much. In fact, it seems that the Liverpool incident of 1911 can be forgotten." He picked up a sheet which, Kitchener saw, was stamped "CONFIDENTIAL" across the top. "The constable, it turns out, was not as badly injured as it was first feared, and he returned to duty shortly afterwards. The Chief Constable then took the view that as there were allegations of brutality on both sides— by our people as well as the trade unionists—it would be a public relations error to have the matter debated in open court." He looked up again. "Miss Bridgeman has, therefore, been as free as a bird for the past two years or more."

"But she doesn't know that, sir."

Quinn grinned—not quite a smile—and waved a finger at Kitchener. "Oh, you're very naughty, Detective Constable. Yes, it might in theory be possible for us to make use of that circumstance, but in all honesty it's a bit like her file: very thin. Slim though it may be, however, the file *does* make interesting reading. Comes from a rich family, does our Miss Bridgeman: father's a shipping magnate, would you believe." His eyes turned from one sheet to another. "Joined the British Socialist Party shortly before her Liverpool adventure." He scooped up the pages and reinserted them into the file, closed it and smacked it with his palm. "Nothing there of real use to us, I suggest, unless the opportunity arises. Of far more interest to me, Detective Constable, is the current circumstance that you, by your ingenuity, have unveiled."

Kitchener did not know whether Quinn was making fun of him, and was not even particularly sure what he meant. "Current circumstance, sir?"

Quinn sighed, and it was difficult to tell whether he was pleased or disappointed that his young subordinate had not seen it. "Her lover is a busman, and this socialist extremist works, under an assumed name, at the headquarters of his employer! There must be something going on there, Kitchener."

"Ah, yes."

13

Albert Stanley was, ostensibly, on his lunch-break. Leaving Electric Railway House dressed in a light overcoat and carrying an umbrella, he walked down Broadway to Victoria Street, where he hailed a cab and directed the driver to take him to the Victoria Embankment. It would have been far easier to have undertaken the journey in his chauffeur-driven car, but Quinn had emphasised the need for discretion. The Superintendent had also explained that, for reasons he would make clear when they met, he was unable to see him at Electric Railway House.

Stanley sighed and sank back into the passenger seat, gazing out of the right-hand window. The rain of the previous evening was nowhere to be seen, and it was a pleasant mild day, and as the cab, having crossed Parliament Square, turned left from Westminster Bridge onto the Embankment, weak sunlight sparkled on the Thames. He was suddenly grateful for Quinn's call, as it had given him a reason to leave the office—something he rarely did while the sun was high in the sky. He must, he resolved as the cab pulled up opposite New Scotland Yard, get out more.

*

"Ah, Mr Stanley!" Quinn stood up at his desk and extended a hand as his visitor was escorted into the office by Detective Sergeant Delany. "A great pleasure to meet you! I have, of course, heard so much about you."

Stanley seated himself opposite the Superintendent and raised an eyebrow. "Oh? Do I have a file, Superintendent Quinn?"

Quinn, unused to banter, was momentarily stumped. "A file?"

Then his frown was banished and he forced a laugh. "Oh, very amusing, Mr Stanley." He raised a hand towards the coat stand in the corner of the room. "Sergeant, take Mr Stanley's coat."

Stanley raised a hand. "That's quite alright, Superintendent. I have only a few moments to spare."

"Well, at least your umbrella..."

Stanley sighed and handed his umbrella to the sergeant. "Now, Superintendent, perhaps you can tell me why I am here."

Quinn sat and placed his forearms on his desk. "Tell me, Mr Stanley," he began, having assumed control, "does a Miss Richardson work at Electric Railway House? I understand, of course, that you have a large complement of staff and may not be familiar with every individual."

Stanley's mouth dropped open. "Miss *Richardson?* Why, yes, she works in my office as a member of my secretarial team. But why on earth should you be interested in Miss Richardson?"

Quinn ignored the question for the moment. "Has she been with you long?"

"Six or seven months, I suppose. Yes, she started with us last June."

"And she is therefore, one must assume, a satisfactory employee."

"Highly satisfactory." Stanley drew himself up. "Come now, Superintendent, I must insist that you explain yourself."

Quinn was silent for a moment. If, however, he resented Stanley's attitude, he was forced to concede that men of this stature were allowed to address the head of Special Branch in such a manner. "Richardson," he said, "is not her real name. She is Dorothy Bridgeman, and in 1911 she attacked a policeman in Liverpool, during a demonstration in support of the transport strike."

Stanley now relaxed, a small smile on his lips. "Well, I *do* remember reading about that demonstration, Mr Quinn," he said. He cleared his throat. "From what I recall of it, I think we might safely assume that Miss Richardson's actions were not entirely unprovoked."

Having lost the initiative once more, Quinn glanced briefly at his desk before returning his gaze to Stanley. "Perhaps not entirely," he conceded. "But that is neither here nor there. Of more immediate relevance is the fact that she is a member of the British Socialist Party."

Stanley considered this for a moment. "Well, while we would find it regrettable if any of our staff held socialist views, we do not yet vet our employees on political grounds, Superintendent."

Quinn was close to losing his patience. "You're simply not

concerned that a member of the BSP is working for you—in your own office!—using an assumed name?"

"But you have explained the need for an alias, Mr Quinn," Stanley responded gently. "Do you, by the way, intend to arrest her for the Liverpool offence?"

"We do not!" Quinn blurted out, and immediately regretted it.

"Then I really fail to see why we should be concerned." He spread his hands. "It's not, after all, as if Miss Richardson has been attempting to convert the rest of my staff to the cause of socialism."

"Would you concede the possibility that she has been placed in your office to gather intelligence, Mr Stanley?"

"On behalf of whom, for heaven's sake?"

It was Quinn's turn to spread his hands. On firmer ground now, he smiled. "The union, of course. Your Miss Richardson is acquainted with George Sanders, one of the red-button union's full-time organisers, and even better acquainted with a young busman called Rice."

This had its effect. "Rice? Young Rice from Middle Row?"

Quinn took a pencil from the pot on his desk and hastily scribbled on his blotter. "Middle Row, you say. Is that the name of his garage? You might be interested to know, Mr Stanley, that Rice spent last night in Miss Richardson's flat in Clapham."

Stanley bristled, reddening. "And how could that possibly interest me? Or you, for that matter, unless Special Branch is now policing morals as well as politics?"

Quinn was unflustered. "In all honesty, it doesn't concern me in the least. What does concern me is the possibility that the British Socialist Party is engaged in activity which might at some stage imperil the smooth running of our capital's transport system." He fixed Stanley with a hard stare. "One would like to think that such a possibility would also be of concern to the managing director of London's largest omnibus operator."

*

It was an angry managing director of London's largest omnibus operator who rode a taxi back to Electric Railway House. He had found Quinn quite insufferable, his approach invasive. The last thing the LGOC needed was a labour war like those waged by the Pinkertons in the USA; and Special Branch, it seemed to him, was in danger of becoming little more than a state-owned version of the Pinkertons if it was now to act against legal political parties and trade unions. Of course, the state needed to protect itself against bombers, whether of the Irish republican or anarchist variety, and those who threatened violent revolution. The actions Special Branch was taking against the suffragettes was surely reasonable, however logical their demands, given their violent tactics. But the British Socialist Party was small and had not, to his knowledge, undertaken any terrorist activity, and the notion that the LPU might be a danger to the state was, given his experience of its general secretary, ludicrous.

But Quinn had hit home when it came to the suggestion that Emily Richardson might be involved in some kind of industrial espionage. This was, indeed, a possibility. As he had sat in Quinn's office, he had recalled the telephone call he had received from Bywater just before the Board of Trade arbitration hearing last September. Someone, he had complained, had leaked the news of his visit to Stanley's office in June; George Sanders, in confronting him with this, had claimed that the information came from a police friend, who in turn claimed that a Chief Inspector Griffiths, who had heard it from Stanley himself, had talked about it openly at the Yard. It was certainly true that he had told Griffiths of Bywater's visit, but Emily had been present...

*

Back in his office that afternoon, Stanley replaced the receiver on his telephone, sat back in his chair and uttered a long sigh. So that was it. He was left with no alternative. Using his intercom device, he asked Miss McKewan to send in Miss Richardson. She gave him a tight grin as she entered and sat opposite him, pencil poised over her shorthand pad.

"No, Miss Richardson, you may put down your pad and pencil," Stanley advised, not unkindly.

She did as he suggested and, raising her eyes, saw that he was regarding her with what might have been a mixture of irritation and regret. "How can I help you, Mr Stanley?" she asked, and was aware that she seemed to be short of breath.

He shook his head. "I'm afraid you cannot, Miss Richardson." Another shake of the head. "Not anymore."

"Is anything wrong, sir?"

He sat silently for a moment, as if unsure how to proceed, and then rose from his chair and strode to the window. Now he turned to her.

"Yes, Miss Richardson, something is wrong, very wrong." He stepped to the side of his desk, placing his left hand on its surface and leaning towards her. "In June, you will recall that Chief Inspector Griffiths was here for a Traffic Liaison Meeting. Before the meeting commenced, and in your presence, I told the chief inspector that I had received a visit from a leader of the red-button union. Do you have any recollection of that?"

Emily managed to look puzzled. "Well, I can recall the meeting, but any preliminary remarks you may have made...I was, after all, not required to take a note, and so I probably paid little attention to anything you may have said at that stage."

This, he thought, sounded perfectly believable. Perhaps he needed to adopt a different approach. "Are you acquainted with Mr George Sanders?"

"George Sanders? I am acquainted with his name, of course. I recall reading about him during the cabdrivers' strike in January last year."

"But I understand, Miss Richardson, that you were with him last night at the Hackney Empire."

"I..." The colour had drained from her face and she found herself unable to respond.

He whirled away from her and returned to the window, where he placed his back to the sill and crossed his arms. "At lunchtime today, I was called to New Scotland Yard by Superintendent Quinn of Special Branch. There, I was told that you were a member of the British Socialist Party, and that last night at the Hackney Empire you conversed with Mr Sanders. Furthermore, I was advised that in 1911 you had assaulted a policeman in Liverpool, when your name was Dorothy Bridgeman."

"But I fail to see..."

"Last night, you were identified by a Special Branch officer, Miss Richardson, who also followed you home to Clapham."

Her head fell, and she spent a few seconds regarding her hands, which she had folded in her lap. When she lifted her head once more, however, she had regained her colour and appeared perfectly composed. Unflinchingly, she locked her eyes with his and took a breath. "Yes, it's all perfectly true, Mr Stanley; and, yes, I told George Sanders about the visit of Mr Bywater to your office."

"But unless I'm mistaken, Miss Richardson, I did not mention the gentleman's name to Chief Inspector Griffiths."

"No, but you indicated that he was not particularly clever."

Despite himself, Stanley laughed. He relaxed and returned to the chair at his desk, where he sat and contemplated her silently. She was, he thought, quite wonderful.

"I would also like to say, Mr Stanley, that my alleged attack on the policeman was not as it might sound."

He held up a palm. "Oh, have no fear on that account, my dear. I remember reading the newspaper accounts at the time, and am quite prepared to believe that you acted in self-defence." Although there was no possibility of him being overheard, he now lowered his voice and leaned forward. "And I can advise you, Miss Richardson, that Superintendent Quinn—who appears to be only marginally more intelligent than Mr Bywater—let it slip that the police do not intend to prosecute you for that incident."

Her mouth fell open and there then blossomed that enchanting smile. "Oh, that's wonderful. Thank you so much for telling me, Mr Stanley...But tell me: am I dismissed?"

He bit his lip. "You should be, shouldn't you? What would you do, were you in my position?"

She did not hesitate. "Oh, I would dismiss me."

"For being a dangerous revolutionary?"

She grinned, aware now that the situation was not as serious as it might have been, and that they were almost playing a game. "No, for betraying your confidence in the matter of Bywater. It does seem to me, however, that I was a little rash in confessing my guilt. I could, for example, have suggested that Chief Inspector Griffiths had been indiscreet..."

He smiled. "Wouldn't have done you a bit of good, I'm afraid." He nodded at his telephone. "As soon as I returned to the office, I called Mr Griffiths, and he is absolutely sure that he spoke to not a soul."

"Dismissal it is, then."

"Dismissal it *should* be, but I am for some reason inclined to be lenient. Needless to say, you can no longer be employed in this office: this May, we will be negotiating terms and conditions with the union, and it simply would not do to have one of their sympathisers—and possibly, an informant—on our team. I would therefore suggest that you give it to the end of the week and then hand in your notice. In the meantime, I will find an alternative post for you."

A tiny smile. "I'm very grateful, Mr Stanley. But why, if I am merely to be transferred, do I have to resign?"

"Because you can now be employed as Dorothy Bridgeman. I thought you would like that. And because, Albert Stanley not being *entirely* soft, you will commence a six-month period of probation in your new job."

She nodded. "Well, thank you. I know it's more than I deserve. But I hope you won't be affronted if I should happen to find an alternative post."

Albert Stanley turned down the corners of his mouth, a gesture with which trade union negotiators in the decades to come would become familiar. "Affronted, no. But I *would* be disappointed, Dorothy, because I should hate to lose you from the company. It has been a pleasure working with you."

"And I think you know that I have enjoyed my time here, Mr Stanley."

"Yes, I can tell that. Now, before you go, one piece of advice: change your residence, Dorothy. Now that Special Branch know where you live, it's possible that they will pester you."

Her smile now had genuine warmth in it. "Yes, that would make sense. It will depend, of course, on the location of my new job." She rose from her chair. "If there's nothing else, Mr Stanley..."

"Only one thing, Dorothy."

"Yes, sir."

He gave her a wry grin. "Young Mr Rice is an extremely lucky man."

*

Albert Stanley fell back in his chair, exhausted. What was happening to him? What was he thinking of? Not only had he not dismissed her, but he had called her "my dear" and had used her forename. Was he becoming besotted with Emily/Dorothy? Well, yes, there was obviously a danger of that happening. Should he proceed further? No, that would be lunacy, because if she had threatened the company's security by working in his office, what a greater threat she would be if he went to bed with her!

So what must he do? He could, of course, reconsider the decision not to dismiss her. But, no, he would not wish to do that. He would simply keep her at arm's length, ensuring that he did not allow himself to be anywhere near that charming smile of hers, which more than anything else would surely captivate and capture him.

14

A few days after her interview with Albert Stanley, Dorothy, as Mickey was now free to call her, announced her intention to move from Clapham.

The news brought a grin to his face. "Good: perhaps we can kill two birds with one stone."

There was no mystery to his remark: she knew that he was resolved that they live together. Although she welcomed this, she was nervous of the further implications of such a development. She raised one eyebrow, asking pleasantly enough, "You think we should look for a flat together?"

"Okay, three birds: I've been taking up space in Eric's flat for far too long, but yes, we can get a place together. Or even get married, Dorothy, if you would like that."

Goodness! Although they have been together for almost nine months, this was the first time that either of them had mentioned the possibility of marriage. She found herself looking lovingly into his face, straining to keep her eyes open lest her lids should close and propel a tear down her face. She tried to make light of it. "Aren't you supposed to be on one knee, Mickey?"

Her use of that name told him that there would—for now, anyway—be no marriage. "Not really, because I thought we'd left the Victorian age behind us. We're comrades as well as lovers, and comrades don't kneel." He sighed, feeling his heart flutter and, regardless of his misgivings, plunged ahead. "But I'll kneel if that's what it takes. On both knees, even."

She smiled and stepped closer, taking his face in her hands, kissing his eyes and mouth. "Oh, Michael. Yes, let's live together, but we should see how we get along before we discuss marriage." She drew back for a second, smiling and breathing "My very own Michael" before kissing him urgently on the mouth.

He had been waiting for her at the Clapham flat and she, having arrived home in the last few minutes, was still dressed for the office. With her use—twice!—of the name Michael, he knew what was expected of him, and now gathered up her skirt until he could place a hand between her legs. She cast off her jacket and then, breaking off from the kiss, placed her mouth next to his ear, whispering her directions.

*

After that first round, they undressed and withdrew to the bedroom.

"What exactly do you mean when you say we should see how we get on?" Mickey asked. He was stroking her head as she lay half on top of him. "I was thinking that we get on rather well."

She took one of his fingers and placed it in her mouth, nipping it

144

playfully. "Sexually, my love, we get on extremely well. But there is, I am reliably informed, rather more to marriage than that."

He sighed. "Yes, but I don't think that's what you mean at all."

At this, she sat up and looked down at him. "Really? Tell me what I mean, then."

"Well, I think you want to see how we get on politically."

"But aren't we agreed on most questions?"

"We are, but that's mostly analysis. You want to see whether we agree when it comes to, for example, taking a course of action."

"Ah." She laughed. "To be honest, Michael, I think you've given this rather more thought than have I. I'm not at all sure I know what I meant." This was not true: she suspected that Mickey knew that she wanted to see how they would fare in the event of another flare-up such as had occurred at the Hackney Empire. And Mickey was right.

They regarded each other in silence, he on his back, she now sitting at his side.

"We could, if you like, test each other now and again."

"And how would we do that, dearest?"

"Well, we could discuss a recent political action that someone had taken and see if we agreed that it was either good or bad, right or wrong."

"For example..."

"For example—and I've been wanting to see how you felt about this anyway—there was a report in the papers yesterday about a suffragette who took a meat cleaver to a painting in the National Gallery. She was protesting, so they say, about the imprisonment of Emmeline Pankhurst."

"Ah, Velasquez: the Rokeby Venus, so called because when it first came to this country it was hung at Rokeby Hall in Yorkshire."

"Do you know the woman who did it?"

"Mary Richardson? No."

"Have you seen the painting?"

"I have. The nude Venus lies with her back to us as Cupid, her son, holds a mirror to her face. It's a very nice, slender Venus, not like that horrible thing Rubens painted."

"Can we go to the National Gallery some time? You may have noticed that my education still has a few gaps in it."

She smiled. "Yes, that would be lovely. I would like that very much." She paused. "So tell me, do you agree with Mary Richardson's act?"

"To be honest, I think she had a bloody nerve. I hope she gets what she deserves."

Interested, Dorothy leaned forward. "Why do you think that, my love?"

"Well, I suppose she did it because the painting is owned by the state, and the state has banged up poor old Emmeline in Holloway. But this is not the same as smashing windows at the House of Commons, or blowing up a house being built for Lloyd George. The state bought that painting for a reason: so that people could *see* it. Now, I know that most people who go to the National Gallery are probably toffs or middle-class, but this painting was owned by all of us, so that workers like me could also go and see it. Now I won't be able to." He looked up. "So what do *you* think, my Dorothy?"

She smiled and stroked his face. "If you had asked me first, I would have said that I deplored her act, although I'm not sure I would have been able to tell you exactly *why* I felt that way. Now, thanks to you, I know."

"We agree, then."

"We agree."

"So when shall we get married?"

She laughed and slapped his leg playfully. "I have to say, my love, that you don't appear particularly distraught that I have declined your very nice, if unorthodox, proposal."

"It's very difficult to feel distraught, my darling Dorothea"—his pet name for her, equivalent to her use of Michael—"when you're dangling your pretty tits in front of my face."

"Oh, Michael."

"And have you heard, by the way, that the woman in that painting was not really the goddess of love?"

She frowned at him. "No?"

"No. Because you are."

"Michael, Michael, Michael."

*

"So that's settled, is it?" he asked after the second round.

"That we'll discuss marriage after we see how we get on together?"

"No—yes, rather; but also that we'll live together now."

She nodded, "Yes, let's do that."

"Do you have any ideas? Is there anywhere in particular that you'd like to live."

"Oh, several places, but it's a question of practicality—by which I mean affordability. It also depends on where my next job will be, of course."

"So the fact that my job is in North Paddington doesn't count?"

"Well, of course it does, darling. But the fact of the matter is that you could get a transfer to any bus garage in London."

"I could, but I wouldn't want to leave what I've started on the union front at Middle Row."

"No, I can see that, Mickey: you can't just walk away." She sighed. "Alright, do you have any ideas?"

"How about Bayswater?"

"Are you completely mad? We could never afford that!"

"Well, we could if we had a generous friend."

She propped herself up on an elbow. "Do we have a generous friend?"

"It seems we do. Do you remember I told you that Dick Mortlake inherited a rather posh flat from his mother? Well, it turns out that he owns the whole bloody house, and one of the other flats has just become vacant. He's offered it to me for a song."

"But then there's furniture..."

"It's fully furnished."

She threw her arms around him and pressed her face to his. "Yes, yes, yes, yes, yes."

"Oh, Dorothea."

*

"You are aware, of course, that I am a married man, Miss Richardson."

"Of course, Mr Stanley."

They sat in his office, he behind his desk with his head tilted back, she opposite him, erect and watching him carefully. It was three days before her notice expired.

"I...I'm not at all sure how to proceed, Miss Richardson."

He was pale and apparently nervous, something she had not expected of him. She was, although intensely curious to see how this unorthodox interview developed, perfectly calm.

"Oh, I'm sure you do, Mr Stanley."

"My god, but you're a strange woman." He shook his head, breathing softly: "So strange, and so beautiful."

She smiled. "But that takes us no further, does it, Mr Stanley?"

Somewhat tentatively, he returned her smile. "No, it doesn't. You see, I've never done this before."

"Oh, come now."

His mouth turned down at the corners, in that gesture of his.

"Well, not here, not at work."

"Ah, that's more like it. You know perfectly well that it's not inexperience that makes you hesitate, but fear."

"Fear, Miss Richardson?"

"Yes. That I will say no."

"And will you?"

"Ask me, Mr Stanley, and you'll see."

"Miss Richardson, if I offer you a new post, will you have dinner with me?"

"Certainly not, Mr Stanley."

"Might I ask why not, Miss Richardson?"

Emily looked affronted. "Having thought about it, I am no longer inclined to accept your offer of alternative employment, Mr Stanley."

He was nonplussed. "Oh. But what will you do?"

"I don't know yet."

"How will you live?"

"I have some savings."

"Would you like me to help you?"

"Just now, Mr Stanley, you asked if I would have dinner with you if you offered me a new post. That sounded rather like a transaction. You now ask if I would like you to help me." She gave him a sideways glance. "I cannot help wondering what form *that* transaction would take."

He leaned forward, flustered, bringing a knuckle to his mouth. "Oh, I'm so sorry. That was…"

"Crass."

"Yes, indelicate, on both occasions. But if it were *not* a transaction…Would you still decline my assistance?"

"Of course."

He raised his shoulders. "But why?"

"Because I should not want to be dependent on you."

"Ah, I see. I daresay that, as well as a socialist you are also a feminist."

"I suppose so, but you should understand that it's first and foremost something I *am* rather than an ideology to which I have been won."

He nodded. "I think I understand."

"Maybe you do, although I have to say that, as experienced as you might be in some ways, you are obviously not used to dealing with a working woman of a certain outlook."

He laughed. "Well yes, I think you've demonstrated that." This sparring contest seemed to have relaxed him, for he now leaned across his desk and looked into her eyes as he asked the question he had wanted to pose the moment she had sat down. "Now please tell me, dear Miss Richardson, will you give me the immense pleasure of dining with me."

Emily's smile was dazzling. "I would be delighted to have dinner with you, Mr Stanley."

"Oh, Miss Richardson, you have no idea how that makes me feel!"

"Oh, I probably do. But there is a problem, is there not?"

"A problem?"

"Of course. "Where could we possibly dine where you were not known, or in danger of being recognised, as Mr Albert Stanley?"

"Ahhh..." At a loss, Stanley held up his hands.

"Unless, of course, we used room service."

15

Superintendent Quinn, sitting behind his imposing oak desk, looked up as Kitchener entered his office. He did not invite the younger man to occupy the chair on the opposite side of his desk but, resting his chin on a fist, looked up and demanded, "Well? It all went well, I take it?"

Quinn was referring to the previous day's operation to re-arrest Mrs Emmeline Pankhurst's daughter Sylvia and return her to Holloway Prison. Earlier in the year, Sylvia had been expelled from the movement created by her mother for associating herself with the working-class movement, and she had now established the East London Federation of the Suffragettes. Recently, serving a term in Holloway, she had been released on licence due to her determined conduct of a hunger strike. It was common practice, under the terms of the "Cat and Mouse" Act, to release such women, usually for fourteen days, until they had regained their strength, and then re-arrest them. On this occasion, Sylvia had been more than usually provocative, announcing her intention, within a week of her release, to attend a mass rally in Victoria Park. Quinn had therefore ordered her arrest.

"It went like clockwork, sir," reported Kitchener. "When the time of the demonstration came, a long procession was assembled in front of the house where Miss Pankhurst had been residing, and she was brought out on a stretcher and given a place in the middle of the procession. Meanwhile, the uniformed officers had placed a car at a strategic location on the route the procession was to take, and as soon as the marchers reached this point, the procession was cut in two by mounted men and we Branch detectives stepped in and swiftly transferred the stretcher and its burden to the car and drove off with them to the women's prison at Holloway."

"Excellent, Kitchener. No injuries at the demonstration?"

Kitchener's eyes wandered. "That I couldn't say, sir. We were, after all, in and out of there before you could say Jack Robinson."

Quinn grinned grimly. "Alright, constable, let's not pursue that." He slapped the top of his desk. "A job well done, Kitchener!"

*

"This must be a joke!"

A few months earlier, scrutinising the list of payroll number changes posted outside the output, Mickey Rice had found good news and bad news. The good was that he was finally about to graduate from the spare list, and so would now be able to note his scheduled duties and rest days weeks in advance; the bad was that he had been paired with Ted Middleton on route 7.

"Well, you can guess who's responsible for this, can't you!" remarked Dick Mortlake, peering over Mickey's shoulder.

"Butcher?"

"Who else?"

"Yeah, I suppose so." Mickey groaned. "Well, how do I sue for divorce?"

"Easy: you just put Middleton in the hat." Seeing his friend's frown, he went on to explain that all Mickey had to do was apply for a change of payroll number and, assuming he was first in line, the next time a conductor vacancy appeared on the rota, he would be assigned that slot and the most senior spare conductor would be paired with Middleton. "In fact, I'm probably being a bit unfair to Butcher, because this is probably how you've ended up with Middleton: his previous conductor may have put him in the hat. The only problem with doing it this way is that you might have to wait weeks—months, even—before there's a vacancy."

"Is there another way?"

"Yes, you could see if there's anyone willing to do a mutual with you."

"Find someone willing to work with Ted Middleton, you mean? Fat chance, Dick."

No chance, in fact, and so for seven long weeks Mickey worked with Middleton. To begin with, the older man affected a friendly demeanour, but Mickey found that this was used in an attempt to

150

wheedle information from him about union plans and proposed tactics, and so he told him nothing; thereafter, he had to endure Middleton's morose silences whenever they came together on their meal relief or at the end of a trip, biting his tongue whenever the older man tried to provoke him by dropping a reactionary remark.

Finally, when an alternative slot fell vacant, the ordeal was over, and Mickey sensed that Middleton was just as relieved as he when he was assigned to stand behind Lenny Hawkins, who had sometime earlier elected to transfer to route 31.

The territory traversed by route 31 was more sedate than that crossed by route 7. From the World's End pub in Chelsea, their B-type—another bonus!—travelled along Edith Grove and Earl's Court Road to Kensington High Street and here, particularly during shopping hours, Mickey often became busy; turning left into Church Street, they climbed to Notting Hill Gate before pushing on to the more proletarian Great Western Road, across the Harrow Road into Walterton Road, up through Kilburn and then to the middle-class area of Belsize Road to Swiss Cottage. Mickey had liked the route on the several occasions he had worked it while on the spare list, and this affection was confirmed during the first few weeks he worked with Lenny; but he also found that he missed the vibrancy of the West End—something to do, he suspected, with his provincial background. It was during this period, much as he enjoyed working with Lenny, that he began to consider applying for training as a driver.

*

Life in Alexander Street was also less hectic, more peaceful, than in Eric's small flat across the Harrow Road. Mickey often wondered what the neighbours thought as he made his way to and from the flat in Dick Mortlake's house, dressed in his busman's uniform; but they had probably become accustomed to seeing Dick similarly attired, and perhaps concluded that, rather than the neighbourhood as a whole becoming more proletarian, this particular house had become an outpost of eccentricity.

Furnished though the flat was, the one thing it lacked was a bookcase, and after moving in Mickey and Dorothy bought one second hand from the shop on Golborne Road owned by Andy Dixon's father, arranging for it to be delivered on a horse-drawn cart. Dorothy placed their books in it, and Mickey was pleased to see that she arranged them by subject or author rather than owner.

Temporarily out of employment, she had more time to read than he, and she seemed to make the most of it, devouring the Marxist classics and often making extensive notes which she then used as the basis for the occasional article, explaining that she was considering a return to left-wing journalism.

The evening Dorothy had announced her decision not to remain in the employment of the Traffic Combine almost brought them to their first crisis since the evening at the Hackney Empire. When Mickey arrived from work, he was surprised to find her home.

"I thought you were out with friends this evening."

She gave him a tight grin. "Fell through."

When, having washed and changed, he came back into the living room, she looked up, lay down the newspaper she held and announced: "I have decided that it would be a mistake for me to continue to work for Mr Albert Stanley."

"Oh? But how will we survive on my wage, sweetheart?"

Momentarily diverted from the discussion she had planned, she was forced to laugh. Mickey: so practical, so trusting and unsuspecting. "As I told you, my father still sends me money from time to time."

"But you said you were saving that in case it was needed for the movement."

"Yes, that is what I have been doing, and the way I look at it, if I use it to keep us together so that you can continue your trade union work and I can do some writing, that *will* be using it in the service of the movement. But I have no intention of emptying my bank account, Michael. Soon, I hope to be earning again, although probably not as much as previously. Anyway, my love, you should not worry yourself about it."

He relaxed somewhat. "What's brought this on, sweetheart?"

Seated on the sofa, she patted the place at her side. "Come and sit with me, Michael."

At the time, the repeated use of this name in connection with her employment struck him as strange. Later, he would understand. Wearing a dressing gown, she placed a hand on his arm.

"I'm afraid I've been a little silly, Michael..."

Immediately, he felt alarm. "Oh, Dorothy...No, please no..."

She shook her head. "No, Michael, don't fret. It wasn't that—well, not quite." She sighed. "Mr Stanley often flirted with me, and to be honest I rather liked it. He is, as I may have told you, a very nice man. Anyway, the last time I saw him, he was somewhat bolder than previously..."

"He touched you?"

This was proving more difficult than she had anticipated, and she found his...proprietorial stance most unappealing. "No, of course he didn't touch me! He asked to meet me, and I am afraid that I led him on."

"You did what?"

She saw both anger and desolation in his eyes and for a moment doubted her ability to go through with this without damaging their relationship.

"You betrayed me?"

It was her turn to be angry, gripping his arm and looking into his face. "Michael, if you will listen to me you will soon see that I did *not* betray you! Far from it, in fact. *Will* you listen to me, Michael? *Michael!*"

He closed his eyes and nodded. "Go ahead."

"I once told you—in fact the first time we made love—that my experience was not as extensive as you might have thought. That was true. It was not extensive, but it *was* diverse. During that period, I was very taken by something said by an ancient playwright called Terence: 'I am a man. I consider nothing that is human alien to me.' Now, that did *not* mean that I was intent upon experiencing the whole range of human behaviour, good or bad. It *did* mean, however, that I was very open to relationships, both social and sexual, with people from various walks of life."

"People? Men *and* women?"

She allowed the question as, given her choice of words, it seemed a reasonable enquiry. "I am being completely honest with you, Michael, because of what you have come to mean to me, so yes, once or twice. Twice. So we come to Albert Stanley, a man of my own class. I have, believe it or not, never had a relationship with a specimen from that class. Mr Stanley, of course, is somewhat different in that he was not born to the class but has worked his way into it. He is an achiever. And, yes, I found that attractive." She paused, sighing. "And so when—very nervously, very falteringly—he worked his way around to asking me to meet him, I must admit that I helped him. Partly, I suppose, I was enjoying his discomfort, seeing how this powerful man was totally at a loss then it came to talking frankly with a woman. Nevertheless, I agreed to meet him in a hotel room."

This brought a gasp from him. "How...? Why did you do this?"

She was abrupt with him. "I've just told you how and why I agreed to it! If you promise to listen, Michael, I will now tell you how and why I did *not* go through with it." She paused and swallowed before continuing. "The arrangement was that he would arrive at the hotel at seven o'clock and go to the room he had booked. I would arrive twenty minutes later and join him. I *did* go to the hotel, but I sat in the reception area and thought about what I was doing. More to the point, I gave careful consideration to *why* I had come to this hotel, and *why* I was going to walk out of it without seeing Mr Stanley. For that, Michael, as soon as I sat down, was what I knew I was going to do."

Seeing that he was no longer upset or angry, but was now listening with great interest to what she was telling him, she reached up and stroked his face.

"I found myself thinking, Michael, of our...intimacy. You know, I cannot think of a better word to describe what you and I have. When most people say that A has an 'intimate relationship' with B, all they really mean is that A and B copulate. Well, to my mind, copulation is not necessarily intimacy. To me, intimacy means that *closeness* which Michael and Dorothea share every time they make love, that complete absence of barriers that allows them access to each other's bodies; they see all, they touch all, and they love all they see and touch."

He took her hand and pressed it to his mouth, looking into her eyes and nodding. "Yes," he whispered, "that is exactly what we have, Dorothea."

Seeing that his eyes were damp, she was suddenly aroused, and was forced to rein in her desire so that she could complete her confession—for confession it was: not of guilt, but of love.

"And what could I possibly have with Mr Stanley? Certainly not intimacy." She sighed. "It seemed to me then that my interest in diversity, while it may have had value at one time, had been transcended, because now I knew that I could embrace all that is human in my relationship with you, Michael." She sniffed. "So I asked the receptionist for notepaper and an envelope and I dashed off a note to Mr Stanley—or, as he was calling himself at this hotel, Mr Ashfield, which is apparently the name of a village near his birthplace—and requested that it be delivered to his room. In the note, I apologised for both my non-appearance and for having led him to believe that I *would* appear, and explained that I was in a deeply loving relationship and had made a terrible mistake. Then, resolving to tell you everything, Michael, I came home."

*

Opening the door in his shirtsleeves, Albert Stanley's face fell as he found himself facing not the exquisite Emily Richardson/Dorothy Bridgeman, but an acne-ridden bellboy proffering a tray on which lay a small envelope. From somewhere, Stanley summoned a grin, reached into his trouser pocket for a coin, and exchanged it for the envelope. He walked to the small table where he had planned to dine with his guest and sat, tearing open the envelope.

Dear Mr Ashfield,

I must ask you to accept my sincere apologies for my failure to keep our assignation,   and even more so for having led you to a contrary expectation. This was a horrendous error on my part, but at least it has brought me to the realisation that the loving relationship I have is far too important to jeopardise.

Incidentally, I believe I was incorrect when I said that you were reluctant to ask to meet me because you feared that I might decline. On the contrary, I believe your reluctance was due to the fear that I would agree. If this was indeed the case, my failure to arrive this evening will perhaps be something of a relief to you.

Under the circumstances, I trust you will agree that it would hardly be appropriate for me to work the brief remainder of my notice period, and I would therefore be grateful if you would arrange to have any outstanding wages forwarded to me.

Yours most respectfully,

D. B.

Having read the note a second time, he felt a smile spreading across his face. What a woman! Yes, part of him had feared that she would agree to the assignation, and the hours since she had done so had been filled with terrified speculation regarding the turmoil into which his life might be pitched if he became attached to her.

Yes, he was feeling relief, so thank you, Dorothy, and my very best wishes to Mr Rice. He tore up the note, let the pieces fall into the wastepaper bin at the dressing table, and reached for his jacket.

*

At first, black dread had gripped his mind, followed, as she mentioned the agreement to meet in a hotel room, by a tearing sense of betrayal and loss; his vision had blurred at this stage and he thought he must be dreaming, having a nightmare. But then she had once again urged him to just listen, and he came to see that she was being as honest with him as any woman would ever be, and that he was the beneficiary of this confession. From feeling the urge to scream to the heavens and throw the furniture around, he became very calm and wanted to kiss her face and throw his arms about her or in some form pledge himself to her. Instead, he just told her that he loved her. And then, amazingly, he found himself risking a joke, asking, "Does this mean, Dorothea, that you're becoming more conventional?" to which she replied, "Not totally, Michael, as I shall now proceed to demonstrate."

16

Mickey read that the title of Sylvia Pankhurst's new newspaper, *The Woman's Dreadnought*, had been chosen as being symbolic of the belief that "the women who are fighting for freedom must fear nothing." The inaugural issue, dated 8 March, 1914, had come out some weeks ago and was sold for a penny, although it was hoped that in future the costs of its production would be borne by advertising, so that its weekly print-run of 20,000 copies might be distributed free of charge. Published by the East London Federation of the Suffragettes, composed largely of working women, it promised to deal with the franchise question and "the whole field of the women's emancipation movement."

Reading the main article, written by the editor herself, he saw, as she summarised developments of the recent period, that fear and Miss Pankhurst certainly seemed to be strangers. He also saw that the often-violent events in the East End had been treated inaccurately in the Fleet Street press.

The Liberal government, having earlier given assurances to the suffragette movement that its cause would soon succeed, had in 1912 withdrawn its Reform Bill, telling the women that it must henceforth rely on private members' bills, with no official support. Until this time, wealthy branches of the organisation led by Sylvia's mother, the Women's Social and Political Union, had aided work in the East End, but finance was now withdrawn. Nevertheless, in early 1913 Sylvia and her supporters opened an East End headquarters at 321, Roman Road in Bow. At this stage protest activity tended, with the exception of periodic marches and rallies, to take the form of breaking windows—hardly more imaginative than the actions of the WSPU's more comfortable members. This led to imprisonment, hunger strikes and forced-feeding in Holloway Prison, the North London penitentiary which had, since 1902, catered solely for female offenders. In this brief period, Mickey read, there had been no less than eight sizeable protest marches from the East End to Holloway.

The government then cracked down on the movement, sentencing Sylvia's mother Emmeline to three years' imprisonment, attempting to prevent the publication of the movement's newspaper, *The Suffragette*, and banning WSPU platforms from Hyde Park. Even so, suffragettes continued to speak there, and when attacked by police or hooligans they were protected by East End dockers. This was new to Mickey, as was the violence employed by the police when breaking up meetings at which, in July 1913, Sylvia spoke, having been released from prison on a licence which had now expired, under the "Cat and Mouse" Act.

It was now, also, that he became familiar with the regularity with which the people of the East End, a community in which Sylvia had by now become a well-regarded fixture, acted to shield her and her comrades from the police. In October 1913, she was arrested at Poplar Town Hall, jailed and released on licence after nine days. So debilitated by her hunger strike that she had to be transported by stretcher during the period of her licence, following its expiry, at which point she should have been returned to Holloway, she spoke at the Albert Hall and Hackney Baths and "was so well protected by the people that I was able to get away in safety."

The ELFS was founded in early 1914, and although Sylvia explained this as merely a change of name, "made at the request of others," Mickey had learned from Dorothy that this stemmed from the 10,000-strong rally at the Albert Hall on 1 November, 1913, when Sylvia, speaking alongside James Connolly, had defended the 20,000 Irish workers involved in the Dublin Lockout. Summoned to Paris, where her older sister Christabel lived in virtual asylum, Sylvia found herself expelled from the WSPU for the high crime of associating the group with organised labour. That she chose not to mention this in her article was, Mickey thought, somewhat troubling, but doubtless due to family—almost certainly "the others" mentioned by Sylvia—considerations.

"Our policy," Sylvia concluded her article, "remains what it has always been. We are still a Militant non-party organisation of working women." Some argued that it was not important for working women to agitate for, or even receive, the vote. "They forget," said Sylvia, "that comparatively the leisured comfortably situated women are but a little group, and the working women a multitude."

He had found the newspaper on their small dining table, where Dorothy had doubtless left it in the hope that he would pick it up. He left it where he had found it and went out to work, knowing that when he returned she would expect a discussion.

During this brief hiatus in her employment, Dorothy had, despite her earlier assertion of equality on this issue, taken to cooking their dinner whenever Mickey was working, although he was expected to prepare meals whenever it was convenient. During dinner on this particular evening, they first discussed the prospects for left unity. On 13 April, the Independent Labour Party, the Fabians and the British Socialist Party, to which Dorothy and Mickey belonged, had been brought together by the International Socialist Bureau in the hope that they could be persuaded to work together more closely; it was recommended that the three form a United Socialist Council if the BSP would agree to affiliate to the Labour Party, and the BSP annual conference had now agreed to subject this proposal to a referendum of its members. Neither Dorothy nor Mickey were optimistic of the prospects.

"George thinks the vote will be close," said Mickey.

"And even if it goes through," Dorothy followed, "what can we expect from the Labour Party?"

"Socialism by legislation," Mickey snorted derisively, "while the bosses sit back and let it happen."

Dorothy placed her knife and fork on her plate. "Your turn, I believe," she said, nodding at the cutlery.

He held up his palms. "I know, I know, sweetheart. Don't worry, I'll do it."

She smiled. "And talking of women's issues, did you have a chance to look at that copy of Sylvia's newspaper I left on the table?"

"I did. Strong stuff, I thought. Where did you get it?"

"From Dick. He passed it to me after he had finished with it." She paused. "What did you think about it politically?"

He sighed. "Sylvia Pankhurst is obviously very brave, and it's good that she's decided to organise working women. But organise them for what? She said in her article that, particularly after that woman threw herself under the king's horse, there was a need to act rather than just talk. But I honestly don't see that breaking windows is going to persuade too many MPs to change the law."

"Well…"—she inclined her head, with half a shrug—"I suppose she has inherited that kind of action from the wealthier suffragettes associated with her mother."

"And they suffer from a lack of imagination—not surprising, given their background. But you'd really expect more from Sylvia."

Interested, she narrowed her eyes. "What do you mean, exactly, Mickey?"

"Because she already knows that it's not just the suffrage question that needs to be tackled, and she understands that working women have the numbers. She was kicked out of the WSPU because she associated with the labour movement, but can't she see that her way forward is to move even closer to it? She needs allies in the trade unions, Dorothy."

She nodded. "You know, that's also my thinking, Mickey." She cleared her throat. "And that's why I'm thinking that I might have something to contribute to her group."

This gave him pause. "You mean by writing for her newspaper?" he suggested tentatively.

"At first, yes, and I have contributed several pieces. But this might lead to some kind of organisational involvement." She rearranged the cutlery on her plate before glancing up. "Why that look of concern, darling?"

"Probably because I *am* concerned."

"But why, Mickey?"

He counted off his fears on the fingers of his left hand. "Police beatings; Holloway; hunger strikes…"

She smiled, touched by his anxiety. "But I do not intend to break windows, darling."

"Not all of the women who've had their skulls cracked or arms broken were breaking windows, Dorothy; just being in the way of the police was enough."

"You're so sweet, Mickey. Come, I'll help you with the washing up."

*

George Sanders surveyed the recent entries in what he called his

159

"war diary"—a list of developments in Europe and elsewhere that indicated that a major war was on the way. Whenever possible, he shared its contents with those branch meetings to which he was invited, using the data to demonstrate that this war would be detrimental to the interests of working people and urging the members to prepare to resist it.

On the home front, the result of the BSP referendum on Labour Party affiliation had been announced: 3,263 to 2,410 in favour of affiliation. He could see little future for this endeavour, however, for too many Labour MPs had been waxing patriotic when it came to the arms-building programme, and he suspected that when the war came, as it surely would, they would abandon the commitments made at Basel and Stuttgart and wrap themselves in the Union Jack, leaving the BSP, along with a few allies in the Independent Labour Party, to carry on the anti-war struggle virtually alone.

A similar fate, he felt, would befall the WSPU wing of the suffragette movement, which at present was maintaining its campaign of destruction and damage: in late April, two women had been arrested and promptly sent to prison for burning down an empty Felixstowe hotel; a month later, following the House of Lords' rejection of the suffrage bill, two suffragettes had somehow, despite the presence of sentries, broken two windows at Buckingham Palace. To Sanders, it all sounded a bit like children stamping in puddles.

His phone rang and he reached for the receiver.

"*A lady for you, George,*" Rose announced, and he could hear the smile in her voice.

"You'd better put her on then, Rose...Hello, Sanders here."

"*Good afternoon, George.*"

"Dorothy?"

"*Yes, George. I'd like to have a word with you, if you've time.*"

"Will you come to the office?"

"*I can hardly do that if Bywater is there, can I? I may no longer work for Mr Stanley, but I'm sure he would recognise me.*"

"Do you know the Italian café down the road from the office?"

"*I think so. I can be there in forty minutes.*"

*

As she walked into the café, Sanders nodded to the chair opposite him and, as she sat down, pointed at the mug of tea awaiting her. "A bit more proletarian than Lyons, I'm afraid Dorothy."

She smiled. "I'm sure it's perfectly acceptable, George. I'm quite partial to strong tea."

"Mickey given you a taste for it?"

"I suppose so, yes."

"Can I get you something to eat, Dorothy?"

"No, no, I had a late lunch. Thank you."

He took his Gold Flake packet from his pocket, looked at her enquiringly and, at her nod, took out a cigarette. "What are you up to these days, Dorothy?"

"Well, I've started writing for Sylvia's paper."

"The *Dreadnought*?"

"Yes," she nodded. "I can see you don't think much of the name. Neither did I at first; it sounded like some weapon of war, a battleship. But then I realised that it merely meant that women should be fearless in the pursuit of their cause. That's not so bad, is it?"

"No, it's not. I hadn't realised that."

"So you haven't read it?"

Sanders grimaced. "Afraid not. Should I?"

"Yes, you should. I think you'll be pleasantly surprised. Mickey is quite impressed."

"Is he, now? Well, I'll take a look at it." He glanced at the tip of his cigarette and knocked the ash into the ashtray. "But I'm sure that's not why you asked to see me."

Dorothy took a sip of her tea. "Well, in a way it is. Not the paper, but Sylvia herself."

"I see." He regarded her through narrowed eyes. "Thinking of joining the suffragettes?"

"Well, that's just it, you see: Sylvia seems to be somewhat more than a mere suffragette. Oh, yes, her organisation is called the East London Federation of the Suffragettes, and she still campaigns for votes for women, but the people she's mobilising are working class women—and men, incidentally—and she's also taking on other working-class issues." She paused, pursing her lips. "You ask if I'm thinking of joining them. Yes and no, George. Not quite yet. As she's published a few of my pieces, I thought I'd go and have a word with Sylvia. I'd appreciate your view before I meet her, though."

"Ah, I see." He stubbed out his cigarette. "But don't you find enough to do in our party, Dorothy?"

"You mean like stuffing envelopes?"

Sanders' eyebrows shot up. "Oh, come, Dorothy, it's surely not as bad as that."

"Isn't it, George? Name me one woman leader in our party."

"Zelda Kahan."

"And do you know why you were able to reply without thinking, George? Because she's practically the only one. And some of our male leaders are actually anti-women—Belfort Bax, for example. A man who thinks that current legislation favours women at the expense of men. And to think that he was considered the party's leading theoretician!"

"Bax hardly spends any time on the party nowadays, Dorothy; he's almost a full-time barrister now." He tapped the table with his fingertips and grinned. "And if he had decided to spend more time on party work, who would you have put your money on—him or Zelda?"

Dorothy chuckled. "Yes, that would have been a sight to see. But George, he's not the only one. There's Harry Quelch, for instance."

"Died last September."

"Yes, I was sorry to hear that, George, but on the question of women he was just *terrible.*"

"Yes, I know, Dorothy, I know, but just step back and spend a few moments taking a good look at our party. What is the BSP? It would be a unique and wonderful organisation if it didn't reflect any of the less healthy ideas and attitudes of this capitalist society. Just think of the two men you've mentioned. Ernest Belfort Bax, born into a capitalist family, became a journalist, then a barrister. Wasn't it practically inevitable that he would be affected in one way or another by bourgeois prejudices? But, on the positive side, he played a very valuable role in spreading Marxist ideas in this country. And Harry Quelch, a blacksmith's son from Hungerford—just down the road from where Mickey comes from. Harry turned himself into a genuine working-class intellectual, and like Bax he did a great deal to disseminate Marxist ideas. But it turns out that he was not the all-round Marxist superman we would have preferred him to be. He had blind spots, and one of them was on the question of women. It's to be regretted, Dorothy, but it's hardly surprising, considering the kind of society we have here and the kind of background he came from. Our party has to play with the hand history has dealt it, but we also need to work at improving that hand, and that means improving the ideological level of the membership." He threw up his hands. "And that's why, Dorothy, I can't understand why one of the most forthright, outspoken women we have would be thinking of decamping to Sylvia's group."

It was Dorothy's turn to raise her hands. "Oh, wait, George, just wait. You've jumped to the wrong conclusion entirely. Alright, it's partly my fault, because I said I might be thinking of *joining* them, whereas what I meant was that I was thinking about the possibility of working *with* them. I badly need to get involved in some political activity, George, and if the BSP cannot currently accommodate that, I'm prepared to look elsewhere. But that should not be taken to mean that I am considering terminating my party membership. Not at all." As she paused for thought, a smile appeared. "In fact, George, in view of what you've just said, isn't it the case that the BSP would benefit from a healthy infusion of the kind of women Sylvia is organising? Isn't it possible that if I were to work with Sylvia for a while—with no attempt to conceal my party membership, this might in time lead to joint work by our organisations, and then...who knows?"

Sanders remained silent for a while, studying his hands which lay, fingers splayed, palms down, on the table before him. When at last he raised his head, there was a grin for Dorothy. "Oh my," he said, chuckling, "now that would be something, wouldn't it? But,"— his expression now hardened as he lifted a hand from the table, one finger extended in Dorothy's direction—"this could only work, and it might not work anyway, if you..."

As previously, Dorothy's hands came up defensively. "I know, I know, I know, George. I will have to curb my temper, wrestle with my ego and think before I speak."

Sanders uttered a long sigh, nodding. "That about covers it, Dorothy." Quite dramatically, he reached across the table, clasping her left hand in his right as he looked into her eyes. "Seriously, now, Dorothy, that is the only way you can do this, and you have to be absolutely sure of your self-control before you attempt it." He relaxed, releasing her hand with a gentle smile. "But first things first: you go along and meet Sylvia and see how she and her organisation strike you."

"I'll do that, George."

"I think this calls for another round of teas, Dorothy." He raised a hand and waved at Emilia.

"So, George, what is your view of Sylvia? What should I expect?"

Sanders directed a thoughtful gaze at the window and then sighed. "If you've been reading the *Dreadnought*, you probably have a better idea than I do. I've never met Sylvia, and I only know what I've heard. I suppose I have a fairly positive view of her, in that, as you've said, she's campaigning with working-class women, and encourages the involvement of men. But I'll be surprised if there aren't a few problems along the way. Given her background, she obviously has no first-hand experience of working-class life, and I just wonder whether this will prove to be a bit of a drawback at some stage."

Dorothy inclined her head to one side, almost smiling. "In what way, George?"

"Well, people from her background are used to getting their own way: what they say goes. You can see that, of course, with her mother and sister. But working-class women in the East End, particularly if they're sufficiently independently-minded to have joined the movement, probably won't stand for that."

Dorothy shrugged in mock resignation, pretending to be downcast. "Oh well, that counts me out as well, I suppose, so perhaps we had better forget the whole thing."

But Sanders merely smiled. "Nice try, Dorothy. I'm not saying that everyone from such a background is bound to be like that. If that were the case, Marx and Engels wouldn't have made much progress, would they?"

"So why do you fear it might be the case with Sylvia?"

"Because she has, so I've heard, a bit of her mother's egotism."

"Oh?"

He nodded. "For example, when did the women's movement get underway in the East End?"

"According to Sylvia, two years ago, in 1912."

"Exactly: according to Sylvia. But it's not true, Dorothy. There was activity for at least five or six years before she came on the scene. WSPU branches were formed in a number of places—Canning Town, Poplar, and Bow, I believe. And those branches worked in and with the labour movement, just as Sylvia's group is doing now. In 1907, of course, the WSPU broke with the Labour Party, following which the leaders like Mrs Pankhurst tended to ignore or denigrate those branches, but they continued their work. Sylvia herself tends to ignore the contribution made by those women, dating the start of the movement from her arrival in Bow. You see what I mean?"

"I do, George," Dorothy nodded, "I do."

*

The morning she travelled by bus and tram to 400, Old Ford Road, where Sylvia had established her new headquarters, Dorothy wore one of her oldest skirts and the white blouse she had worn on her journey to Paddington in June 1913; had she been visiting the WSPU, a finer outfit might have been appropriate, but this would hardly have been appreciated by Sylvia. The premises of the East London Federation of the Suffragettes was situated next to the Lord

Morpeth public house, and as Dorothy entered a pale woman in her mid-thirties, carelessly dressed and her hair dishevelled, looked up from her desk.

"Miss Pankhurst?"

The woman got to her feet, stepped around her desk and took a tentative stride towards Dorothy. At first, she appeared to be squinting, as if short-sighted, but Dorothy realised that she was evaluating her, wondering whether her visitor might have come to augment her forces and, if so, in what capacity she might serve the cause. "Yes, I'm Sylvia Pankhurst. How may I help you?"

Dorothy gave her what she hoped was a modest smile and extended a hand in greeting. "Good morning, Miss Pankhurst. I'm Dorothy Bridgeman. You have been good enough to publish one or two of my pieces in the *Dreadnought*."

Miss Pankhurst's full features blossomed into a broad smile as she stepped slowly, as if she were ill, to Dorothy and, ignoring her extended hand, threw her arms about her; as she did so, Dorothy detected a slight odour of perspiration, but willed herself to ignore it. "Oh, Miss Bridgeman, welcome, welcome, welcome! How nice of you to visit us!" She stepped back, clasping both of Dorothy's hands in her own. "Come, we must have some tea!" Miss Pankhurst's accent, Dorothy noted, was quite ruling-class, containing only the slightest hint of Mancunian; the Pankhursts hailed from Manchester, had lived in London between 1887 and 1892 before returning home after a failed commercial venture, and had come south again when Emmeline estimated that the movement she led would flourish in London.

"Forgive me for saying so, Miss Pankhurst, but you do not appear to be quite well. Are you sure this is convenient? Would you prefer that I came another time?"

"Oh," she sighed, "I was released from Holloway a few days ago, and I'm still recovering. But I *am* recovering and I do so want to make your acquaintance, so a brief visit will do me no harm—quite the contrary, in fact."

Dorothy was led to a small kitchen at the rear of the building, where she sat at a small stained table while her hostess lit a gas ring under a large kettle, emptied the contents of a blue china teapot into a sink cluttered with unwashed crockery, swilled it out under the tap, and threw in a handful of tea from a cheap tin caddy. Sylvia opened a small pantry door in the corner of the kitchen, reached in and drew out a half-full milk bottle but, raising it to her nose, frowned and replaced it.

"Have to be black, I'm afraid, Miss Bridgeman. Milk's on the turn," she explained without embarrassment.

"That will be perfectly fine. And please call me Dorothy."

Again that broad smile. "And you must call me Sylvia."

Dorothy watched in mounting alarm as Sylvia, having searched in vain for clean cups, picked up two mugs from the sink and, after the most perfunctory of rinses under the cold tap, proceeded to dry them with a tea towel which might once have been white.

At this point, a stern-faced woman in her middle twenties entered the kitchen, laid her basket on the table and, arms folded, frowned with obvious disapproval upon the activity of Miss Pankhurst.

"Ah, Mrs Elkins!" cried Sylvia. "I'd like you to meet Miss Dorothy Bridgeman. Miss Bridgeman writes for our paper. Dorothy, say hello to Molly Elkins; Molly's husband works on the West India docks."

Mrs Elkins nodded at Dorothy, murmuring "Pleased to meet you, I'm sure" before turning once more to Sylvia, to whom she issued the order, pointing to the chair next to Dorothy: "Sit!" She picked up the two mugs that Sylvia had placed on the table, peered into them, grimaced, and returned them to the sink. Holding the tea towel gingerly between thumb and forefinger, she dropped it into a laundry basket before opening a drawer next to the sink and taking out a clean one. She then turned her attentions to the sink, glancing over her shoulder as she suggested that Sylvia might like to return to the office with her guest; she would bring their tea when it was ready.

"I'm afraid," said Sylvia as she ushered Dorothy into a chair in the office, "that Mrs Elkins can be a little abrupt."

"Oh," smiled Dorothy, her confidence in the East London Federation of the Suffragettes partially restored, "she seems an admirable woman."

*

"So you came to the East End in 1912, Sylvia?" prompted Dorothy as they began their discussion.

"That's correct, although at that time, of course, I was a member of the Women's Political and Social Union."

"You must have greatly admired George Lansbury for his action in resigning his seat in order to fight a by-election on the suffrage question."

Sylvia hesitated. "Well, George is a very dear friend, and of course his action was most courageous." She sighed. "But I felt, if I'm honest, that it was somewhat rash and premature."

"Really? How so?"

"The links between the suffrage campaign and the labour movement in the East End were at the time insufficiently developed. True, there *were* such links, but nothing like those that existed in the industrial north. Then, again, George had not even discussed his intentions with his constituency party, and, as you can imagine, they were not best pleased, being thrown into an election quite unexpectedly. It's hardly surprising that George failed to recapture the seat. I am also unable to accept George's view that the Labour Party should vote against the government on all matters—even Home Rule, would you believe—until suffrage is conceded."

"So there had been activity here before your arrival?" Dorothy, not daring to look her in the eye as she asked this, pretended to busy herself with a piece of stray cotton that had attached itself to her skirt.

"Oh, yes," conceded Sylvia, "for some five or six years." She waved a hand dismissively. "But, of course, the sole question for them was the vote, despite the fact that so many of the active women here were from the working class. In a sense, I had to start all over again." Inclining her head, she fixed Dorothy with an earnest gaze, as if anxious that she should clearly understand her position. "You see, Dorothy, I view our work here as being concerned not merely with votes but as working towards an egalitarian society—an effort to awaken the women submerged in poverty to struggle for better social conditions and bring them in line with the most advanced sections of the movement of the awakened proletariat."

"Yes, I quite see that, Sylvia: your orientation is as much socialist as it is feminist."

Sylvia raised an eyebrow, as if her visitor had pleasantly surprised her, and a small smile came to her lips. She nodded. "Precisely, Dorothy. Are you a socialist yourself?"

Dorothy grinned. "I thought that would have been obvious from my writing, Sylvia."

"No necessarily. You see, many people write or speak in a socialist vein without having the first idea about socialism. Sometimes, they adopt a moral stance and believe that they are socialists."

"Yes, I know what you mean." Dorothy cleared her throat. "Actually, I'm a member of the British Socialist Party."

Sylvia's face fell. "Oh dear. Poor you." She chewed her bottom lip as she considered this information, then glanced up sharply. "Then I suppose the question I should be asking is whether you're a feminist."

Dorothy sighed. "Again, that should be obvious from my writing, Sylvia. And yes, I know some of the men in our party are incredibly backward, but they are not all like that, and I am perfectly confident that our party will be won for the cause; otherwise, I would not be a member."

Sylvia nodded silently. "Well, I hope you're right in that, dear." She shuddered. "But Belfort Bax and Harry Quelch! They should belong in the Tory Party!"

"On the women's question, maybe, but otherwise..."

"Tea up!" Mrs Elkins entered, bearing a fully-laden tea tray. "Where would you like it?"

"Oh...just put it on the desk over there, Molly, and I'll see to it."

"No you won't, Sylvia," responded a firm Mrs Elkins—who, Dorothy now realized, must be rather more than the cleaner she had initially taken her to be. "If I leave it to you, you'll let it get cold." Having placed the tray on the desk indicated by Sylvia and established that Dorothy would take milk but no sugar, she now proceeded to serve the tea.

"But Molly, the milk is..." Sylvia objected as Mrs Elkins raised a small milk jug over Dorothy's cup.

"You may've let the last bottle go off, Sylvia, but this is from the fresh bottle I brought with me this morning." She winked at Dorothy as she placed her cup before her and returned to the tray to pour a cup for herself, then sat at the desk. "In case you're wonderin', Miss Bridgeman..."

"Dorothy, please."

Molly Elkins gave her a pleasant smile. "In case you're wonderin', Dorothy, I'm not the domestic, although it's true I once worked as one. It's just that Miss Pankhurst, as you may've noticed, is lackin' in practical skills, so the rest of us have to muck in."

Sylvia took this is good part and chuckled, her shrug acknowledging her uselessness in these matters. "Molly is one of our founder-members, Dorothy, a very active member of the committee, and she will be on the delegation to see Mr Asquith."

"The Prime Minister?"

"Well, it won't do us much good goin' to see Asquith the greengrocer, will it?" Molly quipped, causing all three to laugh.

"I told you Molly can be a bit abrupt," said Sylvia.

"That's why I'm on the delegation," said Molly. She wagged a finger at Sylvia. "Don't forget we've got the meetin' this afternoon."

"Plenty of time," said Sylvia after a glance at the wall-clock.

"So how did this come about?" asked Dorothy.

It was Molly who answered. "Sylvia wrote to him weeks ago, didn't she, right after she came out of Holloway on 30 May? Did she get a reply? Not for a long time. And when he did reply, he turned 'er down. So she threatened to go on an 'unger, thirst and sleep strike, didn't she? Indefinite, mind you, not just for a day or two. Said she'd die on the steps of the 'Ouse of Commons. An' they knew she'd do it, too! In fact, she very nearly carried it through. Gettin' on for a fortnight ago, the police nabbed her on a demonstration and whipped her back to Holloway—even though she was on a stretcher! Well, needless to say she continued her 'unger strike there, and so they 'ad to let her out a few days ago." As she turned her gaze to Sylvia, it was obvious that, no matter what her views on her practical skills, Molly viewed her with deep affection and profound admiration. "Soon as she gets 'ome, she tells us she's goin' to the 'Ouse of Commons to carry out her threat. Well, she could neither walk nor stand, 'ardly, so we put her in a cab and took 'er there."

Sylvia nodded. "I lay down near the Cromwell statue. When they heard about it, Keir Hardie, George Lansbury and the journalist Henry Nevinson, who happened to be in the House, came out, and then went to see Asquith. And he gave in. So on Saturday Molly and six other members will see Asquith. They'll all be here this afternoon for a bit of a rehearsal."

"You're not going yourself?"

Sylvia shook her head. "No, because that would allow Asquith to dismiss the arguments as the ravings of a silly middle-class woman." She inclined her head towards Dorothy. "And that, if I may say so, Dorothy, is something you'll have to be careful of as well. Far better that he hears it direct from the people who will benefit from the vote."

"And far better that a group of working-class women discover that they can hold their own with a prime minister," suggested Dorothy.

A delighted Sylvia brought a fist down onto her desk, causing her tea to slop into its saucer and Molly to make a tutting sound. "Exactly!"

"So where are you working now, Dorothy?" asked Molly, leaning back in her chair, arms folded, as she regarded Dorothy with an evaluating gaze.

"I'm not, although until recently I was working for Albert Stanley."

"What, the transport king?"

A smile tugged at the corner of Dorothy's mouth as she turned to Molly. "Well, it wasn't Albert Stanley the greengrocer, was it?"

They all laughed, and Dorothy felt at home.

17

The time had come. Negotiations with the General and Tilling's had been completed and the Executive Council was meeting at Gerrard Street to consider the results of the negotiating sub-committee's efforts and decide on a recommendation.

Sanders looked around the table in the meeting room. Harry Bywater sat licking his lips, a pile of documents in front of him, waiting for Tich Smith to open the meeting. The lay members looked apprehensive. Barney Macauley, when Sanders caught his eye, shook his head and grimaced, obviously unhappy with the proposals. At the back of the room, the "gallery" was full, the rank and file members—today limited to garage reps—chatting noisily as they eagerly awaited the commencement of the proceedings beneath a gathering pall of blue smoke. Sanders caught sight of Mickey Rice, Dave Marston and a number of other likely lads. Given the importance of the occasion, all the full-time organisers, including Larry Russell, were around the table with the executive members.

Tich Smith raised his recently-purchased gavel and brought it down, just once. "Brothers, I declare this meeting open. I would remind the members in the gallery that these proceedings will consist of discussion and debate. It will not be a free-for-all, although sensible comments and pertinent questions will be welcome. Brother Bywater will now distribute copies of the proposed agreement, which will then be considered item by item. Following this, the Executive Council will decide whether the document should be recommended for acceptance or rejection by the LGOC and Tilling's membership."

Bywater stood and passed a copy of the document to each executive member and officer. He then handed the remainder to Larry Russell, asking that he distribute them to the members in the gallery. These were grasped eagerly and the members, as yet unfamiliar with its terms, began to read the twenty items, enumerated A to T. Almost immediately, however, there were gasps and cries of "No!" One rep balled his copy and hurled it in the direction of the table. Sanders and Macauley, considering this reaction wholly predictable, nodded to each other.

Tich Smith now brought down his gavel once, twice, three times. "Brothers! At the end of the day, the whole of our bus membership will have the opportunity to say Yea or Nay to these proposals. Before that time, your elected executive members will debate them without interruption. And the next person who throws the document—or any other missile!—will be asked to leave."

As the tumult subsided, a nervous Harry Bywater cleared his throat. "Mister Chairman, I would like to make a suggestion. In the interests both of creating a peaceful interlude and narrowing down the areas of contention, would it not make sense if we first considered items J to T, pertaining to the garage Inside Staff?"

Shortly after signing the recognition agreement at the Board of Trade the previous September, Sanders had pointed out that the non-skilled engineering staff had no union protection. The Amalgamated Society of Engineers had insisted that it should represent skilled engineers, and as these were a minority at garage level, the LPU had readily agreed, and both companies had shortly thereafter agreed to this extension of the recognition agreement.

Tich Smith looked across at the gallery. "Are there any Inside Staff stewards here today?" When three or four hands went up, he asked: "Do you have any objection to your improvements being discussed first?" As they had none, Smith turned to the executive members. "Agreed?" Agreed. He turned to Bywater. "Proceed, Harry."

This was speedily done, as the handful of stewards indicated their acceptance of every item, followed by the endorsement of the executive members. Washers would receive an extra half a crown a week and cleaners six shillings, and both would be provided with free clogs. Other grades would be paid between five pence and seven pence an hour, with overtime at time and a quarter once a daily nine hours had been worked.

"Item T," Bywater concluded this section of the presentation, "in fact, affects all staff, whether operating or garage hands, so I'll take that next, Mr Chairman. This item reads: 'All regular service employees to receive an allservice pass. Other employees to receive a daily trip ticket.'"

As expected, this sailed through, and Sanders now saw that Bywater was more clever—or crafty—than he had previously thought, because in dealing with the proposals in this order, he had completely transformed the mood in the room. The proposals for garage staff were not, in all truth, that bad, and the free travel pass had cheered up everyone. But he could not prolong this good mood, could he? Bywater now demonstrated that he could.

"Mister chairman, I would further propose that, coming to the proposals for operating staff, we deal with the non-contentious items first. It is my estimate that the earlier display of discontent from the gallery was occasioned by Item B—unless the reps have taken speed-reading courses, that is. So I would suggest that we leave Item B till last."

"Agreed?" asked Tich Smith.

Agreed.

The lead item concerned wages. The amount per service bus mile would be increased to produce an extra two shillings, nine pence and three-farthings per week, based on journeys of 80 miles per day; for staff on routes with heavy traffic, booked at less than 9 miles per hour, the weekly increase would amount to six shillings, nine pence and three-farthings.

"I propose," continued Bywater, "that we take this together with Item C, which proposes that no duty should pay less than six shillings and eight pence per day for drivers and five shillings and eight pence for conductors."

The gallery responded to this with a ballet of tilted heads and a chorus of "Nnnyyyaaa," some of the performers holding up a flat hand horizontally and tilting it from side to side.

"That means we can just about get away with it, Chairman," quipped Macauley.

Tich Smith looked around the table. "Discussion?"

None.

"Agreed?"

Agreed.

"Item D," Bywater continued. "Overtime at time and a quarter for all journeys in excess of those scheduled."

Tich Smith: "Discussion?"

Macauley: "It's a start."

"Agreed?"

Agreed.

"Item E. No deductions for failure to complete scheduled mileage in circumstances beyond the control of the driver and conductor."

A cheer from the gallery. This was nodded through.

"Item F. Staff booked for duty will receive five shillings for drivers and four shillings and two pence for conductors if no bus is available. This will also apply in cases where, due to bad weather, etc., a duty is only partially worked."

Silence. Frowns.

"Agreed?"

"Wait!" Sanders to the rescue. "It seems to me, Chairman, that the companies are trying to take away in Item F what they've conceded in Item E. First of all, there will be no deductions if mileage is lost due to circumstances beyond the members' control; then we're told a driver will receive a flat five bob if mileage is lost due to bad weather, etc. And what the hell does that "etc." mean?" He laughed. "You can just imagine the trouble garage officials would give our members by putting their own interpretation on that. No, we can't have it." He looked around the table. "Can we?"

No, they all said. Not bloody likely, chimed the gallery.

"Alright, I'll grant there's a problem there," Tich Smith acknowledged.

Harry Bywater grimaced.

Spare drivers to receive a minimum of thirty shillings a week, spare conductors twenty-five shillings. Agreed.

No more contributions to the "Accident Club" by drivers and conductors; likewise, no more cash stoppages arising from accidents. Cheers. Nodded through.

Drivers and conductors to receive their uniforms free of charge. More cheers. Nodded through.

Silence now fell as Bywater placed his document on the table and passed his palm over it, as if to smooth it.

"No avoiding it now, Harry," said Barney Macauley, but the laughter this brought had a nervous edge to it.

Bywater looked around the room and then, as if seeking to demonstrate his fearlessness, without further hesitation read in a loud voice: "Item B. An extra payment of one shilling per day to be allowed on all turns on the duty sheets in excess of a 13 hours spreadover."

If he had thought that, by leaving this item until last, the mellower mood he had created would gain a less hostile reception for this measure, he was mistaken, as the gallery now erupted in a display of bitter disappointment, outrage and hostility. Tich Smith raised his gavel but then, possibly thinking that it might be advisable to allow the reps to vent their spleen before the executive members began to debate the item, laid it down and, cupping his chin in his palm, gazed across at the sea of angry, gesticulating, shouting members, their faces contorted with rage. He noted with some interest that one young rep sat, arms folded, in total silence, his expression unreadable. He allowed a full minute for this demonstration and then, as the clamour showed signs of subsiding, brought his gavel down just once. This had the most dramatic effect as—broken only by Tommy Dance of Putney, who shouted "Don't think you can shut us up, Smithy!"—silence immediately descended.

"I have no wish to shut anyone up, Brother Dance. But I would suggest that rather than all bellowing more or less the same thing together, you speak one at a time so that we can understand you and take your views into consideration." Chin held high, Tich Smith looked from one end of the gallery chairs to the other. "Now, who will

173

put your arguments to us?"

The arm that went up was that of the hitherto silent young rep.

"The chair recognises Brother Rice."

Mickey, who occupied a chair in the front row of the gallery, stood and took a step forward.

"Chairman and brothers, the anger you have just witnessed is both very deep and very real. Have no doubt about that. Is that anger directed at you, or at the companies, our employers? Well, obviously we're angry at the companies, because they know how we feel about the long hours we're forced to work. And let me tell you, brothers, that I for one, while I'm deeply disappointed, am not particularly surprised that the employer has ignored our wishes. And let me just say, while I'm about it, that the company has a *very* clear idea of what those wishes are. I know from talking to other reps that before these negotiations started, the garage superintendents made a point of questioning all of us about what we considered the most important goal of the negotiations. The fact that they all did this must mean that they were directed by Electric Railway House. And we all told our garage superintendents the same thing: place a limit on the length and number of spreadovers; place a maximum on the time on duty.

But they haven't, have they?

"Now, the reason this does not surprise me is because I've had some experience of their thinking. At Middle Row, I proved to the garage superintendent that the onerous nature of some spreadovers—and one in particular—had led to accidents. He agreed I had a point! In fact, he went up to Electric Railway House and put it to Mr Albert Stanley that there should be an investigation, with a view to putting it right. And Mr *Stanley* agreed! Yes, he said, there should be an investigation, but it should be conducted at Grosvenor Road, with no union involvement—bear in mind this was before we were recognised. One of his head office managers, he said, would look at the results and make sure they were fair. But what happened? They tackled the worst spreadover, cutting two hours from it. And they just distributed the cut mileage to other duties, worsening them. And, despite the fact that this was supposed to be an investigation into the link between long duties and accidents, not one other duty was touched!

"Why was this? I think there are two reasons, Chairman. First, the people who work at Grosvenor Road and Electric Railway House simply do not *know* what it's like to work a fifteen-hour spreadover five or six days a week! They have *no experience* of finishing work at nine o'clock at night and having to get back to the garage by six the

174

next morning! They don't *know* what it's like to be almost dropping from hunger and fatigue on the second spell of these spreadovers!"

As Mickey counted off these points, his voice rose, becoming hoarse, as he was unable to control his anger, and as he painted a picture which his audience recognised all too clearly, a grave murmur of confirmation rose from the reps. At the table, Sanders, Eric and Ben Smith were smiling.

Mickey paused, breathing deeply, allowing Tich Smith to intervene with "Is that it, Brother Rice?"

"No it's *not* it!" Mickey responded, causing the reps to cheer in encouragement and thus deter any admonition from the chairman. "The second reason why the company is not prepared to move on the question of spreadovers is, of course, financial. Drastically reduce the length of spreadovers and you have to employ more crews. Yes, they'll give us a few more bob a week, we can have a free uniform and travel pass and a few other bits and pieces—but only as long as we continue to flog our guts out on those spreadovers! Reduce those and it'll cost them *real* money.

"And I wouldn't mind betting, brothers, that during the negotiations the company tried to bedazzle you with capitalist economics. 'Oh, Mr Bywater, we can't possibly do that because it would mean we would have to reduce the dividend to the shareholders.' Did they try that one?" He noticed that Macauley was grinning broadly and nodding. "Well, we should point out to them that the wealth they distribute in dividends has been created by *our* labour, *our* sweat, *our* lack of social life! It's not created in the offices, it comes from us, out on the road! And so they need to know that if the price of making this job more humane and civilised is to reduce the dividend, *that's the price they'll have to pay!*"

This gained Mickey a round of applause. Seeing Tich Smith about to speak, he held up a palm and continued.

"So, yes, we're angry at the company. But, Chairman, we're also angry at the executive officers and the Executive." Silence now reigned, and the atmosphere crackled with tension. "If the company was well aware what the membership wanted most of all out of these negotiations, so did you! How many resolutions from the branches did you receive? What did those resolutions demand? A nine-hour day, or a drastic limit on the length of spreadovers! A limit on duty time! And you used these resolutions as the basis for the Busmen's Charter you had printed up and distributed to the branches." He extended both arms in the direction of the table. "And what have you come back with? *No* reduction in duty time! *No* reduction in the length or number of spreadovers! And a shilling a day! Twelve pence a day for continuing to slave away so that the shareholders can maintain their dividend!" He paused, apparently considering carefully how much further he should go. Whatever doubts he may have had were cast aside and he plunged on. "Some of us are now asking, Chairman, if some of our negotiators are unable to understand the depth of our feeling because they have the same problem as the company's representatives. Is it because, like them, some of you have not experienced what we go through six days a week? Driving a cab around London is not the same as hauling the wheel of a fully-loaded X-type or B-type!"

This was too much for Bywater who, red-faced and thumping the table, now intervened. "Chairman, I'll not sit here and listen to such insults! And what would he know? He's not even a driver!"

"I know because I've got eyes in my head!" Mickey came back. "I can see the strain the job puts on the men I work with! *And* I know what it's like to spend all day running up and down stairs!"

"Enough!" cried Tich Smith. "There'll be no bickering here. Brother Rice, if you have any more to say, let's hear it so we can move on to debating the recommendation."

"Thank you, Chairman," said a more subdued Mickey Rice, "and I'm sorry if anyone found my recent remarks unfair. But this, brothers,"—he waved the document containing the proposals in the air—"is not what London busmen joined our union for, and I hope you realise that if their hopes are not met many of them may let go of their membership and we'll be back where we started. That's the danger, brothers.

"It is my hope, therefore, and I think that my comrades here will agree with what I am going to say, that you will recommend *rejection* of these proposals, that the membership will overwhelmingly *vote* against them, sending you back to the negotiating table to bring us what we have asked for and deserve!"

To a man, the reps stood, applauded and cheered, some stepping forward to clap Mickey on the back and shake his hand. At the table, Eric, Sanders and Ben Smith joined in the applause, despite the angry, piercing stare that Bywater directed to each of them in turn.

Having allowed a few moments for the tumult to subside, Tich Smith rapped his gavel smartly and called the meeting to order.

"It seems to me, brothers," he said, "that we have before us something of a dilemma. There can be little doubt that Item B is decidedly unpopular, and left to itself would be thrown out, as perhaps it should be. The problem is, though, that it *cannot* be left to itself, the company having made it crystal clear that these proposals are a package, take it or leave it. So a vote against Item

B..."

"Not forgetting Item F," Sanders interrupted.

"Yes, there are also questions about Item F. But my point is that a vote against either or both of these items are in fact a vote against the whole package. That's our dilemma. So any recommendation can only apply to the package as a whole." He looked around the silent table. "I'm waiting for someone to move a recommendation, brothers."

A tall, slack-jawed executive member called Collins cleared his throat. "At the risk of making myself unpopular, Chairman, I move that we recommend acceptance."

A low refrain of moans came from the reps in the gallery.

"Do I have a seconder?" asked Tich Smith.

"You do," sighed Nichols, co-opted representative of the Tilling's membership. "I second the motion."

"No, Tommy!" cried Dave Marston from the gallery.

Tich Smith wielded his gavel and looked across at the gallery. "Look, brothers, I know that there is much high feeling about this matter. But I cannot allow attempts to influence the votes or the arguments of the Council at this stage. If it is felt that they vote incorrectly, the members at the garages will have the opportunity to show them the error of their ways." He turned to Collins. "Now, Brother Collins, speak to your motion."

"Chairman, I too acknowledge the depth of feeling..."

"What's that, Ted, the depth of the high feeling?" quipped Macauley.

Tich Smith glared. "Barney..."

"But," continued Collins, undeterred, "I honestly do not see that we have any alternative but to recommend this offer to the members. We spent heaven knows how many hours at the negotiating table, and we came away with the best we could get. If some of the reps in the gallery had been with us, they might now be behaving a bit differently. No one on our side pulled any punches. We *did* argue strongly for a reduction in the length of the working day. We pushed the companies as far as they would go." He executed an exaggerated shrug. "What is the alternative? If the members turn down this offer, how will we appear in the eyes of the employers? What will they say of us? I'll tell you: they'll say that our authority to speak on behalf of our members has been weakened. I feel the same way as everyone else with regard to Item B, but I'm afraid we just have to swallow it. So let's vote—and work—for acceptance and get it over with."

Tich Smith turned to Tommy Nichols. "Seconder?"

"I don't have to remind you," he began, "that the Tilling's members joined the union because they wished to see an increase in their earnings and a reduction in the hours. Well, while most of the attention so far has been directed to the question of hours, it seems to me that we've lost sight of the good things in the document. There *will* be an increase in earnings, first of all in terms of pence per mile. Then, as hard as it might be to accept long hours, those spreadovers are now going to generate extra cash to the tune of five or six bob a week. Free travel: what's that if it's not the same as an increase in earnings? Same goes for the free uniform. So I think my members will see that real progress has been made with regard to earnings, and I don't see any danger of them dropping out of the union because of our failure to reduce hours. Rome wasn't built in a day. *That's* what I'll tell my members. One step at a time: this year, we've increased wages; in the next negotiations we'll get those hours reduced. And remember this: when we're recommending acceptance, we don't need to give our members the impression that we think Item B is wonderful. No, we tell 'em straight: we don't like it any more than you, but this time around consider the improvements on the cash side. Next time, we'll do something about hours."

"Contributions to debate?" called Tich Smith.

Sanders feared the worst. A third of the bus representatives had now called for acceptance. Of the remaining four, only Macauley and Shiers could be depended upon to call for rejection. That left Frank Mead and Eamon Quinlan. The other seven members of the Council, six from the cabs and one from the trams, would tend to follow the majority of the bus votes. Macauley, he could see, was biding his time, hoping to come in last and perhaps tip the scales. But no one made a move.

"If no one wishes to speak, brothers, we'll move to the vote," Tich Smith warned.

"No, no, no," Macauley groaned as he raised his hand. "Let's have the other side of the argument before we vote." He glanced around the table. "Looks as if that job's been left to me, Chairman." The burly man threw back his shoulders and cleared his throat. "Brothers, let me take up a couple of points made by Brother Collins. He has asked what the employers will think of us if the members reject this offer. First of all, let me say that they are far more likely to question whether we represent the views of our members if we recommend *acceptance* and the members *still* reject the package." He looked at each of his lay colleagues in turn. "And *that*, brothers, will be the most likely outcome, be in no doubt about it! And *when* that happens, we shouldn't be the least bit upset by it. Albert

Stanley and the Tilling brothers will say we don't represent the views of the members? Well, if we've recommended acceptance, they would be *right*, wouldn't they? But there's a simple reply we can give the employers in that event: our union, Mr Stanley and Messrs Tilling, is a *democracy*, and you shouldn't confuse union democracy with the way you run your companies!

"Now, Brother Collins says that we pushed the employers as far as they would go. I'll surprise you now by saying that I agree with that statement." He paused for dramatic effect. *"As far as it goes!* The biggest mistake we made going into these negotiations was to allow the employers to set the boundaries." He threw a hand in the direction of the gallery. "The lad from Middle Row was right: they *did* tell us that they could go no further without cutting into the shareholders' dividend! Can you show me where it's written that the shareholders *must* have a dividend of fifteen or twenty percent? Of course you can't! Now tell me: if the shareholders' dividend is reduced by a quarter or a third, are they going to suffer hardship, will their children go hungry? Of *course* they won't! But our members, unless those dividends *are* reduced, will continue to flog their guts out on fifteen-hour spreadovers. That's the lesson of these negotiations, brothers! And unless we begin to see beyond—and break through!—the boundaries set by the employers, we'll be going through this year after year after year!" He lowered his voice. "And for those who are prepared to listen and, perhaps, think for themselves, that is also why the public transport system needs to be owned by the community, so that the workers receive a greater share of the wealth they create, and any surplus is enjoyed by the people of London. Reject this motion, brothers."

Shiers, a short man with a sharp voice, now came in. "Just briefly, Chairman, it seems to me that the members will reject this package, whatever we recommend. And if the employers still refuse to reduce the hours, there's the possibility of a dust-up. If that happens, we'll need to be united, standing together, and we'll be far more likely to mobilise the membership if we take a firm lead now, by recommending rejection of the package."

The fair-haired Irishman Eamon Quinlan now raised his hand. "Chairman, a recommendation to reject this offer would be nothing but a pious gesture. Surely, deep down, we all know that even if we go down that route"—he pronounced it "rowt"—"the companies are not going to budge. Brother Macauley says that the rate of dividend paid to the shareholders is not carved in tablets of stone, and maybe that's right, but we need to recognise and accept that this is the world we're living in. The socialist fairyland mentioned by my compatriot Barney is not here yet, so let's not fool ourselves, brothers. Let's make our decision in the light of present-day realities and vote to recommend acceptance. And with regard to the argument put forward by Brother Shiers, I suspect that he's just as much interested in getting re-elected next year as mobilising the members for a fight this year. This is no time to be playing to the gallery." He turned and looked across at the reps. "No pun intended, brothers."

Frank Mead, slow-talking and deliberate, now weighed in. "Most of the arguments have been put, chairman, by Brothers Rice, Macauley and Shiers, and so I had not intended to speak. But Brother Quinlan has said a couple of things that should not go unanswered. First, he's right when he says that socialism—which he calls a fairyland—has not come yet. That's right, it hasn't. And it *won't* come as long as people like him forever tell us that we need to accept the world as it is. Secondly, he has insulted Brother Shiers by suggesting that he is only interested in re-election. Well, let me just say that some of us *are* interested in re-election—not for any perks it will bring us, but so that we can do the job that needs to be done and that certain others are obviously not willing to do!" He thumped the table. "Recommend rejection, brothers!"

Sanders allowed himself to feel a glimmer of hope. It was now evenly split, three-three. The result would be decided by the cabs and the trams.

Dennis Davies, the veteran cabdriver, raised his hand. "I feel somewhat uncomfortable about intervening in this debate, Chairman. This, after all, is the first time our union has negotiated terms and conditions with the bus companies, and I find myself asking what right I, as a cabdriver, have to influence this decision. So maybe we should take a look at our constitution in the near future." He sighed. "Nevertheless, I *do* know what it's like to work a fifteen-hour day, because I've done it in a cab. Would I be able to do it in a bus?" He shook his head. "I think it would kill me, brothers. I therefore vote for rejection."

Jenkins, the tramworker, came next. "I'm not a busworker either, brothers, but I *do* know all about long spreadovers, and I'm bright enough to know that if we can't get a reduction from the London General, we're unlikely to get one from London County Council Trams. So it's partly out of self-interest that I'll be voting for rejection."

That made it five-three in favour of rejection. Five cabdrivers had yet to speak, and it was to them that Tich Smith now turned. "Anyone else?"

180

When no one indicated a desire to speak, the matter was put to the vote. Morris Frankenburg voted for rejection, but his colleagues went the other way, making it seven-six for acceptance.

Sanders took it philosophically. He was convinced that the membership would defy the EC and vote to reject, but he was also self-critical, feeling that he could have done more to influence the outcome of the meeting. He considered it quite likely that Bywater had held an unofficial pre-meeting with Collins, Quinlan and a few of the cabdrivers, with the general secretary advising the lay members on debating tactics, urging that Macauley be forced to make his contribution early on. The key speaker, he saw, had been Nichols, the Tilling's boy. His contribution had undoubtedly made it easier for others to vote for acceptance. Moreover, he had sounded perfectly sincere when he had made his remarks, and Sanders was almost sure that, as an unknown quantity, he would not have been invited to attend a confidential chat with Bywater. If, however, Sanders had asked to speak to him beforehand, or if he had got Macauley to do it, there might have been a different outcome.

The other lesson to emerge from the meeting concerned the question of the dividend, first raised by Mickey Rice and then amplified by Macauley. It went, of course, to the root of the question of exploitation, and if a few more on the Council understood this, the character of negotiations might be transformed. He wondered if there would be sufficient takers for a series of education classes.

After the vote, the reps, partly disconsolate, partly defiant, drifted from the room. Eric caught Mickey before he had a chance to leave and threw an arm around his shoulders. "This calls for a lunchtime drink, Mickey!"

Mickey looked both tired and puzzled. "Why, because we lost the vote?"

Eric laughed. "No, because you're leaving your big brother in the shade! That was fucking brilliant, Mick."

Before Mickey had a chance to respond, they were joined by Sanders, who grasped his hand. "Well done, Mickey," he congratulated him with a warm smile. "I would say that you have a future in this organisation, young man."

As Mickey, who earlier had experienced no difficulty in finding the appropriate words, now struggled to express his gratitude, Sanders winked and nodded. "You've made your mark, son. But don't be too hard on us cabdrivers, eh?"

"You don't seem too upset by the vote, George," remarked Eric.

"The important vote is the one to come, comrades, in the garages." He sent his bowler into the air and, after it had turned two somersaults, caught it on his head. "Also, this meeting has given me a couple of ideas for the future."

Harry Bywater, an insincere smile revealing his uneven teeth, pushed through the milling committee members and reps and extended a hand to Sanders. "See you Monday, George. Bit of a result this morning, eh? No hard feelings, mate."

"No hard feelings, Harry," Sanders responded evenly. "In fact, I have to admire your superior preparation. Nevertheless, I can't help recalling the victory of Epirus over Rome."

Sanders left Bywater with an uncomprehending frown on his face and exited the hall with the Rice brothers and Ben Smith.

*

Days later, the Executive Council was called back to 39, Gerrard Street, where a pallid Harry Bywater confirmed the results, published previously, of the membership ballot.

"For acceptance: 3,820. Against: 4975."

This was greeted with broad smiles from the three organisers, while Macauley, Shiers and Mead actually cheered.

"Yes," said a visibly angry Bywater, "but before you celebrate, it might be sobering to read what the 4 June issue of *Commercial Motor* thinks about this result." He picked up the journal from the table and turned to the second page. "'The leaders,' it says, 'are in a quandary. Our own belief is that the employers will let all the dissatisfied hands go, and will train others. Better shut down for a month or two than accept the imposition of terms that are farcical. Labour may be ill advised by its leaders at times, but here we have a case of men refusing to recognise a success which their leaders have in effect secured.' I couldn't have put it better meself!"

"Oh, really?" said Sanders softly. "So maybe Harry can tell us, Chairman, how this journal knows that the leaders"—his arm swept around the table, identifying said leaders—"are in a quandary, when this is the first time you've met since the ballot. Or is this just Harry's opinion, given when the journal phoned up looking for a comment?"

"Chairman," Bywater spluttered, "I think that, as general secretary, I deserve a little more respect..."

Tich Smith held up a palm. "Look, before this gets out of control let's calm down. Now, Harry, I don't think George has said anything disrespectful." He glanced warily at Sanders, as if suspecting that a display of disrespect might not be delayed much longer. "He simply wants to know how this magazine could have arrived at the conclusion that we are in a quandary."

"Alright, they *did* telephone. But as far as I recall, I simply said that *I* was perplexed. Not in a quandary: perplexed."

Tich Smith looked at Sanders and raised his eyebrows.

"If Brother Bywater says that, to the best of his recollection, those were his words, then we must accept that explanation," said Sanders. "I would say, however, that it's hardly a hallmark of leadership to state in public that one is perplexed by a democratic decision of the membership. I dread to think what the members would think of us if they read that."

"The bloody members don't read *Commercial Motor*, do they?"

"Language, Harry," counselled Tich Smith. "And maybe the members don't read *Commercial Motor*, but I think we have to assume that the employers do. Does it make sense to tell *them* that we're perplexed? It hardly gives the impression that we're ready to return to the fray, does it?"

Bywater sighed and dropped his head. "Point taken, Chairman."

"Chairman, even more...ah...*perplexing* is how the journal came to the view that the employers might let go those staff who voted to reject the proposals," Sanders continued. "Has Mr Stanley given any intimation to our general secretary that this is his intention?"

"He has not," Bywater snapped.

"Have you been in communication with him?" asked Tich Smith.

"I advised him of the ballot result by telephone."

"And what was his reaction?"

"He was..."

"Perplexed?" This from Barney Macauley.

"Well, you may make a joke of it, but yes, that is exactly what he was."

"So are we expected to believe, chairman," said Frank Mead, "that the company told *Commercial Motor* that it was thinking of letting thousands of staff go but hasn't bothered to tell us?"

Sanders now relented, perhaps feeling that Bywater had been sufficiently discredited for the time being. "There is an alternative explanation, chairman. It might be a mistake to think that the people who write these stories are really in the know. For example, when this story talks of 'farcical terms' it can only be a reference to a reduction in hours. Anyone who finds that farcical has, like the LGOC directors, never sweated on a fifteen-hour spreadover. In fact, this line possibly comes from the company, which believes that a reduction in the dividend would be farcical. Similarly, anyone who believes it likely that a major company is going to close down for a couple of months because of a ballot result has probably never sat on a board of directors. It's also possible, of course, that Albert Stanley fed them this line in order to frighten us."

Bywater looked almost grateful.

"Chairman," intoned Frank Mead, "I am neither perplexed nor frightened, and I move that, based on this clear rejection of the previous proposals, this committee seeks an early return to the negotiating table with a view to the radical amendment of Items B and F."

"Seconded!" said Macauley.

"Agreed?"

Unanimous.

After the meeting, Bywater came to Sanders, proffering his hand. "I'd like to thank you, George."

"Good ballot result, Harry," said Sanders, ignoring the hand. "No hard feelings, eh? And remember what I said about Epirus and Rome."

*

"The situation," Bywater said to Tich Smith as they sat in the general secretary's office, "is becoming intolerable."

"The situation, or George Sanders?"

"As far as I can see, Tich, they're one and the same. The situation has largely been *created* by Sanders. Do you think I don't know that he was going around the garages, working for a rejection?"

"Well, maybe not personally, but I daresay some of his followers were doing precisely that. Mind you, I don't think George was any different from the other organisers—Larry excepted, of course. I imagine they've all been at it."

"But you know as well as I do that the others tend to follow Sanders' lead."

"Well, maybe so, but he *does* have a following, Harry. And he's a good organiser." He leaned forward. "And I've told you before, Harry, that you're a fool to give him the ammunition to attack you with. You should think before you open your mouth, man."

"Mm. Maybe so."

Bywater placed his hands, palms down, on his desk and considered them for a few moments before raising his head and posing the question that had been exercising his mind for some weeks. "Do you think, Tich, that there's any possibility of us pushing through a rule change at the next Annual Delegate Meeting, making

184

full-time officers below our level appointed rather than elected?"

Tich Smith grimaced. "Forget it, Harry."

*

"Are they serious, chairman? Do they honestly think this will tip the balance, and our members will now vote for acceptance?"

Unusually, it was Ben Smith who was the first to voice opposition when, after further negotiation, the EC returned to 39, Gerrard Street, bringing with them the companies' agreement to delete the final sentence from Item F, so that it was now clear that *any* failure to complete mileage through no fault of a crew would result in no deductions. It suited Sanders that Ben had taken the lead, as often the other organisers would wait until he, Sanders, had spoken, and then follow him, if they spoke at all. That Ben felt confident enough to take the lead would be an indication to Bywater and his allies of the practical worthlessness of the revised offer.

"Just be thankful," said Sanders with a nod to the empty gallery, "that the reps are not here." Given the shortness of the negotiating meeting, the sub-committee had returned directly to Gerrard Street, where, over the course of the next two hours, they were joined by the rest of the EC.

There was now little discussion. Those who did speak tended, with the exception of Macauley, to repeat the arguments they had advanced previously. Tommy Nichols, who in the past few days had had discussions with Sanders, Macauley and Dave Marston, remained silent.

Macauley restricted himself to a simple observation: "Those who were worried last time that a rejection from the members would tell the world that this committee does not represent their interests have even more reason to be concerned this time around, Chairman. Yes, there's an improvement, but it's so miniscule as to be an insult!"

It was not long before Tich Smith called the vote.

"Those in favour of a recommendation for acceptance, please show."

Collins, Quinlan and four cabdrivers raised their hands, and Bywater's face now showed a clear indication of concern.

"Against?"

Up went the arms of Macauley, Shiers, Meade, Davies, Frankenburg and Jenkins.

Tich Smith frowned. "Abstentions?"

Tommy Nichols raised his hand. Well, thought Sanders, at least he's proved that he was the key man in this vote.

A breathless silence now fell, to be broken seconds later by Sanders' murmured "The chairman has the casting vote, Tich."

Tich had placed both hands on the table, rattling his fingers nervously. He now raised his head abruptly to deliver his verdict. "Brothers, I'm sorry if this disappoints anyone, but this situation threatens to become a complete farce. I recommend acceptance."

Sanders glanced at Macauley and knew what he was thinking: this was yet another sign that Tich Smith could not be considered a reliable ally.

*

In the second ballot the membership once again rejected the package of proposals, albeit by a slimmer margin, and Harry Bywater seemed to be at his wits' end.

"Well, Chairman, there it is: another rejection! Do the wise men have any suggestions as to what we do now?"

"Has the general secretary conveyed the result to Albert Stanley, chairman?" Sanders asked, careful to give his voice a neutral intonation.

"No, I have not."

"Well, Chairman," said Macauley, who seemed to be enjoying Bywater's discomfort, "that's the *first* thing our general secretary has to do."

"And *then*?"

"And then you tell him to agree a date for the resumption of negotiations," said Meade.

"You think this is so simple, don't you? God, it's so embarrassing! I feel like Oliver Twist, 'olding me plate out for more!"

If, just moments ago, Macauley had been amused, he was now angry. "It is regrettable, Chairman, that Brother Bywater finds a democratic decision by our members to be embarrassing. *Embarrassing?* I'll tell you what *I* find embarrassing, chairman: that our general secretary hesitates to demand a resumption of negotiations because it makes him feel like Oliver Twist! We're not *begging* here; we're *demanding*! So if he's not up to making the call to Albert Stanley, maybe you should do it, Chairman. Or, better still, let him clear out and let someone who genuinely champions the members do the job!"

There was a short, stunned silence in which those who agreed with Macauley's sentiments were surprised, and those who usually sided with Bywater were shocked and appalled that he had actually voiced thcm. Bywater himself simmered, ready to explode—something to which the Sanders-Macauley camp looked forward, as he was almost certain to utter something recklessly indiscreet.

Perhaps sensing this, Tich Smith laid a hand on Bywater's arm as he quietly addressed the committee. "This has gone far enough, brothers, and I suggest that you, Brother Macauley, have gone a little *too* far. Brother Bywater will call Albert Stanley as soon as this meeting is concluded, and he will arrange a further negotiating meeting." He turned to Bywater. "Yes, Harry?"

"Of course!" Bywater's face was red, his lips speckled with saliva, but he appeared somewhat mollified.

"And I suggest," said Shiers, "that Mr Stanley be left in no doubt that we will be discussing Item B."

It was Tich who replied. "Yes, that will be done. In fact, I would suggest that we release Brother Bywater from the meeting now so that he can make the call and advise you of the date of the negotiations before you depart. Agreed?"

Agreed.

*

As the final negotiating meeting concluded at midday, it was agreed that the sub-committee would take a lunch break before joining the rest of the EC at the Gerrard Street office to discuss the recommendation. Macauley travelled directly to Gerrard Street where, as previously arranged, he met Sanders in the little café down the street from the office.

"Hail, Barney," Sanders greeted him as he came through the door. "Are you the bearer of glad tidings?"

Macauley grinned and took a seat. "Well, we certainly discussed Item B," he said, "but they refused to make any movement on hours. What we got instead was agreement that the one shilling allowance will be paid for spreadovers in excess of *twelve* hours, not thirteen."

"Ah, well..." Sanders waved to the waitress. "I suppose that's it, then."

Macauley nodded. "Yeah. I don't see any further movement."

"What mood were the employers in?"

"They weren't too happy," Macauley laughed, "but there was no talk of laying off dissenters and shutting up shop."

Sanders looked over his cup and narrowed his eyes. "Well, there

187

wouldn't be, would there? You know, I think it might have been Harry who gave that to *Commercial Motor*—not as what the companies might do, but what *he* would do in their position."

"I have to admit that's a possibility. Imagine, have all the 'no' voters sacked and what have you got? One hundred percent for acceptance!"

"Still, that's by the by. What do you intend to do this afternoon?"

"This thing has run its course, George, so I reckon we go for a unanimous vote for acceptance. Time for a bit of unity, I think."

"That makes sense, Barney. Have you put this to the others?"

"They're on board, George."

Sanders leaned back in his chair and gazed reflectively at the ceiling. "And, do you know, Barney, if you take a cool look at the package as it now stands, it's not half bad."

Macauley laughed. "Oh, I know, you're right. It's just a pity about the bloody hours."

"Their time will come, Barney."

After lunch, the EC convened and, on Macauley's motion, voted unanimously to recommend acceptance. The meeting lasted just fifteen minutes.

*

As was their practice, Tich Smith and Harry Bywater held a brief post-meeting discussion in Bywater's office.

"Fancy a snifter, Tich?" Bywater pulled a half-full whisky bottle from his desk, followed by two glasses.

"Not for me, Harry, but you go ahead."

Bywater poured a generous measure and lifted the glass to his mouth, drank, swallowed and, closing his eyes, smacked his lips. "Ah, that's better!" He sighed and leaned back in his chair.

"Well, Harry, it seems we can forget about wage negotiations for a while—at the General and Tilling's, anyway. You confident that this offer will be accepted?"

"Oh, yes." He laughed self-deprecatingly. "But don't take my word for it—I've been wrong twice before. But, yes, I think you're right." He sighed. "And do you know, I just don't know how much more of this I can take."

Tich Smith frowned. "What, you mean the argy-bargy with the lay members and Sanders?"

"Not *just* that: the whole circus. You know, it's almost impossible to build a constructive relationship with an employer when the members can come along and kick out a perfectly fair offer. I'm not sure that I can go on doing it."

"You're surely not thinking of jacking it in, Harry?"

Bywater took a large swallow from his glass. "Put it this way, Tich: if something else came along, I'd have to think about it seriously."

"I'm not sure I know what to say, Harry..."

Bywater used his free hand to point a finger at the president. "And I'll give you a little advice, Tich: if I'm not here when the next London busmen's wage negotiations come around, you want to think seriously about the possibility of having the executive take the decision on whether to accept or reject, rather than balloting the membership. That way, you'll avoid the anarchy we've just been through."

Tich Smith looked at the general secretary ruminatively. "I've changed my mind, Harry," he said after a few moments. "Splash me a little whisky in that glass."

18

"There is nothing," Sylvia Pankhurst, stronger now, advised Dorothy Bridgeman at their second meeting, "like a hammer for smashing plate glass; stones, even flints, are apt to glance off harmlessly."

"Here, Sylvia," Dorothy replied cautiously, struggling to keep her gaze steady, "I am afraid I must disappoint you."

"Oh?" There was no disappointment in Sylvia's tone, merely curiosity.

"I was under the impression that you disagreed with the violence of the WSPU's current campaign." She pursed her lips. "And if I'm perfectly honest, I really fail to see the point of breaking windows."

Sylvia considered her hands, which were folded before her. "Oh, I see." She sighed and her eyelids fluttered closed, giving Dorothy the impression that there was a struggle within her. "Well, yes," she said finally, "it's perfectly true that I disagree with the violence of the WSPU campaign." Her eyes sprang open, as if a thought had suddenly occurred to her. "In fact, however, I said nothing at the time; indeed, I was on a speaking tour of the United States when the campaign was launched. The Pethick Lawrences certainly objected, however. You are familiar with them?"

"I know they were, along with your family, founder-members of the movement, and that they contributed generously, but little more than that."

Sylvia inclined her head and, lost in thought for a moment, her gaze lost its focus. "Yes, Franklin and Emmeline..." She grinned. "Another Emmeline. They put an awful lot of money into the WSPU, and funded the newspaper, *Votes for Women*; and, along with my mother, they were sentenced to nine months' imprisonment for conspiracy. But when they voiced their disagreement with the arson campaign—like me, they were out of the country, in Canada in their case, when it was launched—they were expelled. That was two years ago." She snapped her fingers. "Just like that! Needless to say, they took the newspaper with them and a few months ago they formed a new organisation called the United Suffragists." She sniffed. "Well, when I say *they* formed it I do an injustice to others: George and Bessie Lansbury, Louisa Garrett Anderson—daughter of Elizabeth, niece of Millicent Fawcett—among them. They admit men into membership, which I suppose is a step forward."

"Were there no protests at the expulsion of the Pethick Lawrences?"

Sylvia laughed scornfully. "Only in the sense that some members decamped; to have protested *within* the WSPU would have been to court the same fate as that of the Pethick Lawrences." She grimaced. "You may have seen recently that my sister Christabel has made it clear that within the WSPU, to use her words, the 'word of command is given by Mrs Pankhurst and myself' and that 'those who wish to give an independent lead must necessarily have an independent organisation of their own.' Now, that edict was issued with reference to me, but it has long been the manner in which the WSPU has been administered." She shook her head—Dorothy was not sure whether in disbelief or despair—and when she looked up Dorothy could see that there was a danger of tears.

Thinking that she had better proceed with care, Dorothy beat a small tactical retreat, reminding Sylvia of a shared confidence. "Oh dear," she mused. She paused, then sighed. "Well, I believe I told you something of the problems I had with my own parents, so I'm well aware that family relations can be very difficult when one seeks to break with conformity." She had, in fact, repeated to Sylvia the account of her earlier years that she had first given to Mickey. Her reminder now had the effect she had hoped for, putting Sylvia at her ease and encouraging her to open up.

"Yes, dear, you did,"—she placed a comforting hand on Dorothy's forearm—"and I was very gratified that you felt able to trust me with such a painful recollection." It was now Sylvia's turn to pause. She bit her lower lip, closed her eyes and, opening them once more, had obviously determined to be equally frank with Dorothy.

"I think you probably know that I was called—summoned!—to Paris in January." She nodded in confirmation of this fact, as if Dorothy, despite previous knowledge, might still have difficulty in believing that such an outrageous procedure had been followed. "Yes, by my sister Christabel, who lives in virtual exile in Paris."

"So no Holloway for her? No hunger strike or forced feeding for Christabel?" Dorothy interjected.

Sylvia now appeared defensive, leading Dorothy to fear that she had gone too far, but her response was measured enough. "Well, it's true that she fled to France in order to avoid re-imprisonment under the Cat and Mouse Act, but she had, to be fair, been imprisoned on a number of occasions in the past.

"Anyway, we met in her apartment. I stood before her like an errant child, while she sat in an armchair, nursing a wretched little dog—a Pomeranian, I think." She sighed, a form of punctuation separating the restraint with which she had responded to Dorothy's interjection from the pain and anger now evident in the set of her jaw and the way, perhaps unconsciously, she drew her fingers into fists. Her eyes misted. "And she laid down the law: the movement could have but one centre of power, and that resided with her and our mother; in particular, independent activity by a group composed mostly of working-class women would not be tolerated, as such women were weak and unintelligent and, therefore, of no use to the movement, which should be based on women of our own class, who would, in Christabel's words, 'take their instructions and walk in step like an army.'"

"Was your mother present, Sylvia?"

Sylvia, perhaps welcoming this new question, nodded, delaying her reply while her anger subsided. "Yes, and she appeared a little upset. Oh, and Norah Smyth was with me, but she said nothing during that initial encounter. In the afternoon, however, the four of us went out walking, and it was then that Norah challenged Christabel with the fact that donations to our federation had found their way to Lincoln's Inn, where Christabel and my mother were based. Mother then began to talk of the possibility of compensation—not to me but to the East London Federation, which, even leaving aside the diverted donations, had spent a great amount of energy in raising funds for the WSPU, of which it was then a branch. Christabel doubted, she said, whether such a 'simple' organisation as ours would require funds. I don't know how Norah managed to control herself; that poor woman has poured much of her inheritance into the federation. Anyway, Christabel insisted on a clean break, with no financial settlement." She shrugged, and a wan smile touched her lips. "And thus it was, Dorothy." She spread her arms, palms upward, indicating her surroundings. "And here we are."

"And so you gave the name a slight tweak and became the East London Federation of the Suffragettes."

Sylvia smiled. "Yes. My mother was most unhappy with our use of the word 'suffragettes,' as it was so closely associated with the WSPU. She suggested alternatives, but our committee took the view that it was not going to be dictated to by Mrs Pankhurst."

"Indeed." Dorothy cleared her throat. "You were saying, Sylvia, that you disagreed with the violent tactics of the WSPU..."

"Profoundly. It was—and is—my view that the old methods had not been exploited to their full capacity. The new tactics tended to introduce new elements of doubt concerning the movement's methods, with the result that enthusiasm was diluted. They retarded a wonderful movement which was rising towards a great climax when this secret militancy was introduced. What the movement needed—and needs—is not more militancy by the few, but a stronger appeal to the masses to join the struggle."

"And yet—forgive me—you still smash windows, Sylvia."

"You feel there is a contradiction here?"

"It seems so to me, Sylvia."

"Well, yes, you are right." A thoughtful silence. "And I suppose there are two reasons for it. First, of course, one courts arrest and imprisonment in order to gain public sympathy for the cause. I think you have seen in the *Dreadnought* that this has been successful: huge marches by working-class men and women to Holloway. But to get arrested and sentenced to prison, one has first to break the law. Now, often this can be done, when released from prison under licence, by simply breaching the terms of the licence—by, for example, speaking at a rally or public meeting. When, however, one's sentence has been served, the cycle must begin again, and so obviously a window needs to be broken." She shrugged. "As simple as that, really."

"How many times have you been in prison, Sylvia?"

"This year? Nine times since February."

"Oh, my goodness," Dorothy breathed, aghast.

"I would much rather you were angry at the British state, Dorothy, than sorry for me."

"Yes, of course." Dorothy was filled with admiration for this brave woman. "And the other reason?"

"To be honest, I'm not at all sure that I can adequately explain

192

the other reason." She closed her eyes in what Dorothy now recognised as a characteristic gesture and brought a hand to her mouth as she sought the words. "Sometimes!" As the answer came to her, it was if she had been startled awake from a nightmare, and the word was almost shouted, alarming Dorothy. "Sometimes, on a march or demonstration, I will be thinking of the injustice against which we are campaigning...Even more, the *several* injustices to which we are opposed—yes, the denial of the vote to all women and most working-class men, but also the exploitation and deprivation in the East End—and I will be filled with such a...fury, yes, a *fury* that, presented with a clean, shiny window I am simply unable to restrain myself."

Dorothy watched her closely as she spoke, noting that her demeanour, most of all her anger, was as it had been when she had spoken of her interview with Christabel, although now she did not mention that particular injustice. And Dorothy thought she knew how Sylvia felt as she smashed those windows, for was this not the same emotion that took control of her from time to time, causing her to unleash an outrageous and usually undeserved tongue-lashing on whoever happened to have unknowingly provoked her?

*

"I do have to say," said Mrs Elkins when, having arrived at 400, Old Ford Road that afternoon, she responded to Dorothy's enquiries about her recent visit to 10, Downing Street, "that Mr Asquith is a tolerably 'andsome man."

Tolerably handsome for all his 61 years and white hair, Asquith had stood as the women were led into the small room where they were to meet, stepping forward to shake each of them by the hand and bidding them welcome. One of his officials then waved the women into a line of chairs before an oak table, behind which sat Asquith with two officials.

"Well, ladies, welcome to Downing Street," Asquith began. Unused to the company he was now keeping, he seemed somewhat diffident. He looked down at the blank notepad before him as if hoping that he might see his next line written there, then brightened as the line came to him anyway. "I daresay this is the first time you have visited Downing Street..."

"That's not strictly true, begging your pardon, because," interjected Molly Elkins with a nod in the direction of Julia Scurr, "this is Mrs Scurr's second visit."

Asquith's mouth fell open and he spent a moment blinking at Julia Scurr. "Is that so?" he managed eventually. "And what was the occasion of your first visit, Mrs Scurr?"

Julia Scurr, a greying 43-year-old, was the leader of today's delegation, chosen by Sylvia because of her experience. In fact, although she worked closely with Sylvia, the main focus of her activity was with the recently-formed United Suffragists, of which she was a vice-president. "I was here to meet Mr Balfour," she replied calmly. "This was in 1905, after I had organised a deputation against unemployment. Keir Hardy and George Lansbury were also members of the deputation."

"And how," asked Asquith in a patronising tone, "did you find Mr Balfour?"

"Rather too full of himself for my liking, sir."

The officials at either side of the prime minister suppressed their smirks but, surprisingly, Asquith smiled openly. "Well," he said, "I suppose I had better watch my step," and this served to relax the members of the delegation, who chuckled, and Asquith himself. He folded his hands in front of him and regarded the women with a new respect, grudging though it might have been. "Now, ladies, you are here to discuss a matter about which you feel deeply and which, regrettably, has divided the nation. Lest you be in any doubt, I must tell you that I have long opposed women's suffrage, but today I am here to listen. So who will begin? Mrs Scurr?"

Julia Scurr delivered a speech partly written by Sylvia, in which she pointed out that although Parliament presided over many areas of women's lives, women themselves had no voice. Women were subject to the same laws as men, and were taxed on the same basis as men, and yet they were allowed to make no contribution regarding these matters. Tactfully, she presented this almost as on offer to assist in the burdensome task of law-making: women should be given the opportunity to *help solve* the problems of working women; it was not only unjust but unwise to legislate *without the help* of women. And, finally, there was the poverty of the East End, the barely-affordable rents, and the high unemployment amongst men, which meant that often women bore the children, kept the home and acted as breadwinner. Such women, concluded Mrs Scurr, had more reason than most to desire to help in securing the welfare of the state.

She was followed by Mrs Hughes, a brush-maker who unintentionally introduced an element of comedy into the proceedings as she walked to the table and placed a sample of her product on it. The officials sitting beside Asquith were immediately alarmed, shifting their chairs back and looking closely at the object on the table as if it might be an explosive device.

"There is no cause for concern," laughed Mrs Scurr. "We no longer follow Mrs Emmeline Pankhurst, and so Mrs Hughes's brush will do you no harm."

"I wish I could say the same," said Mrs Hughes, holding up her scarred hands. "This is what I get for making these brushes ten hours a day, from eight in the morning until six at night." She grinned grimly. "Well, these and the tuppence per brush they pay me. Then they sell the brush for ten shillings and sixpence. On top of that, I have housework, so I work fourteen hours a day. I do not like having to work fourteen hours a day without having a voice on it, and I think when a woman works fourteen hours a day she has a right to a vote. We want votes for women."

Mrs Ford told them that she had been eleven years old when she started work in a jam factory. "More than anyone, we know what sweated labour is, and so we should be the ones able to bring forward reforms, because we know what is really wanted." She pursed her lips and looked briefly in the direction of Julia Scurr, as if seeking permission, or announcing a new departure. "It's important that you gentlemen know as much as possible about how we live, and so I want to say something about unmarried mothers: they face an impossible situation because of the way the laws are and the way people look on them. I'd like to tell you about a young friend of mine." She sniffed, swallowed hard and touched the corner of her eye with a finger. "She had to go to the workhouse to have a baby. When she came out she had no mother and no home to go to. I took her with me, and she shared my bed and my room, where there was five of us. Money was very short, and sooner than take the food, as she felt she was doing, out of my children's mouths, she went away, and I did not see her until three days afterwards, when she was drawn out of the River Lea with her child."

Mrs Elkins was to have been next but, affected by Mrs Ford's account, she sat silently and shook her bowed head. Julia Scurr then nodded to Daisy Parsons to indicate that she should now speak, but very cleverly, Daisy paused before she came in, allowing the thought of that dead child being pulled from the river to sink in; and it was clear that Asquith was moved. "I went to work in a factory in Aldgate and there I was a cigarette packer. We used to pack a thousand cigarettes for thruppence and in the morning when we were quite fresh we could pack 2000 cigarettes, but as we got tired after dinner we could only pack a thousand and a half. There you see that the wages some days we earned were less than a shilling a

195

day. At dinner time, the men had a set time and a place they could go, away from the line, but we women and girls had nothing like that. If the men were working under those conditions, through their trade unions, and through their votes, they would say they would not tolerate that sort of thing."

She cleared her throat, squaring her shoulders. "But there is another matter. We *do* protest when we go along in processions that suddenly without a word of warning we are pounced upon by detectives and bludgeoned, and women are called names by cowardly detectives when nobody is about. There was one old lady of seventy who was with us the other day, who was knocked to the ground and kicked. She is a shirt-maker and is forced to work on a machine, and she has been in the most awful agony. These men are not fit to help rule the country while we have no say in the matter."

Jessie Payne, who had cared for Sylvia at her home in Old Ford Road when she was suffering from the effects of her hunger strike earlier in the year, spoke of her daughter, who had learning difficulties.

"Once, when my girl was taken bad, she went into the Poplar workhouse, because I thought I was compelled to let her go. When I got there the next morning they had placed her in a padded room, and I asked the doctor why she was there. He told me I had no voice, I was not to ask why or wherefore, only the father had the right. If my girl had not had a good father to look after her, the same as her mother, I could not have got her out of the workhouse.

"I think we ought to have a voice in the different laws for women, because when you make laws, such as this Mental Deficiency Bill, it is all very well to make them; but unless you have had dealings with the mentally deficient people you do not know what they really need.

"We come from the East End," she concluded, raising her voice, "and we have the voice of the people. They want us to ask you to give the vote for every woman over 21."

Asquith spent a few moments silently regarding his hands, which lay folded before him, before raising his head and looking across the table at his six guests. He nodded several times. "Thank you for coming," he said. "Your visit has been very helpful to me." He sighed and cast his eyes to the ceiling, as if trying to recapture a memory. "You know, I think it was last year that I made what now seems to have been an insufferably flippant remark to the House of Commons. I said that I was tempted to think, as one listened to the arguments of *supporters* of women's suffrage, that there was nothing to be said for it, and that as one listened to the arguments of the *opponents* of women's suffrage, there seemed to be nothing to be said against it. That was before I listened to you, dear ladies. Having done so, I think I can say that I no longer feel that way. I have listened very carefully to what you have told me, and I will take all these things into consideration. On one point, I am glad to say that I am in complete agreement with you: if we are going to give the franchise to women, we must give it to them on the same terms that we do to men. That is, make it a democratic measure. If the change has to come, we must face it boldly and make it thoroughgoing and democratic in its basis."

"And do you think he was sincere?" Dorothy asked when Molly Elkins had finished her account.

"That I wouldn't like to say," she replied, "but I will say this: he was shocked by some of the things we told him, and moved. I don't think for a minute that it was time wasted as far as we were concerned."

Dorothy turned to Sylvia. "So can we hope for legislation in the near future? Is it possible?"

Sylvia was phlegmatic. "It *is* possible," she said, "but not, I fear, very probable. There is, after all, a war on the way."

*

It would arrive six weeks later, on 4 August.

By that time, Dorothy would be working for the ELFS as a paid organiser, although to call the post "paid" was to stretch a point. In discussing this delicate subject, Sylvia made much of the fact that when she began work for the WSPU in East London she had refused remuneration as, not being in total agreement with the policies of the organisation, she had wanted to preserve her independence.

"Well, yes," said Dorothy, "I can understand that, but I'm not really in that position, am I? I understand, Sylvia, that you can hardly afford to pay me what I hope to be worth to the organisation, but I must have something. I have to contribute to the rent and the household budget after all."

"But why don't you rent accommodation in this area, Dorothy? You'll find it much cheaper."

"I daresay, but I'm afraid it's not that simple. I have a young man, you see."

"Oh." They had not previously discussed Dorothy's domestic arrangements, and Sylvia's eyes now widened in realisation. "Is he in well-paid employment?"

Sylvia was obviously keen to seek out any circumstance which would enable her to pay Dorothy as little as possible, and Dorothy, finding this ruthlessness an unlikeable trait, decided to stop her in her tracks. "He is," she said, "a bus driver, Sylvia."

"Oh." This "Oh" was different in tone from the previous one, and Sylvia was looking at her wonderingly. "How wonderful."

"Well, I'm not at all sure that he would agree with that assessment, but..."

"No, I mean that you should have such a relationship with a working man. You must bring him here so that he can see the work we do." She gave Dorothy a questioning glance. "Why didn't you tell me before?"

"This may sound silly, Sylvia, but I was not at all sure that you would approve."

"That you live with a man, or that you live with a working man."

"The former, of course."

Sylvia laughed. "Oh, so you suspected that I might harbour a vestige of bourgeois morality! Well, there's something else we agree on: it *does* sound silly." She gave Dorothy a playful nudge with her elbow. "Do you know what my late father once told us children? 'If you ever return to religion,' he said, 'you will not have been worth the bringing up.'"

"How lucky you were to have a father like that, Sylvia."

"He was a wonderful man, Dorothy." She shook her head. "I dread to think what he would think of Christabel's beliefs these days. She has taken to studying the Bible in Paris, and she also has this bizarre belief that eighty percent of British men are infected with venereal disease, hence her slogan 'Votes for Women—Chastity for Men.'"

To begin with, Dorothy's duties were not particularly well-defined: predictably, her input into the *Woman's Dreadnought* increased, but she also played a role in the layout of the paper, liaised with the printer and sold the finished product in the Roman Road market— the original aim of distributing the *Dreadnought* free of charge had not been realised, although its price was reduced to a halfpenny; she drafted leaflets and arranged their production; in July, she played a substantial role in organising a march and rally at Canning Town public hall and library.

It was on the march to the hall that Dorothy experienced her first tremor of fear since entering the East End.

"Who are those men marching a few rows back?" she asked Sylvia.

Sylvia glanced over her shoulder and smiled. "A rough-looking lot, aren't they? Those are some of our regular male supporters." She laughed. "They call themselves the Rebels' Social and Political Union—a satirical variation of the WSPU."

"But they appear to be carrying weapons."

"Yes, dear. They take a nice length of thick rope, twist it and knot the end, then coat it with tar; sometimes they add a piece of lead to weight it down further. They call them Saturday Nights. They're only used for protection, Dorothy, so you needn't worry."

"Whose protection?"

"Their own—and ours."

"But protection from whom?"

"Most usually from the police. You will have seen from the accounts I have published in the *Dreadnought* from time to time that the police can be most wickedly brutal. Not only do they crack heads and ribs, but often they manhandle us, in the quite literal sense of that word, using our apprehension as a pretext to grab our breasts, and so on."

"And so on?"

Sylvia turned to her and nodded. "And so on, depending on whether there are witnesses." She smiled. "You're not afraid, are you, Dorothy?"

Dorothy, concerned that she might be failing a test, shook her head. "Not really," she said, although this was not the truth. "More curious, really."

"Well, I do not think the police will dare attack us today, dear, so you can relax."

"Why, because of the Saturday Nights?"

"That, and the fact that your young man has apparently mobilised several of his comrades."

"Why should the presence of busmen deter the police?"

"Because, dear, only the most foolish policeman would run the risk of provoking a bus strike."

In helping to organise the march and rally, Dorothy had called upon the assistance of the BSP and, in particular, Mickey, who took a supply of leaflets and passed them onto Eric, who gave them to Sanders; he, in turn, divided them among the reps at the East End garages. Sanders also had a word with Theo Rothstein, who ensured that the forthcoming event was announced in *Justice*, the BSP paper. On the day, Mickey turned up with Dick Mortlake, both in their uniforms, and if Mickey had expected that he might be surrounded by a horde of militant women, he was surprised to find that half of the people crammed into the hall were men, mostly workers, and there were several other busmen's uniforms to be seen.

During the march, Dick, who had lived in the area before the death of his mother, pointed out the local landmarks to Mickey who, on his first visit to the East End, was more impressed by the dire poverty of some of the neighbourhoods through which they passed, where ill-clad and underweight children stood on the kerb to watch them pass, their eyes uncomprehending; he was reminded of Jack London's *People of the Abyss*, which he had now read. Mickey waved whenever he spotted a busman's uniform, even though he had never met the man concerned. Several women were selling *The Woman's Dreadnought*, and now and again they came upon someone selling *Justice*; it was impossible to tell whether, apart from these, other BSP members were in attendance.

At one point, on a straight stretch of the Barking Road, Mickey found that he had a full view of the march ahead of them: thousands of people, many unknown to each other, marching with a common purpose. Although over a year had passed since his arrival in London, this was his first march, and as he gazed upon the long ribbon of heads and shoulders, marching five or six abreast, interspersed with banners, he felt his heart lift. He must have given some indication of this because Dick, marching at his side, turned to him and asked: "You getting that feeling again, Mickey?" He nodded.

*

Unknown to the participants, on the following day the march was briefly the subject of consideration by Albert Stanley. It was just before 10.30 when his telephone rang.

"You have a call from a Mr Quinn, sir."

Stanley sighed. "Put him through."

"Mr Stanley? Superintendent Quinn here. Earlier this morning, I had one of my men nip down to Electric Railway House with an envelope for you. May I assume that it arrived safely in your office?"

"Good morning, Superintendent. Yes, you may. It contained a copy of this morning's *Daily Herald*, which I have open before me on my desk."

"And was it of interest to you, Mr Stanley?"

"Well, I suppose it's always interesting to have the other chap's point of view, but I have seen nothing that would justify Special Branch drawing my attention to it. Or am I being obtuse, Superintendent?"

200

"You saw the report of the march and rally in Canning Town?"

"I did, but I fail to see..."

"And you saw nothing of interest in the photographs accompanying it?"

"Just a moment. I'll take a second look." Having previously lied to the Special Branch man, Stanley leaned over and retrieved the newspaper from his rubbish bin, placed it on his desk and opened it at the page in question. "Now tell me, Superintendent: what have I overlooked?"

"Do you not see that in the first photograph there are clearly visible several men wearing the uniform of the London General Omnibus Company?"

"Well, now you mention it..."

"And is it not a rule of your company that men should not wear the uniform in circumstances likely to bring the company into disrepute?"

"Is the purpose of this call to alert me to the possibility of a disciplinary offence, Superintendent?" Stanley asked brusquely.

"Not entirely, Mr Stanley," Quinn replied, taking the rebuff in his stride. "You will recall that earlier this year I alerted you to the fact that a member of your staff, employed in your own office, was a member of the British Socialist Party, and that she was involved in an affair with one of your drivers. Now we see some of your drivers taking part in a march and rally organised by Miss Sylvia Pankhurst's East London Federation of the Suffragettes." He paused. "It may interest you to know that Miss Bridgeman, formerly your employee, has recently attached herself to that organisation."

"So she is no longer with the British Socialist Party?"

"Oh, I think she is, Mr Stanley. Our men report that several known BSP members attended the Canning Town event." He sighed. "It therefore seems possible that the left wing of the socialist movement is contemplating a marriage—or at least a courtship—with the socialist wing of the suffragette movement, and that several of the people involved have—or have had in the past—links with your company."

"Ours being a large company, Superintendent, that is hardly surprising." How to get rid of this man? "However, there may be something in what you say, and I thank you for drawing it to my attention. I'll keep my eye on the situation."

That did the trick. Having replaced the receiver, Stanley leaned over the newspaper, noting as he had done earlier that in the second photograph, taken inside the meeting hall, Dorothy Bridgeman stood at the side of the stage, looking upwards as she conversed with Sylvia Pankhurst. His eyes then moved up to the first photograph and he wondered, as before, whether either of the men in busmen's uniforms was Mickey Rice.

19

On a late September evening, the meeting room in Gerrard Street was full as George Sanders prepared to introduce Theo Rothstein to those officers, executive members and lay activists who had come to hear him speak on the seven-week-old war. Although he had grudgingly given his consent to the meeting when Sanders had proposed it, Harry Bywater was absent, as was Larry Russell, but the Smiths and Eric Rice sat with Barney Macauley, Frank Mead and other left-leaning executive members at the top table, while Mickey Rice, Dick Mortlake, Dave Marston, Lenny Hawkins and other lay members from a number of garages across London occupied the gallery seats.

"Comrades and brothers," Sanders began, "in the past few months I have spoken at a number of branch meetings about the danger of war that threatened us—and when I say 'us' I mean not just you and me as individuals, but our movement. Now war is upon us, and in France and Belgium and elsewhere in the world worker fights worker because of the accident of birth. Workers who happened to be born in France or Britain fight workers who happened to be born in Germany or Austria."

He threw open his arms, palms upturned, indicating that such a state of affairs might be beyond his comprehension. "Why do they do this? They do it because their minds have been captured, because those who rule their nations have persuaded them that their first duty is to the country in which they happened to have been born. And that, comrades, is bunk! *Our* first duty is to our class, the working class—whatever its nationality.

"However,"—he held up a finger in warning—"don't for one moment think that the politicians and the bosses are insincere in their patriotism, comrades. Oh, they mean it, believe me. Why? Because they *do* have an interest in this war. It's in *their* interests that Britain should hang onto its colonies and if possible take a few others from Germany. Similarly, it's in the interests of German capitalists that *their* country should expand its empire. Why? So that new markets, and new sources of raw materials, and a new supply of cheap labour, can be gained for the capitalists, be they German or British. But capitalists are not going to *fight* the war, are they? Of course not! They need people like you and me to do that for them, and *that* is why they try to convince us that *our* first duty is to put on our kitbags, grab our rifles and line up behind the Union Jack."

As this brought a wave of applause, Sanders bowed his head until it had passed and then considered his audience, looking first at those around the table and then at the occupants of the gallery. "To tell the truth, comrades, we have our work cut out for us here. In this country, just as in Germany and France, there is war hysteria. Everywhere you look, you see bunting, the red, white and blue. And everywhere else you see that poster with Lord Kitchener pointing his finger at you, telling you that your country needs you. Lord Kitchener, appointed Secretary of State for War the day before war was declared! Kitchener, the man who conducted the scorched earth campaign in South Africa, burning farms and placing the displaced families—men, women and children—in concentration camps, where over 25,000 of the women and children died. What better candidate for Secretary of State for Imperialist War than the imperialist Earl Kitchener of Khartoum!"

This was greeted by a wave of scornful laughter.

"Sorry, boys, I was wandering a little there," Sanders said with a self-deprecating grin. "The point I was about to make is that those of us who see this conflict as an inter-imperialist affair are in the minority, so if we are to convince the rest of our class to see things our way and somehow end this war, we are going to have to work damned hard, and to do that we need to be equipped. Equipped not with kitbag and rifle, but with understanding, and it is for that reason that I have asked Theodore Rothstein of the British Socialist Party to speak to us this evening. He, more than anyone I know, *understands* this war and the reasons for it. Some of you will have heard him speak at the Hackney Empire back in February." He extended an open palm towards Rothstein. "Theo, they're all yours."

"My dear friends and comrades," Rothstein began, smiling around the room, "let me say at the outset how grateful I am for the invitation to speak to you this evening, and what a privilege it is to address members of the London and Provincial Union of Licensed Vehicle Workers. Now why do I say that? Is it just empty flattery, an attempt to get you to like me and, if I am successful in this, to persuade you to like what I have to say? Not at all." He held up a finger, picking up a newspaper with the other hand. "Let me begin by reading you something. You have no need to worry,"—grinning, he peered at his audience over the top of his glasses—"as it is very short." He cleared his throat and, adjusting his glasses, lifted the newspaper.

> "The workers of the world are now faced with the greatest calamity ever known in the history of civilisation. At the present moment all our Continental trains are crowded with men of various nationalities who are hurrying back to their own country to take part in the coming fight. Many of these men have been working side by side, and are on terms of the closest intimacy and friendship, and yet in a few days' time they may be shooting each other in cold blood. For what reason? Why, simply to satisfy the ambition and lust for power of the governing classes."

A number in his audience nodded or murmured in recognition.

"This appeared, my friends, in the 5 August edition of the *Licensed Vehicle Trades Record*, written by Lawrence Russell." He glanced around the table. "Is Brother Russell here, by any chance?" Discerning from the nature of the laughter this elicited from some quarters that this was not an enquiry he should pursue, Rothstein replaced the newspaper on the table, continuing, "Regardless of the author, I think this is an admirable piece for a British trade union journal to have published, particularly at a time when so many are abandoning what for so long we mistook for their principles, and this is one of the reasons why I am proud to stand before you this evening."

Rothstein removed his glasses, folded them and placed them in the top pocket of his jacket. "And so to business," he sighed. "In years to come, if you ask people what started this war, I am sure that eight or nine out of ten will tell you that it was the assassination of Archduke Franz Ferdinand in Sarajevo on 28 June. Indeed, I think you will find that this is what people believe today. But, of course, it is not true. Now, I do not deny that it was a contributory factor, but it was not the *cause* of the war, but a *pretext*. How can I state this with such confidence? Well, you only have to look at the events in the months *before* the assassination to see that various nations were preparing for war. I know that my good friend and comrade George here has addressed many branch meetings on the war issue, and that he based his remarks on a diary of such events, so I will not tax your patience by repeating what he may already have told you. I will confine myself to discussing the occurrences during the *weeks* before the assassination.

"June was an eventful month. At the end of the second week, Kaiser Wilhelm met Austria-Hungary's Archduke Franz Ferdinand to discuss the Balkan balance of power, and a day later Austria-Hungary's foreign minister made public a memorandum in which he suggested that this balance would be better served if Serbia ceased to exist as a nation." He threw up his hands. "Hah! Here we have the Austro-Hungarian Empire proposing the assassination of an entire nation! Isn't this a more likely cause for the start of the war than the assassination of a mere individual?

"At this time, there was a summit meeting in Constanta, Romania, where Russia worked towards an alliance with Romania, Serbia, Greece, Bulgaria and Montenegro against Austria-Hungary. What was this if not preparation for war? Over a week later Austria-Hungary suggested an alliance with Germany, the Ottoman Empire and Bulgaria—poor little Bulgaria, torn between two suitors!—against Russia. Again, to me this sounds like war preparations." He gave an exaggerated shrug of his shoulders. "But what do I know? I am just an ill-informed Russian, actually Lithuanian, journalist."

When this was greeted by silence, Rothstein looked around sharply, adding, "That was a joke, by the way." Then the laughter came.

"And then, of course, Archduke Franz Ferdinand and his wife were assassinated during their visit to Sarajevo by the Bosnian Serb nationalist Gavrilo Princip, a member of an organisation dedicated to removing the influence of the Austria-Hungarian Empire from its country. The immediate result of this was the outbreak of anti-Serb pogroms while the police stood by.

"In the longer term, of course, there would be war, but first preparations were necessary. If it had been left to the German army, war would have broken out immediately, but of course the decision really lay with Austria-Hungary, and here various disagreements had to be resolved. Hungary was at first reluctant to go to war, and it was not until the middle of July that, fearful that Germany might renounce the Dual Alliance pledging the two empires to mutual support in the event of a conflict with Russia, that war was decided upon. And then there was the question of tactics. Should there be a surprise attack on Serbia? No, public opinion had to be prepared, and a means should be concocted that would give an attack the appearance of legitimacy. And so it was decided to present Serbia with an ultimatum which it was bound to reject. It was not until 19 July that the wording of the ultimatum was agreed, and a further four days before it was presented to Serbia. Meanwhile, Germany mobilised its navy.

"As I have said, the terms of the ultimatum were designed to be rejected, and so Belgrade now learned that it was expected to suppress all publications inimical to the Austro-Hungarian empire, ban all nationalist organisations, censor anti-Austro-Hungarian sentiments from schoolbooks and public documents, dismiss civil and military officials on a list to be provided by the Austro-Hungarian government, allow representatives of the Austro-Hungarian government to assist in the suppression of subversive movements in Serbia, permit Austro-Hungarian police to participate in the investigation of suspected accessories to the assassination and to bring such accessories to trial, arrest a military officer and a civil servant named as participants in the assassination plot, crack down on the cross-border traffic in arms and explosives, provide explanations regarding Serbian officials quoted in the press as having made comments hostile to Austria-Hungary, and, finally, to notify the Austro-Hungarian government once these measures had been implemented."

Rothstein paused and considered his audience. "Is it possible, comrades, to imagine that *any* country would agree to such terms?" He shook his head. "No, of course not."

"Austria-Hungary declared war against Serbia on 28 July. One by one, the European countries declared for war, with Britain issuing its own declaration on 4 August, as a result of Germany's violation of Belgian neutrality after the latter refused to allow German troops passage into France. Britain, by the way, was pledged to defend Belgium's borders"—he paused for effect—"by a treaty signed in 1839."

This revelation brought the laughter and gasps of amazement he had anticipated. He smiled at his audience. "So, can it really be possible that the assassination of Franz Ferdinand caused the war? Does anyone really believe that Britain has declared war because of a treaty it had signed three-quarters of a century ago?" He grimaced and shook his head. "Of course not." He extended a hand towards Sanders. "George was correct when he said in his introduction that this war is an imperialist one, with the capitalists of one imperial power anxious to grab territory and markets from their competitors."

He held up a hand, indicating caution. "However, we cannot leave it at that, because this can be interpreted as saying that the war is caused by German aggression. That may be true, but we need to dig deeper and ask the *reason* for this aggression, discover *why* it is so important for Germany to expand its colonial possessions. And such an inquiry, comrades, will lead us to the conclusion that it is a mistake to apportion blame to this country or that when the *real* culprit is none other than the capitalist system. This will entail, I am afraid, a detour into the realm of political economy, but fear not: I will be brief, and I hope, deliver my explanation in plain English— despite being merely a poor Lithuanian journalist. *And*, I should tell you, comrades, I was severely—and I believe correctly—criticised for omitting this explanation from my speech at the Hackney Empire. There are two comrades here who will know what I'm talking about." He turned to Sanders and grinned and then, peering into the gallery seats, sought out Mickey and gave him a broad wink.

"Let us imagine, comrades, a factory worker. Every day, he must earn at least enough to reproduce himself. That is to say, enough to keep him and his family in food, clothes and accommodation, and for those other things which society considers necessary to the life of a worker. Now, let us say that, working at his machine, he creates enough new value to cover these expenses in six hours. Good! But what does he do now? Does he wave goodbye to the foreman and go home? No, of course not, because he has contracted with his employer—the owner of the machine on which he works, the factory in which it is housed, and the material upon which he works—to labour for a total of ten hours each day. So he remains at his machine for a further four hours, until the hooter blows. And what does he create during those four hours?" He looked around at his audience. "Can anyone tell me?"

He chuckled as Mickey and Dick Mortlake raised their hands. "No, no, let's have someone who has not read Marx. Yes! The comrade behind Brother Rice."

It was the Tilling's man, Tommy Nichols, who had raised his hand. "Well, he creates more value, doesn't he?"

Rothstein nodded enthusiastically. "He does indeed, comrade. Now, we saw that the new value created in the first six hours was for the upkeep of the worker himself. So what will happen to the new value created in this four hours? Anybody?"

Lenny Hawkins raised his hand. "Well, some of it must go to pay for the raw material, the wear on the machine, the upkeep of the factory."

Rothstein struck his forehead with a palm. "Ah! Idiot! No, comrade, not you, *certainly* not you! Me! *I* am the idiot. Why? Because I try to keep the explanation simple, but it turns out to be *too* simple, so that an intelligent worker—that's you, comrade—has to point out that I have omitted any mention of machinery, overheads, raw materials. These things *do* add value to the commodities which our worker is creating, comrades, but it is their *own* value, or a part of it. Let's say that the life-span of the machine upon which he is working is ten years. Every working day, then, it will transfer a very small part of its value to the commodities being

207

produced on it, and at the end of the ten years its working life will be over, as all of its value will have been used up, transferred to the thousands of commodities which have been produced on it. So the machinery, the electricity, the raw material and so on *do* add value to the commodities being produced, but it is not *new* value.

"Only the worker can create *new* value.' He looked around with an impish grin. "You can all test this if you like. Tomorrow, stand next to your buses and tell them to create new value. Talk to your bus as you would to a horse. 'Come on, now! Giddyap! Let's see you create some new value!'" He looked around at his laughing audience and raised his shoulders. "Will it work? No! It's not until *you* climb on the bus, turn on the engine and take the steering wheel in your hands and begin picking up passengers that new value begins to be created. Meanwhile, the engine, the tyres, the gasoline, etc. all begin to *transfer* a little of their *already existing* value to the commodity you are creating, the commodity called, in this case, transport. Only the workers create new value, comrades."

As his audience, delighted with this simple and apposite explanation, laughed and applauded, Rothstein drew a large white handkerchief from his trouser pocket and mopped his brow before turning with a smile to Sanders. "George, I fear I must ask you to act the part of regulator or inspector, for I am like a bus driver on an unfamiliar route. I have turned so many corners that I have quite lost my way."

"I don't believe that for a minute," chuckled Sanders, "but you were asking about the four hours."

"Ah, of course!" he exclaimed, turning back to his audience. "Now, comrades, if the new value—note *new* value—created in these four hours does not go to compensate the capitalist for electricity, wear and tear and so on, where can it possibly go?"

Tommy Nichols, the man who a few months earlier had so eloquently argued that the question of hours could be postponed until the next negotiations, seemed to have undergone a Damascene conversion as, almost trembling with rage, he called out, "Into the boss's pocket!"

"There you have it!" Rothstein concurred. "The new value created in those four hours—which, by the way, we call surplus value—goes into the pocket of the capitalist, or at least, into his company's bank account."

He paused, then dropped his voice. "Now, I know you are all probably getting a little impatient, because you want to get home for a good night's sleep before you have to go and create more surplus value tomorrow. 'What,' you must be asking yourselves, 'has this to do with war?' When will this long-winded Lithuanian journalist get to the point?"

This provoked a chorus of dissent, causing Sanders to assure him: "Don't worry, Theo, they're still with you."

"Good! Because now we come to a very thorny problem. So far, we have talked of one factory worker. But you must understand that *every* worker in that factory is *also* producing surplus value. If there are five hundred workers, they will produce surplus value for, on average, two thousand hours a day. But we have to broaden our vision still further, for *every single workplace in Great Britain where new value is created will be creating surplus value.* Now, the major question: what will be the inevitable consequence of this?" He leaned forward, placing the knuckles of each hand on the table, and slowed his pace. "If every worker receives only a proportion of the value of the commodities he creates, who will buy all these commodities? Who *can* buy all these commodities? Clearly, the British market cannot afford to buy them all. So from time to time there will be what we call crises of overproduction when, the market flooded with goods that cannot be sold for their full value, companies begin to cut back, some factories close, and workers are thrown out of employment. Curiously, the situation is exacerbated by the fact that the capitalists will use some of the surplus value they have appropriated from the workers to expand their operations, building new factories, making new products, and, in the process, having their workers create yet more surplus value, with the same result.

"There are, of course, ways in which these crises can be alleviated somewhat, or postponed. Goods which cannot be sold here can be exported. Here, Great Britain is very favourably placed because of its enormous empire and all that goes with it. For example, no less than forty-five percent of all merchant shipping in the world is British. A British capitalist who wants to become an exporter, therefore, starts off with a very big advantage compared to his international competitors.

"But it is not just that the British market cannot consume all that is produced within its borders. The time comes when all of British *capital* cannot be profitably *invested* here, because of the problems of overproduction, so some of it too must be exported. At this stage, colonies become vitally important to the capitalist system, because British capital can be most safely invested in territories where the Union Jack flies, where Britain has political control and can keep out foreign competitors.

"But this forms a problem for competing imperialisms, for their accumulation of surplus value means that they too must export both goods and capital. The problem is even greater for Germany, because it arrived late on the scene. Along with the rest of the capitalist world, it too suffered from the Great Depression which began in 1873. This was caused by an excess of investment capital. Once surplus value created by the workers has been transformed into capital, it cannot be left to sit around but must be invested, but on this occasion there was so much capital that it simply could not all be absorbed profitably. In the USA, many of the railroad schemes ended in bankruptcy, and the same kind of thing happened in Germany. A temporary solution was found, in the case of Germany, by emigration: in the 1870s, some 600,000 Germans emigrated to the Americas, and in the 1880s this number was doubled. But what Germany really needed to do, of course, was to export capital, not people, and in the mid-1880s it gained a few colonial possessions.

"Few of you will have heard of Max Weber, a German sociologist. In 1895, he argued that Germany, unless it was to end up as merely a larger version of Switzerland, must follow the example of the other great capitalist powers and establish its own colonial empire." He shrugged. "With what result? Cameroon, Togo, Southwest Africa, East-Central Africa, part of New Guinea, a few Pacific islands. In 1905, Germany tried its hand in Morocco, but Britain and France stood against it, forcing it to settle for a few concessions.

"And this, comrades, has been the problem for German capital. It may be the most powerful economy in Europe, but it has arrived too late at the table where the imperialist nations carve up the world between them. So this war, my dear friends, is the inevitable outcome of the growth of the capitalist system, and its development into imperialism. In one sense, it all begins with that worker standing at his lathe for ten hours a day, during part of which he creates surplus value which the capitalist appropriates for himself.

"Comrades, I have an acquaintance, a fellow journalist—I cannot say that he is a friend, exactly—called John Spender, who edits the *Westminster Gazette*. The day before Britain declared war, Spender was in the office of his friend Sir Edward Grey, the Foreign Secretary, who, while gazing from a window at twilight, said something like 'The lamps are going out all over Europe; we shall not see them lit again in our lifetime.' Well, I suppose we must allow him his poetic moment, but I feel he would have been more accurate if he had said that the lights in the stock exchanges are going out all over Europe— and New York. Most of them are closed! Does that mean that capitalism is closed? Of course not! You are still working. Everyone else—unless they have volunteered or been called to their regiments—is still working. So we see again, comrades: you, not the

210

stock markets, are the ones that create value."

A conductor from Battersea threw up his hand. "Brother Sanders, I thought I was probably wastin' me time when I came along 'ere this evenin', but I 'ave to say that I've found Brother Rothstein's talk very interestin'. It's true that by the time I get home tonight I'll probably 'ave forgotten everythin' he said, but at the moment I feel as if I understand things that've been botherin' me for a long time." Grinning, he nodded as his frankness drew laughter and applause. "My question is, though: what are we gonna do about it? What *can* we do about it?"

Rothstein nodded and beamed at the little conductor. "That, comrade, is the most important question. Whether you know it or not, you are following in the footsteps of Marx, who said, 'The philosophers have only interpreted the world in various ways; the point, however, is to change it.' Brother Sanders, however, has really already answered the question: we must first arm ourselves with understanding, and then use that understanding to win others to our cause. How do we want to change the world? Well, first we want to bring this imperialist war to an end. Realistically, we are unable to do this on our own; it must be an international effort.

"But here we have a problem, because many of our comrades in the International have, of course, reneged on the commitments of Basel and Stuttgart. It was also on 4 August that the strongest of our socialist parties, the German, voted with every other party in the Reichstag to support the war, abandoning its class position. Here, the Labour Party, followed by the Trades Union Congress, has declared an 'industrial truce.' In Russia, of course, the Bolsheviks remain firmly against the war, but they are unfortunately not yet in a position to decisively influence events. In France, our comrade Jean Jaurés was in fact preparing to attend a meeting of the International, where he would have argued against France's participation in the war, when he was assassinated by a French nationalist on 31 July.

"From this, we can assume that this war will be a long one. That being the case, however, who can say how the situation might change in one year, or two years? I think one thing that will change will be that the support by the majority of the British people for this war will diminish the longer it goes on. It is probably true that the same will be the case in the other warring countries. In the meantime, we must use every opportunity to get our message across, speaking to other workers, using our newspapers, holding meetings, building the opposition to imperialist war and, where possible, pressuring the politicians—and, of course, the leaders of our own movement.

"In the longer term, of course, whatever the outcome of the war, or of our efforts to stop it, we must rid ourselves of the economic system that is its root cause. And that also will require us to deepen our understanding of the system, to communicate that understanding to others, and to organise. This war, I suspect, will provide us with many opportunities to do that, and we must grasp every one of them with both hands. In fact, the struggles for peace and socialism are deeply connected: if we are successful in our struggle against imperialist war, the struggle for socialism will be that much easier." He paused, smiling at the audience. "If, on the other hand, we succeed in our struggle for socialism, there can be no question of imperialist war."

This, thought Sanders, would be an ideal note on which to end the meeting. He had been examining the gallery closely, attempting to gauge to what extent the activists were prepared to accept Rothstein's socialist prescription. Apart from the converts like Micky Rice and Dick Mortlake, some were nodding thoughtfully, others frowning in concentration, still others studying the floor. Only three or four, he thought, had been fully won over. Then the little conductor from Battersea leapt to his feet.

"Ok, where do I sign up?"

PART THREE

1915

20

Things changed in the suffrage movement after war was declared. "It seems," Dorothy told Mickey one rare evening when they were both at home, sitting at the table after dinner, "that Christabel Pankhurst began studying the Bible while she was in Paris, and she now claims that the war is God's punishment on those who have held women in chains for so long. She and Emmeline are touring the country to aid the Army recruitment campaign and pressing white feathers on those men who resist their advances."

Mickey lifted an eyebrow. "So the demand for women's suffrage has been dropped?"

"By the WSPU, yes. Christabel and Emmeline seem to think that having workers kill each other is far more important than winning the vote for women."

"So they're not putting forward any women's demands now?"

"Well, hardly any: they do believe, however, that women should be allowed to join the Army."

Mickey spluttered and returned his cup to its saucer. "You're making this up, Dorothy."

"I wish I were, but it's perfectly true, unfortunately."

"And how is Sylvia taking this?"

"Needless to say, she's appalled, and wrote to her mother to criticise her reactionary position. Emmeline replied, saying that she was ashamed of Sylvia, given her anti-war position."

"So when it comes to suffrage, Sylvia and Mrs Despard pretty much have the field to themselves, don't they?"

Dorothy fell silent, contemplating her hands as they lay on the table and tightening her lips.

"Sweetheart?"

Dorothy forced herself to look up, and there was a hardness in her eye which, Mickey could see, presaged an outburst. "The largest suffrage group, the National Union of Women's Suffrage Societies— 100,000 members by the outbreak of war, has turned to relief work and became the Women's Active Service Corps. There are some smaller groups, like the United Suffragists, but we work fairly closely with them. So, yes, the ELFS has the field pretty much to itself, Mickey, but Sylvia's attention, frankly, is elsewhere. All we seem to be doing these days is *relief* work!" She sighed and crossed her arms on the table. "First, there was the milk distribution centre at 400

Old Ford Road, followed by a clinic for the children at the same address. Then, before the war was a month old, we had opened the cost-price restaurant: two pence for a two-course meal, a penny for children. Soon, we were serving hundreds of meals a day—*hundreds*, Mickey, you have no idea."

Her right hand went to her forehead, as if brushing away a stray hair; but there was nothing there, and Mickey assumed that this was an action she often employed when, dashing about the various East End premises, there *was* a stray hair. What should he do? Merely sympathise with her, or offer a reasoned justification for the shift of emphasis in the work of the ELFS? He decided to risk a combination of both.

"Well sweetheart, I can see how you would find that kind of activity frustrating. But isn't something like that necessary? I mean, as husbands and fathers volunteer for the Army—no matter how mistaken that might be—more and more East End women have to be breadwinners. And if they have children, they must be finding it almost impossible to cope."

Dorothy uttered a ragged sigh, an exaggerated show of patience that did a poor job of camouflaging what was in fact *im*patience. "Yes, I *know* all that, Mickey, of *course* I do. Yes, these schemes are necessary. But they should be carried out by the government and the local authorities, not by an organisation that is supposed to be campaigning *for* the vote and *against* the war! I'm supposed to be an organiser, for God's sake, but what do I organise? Yes, I grant you that I help organise the occasional public meeting, and I've put quite a bit of effort into organising the forthcoming annual conference, but more often than not I'm running around to ensure that sufficient milk is available at the distribution centre, the doctors are available to take the clinic, and the local butchers and greengrocers have enough supplies for the restaurant.

"And then!" She threw out a hand, as if to signify that this next development had severely tested the limits of her tolerance for relief work. "And *then* in October came the Norman Road toy factory! Yes, it's a cooperative and there are jobs for almost 60 women, but all of these projects take up time and energy—and funds!—that might otherwise be spent on activity of a more directly political nature. And to the toy factory is added a nursery, graced by the presence on four days a week of Lady Sybil Smith."

Dorothy was now going over old ground. Each of these developments had been reported to Mickey before, but whereas previously they had been individual news items, mentioned for information purposes only, now she appeared to be assembling a case. But a case for what? For bolting the East End, or for engaging Sylvia in a major political disagreement? He suspected the latter.

"And for the first two weeks of the nursery, who was assigned to look after it with Lady Sybil?" She struck herself on the chest with her palm. "*Me*, on the basis that I had some experience as a nanny in Swindon, and so that, given the elevated circumstances of my upbringing, her ladyship would not succumb to feelings of social disorientation. You know who she is, don't you?"

Helpless, Mickey raised his palms. "Not a clue, I'm afraid."

"Daughter of the Earl of Antrim, married to Vivian, partner at Morgan Grenfell. And so for a whole fortnight, I, who thought my role in the East End was to rally the proletariat, found myself ensconced in Norman Road with a member of the aristocracy!" Suddenly she relaxed, allowing herself to chuckle at her mocking self-characterisation. She looked up at Mickey and smiled, and when she next spoke her tone was softer; no longer the advocate presenting a case, she now, presumably satisfied with that case, offered a more qualified view of Lady Sybil. "Actually, she's rather more than that: she was the treasurer of the WSPU, attacked a policeman at the House of Commons, and was given a short prison sentence. She told me that she came to help in the East End because she found herself bored with the social round among her peers." Bemused, she shook her head. "But I pointed out to Sylvia that while Lady Sybil had escaped—for most of the week, anyway—life with the aristocracy, I had been sentenced to it."

Mickey, glad that her mood had softened, reached across the table and took her hand. "Poor old Dorothy, sentenced to spend four days a week with the aristocracy." He straightened, assuming the role of the outraged Cockney husband. "I'll tell that Sylvia, I will. If she finks I'll let a wife of mine mix wiv such company, she's got anuvver fink comin'. I'll tell 'er, you see if I don't."

Relaxed now, Dorothy, laughed as she rose from her chair. "Washing-up time, Mickey."

"No, not yet, sweetheart." He waved her back into her chair. "Let's finish this discussion."

Visibly pleased by this suggestion, Dorothy smiled the way she had smiled on the Paddington train, and for a moment Mickey considered whether he should curtail this part of the evening by calling her Dorothea.

"You've said that these kinds of activities should be undertaken by some other body, and that ELFS should devote its time and money to suffrage and anti-war activity..."

"Well, I didn't put it quite that way, but yes, that's what I meant."

"Actually, that raises another point: money. Where does it come from?"

"Norah Smyth is using her inheritance to fund a lot of the activities, and there are a few other rich donors—although most of them either went with Emmeline or dropped out. Apart from those sources, the dues-payments are set as a minimum of a penny a month, and there are collections at public meetings."

"Are either the restaurant or the toy factory turning a profit?"

Dorothy shook her head. "I don't know for sure, because I don't see the books—if indeed there *are* books—but I seriously doubt it, even though Sylvia went to see Gordon Selfridge in Oxford Street and talked him into selling our toys in his store."

Mickey nodded grimly. "Doesn't sound too healthy, love."

She grimaced in confirmation.

He paused, careful lest his next question trigger another outburst. "So are you also saying that the ELFS is treading water on the anti-war issue?"

"Yes, I'm afraid that is precisely what I'm saying." She threw back her head. "Oh, to a certain extent it's understandable. Many women have husbands, fathers or brothers at the front, and some of them are therefore reluctant to accept criticism of the war. To begin with, then, the organisation lost quite a few members due to the anti-war stance, but they're beginning to come back—or new members are joining—as news of the war reaches us and people realise just what it's like. But some of those new members have been won by the relief work, of course."

"What discussion has there been on the committee or in the branches?"

"Sylvia has been very cautious. She convened a special meeting at which she put forward three possibilities. First, ELFS could simply continue as before, which would mean pressing for the vote and campaigning against the war. Alternatively, we could do precisely what we're doing now, working to alleviate the problems of those adversely affected by the war. The final alternative would be to use the situation to our political advantage—what might be called the ELFS version of the Basel and Stuttgart line. The members chose the second option."

"Ah!" Mickey was unable to restrain himself. "So the line you've been complaining of was actually arrived at by a democratic decision!"

For a moment, she looked at Mickey steadily, her eyes beginning to smoulder, but then she seemed to ask herself whether it would be worthwhile to develop this into a full-blown argument, for she dropped her eyes and nodded. "Well, yes, technically, but the decision need not have gone that way."

"You mean that Sylvia could have provided more of a lead." Mickey was anxious to let her know that he understood and supported her position, thereby avoiding a needless confrontation.

"Exactly!" She drew in her lower lip, chewing it thoughtfully. "Mind you, in practice the third alternative is also brought into play, as we always make it clear that the war is none of our making and that it should never be assumed that it has our support. So instead of leading with the anti-war demand, Sylvia tends to tack it onto the end of a list of other demands."

Well, thought Mickey, tactically that sounded quite sensible, but the thought was too risky to be mentioned aloud. "If there's one person who is consistently against the war, it's surely Keir Hardie," he ventured instead. "Isn't Sylvia close to him?"

Dorothy gave him a glance which indicated that she was unsure what lay behind his question. "Yes," she replied cautiously, "they are close. Very close."

"You would have thought, then, that he might have persuaded her to place more emphasis on the anti-war activity."

"Ah, I see." She seemed relieved. "Yes, I suppose so, but one can never be sure what goes on between them."

"Talking of which..." Mickey began with a smile.

"Oh, I *knew* it! I'm sorry, Mickey, but I'm not prepared to indulge in that kind of idle speculation."

"Then you're one of the very few people who are not, sweetheart; there have been rumours throughout the movement for ages."

"Yes, I know, but no one—apart from them—happens to know for sure, and so what is the point of speculating?" She sighed. "Alright, if you want my view, they are *not* lovers. He, after all, is almost 60 and he has a wife in Scotland to whom he returns whenever he needs to nurse an illness or rest from his frenetic activity. When Sylvia first met Hardie, she was very young. He was a friend of her parents, and they—difficult though it now might be to believe of Emmeline—were among the first members of the Independent Labour Party. I believe she has always been in awe of him. That's not so difficult to believe, is it? Founder of the ILP, the first Labour MP, a man of principle. And when her father, whom she worshipped, died almost twenty years ago, Sylvia probably looked upon Hardie as a father figure. So I think that their relationship, while certainly affectionate, is platonic, Mickey. Apart from anything else, of course, he was a lay preacher, for goodness sake!"

That, thought Mickey, would not necessarily have stopped him, but he kept the thought to himself, asking instead: "So what do you intend to do? Jack it in, or thrash things out with Sylvia?"

"Well, if I withdraw I'll have to find another job, won't I?"

He shrugged. "I daresay we could manage for a while, but the fact of the matter is that you'd be spoilt for choice. They're crying out for women to replace men all over the place."

"I should play a part in dilution?"

"Not necessarily: at the well-organised workplaces the unions will insist on equal pay for equal work."

"But when you talk of well-organised workplaces, you're also talking of manual labour, where I would be hopeless—and I'm certainly not going to work in a munitions factory, making shells to kill German workers."

"There's plenty office work for women these days. I see it every day, Dorothy, as I drive around London: in the City and Whitehall, there are now hordes of women office workers."

"Unorganised, and therefore paid less than the men they have replaced. Dilution, Mickey."

He grimaced. "You may have a point there, Dorothy."

She cocked her head to one side and regarded him questioningly. "It sounds as if you would prefer it if I left the East End, Mickey."

He held up his hands in self-defence. "No, Dorothy, it's just that you said that if you *did* leave you would need to find a job. I was trying to be helpful, that's all." He winked at her. "The decision will be yours, Comrade Bridgeman."

She nodded thoughtfully. "I think I'll give it a few more weeks and see how the situation develops. If there's no improvement, I'll have it out with Sylvia."

Mickey thought of saying that, given a bit of publicity, she would be able to sell tickets for that confrontation, but he thought better of it.

"You know, Dorothy, I've been thinking while we've been having this discussion, and it seems to me that there might be another angle to this relief work."

She raised a non-threatening eyebrow. "Oh?"

"Yes. You said earlier that these projects are necessary, but that they should be done by someone else—the government or the local authorities. But the point is that they're being done by the working women, and their male supporters, of the East End. Isn't it worth pointing out that working people *can* do these things for themselves, that if they are perfectly capable of running a business or a social service, there's no reason to think..."

"That they couldn't run the whole country!" Dorothy brought her palms together. "Yes! Well, that is indeed a thought, Comrade Rice." But then, as swiftly as her mood had brightened, a cloud passed over it. "But I'm not at all sure that this is Sylvia's conscious intention. If it were, she would be engaged in a socialist project, and if she's too cautious to give any prominence to the issues of suffrage and the war, I'm not at all sure that we can expect her to place socialism on her agenda."

"But it's worth bearing in mind as a possibility."

"Yes, you're right." She sighed. "You know, one of the reasons I've felt so frustrated is that I told George Sanders that I was going into the East End with the idea that Sylvia might be persuaded to work more closely with us, and that some of the working-class women one finds in the ELFS are exactly the kind of women we need in the BSP. I was beginning to despair of even approaching those possibilities, but, as I say, I'll give it a little while longer and see how the situation develops." She smiled the smile. "So I'm very glad we've had this conversation, Comrade." She gave him a nod. "Thank you, Mickey."

He bathed in that smile. "You're very welcome, Dorothea."

"Oh, Michael..."

*

After Mickey had passed out as a driver in June 1914—his appearance at the Public Carriage Office was a brief formality, Sergeant Bascomb treating him with something like respect—, he was placed on the spare list. Whether driving a B-Type or an X-Type, he experienced a torment of aches and pains in the first few days, similar to that he had suffered as a novice conductor; this time the aches were in his shoulders, upper arms and his left knee, consequences of the solid tyres and the constant need for declutching on routes with heavy traffic. By the latter end of the year, due to the absorption of so many of men into the Army, he was off the spare list and driving regularly on route 7, with Steve Urmshaw as his conductor.

As a bus driver, on the road for more hours than most, you tended to notice more than the average member of the public. There was plenty to notice in the first months of the war: mostly things that had changed, but occasionally things that were no longer there. There were now, for example, no horse-buses on the road, as all of Tilling's horses had been commandeered and sent to France. At the same time, the number of taxis had been reduced by 500, as these too had been commandeered and, having been converted into ambulances, sent to France or Belgium. Those transformations had been quite sudden. Rather more gradual were the changes he noticed as he drove through the City during the rush hours. Whereas the office workers crowding the pavements before nine in the morning and after five-thirty in the afternoon as they hurried to and from work had previously been overwhelmingly dark-suited males, after the outbreak of the war the men were not so numerous, and their offices presumably struggling; and then the number of young women sharply increased, swelling as the war progressed. Over the months, he noticed that the demeanour of these women changed: initially gay and vivacious, presumably excited by the new freedoms and responsibilities which had been opened for them by the labour shortage, they became more subdued as the routinism of office life was brought home to them. But hemlines rose.

Some things—and people—became more difficult to notice, due to the blackout. Street lighting was ordered dimmed, and the tops of the lights were painted black, to make them less visible from the air; some streets had few lights at all. London became a dark city, and for Mickey and his comrades driving at night became far more stressful. There was a sharp increase in road deaths.

*

Another thing you noticed if you were a bus driver—and even more if you were a conductor—were the effects of the shortage of both men and buses.

As he drove towards Liverpool Street Station one late afternoon in February, Mickey Rice could see the battleground ahead of him: at Bank, a large and still-growing crowd of office-workers which the X-type, already two-thirds full, would not possibly be able to accommodate, and so there would be the usual battle in which commuters fought each other and, if he attempted to act as referee, the poor conductor. Such battlegrounds were caused by the fact that even though the London General was desperately short of both men and buses, large quantities of both having been despatched to Europe, passenger numbers continued to rise. Most frequently, the battles occurred in areas of white-collar employment like the City and Whitehall where employees, having finished work for the day, were eager to get home through the darkened streets or, in the case of most of Mickey's potential passengers at Bank, arrive at Liverpool Street station before their trains departed. He reached the crowd, casting his eye over the people who intended, come what may, to

222

board his vehicle: a tall, homburg-hatted man of around thirty with a dark moustache who brandished his umbrella as, wide-eyed and baring large teeth, he forced his way forward, hoping to be standing at the bus's platform as it came to a halt; young women who, although using their elbows as best they could, were steadily losing ground; two young office-boys, clever tacticians who ran around the crowd in the hope of pulling themselves onto the bus and disappearing up the exterior staircase before the other passengers could get a foot on the platform.

Having engaged the handbrake, Mickey looked over his shoulder to peer into the saloon. Steve Urmshaw had no chance. He stood on the platform, counting the passengers on, but when the limit was reached and he attempted to prevent others from boarding he was pushed rudely out of the way. Mickey watched as Steve raised his head and remonstrated, knowing from past experience that he was telling them that the bus would not move until the overloaders had alighted. It did no good, of course. Mickey switched off his engine, climbed from the cab and sauntered down the pavement to the rear of the vehicle, where he stood with his arms folded, glaring with disapproval at the sagging platform.

"Ladies and gentlemen, if you calm down and listen very carefully, you will notice that the engine of this vehicle has been switched off. That is how it will remain until those of you who have boarded illegally leave the bus. Now, come on! We all want to get home, but all you're doing is delaying us further. Leave the bus now, please!"

As none of the passengers paid him any attention, Mickey walked away from the bus and leaned against the wall, arms still folded.

"Oi! Driver! Get that bus moving!" Mickey turned to his right and saw a bobby striding toward him. This, he thought with a groan, could go either way.

*

"Take a seat, Mr Rice," said James Shilling as Mickey entered the garage superintendent's office.

"Problem, Mr Shilling?"

"Possibly, Mr Rice, possibly." Shilling lifted an item of stationary from his desk and waved it at him. "Public complaint." He turned the sheet towards Mickey to give him a clear view of the letterhead. "From His Majesty's Treasury, no less."

"Let me guess: late Tuesday afternoon, Bank Station."

Shilling nodded. "Correct." He cleared his throat. "If that were not bad enough, the complainant directed his correspondence to Sir Albert"—Stanley had been knighted in late July, 1914—"at Electric Railway House, who seems to be familiar with the gentleman—or at least with his reputation. It seems that Mr Keynes holds an important post with the Treasury. On the day in question, he'd had a meeting at the Bank of England in the afternoon and then had to travel to Cambridge, where he was due at a meeting of senior economists. This meeting, he says in his letter, was 'of great import to the war effort.' As a result of the delay to your bus, however, he missed his train from Liverpool Street and was therefore late for that meeting." He laid the letter down and looked up at Mickey.

"And I suppose he says that this was my fault."

"Who else would be to blame, Mr Rice?"

"Himself—and the others who overloaded the bus."

"He says that he patiently explained his difficulty to you and your conductor, and yet you still refused to move the bus."

"Of course I did." Mickey sighed and leaned forward, placing his forearms on the desk. "Look, Mr Shilling, you know as well as I do that a bus carrying that kind of weight would be almost impossible to steer. If I had been daft enough to get back in the driver's seat, it's doubtful whether this chap would have lived to see Liverpool Street, let alone Cambridge. It seems to me that the only reason we're having this discussion is because the complaint comes from a man with an important job and Sir Albert has heard of him."

Ignoring this suggestion, Shilling glanced down at the letter. "He also says that you defied a policeman who had specifically ordered you to get back in the cab."

"He did order me to move the bus, but I then gave him the same explanation I've given you, following which *he* ordered the people off the bus—including the man in the homburg."

Shilling sighed and scratched his head. "You know what puzzles me about this, Mr Rice?"

"I believe I do, Mr Shilling: you're wondering why, if he was in such a rush, he didn't nip down the Underground. I told him in front of the bobby. 'Look,' I said, 'we're right outside the station. Liverpool Street in one stop on the Central Line.'"

"And what did he say to that?"

"Nothing. He just rolled his eyes as if he'd just realised what a prat he'd been and shot off into the station."

Shilling grinned and nodded. "Alright, Mr Rice."

Mickey leaned across the desk for a closer look at the letter. "What did you say his name is?"

Shilling pointed to the foot of the letter. "Signs himself J.M.

Keynes."

Mickey shrugged. "Never heard of him."

"Neither have I. Off you go, Mr Rice."

21

"Do you remember," Sanders asked as he drove Eric Rice into Southeast London, "what Larry Russell wrote in the *Record* last month about the National Steam Car strike?"

"He called for support as far as I remember," Eric replied from the passenger seat.

"That's right: support for those 'three hundred men who are fighting in the interests of all licenced vehicle workers to enjoy a living wage.' Those were his words. A fortnight later, in the next issue, he promised that however long the dispute lasted, the red-button union 'shall never be a party to lowering the standard rate of wages, which have only been obtained through the unity of the busmen of London.' Again, his words."

"Yeah, I remember that, too. George, is that some kind of clue to our destination this morning?"

"Oh, yes," said Sanders.

Originally based in Chelmsford, the National Steam Car Company had entered the London bus market in 1909 and, with the exception of Tilling's, which was tied to an agreement with the London General, was now practically the latter's only competitor. Having started with just four buses, which used paraffin to generate their steam, in Hercules Road, Lambeth, the company now, in April 1915, operated just under two hundred vehicles, many of which ran out of Nunhead garage in Peckham, and others from Putney. As the Steam Car staff expanded, its members—several of whom had either failed to meet the requirements for employment by the London General or had been dismissed by that company—began to compare their wages and conditions with those of the men working for their giant competitor; and, disappointing though many of the London General crews found their 1914 agreement, the Steam Car men could clearly see that their own terms and conditions were inferior. In late January, the Nunhead men had struck in support of their demand for improvements, and on 1 February the LPU Executive Council had called out the Putney membership; but the company had proved intransigent, withdrawing several routes and selling some of its buses to the provinces. Effectively, the Putney men were locked out.

Meanwhile, there had been dramatic developments at the leadership level of the union. The War Office having made an appeal to the LPU for more drivers for the transport section of the Army Service Corps, General Secretary Harry Bywater had, despite the strength of anti-war feeling among the activists, enlisted, followed by Larry Russell. Both were now recruiting sergeants, and a few nights ago Bywater had addressed a meeting of cabdrivers at which fifty had responded to his call. President Tich Smith had made what Sanders considered to be a feeble and mealy-mouthed attempt to justify what the anti-war activists considered an act of betrayal. "From a trade unionist's point of view," he had told the press, "it is humanitarian work that they are called upon to do, carrying supplies to trade unionists who are in the fighting line and conveying wounded to the base hospital."

"So why do you think Larry joined up?" Eric asked.

"Well, if you ask him he may tell you that the future of the country is at stake and so, regardless of the fact that this is a bosses' war, he felt duty bound to respond to the call. The truth of the matter is that he probably didn't fancy life in Gerrard Street without Harry to protect him. It's also possible that as, regardless of our anti-war activity, more of our members joined up, he felt under a bit of pressure to do the same. Just think, Eric: as of two months ago, around a fifth of London bus and tram workers had enlisted. Jesus!"

"And next it'll be conscription. They're already talking about it."

"That's right. So we need to build up a head of steam on that issue. With Bywater out of the way, I've had a word with Tich about a couple of proposals; he likes one of them, but is not keen on the other."

Eric laughed. "You mean the branch referendum on conscription?"

"Yeah, he's okay with that. When I mentioned the formation of an Anti-Conscription Committee, though, he went quiet; probably sees it as a rank-and-file threat to the authority of officialdom. But we need to go ahead with it anyway, because it's pointless holding a branch referendum if we're going to give government and Fleet Street propaganda a free run."

"George, are we going to Nunhead garage?"

"We are, Eric."

"So what's that got to do with Larry Russell now?"

"You'll see soon enough."

And there he was. As they drove along Nunhead Lane, their attention was drawn first to the pickets lining the pavement outside the sizeable bus garage, with its three large doors, then to the uniformed soldier, a sergeant's stripes on his arm, moving among them: Lawrence Russell.

"Well I'll be fucked." This from Eric.-

"Thought you'd say something like that, Eric," said Sanders with a wry grin. "Now listen: I see there's a copper across the street, so if he asks, we're here to boost the morale of our members, not to harass a member of His Majesty's Armed Forces. Okay? Let's go."

As they crossed the street, it became apparent that Russell had been distributing leaflets, although only a few of the twenty or so pickets had accepted them. It was not Russell who first approached the two union officials but one of the pickets, a large, untidy man whose name, Sanders seemed to recall, was Beard.

"Ah, Mr Sanders!"

Usually a bad sign when they call you mister, thought Sanders.

"Yes, Brother Beard?"

"I thought the union was supposed to be on our side."

"As it most assuredly is, Brother Beard."

"Then what is this clown doing?" he demanded gruffly, jerking a thumb in the direction of Russell.

Sanders turned to Russell and looked him up and down before responding: "Never seen him before in my life. He's nothing to do with the union, anyway."

Russell now came forward, giving no impression of authority or confidence. "George, I know we don't agree on much, but this is about defending our country."

Sanders whirled on him. "Oh? Who's defending our country, Larry? You? No, you've slunk into the enemy camp, but you're not prepared to go that far, are you? While you hide behind your recruiting sergeant's stripes you want these poor buggers to go and do the fighting—and the dying!—for you! And here's another thing: aren't you the one who wrote in the journal a few weeks ago that our union will never be a party to lowering the rate of wages, and yet here you are, trying to recruit..."

"He's trying to *what*?" asked an astounded Eric.

Sanders reached forward and ripped a sheaf of leaflets from Russell's grasp, causing some to scatter on the pavement. "Here, take a look, Eric."

Eric held a leaflet before him and saw that it advertised an Army recruitment meeting that afternoon at a public hall a few streets away.

"And yet here you are, Russell, attempting to recruit men who are on strike for better wages. What are you offering, eh? You want them to give up their busmen's wage—as poor as that might be—and become a soldier for not much more than a shilling a day! You, Russell, are worse than a scab, so fuck off!"

Russell, colouring and blinking hard, turned to Eric. "You'd better tell him, Eric, that under the Defence of the Realm Act…"

"You heard him," said Eric with an expression of extreme distaste. "Fuck off."

"Now, gentlemen," said the bobby, attracted by the raised voices, "what's all the excitement here?"

"These two," Russell blustered, "are attempting to dissuade these busmen from joining the Army, and under the Defence of the Realm Act…"

"Yes, yes, yes," cooed the bobby, a man of mature years, "but I suspect that the gentleman here might have an alternative view." He turned to Sanders, "Good morning, Mr…"

"Sanders, George Sanders, and this is my colleague Eric Rice." He extended a hand to the policeman, who shook it. "Good morning, Constable. There certainly is, as you say, an alternative view of what is occurring here. As you are obviously aware, these men are involved in an industrial dispute with their employer, the National Steam Car Company. Mr Rice and I are officials employed by their union. As you will have observed, we have only recently arrived on the scene. Nevertheless, it was immediately obvious to me that this…soldier was, by attempting to recruit the men into the Army, intervening in the industrial dispute. I am aware, of course, that the civil authority can, on occasion, order such intervention, but I would be very surprised to learn that the National Steam Car dispute is causing sufficient national concern to give rise to the issue of such an order on this occasion. If I am correct in that assumption, then it surely must be the case that this…soldier has overstepped his authority, and is probably guilty of an offence. We, however, are not vindictive men, and therefore…"

"Yes, yes, yes, of course," said the bobby with a bright smile. He turned to Russell. "I have to say, Sergeant, that this version of events is rather more convincing than your own. It might be best, therefore, if you just…"—he waggled the fingers of his right hand in the direction of the centre of Peckham—"toddle off and let these gentlemen conclude their business with the strikers."

The two union officials, the policeman and the twenty strikers watched as a disconsolate Sergeant Russell walked towards the nearest tramline.

"Or," the bobby said in hushed tones, leaning towards Sanders' ear, "as you so eloquently put it yourself, Mr Sanders: Fuck off,

Sergeant."

Hushed though the policeman's tones may have been, the comment was overheard—as, of course, was intended—by the picket line, which now erupted into laughter.

The big man called Beard approached Sanders once more, hand extended. "Brother Sanders…"

22

That Easter weekend, a note of tension was detectable as the red-button delegates filled the Club and Institute Hall, Clerkenwell Road, for the union's Annual Delegate Meeting. Upon Mickey Rice's nomination, the Middle Row branch had elected Dick Mortlake to represent them. He sat among the bus delegates in the hall, half-dozing, having finished a late turn at 12.30 a.m., as Tich Smith, president and acting general secretary, somewhat monotonously ran through the Executive Council report for the year, recounting the successes and failures—a loud cheer from the bus section as its organising successes were mentioned, a murmur of concern regarding the unresolved situation at the National Steam Car Company—and winding up by outlining the union's financial position, which was neither flush nor precarious. This report generated little debate and its adoption by a show of hands was a mere formality.

Next on the order of business was the announcement of the results of the annual elections to the Executive Council, following which Tich Smith called upon the successful candidates to take their seats on the platform. As they did so, Dick noticed few changes from the previous year, although he was pleased that Frank Witcher, the Hendon branch secretary, had beaten Eamonn Quinlan for a seat. Tich, as he intended to spend the rest of the conference as acting general secretary, now handed the duties of chairmanship to Dennis Davies, the longest-serving member of the EC, while he took the adjacent chair, next to Ben Smith, acting organising secretary.

Several of the motions which followed were of great importance to the delegates concerned, and were moved, seconded and debated with considerable feeling. Who could be complacent about the rising toll of road-deaths due to a combination of darkened streets and fatigued drivers, and the consequent disciplinary hearings at which the companies' approach to justice often appeared to be determined by whether they could afford to let a man go? This motion was also of interest to the cabdrivers, one of whom said that in his trade, it was not only accidents that drivers had to worry about, as several drivers had been "bilked" in ill-lit areas—and that often the passengers who ran off without paying were Army officers!

The motion on onerous working conditions was moved by Dick, who walked unsteadily to the rostrum and placed his written speech before him.

"Chairman, brothers," he began a little nervously, having never before addressed a gathering of this nature, "I fear there is little I can say on this subject that you don't already know, so I intend to keep it short."

This occasioned a flutter of appreciation and good-natured ribbing.

"Soon be dinner time," joked the West Ham delegate. "Time for a pint."

"Or you could just play us a tune on your flute," suggested a cab delegate.

"Delegates!" Dennis Davies brought down his gavel with considerable force. "You'll have the dinner-break when I say so, and if anyone comes back the worse for wear they'll be spending the rest of the weekend with the wife and kiddies! Now, no more interruptions! Brother Mortlake, please continue." He grinned mischievously. "And if you have time, you might explain what the brother from the cab section meant by that remark about the flute."

"Thank you, Chairman." Dick looked around at the conference, feeling a strange calm descend upon him. He realised that his nervousness had been due to his *difference* from most of the other delegates, and his fear that this would be detected and resented. But now that his secret was out, the fear disappeared and he decided to use the cab delegate's disclosure to his own advantage. "Chairman, in a previous life, I was classical musician, and while I thought that this knowledge was confined to just a few friends and comrades at Middle Row, it seems that word has spread—although not as far, apparently, as the exalted heights of the Executive Council." He shrugged. "Well, so be it. However, I fear that I must disappoint the cab delegate—and, who knows, maybe many more of you—and decline his invitation to play you a tune on my flute."

From the conference there arose moans of feigned disappointment, which the chairman tolerated with good humour.

"And do you know why, even if the chairman allowed it, I would have to decline the offer, brothers?" Dick cried. "Because I wouldn't have the energy! I'm knackered, comrades, completely knackered! It was one o'clock before I got home this morning, and it's been the same every day since last weekend. And I know it's the same for many of you. What time or energy do any of us have for culture or entertainment? None! When was the last time you went to a picture palace or a music hall? You know what happened the last time I went to a picture palace? Within ten minutes, I found my eyes closing. I was dozing off, but I was unable to sleep, brothers. You know why? Because I was kept awake by the snores coming from all over the theatre!" Dick had completely abandoned his written speech now and was enjoying himself, and he could tell that the delegates appreciated it. "And then, on top of the snores came the complaints from those who wanted to enjoy the picture. 'Sshhh' from here, 'Be quiet!' from over there, 'Get home to your bed!' from behind me. 'Leave them alone!' I shouted. 'They must be vehicle workers!'"

Even the chairman joined in the laughter and applause which greeted this.

"And Chairman, I fear that some of the delegates might be tempted by your threat to send some of them home to the wife and kiddies if they have too much to drink during the dinner-break. They'd probably think you'd be doing them a favour! What time do they get to spend with their families? Precious little, I fear."

Leaning on the rostrum, he felt the three pages of his speech under his elbow and lifted them up and, with a shrug, waved them at the conference before placing them in his pocket, causing another ripple of laughter.

"But it's not just the hours, is it, brothers? It's also the sheer *intensity* of the job: the traffic, the overloading, the late running so that you don't have time to grab a cup of tea at the end of the road, the feeling in your head and in your stomach that if you don't have a break soon you'll pass out. Every fibre of your being cries out for rest and refreshment, for the chance to close your eyes or put something in your stomach. And then there are the additional hazards of the dark streets, which have already been deal with."

"Brothers, if you're the same as me there's another feeling that caps it all. In fact, it's not so much a feeling as a cast-iron certainty. As you slave over the wheel of your vehicle, or dash up and down the stairs if you're a conductor, it becomes clear to you that every drop of sweat that falls from your brow is converted into pounds, shillings and pence for the benefit of the company you work for and its shareholders!"

It did not matter now how many delegates knew of his background, because he had won them over. Standing at the rostrum, cultured voice and all, it was obvious that he was more than a flute-player: he was a vehicle worker and a trade unionist, and his feelings and his instincts were the same as theirs. He was one of them.

"Bearing that in mind, brothers, it may be thought that our motion falls a little flat when it comes to the demands: we call on the employers to exhaust every possible avenue to bring about a shortening of the hours and the length of spreadovers, and to provide adequate rest-breaks; and we call upon the government to make available the industrial capacity to provide us with the vehicles we need and, at the very least, to drop all thoughts of military conscription, which will only worsen our plight and add to the intensity of the job; more than that, the government should examine the possibility of combing the country for potential drivers and conductors and, where necessary, giving them the assistance to move to London and help keep the wheels of the capital turning. I'm sure they'll tell us that London has no claim to special status." His fist came down on the rostrum. "Well, they'll be wrong. London is the largest city in the world and if its transport system fails, the whole city fails. If the government and local authorities can put up temporary dwellings to house women munitions workers, which is what they're talking about, they can do the same for vehicle workers!"

He won a generous round of applause, and as he made his way back to his seat the cab delegate who had made the joke about his flute stepped forward to shake his hand. "Well done, brother," he said warmly, "and I apologise for the stupid crack about the flute."

"Not at all, comrade," Dick responded, pumping his hand vigorously. "You did me a great favour. Thank you!"

*

George Sanders and Eric Rice sat at the side of the hall, observers today, as Dick Mortlake was followed by a South London tramworker who, in speaking to a motion deploring the rampant inflation since the beginning of the war, issued a desperate call for action by employer and government. Everything about the man spoke of desperation as, tall and gaunt, he stood before the conference and confessed his inability to adequately feed and clothe his family, unashamed because he knew that the same was true of many delegates in the hall.

"And at least one of the officers," Eric murmured to Sanders. "Fucking landlord's just put the rent up."

"This ADM must call upon the Parliamentary Committee of the

TUC to demand that the Board of Trade cracks down on the war profiteers!" the tramworker concluded. "And this union must demand that London County Council Tramways grants us the increase we deserve and need. Failing that, we need to drag 'em to the Board of Trade to get a war bonus. Believe me, brothers, this pot is about to boil over!"

Rather than have the motions debated and voted on one at a time, the chairman was allowing all those on industrial matters to be moved, following which they would be debated in a lengthy session, and then put to the vote individually. The next speaker was the portly George Blundy, secretary of the Owner-Drivers' Branch of the Cab Section, whose carriage as he made his way to the rostrum was somewhere between a waddle and a swagger. A member of the union since it had first seen the light of day as the London Cabdrivers' Union in 1894, Blundy made no attempt to disguise his patronising gaze as it swept the hall. This, that gaze inferred, is my domain, and were it not for the pioneers like me, you newcomers would not be here.

"Chairman," he began, unbuttoning his tight jacket and removing an envelope from his inside pocket, "I believe I can be of assistance to the tramway delegate who has just spoken." He peered into the centre of the hall, where the tramworker was sitting. "You short of cash son?" He removed a wad of pound and ten-shilling notes from the envelope and threw them into the air. "Here: take 'em! They're yours!"

Sanders placed his face in his hands, moaning "Welcome to the George Blundy school of diplomacy."

The conference was in uproar as the tram delegates roared their disapproval of this mockery of their colleague's heartfelt speech and others reacted to Blundy's bewildering behaviour with laughter. "He must be drunk!" shouted one delegate. "Send 'im 'ome to the wife and kiddies, Chairman!"

Dennis Davies, who had joined the London Cabdrivers' Union in 1897, got to his feet and swung his gavel. "Brother Blundy, what do you mean by this outrageous display? Can't you see that you have insulted the previous speaker?"

"That was not my intention, Chairman..."

"Well, you did, whether you intended it or not. Brother Blundy, I've worked with you for almost twenty years, but you've gone too far this time. Now, before you proceed—*if* I allow you to proceed—two things are going to happen: you're going to apologise, and a couple of volunteers are going to pick up these notes."

Three delegates from the front row set about gathering up the notes as Blundy, seemingly far from contrite, gave an exaggerated shrug. "Chairman, conference, I think you heard me say that it was not my intention to insult the previous speaker. If, however, I have given offence, please accept my humble apology." He bowed his head, then turned to the chairman. "Alright?"

"No, it's not alright! Now I want you to explain what you think you were doing, Brother Blundy."

"But you know what I was doing...Oi!" He pointed a short, stubby arm at the three men scooping up the notes from the floor. "I'm watching you, so don't be putting any of those in your pockets. They've been counted."

This gave rise to a further outburst from the conference, and one of the note-gatherers looked up at Blundy, threw the notes back on the floor and walked away. The chairman placed a hand over his face, shaking his head; but his shoulders were clearly rocking.

"Shall I continue, chairman?"

The chairman, face still concealed, indicated by an exasperated wave of the hand that he should proceed.

"Brother!" Blundy called to the man he had offended. "Come back, brother, it was just a joke. In fact, it was *all* a joke—although, believe you me, it's not really a laughing matter. Now, Chairman, as I was about to say, you, having read the motion I'm about to move, know only too well what this is all about." Stretching on his toes, he waved an arm, encompassing the whole hall. "And so, if you've read the motion, brothers, do you!" He now emphasised each word by bringing his right palm down onto the rostrum. "Every. Single. One. Of. Those. Notes. Is. A. FORGERY!"

The conference erupted in laughter, genuine mirth combining with relief that the apparent crisis brought about by this speaker's behaviour had turned out to be no crisis at all.

Blundy, for all his union experience, continued to give the impression that he was a better music-hall comedian than orator. He frowned at his audience, feigning offence. "You laugh. You think this is funny? Well, it's not.

"In August last year, after the declaration of war, the Welsh Wizard, Chancellor David Lloyd George, ruled that no further gold coins would be issued and that, instead, we would have to make do with paper money—pound notes and ten-shilling notes. Well, the criminal underworld must have been celebrating that night, and the following morning, hangover or no hangover, they got to work copying those notes. And where do they get rid of 'em? They can hardly pay 'em into their bank accounts, because bank staff know what a pound note is supposed to look like. No, they use 'em to buy pricey items in Selfridges and they presumably pass a few to shopkeepers. AND CABDRIVERS!

"Now, believe it or not, brothers, cabdrivers also suffer many of the stresses and strains you've been talking about this morning: long hours to make a living, the darkened streets, traffic congestion, high prices and so on. But *on top* of all that, now and again you'll get home, or return to the garage, and when you total up your takings you find that someone has passed you a dud note. Please note, brothers, this is *after* you've already been through a full day— or day-and-a-half—of those other stresses and strains. It's *now*— when, to use the language of the Middle Row delegate, you're completely knackered—that you discover you're ten bob or a quid short. How do you think that makes you feel? I'll tell you how it makes *me* feel, brothers." He held his hands above the rostrum in a strangling position and gave the conference a silent snarl.

"But Gerrard Street told us our motion couldn't call for the murder of forgers, so it now instructs our leadership to urge the TUC's Parliamentary Committee to put all possible pressure on the Treasury to make the new notes more difficult to forge, and for Gerrard Street to liaise with Scotland Yard on a regular basis until these forgers are tracked down and put away." He nodded to the delegates. "Thank you for your support, brothers."

As Blundy made his way back to his seat, he glanced at the chairman, who wagged a finger at him. Blundy grinned. "Got their attention though, didn't I, Dennis?"

*

"You know," said Sanders as he sipped his tea in the café—Eric had suggested a pint, but Sanders had pointed to the need for a clear head during the afternoon session—, "I was wondering during this morning's debates whether we were on the right track."

"About what, George?"

"Our approach to socialism. Our Rule Book calls for control of the industry, but would that be enough? Practically every one of those motions ended with a call for government action. What would be the good of controlling the industry if we didn't also control the state?"

Eric grinned. "You sound as if you're beginning to doubt the syndicalism you learned at Tom Mann's knee."

"Not for the first time, to be honest. To tell you the truth, I've often wondered whether it wasn't an over-reaction to the neglect of the trade union movement by people like Hyndman."

Eric grimaced. "Mmmmm…yeah, I can see what you mean, but aren't you the one who's forever moaning about the careerists in the Parliamentary Labour Party?"

"True. There'd have to be a few changes there."

Eric looked towards the counter to see if their orders were on the way. Usually closed on a Saturday, the café had opened upon the request of the union, and every table was taken. "If it takes much longer, we'll be late."

Sanders shrugged. "We're not delegates, Eric, so no need to worry."

"I know, but I don't want to miss anything." He frowned. "I've got a funny feeling about this ADM. I think something's going to happen."

Sanders considered him for a moment. "I know what you mean, Eric. I can feel it too." He spread his arms. "But what can happen? It's an odds-on certainty that the call for nominations will go through."

"I know, I know, but I can't help thinking that they're up to something." He looked around the café. "And, come to think of it, where's Ben? I thought he was coming over to join us."

Sanders nodded. "He said he was, but it might be a mistake to read anything into that. Maybe he looked in the window and saw the place was full."

"Yeah, maybe." He sniffed. "Anyway, what do you think of the EC results?"

"Well, no surprises, were there?" He sighed. "Our people will have to work a damn sight harder if we want to ensure that this union is progressive." He winked at Eric. "When will that brother of yours be throwing his hat in the ring?"

"When he feels he's ready, I suppose, George."

Sanders nodded. "Yeah, it's early days."

Eric chuckled. "Now don't laugh, George, but do you know what crosses my mind from time to time?"

"Well, I probably do, but there's so much to choose from, mate."

"I often wonder whether he might try to get adopted as a parliamentary candidate a bit further down the road."

"Has he mentioned it?"

Eric shook his head emphatically. "No, no, no. The boy hasn't got an ambitious bone in his body as far as I can see. He hasn't even mentioned the EC as a possibility. It's just that I can, you know, picture him up there."

"Mm," Sanders mused, "maybe, although I would have thought his future lies on the industrial side."

"You see him as an officer, then?"

"Oh, yes. And, young as he is, he could go a long way."

"On the other hand," Eric said mischievously, waving a finger at Sanders, "if I'm right, he and a few like him could be the answer to your dilemma about parliamentary action."

Sanders grinned. "Well, maybe, but that, as you say, would be a bit further down the road. In the meantime, I would have thought that it would be your landlord that's crossing your mind rather than Mickey's future."

"Well, that's true: several times a day, the bastard is present in my thoughts."

"Will you manage?"

"I suppose we'll get by, George, so don't go putting your hand in your pocket."

"Ha! I wasn't about to. You're not the only one with a landlord, you know." He winked again. "I think we'll see a little action on the rent issue before this year's much older, Eric."

"Rent strikes?"

"Bound to be, mate, bound to be. When people have to choose between feeding their kids and paying the rent, the rent's bound to come a poor second. And that point can't be far off, in my view."

"And talking of feeding," said Eric, peering towards the counter, "here it comes."

*

"Don't like the look of that, George," said Eric as they walked back to the conference venue, nodding down Clerkenwell Road to where Ben Smith, Tich and a number of EC members were strolling along in a group. Of the five EC members, three were from the cab section, while the other two were busmen known for their moderation.

"Well, Eric," Sanders replied, "maybe you were right. Maybe something's going to happen, although I'm blowed if I can think what it might be."

The tension that had been apparent as the conference had opened that morning had sprung from one cause: delegates knew that this was the ADM which would debate whether the positions of general secretary and organising secretary should be declared vacant, the incumbents having enlisted in the Army, with nomination papers being issued in the event of an affirmative vote. Much of that tension had been dissipated by midday, no doubt due to the quality of the morning's debates, but it was undeniable that it had now returned, stronger than ever. Most of the afternoon's business concerned non-industrial matters, the motions generating little controversy. This lasted until, the voting on these motions being completed, Dennis Davies looked around the hall, cleared his throat and announced:

"Brothers, a week ago, a motion in the names of three bus branches was received at Gerrard Street. The motion reads as follows:

> "'That this Annual Delegate Meeting, aware of recent speculation in the press that the government is considering the introduction of military conscription, hereby declares its unalterable opposition to such a proposal and agrees:
>> 'a) that a referendum on this matter be submitted immediately to the branches and
>> 'b) that sanction be given to the formation of an Anti-Conscription Committee on a strictly voluntary basis in order to conduct educational and agitational work among the branches on this matter and, if the aforesaid branch referendum results in a vote of opposition, in the wider community.'

"Conference, before we proceed any further, the acting general secretary wishes to address you on this matter."

"Point of order, chairman!" Heads turned to Dick Mortlake, who now stood in the centre of the hall. "I realise that, this being an emergency motion, it was not possible to include it in the printed agenda, but surely it would have been possible to type it on a single sheet so that delegates would be fully aware of the matter under debate."

Davies grinned. "Well, at the moment, brother, nothing is under debate, because as I said the acting general secretary wishes to address you on the matter. But you have a point." He looked to his right. "Brother Smith?"

Tich Smith shrugged. "A simple oversight. Please accept my apologies, brothers."

"You've heard the acting general secretary's explanation, Brother Mortlake. Any further comment?"

"Yes, chairman. Fortuitously..."

Dick paused while various delegates issued "Oohhs" and "Aahhs" at his use of this five-syllable word.

"Fortuitously, Chairman, I and the delegates from the other two branches concerned have copies with us, and there should be a sufficient number, so if you would ask the tellers to assist..."

Tich Smith leaned toward the chairman and muttered furiously.

"The acting general secretary," said Davies with a smile, and to the amusement of a good proportion of the conference, "thanks you for your foresight, Brother Mortlake. Tellers!"

After a brief delay while tellers collected the copies from the Middle Row, Willesden and Dollis Hill delegates and distributed them to the conference, Tich Smith rose to his feet.

"It is my considered view, conference," he began, tugging on the lapels of his jacket, "that the motion should not be adopted in its present form. A referendum of the branches? Certainly! But a voluntary Anti-Conscription Committee? No, I think we have to draw the line at that, because it trespasses on the role of the Executive Council. Surely, if this ADM adopts an anti-conscription stance, it is for the EC to form such a committee—if, indeed, it finds the formation of such a body to be desirable." He lifted his chin and looked across at Sanders who, as he had during the morning session, sat at the side of the hall with Eric Rice. "No, brothers, I believe this idea originated with one of our officers and, if adopted, would be a recipe for mischief-making."

Heads were turned in Sanders' direction; he sat with arms crossed, his face expressionless.

"Equally," Tich Smith continued, "I think we must question the proposal that, following a positive vote in our referendum, this Anti-Conscription Committee should campaign in the broader community on the matter. Isn't that the job of the Labour Party to which we are affiliated? So, conference, unless the motion is amended, I must ask that you vote against it." Dennis Davies looked about the hall and was initially greeted with silence. "Well, brothers, is there a move to amend the motion, or do we debate it as it stands?"

A cab delegate, one of those who had been walking back to the conference hall with the Smiths after the break, raised his hand. "Chairman, I move the deletion of item b)."

"Is there a seconder for that amendment?"

"Seconded." This from Eamonn Quinlan, recently reduced in rank.

"Alright," said Davies, "we're almost ready to go. But first let's get clear who will move and second the substantive motion. It's been submitted by three branches, after all."

"Moved by Willesden, seconded by Middle Row," announced Reuben Topping of Willesden.

"Alright, Brother Topping, as mover of the original motion, you're on first. Off you go, lad."

Topping, a short, thin man of around thirty, walked swiftly to the rostrum.

"Chairman, conference, it seems to me that the proposal for a branch referendum will go through whatever else happens…"

A rumble of agreement came from the conference floor.

"So I don't really need to say very much about it. However, I would urge delegates to ensure that their branches do not treat the referendum as a mere formality. If the proposal is adopted today, this will be the policy of the ADM, the parliament of our union, and that means it should be given the serious consideration and discussion it deserves. We need to explain to the members *why* the policy has been adopted, deepening their understanding of what this war is about and whose interests it serves.

"Now, as regards item b), I find myself pitted against the acting general secretary." He shrugged. "So be it, brothers. First of all, conference, Brother Smith advises us that the formation of a voluntary Anti-Conscription Committee would encroach upon the authority of the EC. I don't know how that can possibly be, brothers." He held up his arms. "Isn't the ADM the paramount policy-making body of our union?"

An emphatic rumble of assent rolled off the floor.

"Then it seems to me that if we accept Brother Smith's argument, the EC would be encroaching on the authority of the ADM! The EC makes and interprets policy *between* ADMs. So the decision is ours to make, brothers, and no one else's."

The rumble was yet more emphatic.

"Now, should our voluntary Anti-Conscription Committee be able to campaign in the community, or should we leave that job to the Labour Party?" Topping turned to his right and addressed Dennis Davies. "Have I missed something, Chairman? Has the Labour Party had a change of heart? Because to the best of my recollection, shortly after the ink was dry on Mr Asquith's declaration of war, the Labour Party was waving the flag and calling for support. Is *this* the party that's going to campaign against conscription?"

The conference erupted in laughter and applause.

"No, I don't think so, Chairman. Mind you, we know that there are staunch anti-conscription—and anti-war!—people in the Labour Party and its affiliates. People like Fenner Brockway and Keir Hardie in the Independent Labour Party. Even Ramsay McDonald! If they want to campaign with us in the community, they'll be more than welcome and, needless to say, I'm sure our Anti-Conscription Committee will join with them whenever they arrange anti-conscription activity.

"One final thing: is this motion the handiwork of a full-time officer? Conference, in our union we do have several officers who are in touch with rank-and-file sentiment, but they don't need to lead us by the hand. In fact, it's the other way round: we provide the lead for them. And I resent the implication that someone like me—not to mention the Middle Row and Dollis Hill delegates—is incapable of putting together a motion of this nature.

"As for mischief-making, let me tell you straight, brothers." He struck his chest with the flat of his hand. "If conscription is introduced, I will be one of those called up. I'm a conductor, and I don't believe the government will agree to leave us in place. Drivers probably, but not conductors. But I tell you this!" He drew his shoulders back. "If they call me, I will not go! I will not throw away my life for a war I don't believe in, neither will I kill German, Austrian or Turkish workers for that cause! So please, brothers, when the time comes, by all means create some mischief on my behalf!"

As Reuben Topping made his way back to his seat, he was cheered and applauded. On the platform, Tich Smith was not a happy man.

"Seconder?"

Dick Mortlake was already at the rostrum, far more confident than when he had first stood there in the morning.

"Chairman, just a few words. First, I would like to add emphasis to something Brother Topping said. I would urge delegates not to treat the branch referendum in a perfunctory manner..."

"A *what* manner?" the chairman asked, to chuckles from some of those on the platform.

"Perfunctory, chairman. I'm asking delegates to ensure that their branches don't simply go through the motions but discuss the matter thoroughly. Let the members know precisely what conscription means: even if a man doesn't believe in the war, even if he is opposed to it, he will be torn away from his family and forced to fight it—forced to kill or be killed. That cannot be right!

"And secondly, conference, we want the Anti-Conscription Committee to be voluntary because it needs to be largely composed of people who deeply believe in the cause and are keen to fight for it and make it the main focus of their activity. With the best will in the world, members of a committee formed by the EC would probably have many other calls on their time."

Dennis Davies smiled. "Very diplomatically put, Brother Mortlake. Now the amendment: does the mover wish to speak?"

"I move formally," said the cab delegate, perhaps accepting that he could do little to counter the arguments of Reuben Topping.

"And the seconder? Are you seconding formally?"

Quinlan got to his feet and walked slowly to the rostrum.

Dennis Davies awaited his arrival and then posed his next question. "I take it that your reply is in the negative, Brother Quinlan?"

"Yes, I'm afraid it is," the Irishman replied in a soft lilt. "You see, brothers, I can't help thinking that the acting general secretary might have a bit of a point"—he pronounced it *pint*—"when he mentions the potential for mischief-making. I think as a union we have to be very careful, Chairman. We're a young union and, to be honest, we're still quite small, and unless we're very careful I see the danger of us breaking into cliques, of politics coming to divide us. Believe me, as you might appreciate from my accent I have plenty of experience of how politics can divide rather than unite. Just lately, I've noticed that there's a lot of hole-in-the-corner meetings and discussions, and matters that should be discussed in the branch or this ADM are instead discussed elsewhere. Plots and plans, brothers, plots and plans. We need to adhere to the Rule Book, and for that reason I believe we should heed the advice of Brother Smith and leave any question of an Anti-Conscription Committee to the EC that we've all just elected. We need to speak with one voice"—*vice*—"after debating our differences out in the open."

This was greeted with murmurings about the hall, but otherwise silence reigned as Eamonn Quinlan returned to his seat.

"The motion and the amendment are now open for discussion," announced the chairman.

"I move we go straight to the vote, chairman. The issues are clear enough," called a delegate from the back of the hall.

As this was greeted with a roar of approval, the chairman held up a hand. "Alright, if that's the wish of this ADM. Does the mover of the motion wish to reply to the remarks of Brother Quinlan?" He grinned. "We have to do this by the Rule Book, after all."

"Yes, chairman," said Reuben Topping, "But it's so brief that with your permission I can do it from here."

"Go ahead."

"You know, I tend agree with Brother Quinlan when he speaks about hole-in-the-corner discussions. I got the impression there were one or two of 'em going on during the dinner-break. Eh, Brother Quinlan?"

A certain amount of knowing laugher greeted this, and the fate of the amendment was sealed.

"And I hope, Chairman, that conference will speak with one voice when delegates vote against the amendment and for the motion."

And so it was—a sparse scattering of hands went up to support the amendment, followed by a forest to vote it down; when the motion was put to the vote, even one or two delegates who had voted for the amendment raised their hands.

*

Sanders turned to Eric Rice, palms upturned. "So is that what they were planning during the break? Is that the best they can do?"

"Seems it is, George," replied Eric.

But it was not.

*

The moment had arrived, but the tension had lessened—a result of the manner in which the platform had so easily been defeated in the previous debate. Given the numbers which had rallied to the anti-conscription motion, it seemed likely that the proposal to issue nomination papers to fill the posts of general secretary and organising secretary would sail through. It would, surely, be hardly worthwhile for the allies of Harry Bywater to put up a fight.

"I can't for the life of me work out what's going on here, Eric," Sanders confessed. "Have they given up?"

"Well," replied Eric, "one thing's for sure: this is going to be easy."

And so, at first, it was.

Dave Marston from Lewisham moved the proposal, seconded by Ernie Sharp from the New Cross tramshed. Both avoided speaking of personalities, pointing out that the issue was simple: Bywater and Russell had, by enlisting in the Army, effectively resigned their positions in the union; had they been conscripted, it might have been a different matter, but they had volunteered. Now more than ever, due to the wartime pressures, the union needed a permanent leadership; if, when peace was finally declared, Brothers Bywater and Russell wished to stand for election again, they would be welcome to do so, as long as they had not fallen into arrears with their contributions. Those who spoke in opposition were mainly from the Cab Section, and their only real argument was one of personal loyalty to the individuals concerned, although one speaker maintained that Bywater and Russell had not resigned but had taken leave of absence. A good spread of delegates from the buses and trams, and even a couple from the Cab Section, spoke in favour of the motion, and when Dennis Davies called the vote the proposal won the support of an overwhelming majority of the delegates.

Strangely, however, it was at this point that tension returned to the conference; it was as if the delegates were unable to believe that this controversial issue had been decided without disruption or rancour, that the Bywater loyalists, having lost the vote, were going to leave it at that. Surely they had planned for this eventuality.

Then it came: the chairman announced that before he closed the conference the acting general secretary wished to address the delegates.

Tich Smith, who had followed the debate with a dark and brooding countenance, making no effort to intervene, now stood.

"Brothers," he said, "I believe this to be a sad day in the life of our union. I have known Brother Bywater for more years than I care to remember, and despite our occasional differences, I believe you have today done him a disservice. Therefore, conference, out of loyalty to my comrades, I must tender my resignation."

There was a stunned silence within the hall as delegates attempted to come to terms with this new development. What did it mean? Would there now be three sets of nomination papers issued? Was this a trick whereby Tich Smith was attempting to make them feel guilty for the decision they had just taken? After a few seconds, the silence was broken by a groaning of discontent.

Sanders turned to Eric. "So this is it. But where does it get them?"

The second bombshell came when the chairman announced that the acting organising secretary would also like to say a few words. As Ben Smith stood, there were cries from the body of the hall. "No, Ben! No!"

"Comrades," said Ben Smith, "I also feel that I have no alternative but to tender my resignation."

More cries of "No, Ben! No!" Someone shouted, "Your loyalty is to us, Ben, not Harry Bywater!"

Ben Smith nodded at this latter outcry. "Yes, Brother, that is correct, and to be of service to you I must have credibility as an officer of this union. One of my tasks as an organiser is to make sure that employers keep open the positions of those men who have joined the forces." He threw out an arm. "How can I possibly do that when I know that the employer will turn on me and demand to know why my union doesn't practice what it preaches? I'm sorry, brothers, but I see no alternative."

Dennis Davies now got to his feet. "Brothers, our business having been completed, I declare this ADM closed. It would be greatly appreciated if you would vacate the hall as swiftly as possible, as the acting general secretary wishes to call the first meeting of the new EC."

"I thought he just resigned!" called out Reuben Topping.

Davies smiled patiently and extended both hands, palms downward, as if urging calm and understanding. "Technically, no," he said. "He has *tendered* his resignation, but it will be for the EC to decide whether that resignation is accepted."

There were jeers and catcalls in response to this, but nevertheless there was movement towards the main doors.

"So," said Eric Rice, "there will be four elections. But as you say, George, where does it get them?"

Sanders, who had been shocked by Ben Smith's announcement, scowled. "They haven't finished with us yet, Eric. Believe you me, there's more to come."

That was the first time that Sanders had been right that afternoon.

*

Sanders, accompanied by Eric, Reuben Topping, Dick Mortlake and Ernie Sharp walked around the corner to a pub on Clerkenwell Green. Sanders nodded to a building just before the pub. "You blokes know this place?"

"Twentieth Century Press," said Eric.

"Well, anybody can read the bloody sign!" said Reuben Topping.

"It's where *Justice*, the party newspaper, is published," said Eric with a sigh. "They also print our *Record*."

"And where, twelve or so years ago, Lenin worked on his newspaper *Iskra*," said Dick.

"Is that right?" said Reuben. "Bloody hell."

In the pub, they walked to the bar and Sanders pulled out a handful of small silver as the barman approached.

"Five pints of bitter, please, mate."

The barman, a large man with braces over his shirt, grimaced. "Sorry, sir, no treating. You can have a pint each, but you'll have to pay for 'em separately."

The "no-treating order" had recently been introduced by a government seemingly intent upon extinguishing pleasure from public life, especially if it involved alcohol and held the possibility of adversely affecting the work of common toilers.

"Come on, mate, we've had a long day, and three of these blokes are working men. Just give us five pints and let me pay."

The barman frowned at him. "But you might be a copper for all I know. You know, a plain-clothes man."

The five intending customers laughed, and Sanders pinched his lapel, pulling it out so that the barman could see the badge.

"Oh, red-button men." He leaned closer and lowered his voice, even though the bar was empty. "Alright, guvnor, but if any suspicious-looking customers come in, you'll have to pay separately."

"Alright, barman, thanks." Sanders winked at Eric as the barman bent to the taps. "Oh, and have one yourself."

The barman looked up, grinned, and waved a finger at him.

Sanders took out a Gold Flake packet and selected a cigarette, tapping it on the bar before placing it in his mouth. He struck a match and held it to the cigarette, looking over the flame at the other four. "So what the hell do you think has got into Ben?" he asked.

"Well," ventured Eric, "at least he didn't plead loyalty to Bywater and Russell the way Tich did. Besides, he had a point with what he said about the employers."

"Oh, come on. If that was a valid argument, we'd all be resigning, wouldn't we?"

"Maybe they offered him something," suggested Ernie Sharp, a middle-aged man with the thin chest and deep voice often associated with tuberculosis.

"Yes, I know that would make sense, but this is *Ben*, for Christ's sake. Ben Smith—a comrade."

"And what has he resigned from—his position as acting organising secretary or his original job as organiser?" queried Dick. "Similarly with Tich Smith. Is he going back to his position as president, or is he out completely?"

They stood at the bar drinking and attempting to make sense of the drama they had so recently witnessed at the ADM. Halfway into the second pint, Sanders confessed defeat, suggesting that it would be a day or two before all became clear. But then Dennis Davies arrived.

"Thought I'd find you lot here," he said, shrugging out of his jacket and throwing it over a stool at the bar. "My, this resigning is hot work, brothers."

"It might be," said Sanders, "but you haven't resigned, Dennis."

"Yes, I have."

"*What?*"

He shrugged and looked around at the five of them. "I've resigned."

Dick narrowed his eyes. "As what?"

"As a member of the EC."

"Oh, that's clear enough. You see, we were wondering earlier about Tich and Ben—you know, what exactly have they resigned *as*?"

"I see." Davies, his dark hair streaked with grey, was surrounded by the other five who were as eager to get an explanation from him as he was keen to drag it out for the maximum dramatic value. He peered over their shoulders. "Barman, could you pull me a pint, please? I did drop a hint when I first came in, but no one seems to have picked it up."

"So what *did* they resign as?" Dick persisted.

"That's somewhat academic now, brother." He stuck out his hand. "Dennis Davies, by the way."

"*Dennis!*" This was Sanders.

"Alight, alright." He reached out to take the pint the barman was handing him over the counter and took a long drink. "Tich and Ben have withdrawn their resignations because the EC—or a majority of its members—has decided that it will not implement the decision of the ADM. And *that* is why I have resigned!"

The silence that followed was rather like that which had greeted Tich's resignation.

"What—they won't issue the nomination papers?" It was an incredulous Reuben Topping who broke the silence.

"Correct."

"Jesus Christ," Sanders uttered through clenched teeth. He glanced at Eric. "So that's what they were hatching."

"But," growled Ernie Sharp, "it's an ADM decision. They can't do it."

Davies shrugged. "They've done it."

"Well, we have to get it overturned!" Dick stated the obvious.

"And what is the body that can overturn a decision of the EC?" Davies asked rhetorically.

"The ADM."

"And the ADM has just closed for another year."

"Or a Special Delegate Meeting," Sanders suggested calmly.

"And Special Delegate Meetings are convened by decision of the EC."

"Or," countered Sanders, still calm, "upon the demand of a third of the branches."

"And how do we organise that?"

"We're going to have a voluntary Anti-Conscription Committee, aren't we? That can kill two birds with one stone: as it goes around the branches, ensuring that we turn out the anti-conscription vote, it can encourage them to submit resolutions calling for a Special Delegate Meeting." Sanders smiled. "In fact, I hereby volunteer for the Anti-Conscription Committee."

Dennis Davies laughed. "Ah, I knew I'd come to the right place! Put me down as well."

There were four other volunteers.

"In fact," Sanders suggested, "if this is the way Tich and the EC are going to behave, after the anti-conscription vote is in I think we'd better turn the committee into a Vigilance Committee."

*

"Time we had a chat, Ben."

A few days after the ADM, Sanders came upon Ben Smith in the kitchen at Gerrard Street and Ben, jerking around at the sound of his voice as he poured boiling water into the teapot, looked first at Sanders and then at the open door behind him, possibly in the desperate hope that someone else would be joining them. Seeing no one, he sighed in resignation and nodded.

"I suppose so, George. I can't say I've been looking forward to it."

"No, I suppose not." He pulled out a chair and sat at the table. "Take a seat, Ben."

"You having a cup?"

"Later. Let it brew a while. Let's talk first."

Ben Smith sat opposite Sanders and for a few moments they just looked at each other, Sanders seeking a clue to his comrade's action at the ADM and Smith attempting to show no sign of weakness.

"Why, Ben?" Sanders asked at last, removing his eyes from the man before him and taking out a cigarette.

"I gave my reason at the ADM, George."

Sanders gave him a penetrating look and noted that Ben was unable to hold his gaze. He shook his head. "No, Ben, that couldn't have been the reason. As I said to the lads, if that was a valid reason we'd all be resigning. And besides, if that was all there was to it, you would have discussed it with us beforehand." He raised an eyebrow. "Wouldn't you?"

"Normally, I would have, yes." Ben was now looking at his hands, which lay on the table before him.

"So why didn't you?"

It was Ben Smith's turn to shake his head. "I don't know. I wasn't thinking."

"Ben." Sanders touched the other man's hand with his own, causing Ben to raise his eyes once more. "You must know that the truth will come out, and probably sooner rather than later. Now, I know that you would never do anything dishonourable, and that there must have been a lot of pressure on you. So come on, Ben, give it to me straight so that we can go back to being friends and comrades."

Ben Smith placed a hand over his eyes and, for now, maintained his silence.

"In your own time, Ben." Sanders was persistent, but calm and quietly-spoken.

When Ben Smith tore his hand away from his eyes, his face was that of a desperate man. "We can't cope, George! It's as simple as that! Mildred and me can't bloody cope!"

"You mean financially, Ben?"

"Yes, of course financially, what with the prices and the bloody rent."

Sanders grunted sympathetically. "I know, Ben, I know. Young Eric has got the same problem."

"But he's only got one small kid, George, and we've got two strapping lads with healthy appetites and a need for new clothes every six months!"

"Yes, I can see how that would be a problem, Ben, but I'm still having a little trouble following the logic here."

Ben Smith was an angry man—angry at the war, angry at the profiteers, angry at his landlord, angry at the men who had pressed him to act with them at the ADM. One of the people he was not angry with was Sanders, but if anyone else had entered the kitchen at this point, they would have thought otherwise. "They told me that whichever way it went at the ADM—or afterwards—they would make sure that I remained as acting organising secretary."

"And so for the few extra bob a week..." This is what Sanders was tempted to say but, not wanting to humiliate Ben, he restrained himself and encouraged the other man to reveal the final piece of the jigsaw. "But, Ben, your role at the ADM was to resign..."

"Yes, yes, yes, but on the understanding that the resignation— and Tich's—would be withdrawn later, when the EC refused to implement the decision. It was all worked out beforehand, George."

Sanders uttered a long sigh. "So there we are, then; I knew it had to be something like that. And the people behind this were Tich and..."

"And the more right-wing members of the EC, led by the cabdrivers—although they kept Davies and Frankenberg out of it."

"But now they have to face a Special Delegate Meeting."

"Maybe."

"What do you mean?"

"They'll drag it out, and maybe the war will be over before they call it, with Bywater and Russell back to work."

"Ha, fat chance!"

"But they'll delay it."

Sanders, paused, stroking his moustache with thumb and forefinger. "So what are your plans now, Ben?"

Ben Smith cleared his throat. "Well, I suppose I should be looking for redemption. Any ideas, George?"

"Well, it will be difficult for you to mobilise branch resolutions calling for the SDM…"

"Unless I was to say it was needed to put the issue to bed…"

Sanders thought for a moment and then pointed a finger at Ben Smith. "Good thinking, Ben. Yes, you could do that. But I was thinking of something else too. You'll remember that Bywater met Albert Stanley behind the backs of the members on two occasions. You and I are still the only two people in the union who know that. At some point, maybe at the SDM, it may be necessary to acquaint the members with that information." He paused and looked seriously at Ben Smith. "In the circumstances, it might carry more weight coming from you, Ben."

Ben Smith considered this and then held up both hands. "If that's the price, I'll pay it."

"Good man. And thanks, Ben, for being so frank with me. I know it can't have been easy for you." He grinned. "You know, I reckon that tea has brewed by now."

Ben Smith began to get to his feet, but changed his mind, sinking back into his chair and leaning across the table. "George," he almost whispered, "the other thing that has come out of this is that you have to watch your step. They'll do almost anything to take you down a peg or two, or even get rid of you."

Sanders grinned. "I thank you for the warning, Ben, but I'm well aware that moves are afoot. Talk of amalgamation with the AAT, for example, in the hope that their numbers would swamp us."

"Then we've got the merger ballot with the National Union of Vehicle Workers coming up in June…"

Sanders waved his hand dismissively. "I'm not too worried about them; they're smaller than us and mostly London-based, so it wouldn't be beyond our means to influence their members. That, in turn, would stand us in good stead if a merger with the AAT ever came onto the agenda in a serious way." He struck his mouth with two fingers of his right hand. "And do you know, it strikes me that this might be why Tich and the EC are acting so casually with regard to the NUVW merger."

Ben Smith nodded. "That's a fair point. And then there's talk of making organisers appointed rather than elected. Did you hear that one?"

Sanders shook his head in disbelief. "Has it really come to that, Ben?"

"They'll never get it past the members, of course." Seeing that Sanders, despite the probable truth of this assertion, was concerned, Ben changed the subject. "I'll pour the tea."

23

The first half of 1915 was busy enough for Dorothy. At the turn of the year, the ELFS held its annual conference at Bow Baths, and the *Dreadnought* emphasised the democratic aspect of this, pointing out to its readers that it was "essential that every member should be present to vote for the officers of the Federation," thereby clearly demonstrating its difference from the defunct WSPU. In the event, however, Sylvia was elected unopposed as secretary, as was Norah Smyth as financial secretary, although seats on the general committee were hotly contested. It was decided that men would be admitted as associate members and that subscriptions would be a minimum of a penny per month, thus ensuring that working-class women could afford to join; again, these decisions clearly distinguished the federation from the organisation previously led by Sylvia's mother and sister, as did the organisation's major aim, which would be stated on the membership card as "to secure the votes for every woman over 21," thus opposing any property qualification.

On Sunday, 24 January, Dorothy was among the hundreds of ELFS members and supporters who attended a Trafalgar Square rally called to protest the recent government order whereby separation allowances and pensions might be withdrawn from those servicemen's wives and widows who were thought to be living dissolute lives. Among the banners displayed in the square were those of, apart from that of the ELFS, the Women's Freedom League, the United Suffragists, and the Northern Men's Federation for Woman Suffrage; a large number of supportive soldiers were also in attendance, and George Lansbury was one of the male speakers.

The following Tuesday, Sylvia and Dorothy were members of the delegation led by Charlotte Despard, which, following the agreement of Lord Kitchener, attended the War Office to protest on the same issue to Assistant Secretary of War B.B. Cubitt. "We cannot accept for one moment," Sylvia told him, "the view that either separation allowances or pensions should be withdrawn for any failure of the recipient to live up to accepted standards."

This agitation led to the formation in early February of the League of Rights for Soldiers' and Sailors' Wives and Relatives by Sylvia, the 70-year-old Mrs Despard and, among others, George Lansbury, and in the following months both Sylvia and Dorothy spoke at local meetings aimed at rallying support for this cause. Dorothy noted a curious anomaly here, for whenever an ELFS meeting was announced, Sylvia was always promoted as the main speaker, but when she was advertised to speak at an East Ham Town Hall meeting to form a local branch of the League of Rights, her name appeared in the fifth and last place.

"So is there a bit of infighting in the East End?" Mickey asked when Dorothy drew this to his attention.

"Well, not quite infighting, Mickey, but I sometimes get the feeling that there is a degree of resentment when Sylvia bruises the sensibilities of others by always placing herself in the front rank. She seems to think that no one should be allowed to outshine her." She looked up from her book. "Do you know, last year when I told George that I was thinking of working with Sylvia, he warned me that this sort of thing should be expected."

"So how did she end up fifth in the list of speakers for the League meeting?"

She shrugged. "The other women's groups were involved in the organisation of the meeting, and so I suppose someone was trying to teach her a lesson." Dorothy raised a finger. "And there's another thing that I simply do not understand. The other Sunday, she spoke at the Trafalgar Square rally against inflated food prices. Quite a good turnout, as you will have heard, with the local Labour Party and trade union branches out in strength. There she was, speaking alongside Ben Tillett and Harry Hyndman. *Then* she rushes back to the East End to chair a meeting at Bow Baths where Lady Emily Lutyens was speaking on 'The Theosophic Ideal.' What *can* be going on in her mind?"

Mickey frowned. "You think she's going religious on you?"

Dorothy chuckled. "Well, I doubt it, as her mind seems quite made up on that matter. And to be honest, I'm not even sure that theosophy *is* a religion. While its adherents apparently believe in reincarnation and that kind of thing, they also place a great deal of emphasis on the brotherhood of man and the improvement of social conditions, so I suppose Sylvia might be attracted to this aspect of it."

"And Lady Emily?"

"One of the Bulwer-Lyttons, married to the architect Sir Edwin Lutyens, although it's said that their marriage is practically dead, as Her Ladyship is deeply involved not only with theosophy but also, apparently, with Jiddu Krishnamurti, a leading practitioner and some twenty years her junior—quite a comely youth, by all accounts."

"Oh, she likes younger men; you're on thin ice here, Dorothy," he joked, wagging a finger at her.

"But none of that explains Sylvia's involvement—although that might be too strong a word."

"Would you like a crude, working-class view?"

"You know I would."

"Is Her Ladyship worth a few bob?"

"One assumes so."

"There you go, then: the ELFS needs money; Her Ladyship *has* money; Sylvia invites her to speak at Bow Baths, offering to chair the meeting herself in order to guarantee an audience; Her Ladyship is impressed by what she sees and hears of the work of the federation and so takes out her cheque book before she returns to civilisation. Why look any further?"

"Why, indeed?" she sighed. "They can say what they like about crude, working-class logic, Mickey, but it does have its strengths."

While much of the activity of Dorothy and the other paid organisers and activists revolved around meetings, conferences and rallies, there were occasionally bolder initiatives that brought both excitement and entertainment. In February, Sylvia led Norah Smyth, Dorothy and thirty others on an expedition to the West End, where they purchased bacon, coffee and sugar at Harrods and the Army & Navy Store and then made their way to the House of Commons, where they demanded to see Herbert Asquith, the Prime Minister. Once in his office—entry into which was an achievement in itself— they placed their goods on his desk and stood back to allow Sylvia to speak. Asquith's gaze ran over the assembled women and Dorothy was certain that his eyes lingered on her before passing on; he was, as Molly Elkins had said, "tolerably 'andsome."

"Here, Mr Asquith," Sylvia began, "we have sugar, coffee and bacon which we have purchased in the West End. Why?" She brought her fist down on Asquith's desk. "Because they are not available in the *East* End! Why is that? Because the suppliers know full well that they would be unable to achieve the prices they desire! So working people and their families must go hungry while the well-off in this part of London continue to be well-fed. Such a situation is *not* acceptable, Mr Asquith, and unless adequate food supplies for the East End are organised forthwith, we will return with 300 angry women; and if they are unable to persuade you to address their hunger, we will be back with 3,000!"

Oh, Dorothy would think in the days that followed, this was fine theatre, but what did it achieve? There was a barely perceptible increase in the availability of certain foodstuffs, but not sufficient to make a real difference. Possibly the most significant result of the episode was the raised stature of Sylvia Pankhurst throughout the East End, as the thirty activists who had accompanied her told all who would listen of her boldness and courage before the Prime Minister. Had that been the point of the exercise? No, Sylvia was surely above that sort of thing. Or maybe she hadn't realised she was doing it.

All of the causes—against child labour and the ongoing trial of escalating food-prices—for which the ELFS worked were worthy and needed to be fought, but these were symptoms, not the root causes, of working-class misery. And even on such a matter as food prices, Sylvia, in focusing on the one issue, seemed to lose sight of the broader picture. Writing in the *Dreadnought* on 20 February, for example, she righty criticised Asquith's weak response in the Commons and complained that Labour had presented "no clear, definite scheme." All true enough, but she also commented that the Tory Bonar Law sounded more "human" than Asquith. Well, thought Dorothy, maybe this was true as well, but did Sylvia seriously think that the Conservative Party would come to the aid of hungry East Enders? There was no attempt at a class analysis of these problems.

In the meantime, the longer-term relief projects of the ELFS continued. In April, further premises were acquired at the Gunmaker's Arms, a former pub. The name was swiftly changed to the more appropriate Mother's Arms, and here the children's clinic and the nursery would be brought together under one roof. Finally, and partly at Dorothy's urging, this project obtained public support from the Ministries of Education and Health and the Corporation of London.

Sylvia's policy on the war amounted to a call for a negotiated peace, but the one major initiative in which she attempted to involve herself on this issue in April came to naught. In this month, some 1,200 women from a host of countries came together for the Women's International Conference in the Hague. Although 180 British women, including Sylvia, had applied to attend, the British government, which did not look kindly upon the initiative, at first denied passports to all, but then agreed to grant them to two dozen women, of whom Sylvia was not one, selected by the Home Secretary. But even these did not make it to Holland, as the Admiralty closed the North Sea. Thus, the only British women who managed to attend were two who, having helped organise the conference, were already in the Hague, and Emmeline Pethick Lawrence, who travelled from the USA.

In stark contrast, it was in this month that the new journal of Emmeline and Christabel Pankhurst finally appeared. Reflecting their jingoistic, pro-war stance, they called it *Britannia*.

In mid-May, Sylvia wrote of the sinking of the *Lusitania*, which she condemned, but she was just as harsh on the "cowardice" of those who, seeking some form of ill-thought-out revenge, attacked the homes of German civilians living in London

Increasingly, the issue occupying much of the time and effort of the ELFS' organisers was that of women's war work and pay. This, Dorothy told herself, at least brought the federation into close proximity with the class struggle, leading her to the decision to remain with the ELFS a while longer.

On 13 April, a host of women's and suffrage organisations, both pro- and anti, attended a meeting with Walter Runciman, President of the Board of Trade, who announced that the piece-rates for women would be the same as for men.

"But we are here to demand equality for time-rates," protested Sylvia.

"No," replied Runciman with a shake of his head, "there are no special conditions laid down for time-rates."

"Presumably," commented Dorothy with a curl of her lip, "because you cannot bring yourself to believe that a woman can work as speedily as a man."

Runciman spread his hands, as if to suggest that this might well be the case, although he did not intend to be so rash as to say it aloud.

From then onward, week by week, the *Woman's Dreadnought* carried reports of "sweating" by major companies with government war contracts: in Sheffield, Vickers was opening workshops where women were paid a mere eight shillings a week; in the same city, an electroplate maker on a government contract was paying women twelve shillings a week, whereas men had been paid 32 shillings.

Three days after the Board of Trade meeting, the Caxton Hall was host to a National Conference on War Service for Women called by the Workers' National Emergency Committee. Here, there were calls for trade-union membership for all women who registered for War

Service, equal pay, and, in one resolution, early universal suffrage.

In May, the ELFS hired the Caxton Hall for a three-day Women's Exhibition that illustrated the meagre pay and wretched conditions of East End women employed on government contracts. Largely as a result of this and similar activity, the term "sweating," while it did not pass into common usage, gained greater currency, and later in the year protests on the issue would be held by sections of the labour movement.

The month would be crowned by the Women's May Day rally in Victoria Park on 30 May, where the resolutions to be put forward, representing the major concerns of the federation, would discuss international solidarity, equal pay for War Service, and suffrage. Dorothy would have attended this major event, had she not been arrested outside Holloway tramshed that same morning.

24

Just after midnight on 13 May, Brixton's Gaiety Theatre was packed with angry tramworkers. Archie Henderson, tall and slim with bushy red hair, found a seat in the rear stalls and settled down to listen. Being a full-time organiser in the Amalgamated Association, the blue-button union, he would not be speaking at this meeting, as it was a red-button event. His friend George Sanders had told him that the London and Provincial's tram membership was at breaking point, a strike inevitable. This was the second of a series of mass meetings being held all over London, and he might like to attend.

"*All over* London, George?" he had queried. "Including north of the river, where the AAT has most of the membership?"

Sanders had nodded grimly. "Yes, mate. It seems the feeling is just as strong at the AAT sheds, but your leadership shows no interest in discussing a strike with us. That being the case, we'll give your members the opportunity to let off some steam at our meetings. Then we'll see what happens."

"Oh, you know what'll happen, George, as well as I do."

On the stage, two men sat at a table. The shorter of the two now stood up and silence fell.

"Brothers, for those of you who don't know me, my name is Albert Smith, usually known—don't ask me why—as Tich"—this was greeted by a wave of laughter—"and I am the president, and acting general secretary, of your union. Seated beside me is George

Sanders, one of our full-time organisers." Cheers from some quarters, causing Tich to turn to Sanders. "Seems you're not a stranger in these parts, George." If there was any ill-feeling between the two men as a result of the recent Annual Delegate Meeting, it was well concealed.

"Brothers, in the recent weeks, our office has been bombarded by letters and resolutions from the tram membership. And they all say the same thing: the hours are killing us, we can no longer live on the wage we receive, and we want you to do something about it! So we went to the London County Council to speak to the chief officer for tramways, Mr Aubrey Llewellyn Coventry Fell. His answer was short and sweet: No. Wait until the expiry of the current agreement."

Catcalls and boos.

"At that point, Brother Sanders"—he placed his hand on George's shoulder—"banged the table and shouted at Aubrey Llewellyn Coventry Fell: *'But our members—your staff—can't take any it more! Can't you understand that, man?'*"

Cheers, cries of "You tell 'im, George!"

"Yes, George *did* tell 'im. And the answer that came across the table was the same: 'Wait until the expiry of the current agreement.' It being now clear that not even an angry man like George Sanders can move Mr Aubrey Llewellyn Coventry Fell, it occurred to us that the only alternative is to see how he deals with *several thousand angry men!*"

More cheers. Cries of "Yes, let us at 'im!"

"Well, brothers, I think you will get your opportunity. We have called these meetings, of which this is the second, to gauge your feelings. The last thing we wanted to do was to call an official strike until we were absolutely sure that this is what you want."

"Call it!" came the cry. "We do! Call it now!"

"Our executive will meet on Saturday, brothers, in order to take that decision, so I don't think you'll have long to wait. In the meantime, however, we all need to understand just why you're suffering. Now George is sitting here, and he hasn't said a word yet, so some of you may be thinking that I've brought him along as a pretty face. Not at all, brothers, not at all. He'll now say a few words, and if you listen very carefully, you may leave this theatre with a much better understanding of what has caused your distress and anger." He turned to Sanders. "George."

Sanders stood and regarded his audience, waiting for the applause to die.

"Comrades and brothers!" he began, his voice strong and loud. "Those who regularly attend your branch meetings may already have a pretty good understanding, because even before this bosses' war started we were sending out circulars explaining the probable consequences of this conflict. And, unfortunately, events have shown that we were right!

"Most of you know that your union has from the very start campaigned *against* this war. As far as we're concerned, it's a war between the ruling class of this country and the ruling class of Germany—the bosses, the employers and those in government who represent their interests. The bosses of this country have the largest empire the world has ever seen, gained by robbing the colonial peoples of their own lands and the wealth they produce, and at the expense of countless deaths. The German bosses want a slice of that loot. Germany has developed as a capitalist nation, and its rulers face the same problem the British ruling class faced: because the capitalist system robs its workers of a good part of the wealth they create, it obviously cannot sell at home all that it produces. It needs foreign markets, just as it needs foreign sources of raw materials, and so it takes foreign lands by force in order to get them. Germany has come into the game a bit late, and finds that the world has pretty much been divided up already, by Britain, France, Belgium and lately the USA. So the British and German ruling classes send their workers to kill each other—not to serve their own interests, but the interests of capital. *That* is what this war is all about, brothers.

"And it's *also* the cause of your current problems. Now, as clear and as firm as this union's policy has been, we obviously have not been as persuasive as the jingoists and the capitalist press, because five thousand—*five thousand*, comrades!—of your fellow London tramworkers volunteered to go to this war, and we can't claim that they were all blue-button men. And that has left seven thousand of you to do the work of twelve thousand. Oh, yes, whenever it can, the LCC will take on a new man. Whenever it can, I say. But where are these new men to come from, when if a worker hasn't gone off to the war, he's able to step into a job that pays a damn sight more than this one? Yes, come and be a motorman, mate. What does it pay, he asks? You tell him six and a tanner a day—after two years! So what does he say to that?"

"Fuck off!" shouted some. "On yer bike!" cried others.

"So, comrades, you're overworked and underpaid. Fifteen-hour spreadovers are now the order of the day. And I know—because so many of you have told me—that body and brain won't stand it!"

More cheers came from the tramworkers, not just because of what Sanders had said, but in recognition that someone understood.

"And how far do your wages go these days, comrades? If you had a pound a year ago, what would it be worth today? Fourteen shillings! And why?" He reached into the inside pocket of his jacket and drew out a single sheet. "Compare the prices a year ago with the prices today: a sack of flour used to be between twenty-four shillings and sixpence and twenty-seven shillings, and it's now between 48 and 53 shillings; butter was 115 shillings a hundredweight, and it's 145 shillings; Canadian cheese that was 60 shillings a hundredweight has gone to 98 shillings; sugar used to be 16 shillings a hundredweight and it's now twenty-eight shillings; bacon's gone from 70 shillings to 95 shillings; Scottish beef was sevenpence and now it's elevenpence; Argentine beef was fivepence-halfpenny and now it's ninepence-halfpenny." He threw down the sheet of paper onto the table. "How can a person survive with those price-increases, brothers?"

"We can't!" came the response, "We can't!"

Sanders paused and thoughtfully stroked his moustache. "Well," he said, "there are two ways you *could* survive. You *might* be able to survive if you had a wage-increase, for example."

A roar of approval.

Sanders picked up his single sheet of notes. "There's a bit of a problem here, though, because when this was put to the government its spokesman replied—and I forget which newspaper this comes from—that 'the rise in the cost of living is not by itself sufficient reason at the present time for increasing the wages of their employees. They regard this rise as a burden which must be shared in common by all classes in the country.'"

A tumult of insults, curses and commands: "Bastards!" "May they rot in hell!" "Strike now!"

"Now, it's true that you work not for the government, but for the LCC. Your industry is funded not by the tax-payer, but by the rate-payer. But I think we can rest assured that Mr Aubrey Llewellyn Coventry Fell is under instruction from the government. Any success you might have will be an inspiration to other workers in the public sector, and that's the last thing they want.

"But let's turn to the other half of that statement: 'a burden which must be shared in common by all classes in the country.' What utter tripe! What lies and hypocrisy! In fact, the *second* way you can survive the price-increases is if you're rich! The rich may see their pile of cash reduced a little, but they won't be hungry. And if they got rich by owning a business, the chances are that their pile will actually increase rather than reduce. I'll show you what I mean in a minute.

"First, though, and just before I wind up, I want to talk about another question. If you read the papers, you will have seen that, around the country, a number of shops owned by Germans, or people with German names, have been attacked. In fact, you probably don't have to read the papers to know about this, because some of the attacks have been in New Cross and Deptford. In the New Cross Gate area, several bakers' shops have been attacked, so there's now a bread shortage!"

The theatre was silent, and Sanders was unable to tell whether this was due to the seriousness of the matter or guilt; he hoped the former.

"Comrades, if we can accept that German and British workers have no genuine interest in this war, and should not be killing each other, isn't it even truer that someone with a German name who owns a family business is also not our enemy? I would therefore ask everyone here to dissuade anyone who talks of attacking Germans or German businesses on the streets of this country, and try to convince them that their real enemies are to be found elsewhere.

"And where might that be? I said just now that the rich would not suffer from the price-increases, particularly if they owned a business. It goes further than that, brothers, because some of those people are *responsible* for the price-increases. What we're seeing throughout this country in industry after industry is *war-profiteering*! As just one example, before the war, the annual profit of Spillers and Bakers of Cardiff amounted to £89,000. Now? £367,655! That massive increase in profits, comrades, is—I have it on very good authority—almost *all* due to the war. These are the kind of people who benefit from this war. These are the kind of people on whose behalf the war is being waged. The enemy of British workers, comrades, is not the German working class but this capitalist system!"

The meeting continued, with one worker after another climbing onto the stage to call for a strike, sometimes illustrating the need for this by an account of their own experiences or those of a comrade. Archie Henderson left before the end, sure that there would be a strike and that the AAT men would join it.

*

The strike begun by the tramworkers of New Cross quickly spread to other red-button sheds. So far, however, the strike was unofficial, as the Executive Council of the LPU had yet to take a decision; in the course of a telephone interview, Tich Smith mentioned this fact to the *Daily Telegraph*, only to find his comment distorted to give the impression that the union had washed its hands of the strike. Although the blue-button membership clamoured for inclusion, at this stage all they had to do to make this a reality was to walk out.

The offices of London County Council Tramways were on Belvedere Road, running between Westminster Bridge Road and Waterloo Bridge Road on the south bank of the Thames. On 14 May, in one of those offices Chief Officer Aubrey Llewellyn Coventry Fell monitored events. Fell was 45, an engineer by training and a manager by promotion; after training at the School of Electrical Engineering, he had worked for Laing, Wharton and Down, which in 1896 became British Thomson-Houston, a subsidiary of the US firm General Electric; in 1898, he had moved north to join Sheffield Corporation Tramways, first as Electrical Engineer and then as general manager until, five years later, he was recruited to his current position in London.

There came a buzz on his intercom machine.

"Yes?"

"There is a delegation from the trade union here, sir."

Oh no. "The trade union?"

"Yes, sir, the Amalgamated Association: Mr White and two other gentlemen."

"Ah, I see. Send them in."

Clifford White, London District Secretary of the blue-button union, was a former conductor, having failed in an earlier endeavour to enter the field of art and design; still only thirty, he sported a thin blond moustache, and, perhaps as a memorial to his artistic ambitions, dressed with a studied shabbiness that endeared him to his friends in the Fabian Society. He was accompanied by two lay members, both motormen, who, despite their low wages, managed to appear smarter than him.

Anxious to appear the harried, crisis-ridden manager, as the trio entered his office Fell looked up sharply, snapping: "Good morning, Mr White. Good morning, gentlemen. Please be seated." He glanced at the clock on the wall opposite. "I can only give you five minutes, I'm afraid; as you may have gathered, we have a few problems this morning."

"And that, Mr Fell, is what brings us here." White gestured to his two colleagues. "You know Mr Johnson and Mr Dale."

"Yes, yes, of course." He raised an eyebrow. "You say you are brought here by the strike, Mr White?"

"Yes, sir." White spoke with the lisp of a worker who believes he has risen above his class, the word "yes" ending, just as "sir" began, on a whistle between the upper teeth and the lower lip. "We wish to advise you that our union is not involved in it and has no intention of becoming so."

*

As the door closed behind his three visitors, Aubrey Llewellyn Coventry Fell clapped a hand to his forehead and uttered a long, shuddering sigh. Being shouted at by George Sanders was, he felt, almost preferable to receiving the pious assurances of this fop White. Did the man really believe that the AAT would not join the strike? If so, he was a fool. Was a man's toleration of long days and short rations regulated by the colour of his union badge? White certainly seemed to think so. Fell was well aware that there was just as much anger north of the river as there was at the red-button sheds to the south, and he would be extremely surprised if the AAT membership failed to join the strike. Not for the first time, he was struck by the fact that the more opportunistic trade union leaders seemed to be completely out of touch with—or oblivious to—the feelings and wishes of their members.

Fell picked up his telephone and called George Hopwood Hume, Municipal Reform Party, chairman of the LCC's Highways Committee, and reported the assurance he had received from White, making no mention of his private doubts. A little later, Hume spoke to *The Globe* newspaper, telling the reporter from the evening daily that the Council regarded the strike as no more than an isolated eruption of discontent by some members of the LPU. "Most of the men," he said, "belong to the older Amalgamated Association, and we regard it as inconceivable that they will violate the contract with the Council at a time when a full and effective service is essential."

*

The Chief Officer's telephone rang.

"I have Mr Reginald McKenna on the line, sir."

"Oh, good. Put him through, please."

"Mr Fell?"

"Good morning, Home Secretary. So good of you to return my call."

"Good morning, Mr Fell. Would I be correct in assuming that you wish to discuss the tram strike which appears to be spreading across London?"

262

"You would, sir."

"*Strictly speaking, of course, this is a matter for the Board of Trade.*"

"Ordinarily, yes. But in time of war, Home Secretary..."

"*I'm with you. How will this strike impinge upon the war effort, Mr Fell?*"

"In two ways, sir. The most obvious one, of course, is that war production will be adversely affected. In particular, the munitions workers at Woolwich depend upon our trams to get to and from work."

"*Have you spoken to the strike leaders regarding this?*"

"The problem there, sir, is that at the moment the strike is unofficial. That being the case, we have no one to talk to."

"*I see. Is it likely to be declared official?*"

"Possibly tomorrow, sir."

"*Well, when that happens I suggest you talk to the leaders and ask them, at the very least, to make an exception in the case of the munitions workers.*"

"But aren't you empowered to order a return to work under the wartime regulations?"

"*Ah. Now I see why you have asked to speak to me rather than the Board of Trade. No, Mr Fell, I am afraid I do not have that power, much as I would like it. As you may know, we met with the leaders of the major trade unions in March and arrived at a voluntary agreement whereby, among other things, industrial disputes will be settled by arbitration rather than strike action. But it's entirely voluntary. Now, we realise that this is proving unsatisfactory, and so you can expect further legislation in a month or two.*" He paused. "*But that's no help to you today, is it?*"

"Regrettably not, Home Secretary. However, the strike is possibly affecting the war effort in a second sense. The action itself was preceded by a mass meeting in Brixton during the early hours of this morning..."

"*Yes, at the Gaiety Theatre. We have a report on that.*"

"You do? Oh well, then you will know that at least one of the speeches was extremely unpatriotic. Almost seditious, in fact."

"*And your point, Mr Fell...*"

"Is that the Defence of the Realm Act surely allows prosecution in cases like this. 'To prevent the spread of false reports or reports likely to cause disaffection to His Majesty or to interfere with the success of His Majesty's forces by land or sea.' That, I believe, is one of the provisions of DORA, Home Secretary. Furthermore, if you care to peruse any issue of the union's journal, you will see..."

"Let me assure you, Mr Fell, that our security forces are most avid readers of the Licenced Vehicle Trades Record. I take it, then, that you are suggesting that we prosecute Mr Sanders and those responsible for the union's journal under the Defence of the Realm Act."

"That would appear to be a realistic course of action, Home Secretary."

"Realistic, Mr Fell? Yes, realistic in the sense that we could do it and a prosecution would be successful. But politically realistic, Mr Fell? I hardly think so. As we speak, you have the beginnings of a tram strike. If we act as you suggest, however, London would be entirely without public transport: no trams, no buses, no cabs and, although they have a different union, probably no Underground trains either. No, Mr Fell, I am afraid you will have to manage your tram strike as best you can. Do not think for one minute, however, that we are unsympathetic to your case. If the strike develops, we may have advice to offer. But DORA, I am afraid, will not be invoked in this instance. Good morning, Mr Fell. I may be speaking to you again soon."

Aubrey Llewellyn Coventry Fell replaced his receiver.

*

"How did it go?" Archie Henderson asked as he walked into the AAT office's small kitchen.

Eddie Johnson replaced his mug on the table. "Oh, famously, Archie, famously."

Archie's red eyebrows clenched in a frown. "Go on."

"Well, Cliff told him we wouldn't be getting involved in the strike."

"He fucking *what*?"

"You heard."

"And what did Fell say?"

"He said thank you very much. Then he told us that he's having notices posted in all the sheds saying that anyone who doesn't turn up to work tomorrow will be sacked."

"Fuck!"

*

Early on the Saturday morning, Sanders toured the South London tram sheds where, despite the notices posted by Fell, not a tram stirred. Although the shed at New Cross, where the action had begun in the early hours of Friday, was more heavily picketed than most, a sufficient body of men stood at the entrance of them all. Wherever he stopped to talk to the strikers, the message they gave him was the same: "Fell? How's he gonna sack us? Who will he get to operate the trams? No, mate, we're out and we're stayin' out until we win. We've had enough!"

There was, Sanders pondered gloomily, something of a contradiction here: chief among the red-button members' demands was a reduction in hours, and yet how would this be won when the war had created such a shortage of labour that these same members were confident that they were indispensable and could not be sacked? If that were so—and it probably was—where would the extra men be found to plug the gaps created by reduced hours?

When he asked the strikers what the union leadership should be doing, the reply he received to this was also the same: "Get the blue-button boys across the river to join the strike!"

Conscious that the Executive Council would be meeting at ten o'clock, he returned northwards. Having parked the Unic outside the Gerrard Street office at 9.30, he walked down to the café where, as soon as he opened the door, he was greeted by a shout. "George!" He turned in the direction of the speaker and saw, over the heads of several EC members, Archie Henderson sitting alone in the corner. Having stopped at the counter to order a sandwich and a tea, Sanders joined the blue-button man.

"I was hoping I would find you here, George," said Henderson as Sanders sat down. "Didn't think I should risk being seen entering your office."

Sanders grinned. "Why's that, Archie? You thinking of jumping ship?"

"It *has* crossed my mind, George."

Sanders took out his cigarettes and matches. "This calls for a fag, Archie. So what's brought this on?"

"Can't you guess? Bloody White, of course! He only went to Fell yesterday morning and told him that the blue-button had no intention of joining the strike, didn't he!"

"Get away." Sanders extracted a flake of tobacco from his tongue and shook his head. "Well, I never. He sounds a bit like Harry Bywater."

"Talking of whom, now that he and Russell have gone to aid His Majesty's war effort, you must be a bit short-handed."

Sanders looked at him and nodded. "A bit, yes. But, of course, some are pretending that we don't really have any vacancies, as Tich is holding the fort on the general secretary front, and Ben is acting as organising secretary. The right wing wants the two posts held open until our two heroes return from the war, and the Executive Council has refused to carry out the Annual Delegate Meeting's instruction to issue nomination papers. So any berth we might find for you—and it would make sense to slide you into Ben's old slot—would at the moment be temporary." He drew on his cigarette. "In the meantime, of course, we have a tram strike to win."

"How are things looking?"

"Did a bit of scouting around this morning, and the south is solid. But the boys want your members to join 'em."

Henderson nodded. "Don't worry, they will. There's a mass meeting tonight at the Euston Palace of Varieties, and they're bound to vote to come out."

Sanders was bemused. "You mean that White, having told Fell that your union was having nothing to do with the strike, agreed to a mass meeting?"

Henderson smiled. "Didn't have much choice, did he? After word got out about his trip to Fell's office, his phone started ringing and members were blocking the pavement outside the office. He had to give 'em something so he could get through the crowd to get home last night."

"And," laughed Sanders, "I wouldn't mind betting that a certain red-haired organiser had something to do with that."

"You could be right, George, you could be right. But listen, I didn't come here just to bellyache and discuss my future career prospects. If your executive declares the strike official this morning, you have to make sure that there's a joint strike committee—red-button and blue- button—because if White is left to his own devices he'll drag his feet. He has to be subject to some discipline. So if your executive can agree that this morning, I'll make sure that it's proposed at our mass meeting tonight."

Sanders nodded. "Agreed, Archie. And what about your future prospects, mate?"

"Let's see how we go in the next few days. But I'll tell you one thing, George: if I put on the red button, you can be bloody sure I won't be the only one."

*

Mass meetings were not to the taste of Clifford White, and the current meeting at the Euston Palace of Varieties was, from his point

266

of view, the worst he had ever experienced. This was more like a riot than a meeting, with members shouting insults at the platform and demanding a vote on strike action even before the matter had been properly discussed. Finding the stench of tobacco smoke and human sweat overpowering, he drew a handkerchief from his pocket and pressed it to his face.

"Aahhh, don't cry Mr White!" called a member in one of the front seats. "Give us the vote, then we'll let you go home."

White turned to Eddie Johnson, who was supposed to be chairing the meeting, hissing: "Can't you control them, man?"

Johnson grimaced. "You want to give it a try?" Nevertheless he stood, pounding his gavel.

"Alright, now! Let's have some order. Let's have your questions and comments one at a time. You don't want to be here all night, do you?"

"It's all the same to us, Eddie," shouted someone in the gallery. "We don't have to get up in the morning!"

A tide of laughter rolled off the audience. Johnson allowed this to subside and then called again for questions or discussion contributions.

A bearded man in the middle of the audience stood, declaring in a booming voice, "You know what we want, Brother Johnson, so why don't you get to it? Call a vote for strike action!"

"No!" This from a stocky, clean-shaven character at the back, close to where Archie Henderson leaned, arms folded, against the wall by the centre doors. "There are some questions that need to be answered. First, has our union received any request from the red-button to join the strike?"

White seemed quite comfortable with this question. He stood. "Yes, I was"—whistles on the esses—"contacted today by Brother Albert Smith, but I had to tell him that I had no power to take a decision of that nature."

"Okay, *second*: did Brother White tell the LCC Chief Officer yesterday that our union would not be joining the strike?"

All of a sudden, the theatre was hushed. Johnson took it upon himself to reply. "We went to Mr Fell's office in order to..."

"We want to hear it from Brother White. Let *him* answer the question!" cried the same man.

Johnson turned to White, holding out an open palm to indicate that he had the floor.

Scowling, an ashen White climbed to his feet. "No! I told Mr Fell that our union *was* not involved. I said nothing about the future." Before he resumed his seat, the look he gave Johnson was half threat, half entreaty.

"And you went to his office just to tell him that?" called a man standing in the left-side aisle. "You could have done that over the telephone, couldn't you?"

White stood once more, casting a further glance in Johnson's direction. "I also asked him whether the dispute might be settled peacefully, with agreement on a reduction in hours and an increase in wages. He said that nothing could be done until the current agreement expired."

"So call the bloody vote!"

A chant, accompanied by the stamping of feet, begun at the back stalls, quickly spread throughout the theatre. "Call the vote! Call the vote! Call the vote!" Johnson sat and watched as the anger, the raised fists and the snarled demand rippled down to the front stalls. At his side, White sat with his head lowered. And then the stage, and the table at which they sat, began to be struck with small missiles. White looked up, reached to pick one up, and realised that some of the men were pelting the stage with their blue buttons. With a sigh, he turned to Johnson. "Call the bloody vote," he said, "while we still have some members left."

Johnson got to his feet and employed his gavel to compel silence. "Brothers, I will now put the issue to the vote."

"Ooohhh, can't we have a few minutes to think it over?" asked a clown in the front row, frowning and extending a finger to his cheek.

Despite himself, Johnson spluttered with laughter, then collected himself. "All those in favour of immediate strike action against LCC Tramways, please show!"

Throughout the stalls, a sea of hands waved, and a roar of approval echoed about the building.

"Those against?"

None.

"Any no votes hiding upstairs in the circle?"

"None up here!" came a voice.

"The motion," Johnson announced, even though there had not actually been a formal motion, "is carried unanimously. Now, before you leave..."

"Chairman!" came the call from the back stalls as a man left his seat to stand in the aisle. "Chairman, I don't think we're finished yet."

Johnson resumed his seat. "Let's hear it, brother."

"I move that our union form a joint strike committee with the red-button union, and that no meeting with the company takes place unless both unions are represented."

An angry White sprang to his feet. "This is where I draw the line..."

"No it's not," said Johnson, finally asserting his authority. "You can draw it when the motion is debated." He turned to the audience. "Is there a seconder?"

Countless voices seconded the motion.

"It's open for discussion, brothers," called Johnson.

White was back on his feet. "Brothers!" he began, and for the first time there was a note of conviction in his voice. "The Amalgamated Association of Tramway and Vehicle Workers is a proud union—proud of its record, and proud of its independence! When we have a problem, we sort it out ourselves. It would be entirely wrong to abrogate our responsibilities by sharing our decision-making powers with another union—and a union, moreover, that did not exist until two years ago!"

"There's a hand up at the back. Yes, brother, I'm calling you."

The stocky man who had questioned Watson about his meeting with Fell now stood up. "Chairman, Brother White is a liar! He told us earlier that he gave the Chief Officer no assurances regarding the future. A lie! I know for a fact that he told Fell that our union had no intention of becoming involved in the strike. That's *one* reason why we need a joint strike committee, and why both unions must be present at any meeting with the company: because we can't trust our own London District Secretary!"

White was apoplectic, demanding a retraction, but Johnson waved him down.

"Any further discussion? No? All those in favour?"

Once again, the theatre was filled with a roar of voices.

*

A few days later, Mickey came across Dick Mortlake in the canteen at Liverpool Street.

"Hello there, Dick. What you reading?"

Dick lifted the journal from the table so that Mickey could identify it as the *Record*. He hurriedly leafed back through the pages. "Listen to this, Mickey. This is from a New Cross tramworker:

> "We have had the screws put on us for a long while...Walking home from Brixton after a midnight mass meeting, we decided to call out the men, and at three o'clock we started. In an hour over a hundred men were out with us, and by seven o'clock the pavement was blocked with strikers. We began to

269

feel a new sense of freedom and manliness come over us.

"That ring any bells with you? Remember that day outside the garage at Middle Row last September?"

Mickey nodded. "'A new sense of freedom and manliness.'" He grinned. "Yeah, that was the feeling, alright."

*

By 16 May, the AAT leaders had still not agreed to meet with the red-button union. The following day, the Metropolitan Electric Tramway men came out, partly in sympathy but also in the hope of settling their own grievances. By this time, many of the red-button strikers were saying that they wanted a permanent wage-increase and not, as had been demanded, a war bonus and, picking up something from the busmen's agreement the previous year, an extra shilling a day for spreadovers exceeding twelve hours.

The employer, however, stood firm. Meeting at Finsbury Pavement, the LCC's Highways Committee insisted that the current agreement must first expire. Following the expiry date on 26 June, the strikers' demands would be considered by the council's Tramways Committee on 29 June, its Highways Committee on 1 July, and by the full council on 6 July. A meeting of the Board of Trade's Conciliation Board would be arranged for the following day or any time convenient for the unions—a clear indication, thought the red-button leaders, that the council had no intention of reaching an agreement on its own.

On 18 May, several red-button men, Eric Rice and Ben Smith among them, were able to gauge the mood of the employer as they sat in the gallery during a full council meeting at County Hall in Spring Gardens. George Hopwood Hume, chairman of the Highways Committee, had the floor.

"Quite apart from the main issue—the demands of the strikers— we have not even been able to come to a satisfactory arrangement for the transport of munitions workers!" Hume told the councillors and aldermen as he ran through recent events. "At the Board of Trade, it was agreed that the munitions workers would be conveyed to and from the arsenal at Woolwich, but this was so exceedingly difficult that at one stage I suggested in all seriousness to the Board of Trade that the government must take over the running of the tramways. The London and Provincial Union of Licensed Vehicle Workers insisted that if munitions workers were to be conveyed, they must travel free."

Cries of "Shame!"

"Then we must guarantee that *only* munitions workers were carried. We must also ensure that inspectors or regulators were not used instead of the regular motormen and conductors, or they would run the cars back into the depot. And when Mr Fell deployed the inspectors and regulators on other lines, the red-button men ran the cars in anyway!"

More cries of "Shame!"

"And so, faced with this, the Board of Trade recoiled in horror, telling me 'No, Mr Hume, you must run the services yourself, and do the best you can to get the workers to the Arsenal and other big shops.'"

In the gallery, Ben Smith turned to Eric Rice. "See? *And* other big shops! This is not just about munitions workers."

During the following discussion, Harry Gosling, Labour/Progressive, rose from his seat and here, thought the red-button men, they would surely receive some comfort. Gosling, now a member of the Port and Transit Executive, had, in the wake of the Dock Strike of 1889, been a founder member of the Amalgamated Society of Watermen, Lightermen and Bargemen, becoming its general secretary at the age of 32, and surely would not side with those condemning the strike action. But he came close, for while he avoided an attack on the demands of the strikers, he proclaimed that their action was "precipitate."

"Not a word he would have heard very often on the river," Ben Smith remarked caustically to Eric Rice, "and notice how he avoids looking up at the gallery."

At the conclusion of the debate, the council agreed unanimously that the tramworkers must end their strike before their demands could be discussed.

"So what do you think?" asked Eric Rice as they walked away from County Hall towards Trafalgar Square.

"I think," said Ben, glancing over his shoulder to ensure that he would not be overheard by any of the strikers who followed them, "that we're fucked."

*

By 19 May, the AAT told *The Times* that it was still considering a joint arrangement with the LPU; but at least it declared the strike of its members official. The LCC declared that the men must return to work before the dispute went to arbitration. Hope began to fade. Walter Runciman, President of the Board of Trade, had said in the Commons that the government would intervene, but as the days passed that seemed even less likely than the prospect of the blue-button union forming a joint strike committee with the LPU. Police Commissioner Henry relaxed the conditions attached to the training of motormen, a process which usually took a month.

Whenever it could, the LCC played the patriotic card, Aubrey Llewellyn Coventry Fell producing a letter he claimed to have received from three soldiers who called upon the strikers to "act like Englishmen."

"Strange, that," Sanders commented as the officers sat in the Gerrard Street office.

"In what way, George?" asked Tich Smith.

"Well, I would have thought that if a soldier wanted to persuade our members to return to work, he would write to us rather than the employer."

Tich chuckled along with the rest. "Fair point, George, fair point." Then he shook his head sadly. "But for the life of me I can't see a way to win this dispute."

Sanders sighed and reached for his Gold Flake packet. "I have to admit," he conceded, "that the odds are against us."

"And that's only part of the problem," said Ben Smith. "The other side of the coin is that the men are adamant for sticking out. If the Executive Council recommended a return now, they and not the LCC would be seen as the villain."

"I suppose we should be asking ourselves," said Tich soberly, "whether we were right in encouraging the strike in the first place, and if the EC was right in declaring it official."

Sanders shook his head. "I don't think we had a choice but to ride this one, Tich. The strike was inevitable, and nothing we could have said would have prevented it. The men had simply come to the end of their tether. When they reach that stage, men simply have to be allowed to release their anger and frustration."

Tich Smith nodded. "Aye, that's probably right, George. Well, we'll see how the Trafalgar Square demonstration goes on Sunday. That should give us a measure of the members' temper."

*

"Mr Fell."

"Good morning. How may I help you?"

"More of a case of how I can help you, I fancy. Lloyd George here, Chancellor of the Exchequer."

"Oh, really? I was expecting to hear from the Home Secretary, Chancellor."

"Strictly between the two of us, Mr Fell, Mr McKenna will only be in that post for a few more days. A Cabinet reshuffle looms, in which I will be leaving my current post to become Minister of Munitions. That being the case, I feel duty bound to advise you on the conduct of your tram strike."

"You have my attention, Chancellor."

"It just seems to me that we might kill three birds with one stone here. You need to end the strike, I will need to ensure that munitions workers can get to work, and the Army constantly needs to replenish its ranks. I would therefore suggest, Mr Fell, that you post a notice announcing that, failing an immediate return to work, all men of military age will be dismissed. Should they choose to enlist, they will receive favourable consideration for re-employment after the war. That kind of thing. Can I leave that thought with you?"

"You may, Chancellor."

*

That Sunday afternoon, Trafalgar Square was not quite full. Many of the strikers, being practically broke, would have travelled here on buses where the conductors, seeing their red buttons, had allowed them to travel free. As Tich Smith made his introductory remarks, Sanders allowed his gaze to wander over the gathering.

Men began to take off their caps and use them as fans as the afternoon bathed them in its sunlight. Some used newspapers for the same purpose, and among the crowd were a small number of British Socialist Party activists selling *Justice*, the party newspaper, although few strikers bought it because they were penniless. Sanders gazed across at the columns at the facade of the National Gallery and, his mind wandering, wondered when he would get the time to visit once more, viewing the Turners and the impressionist exhibits which had caused so much controversy among the members of the art establishment when they had first arrived.

At the back of the crowd, Dorothy Bridgeman stood with Mickey Rice, watching as Tich Smith sat down and Sanders stood, removed his bowler, and placed it on the table in front of him.

"Comrades, brothers"—Sanders paused and seemed to cast his

eyes about the square—"and sisters!" This brought forth a cheer of gratitude from the women, joined by some of the men. "To those who have not been here before, allow me to welcome you to Trafalgar Square, the home of British dissent and protest! Where you now stand once stood the Chartists who, campaigning for democracy for the working class, began their great demonstration of 1848 in this square. After that, our masters outlawed such activity in this place, and it was not until the 1880s, when the labour movement began to awaken from its slumber, that the Social Democratic Federation and others reclaimed the right to state their case here. More recently, of course, it was here that the great demonstrations against the imperialist war were held. So you, comrades, sisters and brothers, are part of a long and noble tradition!

"A few days ago, you may have seen in the press that Mr Aubrey Llewellyn Coventry Fell claimed to have received a letter from three soldiers, calling upon you men to 'act like Englishmen.' Let me tell you, comrades, that in standing up for your rights and fighting for a better life you *are* acting like Englishmen!" Here, he was interrupted by cheers. "I should correct that, because those soldiers, brave though they might be, strike me as being very backward. 'English*men*?' What are 'English*men*?' You are behaving like English *workers*!

"Mr Aubrey Llewellyn Coventry Fell, on the other hand, behaves like an English *employer*, and on Friday he tried to get West Ham trams to run on the LCC lines. And what happened, comrades? The West Ham men behaved like English *workers* and announced that if any such attempt was made they would be on strike!"

More cheers.

"That was Friday. On *Saturday*, Mr Aubrey Llewellyn Coventry Fell had a notice posted in the sheds telling every striker of military age to hand back his uniform, as he would not be accepted back. *Unless*, of course, he enlisted in the Army, in which case he would, if he returned from the bosses' war in one piece, be considered for re-engagement when that war was over. Is that how an Englishman behaves? No, it's how an English *employer* behaves!

"Comrades, some of you—most of you, I think—engaged in this strike thinking only of winning the dispute, of having less time to work and more for your family to eat. That's perfectly understandable, and perfectly acceptable. That is why trade unions exist. But there are some who look forward to a time when the things of work—the factories, the buses and trams and the fields, the tools and the raw materials—will be owned collectively by their class. *Your* class. *Our* class. They look forward to a society where there will be no place for a manager like Mr Aubrey Llewellyn Coventry Fell, and where their government—*your* government, *our* government—will more often order the raising of wages rather than their erosion by inflation, the shortening of hours rather than their extension.

"I make this point, brothers and sisters, because in such a society the state will be in the hands of the working class, defending the working class, representing the interests of the working class. What kind of state do you have at the moment? A state that is in the hands of the capitalist class, which defends the capitalist class and represents the interests of the capitalist class. And the longer this strike goes on, the clearer it becomes that you are facing not just Aubrey Llewellyn Coventry Fell and London County Council Tramways but the whole apparatus of the capitalist state: the Board of Trade refuses to intervene, apart from making sure munitions workers can get to work; the Metropolitan Police Commissioner relaxes the training regulations so that scabs can be given your jobs; the House of Commons criticises your strike but says not a word against your employer; the millionaire-owned press poisons the public mind against you; and now your employer—acting, I am sure, on the instructions of the government—wants to send as many of you as possible to fight in the bosses' war.

"It may not be like this in every strike, but in an important one like this, in a key industry in the capital, at a time when the government fears that a victory for you will lead to demands from other public sector workers, the whole force of the British state, the *capitalist* state, is brought to bear against you. And that is why, comrades, that more workers need to be thinking beyond wages and conditions, important as they are, to a society where the working class rules and the capitalist state is no more! Socialism, comrades, socialism!"

The strikers cheered Sanders because he was, after all, George Sanders, and some, although not the majority, because they shared his vision or had been inspired by his words. "Well" said Dorothy, turning to Mickey, "George is certainly doing his best to implement the decisions of Basel and Stuttgart, but I'm not sure that the conditions are ripe yet. He's also running the risk, of course, of prosecution under DORA."

Mickey smiled and shook his head. "They won't lay a finger on George, Dorothy."

"And why not, Mickey?"

"Because they'd have to deal with us."

After Sanders had resumed his seat, a tall, bushy-haired man stepped up.

"Brothers and sisters!" he called. "My name is Archie Henderson, and I'll not keep you long. Are there any AAT members here?"

He looked about the audience and saw only a few hands raised.

"Come on, lads, are there any blue-button members here? Don't be shy."

More hands were raised.

Henderson placed his hands on his hips and, leaning forward, shouted rather than spoke. "Until yesterday, brothers, I was an organiser for the blue-button union. Today, I wear the red button and organise for the London and Provincial Union of Licenced Vehicle Workers!"

A cheer went up, although some of the blue-button men maintained a puzzled silence.

"And I'll tell you why! The London District Secretary of the blue-button had to be dragged kicking and screaming into this dispute. The very day you red-button lads began to stop work, he was in the office of Chief Officer Fell, assuring him that his members were not, and would not be, party to the dispute. Then, at the mass meeting on the Saturday night, there was a decision that the AAT would form a joint strike committee with the LPU. And now, eight days later, where is it? Nowhere! Because the blue-button leadership doesn't want it! For the first week of this strike London District Secretary White did nothing! It wasn't until 19 May that the AAT leadership declared the strike official. And even now, comrades, that leadership has sanctioned the use of its members in the conveyance of munitions workers to Woolwich—but with none of the conditions demanded by the LPU!

"So this organiser"—he jabbed a thumb at his own chest—"has had enough, and I have taken off the blue button and put on the red, the badge of a truly democratic union where the members rule. And to our AAT brothers I say: Follow me! Off with the blue button and on with the red! Off with the blue and on with the red! Off with the blue and on with the red!"

Soon the square rang with the slogan as the strikers took up the chant. "Off with the blue and on with the red!"

Archie Henderson threw back his head and laughed in exultation, doubtless sharing the feeling, now that he had left the AAT behind, that had descended on the New Cross strikers on the first morning of the strike. He turned to leave the rostrum and regain his seat, but then returned, gently waving his palms to request silence.

"Okay," he said, "I can see you lads like a good slogan, so here's another one for you. In fact, you'd be better off using this one outside the Tramways office in Belvedere Road—or, better still, get your kids to chant it to the Chief Officer:

> "Aubrey Llewellyn Coventry Fell
> "Sacked the strikers and sent them to hell!

"Come on, let's hear you:

> "Aubrey Llewellyn Coventry Fell
> "Sacked the strikers and sent them to hell!

> "Aubrey Llewellyn Coventry Fell
> "Sacked the strikers and sent them to hell!"

And, despite the couplet's gruesome message, the audience laughingly took up the chant, and for now looked at each other rather than the platform on the plinth, drawing closer together and giving release to their feelings about their employer; their defiance was rekindled as their individual voices joined together to form one mighty voice that one day would be heard.

Tich Smith, having slapped Henderson on the back as he walked from the rostrum, now turned to the audience. "Comrades, I'll bet a pound to a pinch of snuff that you'll not read a word of that—or of George's speech—in tomorrow's newspapers!"

"It seems," Dorothy remarked to Mickey, "that your union has acquired a music hall comedian."

"Oh," he replied, wiping tears of laughter from his eyes, "we can certainly use someone like him. While everything George said had to be said, it was a bit dry, leaving the men in a serious mood and maybe even a bit worried." He gestured towards the crowd. "Look at 'em now!"

The rally ended with the LPU reiterating the call for its demands to be immediately submitted to arbitration, given which there would be a recommendation for a return to work.

*

But there was no promise of arbitration and, following the dismissal of men of military age, many now returned to the sheds, some to work and some to hand in their uniforms. At one shed on Monday, men were told to keep their uniforms, as they would be given work if they left the ranks of the strikers. This led to the notion that Fell's notice of 22 May was merely bluff, leading some who had returned to rejoin the strike. The LCC did not budge, and thus it appeared likely that the promise of work to military-age men had been an initiative of a local official, aiming at tricking men into returning to work.

On 25 May, after an interview at the Board of Trade, two mass meetings—the LPU's was at the Shoreditch Empire, presided over by George Sanders—called on the two unions to negotiate an end to the dispute, a clear sign that support for the strike was fading—not surprising in the case of the AAT members, as they had still received no strike pay. At the same time, the patience of the red-button members with the leadership of their blue-button counterpart was obviously wearing thin, as their demand for negotiations was qualified by the term "with or without the AAT." That evening, the LPU agreed to ask the Board of Trade to broker an agreement.

The following day, as Archie Henderson arrived at Gerrard Street he was told that a visitor awaited him in Tich Smith's office.

"Come in, Archie," said Tich as Henderson opened his door. "I think you probably know this colleague."

As the visitor rose from his chair and turned, Archie saw that it was Stanley Hirst, Assistant General Secretary of the AAT, and a former tramworker himself.

"I do," said Archie, extending his hand. "Good morning, Brother Hirst. A pity we have to meet again in these circumstances."

Hirst, a lean man of medium height, just under forty years of age, stepped forward and took Archie's hand. "Maybe, maybe," he said, affably enough.

"Listen," said Tich, "I have a few things to discuss with George down the corridor, so I'll leave you two to have a chat. Alright, Archie?"

Archie nodded. "Alright, Tich."

When they were alone, they each took one of Tich's visitors' chairs, appraising each other.

"Just down from Manchester, Brother Hirst?"

"Last night. And you can call me Stan."

"The lads could have done with you earlier."

Hirst nodded. "Aye, I can see that now, Archie." He passed a hand over his mouth. "Let's get straight to the point, shall we? Archie, I want you back in the AAT."

Archie sighed and shook his head. "It's too late for that now, Stan. Sorry, but there it is."

"You want to tell me why you jumped ship, Archie?"

Henderson threw back his head. "Good god, do I need to?"

"I think you do, Archie."

"Well, for a start there's White..."

"Yes, Eddie Johnson has given me chapter and verse." He looked Henderson in the eye. "As soon as this strike is over, Brother White will face an investigation. You have my word on that. For the moment, though, that's between you and me. Anything else?"

"The strike has been on for almost two weeks and the lads have received no strike pay."

"They'll receive it today, Archie."

"It was agreed that a joint strike committee would be formed..."

"Yes, it was. And it will be, Archie. That was the other thing I came here to discuss with Tich Smith. Is that it?" He spread his hands. "It seems to me that all your grievances flow from the White problem. That being the case, what's to stop you coming back to the AAT?" He grinned mischievously. "And, while you're about it, bringing back the hundreds of our members that jumped ship with you?"

"Many of 'em jumped before I did, Stan. And it's not just White. Why, for example, did it take until 19 May to declare the strike official?"

Hirst shrugged. "You know our executive, Archie..."

"I do, Stan, and that's really my point. And, the red-button elects its officers rather than appointing them; that's something that has always attracted me, to be honest."

Hirst regarded him in silence for a long while. Eventually, his mouth fell open and his eyes widened. "Well, Archie, there can be no meeting of the minds there, I'm afraid. By the sound of it, you may have crossed over even if this strike had never happened."

"Maybe so, Stan, maybe so."

Hirst gave him a tight grin. "Well listen, let's you and me not fall out." He held out his hand. "No hard feelings."

"No hard feelings, Stan."

"And you know," said Hirst, waving a finger at Henderson as he got to his feet, "I have a feeling that it won't be too long before you and I are under the same roof again."

*

Hirst's intervention came too late to influence the course of events. While the LPU claimed on 26 May that 3,000 men were still on strike, the LCC opened new training schools, announcing that it would not be recruiting men of military age, leading Hirst to tell *The Times* that the company was quite cynically clearing the decks in anticipation of conscription: come that day, with no eligible men in its employment the company would be completely unaffected. Others, notably Sanders, put a darker interpretation on the matter, reasoning that Aubrey Llewellyn Coventry Fell must know that tramworkers—or at least motormen—would, like munitions workers and others in crucial occupations, most likely be exempted from national service, in which case he was now acting as an Army recruiting agent.

With nothing of note heard from the Board of Trade, more tramworkers returning to the sheds, and more blacklegs being taken on, the red-button union on 28 May assigned executive members to address meetings of the members in various parts of London in an attempt to persuade them to stand firm, but the only good news brought to those meetings was that the Joint Strike Committee, chaired by John Stokes, secretary of the London Trades Council and a member of the British Socialist Party, was finally meeting. And meet it did, for almost eleven hours, after which the most it could announce to the world was that both unions were now working in unity and that progress was being made.

*

While the unions had been attempting to forge their own reluctant coalition, Herbert Asquith had put together one of his own on 25 May. Subject to intense criticism by the Conservatives for the conduct of the clearly failing Gallipoli campaign in Turkey for which his First Lord of the Admiralty, Winston Churchill, was largely responsible, Asquith, reluctant to fire him, was forced to form a new government with Conservative participation as the price of Churchill's retention in the Cabinet—although he was demoted to Chancellor of the Duchy of Lancaster, a sinecure. Further criticism was levelled at the government for the severe shortage of high-explosive shells as a result of its shift in military tactics, now believing that a battlefield could be controlled by heavy artillery, which had led to an unanticipated rate of fire. Thus, the Liberal government was no more and Britain was governed by a wartime coalition in which David Lloyd George, having campaigned for the creation of the post, became Minister of Munitions.

"I'm surprised they didn't blame the shell shortage on the tram strike," Sanders remarked in an informal discussion with other officers and EC members just before the start of a meeting.

"Oh, I'm sure they would have if they could have got away with it," said Archie Henderson. He sighed. "Anyway, so the Tories are back."

Sanders grimaced dismissively. "Yes and no, Archie. The Liberals have kept all the major posts."

"And Labour's in government for the first time," chipped in an EC member, who seemed to believe that this might be this particular cloud's silver lining.

"He's appointed nine Tories and one Labour," said Sanders, "so we can hardly say that Labour is in government."

"Who's the lucky man?" This from Barney McCauley.

"Archie's namesake."

"Arthur Henderson? And what ministry did Asquith give him?"

"Education. What did you expect—Foreign Secretary?"

Macauley shook his head in disbelief. "First they ditch their principles and support the war, now they join the government in return for scraps."

"And we," said Sanders, "go on financing them."

*

Saturday, 29 May brought a false dawn, when a letter was received from Harry Gosling, writing on behalf of the LCC to John Stokes, chairman of the Joint Strike Committee, saying that if the men returned to work their claims would now be considered, with an immediate submission to arbitration if no agreement could be reached. Thinking that this meant that the men of military age would be reinstated, a return was agreed, and Stokes issued a telegram: "I am instructed to inform you that all men out in dispute are instructed to return to work on Sunday at 8 a.m. All men required for night work to prepare cars are instructed to resume work at 9 p.m. this Saturday." On Sunday, however, when men of military age marched to the sheds with the older men, it was found that the former were not allowed to work; some of the older men now refused to take the cars out, and the JSC met again and called the whole workforce out. At Holloway, there was violence.

25

On the Saturday evening, Dorothy Bridgeman and Mickey Rice attended a fund-raising social for the British Socialist Party at the house of a middle-class couple just a short distance up Highgate

Hill from Archway. As they entered the large house, Dorothy noted that Mickey, who was by now able to hold his own in most discussions, seemed perfectly relaxed in these petty bourgeois surroundings.

"Ah, Comrade Bridgeman!" she heard as they entered the living room.

Turning, she saw Theo Rothstein, his son Andrew at his side, beaming at her. He placed his glass on a sideboard and came to her, nodding a greeting to Mickey as he extended a hand.

"Dorothy, how nice to see you again! I was afraid that after our last encounter you had cast me into the wilderness."

She laughed and took his hand. "Oh Theo, I owe you an apology for my behaviour that evening. It was unforgiveable and I am truly sorry."

With a wave of the hand, he dismissed the matter. "As I told Comrade Rice and my son Andrew—Andrew, come and join us," he interjected—"you were correct in your estimate of my performance, so there is nothing to forgive."

"My rudeness, Theo, my rudeness."

A more emphatic wave of the hand. "Enough! Andrew, I believe you know these two comrades. I am hoping that Comrade Rice, although he is a busworker and not a tramworker, will be able to give me some news of the tramways strike." He turned to Mickey and raised an eyebrow.

"As you say, Comrade, I am not a tramworker, but from what I've heard from my brother Eric,"—he grimaced and shook his head—"it seems that the strike is lost."

"Ah!" Rothstein nodded sagely. "This is what I thought. You know, I was at Trafalgar Square last Sunday, and it struck me that George Sanders in his speech made no attempt to urge the strikers to stick to their guns, and he said nothing about the prospects of a settlement. He must have known, I thought, that the strike was doomed to failure." He shook his head sadly and then, brightening, turned to Dorothy. "And I see that you, dear Comrade, are writing for Miss Pankhurst. How is that going?"

"You disapprove of Sylvia, Theo?"

"Why do you say that, Dorothy?"

"Because you call her Miss rather than Comrade."

"Ah!" He struck his brow with the heel of his hand. "You have me again, Dorothy! You're right: I should have referred to her as *Comrade* Pankhurst. And disapprove of her? No, of course not." He grinned mischievously. "Not entirely, anyway. Compared to her mother, she is a giant. Where is the Women's Social and Political

Union now? Nowhere, its activities suspended in order that these bourgeois women can support the war, its journal *The Suffragette* dropped and replaced by something called *Britannia*. But Sylvia? She fights on, she mobilises working-class women, and her journal *The Woman's Dreadnought* is on the whole excellent." He paused, wagging a warning finger. "However, I would be grateful, Dorothy, if you would tell Sylvia to stop intercepting material intended for me and publishing it in the *Dreadnought*! That, I find, is most...un*comradely*."

Dorothy smiled and nodded. "I will tell her, Theo."

*

After the encounter with the Rothsteins, Dorothy left Mickey to insert himself into whichever discussions appealed to him while she moved about the room, renewing acquaintances. As Mickey started a week of late turns the next day, she was not concerned with the time, but then found that they had missed the last 27 bus, which would have taken them to Westbourne Grove. When she told Mickey that the owners of the house, John and Alexandra Kirby, had invited them to use a spare room for the night, he readily agreed.

As they walked down towards Archway the next morning, it struck them both that something was afoot. Two police vehicles passed them, and from the Holloway Road came the sound of many angry voices. Deciding to postpone their journey home, they proceeded down Holloway Road. Outside Holloway tramshed stood a small detachment of policemen, while on the opposite side of the road three to four hundred people were gathered on the pavement. Mickey took Dorothy's hand and led her across the street where, pointing to the red button on his lapel, he walked into the crowd.

"What's happening, mate?" he asked a man who moved to let him pass.

"Last night, we gets a message to say that the strike's over, don't we? If we goes back to work, the company's gonna look at our demands and they'll take back the men they sacked. So some of us go in this morning, and they tell us to go and join the fuckin' Army don't they? Bastards!" He turned from Mickey and directed his anger at the tramshed. "BASTARDS!"

The man turned back to Mickey, his pale, freckled face close, his rank breath in Mickey's face. "Are you an official?"

"No, mate, I'm a busman."

"That's no good to us, then." He returned to the job in hand.

"BASTARDS!"

All the men were shouting, but there was no uniformity in their shouts, no apparent leadership in their ranks. Mickey noticed that some in the middle of the crowd had gathered stones from a neighbouring patch of waste ground and were passing them out to their comrades. Others asked where these missiles could be found and were directed to the waste land, from where they soon returned with their pockets loaded. Somebody needed to do something. Mickey thought back to Trafalgar Square, desperately trying to recall the words of Archie Henderson's couplet. Finally they came to him and he considered the best course of action, quickly deciding that it would be a mistake to step out in front of them because they would probably not follow a man, badge or no badge, dressed in civvies. He raised his head and called from the back of the crowd, feeling Dorothy behind him place a hand on his shoulder, encouraging him.

"Aubrey Llewellyn Coventry Fell

"Sacked the strikers and sent them to hell!"

No response. Louder and slower this time:

"Aubrey Llewellyn Coventry Fell

"Sacked the strikers and sent them to hell!"

Only a handful—maybe they had been in Trafalgar Square a week ago—joined in.

"Come on! All together!

"Aubrey Llewellyn Coventry Fell

"Sacked the strikers and sent them to hell!"

At last they had it, and around four hundred voices came together. Over and over they chanted it, and even the coppers outside the shed seemed to see the funny side of it, grinning broadly. The men were more unified now and the threatening atmosphere, born of the anarchy of individualism, seemed to recede.

But this lasted only until the company attempted to bring the first tram onto the road, driven by a regulator from the look of his uniform, and then the chant was dropped in favour of oaths and curses and the stones began to fall, raining onto the tram, which now accelerated. At this, one man ran from the crowd, leapt aboard the vehicle and threw his fist into the regulator's face. Now the police went into action, dragging the striker from the tram as it slowed again, using their truncheons on his head and arms, and dragging him to a vehicle parked at the side of the shed. Apparently without serious injury, the regulator swung the tram onto the eastbound rails and accelerated down the Holloway Road. A second tram now emerged from the shed and once more the stones sailed through the air. Mickey turned, intending to shepherd Dorothy away from the scene, only to find that she was no longer behind him. Later he would try to define the freezing sensation that passed over his whole body: was it fear, horror, panic? Then he was trembling as he turned from side to side, trying to catch sight of Dorothy. But she was not in the crowd.

He began to shout "Dorothy! Dorothy!" but it was a feeble sound that came from his mouth.

"Look! Look!" cried the man with the bad breath in front of Mickey, grasping Mickey's arm and pulling him forward. "There she is! Can't you see her?"

Yes, he could. She was in front of the crowd, bending to scoop up stones as she ran, and now anger restored his voice—anger at this crowd which had allowed her to run onto the road, but most of all anger at Dorothy herself for once again letting loose the demon he had first seen over a year earlier at the Hackney Empire.

"Dorothy! Come back here! Don't do it! PLEASE!"

She heard this, and when she turned to him—if she could see him at all—her face was as it had been in February 1914, a mask of fury that would not succumb to reason. Then, inexpertly and awkwardly, but still finding her target, she was hurling her stones and the police were advancing on her.

*

"Morning, sir!"

Superintendent Patrick Quinn looked up from his desk as Ralph Kitchener entered his office on 1 June, waving a newspaper. "Good morning, Kitchener. I see you've forsaken the *Sporting Life* for *The Times*."

"Haha. Most amusing, sir. During working hours, Superintendent, I only read newspapers in the line of duty."

"Of course, Kitchener, of course. You must forgive my little joke. Now, what do you wish to show me? Or, better still, read to me? Yes, Kitchener, read me your news story."

Quinn leaned back in his chair and closed his eyes, like a child awaiting a bedtime story, while Kitchener shook out his newspaper, folded it twice, and cleared his throat.

> "A milestone was passed on Sunday with the first arrest of a lady in connection with the protracted London tramway strike. Miss Dorothy Bridgeman, 32, was apprehended outside Holloway tram depot, where a crowd of approximately four hundred strikers

maintained an intimidating presence. Along with many of the strikers, and in full view of the police officers in attendance, Miss Bridgeman attempted to prevent trams from leaving the depot by pelting them with stones, causing minor damage. Appearing before magistrates yesterday, the latter-day Amazon was charged with causing malicious damage and resisting arrest. Miss Bridgeman, who was unrepresented, offered no defence. Fined £10, she told the court that she had no intention of paying this, and was therefore sentenced to eight weeks' imprisonment."

Quinn opened his eyes and slapped his desktop. "And who was it," he laughed, "who claimed that justice delayed is justice denied? Better late than never, Kitchener, better late than never!"

"Should I have a word with the prison chaplain, sir, see what he can get out of her?"

A satisfied Quinn nodded. "Yes, do that, Kitchener. May lead to nothing, but she might know of the BSP's plans. We need to know about anything that breaches DORA. Then again, she's writing for the Pankhurst girl now, so anything we can learn about her designs would also be useful."

*

Holloway Prison, less than a mile from the site of Dorothy's offence, was constructed in the early 1850s in imitation of a mediaeval castle, its crenelated turrets easily visible from Camden Road, despite the eighteen-foot wall. Confined in a windowless police vehicle, Dorothy saw none of this as she was conveyed through the entrance gates and then, along with her fellow prisoners, hurried into the reception area. Here, she stood in a line and waited to be booked in, noting, as she overheard others undergo this process, that most of the women ahead of her had been sentenced for prostitution and drunkenness and that many, from their accents, were from the East End.

Although it was only just over a day ago that she had thrown rocks at the tram emerging from the Holloway depot, it seemed to her that half a lifetime, with mood following mood, one level of consciousness after another, had passed since then. The images from the minutes outside the tramshed were the most vivid. She could still picture the faces of the men turned in her direction as she peered over Mickey's shoulder. The man to whom Mickey spoke was ugly, and she could still see his pale, freckled face, cracked lips and uneven and discoloured teeth; and, yes, the grimy collar of his blue shirt. Others were more presentable, evenly featured, but they all had the same tired, anxious appearance, and when the trams began to emerge from the shed that tiredness and anxiety fused into desperation as they gave vent to their anger. With great clarity, it came to her as she stood there that their ugly and unkempt appearances were products of their conditions of life, conditions from which they so urgently wished to escape, even if they did not really know *how* to escape them with any finality. It was then that the anger they were feeling was communicated to her, like a contagious virus, and she saw that the men driving those trams, those scabs and blacklegs, were by their treachery, weakness, or merely lack of understanding, conniving in the prolongation of the servile status of those men on the pavement. She had no choice: she must act. And so she drew away from Mickey, making her way around the back of the crowd until the way was unimpeded, and then all her senses sprang to life as she ran forward: the smell of unwashed bodies and clothes as she passed the edge of the crowd, the sparkling maroon and cream livery of the tram as it came from the shed, the silver tramlines shining in the early summer sunlight, then the shape and texture of the first rock as she bent to pick it up. She threw once, picked up another and threw again, only to see them fall short of the tram. A bitter, foolish thought came to her then: in her childhood her parents had denied her not only a proper education but also the ability to throw! She sought the image of her brother playing cricket on a Sunday afternoon, saw how he threw when fielding, then picked up a third rock and hurled it, crying out in delight as it hit a window on the lower deck of the tram, watching enthralled as the glass splintered but did not break. As she scooped up her fourth rock, she was conscious of a voice from afar, calling to her, imploring her, and turning her head she saw Mickey, in the middle of the crowd now, shouting her name. It was very apparent that he wanted her to stop, to turn and run. How *could* he? How *could* he seek to stop this fine feeling that was electrifying her whole body, calling it into life? Didn't he understand her at all? She felt her face harden, her eyes narrow, and she turned back to throw her final rock, chipping the paint on the side of the tram. Then the police were all about her, blocking out the sharp colours with their dull blue uniforms, and when they put their hands on her she kicked and struggled but was overcome, sustaining a graze on her forehead—probably caused by an accidental blow, she later conceded—and losing her hat.

Her arrival at Holloway Police Station was the cause of some puzzlement, as some thought that, given her accent and obvious class origin, she must surely be a suffragette. She remembered little of the encounter now, except the indelible impression that she had entered an *institution*, one of the outposts established, usually well away from its own territory, by the ruling class for the training, care,—in the loosest sense of those terms—apprehension or punishment of those who fell under its rule.

Dorothy also had a very clear picture of Maisie Doyle, one of the two women already occupying the cell into which she was placed. Maisie was a portly, shabbily-dressed woman in her mid-forties with a florid complexion and dark hair streaked with grey.

"We'll be here until tomorrow—you realise that, don't you dearie?" she greeted Dorothy, revealing gaps in her teeth as she smiled at the new prisoner. "Always a mistake to get arrested on a Sunday—or a Saturday night, like we was." She nodded in the direction of the cell's other occupant, a thin, grey-faced woman of about her own age. "I'm Maisie Doyle and this one's Doris Hartley."

"Ah, of course," Dorothy replied, "Saturday night."

"Mm," said Maisie, wondering whether Dorothy's utterance constituted a realisation of how she and her companion came to be here in the first place or an explanation of why they were *still* here. She appeared to decide which was the more probable, for after a few seconds she nodded. "Yes, Saturday night. You got it, dearie: we was pissed again." She pointed to the graze on Dorothy's brow. "Looks like you been in the wars, duck."

Dorothy's hand went to the graze and stroked it gingerly, having not previously been aware of its existence. She smiled. "Well, not quite the wars. The class struggle, actually. Oh, my name's Dorothy Bridgeman."

"So what they got you for, Dorothy?" Maisie asked.

"Oh, the class struggle," she replied, with a shrug, sounding as if she thought this might have been obvious. Then she began to laugh. "I threw some stones at a tram," she explained. "And I may have kicked a policeman."

Maisie joined in her laughter. "Good for you, Dorothy, good for you."

"What will happen now?"

"Well, dearie, nothin' will 'appen *now*, but tomorrow mornin' they'll bring us before the magistrates, then we'll 'ave the choice of payin' a fine or spendin' a few weeks in 'Olloway."

"Lookin' the way she does," said Doris, "they'll have her knickers off in no time in that place."

Maisie waved a hand dismissively. "Don't listen to 'er. I been in there enough to know that there's precious little chance of that kind of thing." She frowned reflectively. "'Less it's one of the wardresses, o' course."

A short while later, she had visitors. She was released from the holding cell and, turning right, saw Mickey and John Kirby, a lawyer, their host of the previous evening, awaiting her. Over her shoulder, she could hear the comments from Maisie and Doris.

"She'll be out of here like a shot, you take my word for it," said an unimpressed Doris.

"I wouldn't be so sure of that," countered Maisie. "There's somethin' about that girl."

"I'm afraid you'll be here until tomorrow morning, Dorothy" said Kirby.

Doris: "'E sounds posh, just like 'er."

"Yes, I know," said Dorothy. "Then the magistrates' court and the choice of a fine or Holloway."

"You needn't worry about that. We'll make sure your fine is paid, and you'll be home by lunchtime."

Doris: "See, what did I tell you?"

"I'm not at all sure that I want my fine to be paid."

"Jesus Christ, Dorothy!" exploded Mickey. "What can you be thinking of? And what made you do this anyway? What purpose did it serve?"

Maisie: "Now 'e sounds as if 'e might work on the trams."

"Let's not go into that now, Mickey. I acted as I thought I had to, and I have no regrets."

"Well, you will if you end up in in prison, Dorothy. Why would you want to spend time in Holloway?"

Doris: "Maybe somethin' I said."

Dorothy lowered her head and placed a hand over her eyes, leading the two men to think that she was crying, but as she straightened once more and turned to call over her shoulder they saw only laughter. "*Do* shut up, Doris!"

"I don't know what to say, Dorothy," said Mickey. "You seem to think that this is some kind of joke."

"Well, it's not a major tragedy is it? Listen, Mickey, you have no need to worry. Sign on for your late turn this afternoon as if nothing has happened. I'll be alright. But do *not*, do *not*, Mickey, pay my fine tomorrow."

"We'll be in court in the morning."

"*No!*"

And they were not. She remembered little of the proceedings, short though they were. At one point, the elderly magistrate asked if she had, indeed, struck one of the policemen involved in her arrest.

"I did, but not deliberately."

"Are you saying, Miss Bridgeman, that you *accidentally* kicked the constable?"

"Not accidentally, no, but possibly as a reflex action after I sustained a blow to the head."

"The policeman struck *you*?"

"Yes, although it is perfectly possible that this *was* an accident. My reaction was, I believe, automatic—a reflex action, as I say."

A little before midday, she was placed in a Black Maria with several other women, each in a separate compartment to prevent communication between them, and driven to Holloway.

And here she was, gazing up at the central concourse from which radiated the four blocks of cells, each four stories in height, and if she had been struck by the institutional nature of the police station, that impression was now multiplied. Here was the power of the state. As she reached the head of the line, she was led to a reception cell, from where, after a lengthy wait, she was sent to a doctor who weighed and examined her. She was then asked to discard her clothing and her personal details were recorded.

"Religion?" demanded the wardress.

"None."

The wardress blinked in incomprehension. "What did you say?"

"I said that I have no religion."

The wardress now smirked. "Don't think that you'll get out of morning chapel that way, my lady."

"*Every* morning?"

"From ten past eight until nine." She looked up at Dorothy with an insincere smile. "And I've put you down as C of E."

Having been divested of all that was hers and assigned a consciousness that was not, she was told to take a bath in grey, cool water while a wardress observed her over a small door. After drying herself, she was directed to a pile of clothing on the floor and told to choose a uniform that fitted her. None did, quite, but she was soon clothed in a dress of green serge, a white cap, a checkered apron and stockings that immediately began to slip down her legs. The rough underwear was too large, and the clumpy shoes of different sizes. Each item was marked with a number of broad arrows to indicate that both the clothing and the person who wore it were property of the Crown.

Once she had collected her bedding, religious reading matter and toothbrush—this was voluntary, while she was given no choice regarding the first two—she was led to a whitewashed cell on the second level. This measured thirteen feet by seven and was nine feet high, with a high window at one end and a heavy door at the other; it was furnished with a small table and chair, a cupboard, and a narrow bed; there was also a washbasin and a toilet. Here, at least, she thought, is privacy and somewhere to think, but this soon proved to be not totally correct, as she noticed that the door contained an inspection panel through which she could be observed by anyone who cared to look through it. Here also, she would work and eat. She would rise at 5.45 a.m. and sleep at 9 p.m. The only time she would see another prisoner was when she attended the chapel service or took exercise in the prison yard, but even then communication was prohibited.

She had nothing to do until supper was brought at around 7 p.m., as she had been told that her prison regime would begin in earnest on the following day, when she would be expected to weave baskets in her cell. So now, there being nothing worthwhile to read, she could at least think. Gradually, the fog surrounding so much of her thoughts and actions during the past thirty hours or so was beginning to clear. Just as, in time and under Mickey's criticism, she had realised that her action at the Hackney Empire had been foolish and unacceptable, so now she was coming to see that her stone-throwing had, while it may have satisfied some impulse within her, been productive of nothing whatsoever. Mickey had already told her that the strike was practically defeated, so she cannot have hoped to influence its course. Nor can she seriously have sought to set an example for the strikers to follow, for what kind of example was hooliganism? She remembered now hearing George Sanders, at a meeting several years earlier, condemning hooliganism as "vandalism with neither clear-cut aim nor prospect of success."

What had she been thinking? Truly, of course, she had not been thinking at all. *Feeling*, maybe, but certainly not thinking. But there must, somewhere in her consciousness—or perhaps in her unconscious—have been a desired outcome. Had it been the desire for arrest? But why would she have wanted that? Or had it been a desire for that which often followed arrest—imprisonment? Ah...now we're getting warmer! Why had she decided on the spur of the moment, during the visit by Mickey and John Kirby yesterday, having not previously given it conscious consideration, to go to prison rather than pay a fine? Was she seeking to emulate Sylvia, or perhaps to demonstrate to her that, although she might disapprove of her methods, she too had her kind of courage? If so, it was a strange thing to have done, for she had actually *adopted* her methods! That is what happened when one allowed feeling to dominate thought. But yes, that must have formed part of her motivation, and she remembered now how, upon her arrival, she had looked at the interior of the prison with a writerly eye, half-consciously composing descriptive sentences for an article she might write for the *Dreadnought*.

Well, she might still write such an article, although she now knew that it could hardly be as comprehensive as she had, in odd moments during the past day or so, hazily envisaged it. Initially, she had assumed that she would be able to make contact with other prisoners, encouraging them to talk of their backgrounds, of the circumstances that had led them to Holloway, only to discover that the prison was run along similar lines as an order of Trappist nuns. Hah! And to think that she would be here for two months, a wasted one-sixth of a year in which she would be able to achieve nothing. She should have paid the bloody fine.

At six o'clock the next morning, a wardress entered her cell carrying a sheaf of slender white canes, a number of hexagonal plywood bases and a wide enamel bowl.

"Ah," Dorothy exclaimed in recognition, "the subject of my labour!"

The wardress ignored this and swiftly showed her how to render the cane pliable by soaking it in water, and then inserted six of the canes vertically through a base before commencing the weaving. Breakfast arrived shortly after this demonstration: tea so sweet that it caused Dorothy's teeth to scream, a small wholemeal loaf, and two ounces of butter which, the wardress informed her, would have to last her the whole day.

And then, of course, came the chapel service where, for the first time since her arrival, Dorothy saw other prisoners—all the prisoners, in fact, as the chapel accommodated the whole prison, including staff, who sat among the inmates. She spent the entire forty-five minutes, which otherwise would have seemed interminable, studying as many of her fellow prisoners as she could manage without turning her head—anyone appearing to ignore the chaplain was instructed "Eyes front!" by a wardress who patrolled the aisles on the lookout for such signs of inattentiveness or rebellion. Given that all wore either green or brown serge dresses, depending on their prisoner-classification, it was impossible to detect any suggestion of individuality from their wardrobe, and the few faces visible to her were either vacant-eyed or pretending interest. As the governor sat to one side of the pulpit, his eyes able to scan the whole of the chapel, there were few opportunities for furtive communication, although Dorothy suspected that notes might be passed. The chaplain, a fiftyish, red-faced man whose name she never learned, gave several readings from the Bible interspersed with his own thoughts concerning the valuable lessons which the prisoners, if they were sincerely desirous of improvement, might take away from this temporary home; he said a great deal about the dignity of labour, and Dorothy was reminded of that Sunday afternoon on Clapham Common when she had enlightened Mickey on the theme of Percy Fletcher's "Labour and Love." The chaplain, she thought, was probably like those doctors one sometimes came across on Mediterranean cruises: not sufficiently competent or energetic to occupy a post where they might be called upon to treat illnesses more complex than mal de mer, enjoying a form of early retirement. She was forced to concede, however that, as he was called upon to preach seven days a week, he must find it quite challenging to come up with something interesting every day; although on the current evidence he was failing to rise to that challenge.

More basket-weaving was followed by an hour's exercise in the yard, where Dorothy found that communication between prisoners was prevented by the stricture that they walk three paces apart. By the time it was over, her stockings had slid down to her ankles. Just before midday, when lunch was to arrive, her weaving instructor returned to her cell and made some very uncomplimentary remarks about the six-inch cylinder she had constructed which, listing heavily to one side, was beginning to resemble the Leaning Tower of Pisa.

"Well," shrugged Dorothy, "you can just withhold my wages."

This earned her a withering look as the wardress pointed a finger and hissed, "Just you mind your words, young lady."

As she completed her meagre lunch, another wardress arrived in her cell and Dorothy lifted her plate.

"No, no, leave that here. You're wanted in the governor's office."

Walking along the gallery and down the stairs at the central concourse, she wondered whether her sarcastic remark to the weaving instructor had earned her some form of punishment, but when she and her escort arrived in the governor's office, he looked up from his desk with a smile on his face.

"Ah, Miss Bridgeman. Do take a seat, although I think this will be a very short interview."

This could mean anything, of course, and so it was a still-cautious Dorothy who eased herself into the chair facing the governor. He, luxuriously moustachioed, clasped his hands before him and beamed at her. "Tell me, Miss Bridgeman, before we get down to business, how have you found our little hostelry since your arrival yesterday." He displayed his palms. "Please feel free to be as frank as you wish."

Dorothy's lips twitched with the beginnings of a smile. "Well, since you ask, I am reminded of the occasion when my father booked our family into a holiday hotel, sight unseen, only to find upon our arrival that it fell considerably short of his expectations."

The governor blinked and pursed his lips as he considered this, then burst into laughter which may or may not have been genuine, displaying a mouthful of strong if somewhat tobacco-stained teeth. "Oh," he boomed, "that's very good, Miss Bridgeman, very humorous." He looked across at the wardress who, not having been invited to sit, stood just inside the door. "Don't you think that was terribly amusing, Parker?"

"I daresay, sir," came the sullen response.

"Oh," continued the governor, looking across the desk at Dorothy, "in one way it's a pity we have to lose you, Miss Bridgeman. It's rare that we find such wit within these walls."

"You might find it less of a rarity, Governor, if you allowed the prisoners to speak."

The governor's expression now indicated that, had it not been for the news he had yet to impart, this would have been considered a step too far. But he forced himself to relax, and with a shrug said, "Ah! Regulations! One's hands are tied, Miss Bridgeman."

"Would I be correct in assuming, Governor, that the business we are yet to get down to involves my leaving your little hostelry?"

He now sprang it on her. "Yes! Your fine has been paid! You are free!" He raised both arms, fingers extended, in the direction of the door. "Go thy way; and henceforth sin no more!"

Dorothy was momentarily silenced by this news. Mickey! Thank you for disobeying me! "As you might imagine, that it very welcome news," she murmured finally. A mischievous smile now touched her lips. "However, I think you will find that the woman to whom Christ is said to have spoken those words had committed adultery rather than malicious damage, so you might like to leave that kind of thing to the chaplain."

The governor shrugged off any embarrassment he might have felt as he realised that Dorothy had handed him his next line. "Ah! The chaplain! So glad you mention him." Once more, his hands were earnestly clasped before him. "It had been the chaplain's intention to interview you, as is his custom with new arrivals. You are now under no obligation to do so, of course, but I wonder, as it will take a little time for the staff to gather together your belongings, if you would mind giving him a few minutes of your time."

As a free woman, Dorothy now stood. "But what possible purpose would that serve, as I will now longer be, so to speak, a member of his flock?"

"Oh, our chaplain is interested in humanity as a whole rather than merely the small proportion of it that shelters beneath this roof, and he finds your case...interesting."

"Does he now?" Dorothy sniffed and gave him a curt nod. "Very well. Where do I find him?"

The governor peered around Dorothy at the wardress. "Parker? Please convey Miss Bridgeman to the chaplain's office."

As she entered his office, the chaplain rose and beckoned her towards the chair on the opposite side of his desk. After she had seated herself, he spent a few moments contemplating her, fingers laced over his stomach. "The governor tells me," he said finally, "that your fine has been paid and that you are now leaving us, Miss Bridgeman."

"That is correct, and I am therefore somewhat puzzled," she replied with a polite smile, "by your request to interview me."

"Why, I thought I might be of assistance to you, Miss Bridgeman. You are, as one can plainly see, a woman of good family. Of course, we have in the past had a good number of women of your social standing in Holloway, but they have usually been suffragettes. Your own case is quite unique, I think. I just found myself wondering how a woman of your background came to be involved in this recent tram strike, and whether you might need some spiritual advice."

"Oh really." Dorothy had decided to be quite cold with him. "And what, may I ask, do you know of my background?"

"Why, nothing concrete, if you insist on the word 'know,'" he replied, flustered, "but one must assume, from the way you speak and the way you deport yourself..."

"You say you wonder about my involvement in the tram strike, Chaplain, but I rather suspect that you have also made assumptions regarding this. Would that be correct?"

He ran a palm over the surface of his blotter, as if he were stroking a pet, although when his eyes returned to hers all signs of confusion or diffidence were gone and he seemed to have determined on a more direct approach. "You are right. And my assumption is that, having associated with socialists and trade unionists, you have lost your moral bearings. It is my hope that I may assist you in finding them once more."

"So you consider socialists and trade unionists to be immoral?"

"Is it not true that they seek to take what they have not earned from employers, and to take what is not theirs from the more prosperous and enterprising members of society?"

"No, it is not," she said flatly, holding his gaze as she awaited a reaction. "And even if it were true," she continued when no reaction came, "didn't Christ associate with thieves and prostitutes?"

At last, he smiled. "Are you saying that you are engaged in some form of missionary work?"

"Not in the way you would understand it, no."

Apparently at a loss to know which way to proceed, the chaplain tapped thoughtfully on his desk before putting a simple question. "Who would you say, Miss Bridgeman, has had the greatest influence on your thinking in the recent past—let's say the last five years?"

"My political thinking, do you mean?"

"Yes, yes, your political thinking and your outlook on the social questions of the day."

It could only be a matter of time, thought Dorothy, before he began asking her for names and addresses, and the governor's extraordinary behaviour was now explicable: he had been relaxing her, softening her up for the chaplain. "Well, I think I would have to say Marx and Engels, Chaplain."

"No, no, no, I mean among people who are living—English people."

"You are presumably unaware that Marx and Engels spent a good part of their lives in this country."

"Really? No, I was not aware of that. But I was thinking more along the lines, Miss Bridgeman, of George Sanders and Sylvia Pankhurst. I understand that you write for Miss Pankhurst's newspaper."

"Do you, indeed?" Dorothy got to her feet. "Well, it seems that you know rather more about me than you do about Marx and Engels." She leaned across his desk, whispering: "But if you think that I'm going to give you information that would be of use to Special Branch, you're going to be disappointed, you wretched little man." She straightened. "Now, kindly ask the wardress to lead me to my clothes and belongings."

"How long," the chaplain called as she approached the door, "have you known Mr Stanley Ashfield?"

She halted, appalled by the possibility that the authorities had somehow managed to gain knowledge of the hotel room reserved by Albert Stanley over a year earlier. She turned to confront the chaplain. "Who?"

"Ashfield, Stanley Ashfield." Seeing her discomfiture, the chaplain was pleased with himself.

"I know no one of that name," she stated coldly and truthfully.

"Well, he certainly knows you, Miss Bridgeman."

"What can you possibly mean by that?" she demanded.

The chaplain spread his palms. "Mr Ashfield is the gentleman who paid your fine, Miss Bridgeman."

26

Arriving home at almost one o'clock after his Tuesday late turn, Mickey Rice found Dorothy asleep in her usual armchair in the living room; a reading light threw a yellow arc over her and the book which lay open on her lap. He stood for a moment, confused after two days in which he had spent every waking moment, whether at work or at home, worrying about her. And yet here she was, apparently unscathed by her ordeal. He leaned over to kiss her brow and watched as her eyelids fluttered open. Her eyes darted about the room. Then she frowned and looked to her right and upwards and, seeing him looking down at her, smiled in recognition and reached for his arm, pulling him down. He fell to his knees and took her face in both hands, kissing her cheeks, eyes and mouth.

"You gave me a scare, Dorothy."

"I'm sorry, Michael."

"Michael?"

"Yes. Michael."

"But you've still got your clothes on."

"Then take them off."

"All of them?"

"Just as many as necessary, Michael."

"I'll take your knickers down while you take off your blouse."

"Why my blouse, Michael?"

"You know perfectly well why, Dorothea."

*

"I don't want to soil your dress, my love…"

"It's not exactly soil, Michael. On my leg, on my leg, Michael."

*

297

For some minutes, they lay on the floor, Mickey's head resting on Dorothy's breast.

"I must confess to a little disappointment, Michael."

"Oh?" What could this mean?

"You have yet to bite my tits, my sweet."

"Ah." He propped himself on an elbow, took one of her breasts in his hand and bent to it, taking the nipple into his mouth.

"Mmm, that's nice, Michael." She took his hand and placed it between her legs, then gripped his wrist, urging him to insert his fingers in her vagina.

"Do you remember the first time we did this?" she breathed, her eyes closed.

"Of course: at your Clapham flat."

She thrust her vagina onto his fingers. "Do they have a name for this, Michael?"

"I'm not sure...Finger-fucking?"

"Oh, that's lovely: finger-fucking! Do you know, that time in Clapham was the first time I'd been finger-fucked?"

"Why do you think that was?"

She sighed, all the time urging his fingers to greater effort. "I'm not at all sure. Maybe I gave an impression of inviolability in this regard."

He chuckled.

"You find it funny? I've never been this way with anyone before, you know."

"And nor, needless to say, have I, my Dorothea."

She paused, and then looked him in the eye, her face close to his. "Tell me truly, my love. Do you really like all the things we do?"

"You know—or I hope you know—that I love the things we do." He kissed her on the mouth.

"And you're never ashamed? You know, if I ever saw a look of distaste on your face, if you thought I'd gone too far, I would be absolutely devastated, Michael."

"That will never happen, Dorothea. Never." He touched her face. "We're in our own world here, my love, our own world. No one else can come here. It's just us, me and you. You used the word yourself some time ago: *intimacy.*"

"Sexual love, Michael, sexual love." Her smile was radiant. "Oh, please, please, please, Michael, don't let anything—anything!—come between us."

"But there is something between us, sweetheart."

She sat back, alarmed. "What?"

"You've got your hand on it, Dorothea."

She laughed, joyous, then became serious and once more regarded Mickey very closely, seemingly watching his face for the first flicker of dissent. "Alright, Michael, I am now going to make a few outrageous suggestions for this next round." She did so, and was rewarded by a smile that slowly lifted his lips. "Does this meet with your approval?"

Mickey stood up.

"What are you doing, sweetheart?"

"No clothes for this one, Dorothea."

*

After a joint bath, it was 3.30 before they got to bed.

"I suppose," said Dorothy as she laid down, "that my gesture outside the Holloway tram depot was entirely without value."

Mickey laughed.

"Why is it funny?"

"What's funny is *us*," he said. "I imagine that most normal couples have their political discussions in the living room, and then they go to bed, sometimes to make love. We seem to do it the other way around."

She joined in the laughter. "But it *was* an empty gesture, wasn't it?"

"I'm afraid so. On Monday, the executives of both unions recommended that all men above military age go back to work. Our union is paying victimisation pay to those not taken back, while the AAT is paying fuck-all. According to the LCC, staff numbers are down by over 1,300 as a result of the strike. Many of the men are working seven days a week to try and plug the gaps in service and make up for what they lost during the strike."

"Thirteen hundred? My goodness, that's a lot of victimisation pay."

Mickey nodded, impressed that she had seen this implication. "Yes, it is, although the rest of us are putting our hands in our pockets, because it's doubtful whether the union's general fund could manage on its own."

"And how is the AAT behaving?"

"Two-faced. On the one hand, it's sniffing around for the possibility of amalgamation. For some in the leadership of our union, that's attractive because of the strain on our finances. They— people like Tich Smith, I mean—also see it as a way of getting the left off their backs."

"How would that work, Mickey?"

"The AAT outnumbers us, simple as that. In any amalgamation, we'd be fighting for our lives."

"Oh dear. Bad news for people like George, I suppose."

"You can say that again. At the same time, the AAT has written to the LCC to say that they've withdrawn from the joint committee and that from now on they will negotiate on their own."

"Oh my god, that's awful."

He leaned closer to her, nuzzling her cheek. "I'll tell you what's awful, Dorothy: we've been fucking our brains out and now we're discussing union business, and I've not even asked you about your experience in Holloway."

She reached down and gave his soldier, now fallen, a tender squeeze. "A question of priorities, my love."

"Alright, sweetheart," he breathed gently. "What happened outside the tramshed?"

"I simply lost control, Mickey. A little while ago, Sylvia told me how she feels just before she smashes a window. She said that it's as if all the causes we're fighting for, and all the things oppressing us, present themselves to her mind at once and, confronted with a window owned by a bourgeois or the authorities, she becomes possessed by a fury that simply has to be given its head. That was how I felt on Sunday morning, Mickey. I know now and probably knew then that it was a futile gesture, but I just couldn't help myself."

"But if there had been a more productive outlet for your aggression..."

"Yes, then it probably wouldn't have happened. Yes, you're right! My action was an indication of frustration, of powerlessness." She drummed her fingers on his stomach. "I must make this point to Sylvia."

"And Holloway Prison?"

"Mickey, if anyone tells you that a custodial sentence gives one the opportunity to conduct political work with the other prisoners, please tell them that they're talking rot, absolute rot." She sighed. "Well, that kind of activity might be possible in some prisons, but I can tell you that it is quite *im*possible in Holloway. They don't allow you the opportunity to even *talk* to the other prisoners, let alone anything else. Anyway, I could see within my first day that my time there was going to be wasted. It became very clear to me that if I am to make a contribution to the movement, I must be free, and so I immediately regretted my rash decision not to pay the fine..."

"And so you paid it."

"No!" She sat up, agitated. "You will never guess what happened, Mickey! After I had been told that I was to be released, I was encouraged to see the prison chaplain. He just wanted to pick my brains so that he could pad out his report to Special Branch, I suppose. Anyway, he told me that my fine had been paid by a gentleman called Stanley Ashfield..."

Mickey frowned. "Stanley Ashfield?"

"Yes, don't you remember? I told you that this was the name Mr Stanley used when he booked that hotel room."

"Stanley!" Mickey laughed. "My, he's a persistent bugger, isn't he?"

"Well, it's entirely possible that, having read the report in *The Times*, he simply paid it because he wanted to help."

"It was in *The Times*? Dorothy, how will I ever show my face in Reading again? They all read *The Times* down Tidmarsh Street!"

"Seriously, Mickey, he was probably just being kind."

He looked at her questioningly. "Do you think he's really capable of that sort of gesture?"

Dorothy thought for a second and nodded. "Yes, I think he probably is. I'll drop him a note, returning the money and thanking him."

"He's not going to be happy with that, is he?"

"What do you mean?"

"Writing to him at Electric Railway House for all to see."

"Oh, I'll mark it 'Private and Confidential.'"

He patted her leg. "Leave it to me, sweetheart."

*

It was a week later when, having signed on for a middle turn, Mickey asked the garage inspector whether James Shilling was in his office.

"He is, young Mickey," chirped Sid Phillips. "You want a word?"

"If he can spare a few minutes, Sid." In the past eighteen months, the atmosphere between the garage officials and the union branch officers had relaxed to the point where first names were the rule, although there were some exceptions: Mickey didn't know anyone who referred to Mr Butcher by his first name—if they knew what it was—and as a matter of principle he never referred to Mr Shilling as Jim for, likeable man though he was, he was the local boss, and Mickey felt that a certain distance must be maintained.

"Mickey!" James Shilling beamed up at him as, having knocked, he put his head around the door. "Come in, come in. What can I do for you?"

"I understand you're expecting a visitor in an hour or so, Mr Shilling."

"You mean Sir Albert? Yes, he'll be here in a bit. He's on one of his periodical tours of the garages."

"How long do you expect him to be here?"

"Why, do want to meet him?" James Shilling frowned. "You really should leave this sort of thing to your leaders, you know. Don't want to get into trouble with Gerrard Street, do you?"

Mickey laughed and almost called him Jim. "No, it's nothing like that, and it will only take a minute."

"What are you on today, Mickey?"

"Just signed on for a middle."

"Anyone on stand-by in the output?"

"One or two, I think."

James Shilling held up a finger. "Give me a minute."

The garage superintendent pushed back his chair and walked to the door leading to the allocation office, where he called over Sid Phillips and conversed briefly with him. Then he was back at his desk, grinning across at Mickey.

"Your first half is covered, Mickey, so you can relax. Sir Albert will be here at around ten, and I expect he'll want a word or two with me, then we'll call you in. In the meantime, you can get yourself a tea in the catering vehicle. Oh, and don't let on that we've covered half your duty, because that will probably be money out of the company's pocket, what with the staff shortage."

"Oh, now look, I wasn't looking for favours, Mr Shilling..."

"I know you weren't, Mickey, but it's just occurred to me that Sir Albert would probably like to meet you anyway. In fact, I should have thought of it meself."

"Why would he want to meet me?" asked Mickey with a frown.

"Because he's heard a lot about you. You know, during the time when we had that business with the long spreadover on route 7..."

"Oh, I see... But I'll make up the lost mileage if there's anything going..."

James Shilling leaned back in his chair and shook his head as he scrutinised Mickey. "Mickey Rice, will you please learn to relax. I've stood you down so you can meet the managing director, so just accept that."

Mickey grinned. "Oh, so it's rostered earnings for my lost first half, then."

"Of course it is." He waved an arm. "Now go and get a cup of tea."

"Oh, and another thing," James Shilling called as Mickey reached the door. "Don't let him hear you call me Jim."

Mickey frowned.

"It's a joke, Mickey, a joke."

*

The catering vehicle contained four small tables, each of which could, at a squeeze, accommodate four people. Mickey chose one of those furthest from the counter and sat there, sipping his watery tea until he saw the black Daimler Cranmore Landaulette roll almost silently into the garage. It stopped outside the garage superintendent's office, where the chauffeur alighted and opened the rear door of the car.

"That'd set you back a few bob," observed the operator of the catering vehicle, peering out of the grimy window above his stove.

"About a thousand quid, I reckon, Tommy."

"Mm. Must be one of the nobs."

"Not just *one* of 'em, Tommy. That is *the* nob, Sir Albert Stanley."

Mickey watched through his own window as Stanley emerged from the passenger door. The tall, grey-haired man wore a charcoal lounge suit, collar and tie—no cravat or diamond pin today—and carried a folded copy of *The Times* with his black leather document case. He cast an eye around the almost deserted garage, frowned at the catering vehicle and, issuing a brief instruction to the chauffeur, walked around the Daimler and rapped on the garage superintendent's door. The chauffeur got behind the wheel and drove further into the garage, where he executed a U-turn and parked facing the exit. He left the Daimler and walked towards the catering vehicle. Two bus mechanics, hands in pockets, sauntered over to the executive car and began to slowly circle it, nodding at one feature or another and making appreciative noises.

The chauffeur, a man in his late forties, placed a penny on the counter and asked Tommy for a tea. As the tea was being poured, he looked down the vehicle and, seeing Mickey, winked. He brought his tea to the table in front of Mickey's and sat facing him, removing his cap and placing it on the table, next to the window. His dark hair was turning grey.

Mickey let ten minutes pass before he decided to be friendly. "Looks like a sweet job," he said.

The chauffeur nodded. "Can't complain," he said. "A few late nights, though."

303

"What's he like to work for?"

"Who?"

"Albert Stanley."

The chauffeur, having tested Mickey's knowledge, grinned. "I've known worse."

"How many chauffeurs do they have at Electric Railway House?"

"There's five of us. Got our own little garage around the corner."

"You all in the union?"

The man chuckled and shook his head. "You're a boy, you are. Why do you ask that?"

"I'm the union rep here." Mickey stood up and crossed the short distance between them, extending his right hand. "Mickey Rice."

"Ah, I see." The chauffeur looked at Mickey with renewed interest. "Well, Mickey, what would you say if I told you we're *not* in the union?"

"I'd give you some forms and ask you to join."

The chauffeur laughed and took Mickey's hand. "Alf Gordon. You needn't bother, son, because we're all members. George Sanders dropped by late last year and recruited us. I've known George for years. Used to be a cabdriver."

"Why'd you give it up?"

"I was working for a garage. When the government took over a lot of cabs and sent 'em to France, I was only able to get work three or four days a week. Then there was the darkened streets, of course. So when a mate told me this job was goin', I applied and got it." He winked at Mickey. "Best thing I ever did."

"Mickey!"

Mickey turned and saw that Sid Phillips had poked his head into the doorway of the catering vehicle. Mickey offered his hand to the chauffeur once more. "Have to go now, Alf. Nice meeting you."

"Off to work, Mickey?"

"No, mate, I've got an audience."

*

"Ah, Mr Rice, we meet at last!" Albert Stanley, who had been sitting at the left corner of the visitor's side of James Shilling's desk, got to his feet and shook Mickey by the hand, waving him into the chair at the right corner. "Encountered any economists lately?"

All three laughed together.

"Not lately, Sir Albert."

A mildly awkward silence, during which the bus driver and the

304

business leader sized each other up, was broken by James Shilling. "Sir Albert has been asking me about staff morale," he said to Mickey. "I'm sure he would be interested in your view on that question."

Mickey raised his eyebrows at Stanley, seeking confirmation. "Yes," Stanley nodded, "I certainly would, Mr Rice."

Mickey uttered a long sigh and offered up his hands, palms upward. "But what purpose would that serve, Sir Albert? I can't tell you anything you don't already know. You must have heard the same song in garage after garage."

Stanley's face was imperturbable. "Tell me anyway, Mr Rice."

"Alright. To be honest, the general level of morale is not as low as it might be. But that's because we've tried to give the men a degree of political understanding. Now you won't agree with our way of viewing the current situation—the problems caused by the war, the problems that caused the war itself—but you should know that it is this understanding that gives them hope.

"What understanding?"

"The understanding that while men must suffer the defects of the society in which they live for the time being, there will come a time when they will have the opportunity to change that society for something better. If they didn't have that hope, they would sink into despair, and then you would see how low morale *can* sink."

"And what are these problems you talk about?"

"You know, Sir Albert, you know: the length of time on duty, the length of the spreadovers, the inadequate rest breaks, etc. And all of this has been made worse by the war—the fact that so many have enlisted in the Army, the fact that there are gaps in service because so many buses have been sent to France, and the fact that at the same time passenger-numbers are increasing month by month."

"I recognise that all those problems exist, Mr Rice, but if they are as onerous as you suggest, how do you explain the fact that the level of absenteeism at Middle Row is comparatively moderate—Mr Shilling has just shown me the figures, and I must confess that I was surprised."

Mickey smiled. "Did you ask Mr Shilling to break down those figures for you?"

"In what way, Mr Rice? You mean by route, by length of duty? Are you suggesting that absenteeism is partly determined by the same factors that, as you argued some time ago, contribute to accidents?"

"That might be an interesting exercise, Sir Albert, but I was thinking more of marital status." He gestured to James Shilling with his left hand, inviting him to contribute to the discussion.

"Yes, go ahead, Mr Shilling." Seeing that Shilling was not entirely comfortable with Mickey in the role of chairman of the discussion, Stanley felt it necessary to offer him encouragement.

Shilling nodded. "It's true, there's a fairly clear picture, Sir Albert: absenteeism is much higher among the single men."

"And why would that be?"

Shilling nodded in Mickey's direction. "Mr Rice has a theory."

"It's common sense: with prices as they are, a married man, especially if he has children, can't afford to be absent, even if he's dead on his feet. So, the war again."

"Talking of which, Mr Rice," said Stanley, placing a finger on his chin, "if conscription is introduced and the government fails to designate bus driving as a reserved occupation, will you go?"

"I will not."

Stanley turned to Shilling. "No hesitation there. Why not, Mr Rice?"

"Because it's a war between empires. I will not kill German workers in order to preserve the British Empire, or to help Britain get a piece of the German, Austro-Hungarian or Turkish empires."

"But would you agree that there is such a thing as a just war? For example, I served in the US Navy during the Spanish-American War. We helped to free Cuba from Spanish rule."

"I'm sure the Cuban people would have managed to do that on their own eventually. You surely don't claim that Cuba is free today, Sir Albert? To say nothing of the Philippines, of course, which is now an American colony."

"I think, gentlemen," interjected James Shilling, who had been looking increasingly concerned, "that this discussion is in danger of getting out of hand."

Albert Stanley smiled. "No, it's perfectly fine, Mr Shilling. Discussions only run out of control when one or other of the parties is unable to defend their position knowledgably and logically. So far, Mr Rice has demonstrated both knowledge and logic, even though I might disagree with his conclusions." The smiled was turned to Mickey. "I happen to believe in this war, Mr Rice."

"Oh, I'm sure you do, Sir Albert. So apparently, does the London County Council."

"Do you refer to the recent tram strike, Mr Rice?"

"I do, Sir Albert."

Sir Albert managed to look appalled. "I can assure you, Mr Rice, that I would not have dealt with that dispute in such a manner, no matter how strong my support for the war."

"Then will you permit me to ask an outrageous question?"

Stanley's glance slid to James Shilling, as if he were thinking that the garage superintendent might have an inkling of what was coming. "I'm not sure that I can stop you, Mr Rice."

"I made the acquaintance of your chauffeur outside on the catering vehicle, Sir Albert."

"Ah yes, Gordon. A good man. But go ahead and ask your question."

"Would you have employed him if he had been of military age?"

"Now this has gone far enough!" cried an alarmed James Shilling.

"Calm down, Mr Shilling, calm down," Stanley insisted. "Don't deny me the only opportunity I've so far had to score a point in this debate. Nice try, Mr Rice, but you've missed the target this time." He smiled at Mickey. "Mr Gordon's age *was* a consideration when I took him on, but not quite for the reason you assume. It was not that I wanted to push applicants of military age towards the nearest recruitment office, but because I didn't want a situation where I would have a driver for a year or so, then lose him when conscription came along. Far better, I thought, to hire a man in his late forties or early fifties and be fairly confident that he would be with me permanently." He thrust out his hand towards Mickey. "Do I win this one?"

"You do," Mickey conceded with a smile, shaking his hand.

Stanley sprang to his feet. "Now, I'd best be off to Shepherd's Bush. Oh, wait!" He paused and put a finger to his lips. "Didn't you tell me, Mr Shilling, that Mr Rice wanted a quiet word?"

Shilling rose to his feet. "Yes, Sir Albert, let me get out of your way."

"No, no, we don't want to deprive Mr Shilling of his office, do we, Mr Rice? Surely we can get a cup of tea on the refreshment bus..."

Mickey shook his head doubtfully. "Ahhh, not to be recommended, I'm afraid."

Stanley shrugged and fell back into his chair. "Oh, well, thank you, Mr Shilling, I'm sure we won't be long."

As Shilling closed the door, Mickey took an envelope from his inside pocket and passed it to Stanley. "Thank you, Mr Ashfield. That was a very thoughtful gesture, and we appreciate it."

Stanley narrowed his eyes. "Ashfield? Ashfield?" Then realisation dawned and he pointed to the envelope. "Oh, the fine. But look, I never meant for you to repay it..."

"But we have to, Sir Albert, and I'm sure you know why." He looked Stanley in the eye as he said this but, to save his employer further embarrassment, quickly passed on. "Besides, it wasn't that we couldn't afford to pay it: Dorothy had *refused* to pay it."

"Oh, I see." He chuckled and shook his head. "Emily—I mean Dorothy, of course. What a character! Tell me, Mr Rice, is she in employment at the moment?"

"She's been working with Sylvia Pankhurst in the East End for the past year. I don't know if that will last much longer, though."

"Well look,"—Stanley reached out to pat Mickey's arm—"if she's ever in need of a reference, she only has to let me know."

"Thank you, Sir Albert. I'll tell her that."

They both stood, and Stanley regarded Mickey soberly. "I'd better get a move on. I daresay we'll soon be meeting across the negotiating table."

Mickey smiled and shook his head. "I don't know. I'm making no plans in that direction for the time being."

"Can't say I'd look forward to that anyway," Stanley said with a wry grin. "Oh, and by the way—I think there's almost no chance of you going to prison for your beliefs."

"Prison?"

"Yes, with conscription." He patted Mickey's arm again as they walked towards the door. "I have it on pretty good authority that bus drivers will be exempt. Not so sure about conductors, though."

"Well, that's nice to know, although it hasn't even been decided to introduce conscription yet."

"True, and the Cabinet's not of one mind on the matter. Sir John Simon, for example, is dead against it. He was against the war, originally, and had to have his arm twisted to take the Home Secretary position."

As Stanley opened the office door, he was presented with the sight of the chauffeur standing at the passenger door of the Daimler, hand on the handle.

"Good man, Gordon! How was the tea?"

"Honestly?"

"Of course!"

"Bloody 'orrible, sir."

27

When she returned to the East End, Dorothy was greeted with laughter and playful applause.

"You missed a wonderful Women's May Day," Sylvia told her, "but I daresay your experience was more of an education."

Dorothy took this in her stride. "As a matter of fact, it was, Sylvia. *Very* educational."

"Oh?" Sylvia folded her arms as she awaited the rest of Dorothy's rejoinder.

"I learned, for example, that incarceration is a *complete* waste of time."

"I would say that it depends on the issue."

"I am far from convinced that is the case, Sylvia."

Looking challenged, Sylvia faltered and glanced about the room, where Norah Smyth and Molly Elkins sat, waiting to greet Dorothy. "Well," she said, "let's not spoil your homecoming by bickering. Shall we postpone this discussion while we have a cup of tea?"

Dorothy managed a winning smile. "That sounds lovely," she said, while noting that Norah and Molly exchanged knowing glances.

The discussion did not take place at that time, and a summer of activity was soon underway, with a march to the House of Commons on 12 July demanding equal pay, an end to sweating, and votes for women. Similar demands were in evidence the following month, when the federation held a joint demonstration with the United Suffragists, the Herald League, the British Socialist Party, several Independent Labour Party branches, the Amalgamated Society of Engineers, the National Union of Railwaymen and the Electrical Trades Union.

The same organisations came together for a mass rally in Trafalgar Square, on 26 September, a day when tragedy struck. Dorothy and Mickey stood at the front of the crowd, just beneath the plinth, when they saw an agitated George Lansbury touch Sylvia's shoulder and point across the square. They watched as Sylvia followed Lansbury's gaze, leaned forward to squint at the object, and then brought her hands to her face as a wail of grief escaped her. Heads in the crowd turned in vain towards the west side of the square, but the thing must have been at street level, and was therefore obscured from view; the rallyists on that side of the square were able to see it, of course, and as word passed through the crowd one head after another turned from the west to the south, reminding Dorothy of how, as a child, her brother would stand each tile in a set of dominoes on its side and, having spaced them evenly, set off a chain reaction by tapping over the tile at the end of the chain so that it fell against its neighbour. Instead of waiting for the news to arrive, Mickey dashed to the steps at the foot of the plinth and looked out over the crowd until he spotted a boy bearing a placard for one of the evening newspapers—it looked like the *Globe* from this distance—and could read its message:

KEIR HARDIE DEAD

*

For some weeks after Hardie's death, Sylvia appeared disoriented and prey to self-doubt, wondering to Dorothy whether she should devote all of her efforts to the anti-war struggle, as had Hardie.

Dorothy proceeded carefully. "Well, yes, you might," she said, "although you would risk a falling off of support for the federation—something you have been anxious to avoid."

Sylvia nodded; she looked haggard, and there were dark rings under her eyes. "That's perfectly true, but I sometimes ask myself whether there is much point in keeping the organisation together if we are not going to take on the really major issues."

"But surely women's suffrage *is* a major issue."

"Yes, but if we win it—*when* we win it—we will simply be voters in a bourgeois economic and political system, the same system that has caused this war."

"That's true, but I've thought for some time that it is possible to look upon some of the activities of the federation—even the relief activities—in a completely different way. It's not just that the federation is *providing* services that should really be the responsibility of the state or the local council; it is showing working-class women—and, increasingly, men—that they are capable of organising these things themselves; and if they are able to do this at the local level, should we not be encouraging them to believe that they might one day be able to do it at a more ambitious level?"

"At the level of the whole society, you mean?"

"Of course. Isn't that what we all want to see eventually?"

"Mm. Yes, I suppose so. But how do you suggest that we educate the members as to their historic mission?" There was the faintest note of sarcasm here.

"By precisely that: education. It's surely not beyond our wit to organise a few education classes."

"And who would be their tutor—you?"

"No, I'm not suggesting that at all; we could bring in speakers from the socialist movement." Sylvia, it seemed, was beginning to view her as a possible threat to her leadership—intellectual rather than organisational—of the federation.

"Do you mean from your BSP?"

Oh, and a political threat. "Not necessarily. But if the aim was to school our members in socialism, surely someone from the BSP would be ideally suited to do it."

"But you know that I have reservations about the BSP."

"Regarding the position of some of its leaders on the question of women's suffrage, yes."

"And on the war, Dorothy."

Dorothy forced herself to smile. "But those leaders are becoming increasingly isolated within the party, Sylvia. As you know, we have worked with the BSP in several of our recent activities—the joint demonstration in August, the Trafalgar Square rally on 26 September..."

"Yes, on specific issues..."

"And I think we will see some changes at the BSP national conference next year."

For the first time, Sylvia smiled. "Well," she said, "we'll wait until then, shall we?"

And that was that.

More than ever disenchanted with relief work, and still keen to move the federation closer to the arena of class struggle, Dorothy took the opportunity of Sylvia's frequent absences to canvass the activists and committee members regarding issues that might be successfully adopted.

"Funny you should ask me that," said Clara Turner, "because I've been thinking it's about time we got involved in the rent strikes. Last year, almost as soon as the first shot 'ad been fired, the landlords were puttin' up the rents. You may remember that Shoreditch Trades Council organised public meetings calling for rents to be suspended until the end of the war; they even organised volunteers to keep the bailiffs at bay if they tried to evict anyone." She chuckled. "The landlords went to the Police Commissioner an' asked 'im to step in. It wasn't just in the East, either, 'cause over in 'Ammersmith they was 'avin' trouble collectin' the rents. And in Camberwell, even the Labour Party was callin' on tenants to refuse to pay big increases."

Perfect! "And this year, the strikes are popping up all over the country," said Dorothy, finding Clara's enthusiasm contagious. "Burton-on-Trent and Luton, several of the mining areas, and Edinburgh. Birmingham looks set for a big one, too."

"You don't have to look that far abroad," said Daisy Parsons, who had just entered the office. "There are strikes down the road in Poplar, in Dulwich, Edmonton—there are three strikes there, in fact—and Tooting."

The following morning, having done some research the previous evening by discussing the matter with Sanders, Mickey and Eric

311

after a BSP meeting, Dorothy arrived at the ELFS headquarters eager to continue the discussion. It was, however, mid-morning before Daisy Parsons and Clara Turner arrived, followed by George Lansbury's daughter Annie.

"Yesterday, Annie," said Dorothy over a cup of tea, "we were discussing the possibility of organising a rent strike in the area."

"There already is one in Poplar," said Annie.

"Yes, I know, but one would have thought that there would be far more in the East End. And do you know: I think this struggle will be fairly easily won."

"Why do you say that, Dorothy?" asked Daisy Parsons.

"You would be surprised by how many of the rent strikes around the country are in areas where there are munitions factories, Daisy. In many places, the strikes are led by women—that's understandable, given the fact that their men are away in France—but the trade unions also play a very important part, assembling outside houses where the courts have ordered evictions to chase off the bailiffs."

"You see," Clara interjected, "that's what they were talking about in Shoreditch, like I told you yesterday."

"You did, indeed, Clara. However, the big difference in the munitions-factory areas is that the employers are supportive of the strikes!"

"Well, I'll go to the foot of our stairs!" exclaimed Daisy.

Clara and Annie chuckled at this, while Dorothy frowned. "I beg your pardon, Daisy?"

"Oh, it's something that Sylvia says now and again. It's a Northern saying. Sort of like 'You could knock me down with a feather.'"

"Oh, I see. But when you understand the employers' motives, it isn't really surprising. The munitions factories are desperate for labour, but they can't get enough because there's a shortage of cheap rented accommodation. That's one reason. Another is that if the rents of their workers are increased, what is the next thing those workers will be asking for?"

"Ahhh, a wage increase!" replied Daisy. "Oh, it all makes sense now, Dorothy."

"It does, doesn't it? I think, therefore, that with the munitions employers on the strikers' side, the government will be bound to listen and act. As I say, the struggle should be fairly easily won, but with an extra push from our federation, it will probably come even sooner."

"Well, Dorothy, I don't think we'd have a problem with mobilising for a rent strike in the East End, and the idea certainly appeals to me. But this will have to go before the committee, of course. Which is why we're here today."

"But surely the committee won't meet without Sylvia," said Dorothy.

"Well, in theory it could, I suppose," said Daisy, "but it won't have to, because she intends to be here."

"If that's me you're talking about," came a voice, "she *is* here."

They heard the front door close and Sylvia walked into the office, looking somewhat refreshed and most definitely alert.

"And what is it that the committee is to discuss?" she asked Daisy.

"An idea that we've been talking about with Dorothy, Sylvia: we're suggesting that we organise a rent strike in the East End."

Sylvia's gaze passed from Daisy to Dorothy. "And have they convinced you that this would be a viable proposition, Dorothy? But perhaps it was your idea in the first place." Her manner was studiedly cool, but it was obvious that she resented the notion that policy might be discussed without her presence.

"As I seem to recall," said Clara, "it was my idea. To be honest, Sylvia, I think we missed the boat last year, when Shoreditch Trades Council was holding public meetings on the matter."

"A pity you didn't speak up at the time, then, isn't it, Clara?" Sylvia snapped. "Because you're perfectly right: we *have* missed the boat."

"How can that be, Sylvia?" Dorothy asked, making a great effort to remain calm. "I was just saying that the balance of forces would seem to favour an early victory, but it might be going a little far to suggest that we've missed our opportunity."

Sylvia looked at Dorothy with ill-disguised suspicion. "Might it, indeed? Well, that is *my* view, and it is, I believe, well-founded." She looked around at the four women. "Has Clydeside been mentioned in your discussion at all? No, I thought not. There are currently almost 20,000 tenants on rent strike on Clydeside, dwarfing anything that has been achieved elsewhere in the country—and certainly anything we could manage here. Moreover, the workers in the munitions factories and the shipyards have threatened industrial action, prompting the Secretary of State for Scotland to appoint a committee which will report next week. I have it on *very* good authority that legislation will be introduced before the end of the year. *That,* I believe, means that we *have* missed this particular boat, and that any efforts we might make at this late stage would correctly be seen"—her gaze passed to Dorothy as she said this—"as opportunism. So if you wish to be involved in the rent strikes, you will have to do it with a new secretary. Or with another organisation."

Dorothy was struck by the uncanny similarity that these words bore to those which had been hurled at Sylvia by her mother and sister on the occasion of her expulsion from the WPSU.

"As regards *this* organisation," Sylvia continued, "I believe it *is* time for a new departure, and that we should broaden our demand for women's suffrage into one for *universal* suffrage, thereby drawing men more fully into the federation and its activities. This, of course, will mean that the federation will need to undergo another name-change, as will the *Dreadnought*." She smiled at last, although with little warmth. "Although, of course, this will be for the committee to decide, after a thorough discussion."

It turned out that Sylvia was correct. A parliamentary bill would be introduced in late November and in December the Increase of Rent and Mortgage Interest Act would come into effect, winding back the rents of working-class accommodation to what they had been in August, 1914. Needless to say, Eric Rice and Ben Smith would be among the celebrants.

But the fact that Sylvia might have been right was not so important. More important was that George Sanders had also been right: there was in Sylvia Pankhurst's makeup, possibly due to her class background, possibly as a result of her experience with her mother and older sister, something that made it difficult, if not impossible, for her to yield more than the tiniest portion of control or to accommodate an opinion which conflicted with her own. It was time, Dorothy realised, to leave the East End; better to leave now rather than wait until a major crisis sundered their relationship permanently.

I-will-not-lose-my-temper-I-will-not-lose-my-temper-I-will-not-lose-my-temper. This, on the day after Sylvia's dismissal of the rent-strike proposal, was what Dorothy told herself as she halted at Sylvia's desk and sat down.

"Dorothy." Sylvia looked up from her typewriter with the faintest of smiles. "Tell me what is on your mind, dear." As if she didn't know. As if she had not brought about this moment.

"I feel I must resign from the federation, Sylvia." Afterwards, she would ponder this choice of words. Had she been keen to avoid confrontation, wouldn't she have simply said that she was leaving the East End, implying that an opportunity elsewhere had opened up? Instead, not only was she resigning from the federation, but she felt she *must* do so. What was this if not an invitation to argument? She had, in fact, mentally prepared for both forms of dialogue, and later suspected that she had been provoked along the confrontational path by Sylvia's pretence of innocence.

"Well, I'm sure we'll be sorry to lose you, Dorothy. You have been a great help over the past fifteen-and-a-half months." No attempt at dissuasion. Indeed, she must have prepared for this exchange, for how else would she be able to mention the precise duration of Dorothy's employment without a moment's pause for calculation?

What this form of response aspired to achieve, of course, was to close the door to further discussion. However, in conveying the impression that Sylvia found this resignation perfectly understandable, given that Dorothy had in some way transgressed, thereby igniting the latter's anger, that door was forced open.

"I daresay, Sylvia," said Dorothy, looking her employer in the eye, "that I would have been of even greater assistance if you had learned to trust me. Indeed, the same could be said of your other paid organisers and voluntary activists."

Sylvia's expression was now stern. "What*ever* can you mean, Dorothy? The federation functions on the *basis* of mutual trust and comradeship."

"No, it doesn't, Sylvia. It functions on the basis of your leadership and the admiration felt by the membership for your undoubted courage and energy. But you seem to feel that your leadership must be demonstrated and protected on all occasions and at all costs. This may have been necessary in the early stages of the federation, in order to bind it together, but the organisation is becoming broader and more mature; people are beginning to think for themselves and may not be content to submit to such unyielding control in the future. If you insist of stifling all initiative, the federation will become sterile and incapable of further development. Are you unable to see that?" Dorothy was by now leaning forward, imploring rather than hectoring, her anger seemingly under control.

"Is this all because I rejected your proposal—because I'm quite certain that it *was* yours—for involvement in the rent strikes?"

Dorothy's eyes flared. "It was *not* my idea originally! Did you not hear Clara tell you that she was the one who came forward with it? Do you really believe that Clara would risk your disfavour by protecting me with a lie? And no, Sylvia, it is not *just* that you rejected the idea; your whole manner seemed to suggest that discussion of a proposal before it had been placed before you amounted to mutiny. However, you did make one very pertinent point when you told Clara that she should have raised the matter last year. Why didn't she? *Presumably because she could not be confident that it would find favour with you!* People love and admire you, Sylvia, but they also fear you! Don't you realise that you run the risks of repeating the errors of your mother and Christabel?"

At this, Sylvia got to her feet, fists clenched at her sides, large lower lip trembling. "How *dare* you bring my family into this? How *dare* you suggest that I rule by fear! I know you now for what you are, Dorothy Bridgeman: a woman who has sneaked into our federation with the intention of spreading the doctrines of the British Socialist Party and, for all I know, of recruiting our members into its ranks!"

Despite herself, Dorothy threw back her head and laughed, amazed that Sylvia Pankhurst should resort to such a shallow line of argument.

"Oh," said Sylvia, looking about her as if to locate the cause of this outburst, "have I said something humorous?"

"No, Sylvia, you have said something ridiculous: as far as I know, you have no political disagreement with the healthy forces in our party, and so why would you be concerned if I *were* intent on disseminating the doctrines of the party? It's not our party's doctrines that you wish to avoid, Sylvia, but its discipline!"

Sylvia sank to her seat. "I think you had better leave now, Dorothy."

"I think so too, Sylvia, but before I do, please allow me to leave you this final thought. Do you not see that there is a contradiction in your position? You campaign for the vote for all women, but when it comes to working-class women it seems that you are not prepared to allow them to think or act for themselves. I strongly suspect that this will also be the stance of the authorities once the vote—for working-class men as well as women—is conceded. Do you really believe that such a form of democracy will be much superior to the one we have now?"

Sylvia stood once more, her face stamped with anger and frustration. "*Out!*"

And that was that.

28

Over the months, the Alexander Street flat had become Mickey's castle, his university, and his home—the only one he had truly known. If, however, it was his castle, he was its prince, not yet its king, as he still had much to learn. Some lessons he took from the world outside, and in particular from his life in the union and the British Socialist Party, and others he received from Dorothy, who introduced him to Shakespeare and classical music.

He made a false start with Shakespeare, for as his introduction Dorothy took him to a performance of *The Taming of the Shrew* at the Old Vic thinking, as much as she disagreed with the sexual politics of the play, that, being a simple tale, Mickey would find it accessible. And, when it came to the plot, he did, but being unfamiliar with the Elizabethan language he realised that he was missing more than he grasped.

As they left the theatre, Dorothy, seeing that he was thoughtful and perhaps a little disappointed, ventured a cautious, "Will you come again, Mickey?"

He shook his head. "I don't think so. That is to say, not soon; I'm not ready for it, Dorothy, because as I was trying to understand one line, along would come another just as complicated, and so in the end I gave up trying to follow exactly what they were saying. I got the gist of it, but a lot of it was lost to me."

She placed a hand on his arm. "Oh, Mickey, I *am* sorry. I so hoped that you would enjoy it."

"I did, sweetheart, I did, but I need some preparation. I need to sit down and read the plays, to have a play in front of me so that I can take my time with the language until I've cracked it and *then* watch it on the stage. I suppose I'm a bit on the slow side. Sorry, Dorothy."

She laughed. "If there's one thing you are not it is slow, Mickey. I'm the one who should be apologising. I should have known that the language would be a problem." She smiled. "Well, I have the plays at home, you know."

He nodded. "Yes, good." He glanced at her. "Maybe you can help me."

Again that smile. "If you need helping, Mickey."

As they walked towards Waterloo Bridge, they could not fail to notice the large numbers of prostitutes either pacing the street or, standing stationary at wall or lamppost, awaiting the passing of a potential customer. This came as no surprise to either Dorothy or Mickey, given the area's notoriety, but there was also other women, in uniform, walking the street in pairs and sometimes stopping to harangue a lone woman or, less frequently, a couple.

"Who are these women?" asked Mickey.

"The prostitutes?"

"Nooo, the ones in uniform." He turned to Dorothy and shook his head in mock disbelief. "The prostitutes!"

317

Dorothy, who had been joking, grinned and nudged him with her elbow. "They, Mickey, are the morals police. They patrol the streets to ensure that servicemen on leave do not contract venereal disease and that the wives and widows of servicemen do not lead loose lives, thereby jeopardising their allowances and pensions. Just recently, we had a discussion of the matter in the federation."

"And this is official?"

"The women are all volunteers, but two of their organisations—the National Union of Women Workers and the Women's Police Service—operate with the consent of the authorities; the Women's Police Volunteers, on the other hand, makes a nuisance of itself without official sanction. But you'll be able to make your own enquiries if you're really interested: we're about to be intercepted."

Having crossed the road, two uniformed women, one middle-aged and of substantial build, the other younger, thin and hawkish-looking, stepped into their path. "May we have a moment, sir, madam?" requested the older woman in a tone suggesting that a negative reply was not a realistic option.

"No, you may not!" snapped Dorothy. "Now kindly step out of our way."

The younger woman looked from one to the other of them with narrowed eyes, perhaps noting their age-difference. "What is your relation to this lady, sir?" It was a demand rather than a mere question.

"Very satisfactory, thank you," Mickey replied. "And what is yours to this lady?"

A laugh escaped Dorothy, momentarily ending her planned display of outraged indignation.

Their two interrogators showed no sign of detecting the humour in Mickey's response, the older one extending a hand to him and demanding, "Papers."

Outrage and indignation now returned to Dorothy as she drew herself up and in her most authoritative ruling-class accent, demanded, "Put down that hand, you impertinent creature, and step out of our way. How *dare* you harass respectable, law-abiding people in such a manner! Is *this* how you pretend to be protecting our freedoms? Move, I say. *Now!*"

They moved, and Dorothy and Mickey walked on. "Don't look back," Dorothy advised as they passed beyond earshot of the moral enforcers, "and don't hurry."

"Did you read Jack London's *The Iron Heel*?" asked Mickey.

"Yes, of course. Somewhat crude, I thought. I mean, imagine naming your hero Ernest Everhard!"

"Well, maybe, but if you put all the pieces together, doesn't it seem to you that the kind of dictatorship he foresaw in America is on its way in this country? I mean, those women back there; under the Munitions of War Act, a worker can't leave his job unless his boss is prepared to give him a leaving certificate; if your timekeeping is bad, they can drag you before a munitions tribunal; unskilled workers can be drafted into the jobs of the skilled; strikes are banned. And, of course, soon they'll be using conscription to force men to go and fight the bosses' war for them. Doesn't that sound like the iron heel to you?"

*

Mickey persisted with Shakespeare and was soon rewarded. The first thing that struck him was how much Shakespeare he, albeit unwittingly, already knew:

"All the world's a stage..."

"If music be the food of love..."

"The course of true love never did run smooth."

"The empty vessel makes the loudest sound."

"Parting is such sweet sorrow..."

"What's in a name? That which we call a rose by any other name would smell as sweet."

"There is a tide in the affairs of men, which taken at the flood, leads on to fortune."

"This above all; to thine own self be true."

These and so many other lines and part-lines he thought he had heard before, although he could not recall the contexts. Now, he realised that not only had they all flowed from the pen—the quill!—of one man, but that people had been quoting them for four hundred years. In Shakespeare, then, he discovered a new god, a man of infinite wisdom, understanding and, above all, eloquence.

Like so many others before him, Mickey wanted to appropriate that eloquence, and found himself jotting down quotes that he might use in speeches, but he soon discovered that this could be a risky business. At a meeting of the left wing of the British Socialist Party, a speaker arguing for a break with the Hyndman faction, even if this meant the formation of a new party, boldly enlisted Shakespeare in his cause.

"Comrades, the bard has put it far better than I ever could:

There is a tide in the affairs of men.

Which, taken at the flood, leads on to fortune;
Omitted, all the voyage of their life
Is bound in shallows and in miseries.
On such a full sea are we now afloat,
And we must take the current when it serves,
Or lose our ventures.

"Our time has come, comrades; if we fail to grasp this opportunity now, it may be lost forever!"

This received respectable applause, and it seemed for a while that the tide might well be taken at the flood. But on the platform, Theo Rothstein's eyes were twinkling. "Comrades," he said, rising to reply, "I have always found it essential when quoting Shakespeare to be absolutely sure that the quotation fits one's case. In the third scene of Act 4 of *Julius Caesar*, Brutus and Cassius are in debate over a tactical question in their war with Octavian and Mark Anthony. Cassius is of the view that their own forces should take a little breather in the security of Sardis. Brutus, on the other hand, insists that they should strike now at Philippi, before their enemy has time to gather more forces. Cassius is persuaded, and so off to Philippi they go." He looked around at his audience and shrugged. "With what result, comrades? First Cassius, and then Brutus, is defeated! So, comrades, I urge caution; true, the tide is building, and I estimate that it will be at its flood by the time of our party's conference next year. Let us all prepare for that."

Seeing the Shakespeare-quoter's reddened face as the audience erupted in laughter and applause, Mickey silently thanked him for this lesson.

Initially, he would, whenever the opportunity arose, try out his developing knowledge on Dorothy.

"Do you see the signs of age upon me?" she asked one evening as they lay in bed.

Gently, he ran a fingertip over her face. "A faint line or two at your eyes," he said, "and at the corners of your mouth."

"And you don't mind? I'm almost thirty-three, Mickey."

Seeing the opportunity, he smiled. "Love," he said, "is not love that alters when it alteration finds."

She turned her head and silently regarded him for some time, her brow eventually creasing—more lines!—as she struggled to identify the quote. At last, she sighed in defeat. "No, I have no idea which play that comes from, Mickey, so you'll have to tell me."

"It's not from a play."

Her frown deepened. "But it must be."

"Why must it?" He pretended to be affronted. "Can't you believe that I'm beginning to think and speak like Shakespeare?"

She studied his face closely, looking for the beginnings of a smile. Then her mouth fell open in realisation. "It's from the sonnets! You're reading the *sonnets*, Mickey?"

"Just here and there," he confessed. "To be honest, I don't so much read them as search for lines that might apply to us—or, at least, to you. That was from Sonnet 116."

Just look at her! Oh, she was so pleased that her Mickey was taking Shakespeare seriously. "Say it again," she urged.

"Love," he repeated dutifully, "is not love that alters when it alteration finds."

"Oh, Mickey," she cried, throwing out her arms, "you've set me free! No more worries about my age! So with mirth and laughter let old wrinkles come."

"You've got me there, girl."

"*Merchant of Venice.*"

"Ah, I've not read that yet."

"Michael, you cannot possibly know how often I think back to that summer evening when we glimpsed each other across Oxford Street, and how thankful I am that it happened."

"I *do* know, Dorothea, because it's exactly the same for me."

"There we were, not expecting to see each other—to *find* each other..."

"Love sought is good, but given unsought better."

She raised an eyebrow.

"*Twelfth Night.*"

"Oh, Michael..."

*

Dorothy introduced him to classical music via the concerts which, when they had the price of admission, they would attend.

He did not think he would like classical music, but when he accompanied Dorothy to a performance of Tchaikovsky's Violin Concerto he found himself overwhelmed, feeling a catch in his throat as the orchestra joined the solo violin, the music swelling to a stirring climax. The following day, driving his bus through Central London, he found the main melody swirling though his mind and he was forced to join in, heedless of what the passengers behind him might think as his voice competed with the traffic's roar.

"Da *dah* dah, daddla *da* dah, da *dah* da, da-da-dah, daddla da. Da DA DA DA, DA DA DA-DA-DA…"

Passing Marble Arch on its traffic island, he saw it with new eyes, pushing aside its royal connections and realising with pride that this imposing edifice had been constructed by the working class, just as Tchaikovsky had been able to follow his musical career due to the wealth created by the Russian peasantry and working class. In music, Mickey had discovered a world of previously unanticipated richness, although it might be said that Dorothy had spoiled him by starting him off on Tchaikovsky, for he found that few pieces could produce the tightness in his chest that the Violin Concerto had called forth.

But one even surpassed it, and that was the Organ Symphony of Saint-Saëns. Dick Mortlake sometimes joined Mickey and Dorothy in their concert-going, and this had been his recommendation; it was, after all, another production of the Romantic Period, and it might help sustain Mickey's interest. Having been commissioned by the Philharmonic Society of London, he told Mickey, the symphony had been premiered in London to great acclaim in 1886; tactfully, Dick omitted to mention that in 1871 Camille Saint-Saëns had fled to London to escape the Paris Commune.

The three of them sat in adjacent seats, Dorothy between the two men, in the front row of the western circle of the Royal Albert Hall. Opposite them, but closer to the stage, the boxes were populated with people in evening dress. It was, it seemed, an occasion.

"Look across at the middle row of boxes!" Dick urged his companions just before the performance commenced. "The one at the extreme left. Who do you see?"

And there was Sir Albert Stanley, laughing with his wife, part of a group of four or five couples, several of whom were probably titled, all of whom were doubtlessly propertied.

Mickey nudged Dorothy. "Why don't you wave to him, Dorothy? I'm sure there are a few empty seats in that box. If he notices us, he might invite us across."

Then why don't *you* wave, Mickey?"

"We've only met the once; he probably won't recognise me."

Dick was about to insert the first two fingers of each hand into his mouth. "Want me to attract his attention?"

"No!" This from the couple, both equally insistent.

"Relax, I'm joking."

"Must cost a few bob to sit up there," mused Mickey.

"Three guineas," said Dick.

"Oh, I was forgetting: you've probably played here a few times,

Dick."

"Once or twice."

"So you probably know most of the orchestra."

Dick cast his eye over the stage, where the strings were tuning up. "Quite a few of them, yes."

"Want me to attract their attention?"

"Will you two please stop it!" hissed Dorothy. "You're like a couple of schoolboys."

The lights in the theatre dimmed and the conductor tapped his music stand with his baton. The Sainte-Saëns was preceded by a number of lesser pieces, all well-known and none of them particularly challenging, even to a person of Mickey's limited experience. This first half of the concert was, Mickey conceded, pleasant, but he had an intimation that something much more substantial was on the way.

And, of course, it was. A single oboe opened the piece, then the strings set a cantering pace, seeming to promise an early crescendo which never came; the woodwind section took up the main theme, followed by the whole orchestra; but still no crescendo, the orchestra gradually—almost teasingly—climbing and then falling back. In the second movement, the orchestra laid down the gentlest of backcloths for a voice yet to be heard—that of the organ, which was noticeable by only the faintest of rumblings. Come the third movement, and the orchestra returned to the canter, almost a gallop, with space now given to the piano—another tease? This passage came to an abrupt halt and a beat later the fourth movement opened with orchestra galloping once more until the brass section appeared to announce an arrival of some significance...but no; the strings again, woodwind, and THEN the organ sent out a thunderous chord that struck Mickey in the chest, causing tears to spring to his eyes; he found that he was clutching Dorothy's hand but could tell that she was as affected as he. Comment from the strings and AGAIN that thunder rolled through the concert hall; more strings and for a THIRD time the world's largest pipe organ gave voice. Then, with the organ taking a step back, the strings and piano launched into a rippling passage of such beauty and excitement that, Mickey noticed, some members of the string section were actually smiling. He had never dreamed that music could be like this, and he found himself wondering why, as it had been written four years before his birth, it had been kept from him until now. The whole orchestra now took a step back and slowly, inevitably, gloriously, built for the final climax: cymbals, kettle-drums, strings, brass, woodwind and that commanding organ in a triumphal, triumphant burst of thunder. Mickey sprang from his seat, cheering and clapping, tears streaming down his face, Dorothy and Dick alongside him. Dick smiled broadly as he saw the effect the music had had on his friend and threw his arms around him and Dorothy; it was as if they had just performed the symphony themselves and were celebrating their triumph.

"He's seen you," said Dick.

"What?" Mickey was in a daze, having completely forgotten about Albert Stanley.

"Stanley. Look at his box."

Albert Stanley was also on his feet, applauding, but his eyes were on Mickey and Dorothy, and when he saw them turn towards him he smilingly lifted a palm, which they reciprocated.

"That flautist had a fair bit to do, Dick," Mickey commented as they made their way to the exit.

"He did, didn't he?"

"Any regrets?"

"Of course."

"Seriously?"

"Seriously, I don't know, but hearing that symphony again reminded me of what drew me to music in the first place. Can you imagine what it feels like being part of an orchestra when it delivers a performance like that?"

"No, but you can, Dick. I'm still getting over being part of the audience."

"You do realise, don't you, that tonight's performance was about more than the music?" This from Dorothy, who walked between the two men.

From his expression, it was clear that Dick knew her meaning immediately, but Mickey gave Dorothy a puzzled look. "Such as…"

"I'm sure that climax was supposed to make us believe in the prospect of victory, Mickey. Yes, I know that, as it was written over a quarter of a century ago, this could not have been the intention of the composer, but it *was* the intention of those who arranged the concert. And who is the composer? A Frenchman: an ally."

"I'm afraid Dorothy is probably right," said Dick, who could see that Mickey was still sceptical. "For example, the orchestra took a decision after the declaration of war that they would perform nothing by a living German. Dead Germans like Beethoven are still acceptable."

"Jesus Christ. But surely the players themselves…"

"The players are probably not as high-minded as you would prefer them to be," continued Dick remorselessly, and Mickey suspected that he was being granted an insight into another of the reasons why Dick had abandoned his career. "Just after the start of the war one of the orchestra's founder-members, Adolf Borsdorf, a German, was suspended after the others refused to play with him, even though he had been in this country for decades and had an English family."

"What a bunch of bastards."

"They play well, though."

What could Mickey do? He laughed, but the gloss had certainly been taken off of the evening.

"Mr Rice!"

As they crossed the foyer, Mickey heard Stanley's voice and turned to find him a few paces behind, walking with his party. Stanley turned to his wife and the others and told them to continue without him for a few minutes, although one of the men stayed with him and they walked together to where Mickey, Dorothy and Dick stood waiting.

"Well, this is a pleasant surprise, Mr Rice." Stanley proffered his right hand to Mickey while with the left he gestured to the man at his side. "And this is Mr Walter Runciman, President of the Board of Trade. Walter, say hello to Mr Michael Rice, one of the General's hard-working bus drivers, and Miss Dorothy Bridgeman, who worked in my office for a time. And their friend..."

"Mr Richard Mortlake," said Mickey, "another of the General's hard-working drivers."

"Ah, Miss Bridgeman," said Runciman, a handsome, clean-shaven man in his mid-forties, as he shook Dorothy's hand, "I believe I know your father."

Dorothy was taken aback. "Really?"

"My own father, like yours, is in shipping," he explained, "and of course I have met Sir George during the course of my work at the Board."

"Ah, of course."

Stanley looked from one to the other, perhaps feeling somewhat upstaged. "Well, it seems the surprise is pleasant in more ways than one." He turned to Mickey. "But Mr Rice, I could not help noticing how enthusiastically you greeted the Organ Symphony. What a magnificent finale!" He lowered his voice. "I must confess that I might have acted likewise if my wife had not been with me."

Mickey frowned and inclined his head inquisitively.

"Well, you knooow: some women become embarrassed if one is a little too demonstrative in public."

"One gathers that Miss Bridgeman is not one of those women," Runciman interjected unctuously, giving Mickey the desire to slap him. Stanley, he noted, seemed to be struggling against the impulse to roll his eyes.

"Be careful, Mr Runciman," warned Mickey with a grin. "Though she be but little, she is fierce."

"Oh!" Stanley brought his hands together. "Shakespeare!"

"*A Midsummer Night's Dream*," said Dick.

Albert Stanley's eyes opened wider still. "Is there no end to your surprises, Mr Rice?" He lowered his voice once more, tapping Mickey lightly on the arm with his knuckles. "Oh, but listen: we can't have you and Mr Runciman bickering when you have so much in common, can we?" He looked from one to the other and, seeing that neither man grasped his meaning, glanced furtively over his shoulder and then whispered, "Anti-conscription."

"Of course," Runciman nodded, smiling at Mickey. "A red-button union man."

Well, thought Mickey, maybe he's not such a bad chap after all.

"But tell me, Mr Rice," said Stanley, reverting back to the previous subject, "are you regular concert-goers?"

"Not as regular as we would wish, Sir Albert," said Dorothy, "as I am sure you will understand."

Stanley regarded her thoughtfully, knowing full well that she was making an oblique reference to the wage he paid Mickey and Dick. "Yes," he nodded eventually, "I quite understand." He sniffed. "But Mr Rice, I'm curious as to how you became attracted to music. Do you come from a musical family?"

Mickey threw back his head and laughed. "Not originally, no," he said. He picked up Dorothy's hand in his own. "But I do now."

Albert Stanley smiled sadly as he looked from Mickey to Dorothy and back again. "How very lucky you both are," he said softly. "How very lucky."

Runciman consulted his pocket watch and nodded to Stanley, indicating that the time had come for them to rejoin their wives and the rest of their party. "Well, so nice to have met you all," he said in parting, adding unwisely, "And if there is anything I can do for you chaps, don't hesitate to let me know."

"Well, a nice war bonus would be welcome," said Dick, with little indication of humorous intent.

"Ah, well, I'm afraid that request will have to come from Mr Smith," replied the President of the Board of Trade.

The three watched as the plutocrats marched off briskly to locate their chauffeured vehicles and a dinner in the West End.

Mickey took out his pocket watch and glanced at the other two. "Fish and chips, then?"

They all laughed.

*

Some days later, a cream and green Harrods delivery van, open at the front like the B-type bus and with the royal seal displayed on the side, pulled up outside the Mortlake residence in Alexander Street. The driver, in his long green smock, alighted and rapped on the front door. Receiving no reply, he knocked again and was rewarded by the sound, somewhere above him, of a window opening.

"Yes?"

The driver stepped back, looked up and saw a woman's head at the second floor. "Delivery for Mr Rice, madam."

"From *Harrods*?"

"That's what it says on the side of the van, madam."

"Yes, very droll. I'll come down."

There were, said the driver, two boxes, one on the heavy side and a smaller, flat one bearing a warning: "FRAGILE. DO NOT DROP."

"If you'd like to take the smaller one, madam, I'll bring up the other one.

"No, that's perfectly alright," said Dorothy. "Just leave them inside the front door."

"And if you'll just sign here, madam."

Having handed the receipt back to the driver and taken her copy, she found that he was reluctant to depart. Oh, of course. "I'm so sorry, driver, but my husband doesn't get paid until tomorrow.

"Very well, madam, then I'll bid you good day." Tipless, the driver turned and muttered his way back to his van.

Having conveyed both boxes to the flat, Dorothy continued work on the piece she was writing. By the time she finished, there was still an hour to go before Mickey was due home, and she found herself wandering over to the boxes. Given the shape of the smaller box and the nature of its warning, she had a good idea what both contained. After a few seconds' thought, she began to open the larger box.

Later, as she heard Mickey on the stairs, she rushed to the door and, as he appeared, told him to close his eyes, following which she led him through the living room—"No, a little to the left, Mickey, or there'll be an accident."—and into the bedroom, where she sat him on the bed and instructed him to wait with his eyes closed and his ears open. She returned to the living room, and seconds later the music of Saint-Saëns filled the flat. Mickey appeared at the bedroom door, his mouth agape as he saw the gramophone and wondered at the music coming from its horn.

"But Dorothy...It's wonderful, but we can't afford it, sweetheart. Wherever did you get it?"

"It came this afternoon, Mickey. From Harrods. For you." She handed him a white envelope.

"From *Harrods*? For *me*? But who from, Dorothy?"

"I can guess," she said with a smile, "but if you open that envelope I'm sure you will know."

He tore open the envelope and took out the single sheet of good-quality writing paper. He quickly scanned it, cleared his throat and began to read aloud.

Dear Mr Rice,

I am quite sure that you agree with the advice of Polonius: 'Neither a borrower nor a lender be.' I must therefore insist that you look upon this gramophone and the few records as a gift. Please do not even think of returning them, but 'to thine own self be true.' Polonius again! No one apart from yourself and Miss Bridgeman need ever know that the gift came from me, and you do not need to reply to this brief note.

But why do I make this gesture? I was, in truth, greatly moved by your reaction to the symphony the other evening. You and I will disagree on many things, but that, and our brief conversation afterwards, confirmed a belief that I have held for some time, i.e. that there are no heights to which the human spirit will not aspire. The human spirit, however, must be fed and watered, and it is my earnest hope that the gramophone will play its part in that. May it, as your record collection grows, give you and Miss Bridgeman many hours of delight. Music, as you are obviously discovering, enriches one without impoverishing others. Make of that what you will!

Please give my kindest regards to Miss Bridgeman.

Yours sincerely,

Albert Stanley.

P.S. I had at first thought to send you a collection of Shakespeare's plays, but realised that you would have been unable to quote him if

328

such was not already at your disposal."

Mickey passed the note to Dorothy and ran a hand over his head. "Well, I'll be blowed." He gazed admiringly at the handsome gramophone, shining with its mahogany and brass. "This must have cost a pretty penny, especially coming from Harrods. Is the whole symphony on this record?"

She shook her head. "No, each side only contains about five minutes of music, so there are four records."

"Still...Will you listen to that!"

She smiled, happy that he was so pleased, but worried by the thing that pleased him.

He sensed her ambivalence and sighed. "Alright, sweetheart, let's hear it."

"We can hardly keep it, Mickey."

"And why not?"

"Mickey, you're a union rep. You can't accept a gift from the managing director."

"Who will know?"

"Well, we can hardly keep it a secret from Dick, can we?"

He grinned. "No, he'll be banging on the ceiling before long. But why can't you say that it's a gift from your father?"

She shrugged. "Well, I suppose I could." She thought for a moment before giving the real reason for her doubts. "Look, Mickey, I can't help feeling that this is his way of maintaining some form of contact with me."

"And so the heights to which my spirit aspires...That's just a load of old flannel, then?"

Dorothy chewed her lower lip. "Well, no, he seems perfectly sincere, I suppose. Alright, forget what I just said. But are you sure it's not a bribe?"

He laughed. "Dorothy, my love, there are two reasons why I'm keeping this gramophone. Firstly, because it *will* give us many hours of delight and, secondly, I think of all the hours of surplus value I've created for Albert Stanley and when I look at that gramophone I see that a few of them have been returned to me."

"Ah, well, since you put it like that..."

29

As Sanders had suggested, the Anti-Conscription Committee, or a good proportion of its members, was transformed into a Vigilance Committee, the object of which was to keep the red-button union's leadership under constant surveillance, preventing it from flouting the wishes of the membership and, where possible, to push the union into a still more progressive direction. The first meeting was held in a rented room above the pub on Clerkenwell Green where, after the ADM, the idea had first been broached. As expected, compared to meetings of the Anti-Conscription Committee the attendance was somewhat reduced, as several cab branches, regardless of the involvement of Dennis Davies in the unofficial body, tended to be unquestioningly loyal to the leadership, and some of the branch officers in the bus garages and tram sheds continued to resist the efforts of Sanders and Archie Henderson to give them a political education; still, it was a healthy turnout.

As it was important for the new committee to be seen to be led by lay activists, Dennis Davies was elected to the chair and Dick Mortlake, his reputation for being handy with a pen giving him no rest, was the unanimous choice for secretary.

"Comrades," said Dennis Davies, "judging from the comments I've heard from several of you over the past few weeks, I think there are several matters which require discussion this evening: the progress of our demand for a Special Delegate Meeting; amalgamations; the employment of women; and the National Transport Workers' Federation. Are there any further suggestions? No? Then I'll ask Brother Sanders to give us an update regarding the SDM. George?"

Sanders, who had been sitting in the front row with Archie Henderson and Mickey Rice, got to his feet.

"Brothers, more than six months have passed since our ADM, and something like five months since the branch resolutions demanding a Special Delegate Meeting began to arrive at Gerrard Street. Tich Smith does his best to keep us organisers well away from the issue, but it's obvious to all of us that a majority of branches must by now have called on the EC to convene an SDM. How are they avoiding it? Oh, they claim that the resolutions from this, that and the other branch were never received. Must have been lost in the post, they say. That's what those branches are told when they ask why they've received no acknowledgement. Those branches then resubmit their resolutions, sending them by registered post, so there can be no excuse this time.

"Will they convene the SDM now? They will not. Instead, they say that they've received correspondence from individual members of several branches claiming that their branch didn't meet on the date stated in the resolution, or that the vote went the other way. They then investigate those allegations, which of course are shown to be groundless, but never mind, because it's all time-consuming, and maybe the war will end soon and Bywater and Russell will be back at Gerrard Street before the SDM can be called."

This elicited a number of guffaws, along with a few hissed expressions of contempt.

"To be honest, I wouldn't be surprised to arrive at the office one morning to find that there's been a fire in the room where these resolutions are kept, but so far that hasn't happened. Instead, what they're doing now is seeking legal advice—first on whether the EC has an obligation to convene an SDM if a majority of the branches demand it, and secondly whether an ADM or SDM has the legal right to call for the issue of nomination papers when Bywater and Russell have been granted leave of absence for the duration of the war. And who knows how long the lawyers will take before they come up with their advice?"

"Or how much they'll charge!" said Dennis Davies from the chair.

"Quite right, Dennis. But that's the situation as it stands. It's an absolute disgrace, and only the lay members can force a change." He looked around the room. "It's up to you, brothers, and the members back at your branches."

"OK, comrades, discussion."

"Can't we get our own legal advice?" asked the first man up, a Tilling's driver.

"Sorry, I forgot to mention it," said Sanders. "I ran the case past a lawyer friend of mine, and his view is that in a court case, given a half-way decent judge and a neutral jury, we would win hands down."

"Then why don't we go to court?" asked the same man.

"I can give you three reasons," offered Dennis Davies. "First of all, there's the question of cost: we'd have to pass around the hat, and I can't for the life of me see us raising the amount required, particularly with Christmas coming up; secondly, there's no guarantee that we would *get* a half-way decent judge and a neutral jury, particularly as this whole issue is bound up with our opposition to the war; and thirdly, I think it would be somewhat demeaning for us to go before a capitalist court to sort out a problem in our own trade union." He shrugged. "But that's just my opinion. If anyone wants to take the legal route, let's hear from them now."

No one did.

"Alright, so what's the alternative?" asked the chairman.

Mickey Rice got to his feet. "I would suggest, Chairman, that when the EC holds its next meeting in December, we organise a mass lobby of that meeting and refuse to disperse until they have taken the decision to convene the SDM. That may mean that some of us have to arrange a rest-day exchange, or miss a day's work, but so be it: it has to be done."

A roar of approval came from the meeting.

"No need for a formal vote?" asked Dennis Davies.

"No!"

"Next business!"

*

That same evening, Tich Smith had called a small meeting of his own at Gerrard Street, with George Blundy and Eamonn Quinlan.

"Did we get the legal advice on the SDM?" asked Blundy, Secretary of the Owner-Drivers Branch of the Cab Section. He leaned over Tich's desk and tapped off the ash from his cigar into the china ashtray.

Tich Smith nodded grimly. "We did: not very helpful, I'm afraid."

"What will we do, then?" This from Eamonn Quinlan, keen to learn how to manoeuvre against a recalcitrant membership.

Tich grinned mischievously and shrugged. "I suppose we could suggest to the EC that we seek a second opinion. That should take us through to the New Year."

Not entirely satisfied, Blundy grunted. "And if the second opinion's no better than the first?"

"Then, assuming that the war is still on, I suppose we'll have to give them their SDM."

"This must be costing us dear in legal fees, Tich," protested the small proprietor. "If the outcome's going to be no different, wouldn't it make sense to call the bloody SDM and get it over with?"

Tich shook his head emphatically. "I don't think so. The longer we can string this out, the more the members will get tired of the whole question. Yes, George Sanders and a few of those around him have got the bit between their teeth and they'll never let go, but that's not true of the whole membership." He tapped his desktop with his fingernails. "Don't forget that this question is connected to the anti-war position, and there are clear signs that support for that position is weakening. You'll remember that in mid-September a conductor called George Harvey, a member of the Acton branch, was killed in an air raid. His funeral procession in Hammersmith was 350-strong, led by the branch banner and the union brass band; when the cortege reached the cemetery, there were 2,000 more waiting for them. I wasn't there, but from what I've heard if anyone had called for an end to the war, they would have had a *very* hard time of it." Another tap on the desktop. "Opinion is shifting."

"So you think we can reach a position where we'll win the vote at the SDM?" asked Quinlan, looking up from the cigarette he was rolling.

Tich Smith grinned. "I'm not quite that optimistic, Eamonn, but I think we can get the better of them *after* the SDM, when it comes to the next step."

"And what would that be?" Blundy was not entirely convinced.

Tich smiled. "Just wait and see, just wait and see. I've still got a card or two up my sleeve."

*

"And so to amalgamations. George?"

"To be honest, Dennis, I don't think there's much to be said on the matter at the moment. We had the ballot for amalgamation with the National Union of Vehicle Workers back in June, and the proposal was rejected; or, rather, we failed to get the two-thirds majority required by the law. I think we all know that Tich Smith and a few members of the EC would like to see us link up with the blue-button union, but with feelings still running high after May's tram strike, there's not much chance of that at the present time."

"Well," said Davies, looking momentarily confused, "if there's nothing more to be said..."

"But there is, chairman." Seated next to Davies, Dick Mortlake got to his feet.

Dennis Davies smiled with what appeared to be relief. "OK, lad, off you go."

"Chairman, we're a young union, and I'm concerned that if we're not careful we're going to lose our political identity. First of all, let's look at where we come from. The London Cab Drivers' Union was a *militant* organisation, but I'm not sure that it was socialist. Also, it was not a large organisation. The membership at the end of 1912 was just under 5,000; when the union—now the LPU—balloted the membership on the political levy in 1913, only half that number voted. So only a minority of London cabdrivers were in the union, although it's a fact that this minority exercised leadership over the rest, and when a strike was called they would all be out.

"I think it's quite probably the case, brothers, that within the organised drivers, the owner-drivers had more influence than their numbers might have justified. Why is this important? An owner-driver is a small proprietor; he's not a worker, a proletarian, and this fact will have a big influence on his thinking. He wants to better his own position, certainly, but he won't *necessarily* favour public ownership of the means of production. He won't *necessarily*, that is, be a socialist."

Dennis Davies, a veteran member of the London Cabdrivers' Union, made a great show of clearing his throat.

Dick Mortlake smiled. "In saying this, brothers, please understand that I'm not being critical of anyone. I'm just trying to explain why things are the way they are. And, of course, some owner-drivers *are* socialists, but this is not the general rule. On the other hand, you have the journeyman drivers, those who drive a cab owned by someone else—usually a big company like the British Motor Cab Company. But even these are not proletarians in the true sense, because instead of being *employed* by the owners of their cabs they *hire* the vehicles from them. Like the owner-drivers, they are self-employed, and thus, there is among the journeyman drivers also a degree of the individualism found among the owner-drivers. The dearest wish of some of them is to graduate to owner-drivers.

"In 1913, this was the union that began to organise London busworkers..."

"Brother Mortlake," interjected Dennis Davies, "I thought you were going to speak on amalgamations."

"That is true, Brother Davies," Dick replied confidently, "and that is what I will do, but I feel that this background is important."

Davies was genial enough, waving him to proceed. "As a matter of fact, you're not doing bad. On you go, lad."

"So we come to 1913, when the Cabdrivers' Union started to organise busworkers—and a fine job they made of it, although after a while we were also organising ourselves. But busworkers are a different breed from cabdrivers: we *are* proletarians, and so we're less likely to be individualists, and more likely to think and act collectively. You only have to look at the membership figures to see the truth of this: our union still doesn't have a majority of the cabdrivers in membership, but we achieved a majority on the buses in a fairly short space of time. *And*, it seems, we're more likely to favour public ownership of the means of production. We're more likely to be socialists, although it would be daft to exaggerate this.

"For a time, none of this seemed to matter, as we all got on famously. Now it *does* matter, because we can see our union splitting into camps. On the one hand, there's a right wing led by those with a small-proprietor outlook in the cab section, and the more backward elements of the bus section; this camp is more likely to agree to compromises with the employers, to stifle—or, as recently, ignore—membership democracy, and lack backbone when it comes to opposition to the war. On the other hand, we have a left wing led by the most active and intelligent elements of the busworkers and tramworkers and those cab activists who long ago rose above the small-proprietor outlook; and this camp champions the widest possible democracy within the union, is more likely to take an uncompromising line with the employers, and is firm in its opposition to the war.

"Now when the cabdrivers set about organising the busworkers and tramworkers, they were, in a sense, bringing about an amalgamation, and I hope I've just shown that, positive though they might be, amalgamations also bring problems. It's my view, brothers, that it would be foolish for us to rush into *another* amalgamation until we've secured the position for the healthy forces in our union. Because our position is *not* yet secure: if the EC gets away with ignoring the decision of an ADM, they will also throw away the rule book when it comes to elections in the union.

"Now, George may well be right when he says that, given the bad feeling arising from the tram strike, there can be no immediate prospect of a merger with the blue-button union. But we need to be on our guard, because from what I've heard Tich Smith and some of the EC members are hell-bent on a merger. If the tram strike taught us anything, it's surely that the culture of the blue-button union is very different to our own: the full-timers control that union, and if they merge with the LPU, that's what they'll try to do with us. They'll link up with the right wing of our own union, and they'll have us surrounded: organisers who cross swords with the general secretary or the EC will be sacked. The union journal will no longer play a big role in mobilising the membership.

335

"In conclusion, brothers, let's make sure *this* union is securely won for socialism and democracy first, and then, if a merger proposal arises, we need to be absolutely sure that lay control is guaranteed, and be prepared to campaign for a rejection if it's not."

Dick sat down to thoughtful applause.

"Well, lad," said Dennis Davies, "you've said a mouthful there. And there was me, worrying that we'd never fill the time. Okay, brothers, I think Dick has merely issued a strong note of caution, so there'll be no need for a vote, but I'm opening it up for discussion."

Archie Henderson raised a hand. "Just briefly, Dennis, every word that Dick said about the AAT is true, and if anyone in this room should know that, it's me. But don't run away with the idea that it's only people like Tich Smith in *this* union who favour a merger, because the AAT leaders are just as keen. In fact, towards the end of the tram strike, when Stanley Hirst was down here, he told me that we'd soon be under the same roof again—and this was after he'd been chatting with Tich. So be on your guard, brothers."

Sanders got to his feet once more and sighed, seemingly weary. "First, Dennis, I want to congratulate Dick Mortlake on his thoughtful analysis.

"But I don't think Dick has made sufficient allowance for change, brothers. Things don't stay as they are; everything around us is in constant motion—and that includes the minds of men. Just because an owner-driver has the typical outlook of the petty proprietor, that doesn't mean that he'll never move beyond that. And don't forget, brothers, that when we talk of a cab culture or a bus culture, we're not talking about something that has existed for centuries and so would be that much more difficult to change. These cultures have developed since the introduction of the internal combustion engine, just a few years ago. By and large, the owner-driver of today never owned a horse cab. I'm confident, Dennis, that we in the progressive wing of our union have the ability to secure our position; and I'm equally sure that we can do the same in a merged union, although there is truth in everything that Dick has said. When the time comes, we *will* need to proceed carefully, and insist that any merger proposal is based on the principle of lay control, just as Dick says.

"Of course, Dick also spoke of the culture within the AAT, which is so much different from our own. But shouldn't changing that culture be an easier job than the one we're doing right now? Are there any small proprietors in the AAT? No, they're all workers. And why shouldn't we be trying to change that culture now? Why don't we arrange a few liaison meetings between our progressive activists and some of their leading lay members—meetings pretty much like

336

the one we're having now, where we discuss issues of mutual interest, and familiarise them with the way we do things in the red-button union?"

"I'm sure we all feel a bit more cheerful after listening to George's contribution," said Archie Henderson as he stood up, causing a ripple of assent. He paused, dragging a hand through his hair. "But we need to understand—and, if you don't mind me saying so, George, *you* need to understand—that when it comes to the AAT it won't be *just* a case of winning over a few thousand honest proletarians to our own democratic way of life. That, as George correctly suggests, might be easy enough. In fact, we did it recently in the tram strike, didn't we, when huge numbers of AAT members— me included!—came over to the red-button, so that our Islington tram branch has grown to almost 2,000 members. The *hard* part, comrades, will be to prise control away from the top leadership, the full-timers, and place it securely in the hands of the lay membership. Look at us now: you see the trouble we're having in our attempt to reassert lay control in the red-button. Believe me, it will be a damn sight harder in any merger with the AAT. And make no mistake about it, as it's the larger union the AAT leaders would get the top positions in any merger. It would also be much more difficult to mobilise and coordinate the activities of the progressive forces in a merged union, due to the geographical spread of the membership. At the moment, despite the word 'provincial' in our title, the vast majority of red-button members are in the London area. That's surely one of the reasons we're so successful in mobilising the membership whenever we need to." Archie paused again and emphasised every word with the stab of a finger. "It won't be the same if we merge with the AAT. So please, brothers. Please, please, please take Dick's note of caution seriously."

*

If there was anxiety when this topic arose at the Gerrard Street meeting, it was less to do with the prospects of a merger and more concerned with the perils of continuing to work in an unreformed red-button union.

"It's necessary for a number of reasons," Tich Smith told his small meeting. "This year, our union has been bleeding money, and we're badly in need of an additional source of revenue. Have you noticed how often we have to ask the members for a levy in order to honour our strike-pay obligations?"

"Well, that's one reason," said a mischievous George Blundy.

"Yes," lilted Eamonn Quinlan, "I thought the bigger reason was your need to rein in the organisers."

"It's not as if the two are not connected," said Tich. "George, for example, was the moving spirit behind the tram strike, and that has been a major drain on our finances this year."

"But weren't you on the platform with him at the Brixton meeting?"

"That's true, but I was there because the membership had demanded that the leadership turn up and listen to their case. I couldn't very well refuse. Sanders, on the other hand, was only too keen. And then, of course, the strike was lost, and for a while I thought the membership might turn against him, but no..."

"Well, after the LCC coughed up the three-bob-a-week war bonus in August, the strike didn't look quite so defeated."

"And then," continued Tich, "there are the things he writes in the *Record*, with no respect for the EC...or me, for that matter."

"So why not have the next ADM adopt a rule to cover that?" suggested Quinlan.

"You know damn well why not, Eamonn: they'd never accept it. After a merger with the AAT, however, a lot of things will be possible."

"Will it happen?" asked the practical George Blundy. And when?"

"Oh, it will happen alright," Tich replied. "Stanley Hirst is still very keen; in fact, he wants to rope in a few other smaller unions at the same time. As to the when, well, that's the problem. We'll just have to bide our time until the climate is right and pounce when George Sanders and his cabal are least expecting it."

*

"And that brings us to women conductors," said Tich Smith, shuffling a number of papers on his desk.

"Whatever next!" exclaimed a dismayed Quinlan.

"Women drivers!" responded Blundy. "That's what's bloody next if we allow women conductors in the door."

"Let's not be too hasty," counselled a worried Tich Smith. "What we have at the moment is a resolution from Telford Avenue calling for opposition to women in the trade; that will be before us at the next EC meeting. But we're faced with a *bit* of a problem in that women conductors have been employed in Glasgow and elsewhere since April. As you know, the bus and tram companies have been in discussion with the Commissioner of Police on the matter..."

"But didn't the Home Secretary tell us that nothing of the kind would happen in London?" said Blundy.

Tich Smith nodded soberly. "He did, indeed, George, but I think Sir John Simon has been out-manoeuvred. He is also anti-conscription, and he was probably thinking that if there was to be no conscription, there would be no need for female labour on London's buses and trams. But he and his allies lost the argument on conscription, and the legislation will be introduced shortly." He shrugged. "So that would have put paid to any assurance he'd given us."

"Ah, Jesus!" Quinlan threw up his hands. "So what do we do?"

"The EC will have a choice between adopting the Telford Avenue proposal, in which case we'll be in for a long, costly dispute with little hope of winning much public sympathy, or accepting what I think will be inevitable, but seeking certain safeguards."

"Like what, Tich?" asked Blundy.

"Well, look, I've already drafted a letter to the Home Secretary." He lifted two sheets from the pile of papers before him and passed one to each of them. "Just cast your eye over it and tell me what you think. As you see, I tell him that we've already protested to the companies, telling them that in our view it's not a fit job for a woman, but that if a *real* staff shortage develops we would agree to their employment as conductors on the strict condition that they receive the same wage and allowances as a man doing the same job, and that their employment is terminated once the war is over."

Blundy passed a hand over his mouth. "Well, I suppose that will get us out of a tight corner, but let me give you fair warning, Tich: the moment a woman is licensed to drive a cab, there won't be a taxi on the road."

"I hear what you say, George, I hear what you say. What's your view, Eamonn?"

"Ah well, if we must, we must, I suppose."

"Will my position be accepted by the EC?"

"Aaahhh...Might be a bit close, Tich," replied Blundy.

"Yes," Quinlan agreed, "you might need the chairman's casting vote on this one."

"And what if I sent the letter tomorrow, so that the EC would be faced with a *fait accompli?*"

Blundy chuckled and waved his cigar at Tich. "Oh, you're a wicked bugger, Alfred Smith." He locked onto Tich's gaze for a moment and then brought his hand down onto the edge of the acting general secretary's desk. "Send it."

"Eamonn?"

A sigh. "Yes, send it."

*

"And now, brothers," said Dennis Davies at the Camberwell Green meeting, "the thorny question of female labour. The government has announced that women will be allowed to work as conductors, and so it's for us to decide what we're going to do about it."

This brought forth a few moans, but not enough to deter Mickey Rice from rising from his chair.

"Chairman, I'm probably not going to make many friends by saying what I'm going to say, but it needs to be said."

"In that case," said Davies with a grin, "you'd better say it."

"Our opposition to the employment of women in our trade is based on the suspicion or fear that the employers will attempt to continue their employment after the war, at lower wages. If that was allowed to happen, our position would be undermined and standards in the trade would decline. All of that is perfectly understandable. However, some of the arguments put forward to justify our opposition to the employment of women just don't hold water, and we should have nothing to do with them.

"For example, some say that women wouldn't be able to do a conductor's job. Brothers, I was a conductor before I became a driver, so I know the job. Would a woman be able to do it?" He looked around the room, but no one spoke up. "Yes, a woman *would* be able to do it! Or should I say that *some* women would be able to do it. She would find the hours long and onerous, but the job itself would be no problem for her. Now, don't misunderstand me: ask me if she could do a driver's job and I would give you a different answer, but a conductor's job, yes.

"Now let's ask ourselves a simple question: what is it that makes our job so difficult at the present time? Isn't it the staff shortage, the fact that many men are in the Army? How many conductors are they training up to be drivers at the moment? Hardly any. Why? Because if they gave driver-training to all the conductors who wanted it there would be an imbalance—not enough conductors for the number of drivers. This means that we have to live with the gaps in service and the overloading of our buses." He threw out his arms. "In these circumstances, doesn't it make sense to allow the employment of women conductors, freeing up the men who want to train as drivers? It does to me, brothers.

"So I would suggest, Chairman, that we withdraw our opposition

340

to women conductors as long as the wages and conditions they receive are the same as the men, and on the firm understanding that their employment and the war will be…" He paused, reluctant to use a long word that would get him laughed at, and therefore decided to pass the ball. "What's the word I'm looking for, Dick?"

Dick Mortlake glanced up from his notes. "Coterminous."

*

"You should know, Tich," said Eamonn Quinlan as they prepared to vacate the Gerrard Street office, George Blundy having already departed in his cab, "that some of the bus boys are saying that we should affiliate to the National Transport Workers' Federation."

"Are they now?"

"They're saying we need more muscle at the wage negotiations."

"And we, presumably, would be out on strike whenever, say, the dockers or the seamen wanted a bit of a leg-up with their own negotiations. Well, lad, they're overlooking one thing."

"And what would that be, Tich?"

Tich Smith slammed the front door shut and checked that it was locked. He grinned up at Eamonn Quinlan and winked. "Clause 3 of the agreement between our union, the LGOC and Tilling's."

*

"So we're all agreed that we should affiliate to the National Transport Workers' Federation," said Dennis Davies, drawing this final discussion to a close. "But we'll need a branch resolution to the EC."

"Consider it done," said Reuben Topping of Willesden.

*

"Anything noteworthy in Tich's ashtray from last night, Frank?" Sanders asked the caretaker as he arrived in the office the next morning.

"A cigar butt and three little dog-ends, so small they looked like white rat droppings."

Sanders did his Sherlock Holmes impression, stroking his chin. "Mm, most interesting, Watson. So last night Mr Smith entertained one man who likes to display his wealth and another who hates to

341

part with it."

Frank laughed. "If you say so, Holmes."

"Oh, I do, Watson, I do. More than this, I would say that these offices were visited in the hours of darkness by Messrs Blundy and Quinlan."

30

Late in 1915, Mickey saw two furniture lorries, the backs open, packed with people, pass him on Kensington High Street. The people—of all ages, men, women and children—were surrounded with bags and suitcases, and to say they looked disconsolate would have been an understatement. The faces of some of the children were tear-streaked, and as one ashen-faced man gazed out at one of London's richest streets it was difficult to know what, if anything, he was seeing. Instantly, Mickey knew who these people were, for Eric had told him that two days ago his wife Elsie had seen one of their neighbours, Ernie Schell, a railway worker, dragged from his house across the street and placed in such a lorry by the police. The screams and wails of Ernie's wife and three young children attracted a small crowd, but only Elsie and one other woman berated the police, demanding that they leave the Schell family in the house they had occupied for over ten years. The authorities, Eric had explained, were using commandeered furniture vans due to the shortage of military vehicles. The people in the furniture vans were German civilians and, in some cases, their families. While Mickey, working a rest day on route 31, turned left into Earl's Court Road, the furniture vans carried on, and he knew then that they were driving to Olympia, which had been converted into a transit camp.

Life for London's sizeable population of Germans—many of whom were naturalised, married to English women and had children born here—began to get difficult after the Zeppelin raids started. The first raids had been on East Anglian towns in January, followed by three days of bombing raids on Southend and other towns in the area. There was at this time a rumour that Kaiser Wilhelm had been reluctant to sanction the bombing of England because of his blood-relationship with the occupants of Buckingham Palace, and that in January he had succumbed to pressure and allowed raids outside of London. In May, he relented further, allowing raids to the east of the Tower, and on the final night of that month bombs fell on Stoke

Newington and several East London locations. The next day, there were attacks on bakers' shops owned by Germans. For people with German names, the terror had begun.

Earlier in May, the sinking of the *Lusitania* had led to further pressure on the German population. Mickey knew several drivers who had witnessed the march of hundreds of top-hatted members of the London School of Economics to the House of Commons, where they demanded the internment of all Germans, regardless of whether or not they had taken British nationality, and on 13 May, after a night of rioting, the government announced that all "enemy alien" men of military age would be interned, and the older ones repatriated. The London County Council withdrew scholarships from the children of such "enemies."

Somewhat sporadically, the air raids continued: on 17 August, ten people were killed in Leyton and Leytonstone, and three weeks later there was a raid on the riverside and, the following night, one on Central London, the Kaiser having apparently shrugged at the impossibility of continuing to shield his Saxe-Coburg relatives; the airships returned on 13 October, killing 38 in Central London. By this stage, over 32,000 German civilians had been interned, Alexandra Palace in North London had been converted into an internment camp, and some 5,000 had been repatriated; around 4,500 women, their husbands either interned or deported, had also left, along with 3,000 children.

The whole phenomenon filled Mickey with disgust, anger and frustration, although he realised that the German and Austrian authorities had probably implemented similar measures. He found it completely bewildering that so many working people in England could turn with such hatred on those born elsewhere, simply because the ruling classes of these countries were at war with British bosses. He suggested at one district meeting of garage reps that, if they should hear of one of their own colleagues in trouble because of his nationality, they should mobilise the members to blockade his house, thus preventing his internment or deportation, but this had met with little support. He wondered whether the union's anti-war policy would stand up under pressure. He mentioned his suggestion to Sanders on one occasion, but George just grimaced and told him that "at the moment, that would be a step too far."

But Mickey was defiant. "I disagree, George."

Sanders, about to drink from his mug of tea, returned the mug to the table, and, half-amused, raised an eyebrow at Mickey. "Come on, then: let's hear it."

343

"Just imagine the scene: the coppers outside with the furniture van, our man at an upstairs window, looking as British as you or me; outside the front door, a crowd of bus drivers, British to the core, determined to protect their comrade, who just happens to be German. I reckon that would do two things: first, it would firm up our anti-war line among the members, because after the Zeppelin raids that's no longer as strong as it was. Secondly, if we tipped off the press, it would bring it home to the wider public that this bloke is no different from us, no matter where he was born, and if it's wrong to intern him it's surely even more wrong that people like us should be killing each other in France and Belgium."

Sanders smiled. "That's very well thought-out, Mickey, and I concede that something like that could very well achieve the first of your objectives. As for the second, however... Mickey, I reckon by now that you know the meaning of the word 'dialectical.'"

"You reckon correctly, Brother Sanders." He smiled as he said it, realising that he was responding to Sanders with the kind of cheeky banter he must have picked up from Dorothy.

Sanders held his hands palm-upwards. "And..."

"You consider a thing in its movement, with all of its connections."

Sanders nodded. "And I reckon that, in envisaging the second thing that your proposal would achieve, you've been insufficiently dialectical."

Mickey gave it a moment's thought and then grimaced. "You're right. The press..."

"...being largely a mouthpiece for the ruling class, is either unlikely to print such a story..."

"...or would twist it around and use it against us."

"Bravo." Sanders picked up his mug and finished his tea in one swift gulp.

"Mind you, your suggestion does have another flaw."

"I'm sure you'll tell me what it is."

"I'm not aware that we have a single German or Austrian bus driver in London."

They both laughed.

"So you really think support for the anti-war line is slipping, Mickey?"

"A little, but that's not surprising after the air raids and the *Lusitania* sinking." He cleared his throat. "Bywater and Russell didn't help matters much, of course."

"No, of course not."

"Then there's the fact that most of the movement's leaders are behind the government, and others are keeping their heads down."

"Oh? Who do you have in mind, Mickey?"

"Well, Tom Mann, for example."

"Ah. Yes, well, you have a point there. Tom seems to think that he can't come out too strongly against the war without the risk of isolating himself from the rest of the movement. Believe me, I've done some straight talking to him whenever he's been down in London, but he can't be swayed at the moment." He shrugged. "Anyway, we need to make sure our line is firmed up by the time of the Special Delegate Meeting, so we can dispose of the Bywater and Russell question."

"And will the SDM stand firm behind the demand that nomination papers be issued?"

"I don't see why not, as long as our anti-war policy holds firm. In that respect, the government is doing us a favour with its plans for conscription. The branches unanimously approved the anti-conscription policy, and that in turn will ensure that the SDM is in the mood to send Bywater and Russell packing."

The work of the red-button union's Anti-Conscription Committee had been greatly assisted by the existence of the Non-Conscription Fellowship, which had been founded as early as November 1914 by Fenner Brockway, editor of the Independent Labour Party's newspaper, the *Labour Leader*. Within days of the declaration of war, Brockway had used the front page of that journal for the publication of an anti-war manifesto, writing, "Workers of Great Britain, you have no quarrel with the workers of Europe. The quarrel is between the RULING classes of Europe. Don't make their quarrel yours...The future is dark, but in the solidarity of the workers lies the hope which shall, once again, bring light to the peoples of Europe."

This accorded precisely with the views of Sanders and the other leading anti-war activists in the union, and for a time hopes ran high for a closer relationship between the ILP and the BSP. The referendum of the branches had produced a unanimity of opposition to conscription, and thereafter the members associated with the Anti-Conscription Committee tried to turn outwards, seeking to mobilise the membership to campaign against the war in the broader community.

While the government's conscription plans made it easier to mobilise the peace forces, however, there were two countervailing forces, one internal and one external. Just as the war drew working-class men into its great maw and sent them to destruction so, within the union, it was devouring the energies of the membership as the shortages of both men and vehicles extended the hours, and greatly increased the intensity, of work; at the same time, galloping inflation

345

compelled men, especially those who were married with children, to work their rest days. There was, then, less time and energy for political campaigning.

The other problem was the violence of the patriots, for while anti-war meetings increased several of them were broken up or disrupted by thugs. Mickey was at one meeting in Hackney where, ten minutes after Sanders, who was in the chair, had opened the proceedings, the doors burst open and a crowd of men forced their way in, pushing those at the back to one side and shouting "patriotic" slogans. Dorothy, standing just inside the door with a sheaf of leaflets, staggered into the last row of chairs, toppling one over. Seated to the rear of the meeting, Mickey stood and spun around, mildly surprised to see that the intruders, while containing some middle-class types in boaters, with several brawny lumpen men to provide the muscle, appeared to be led by three or four Australian soldiers. One of the latter, a large moustachioed man with sergeant's stripes, threw out his chest and bellowed, "For King and country!"

To Mickey's dismay, Sanders tried to reason with the intruders, urging them to leave the bosses' war to the bosses and stand with their own class. To this, the sergeant shouted, "You heard me, you yellow vermin! For King and country! This meeting is over!"

Mickey stepped towards him, grabbing a handful of khaki which he hoped contained the man's genitals, and head-butted him. As the patriot slumped to the floor, his nose obviously broken, Mickey caught one of his smaller comrades, moving in to attack, by the collar, pulled him to him and, grabbing his belt with his other hand, lifted him from the floor and hurled him at the invasion force. Glancing over his shoulder, he saw that the younger male members of the meeting were running to assist, and that Archie Henderson, mouth distorted in a snarl and his red hair a war bonnet, was screaming something that had no words; some of the others—Frank Chambers, Malcolm Lewis and Billy Franklin—now joined in this war cry. Turning back to the patriots, Mickey made a move in the direction of the nearest boater, only to see the man back-pedal towards the door, his face a white mask of fear. By the time Archie reached the front line, they had all gone, dragging the sergeant with them. As the tension left him, Mickey began to laugh uncontrollably, falling into Archie's comradely embrace. At this stage, the occupants of the hall had fallen silent, their attention on Mickey; Sanders stood at the rostrum, blinking as if in disbelief at what he had just witnessed.

"You going to let us in on the joke?" asked Archie as Mickey's laughter continued.

"It's just…I was thinking…Oh, Christ…Did you see their faces? Here they were, thinking they were gate-crashing a meeting of pacifists, only to be set upon by warriors of the Red Button tribe! Surprised? They were shitting 'emselves!"

Archie, and most of those in the hall, now joined in the laughter.

At many other meetings, however, things went the other way and the thugs, convinced by propaganda from the government and Fleet Street that in some never-explained way the interests of the British Empire were their own, prevailed. The pro-war message was trumpeted on every possible occasion.

"Listen to this," Sanders, looking up from his newspaper, said one morning as Eric joined him in the Gerrard Street kitchen. "This fellow talks of a 'great crusade…to kill Germans: to kill them not for the sake of killing, but to save the world; to kill the young men as well as the old…and to kill them lest the civilisation of the world should itself be killed.' Who do you think said that?"

Eric shrugged. "Kitchener? Haig?"

"I'll tell you: Arthur Foley Winnington-Ingram, the Bishop of London. This was yesterday at Westminster Abbey." He threw the newspaper onto the table in a gesture of disgust. "Bastard!"

31

After leaving the East End, Dorothy stayed at home for several weeks, writing articles for the socialist press and attempting to stretch the budget in order to avoid having to step into a job previously done by a man for two-thirds of the wage he had received; but it was hard. George Lansbury accepted some of her pieces for the *Herald*, and she managed to place others in small magazines, but before long she was forced to dip into the savings amassed from the occasional cheques received from her father. She did not tell Mickey this, and he did not pressure her to take a job.

But eventually she realised that she must make a move, informing Mickey after the event.

As he came in from work one Saturday evening early in December, she looked up from her typewriter and gaily announced, "I'm starting a job on Monday."

He raised an eyebrow. "Oh?"

She pointed across the room. "The letter's over there on the gramophone. It came this morning."

He looked in the direction of the gramophone. "Do you want me to read it?"

"Of course, darling."

He took two steps, lifted the white envelope from the gramophone and took out the single sheet it contained. His eye went straight to the letter-head. "Bloody hell." He looked across at her, a small smile on his face. "Board of Trade, eh?"

She nodded silently. "Aren't I a clever girl?"

Although still amused, his small smile became a small frown. "Not sure, my love. Weren't you the one who complained earlier in the year about the wages the government was offering women office workers?"

This was true. In mid-June, the Civil Service Commissioners had announced that women replacing men in government departments as temporary assistants would receive between 21 and 25 shillings a week, whereas men received 31 shillings and sixpence; mere typists and routine clerks would receive only between eighteen and twenty shillings. This, Dorothy had pronounced, was a blatant example of dilution, with which she would have no truck.

"Yes, I was that woman," she confessed with a smile. "But if you read the letter, you will see that I will be receiving rather more than that."

He read the letter, then slowly raised his eyes. "You'll be working directly for Walter Runciman, the president. But this is almost the same position as you had at Electric Railway House…"

"Not exactly, Mickey: I'll be his personal secretary."

"But how…?"

*

It had been relatively easy, in fact.

As she would remind Mickey, the idea had its origin in the remarks he had made over the months: how employers of all kinds were crying out for women staff, how the gender of the passengers he dropped off in the City had changed since August 1914…And then there had been Albert Stanley's offer of a reference; this, she thought, might change everything—and it would certainly make a contribution.

She had travelled up to Old Palace Yard on Wednesday, dressed appropriately in a smart grey suit with a skirt that fell a foot below her knee, and was appalled to find herself about to enter a waiting room containing, seated on the left-hand side of the room on several rows of straight-backed chairs, twenty other applicants. The newspaper advertisement she had answered had, it was true, sought applicants for a number of posts, mostly temporary assistants, for which, she assumed, most of the women in the room were applying. But the advertisement had also mentioned senior secretarial staff, and it was upon such a position that Dorothy had her eye. She paused at the door and cast that eye about the room, noting that all of the other applicants were considerably younger than her. At the far end of the room, a sandy-haired, middle-aged man sat behind a desk consulting a single sheet of paper. Sensing her presence, he looked up and squinted at her, before nodding and smiling welcomingly. Now, she realised, was the time to decide upon her demeanour. Demure? Modest? Obliging? She looked again at the other applicants and then at the man behind the desk. No, imperious, definitely imperious. Ignoring the man's smile, she glided past the lines of chairs on her left, turning just once to nod at the heads turned in her direction, as if she were someone in a high supervisory position descending from her eyrie to take a look at those who aspired to be her juniors.

The man looked up as she arrived at his desk. "Good morning, madam. And you are...?"

"Dorothy Bridgeman," she replied loudly and clearly.

The man ran his eye down his sheet of paper, which contained two columns of names, and placed a tick next to hers. There were still several unticked names. "Very well, Mrs Bridgeman. Would you care to take a seat?"

"It is *Miss* Bridgeman; and no, I would *not* care to take a seat."

The man blinked uncomprehendingly. "I beg your pardon, madam?"

"As well you might. I have an appointment"—she glanced at the clock on the wall behind the man—"for an 11.30 interview, and I do not intend to be kept waiting."

The man glanced to his right and gestured at the other applicants. "But all these other ladies..."

"Are presumably too timid to protest at their treatment," she said, leaning towards him and lowering her voice. She fixed him with a glare and then softened. "But perhaps I should give you the benefit of the doubt. Possible, there has been a misunderstanding."

"A misunderstanding, madam?" He was plainly unsure whether he should be amused or intimidated.

"Yes, a misunderstanding. You see, I have applied for one of the senior secretarial positions."

"Ah, I see." The man allowed himself a tiny grin, an incipient twinkle of the eye. "Might I ask whether you are currently employed by the Board, madam?"

"No, of course I am not employed by the Board."

The grin widened somewhat. "Or by any other government department?"

"No."

Amusement having triumphed over intimidation, the grin was full-fledged now, the twinkle in the eye a sparkle. "Then I am afraid, madam, that you will have to take the same tests as these other ladies. In which case, you really should take a seat."

"Tests? Would I be correct in assuming that these would enable your appointments officer—or panel—to gauge my abilities in the fields of typing and shorthand?"

The grinning man nodded. "Quite so, madam, quite so."

"And so," said Dorothy, bringing just a hint of suppressed anger to her performance, "the references I have provided would be completely ignored, would they not? I am sure that Sir Albert would be *most* displeased to learn that his time had been wasted."

The amusement had all but disappeared. "Sir Albert, madam?"

"Yes, Sir Albert Stanley."

"Sir Albert Stanley of the Traffic Combine?" The man was beginning to see that a retreat into intimidation might be prudent.

"Well, he's certainly not Sir Albert Stanley of the corner grocer's shop!"

The other applicants, no longer quite so timid, gave up a ripple of laughter. The man, like a schoolmaster about to admonish an unruly class, frowned and was about to turn in their direction, but the disapproval in the expression of Dorothy Bridgeman gave him pause, forcing him to realise that he was, indeed, intimidated. The nod he now gave her was almost a bow. He lifted a diffident hand. "If I may, madam."

Dorothy handed him the envelope containing Stanley's reference. "I also have another, if you would like it."

The letter was out of the envelope and the man was rapidly scanning it. "I think this may suffice, madam," he said. "Now, if you will excuse me for just a moment..." He got to his feet and walked to a door just a few feet from his desk, entered, and closed the door behind him.

Dorothy turned and, facing the other applicants, extended her arms and bowed, like a magician who has just performed a particularly difficult trick. Her audience, no longer timid but not yet brave, mimed applause.

The sandy-haired man returned to his desk, accompanied by another of roughly the same age, perhaps a year or two older, and from his bearing undoubtedly senior. The former smiled deferentially at Dorothy. "If you would care to go with Mr Rawlins, madam..."

"Good morning, Miss Bridgeman," said Mr Rawlins, extending a hand. He was, she could see now, fiftyish with good teeth and clear hazel eyes. "Kindly follow me."

As Rawlins led Dorothy through the door to the right of the gatekeeper's desk, she saw some ten applicants, half of whom sat at desks copy-typing, while the others held shorthand pads and scribbled as female members of staff dictated their tests. The applicants were, then, tested in batches, of which those she had left in the waiting room would constitute the next two; it all seemed very...industrial. She was led through another door at the far end of this room and into a small antechamber. Mr Rawlins strode across to the lift and pressed a button. When the lift arrived, he ushered her in before him, instructing the elderly male attendant to take them to the fourth floor.

They entered a spacious outer office which reminded her of the one at Electric Railway House. Three typists looked up from their desks and smiled. Rawlins waved her in the direction of a two-seater sofa placed against the wall before which stood a coffee table containing reading material—official reports by the look of them.

"I regret to say, Miss Bridgeman, that Mr Runciman has been delayed in the House, where he has been attending a committee meeting..."

Throughout the journey from the waiting room, Dorothy had displayed a cool, confident demeanour; this was now maintained by an effort of will, as she blinked once and, looking up at Mr Rawlins from her seat on the sofa, she asked, "So I will be interviewed by Mr Runciman himself?" She succeeded, she thought, in making this sound as if she had been asking the time of day.

Rawlins nodded. "Indeed, Miss Bridgeman. For such a position..."

Dorothy tilted her head to one side and smiled. "And that position would be?"

"Personal secretary to the president, madam." A tiny cloud of concern visited his features. "You *are* interested in such a position, I trust, Miss Bridgeman?"

"Of course, Mr Rawlins." By the smallest motion of her head, she indicated the secretaries at the other end of the room. "But I trust that I will not be disappointing the aspirations of other deserving candidates."

He smiled, apparently in relief. "You may have no fear in that regard: the most deserving aspirants have, along with the previous incumbent, been recalled to their regiments."

"Ah, I see." They were, then, all men. She willed herself to silence.

"Now, may I ask one of the assistants to bring you some tea while you wait for Mr Runciman?"

"What time is he expected?"

Rawlins took out his pocket watch. "He should be here within ten or fifteen minutes, I think."

"In which case," said Dorothy, "tea will not be necessary, thank you."

At that moment, the door burst open and Walter Runciman strode towards his office, looking neither right nor left.

"Ah, Mr Runciman!" cried Rawlins.

Runciman stopped, looked behind him and, seeing Rawlins, walked back. He then noticed Dorothy and, recognition dawning, broke into a smile.

"Well, Miss Bridgeman, is it not?" He stepped closer and held out his hand. "How nice to see you again."

Mr Rawlins's eyebrows shot up.

*

Runciman held out a chair for Dorothy on the far side of his desk—which, she thought, might be even more impressive than the one in Sir Albert Stanley's office—before walking around and falling into his own seat.

"Well," he exhaled, throwing up both hands before placing them on the desk, "here you are, Miss Bridgeman! You seem to have leapfrogged the procedure."

"The procedure, Mr Runciman?"

His eyes danced with amusement. "Yes, the shorthand, the typing..."

"Ah, I see. Well, I did explain to your man downstairs that my references should really dispel any doubts regarding my abilities. And Mr Rawlins appeared to be quite satisfied..."

"Yes, yes," he laughed. "A splendid show of initiative, if I may say so, Miss Bridgeman. I only regret that I was not there to witness it. Our poor Mr Johnson did not have the advantage of the advice given me by young Mr Rice at the Albert Hall: 'Though she may be but little, she is fierce.' *The Taming of the Shrew*, yes?"

Dorothy smiled. "*A Midsummer Night's Dream*, actually. What a memory you have, Mr Runciman."

He smiled and then adopted a more sober mien. "You were perfectly right, of course: the reference from Sir Albert is quite sufficient regarding your technical abilities. And he was perfectly happy to confirm this when I spoke to him."

Dorothy's right eyebrow ascended and she regarding him questioningly.

He nodded. "Yes, I telephoned him when I learned that you were among the applicants." He cleared his throat. "Now, may I ask why you decided to apply for *this* position, Miss Bridgeman?"

"But, Mr Runciman, I did not apply for this position."

"I beg your pardon?"

"The advertisement mentioned several senior secretarial appointments. I had no idea that one of these was that of your personal secretary."

"Ah. I see."

"I think that either Mr Rawlins or Mr..."

"Johnson."

"...or Mr Johnson simply *assumed* that I was applying for this position."

"But you would not be happy applying for a lower position."

"Certainly not, if it paid twenty-five shillings a week."

"Twenty...Oh, you refer to the rate for female temporary assistants."

"I do: a quarter or a third less than the amount received by the men they are replacing."

Runciman appeared uncomfortable. "Yes, but that is the rate decided by the government, Miss Bridgeman." He brightened. "But, of course, if your application is successful you will receive rather more than that."

She smiled—rather too sweetly, she thought. "But still less than the man I would be replacing?"

He shrugged. "But, as I said, the government has decided these rates."

Dorothy laughed lightly. "But come, Mr Runciman, you speak as if the Board of Trade has no part in such decisions. It is surely the case that it has a very large part in them. You possibly do not remember this, but I was part of the delegation of women's organisations in April..."

Runciman's fingers came down onto the desk. "Of course! I *knew* you looked familiar, the moment I saw you at the Albert Hall."

"At that meeting in April," she continued, "you announced that there would be equality of wages with regard to piece-rates, but that there were no plans to do the same for time-rates..."

"Yes, yes, I recall that exchange. But piece-rates apply in manufacturing, Miss Bridgeman..."

"Oh, I'm quite aware of that, Mr Runciman. But let me ask you, if I may: have the female temporary assistants you have employed at the Board since June managed, over the last few months, to work as speedily and efficiently as the men they have replaced?"

"Well, in some cases, I suppose that they have..."

"I see." She smiled, seeking to put him at his ease. "However, I have obviously not come here to negotiate on behalf of all your women employees, but I think I would be doing myself less than justice were I not to ask whether—should my application be successful—my own wage would be subject to the appropriate adjustment if I proved to be just as efficient and productive as the man I replaced."

Runciman's head fell and he spent several moments considering his hands on the desk. This interview was not going the way he had anticipated. He shook his head once or twice, but when he raised his head Dorothy could see that he was amused.

"I suppose," he said, "that we might review the situation in the light of your performance. If your application is successful."

"You *suppose* that you *might* review it..."

"We *will* review it, Miss Bridgeman," he declared in a pretence of irritation, "*if* your application is successful, and that will to a large extent depend on the reply you give to my next question." He threw up his hands. "I assume you have no objection if I return to my interview?"

"Well, of course not, Mr Runciman. Please proceed."

"That is most considerate of you. Now." He folded his hands on the desk and met her gaze. "I understand, Miss Bridgeman, that you are a member of the British Socialist Party and that Mr Rice is active in the London and Provincial Union of Licensed Vehicle Workers."

Having prepared for this, Dorothy regarded him evenly and awaited the question he had promised. When it failed to arrive, she shook herself, as if she had perhaps dozed off and missed it. "Oh, I'm sorry, Mr Runciman, I was expecting a question. But yes, your information is correct."

"The question, Miss Bridgeman, is whether you are able to assure me that you would be able to display the integrity and discretion required of the personal secretary to the president of the Board of Trade. Might there not be a conflict of interest? Would your loyalty be to the Board or to the BSP and the red-button union?"

"Surely, Mr Runciman, the only circumstance in which a conflict of interest would arise would be if my position with the Board allowed me to influence policy. That, surely would not be the case. I would be working for the man who makes the decisions—you. Now, it is perfectly possible that I will not, personally, agree with every decision you make." She shrugged. "But that, surely, is quite common in most employment relationships—your own, for example: you are opposed to your employer's policy of conscription, and yet you feel no conflict of interest in remaining in post."

"I am, in particular, concerned with your closeness to the red-button union, Miss Bridgeman. That union is prone to industrial disputes, and the Board sometimes has the task of arbitrating or otherwise intervening. In such situations, we are privy to information provided by the employers."

"But surely it is the Chief Industrial Commissioner, not the president of the Board, who receives that information, Mr Runciman."

He nodded. "That is so…"

"I would have thought, you know, that I might be of assistance to you in some situations. If, for example, you were proposing an action involving the London and Provincial that I knew, from what you refer to as my closeness to that union, to be completely impractical, I would tell you so; it would be entirely a matter for you, of course, whether you heeded my advice."

"Really? Well, that is a possibility I had not considered." He straightened and sat back in his chair. "Well, Miss Bridgeman, I think that concludes our interview. Thank you for coming. I have enjoyed our discussion, and I will give your application very serious consideration. You should receive a letter by the weekend."

"Are there, may I ask, many other applications?"

He smiled. "I am seeing two applicants this afternoon, following which I will make my decision."

*

"Albert?"

"Walter! How good of you to call!"

"I thought you might like to know that I have just spent twenty minutes or so with the delightful, exasperating, outrageous Miss Dorothy Bridgeman."

"Oh really! And did she get the job?"

"Well, *she* interviewed *me*, and I think I've been accepted, at least provisionally, as her employer."

"Ha ha ha! Oh, I wish I could have been a fly on the wall. But what is your decision?"

"I haven't made one, Albert, as I still have a couple of people to see."

"You sound worried, Walter."

"Yes and no, yes and no."

"You sought assurances on discretion, confidentiality?"

"Actually, she came across quite well on that score...But she's so damned *assertive!*"

Stanley laughed. *"She is, Walter, but I think you will find in time that that is to your advantage. And she is extremely bright and now and then comes up with ideas that one has never previously considered. And so, now I think of it, does that young man of hers: they must be a formidable combination."*

"You know, Albert, since she left the office, I've been thinking. When I indicated that I was worried that she would pass information gained in her employment with us to the red-button union, she suggested that she could actually be of use to me; for example, if we were proposing a course of action regarding the union that she thought might prove completely counter-productive, she would tell me so. Now it seems to me that she might be useful as a channel of information—from, say, you to me to her to the union—that, in order to bring us a desirable outcome, might not always be quite accurate."

Stanley was silent for several seconds. *"I hear what you say, Walter, but let me assure you that you would only get away with that sort of thing once."*

"Worth considering, though?"

"I think not, Walter."

PART FOUR

1916

32

"See what I mean?" said Lenny Hawkins as they stood in the output one mid-morning in January. "Give 'em an inch and they'll take a fuckin' yard!"

This was in response to the news that the LGOC had announced that, as it had been unable to recruit male washers, it had no choice but to employ women, and that a special women's wage-rate would be introduced. Mickey thought that Lenny had that arse about face, because, conductors being far more numerous than washers, it surely should have been "Give 'em a yard and they'll take another fuckin' inch." But never mind.

"Don't worry, Lenny. They're just testing us."

"Oh, yeah?" said a sceptical Lenny.

"Most definitely. Watch." Mickey walked over to where the sign-on sheets were kept and called into the allocation office. "Mr Phillips!"

"Yes, Mickey?"

"Kindly tell Mr Shilling that I'm calling the men in and that they'll stay in until the company agrees to pay women washers the same wage as the men."

"Jesus." Phillips's head disappeared and two seconds later he was heard hammering on the garage superintendent's door.

"Bugger!" Although muffled, this expletive could be heard from James Shilling's office.

Within the minute, Shilling appeared at the output window, attempting a smile to mask the concern he was obviously feeling. "Look, do me a favour, Mickey. Give me a few minutes before you call them in. Let me telephone Electric Railway House."

"Ok, but no one else will be signing on until you come back with the good news."

"Oh, that's fair enough, Mickey."

"And could I have the use of your telephone?"

"Of course, Mickey, of course. Do you want to go first?"

"Not a good idea, Mr Shilling. Just let me know when your own call's finished." Sometimes, the man was not very bright: if Gerrard Street spoke to the top brass before him, they would know not only that someone had let Mickey use the telephone, but that they had given him priority.

Ten minutes later, Mickey was in the garage superintendent's office.

"Should I go for a cup of tea on the van while you make the call, Mickey?"

Mickey thought for a moment, then nodded. "Might be best, Mr Shilling."

Almost feeling sorry for him, he watched as the worried garage superintendent made for the door.

"Rose? It's Mickey Rice. Could you put me through to Ben? Hello, Ben? You might like to call Electric Railway House and tell them that I've just informed the garage superintendent that Middle Row won't have a bus on the road unless the company agrees to pay the male wage to the women washers...Jumping the gun?...Yes, yes, I know that's what Tich will say; that's why I'm talking to you...Fuck the procedure! Come to think of it, *what* procedure? They don't have an agreement with us on underpaid women washers, so there *is* no procedure. Or *do* they have an agreement with us? No? Well, that's a relief! Yes, and you can also tell them that as soon as our buses run in, the Bush and one or two others will probably do the same...OK, comrade...Have you got this number?...That's it. Probably speak to you soon, Ben."

Leaving the office, Mickey tapped on the window of the catering van and gave James Shilling the thumbs-up to let him know that his telephone was now free. The output was filling up with crews waiting to sign on for their middles, but Lenny Hawkins had made sure that no one went near the sheets. All the men were in fairly good cheer, apart from Ted Middleton who, glancing at the clock on the wall, complained, "Why should we be losing money for the sake of a few women washers?"

"Because, Brother Middleton, if we didn't there would be a woman doing *your* job before too long, *also* at lower wages."

A rumble of assent came from the other men in the output. Mickey grinned at Middleton. "Look upon it as an investment in your future, Ted."

While they waited to hear from either Gerrard Street or Electric Railway House, the men in the output mainly discussed the whole question of female labour. The union's EC had agreed to women conductors with all the necessary safeguards, and the proposal had been approved at a series of midnight meetings. The first women would soon commence training. In the meantime, the Military Service Bill was before Parliament; this would provide for the conscription of men between 18 and 41, with several exemptions, including married men and clergymen.

"So you won't have a problem working with a woman on the

back?" asked Steve Urmshaw, Mickey's conductor.

Mickey fell silent for a moment as he contemplated Steve. It came home to him that within a few months his conductor could be wearing khaki. "I don't think the question will arise, Steve."

"Oh?"

"You're too fond of a pint, mate. You'll fail the medical."

"And you're avoiding the question, Mickey," accused Lenny Hawkins.

Realising that Lenny had put him on the spot, Mickey decided to show a lead. "If," he said, pointing to the door to the garage, "my conductor is cruelly taken from me, I will volunteer to pair up with the next woman conductor who comes through that door."

The discussion turned to wages and hours, with Mickey pointing out that it was important that the union affiliated to the Transport Workers' Federation; the EC had ducked the question, referring it to the branches, so it was crucial that a big "Yes" vote was returned.

"Mickey!" All heads turned to the hatch, where James Shilling had appeared.

"Yes, Mr Shilling."

"All women washers to receive the male rate of pay!"

The men in the output were jubilant, some cheering and some slapping Mickey on the back, but he was anxious to quieten them. "But there's one more thing, Mr Shilling."

James Shilling frowned, "And what would that be, Mickey?"

"All these men who will be late signing on should be paid for full mileage."

The output fell silent. Where did the man get the gall?

I can read your mind, James Shilling, thought Mickey: If I say no, the whole garage could be on strike for the rest of the day; if I agree, Electric Railway House might think I'm weak, but a moment's thought will show them that an issue which could have brought the whole fleet to a halt has been contained in one garage at the cost of an hour or so's wages for, at most, a score of men; they should give me a bloody medal.

James Shilling sighed, slowly closed his eyes, and then nodded. "Agreed. But let's have you on the road without further delay!"

The output was filled with cheers. Lenny Hawkins grasped Mickey's hand. "You were right, brother. And we passed the test."

Mickey caught Ted Middleton's eye and winked. "Satisfied, Ted?" The little bugger nodded and almost smiled.

*

Politically, the first months of the year were somewhat mixed. In late January, the Labour Party conference in Bristol came out against conscription, although several Labour MPs would ignore the decision and continue their cooperation with the government. Tich Smith seconded the Independent Labour Party motion demanding drastic revisions of the Munitions Act, "with a view to preventing the pretext of war being used for the greater coercion and subjection of labour," which was carried with just one vote against.

"All very well," commented Sanders at the next meeting of the Vigilance Committee, "but the government will simply ignore it. And, of course, it's carelessly worded: you can see Lloyd George tugging on his lapels as he addresses the House, saying, 'Yes, Mr Speaker, I agree wholeheartedly with this motion. Of *course* we should not allow the *pretext* of war to be used to coerce labour, but what we have today is the *reality* of war!'"

Some of those who sought to win the hearts and minds of the populace for wholesale slaughter also attempted to capture their souls or, at least keep their bodies unsullied, as the Church of England organised its National Mission of Repentance and Hope and, a little later, even more puritan types, doubtless egged on by former suffragettes of the Christabel Pankhurst stripe, launched the Crusade of the United Workers for Self-Denial; and after the introduction of conscription in March, often witnessed by drivers or conductors travelling through Theatreland in the evening, there were those seeking to capture male bodies, sullied or unsullied, as the Military Police demanded to see the papers of every man of military age. Mickey found himself wondering just how much longer the pro-war people would continue to believe that they were fighting for "freedom."

In February, the internationalist forces in the British Socialist Party launched a new newspaper, *The Call*. This was a sure sign that a crisis loomed, as *Justice*, under the editorship of Harry Hyndman, was still officially the party's organ, and sure enough, finding their pro-war stance under heavy attack, and seeing that they were outnumbered at the party conference in Salford, Hyndman and his followers—one of whom was John Stokes, who had chaired the Joint Strike Committee towards the end of the previous year's London tram strike—seized upon a minor technicality and walked out of the hall, later to form the National Socialist Party. The BSP, led by the likes of Albert Inkpin, John McLean, William Gallacher, Zelda Kahan and Theodore Rothstein, was now united around its anti-war position.

In January Sylvia Pankhurst's ELFS changed its name to the Workers' Suffrage Federation, campaigning now for universal adult suffrage, and began to attract support from the left of the labour movement. On Easter Sunday, it was part of a broad coalition of forces which mobilised 20,000 to Trafalgar Square to protest against conscription and the Munitions of War Act, but the rally was disrupted by pro-war thugs, among them Australian and New Zealand troops, who pelted the platform with flour and yellow ochre.

*

In March, conscription came into force, and one day Steve Urmshaw was simply no longer there. Rather than serve His Majesty, it seems that Steve, like so many others, had gone on the run, and months later word would reach his erstwhile comrades at Middle Row that, rather than being the coward that some would have painted him, he had, accompanied by his Irish girlfriend, eventually made his way to Ireland. The Rising in Dublin which commenced on Easter Monday had by the end of the week been put down at the cost of 450 dead and some 2,000 wounded, with the city centre reduced to rubble. Steve had not been present for the Rising, for it was the following events which had inspired him to make the move. The leaders were, once in custody, systematically executed. It was, in particular, the treatment meted out to James Connolly, the Marxist founder of the Irish Republican Socialist Party who had spoken alongside Sylvia Pankhurst at the Albert Hall, which fuelled the outrage in Steve Urmshaw. Badly wounded during the battle and not expected to live, on 12 May Connolly was taken to Kilmainham Gaol, tied to a chair and executed by firing squad. The British state had made a major mistake with the executions, which evoked revulsion even in England; in Ireland, however, where support for the Rising had been lukewarm, the executed leaders were now martyrs and a partly dormant nationalism sprang into flame. And Steve Urmshaw and his Kathy crossed the Irish Sea, probably by clandestine means, to join the struggle.

None of this was known to Mickey Rice when, shortly after Steve's disappearance, he signed on one morning and was presented with Gladys Rogers, his new conductor. In her late twenties, Gladys was a large woman—not fat, but big-boned and muscular—with short dark hair and a thin-lipped, determined mouth.

"Look, Mr Rice," she said, "I hope this is alright with you..."

Having placed his signature and pay-number on the sign-on

sheet, he turned and smiled. "And why wouldn't it be alright?" He held out his hand. "Put it there. The name's Mickey, by the way."

She grinned. "Gladys."

He glanced around at the other men in the output, who had been breathlessly waiting to see if Mickey would be as good as the word he had given two months earlier. "How have these blokes been treating you?"

"Oh, they've been fine, just fine. A bit of banter, but nothing I can't handle."

He spent a moment scrutinising her for the first time before slowly nodding. "You're going to be alright, Doris..."

"It's Gladys."

"Sorry. Gladys. But first things first: did you join the union yet?"

"I saw a Mr Mortlake earlier."

"And did he sign you up?"

"He did."

"Then it's *Brother* Mortlake. The misters are all on the other side of this counter."

"You don't have any misters on this side of it?"

"Not a single one."

"Oh, that's a fine thing."

He gave her a broad smile. "Have you prepared your waybill? In that case, Gladys, let's go and introduce you to your public."

On the bus, however, she wasn't alright; she was bloody brilliant. Sometimes, after she had given him the double bell to go, Mickey would glance over his shoulder and there she would be, galloping down the aisle and taking the fares; if she was on the upper deck as they pulled in to pick up a large congregation of passengers, she would hit the platform before the first one boarded, barring the way until any departing passengers had alighted; often, he would hear her issuing instructions to the intending passengers, telling them to stop pushing and fall into line, "and it's the first seven only!"

The real test, he knew, would come during the afternoon rush at Bank, and he warned her accordingly. But she took command, ordering the crowd to form a queue, and they obeyed. After she had allowed the allotted number to board, she dropped her brusque tone and sympathetically advised the person at the head of the queue, "Sorry, love, we can't take any more. There's another one just a couple of minutes behind." Mickey mused that if the introduction of women conductors had come as a culture shock to the men in the trade, the appearance of Gladys Rogers on the platform of his number 7 bus had an even greater effect upon the passengers: by the sheer force of her personality, she made them obey her, respect her and even, in some cases, feel real affection for her. By the end of the week, some were referring to her by name: "Good night, Gladys, see you tomorrow!" "Good morning, Gladys, another long day ahead of you!" And she must have encouraged them to be just as familiar with her driver, for now and then a departing passenger would glance at his cab and shout, "G'night, Mickey!" and on one occasion, "See you tomorrow, Mickey. You've got a real diamond there!"

Yes, he had. Apart from Steve Urmshaw, Mickey had worked with a number of conductors, and none of them—not even Steve—came close to this woman on her first day on the road. He realised for the first time how much easier a conductor could make the life of a driver: due to Gladys's efficiency, they rarely lost time on the road, unless it was due to traffic; time spent wasted while overloading passengers were brought to their senses, during which the driver would count the minutes, anxiously estimating how late they would finish, was mostly eliminated; and the job was lighter because Gladys was entertaining.

That first day, Mickey learned that Gladys was a war widow whose husband had been killed during the second battle of Ypres in May the previous year; she had a four-year-old son whom her mother looked after while she was at work.

"What rank was your husband, Gladys?" Mickey asked as the bus was loading at Liverpool Street for their last trip of the day.

"Sergeant."

"Ahhh, I see."

She gave him a playful dig with her elbow. "No you don't. He didn't give me lessons, if that's what you're thinking."

Back at the garage, Mickey dropped Gladys off outside the output and was then directed onto the pumps by an Inside Staff man. As he climbed from the cab, he saw Dick Mortlake driving in. He stood and waited for him, savouring the smells of oil, petrol and the painted metal of the engine cowlings hot from a long day on the road.

"So how did it go?" Dick asked as they walked from the garage together. "You going to put her in the hat?"

"Comrade," Mickey said with a laugh, "anyone who wants my new conductor is going to have to fight me for her!"

"Is she that good, then?"

"Better."

Dick was having trouble keeping his eyes on one spot. "She's quite nice, too, isn't she?"

*

There had been no definitive outcome of the lobby of the December meeting of the Executive Council as, despite the strength of feeling of the members, and the numbers assembled outside the Gerrard Street office, it had been decided that the Special Delegate Meeting would not be called until further legal advice had been received. The EC, however, had been split, with five of the thirteen members voting against the proposal. The majority obviously could not be held together much longer, and so at its January meeting the EC agreed to convene the SDM. Then there were, or so it was claimed, difficulties with the availability of the venue, and so it was April—almost a year since the demand had first been raised—before the delegates filed into the Club and Institute Hall on the Clerkenwell Road.

Tich Smith had, in detecting a shift in the anti-war sentiments of the membership, been quite wrong to expect that the majority in favour of an election for the positions of general secretary and organising secretary would be reduced; he had also wondered whether some of the more militant spirits might have fallen victim to conscription, and while it was true that some left-wing conductors were no longer present, they had in the main been replaced by others, either married or beyond military age, who were just as uncompromising, and, moreover, the seats of some of the more moderate cabdrivers who had been swallowed up by the Army were now occupied by those of a more extreme opinion. It was not just that the acting general secretary was brought to the gloomy realisation that the vote for an election would be as solid as previously; he was also taken aback by the anger displayed by the delegates. No, it was more than anger: hostility.

"This is the parliament of our union," thundered Willesden's Reuben Topping, "elected as an ADM last year and now reassembled—following one excuse after another from some of those on the top table—as an SDM, and the decisions made here are binding on all. All! That includes *you*"—he pointed at the top table—"and if you ignore our decisions you do not deserve to sit at that table!"

"I would go further than Brother Topping," said Dick Mortlake when he was called upon to speak. "It's not just that you do not *deserve* to sit at the top table: you may rest assured that if you continue to ignore the democratic decisions of this body we will see to it that you *do* not sit there!"

Perhaps the most effective speaker was a tram driver from south of the river. "As a working man," he said, "I own practically nothing.

But one thing I *do* own, together with my fellow members, is this union. For the past few years, it has been the only thing that has given me hope and a sense of pride, and I daresay there are plenty in this hall who feel the same way." The man allowed a warm tide of assent to rise from the floor of the conference and then rode this to his conclusion. "This is *our* union!" He struck himself on the chest. "*Ours!* And if any top official or executive member thinks he can take it away from us, he will have a fight on his hands!"

The tumult following this left Tich Smith in no doubt about the outcome of the vote, but it also strengthened his understanding of the former actions and opinions of Harry Bywater and so, predetermined though the outcome of the vote might be, he resolved to continue to do his best to see that Harry was not too ill-served, giving no thought to the effect this might have on the members who even now had barely stopped short of baying for his blood. So yes, he told the conference, the nomination papers would be issued. "When?" the delegates demanded to know. Immediately, he assured them. "And when will the elections be held?" they insisted on being told, so thinly had their trust in their acting general secretary been worn down. Next month, he told them, in May. "Make sure that's minuted!" called out a delegate to a roar of approval. Yes, yes, it would be duly minuted.

"Well," said Archie Henderson to George Sanders and Eric Rice as the conference broke up around them, "that's a job well done." He frowned. "What's the matter, George? You don't look as happy as you should."

Sanders grimaced. "I can't help thinking back to a year ago, Archie. They had something up their sleeve then, and I wouldn't be surprised if they've got something up there now."

And, of course, they had.

Within a fortnight of April's SDM, nominations were submitted for H.A. Bywater and L. Russell and these were considered valid by the EC.

"Have you taken leave of your senses?" roared George Sanders as, returning to the office after a morning on the road, he arrived just after the decision had been taken. "How can they possibly be considered valid? Why are we having this election? Is it not because Brothers Bywater and Russell, having joined the Army, are unable to occupy these positions?" He looked directly at Tich Smith. "Did you not hear what the delegates were saying at the SDM, Tich?"

"The decision was taken by this Executive Council, not by the acting general secretary," intervened Jack Thompson, who was chairing the meeting. "And if you persist in this tone, Brother

Sanders, I will have to ask you to leave!"

"Then did *you* not hear what the delegates were telling you at the SDM? They think you're stealing their union, and they'll not stand for it. And now you come up with this insane decision that will only make matters worse. Good God, what's the matter will you all? Are you trying to tear this union apart?"

Tich Smith, initially taken aback by the ferocity of this attack, now recovered his composure and fixed Sanders with his gaze. "No, Brother Sanders. Are you? You with your Vigilance Committee and your divisive articles in the *Record*?"

"And you have demonstrated today why there is the need for such a committee!" Sanders retorted as he turned and left the meeting room.

For some time, there was no open clash between the opposing camps. Tich Smith organised an unofficial committee which Sanders would later describe in the *Record* as "private and confidential," the sole purpose of which was to ensure the maximum turnout of the votes for Bywater and Russell; in the event, this body found that it had very little to do, as the Vigilance Committee, condemning the whole exercise as illegitimate due to the inclusion of the two Army sergeants in the ballot, organised a boycott which, particularly in the bus and tram sections, proved very effective. The upshot of this was, of course, that victory was claimed for Bywater and Russell in the illegitimate ballot—a result which large sections of the membership then refused to recognise. However, when at its June meeting the Executive Council granted the two dubious victors leave of absence for the duration of the war, the activists influenced by the Vigilance Committee felt they must take action, and the EC found itself besieged with complaints and threats to withdraw support unless the decision was rescinded—which, in short order, it was.

The decision to grant leave of absence to Bywater and Russell had meant that Tich Smith and Ben Smith would continue as, respectively, acting general secretary and acting organising secretary; the withdrawal of leave of absence would, everyone assumed, have had the same result, but Tich Smith now, as he had after the previous year's ADM, resigned, with the result that Ben Smith, having no further taste for resignation after his previous essay had met with Sanders' scorn, became acting general secretary—to the pleasant surprise, presumably, of the struggling Smith household.

There, for the space of a few months, the matter rested.

There was, during these months of 1916, plenty to occupy the time of the red-button union and its officers. In March, Croydon Tramways rejected the union's wage demand, on the grounds that this would, if conceded, add £10,000 to the annual rates. It could, therefore, only afford to grant a small number of minor requests and advised the Chief Industrial Commissioner that it could see no point in going to arbitration.

In May it was the turn of the cabs, as the British Motor Cab Company proposed to reduce its petrol guarantee of 20 miles for eight pence to 18 miles. After arbitration decided in favour of the drivers, the company asked them to sign a paper waiving the award.

That same month delivered a further body-blow to staffing levels as those married men of military age who had breathed a sigh of relief just a few months earlier now found that, by a new Act, they, too, were to be conscripted. It was not just staffing levels, of course, because union activists were also caught in the net: the branch committee at Middle Row lost Malcolm Lewis and Billy Franklin, and the Willesden rep Reuben Topping was also whisked away although he, as good as his word, refused to fight and would soon find himself in prison. For those who did agree to fight, the future would be grim, as 196,000 British troops would be killed or wounded on the Western Front in July, a third of those on the first day of the Battle of the Somme.

In June, the government introduced petrol rationing. The LGOC announced the withdrawal of some routes and restrictions on others, and the following month Ben Smith, in his new leading role, led a deputation to the Petrol Control Committee where he suggested that bus and cab companies be granted increased allowances. That same month, the union was offered 4 million gallons of petrol by a colonial company independent of the domestic petrol cartel, but this proved too expensive an undertaking. In August, however, George Blundy turned entrepreneur as his Owner-Drivers' Branch secured the exclusive right to sell a petrol substitute within a 60-mile radius of Charing Cross, contracting for an initial 100,000 gallons.

And then came the wage negotiations with the LGOC and Tilling's.

After a vote of the branches, the union had agreed to affiliate to the National Transport Workers' Federation in February, and so hopes were high that this additional source of strength and support would finally convince the companies that hours must be reduced. It was not to be.

Ben Smith wrote to Sir Albert Stanley, advising him that Robert Williams, secretary of the NTWF, would be joining the union team this time around, but the reply he received was not the one he was looking for.

Dear Mr Smith,

Thank you for your recent correspondence regarding our forthcoming negotiations.

I was, of course, aware from press reports that your union had affiliated to the Transport Workers' Alliance. I am afraid, however, that there can be no question of this body being represented at our negotiations. The reason for this is, I think you will agree when you have given it a little thought, obvious. As I understand it, the whole purpose of this alliance is to ensure that each affiliate union will be assured of the support of its fellows in the event of a dispute. In other words, if your union, should our negotiations break down, were to declare a strike, you would, if you saw fit to do so, be able to call upon the seamen's and dockers' unions to also strike in support of your claim. Conversely, if any of those other unions were in a similar position, they would be able to call upon your union to strike alongside them.

This, I am afraid, goes to the heart of our previous agreement, Clause 3 of which states quite clearly: "The companies are not to be affected by disputes with companies with whom they have no direct concern."

I repeat, therefore, that we are unable to agree that Mr Williams, or any other representative of said alliance, should attend our negotiations.

However, we look forward to receiving your submission in due course and trust that an early date for the commencement of negotiations can be agreed.

Yours most sincerely,

Sir Albert Stanley.

There was some discussion of this by the EC, with Sanders, who had made sure he was available for this meeting, pointing out that Stanley's letter was lacking in logic.

"But the LGOC and Tilling's—this time around, anyway—*won't* be affected by disputes with other companies. It will be those other companies that would have that complaint, should we need to call on their unions to take solidarity action."

Ben Smith nodded. "Yes, George, I know, and I've put that to him over the telephone, but he's having none of it."

"So we're on our own?"

"For these negotiations, anyway. Yes." Ben shrugged. "But let's not be too pessimistic; he'll know he's been in a scrap by the time the negotiations are over."

The EC accepted the position and so, a week later, the negotiations commenced. It was late August before the new agreement was announced, at which time the headline in the *Herald* dubbed it "The Busmen's Triumph," seeing it as "a distinct and valuable series of gains." Not all members shared that view, and most were enraged by a certain sting in the tail. At Middle Row, Mickey Rice reported the results at two special meetings.

"The minimum daily rate," he announced at the morning meeting, "will be increased to seven shillings for drivers and six shillings for conductors—an extra four pence a day."

"Plus the war bonuses," said Lenny Hawkins from the floor.

"Of course, plus the war bonuses. Loss of time due to breakdowns will be paid at the full rate. Overtime will be paid at the mileage rate for the road, plus a quarter. Spare drivers who stand by for at least four hours a day will get thirty-five bob a week, and spare conductors will get thirty bob. Bank holidays will be paid at time-and-a-quarter."

"What bank holidays?" shouted Dave Springer, a driver for two years. "The government cancelled the Whitsun and August holidays this year!"

Mickey, knowing that it was too early to make them angry, let such comments pass. "Christmas Day..."

"You sure they ain't gonna cancel that as well?"

"Christmas Day will be paid at time-and-a-half, with an extra bob for duties worked after 6 p.m."

Murmurs of approval.

"General Hands to receive a minimum of five-and-fourpence a day."

Silence: few Inside Staff members, who had their own shop steward, bothered coming to branch meetings.

"To conductors who take out a learner on their bus: a tanner a day."

Cheers from the conductors.

"Paid holidays."

"Whoah! Now you're talking!"

"Three days a year, up to a maximum of seven days a year for those with six years' service…"

"Better than a kick in the pants."

"…At the rate of five-and-fourpence a day for both grades."

Groans.

"If you're declared medically unfit, the union's doctor can take a look at you, and if the two doctors disagree, a referee decides."

Mickey realised that he was following the example of Harry Bywater who, in reporting back on the initial proposals for the 1914 agreement, had saved the bitterest pill until last, although Bywater's aim had been to minimise controversy, whereas Mickey's was to maximise it. There were, moreover, no less than three bitter pills, and he could avoid them no longer.

"Spreadovers."

A tense silence descended on the meeting room.

"There will be two groups of spreadovers, one with a maximum of 14 hours, 20 minutes and the other with the old 15 hours, 10 minutes."

The meeting exploded.

"This job'll be the death of me!"

"No wonder the union's gonna 'ave its own doctor!"

"Are those geezers of the EC fuckin' deaf? 'Ow many times do they 'ave to be told?"

This was too much for Charlie Adams who, Malcolm Lewis having been conscripted, now chaired the meeting. "That's enough! If we're gonna discuss this package, we'll do it in an orderly fashion. And you all know that that kind of language is prohibited at union meetings—particularly now that there's ladies present."

And there were. There were now some fifteen women conductors at the garage and four of them were at the morning meeting. One of them now spoke.

"Thank you for that, Mr Chairman," said Gladys Rogers, fanning herself. "When I heard that, I came over all faint."

Mickey sneaked a glance at Dick Mortlake and saw that he, pretending to be engrossed in his minutes, was not very successfully attempting to suppress a grin.

Gladys's remark caused a chorus of laughter, but Charlie failed to realise that his leg was being pulled. "You're welcome, Gladys," he said primly.

"That's Sister Rogers, if you don't mind."

More laughter, and Charlie, finally getting it, flushed and thumped the table. "Alright, Mickey, finish your report."

"That's Brother Rice, if you don't mind," called another woman in the second row, causing more laughter.

They were in just the right mood, thought Mickey: angry, yes, but still able to laugh; they were not about to turn in their union cards, but should be amenable to any reasonable plan for the tightening of their control over the organisation.

"I'm almost done, brothers and sisters," he told the meeting. "They've agreed to a meal relief of not less than an hour, but have added the condition 'as far as can be arranged,' so that will mean that we'll have to keep an eye on the schedules and make sure that it *is* arranged. And on spreadovers of fifteen hours or more, there'll be a midday break of at least two-and-a-half hours."

"Is that it?" asked Charlie Adams.

"As far as the wages and conditions go, yes," Mickey replied, "but there's more bad news."

Charlie rolled his eyes. "Let's have it, then."

"In cases of dispute, there's a provision for compulsory arbitration."

"Meaning..."

"Meaning that if we have a major dispute with the company, instead of going on strike we go to the Board of Trade, where the Chief Industrial Commissioner will listen to both sides and decide who wins. Like we did when we got the recognition agreement. Oh, and by the way, the agreement I've outlined is for the London General only; Tilling's reckoned they couldn't afford it, and so they're going to arbitration."

"Bear in mind," said Charlie Adams, "that compulsory arbitration is also the law: it's in the Munitions of War Act."

"Well, it may well be," said Lenny Hawkins, "but when have we let the law come between us and a scrap with the employer? It's one thing for compulsory arbitration to be the law, but it's another thing entirely to sign an agreement on it. Look, if the arbitration proposal is gonna tie our 'ands, we have to vote to reject the whole agreement, like we did two years ago."

Mickey paused and studied his audience. This would be the big one. He took a breath. "That brings me to the last item of bad news, brothers and sisters. There's no vote for us this time around. The Executive Council has signed the agreement without seeking our consent."

"Have they got a death wish, Barney?" asked Sanders. As the Middle Row branch was discussing the same matter, Sanders sat with Barney Macauley in the Italian café in Gerrard Street.

"Without realising it, maybe," Macauley replied. "They seem to think that they can get away with anything. In the past, of course, they were following the lead of Harry Bywater and Tich Smith, and while we might disagree with the way they went about things, they at least showed a bit of prudence now and again. This crowd—or most of 'em: I was in the minority of five, so we were outnumbered almost three to one—seems to think that they're untouchable. The way I hear it, by the way, is that the idea of accepting the agreement without referring it to the members originated with Harry. Seems he mentioned it to Tich after the 1914 agreement was finally accepted."

"How did you come to hear about it?"

"Eamon Quinlan. He's a very proper Catholic boy, but he can't take a drink without telling you his life story. Seems Tich mentioned the Bywater story to him earlier in the year. Apparently, Harry also predicted that there would be no Transport Workers' Federation representative at the negotiations. "

Sanders grinned. "And what about Ben? How did he conduct himself when this suggestion came up?"

"George," Macauley assured him, looking him in the eye, "Ben did his level best. He warned them of the consequences and kept the discussion going long after they thought they would have voted the thing through, but they dug their heels in. We know he strayed from the straight and narrow when he played the resignation game last year, but Ben's back on board now, little doubt about it."

Sanders nodded. "That's good to hear. And the arbitration clause: it's in the law, so what was the point of putting it in the agreement?"

"Ben made that very point. But Stanley charmed them into it." He shook his head, chuckling. "He just sat there and fucking *charmed* them! 'Yes, Mr Smith, I am of course quite aware that it's in the Munitions of War Act,' he said. 'But I am also aware that your union thinks nothing of ignoring the law—any law.' He's laughing as he says this, you understand. Then he looks around the table, smiling at us like a kind uncle. 'Look at it this way, lads,' he says—*lads*, he calls us, even though he's younger than some of us. 'When it comes to the London General, I rather wish arbitration was *not* in the law. I would much prefer a situation where, if there was a dispute, the

374

union went to arbitration not because it was forced by the law to do so, but because you had agreed with a decent employer that this is what you would do, at least for the duration of the war.' He clasped his hands as if he was about to break into prayer, put his elbows on the table and said, 'You see, lads, I want there to be *trust* between us, mutual respect and *trust.*'

"Well, fuck me, I look around the table and you can almost see tears in some of their eyes! No point arguing against it after that!"

Sanders laughed at Macauley's mimicry. "But it sounds to me, Barney, as if *you* were charmed as well."

"Funny you should say that, George, because while I wouldn't say that he charmed me, I *did* find myself wondering why we shouldn't give him this, because it was already in the law, and so what harm would it do? And, besides, if we gave him this, he might be a bit more generous on one or two other things."

"And was he?"

"Was he fuck!"

Sanders laughed. He looked about him and sighed. "Well, Barney, what is the EC thinking of doing next?"

"What's left for them to do? They'll seek endorsement of the practice of signing agreements without the members' endorsement, and they'll try to see to it that organisers are appointed rather than elected."

Sanders frowned at him. "You can't be serious. *They* can't be serious."

Barney shrugged. "You watch them, George. But the Cab Section is also making a lot of noise at the moment; they want Tich back."

"But that would only be possible if he let go of Bywater and Russell."

Macauley nodded. "I think some of 'em are working on that, George."

33

Walter Runciman was, Dorothy soon learned, punishingly busy, very hard-working, and often harried and harassed by his critics and political enemies. The presidency of the Board of Trade was not, she came to realise, simply one job, as the holder of that position was also, by definition, an MP and a member of the Cabinet, each of which brought its own duties and stresses. This also meant that she was not *the* personal secretary to Mr Runciman, but one of two; she handled the Board's business, while a male counterpart ministered to the political duties. Even so, she was fully occupied, and soon came to wonder how Runciman was managing to bear the strain; within months, it would become apparent that he was not.

This being wartime, there was no prolonged Christmas break, and 27 December, 1915 found Runciman at a Cabinet meeting in Downing Street, where he and Reginald McKenna, now Chancellor of the Exchequer, opposed military conscription on the grounds that it would dangerously deplete the industrial workforce. In the Commons on 6 January, Runciman voted against the conscription bill, but was not called upon to resign. His father, Sir Walter Runciman, was also an MP and, Dorothy noted, also opposed conscription—but on more idealistic grounds than his son, both his grandfathers having fought at Trafalgar as victims of the press gang.

A fortnight later, the younger Runciman's integrity was being questioned when it was learned that the firm Runciman of London had been used as shipbroker on the Government's behalf to charter ships; asked by Oswald Partington to explain his connection with the company, he told the Commons that he had resigned from the firm a decade earlier and that his only current connection with it lay in the fact that his father was its chairman.

"Don't you find it surprising, Mr Runciman," Dorothy asked him, "that your critics should focus on this rather than the fact that the Government has requisitioned almost half of the Moor Line's fleet?"

Runciman pondered this. The Admiralty had indeed commandeered fourteen of the 33 ships owned by the Newcastle-based Moor Line, of which his father was also chairman. At last he saw her point, and laughed. "Ah, you misunderstand the situation, Miss Bridgeman! When the Admiralty requisitions a merchant ship, its owner receives but a fraction of what he would have earned had it been a straightforward commercial transaction. My critics are well aware of this, and so see no mileage in attacking me on that score."

Runciman's job, Dorothy soon saw, was not one likely to win him popularity. In late January, having received the consent of the Cabinet, he began to prepare a list of "superfluities," the import of which would be either reduced or banned, thus freeing tonnage for activity of more value to the nation. When he announced in the Commons that his list would include paper and paper-making materials, raw tobacco, building materials, woods and some fruits, the reaction was predictable, and thus much of his time in early February was taken up by meeting, and as far as possible assuaging the concerns of, those affected.

Shortly after his announcement, as Dorothy brought him his

morning post, Runciman looked up from his desk and groaned.

"Who is protesting this morning, Miss Bridgeman?" he asked. There were deep rings beneath his eyes. It was no surprise that at the end of January a meeting of businessmen had, while expressing admiration for Runciman's performance, called for the creation of a Minister of Commerce to lighten his burden with respect to the trade war against the Central Powers.

"The Hull fruit trade, the Unionist Business Committee of the House of Commons, the tobacco importers, and the Derry Typographical Association, sir," she replied. "Among others."

"And they all want to send a deputation?"

"I'm afraid so."

He buried his face in his hands for a moment before straightening his back and uttering a long sigh. "Then you'd better bring the diary, Dorothy." He called her Dorothy sometimes.

"I have it here, sir." She removed his diary from beneath the pile of correspondence, which she placed on his desk, and flipped open the pages. "I thought you might be able to see the tobacco importers and the Business Committee on the ninth, while the fruit trade..."

When she had completed the list of suggested appointments, he found it impossible to suppress a smile. "I seem to recall, Dorothy, that when I interviewed you I agreed that we might review your remuneration in the light of your performance."

"Why, yes, I do have a *faint* recollection of that, Mr Runciman."

"How does an extra fifteen shillings a week sound to you?"

She smiled. "It sounds most welcome, sir. Thank you very much."

Despite his tiredness, he grinned playfully. "And having arranged the meetings, you wouldn't like to take them for me, would you?"

"Are you now offering me *your* salary, Mr Runciman?"

He chuckled. "Not yet, Miss Bridgeman, not yet."

"Then I fear that I must confine myself to taking the minutes at the meetings, sir."

The deputations duly came and were dealt with, and, as always, Dorothy found herself impressed by both Runciman's firmness and his ability to listen sympathetically. When, however, he issued a proclamation in mid-February regarding the import of paper, wood pulp and other paper-making materials, the blow was not as heavy as many had feared, for he established a commission to grant licenses for the import as such quantities as the Board of Trade directed and to arrange the distribution thereof. In March, he announced that a total ban would be placed on the import of canned, bottled and dried fruits and preserves, except currants, to be followed by a restriction on fresh fruit, unless from the Empire. His proclamation of 21 March banned the import of motor cars for private use, musical instruments and spirits, with the exceptions of rum and brandy.

The restrictions on imports were a result of the shortage of carrying capacity, as the Admiralty had commandeered such a large proportion of the merchant fleet, and this matter occupied a considerable amount of Runciman's time and energy. At the end of January, a meeting of the North of England Steamship Owners' Association, at which Sir Walter Runciman was present, called upon the government to ensure the speedy completion of those merchant vessels under construction, and a few days later his son toured the Tyne shipyards with M. Clemental, the French Commerce Minister, staying overnight at Doxford Hall, the Runcimans' family home in Northumberland.

Several criticisms were levelled at the government's shipping policy. The deputation from the Business Committee had urged a "more effectual means" for control of the merchant fleet, and in mid-February a number of allegations were voiced in the Commons. Arthur Balfour, First Lord of the Admiralty, was first on his feet in defence of the government, as the Admiralty, rather than the Board of Trade, was felt to be more responsible for the current problems, but Runciman followed him and gave a spirited reply to the criticisms as they affected the Board. Neutral shipping was capturing too great a proportion of British trade? Well, due to the very circumstances under discussion, of course it was, but "drive that away and we shall starve!" British ship-owners were sucking the blood of the Italian consumers? Not so: a glance at the figures would tell you that non-British ships had cornered the major part of the carrying trade to our ally, and that their rates were higher than ours!

It was not *just* that Britain was desperately short of tonnage, argued Runciman. Our ports were congested. And why was that? Forty thousand dockers had been lost to the war. He paused to let that sink in, for this was as much an argument against the extension of conscription as a defence of his department. Some dockers were now returning, and, by agreement with the military, more would come. At one point, almost a third of the horses in the docks could not be taken from their stables because men were unavailable! And was the private sector entirely blameless in the matter of our shipping problems? Far from it: for example, cloth made in the West Riding of Yorkshire was being sent to Pimlico in London to be stored, and then returned to Leeds to be made up. Such foolishness must cease!

In one sense, Runciman got off lightly, for public condemnation of war-profiteering was widespread during this period, but although voices were often raised against high shipping-rates, little criticism was levelled at the £374,000 profit declared by his father's Moor Line in February, allowing it to pay a dividend of 25 percent, double that of the previous year. It was not alone: the Cairn Line, also out of Newcastle, paid a dividend of 30 percent, three times that of 1915, while Liverpool's Holt Line declared a scandalous 106 percent for the fourth time. So while Sir Walter Runciman might from time to time point to the inflated shipping-rates and to the fact that almost half of his own fleet had been requisitioned by the Admiralty, his own company was doing very nicely, even if others were doing better. Dorothy noted that in the office Runciman studiously avoided discussion of shipping matters in the days following the press accounts of the Moor Line's profits.

A significant part of Runciman's duties consisted of dealing with labour disputes and the concerns of both employers and trade unions. He met representatives of the engineering unions, who demanded that the engineering shops be declared controlled establishments, thus guaranteeing safeguards for wages and conditions where dilution was introduced. A week later, he seemed to be putting off a meeting with South Wales miners' leaders, who had a different interpretation of the agreement on Sunday-night shifts than their employers; it was a further week before he met them.

A delegation from the TUC's Parliamentary Committee arrived to express its concern over the employment of women in the engineering trade, urging their speedy replacement by men at the war's end, with the formation in each local area of committees consisting of representatives of the employers, the workmen and women's labour organisations. Runciman smiled at this, remarking that the Government had anticipated this suggestion and was already considering the formation of "restoration committees." Aware that Runciman was periodically glancing in her direction as she minuted this exchange, Dorothy had to struggle to maintain her equanimity, clenching her teeth and exerting rather more pressure on her pencil than was strictly necessary. When the discussion moved on to the restrictions placed on trade union amalgamations, however, she was barely able to avoid bursting into laughter; that evening, she mentioned it to Mickey.

"He reminded the Parliamentary Committee that a Bill had been before the House for quite some time and suggested that opposition to amalgamation proposals might be greatly reduced if they were prepared to accept realistic thresholds."

"Thresholds?"

"Yes, you know: a minimum number of members of each union participating in the ballot, and a minimum majority for an amalgamation proposal to be accepted."

"Got you. And what did he propose?"

Dorothy managed to swallow a guffaw and then rapidly delivered her reply before laughter rendered her incomprehensible. "A-minimum-of-80 percent-participating in the ballot..." She got no further.

"He said *whaaaat?*" Mickey exploded. "Is this boss of yours serious?"

Dorothy wiped her eyes and brought herself under control. She looked at him seriously for a moment. "Do you know, Mickey, I sometimes wonder. I really do."

Snowed under with work as he was, Runciman now and again created problems for himself.

"Do you remember, Miss Bridgeman," he asked her one morning in April, "that during your interview, you said that occasions might arise —if, for example, we were proposing a certain course of action concerning the red-button union—when you could offer me advice?"

"Yes, I *do* recall some words to that effect, Mr Runciman." She raised an eyebrow. "Nothing too drastic, one hopes?"

"Not at all, not at all," he said, dismissing the possibility with the wave of a hand. He leaned forward, placing an elbow on his desk. "In fact, it's something of which you might approve."

Dorothy closed her eyes and sighed. "Women drivers."

Nonplussed, Runciman sat back in his chair. "My goodness, Dorothy, you *are* sharp. But not for the buses. Trams. I think you'll agree that there is no real reason why women shouldn't be trained to drive trams. It's an entirely different kettle of fish. For example, unlike a bus, there is no heavy steering on a tram—no steering at all, in fact." He managed a grin. "What do you think?"

"It might help if you told me what, specifically, you're proposing, sir."

He pressed his palms downwards. "Absolutely nothing major, Dorothy. Just an experiment, really: we thought we might suggest that one of the small tram companies in southeast London should train a couple of women as drivers. Just to see whether they're up to it, so to speak." He smiled. "Personally, I think that it will demonstrate that there is absolutely no reason why a woman should not be a motorman. So to speak." He leaned forward earnestly. "Surely, Miss Bridgeman, you, given your previous activity in East

London, would want to see that."

She sighed. "But you see, Mr Runciman, it really does not matter what I would want. The important thing is what the union will do, should you begin your experiment."

"And what *will* the union do?"

"Strike, of course."

"And if we persist?"

"Then the strike will spread."

Runciman pursed his lips and nodded. "I see."

Dorothy cocked her head to one side and squinted at him. "You intend to go through with it, don't you?"

He sighed. "Well, I would *certainly* like to see the results, yes."

The results were as Dorothy had predicted, and the experiment was swiftly curtailed.

Women workers were, in fact, high on Walter Runciman's agenda. Along with Home Secretary Herbert Samuel, he signed an appeal to employers, beseeching them to release women from unproductive employment so that they might assist the war effort. He also joined Lord Selborne, President of the Board of Agriculture, in signing a Government certificate presented to every woman registered for work on the land. "Every woman who helps in agriculture during the war," this read, "is as truly serving her country as the man who is fighting in the trenches or on the sea." After 30 days of such work, the women would qualify for the official armband.

"What do you think?" Dorothy asked Mickey after she had told him of the scheme.

He laughed. "I assume he didn't ask your opinion of this one..."

"Well, to be honest, it really came from the Board of Agriculture."

Mickey shook his head. "Do these toffs really think that the kind of women who are prepared to work on the land will swell with patriotic pride once they get their certificates and armbands? They know nothing of ordinary people!"

By May, Runciman was showing signs of strain, not least of all because on top of his normal duties he was assigned, along with Bonar Law, Secretary of State for the Colonies, and Billy Hughes, the Australian Prime Minister, to attend a meeting with the Allies in Paris, at which a joint approach to the commercial war with the Central Powers, both during and after the war, would hopefully be agreed.

"And what is my role to be?" Dorothy overheard him ask someone during the course of a telephone conversation. "No, and nor does anybody else! You know how Lord Crewe described our mission in the House of Lords in April? We will attend the conference with no instructions, and once there we will commit the Government to no particular course!" He passed a hand over his face. "It's rather like being asked to take the leading role in a West End play and being told, 'Oh, and by the way, you'll have to write the part yourself!'"

Initially, it was thought that the Paris conference would take place in April, but April became May, the weeks of which slipped away as more pressing matters claimed Runciman's attention; Dorothy thought that he was, in fact, not at all concerned by the delay.

Not least among the issues detaining him in London was the divisions in the Cabinet over the forthcoming Military Service Bill, which would extend conscription to married men. This had been expected in April, but on the seventeenth of that month Asquith told the Commons that he was unable as yet to make a statement, as they were still some "outstanding points." There was really only one, however: David Lloyd George, the Minister of Munitions, was determined to secure all-out compulsion, while many in the Cabinet, Runciman among them, took the view that no further measures were required. Just over a week later, the fall of the government seemed a real possibility, but a "formula" was then found that commanded majority support: unless 50,000 unattested married men enlisted, a Bill would be introduced for the conscription of 200,000 unattested married men. When the Bill had its second reading on 4 May, Runciman and his father were among the Liberals who voted against; Labour dissenters included Ramsay MacDonald, Philip Snowden and J.H. Thomas, the railway workers' leader. But the Bill was passed by 328 votes to 36.

Dorothy had for some time neither the time nor the inclination to write, but the House debate on the Military Service Bill so enraged her that she now felt compelled to put her thoughts on paper and so she surreptitiously used her office typewriter to hammer out a short article which, she thought, she might submit to the *Dreadnought* under a pen-name. This read:

> During the debate on the Military Service Bill on 5 May, Mr David Lloyd George, Minister of Munitions and the leading warmonger in Mr Asquith's Cabinet, remarked that he had never believed that conscription would lead to trouble in the ranks of labour. When it came to patriotism, he claimed, there was no difference between the classes in this country.
>
> Later in the debate, Mr Will Thorne, a founding member of the National Union of Gas Workers and General Labourers, and MP for West Ham South, demonstrated that Mr Lloyd George might be

right when he boldly claimed: "There is no Trade Union executive in the country that will give a unanimous vote against the war or against conscription."

It was the Labour Chief Whip, Mr Frank Goldstone, who pointed out that the railwaymen's executive was against the Bill. He might also have mentioned that the London and Provincial Union of Licensed Vehicle Workers has consistently opposed conscription. The executive of Mr Thorne's own union may not oppose conscription, but his constituency party certainly does — as, indeed, did the Labour Party at its Conference in Bristol earlier this year. It will be recalled that Mr Thorne was one of those who followed Henry Hyndman out of the British Socialist Party when it became obvious that the anti-war forces commanded a majority at its Conference in Salford last month.

It is clear by now that many of the Labour members of the House of Commons have little regard for the democratic decisions of the party which placed them in office or the real interests of the class from which they spring. This was amply demonstrated by Mr Arthur Henderson, secretary of the Labour Party conference, when, during the debate on the Bill, he said that if his position would preclude him from doing his duty to his country, he would choose his country before his party.

Seen in this light, the attraction which syndicalism exercises over important sections of the trade union movement is perfectly comprehensible: what use is parliamentary activity if the end result is the election of men who feel free to ignore the wishes of those who elected them? But this smacks of defeatism, and in reality there is no alternative to the hard work which needs to be expended on reforming the Labour Party, ensuring that the interests of the working class are paramount and that the electors have effective control of the elected.

That evening, as she prepared to leave the office, she took the article from her drawer and placed it on the desk, preparatory to slipping it into her bag. At that moment, Runciman strolled through the office, pausing at Dorothy's desk.

"Off home after another hard day at the coal-face, Dorothy?" he quipped. Despite the lightness of the remark, he looked tired and stressed.

"Yes, sir, unless there is anything…"

He shook his head. "No, nothing…" The single sheet on the corner of her desk caught his eye and he reached for it. "Something for me, Dorothy?"

She cleared her throat. "I'm afraid not, sir. It's just something I dashed off during my lunch-break."

He ran his eye over it, murmuring, "But using the Board's paper and typewriter ribbon, I suppose…"

"Well, yes, but…"

He held up a hand while he finished reading. Finally, he looked up and grinned. "Money well spent, I would say. Well done, Dorothy. If only I had such freedom…" After issuing a wistful sigh, he handed her the sheet and sauntered off.

Sylvia Pankhurst, however, was less easily pleased than Walter Runciman. Being increasingly hostile to the Labour Party she was, Dorothy assumed, opposed to the final paragraph, and so when the article failed to appear in the *Dreadnought*, Dorothy gave it to George Sanders, who found space for it in the *Licensed Vehicle Trades Record*.

Discontent in the South Wales coalfield was still rumbling on, the differences between the two sides having grown, as the South Wales Miners' Federation was demanding a wage-rise, the establishment of a coal selling-price equivalent to the miners' minimum wage, and the appointment of a new, independent chairman of the Coal Conciliation Board with the power to base wage awards only on the selling-price of coal, regardless of any increase in the costs of production. Accompanied by Sir George Askwith, his Chief Industrial Commissioner, Runciman met the union leaders, and said that he would convene a meeting of the Conciliation Board in Cardiff to consider the claim.

After the meeting, he summoned Dorothy to his office in order to dictate the necessary correspondence to the Conciliation Board, but for a long while he simply sat at his desk, having turned his chair sideways, legs outstretched and eyes closed.

"I have no doubt," he said suddenly, as if emerging from a brief nap, "that the miners can see that the coal-owners are making record profits due to the wartime demand for their product, while those at the dirty end of the job are finding it hard to keep pace with the increased cost of living." He looked across the desk at Dorothy. "What am I to do? Industry needs coal; miners and their families need food on the table; the coal-owners need to make a profit."

Dorothy noted that the hand which he passed over his hair exhibited a slight tremor.

"Sometimes, I think that this job is becoming impossible, Miss Bridgeman. Industry must operate at optimum efficiency, and yet the Army drains it of workers. Trade must continue as before, and yet the Admiralty commandeers merchant shipping. Agricultural production must increase, and yet again the Army takes the farmworkers from the land. People look to me to hold prices down, and yet how is that possible in these conditions? I feel, Miss Bridgeman, as if I am at my wits' end."

A few days later, he did not appear in the office, and it was announced that his doctor had ordered a complete rest. While he was indisposed—a period estimated at six weeks—Mr Lewis Harcourt would be acting president of the Board of Trade.

34

After his arrival, Lewis Harcourt immediately began making preparations to attend the Paris conference, which had finally been arranged to commence on 5 June. At 53, he was still slim and handsome, with a carefully groomed moustache and immaculate wardrobe, and able to switch on the charm whenever he felt it might be useful. Dorothy noted that his eyes lingered on her as they were introduced and realised that she would have to be on her guard.

Shortly after Harcourt come over to the Board—he was First Commissioner of Works, having been demoted by Asquith after five years as Secretary of State for the Colonies—Dorothy received a visit from her father. She found this somewhat strange, as Sir George Bridgeman had been to the Board on business earlier in the year and yet had not sought her out. As she entered Harcourt's office, late that morning, shortly before Harcourt was due to leave for the House, she found them at the window, casually chatting.

"Dorothy!" her father exclaimed as he turned from the window.

Dorothy's mouth dropped open, but so also did Harcourt's. "Oh, Miss Bridgeman, why did I not know that your first name was Dorothy? Such a nice name, I've always thought." He smiled in reminiscence. "I knew a Dorothy once." He gave his head a brisk shake. "Years ago now." His mouth dropped open once more and, pointing at the two, who were now embracing, said, "Oh, but of course: *Bridgeman!*"

Sir George, his arms wrapped around Dorothy, kissed her on the forehead and, looking across at Harcourt, assured him: "Yes, Mr Harcourt, Dorothy is my precious, precious daughter."

Harcourt seemed flustered. "Well, Sir George, if there's nothing else..."

"In all honesty, Mr Harcourt, it was really Dorothy that I came to see."

"Well, I must be off to the House—which is presumably what Miss Bridgeman has come to tell me—and so you must feel free to use this office."

Following Harcourt's departure, they sat at a sofa situated opposite the door, holding hands, each searching the features of the other as if they might find there evidence of the lives lived since they had last seen each other. Sir George was a well-built man nearing sixty, but still robust and good-looking, feeling no compunction to disguise his features with whiskers, although his hair was quite grey.

"Dorothy, I have missed you so," he breathed. "And, of course, I have worried about you."

She squeezed his hands. "No need for worry, Daddy. I am healthy and quite safe."

"You are even lovelier than before, although"—he touched her hair with his right hand—"I fancy I see a little grey here."

"The pot calling the kettle black, Daddy."

He laughed. "And your mother misses you also, Dorothy."

She frowned.

He touched her cheek. "She *does* care about you, my precious; you should not doubt that."

"She sometimes has a funny way of showing it, Daddy."

He sighed and dropped his eyes. "I know, dear, I know."

"So, Daddy, tell me why you're here."

He raised his eyebrows, genuinely aggrieved. "Oh, Dorothy, do you doubt my affection as well?"

She gave his hands another squeeze. "No, of course not; and please rest assured that it is returned in full measure." She paused. "But there's more, isn't there?"

He nodded, grinning ruefully. "As perceptive as ever, eh?" A sigh. "Yes, Dorothy, in truth I came to warn you about that creature who has just left us."

"Mr Harcourt?"

"The same. How much do you know about him?"

She pouted. "Well, that his father was Sir William Harcourt, Chancellor of the Exchequer and Home Secretary under Gladstone, and that Lewis delayed his own entry into politics while he served as Sir William's secretary. With the death of his father, Mr Harcourt was elected to Parliament and became First Commissioner of Works, then Secretary of State for the Colonies until last year."

"Do you find him honest?"

"It's far too early to tell, but I think not."

In Sir George's laugh there was both surprise and delight. "Why do you say that, Dorothy?"

"In our first casual conversation, he told me that he had been instrumental in changing the Prime Minister's mind on women's suffrage, in fact that universal suffrage was desirable. I know this to be false, because Mr Asquith reached this conclusion after he had met a delegation of East End women, organised by Sylvia Pankhurst, in 1914. I think Mr Harcourt was trying to impress me."

Her father nodded. "Yes, Mr Harcourt is a poseur. In 1914, he acted as a fierce opponent of war, claiming that he had organised a majority of the Cabinet—including your boss Mr Runciman—in such opposition, and yet he came to support it. This opponent of war, incidentally, is a shareholder in Vickers, the armaments firm. Similarly, he opposed conscription, and yet has accepted it. Six years ago, while claiming to be a Radical, he did his utmost to obstruct Lloyd George's so-called 'people's budget.' So you should place little trust in anything he says, my dear."

Dorothy narrowed her eyes. "But I get the impression, Daddy, that this is merely by way of a preamble."

"You see what I mean? Sharp as ever!" He sighed, dropping his eyes. "To a certain extent, I suppose I'm avoiding the real point, because I don't quite know how to broach such a delicate matter with my own daughter."

"Your daughter is quite wise to the ways of the world, Daddy, so I suggest you just say it."

He nodded, looked up at her and grinned. "Lewis Harcourt— 'Loulou' to his friends— is descended from the Norman family of the same name, Errand of Harcourt and three brothers having accompanied William in his conquest of England; the Oxfordshire land acquired in the late 12th century is still owned by the family. Now, Dorothy, people with such an illustrious background often have a sense of...entitlement, I suppose, especially when it comes to carnal matters."

"Ah, now we're getting there."

He swatted her hand playfully. "You're *such* a naughty girl, Dorothy."

"But tell me about the naughty boy."

"Lewis Harcourt, Dorothy, is not merely a naughty boy. He is a *very* naughty boy. You heard him say that several years ago he knew someone called Dorothy. This was almost certainly a reference to Dorothy Brett, Lord Esher's daughter. Dorothy Brett, my dear, was the victim of an attempted sexual assault by Lewis Harcourt."

"She didn't report it?"

"She was only fourteen or fifteen at the time, my dear."

"Oh, my goodness!"

"Having failed with Dorothy, Mr Harcourt then attempted to seduce one of her brothers. Mr Harcourt's sexual appetites, you see, make no gender distinctions."

"Did Lord Esher not take action?"

"If he knew about it, action would have been difficult, as it is no secret that His Lordship's appetites are similar to those of Mr Harcourt."

Suddenly, and to her father's great surprise, Dorothy burst into laughter.

"Dorothy, Dorothy, what can you *possibly* find funny about this matter? Come now, pull yourself together."

"Oh, forgive me, Daddy, and may Dorothy Brett and her brother also forgive me, but does one laugh or cry when confronted with the reality that this is the class that sits astride the greatest empire the world has ever known?"

Sir George groaned. "Oh, what have I done? I might have known that you would make political capital out of this!"

"But of course, Daddy! If the people who are ruled by these asses—both at home and abroad—were privy to knowledge like this, do you think they would continue to accept their subject status? Of course not! There would be revolutions all over the place! Presumably, this is one of the reasons for the libel laws. Talk about the emperor having no clothes!"

"Yes, yes, yes, that's all very well." Her father waved his hand, as if dismissing such childish imaginings. "But please tell me that you will be careful of this man. *Please*, Dorothy."

"But, Daddy, I can now see that your effusive display of affection when you first saw me—yes, yes, all perfectly sincere, I'm sure—was meant as a warning to Loulou..." She burst into laughter again. "If he has been warned, what do I have to fear?"

"Hopefully nothing, dear, but the cravings to which such men are subject are sometimes...ungovernable." He fixed her with a gaze. "Seriously, now, Dorothy, if he so much as touches you, you must tell me." He nodded. "And then I, believe me, will be the second person in our family to go to prison."

This was the first time they had spoken about her brief visit to Holloway; whatever knowledge her father had of it could only have come from *The Times*. She smiled at him and kissed his cheek. "Don't worry, Daddy. I'm perfectly capable of defending myself. And should I need an avenger, there is one close at hand."

"Ah, your young bus driver, I suppose. Was he also jailed for stoning trams?"

"No, Daddy, he's far more sensible than I."

"Well, that's something, I suppose. I'm glad to hear it, Dorothy. But can a sensible man be relied upon to punish this creature Harcourt if he molests you?"

She nodded. "Oh, I think so, Daddy. And, should it come to that, he will do it sensibly."

*

Rather than feeling nervous whenever Harcourt was in the vicinity, since her father's revelations Dorothy looked upon him as practically harmless, someone not to be taken seriously, or as hardly likely to risk molesting an adult. And he seemed to have taken note of Sir George's veiled warning, for if he ogled her it must have been while her back was turned, for she never noticed him doing it.

As far as the job was concerned, Harcourt appeared to be applying himself with the requisite amount of energy, although he showed none of the concern for his own popularity that had played such a part in bringing Runciman to his knees. There was, however, the occasional questionable decision as when, in July, he conceded the demand of the South Wales coal-owners for an additional half-crown on a ton of coal for domestic use; this looked suspiciously like compensation for the wage-rise granted to the miners, and Dorothy was not at all sure how Runciman would feel about this. At the end of June, it was Harcourt the inconsistent pacifist who proposed that a small plate be placed in the House to commemorate the fact that Lord Kitchener had addressed the Commons on 2 June, before dying at sea three days later; en route to Russia, HMS *Hampshire* had struck a mine just west of the Orkneys.

At the beginning of August, Harcourt stood in the Commons and did what Runciman had so often been compelled to do: convey bad news, in this case restrictions on the distribution of petrol. Although one major cause of the crisis was the shortage of tankers—no sooner was one launched than it was commandeered by the Admiralty—, it was also true that the Army's consumption had increased dramatically, almost the whole of the battle of Verdun having been fought by motor transport. Civilian consumption had also rocketed upwards, from 111 million gallons to this year's 153 million gallons, although the Army was also partly responsible for this, as traders had been forced to switch to commercial vehicles as horses and men had been claimed by the military. The upshot of this was that the Petrol Committee had received 224,000 applications for licenses, but of the 153 million gallons demanded, only 70 million gallons were available.

After an absence of two months, Runciman attended a Cabinet meeting in early August, although he was not yet fit enough to resume his duties at the Board of Trade. It was around this time that Lewis Harcourt, possibly seeing that he would soon no longer have the opportunity, pounced.

*

"He *attacked* you?" This from Mickey as, arriving home at 11 p.m., he noticed Dorothy's grazed knuckles and asked her how she had sustained the injury.

She told him the whole story, beginning with the warning she had received from her father.

"But sweetheart, why didn't you ask for a transfer?" He was kneeling at the side of her chair, still in his uniform.

"Because I wasn't afraid of him, Mickey." She was perfectly calm, not at all upset. "And I'm still not. If anything, I imagine *he* will be a little fearful of *me* after today's encounter."

Torn between admiration and concern, he sighed. "Alright, so what happened today?"

"He had just finished dictating the correspondence, shortly before he was due to leave for the House. I scooped up my shorthand book and pencils and stood up to leave, when he asked me to stay. He came around the desk and laid his hand on my arm. 'Miss Bridgeman,' he said, 'you are quite the loveliest creature I have ever seen, and it breaks my heart to think that I will never see you again once Mr Runciman returns.'

"I looked him in the eye. There was perspiration on his forehead and he seemed short of breath. 'You are making a big mistake, Mr Harcourt,' I told him.

"'Oh, come now, Miss Bridgeman, you don't mean to tell me that Mr Runciman never...'

"'Mr Runciman,' I said, 'is a married man.'

"Still, he persisted. 'And so am I!' he declared. 'Besides, have you ever *seen* Hilda Runciman?'

"'As a matter of fact, I have,' I said. You remember, Mickey, that we caught sight of her at the Albert Hall last year.

"'In that case,' he said, 'you know what I mean. So come, let me show my affection for you.'

"'And how would you propose to do that, Mr Harcourt?' I asked him.

"'Oh, I think you know that well enough, Miss Bridgeman,' he said, and he moved closer to me, so I could feel his swelling penis against my leg."

"I'll kill the bastard," Mickey vowed through clenched teeth.

"That would be a trifle extreme, Mickey. Anyway, I told him, 'I think not, Mr Harcourt,' and took a step away from him.

"And what did he do then?"

"He reached forward and gripped my breast, so I dropped my book and pencils and swung my fist into his face as hard as I could. I caught his teeth, hence my grazed knuckles. He stood there for a moment, apparently amazed that I had dared to strike him. Then I raised my skirt—you should have seen his face, Mickey: the fool seemed to interpret this as me having second thoughts—and kicked him hard between the legs."

Mickey rubbed his hands together. "Good for you, sweetheart, good for you."

"While he was doubled up in pain, I gathered up my book and pencils and stormed into my own office, where I took the letter opener from the desk and went back to him."

"Oh, no..."

She smiled. "No, Mickey. By the time I got back there, he had straightened up and was trying to recover his dignity. I waved the letter-opener in his face. 'If in future you so much as come near me with an erect penis, Mr Harcourt, I shall cut it off with this! Do you understand?'

"'No,' he said.

"'No?' I said. 'What do you mean, No?'"

"That thing is blunt, Miss Bridgeman,' he said, and I suppose you have to give it to him: he's not without humour.

"'That,' I said, 'is precisely the point: it will take a long time and will be extremely painful. This is one of the consequences of assaulting an *adult*, Mr Harcourt.'"

"I'll bet that took him back," commented Mickey.

Dorothy shook her head. "Not that he showed it. He actually grinned and said that he always knew that I would be a challenge."

"So he hasn't learned his lesson..."

"Possibly not, but I can handle him, Mickey."

"But on the other hand, he hasn't sacked you."

"How could he do that, when his reputation is, apparently, not a secret, and I'm not the usual anonymous office clerk?"

"Anyway, tomorrow some of our people will be at the Board of Trade for an arbitration case concerning one of the smaller tram companies. I'll see if I can get myself smuggled in."

"But Sir George Askew is dealing with that."

"Yes, I realise that, sweetheart, but that will get me into the building. How do I find Harcourt's office?"

She told him.

"Does he have a private lavatory?"

"No, but there's one directly opposite his office door."

"Does anyone else use it?"

"Now and again, but rarely."

"How often does *he* use it?"

She sighed impatiently. "How could I possibly know, Mickey?" She passed a moment in thought. "Well, when he first arrives in the morning…"

"Which is at…?"

"Around nine-thirty. Mickey, you realise that you're risking everything? You really don't have to do this masculine thing, you know."

He kissed her hand. "I wouldn't be much of a man if I didn't, would I? And besides, I probably won't be risking as much as you think."

*

At 8.30 the next morning, having left home before Dorothy, Mickey stood in the lobby at Old Palace Yard, talking to Barney Macauley and one or two others, trying to look as if he belonged there and keeping a lookout for Lewis Harcourt in case he should arrive earlier than usual. He received a confused frown as Ben Smith came through the doors, but Macauley simply told him that Mickey was there on private business, despite the fact that he was wearing his uniform, his badge boldly on display on his lapel. No member of staff gave him a second glance, and he began to relax. At five to nine, he stepped into the lift with the rest of the union party, exiting with them but taking the stairs as they were led to the conference room where the arbitration hearing was to be held. Reaching Harcourt's floor, he walked stealthily down the corridor until a door on the right announced itself as the portal to the president's office; he tried the door opposite, marked "GENTLEMEN," and, finding it unlocked, stepped in and bolted himself into one of the cubicles.

Within minutes, he heard the clack-clack of footsteps outside; a woman's gait, probably Dorothy arriving at work. He brought down the seat cover and sat, chin cupped in his hand, hoping that Harcourt's bladder was not more robust than usual. How would he bear it if he was forced to wait here until midday, when Harcourt might come in for a quick slash before nipping off to the House? He took a quick glance around the small cubicle, noting that even toffs were expected to use Izal toilet paper, which tore your arse to pieces if you applied it too firmly. He sighed and took out his pocket diary, leafing through it and checking his duties for the next few weeks; nothing to look forward to there. He turned back to the current week, reminding himself that he was due to sign on at 1300 hours today. Would he remain here even if it meant arriving late at the garage?

He need not have worried, for at nine-thirty-five someone entered the lavatory, coughed once and began to splash the porcelain.

*

As expected, "See GS" was stencilled in blue against his name on the sign-on sheet. He walked around to James Shilling's office, knocked once and opened the door. He grinned at Shilling as he looked up from his desk. "Electric Railway House?"

"Correct, Mr Rice, and on the double. Sir Albert himself wants to see you." He grimaced. "Seems you're in real trouble this time."

Still at the door, Mickey shrugged. "I doubt it."

"Do you, now? You expect to be back for your second half, then?"

Mickey nodded. "I do."

James Shilling fluttered his eyelids, giving his head a barely perceptible shake. "Off you go, Mickey. It was nice knowing you."

*

When he announced himself at the reception desk at Electric Railway House, he was told to take a seat until someone came down for him. After a few minutes, a young man in an ill-fitting suit and a bad case of acne arrived.

"Mr Rice?"

"Yes."

"Follow me, please."

As he followed the young man up the stairs, he wondered if, Sir Albert Stanley obviously having heard that he had had the run of the Board of Trade earlier in the day, the managing director was anxious to ensure that he did not repeat the performance in Electric Railway House. Arriving on the top floor, he was led along the corridor and shown into a small meeting room furnished only with a plain pine table and six chairs. Stanley sat in one of the chairs, a notebook before him. He looked up as Mickey was shown in and got to his feet, indicating the chair opposite him.

"Mr Rice."

"Sir Albert."

They sat regarding each other for some seconds. "Mr Shilling tells me," said Stanley at last, "that you appeared to be not at all worried when he told you that I had summoned you here. 'Cocky young bugger,' is how he described you."

"No, I don't think I was cocky, Sir Albert. Confident, maybe, but not cocky."

"And why, in these circumstances, would you be confident, Mr Rice?" Stanley's tone was even; he appeared to be genuinely interested in what Mickey might say to this.

"Well, as I was being called before you, I knew that this would not be a disciplinary hearing." He shrugged. "The managing director—the man who might need to hear an appeal at the end of the day—doesn't *take* disciplinary hearings. Also, of course, there was no notice and no mention of any charge. Now, if Mr Shilling had started to *question* me about the incident, that would have been a different matter—an investigation which *might* have led to a disciplinary hearing. Then again, here we are: you're meeting me alone without as much as a note-taker." He shook his head. "There's not even a whiff of discipline about this occasion, Sir Albert, because you know that if I did what I've been accused of doing, there must have been a very good reason for it. So my confidence is really in *you*, rather than a cocky kind of *self*-confidence."

Mickey held up a finger. "However, I was a *little* bit worried by the fact that Mr Shilling told me I was in real trouble, because that *could* have meant that you had told him what this was all about. But then I dismissed that thought, knowing that you would suspect that this was the kind of thing which should be kept confidential."

Stanley held up his hands. "Enough, Mr Rice, enough!" He placed his hands over his face for a moment, then sighed and let them drop to the table. "Look, *one* of the reasons I decided to meet you alone, it now occurs to me, is that I never quite know how to *deal* with you, Mr Rice. The usual employer-employee relationship just doesn't seem to *work* with you. While you're never disrespectful, you display absolutely *no* indication that you're in awe of me—or even a trifle nervous. It seems that to you I'm just..."

"Another man," Mickey supplied.

Stanley looked at him for a second before nodding. "Exactly." He thought for a moment and, as if finally understanding the man opposite him, repeated, "Yes, exactly." He straightened his shoulders. "Well, look, let's clear one thing up before we go any further: I did *not* tell Mr Shilling what this was about, but I *did* use the term 'real trouble,' so that's where that came from. And you're right, of course: I suspected, as I still suspect, that this is something which might best be kept under wraps, if that proves possible. You were *also* correct in believing that I might take the view that you must have had a very good reason for doing what you did." He sighed and made eye-contact with Mickey. "Do you realise that the acting president of the Board of Trade has two broken toes?"

"I'm not surprised, the way I stamped on his foot."

"And you also beat him about the face?"

"I *slapped* his face several times—quite hard, it's true—but I was careful not to leave any scratches or bruises."

Suddenly, Stanley became diffident, almost embarrassed. "Now, he also says that you...fondled his genitals." He seemed to look at Mickey hopefully. "No truth in that, I suppose?"

Mickey laughed. "I squeezed his testicles until there were tears in his eyes and told him that next time I would castrate him."

Stanley sat there, blinking. "Yes...quite. But tell me, Mr Rice, *what* next time? What caused you to take this course of action?"

"I'm sure you've worked it out yourself, Sir Albert: yesterday, Harcourt tried to sexually assault Dorothy."

Mickey jumped when Stanley brought his fist down on the table. "Dammit! Dammit, dammit, dammit! I *knew* it! Oh, Mr Rice, I feared this might be the case, and now I feel guilty. I ask myself why I didn't call her and warn her about Harcourt as soon as I heard that he was taking over from Mr Runciman."

"No need to blame yourself, Sir Albert; her father warned her, but still she wasn't afraid of him. In fact, she told me last night that she's not afraid of him now, either."

Stanley leaned forward, concerned. "But tell me, Mr Rice, is she alright? He didn't hurt her?"

"Well, she grazed her knuckles when she punched him in the mouth, but that's about all."

"He didn't retaliate?"

"He didn't have the chance, because she followed that up with a kick in the groin."

Stanley threw back his head and chuckled with genuine delight. He gestured towards his eyes, which were spilling tears. "Forgive me,

Mr Rice," he said. "This is another reason for meeting you alone. It wouldn't do to have this totally inappropriate hilarity minuted."

He gathered himself and, as if remembering a thread of argument he had meant to pursue earlier, became quite sober. He cleared his throat. "Be that as it may, Mr Rice, there is one aspect of this episode which *does* greatly concern me. In fact, I was quite angry, and this was at the forefront of my thoughts when I telephoned Mr Shilling. What *were* you thinking by wearing your uniform? Don't you see that this brings the company into disrepute? And not just your uniform, but your badge. It was almost as if you *wanted* to be identified."

"That's exactly right, Sir Albert. I *did* want to be identified, and so I made sure that Harcourt got a good view of my badge number."

"I'm not sure I understand, Mr Rice."

"Well, quite obviously Harcourt would not complain to the police, and so he would obviously approach the company. In my experience, people in prominent positions tend to go right to the top when they have a complaint..."

"In your experience, Mr Rice?"

"Yes, I'm thinking of that Mr Keynes, who complained directly to you."

"Ah, yes, I recall that."

"Now, if Harcourt had known only that I was a London General driver...what could he have done? A hunt throughout the company for his anonymous attacker would have run the risk of the whole story coming out, and he wouldn't have wanted that. If he could identify me, though, he would have thought that a quiet telephone call to Sir Albert would ensure my dismissal..."

"Whereas in fact..."

"Whereas in fact it would kill the complaint stone dead."

"And do you think it *is* stone dead, Mr Rice?"

"You'll tell me if it's not, Sir Albert."

"How did you ensure that he noted your badge number?"

"I didn't have to, because he told me just as I was leaving him. 'I've got your number,' he said. So I pointed my finger at him and said, 'Yes, Loulou, and I've got yours!'"

Once again, Stanley's head was thrown back and the room was filled with his laughter.

"Now, as far as bringing the company into disrepute, I don't really think I have, because the only person who knows there's a London General connection is Harcourt himself."

"Yes," said Stanley, wiping his eyes with a sparklingly white handkerchief, "but he just happens to be the acting president of the

Board of Trade, a position not without influence on the fortunes of this company."

"But Mr Runciman will soon be returning, won't he?"

Stanley nodded. "That is true."

"How do you intend to respond to Harcourt's complaint, Sir Albert?"

"What I *feel* like doing is going to the Board of Trade and stamping on the other foot."

It was Mickey's turn to laugh.

Stanley, chin in hand, looked gloomily at Mickey. "What would you suggest I do, Mr Rice?"

"If I were you?"

The very thought made Stanley grin. "If you were me."

"I think I would telephone him and say that the case seems rather more complex than I originally thought, and more time is required. 'By the way, Mr Harcourt, are you aware that Miss Bridgeman once worked for me? Yes, I have great respect for Dorothy and was so glad to hear from Mr Runciman that she is flourishing at the Board.' A little later, I might ask him if he *really* wanted me to persist in my enquiries."

He nodded. "Well, Mr Rice, I might very well do something along those lines." He looked up sharply and extended a finger. "But listen, there is another aspect of this situation that we must consider. *Until* Mr Runciman returns, Miss Bridgeman will still be working for Harcourt. Are you absolutely *sure* that she will be safe?"

"Well, she seems to think so—or she did last night—but..."

"But you're not happy with the arrangement."

"No, Sir Albert, I'm not, and I'm wondering whether you could have a word with your friend Mr Runciman..."

"How do you know that Mr Runciman is my friend, Mr Rice?"

"Because he was with you at the Albert Hall."

"Ah, of course." Suddenly, he sat bolt upright. "I've got it!" He leaned forward. "Tell me, Mr Rice, could you bear to be parted from Miss Bridgeman for a week or two?"

"That would depend, Sir Albert."

"Well, before he returns to full duties at the Board, the Government is sending Mr Runciman on a mission to Italy. Now, to a large extent this will be on Board business, so how would it be if I suggested to Mr Runciman that he take Miss Bridgeman with him? There will be meetings with Italian officials, so he'll need a secretary..."

"Sir Albert, that would be very good of you. Thank you very much."

Stanley sat back in his chair with a sigh. He opened his hands as they rested on the table. "Well, I think that concludes…" He looked around the room. "Do you know, Mr Rice, this is only the second time I've used this room, and the first meeting I held here also concerned you."

"Oh really?"

"Yes, I interviewed Messrs Shilling and Butcher in this room." Apparently reluctant to end the meeting, he leaned forward. "Finally, Mr Rice, I must ask you this," he said, having lowered his voice. "Did you have no reservations at all about assaulting a member of His Majesty's Government?"

"Not really," Mickey said with a shrug. "After all, he's…"

Sir Albert Stanley nodded. "Just another man."

35

My Dearest Mickey,

When we arrived in Pallanza, where the conference was to be held, at 7 p.m. on 8 August, we were met at the station by Sir James Rennell Rodd, our Ambassador, and the Prefect, Signor Murftone. As we were driven to the private villa where we were to stay, local people stood by the roadside and cheered us. At that time in the evening, of course, it was still bright, but the air had a lovely balmy texture, and I was quite entranced. I found that one of the melodies from Berlioz's "Harold in Italy" was playing over and over in my head, and even now, days later, it returns whenever I am out of doors in this beautiful country.

Pallanza is just under 30 miles from Como, and quite close to the Swiss border. The town, which is very pretty, sits on Lake Maggiore, and sometimes, as I contemplate the breath-taking view, I have to remind myself that we are here to work.

Perhaps I should make mention of our accommodation. Sir James is staying in the house of Mr Edward Capel-Cure, an Englishman who has lived in Italy for ages and writes novels in Italian, would you believe! It was Mr Capel-Cure's idea that the conference be held in Pallanza, so we have much to thank him for. Having originally volunteered his services to Sir James, he now works in the commercial section at the Embassy. He bought the Villa Misarole in 1913, renaming it the Villa della Quercia after his pen-name, Gian della Quercia. Not only has he provided accommodation for Sir James, but it was he who persuaded the Marchese di Casanova to welcome the Runcimans, myself and the Italian delegates to his beautiful Villa San Remigio. Is the Marchese descended from the famous libertine? I have no idea, Mickey. What I *do* know is that he is a brilliant musician and a very cultured man.

Mr Runciman looks quite recovered, although he is still somewhat pale. Sir James has ensured that the pace of business here will not be very taxing, and the Italians have been, he says, very understanding. I am getting on quite well with Hilda Runciman, although I try to steer her away from her pet concerns back home, one of which is temperance. In the past year, she has spoken at a number of meetings, the aims of which have been to persuade her audiences that victory over the Central Powers will be assured if only British men, and British working men in particular, can be persuaded to resist the temptations of alcohol. However, as her audiences have consisted of those already adhering to this belief, in practice she has converted nobody. Her task in Italy will probably be extremely difficult: refusing every glass of wine that is offered without offending our hosts.

Sir James, although of course very ruling class, is an impressive sort of chap. In his mid-fifties, he is still slim and has an imposing moustache, although this is now white. Aside from diplomacy, he has a scholarly interest in Greece and is a published poet; before he took up his position in Rome in 1908, he travelled to the USA, where President Roosevelt, a great admirer of his poetry, gave him dinner at the White House. Apparently, Oscar Wilde helped to get his first book published—Sir James, I should add, is married with numerous children. He has been Ambassador to Italy for eight years now, and is reckoned by Mr Runciman to have played an essential role in persuading Italy to support the Triple Entente. Sir James himself credits popular opinion with this achievement, and speaks highly of a politician called Benito Mussolini, who, formerly a socialist, abandoned his former comrades in order to campaign for Italy's entry into the war. However, this effort has not yet been crowned with complete success, because although Italy declared war on Austro-Hungary in May last year, followed by Turkey in September, she is still at peace with Germany. This may seem somewhat illogical, but can be explained by the fact that Italy's motives in going to war were, like those of most of the other combatants, completely selfish: she wishes to "reclaim" territories with substantial Italian populations—the word for such a movement is, I am informed, "irredentism"—and they, frankly, lie closer to Austro-Hungary and Turkey than to Germany.

Our first meeting with the Italian officials was not scheduled until 5 p.m. on 9 August, the day after our arrival. The purpose of this was evidently to allow us sufficient time in which to recover from the rigours of our journey, but after breakfast I just could not be restrained, and so, as Mr Runciman would not require my services until the afternoon, Sir James was kind enough to find someone to drive me into the town.

Pallanza dates back to Roman times, and much of its fine architecture was built at various times during the last half-millennium, although the streets themselves were obviously laid much earlier. Oh, Mickey, just to walk along the lakefront and to be confronted with the Borromean Islands on one's right and such a host of colourful, romantic buildings on one's left! From the terrace cafes come the odours of coffee and tobacco, which I find not at all disagreeable. And then, of course, there are the churches. Never mind the backward purpose to which these often magnificent edifices have been put: they were built by men, their frescoes were painted by men, and stand as evidence of the high art of which our species is capable, making one wonder what the world will look like when buildings are dedicated not to the worship of a mythical deity but to the celebration and uplifting of mankind itself. Oh, how I wished that you could have been with me as I walked these ancient streets, Mickey! One day, my love, one day.

I returned to the villa for lunch—and, Mickey, the food, the food! If we were staying here much longer, I fear you would be welcoming me home as a plump Italian matron! At three forty-five, we British gathered around a table at the Villa della Quercia to prepare for the first formal meeting with the Italians. Sir James took the view that there would be a minimum of stiff formality, as the meeting would consist of a brief mention of the topics to be discussed—a "canter around the track," as he described it.

And so it proved to be. The Italians have two major concerns: lacking most of the raw materials required by an industrialising nation, they have no alternative but to import whatever they need, but there is a widespread belief that British shipping companies are robbing them blind; and they fear that they will be unable to secure adequate supplies of coal at reasonable prices. As for the first of these concerns, Mr Runciman said that there was a great deal of misunderstanding, partly due to the efforts of an Italian newspaper, the baseless accusations of which had been repeated in Britain's press and Parliament; he hoped that he would be able to explain the real situation, although he was not hopeful of securing a reduction in shipping rates. With regard to coal, he said that he had a few months ago come to an arrangement with France and, although there would be difficulties, it might be possible to extend this scheme to Italy. The Italians seemed to think this reasonable. So, Mickey, we have come to this beautiful part of the world to discuss the price of coal!

The Italian ministers are, I must say, not particularly impressive. Signor Enrico Arlotta looks the way one would expect a Minister of Maritime and Railway Transportation to look. At around 65, he is a grey man: grey hair, grey moustache, grey face; and, of course, when he goes out he wears a bowler hat. He is not, however, an insubstantial figure, politically or socially. Born of a bourgeois Neapolitan family, he is a member of what is referred to as the Right group, which represents the interests of the northern bourgeoisie and the southern aristocracy. Towards the end of the last century, before he became an MP, he was general manager of the Banco di Napoli, and during his parliamentary career has been known to favour private speculators. Try as I might—and, of course, I do not— I cannot like him.

Guiseppe de Nava, Minister of Industry, Commerce and Labour, is in his middle fifties, with a short, dark beard. He comes from a noble family and is a right-wing Liberal— despite which, he looks far more interesting that his grey colleague.

Over the course of the next few days, the business part of our visit was concluded at a series of fairly short meetings. Mr Runciman was very effective in disposing of the allegations regarding predatory British shipping, although I, to be honest, was perfectly prepared to believe them, pointing out, as he had previously done in the House of Commons, that 75 percent of the trade with Italy is accounted for by neutral shipping, and this being the case it is those shipping lines from neutral countries which set the going rate. What would be the consequence if Britain placed restrictions on the rates charged by its merchant shipping on voyages to Italy? Why, those British lines would simply seek better remuneration elsewhere; there was a shortage of ships but no shortage of customers willing to pay higher rates—in the USA, for example—in order to guarantee a steady supply of goods and raw materials. At times like this, I had to bite my tongue, because the answer to such a conundrum was staring him in the face: rather than accepting that "the market" must rule the waves, the government should step in, take full control of the merchant marine and set the rates it felt were just. But such matters are not the province of a humble note-taker.

On coal-prices, Mr Runciman was quite clever. Yes, the scheme he had agreed with France could be extended to Italy. But England and France were separated by a mere strip of water, and fairly small vessels, mostly French or British, could be used to convey the coal. France's Mediterranean ports were excluded from the scheme, thus ensuring control. The vast majority of shipping in the Mediterranean, however, was neutral, and thus an extension of the scheme to Italy would be attended by great difficulties. In effect, Mr Runciman was using this argument as a mere bargaining ploy, allowing the Italian negotiators to gradually beat him down, as it were, so that at the end of the negotiations they enjoyed a sense of achievement, whereas he only conceded what he had been willing to give them anyway—a reduction in coal-prices along the lines of the French scheme. This, at least, was my perception.

And so, my love, I must guiltily admit that rather more time has been spent on receptions, meals and sight-seeing than on the business that brought us here. To take these in chronological order:

- The reception in Pallanza was at the Passaggio Museum, a lovely 16th century building.

- A morning on Lake Orta—Lago D'Orta. Oh, this place is so romantic, Mickey. I so, so wished that you were with me! The pastel colours of the villas and palazzos at the waterfront brought back vivid memories of Portugal. Orta San Giulio is the main town, and very picturesque, apart from the fact, of course, that one cannot escape religion: there are no less than twenty chapels on the cliffs of Sacro Monte, all dedicated to Saint Francis. Religion again, I'm afraid, but the tiny island of San Giulio has a beautiful Benedictine monastery—that's all it has, in fact—with marvellous frescoes and sculptures. There is something about the light here, as there is in parts of Portugal, which just makes a fresco sing! Although Orta seems to get few visitors, it's not surprising to learn that Balzac, Browning and Byron all came here regularly in the last century.

- An afternoon on Lake Maggiore. Yes an afternoon, i.e. after an Italian lunch which, combined with the August sun and the motion of the boat, ensured that I slumbered much of the time, as did, incidentally, Hilda Runciman and the Signores Arlotta and de Nava. Yes, these sight-seeing trips are attended by the whole conference, and so any guilty feelings I might claim to have are, if I really have them, misplaced. Between slumbers, however, there was the Isola Bella on which sits the 17th-century Palazzo Borromeo, the botanical garden on Isola Madre and, just opposite Pallanza, the smaller island of San Giovanni. These, incidentally, are just some of the Borromeo Islands, so named because the Borromeo family gained ownership of them in the 1300s and still, would you believe, own some of them today. It is, presumably, in the interests of such people that Italy is sending its young men to die. Be that as it may, the islands are, of course, breathtakingly beautiful.

- Our whole party took the train to Milan, where we were received at the station by the local authorities, deputies, senators and the Allied consuls, the crowds cheering Mr Runciman. Once again, Berlioz played in my head. We were driven with Signores Arlotta and de Nava to the Chamber of Commerce building, the street in front of which was choked with cheering people. We were received in the Council Hall by Signor Salmiraghi, President of the Chamber of Commerce, who led the whole party onto the balcony to greet the cheering people. One would have thought that the Runcimans were royalty, Mickey! After the inevitable speeches, we were served the equally inevitable, although rather more digestible, lunch.

- Back to Pallanza for the conclusion of the conference, and then on 15 August—today—we are in Turin, where our party is given lunch at the Hotel de l'Europe by the Prime Minister himself, Signor Paolo Boselli. Aside from the Italian dignitaries, the Russian, French, Belgian, Serbian, Portuguese and Montenegrin consuls were all in attendance. Signor Boselli has a vigorous, short grey beard and moustache and untidy short hair, and his pince-nez gives one the impression that he is wide-eyed and alert. He is, however, absolutely ancient—78, according to Mr Runciman. He is a Liberal and leads the government of National Unity.

Mickey, at the invitation of Sir James I am sending this letter in the diplomatic bag, and so it is quite possible, but by no means certain, that it will arrive in London before me. Needless to say, now that our visit is at an end, I want *nothing more than to fly into the arms of my beloved* ~~Mickey~~ *Michael.*

Will all my love,

Your Dorothea.

36

Runciman was back in the Commons on 21 August, and this heralded his return to full duties. Cabinet meetings now came more frequently, sometimes on consecutive days, interspersed with meetings of the War Committee. When Italy declared war on Germany on 27 August, he found that some parliamentary colleagues were congratulating him, although he was sure that Sir James Rennell Rodd was more responsible for this than he.

At the Board of Trade, business was brisk. Harcourt's decision to allow an increase in the price of South Wales coal brought repercussions, with representatives of municipal and private gas undertakings descending upon the Board to demand that no such concessions be made in future. The Executive Committee of the National Union of Railwaymen came to express its dissatisfaction with the employers, who had offered an extra three shillings a week in response to its demand for ten shillings. Later in September, Runciman also met the managers, who eventually offered five shillings, which was accepted by the union.

Prices were a constant headache, and at first Dorothy thought, as she typed a letter to Mr A.W. Yeo, MP, that Runciman was not as bold as he might be. Although the government had taken action on the prices of sugar, wheat and meat, Runciman stated, it had to be realised that prices were a world problem. Wheat and meat came largely from abroad, and were purchased in competition with others whose needs were as great, or greater, than ours. Britain's enemies were losing this particular battle, for prices had risen 117 percent in Germany, 149 percent in Austria, compared to 65 percent in Britain. A few weeks later, however, there was evidence of a bolder stance when he announced the formation of a Royal Commission, chaired by Lord Crawford, President of the Board of Agriculture and Fisheries, which would have sole responsibility for the purchase of wheat.

Then a step back: there would be no extension of the principle of rationing. When asked in the House if he would consider the advisability of creating Fair Food Price tribunals, he said that he did not think such a step was necessary, although he *was* considering asking the House to grant the Board of Trade further powers to limit food-price increases.

Although outwardly Runciman seemed quite recovered from his breakdown, Dorothy got the impression that he was feeling his way—but to what?

*

"Gladys!"

Responding to the doorbell one evening in September, Mickey skipped downstairs, opened the front door and there stood his conductor, looking somewhat confused.

"What can I do for you, Glad? You want to come in?"

"No, no, Mickey, have I come to the wrong house? I've come to see Dick."

"Ah, of course. Right house, Glad, but you pulled the wrong bell; Dick's is the bottom one."

"Oh, right." She frowned. "What do you mean, 'of course?'"

"Nothing at all, Glad, just that I didn't think you'd be coming to see me. I'm surprised he's letting you walk the streets at night, what with the danger of Zeppelin raids. You coming in, or what?"

She smiled and stepped through the door. "Yeah, that was a bad one last week. What was it, Brixton and Streatham?"

"And Poplar, Shoreditch and Bethnal Green in the east. They seem to be staying away from us, thank goodness."

"Then there was the raid on Woolwich at the end of August."

"That's true. If you give his bell a pull, he'll come to the door."

She looked at him as if unsure whether this was a *double entendre*.

"You want me to do it?"

Gladys returned to the front step and pulled the bell. As she stepped back into the house, Mickey closed the door and they stood there awkwardly. She wore a dark knee-length dress, a light jacket and a blue hat; she had applied a pale shade of lipstick and her eyes were lightly shadowed.

"You're looking very nice tonight, Gladys."

"Thank you, Mickey." Her eyes travelled down his body and she giggled.

"What's funny?"

"Didn't have you down as a carpet-slippers man, Mickey."

"Ah, well. Hidden depths, you see."

Dick came to their rescue. "Sorry I took so long. I was in the—I was busy. Oh, hello, Mickey."

"She pulled the wrong one, Dick."

"Wrong...?"

"Bell."

"Ah."

"Don't worry, I'll pull the right one next time."

"I'm sure you will, Gladys."

"Don't be so saucy, you!"

"Who was that?" Dorothy asked, looking up from the *Herald*, when Mickey returned to the flat.

"Gladys."

"Your conductor?"

"Yes, she seems to have an assignation with Dick. Pulled the wrong bell."

"With *Dick*?"

She had not met Gladys, but Mickey thought that his description of her must have been unflattering. "Yes. He told me some time ago that he likes 'em big."

"Have they been going out together?"

"They've been to the flicks a couple of times, I think."

"Well, well."

"We'll probably be hearing the patter of tiny feet before too long."

"Oh, come on, Mickey! What makes you think he'll get her pregnant?"

"Nothing. She's got a young son, so if she moves in with Dick I suppose he would come too."

"And who would look after him while they're at work?"

"Good point. No, maybe he'll stay with her mother."

Talking of kids, he thought, are we ever going to have one? When they had first moved in together, Dorothy had responded to his marriage proposal by suggesting that they see how they felt after a year, mainly in order to test their political compatibility. That year had come and gone, as had a second one, and the subject had never been raised again, as there simply seemed to be no need; they were happy together and, to all intents and purposes, married, and they seemed to have quietly resolved that their relationship was no business of the state, let alone of a church. But Mickey did sometimes think about the possibility of a child. He had never

408

mentioned it, for fear that this would set off a confrontation that would itself demonstrate the wrongheadedness of bringing a child into a household that might still prove to be dysfunctional. He suppressed the thought now, little realising that, as Dorothy turned the pages of the *Herald*, a major confrontation was about to break.

A report on the annual Trades Union Congress, held earlier in the month in Birmingham, had been given at the last meeting of the Vigilance Committee, and according to this the red-button union had, for a small organisation, performed well. Wally Godfrey, who was unknown to Mickey, had moved the motion to instruct the TUC's "Parliamentary Committee to lose no opportunity after the war to press for the repeal of all Acts of Parliament imposing economic, industrial, and military compulsion upon the manhood of the nation and to re-establish individual liberty with the right voluntarily to refrain from organised destruction." All very well, George Sanders had commented, but a bit on the pious side: if such "individual liberty" was to be decreed by Parliament, the whole movement would need to be mobilised behind the demand, and it was doubtful whether, after several years of war, that could be achieved. However, the motion was passed with only one vote against.

The Parliamentary Committee had also received an instruction in the form of a motion moved by Ben Tillet of the Dock and Riverside Workers, which lamented the exemption of clergymen from conscription. Congress was asked to agree that it viewed "with regret that a large class of able-bodied men, who are engaged in unproductive employment, should not be used for a better purpose during this critical period." At a time when God was being enlisted as not only the protector of loved ones at the front, but as recruiting-sergeant and saviour of the British Empire, Tillet was taking a bit of a chance here, and after a show of hands the Congress president declared the motion lost. Tillet, however, was having none of it and demanded a card vote, which showed that, by 1,378,000 to 1,200,000, the motion had in fact been carried. Seasoned hands at the Vigilance Committee meeting reckoned that, however, the TUC's Parliamentary Committee being as committed to democracy as the current EC of the red-button union, the resolution would now gather dust.

Then there was the red-button union's motion on women vehicle workers, moved by Ben Smith, which called upon the Parliamentary Committee "to assist the London and Provincial Union of Licensed Vehicle Workers to obtain from the Home Secretary a revocation of the Order licensing women to act as conductors on omnibuses and trams, these licenses having been granted as a war emergency measure; that all such licenses issued shall be for the war period only; and that on peace being declared all such licenses shall automatically expire on the date for which such licenses have been issued." This was so lacking in controversy that it was carried without discussion. It would, however, be discussed now.

Mickey sat at the table, Upton Sinclair's *The Jungle* open before him, while Dorothy sat in her usual armchair. She folded the *Herald* in half and leaned over to pass it to him.

"Have you finished with it?" As he looked up, he noted that her jaw was set, and his heart plummeted.

"Not really, but I think you should read the piece by Bessie Ward."

"Alright, I'll get to it in a minute. Let me finish this chapter."

"I think you should read it *now*, Mickey. It's about your union." Her eyes were telling him that he was guilty of something.

What to do? If he insisted on finishing the chapter in Sinclair's novel, he risked angering her, drawing claims that he found her of secondary importance; but it would also give him a little thinking time. And if he read the *Herald* piece first he would be in at the deep end straight away. It was always possible, of course, that he would agree with the article she was so anxious for him to read, although he doubted whether this would count for much, given the gathering ferocity of her expression.

He took the newspaper from her—"Thank you, sweetheart"—and began to read. He was not surprised to see that the article dealt with the motion moved by Ben Smith at the Birmingham TUC. He guessed that Dorothy wished to discuss not the motion itself, but the argument put forward by Bessie Ward, the article's author who, while noting that the LPU had successfully organised women, asked what action it was preparing to take on behalf of them when, if its resolution was carried into effect, they were thrown out of employment at the war's end.

"All Ben did, my love," he said as calmly as possible, "was move something that was already the policy of our union; but you knew that."

Dorothy sighed in apparent exasperation. "Yes, Mickey, I *did* know that. But don't you agree that this article forces one to view it in a new light? For example, when she asks what will become of those who have become widows, or whose husbands are crippled and unable to work. Gladys, your own conductor, is a case in point!"

"The companies agreed to keep open the jobs of those men who had volunteered or been conscripted," he explained patiently.

"But they won't all be coming back, will they?" Her voice was gradually rising. "And those that do may not be all in one piece!"

He nodded. "That's true, but it's thought that once the war ends there will be a recession, with widespread unemployment."

"And so it's the women who must be unemployed?"

"Bessie Ward says that the answer lies in equal pay..."

"But you have that, so why must women be dismissed at the end of the war?"

A sigh. "There's more to it. You know as well as I do that the movement feels that a man's wage should be enough to feed, house and clothe himself and his family. If wives are working, the employers will no longer..."

"Oh, bosh! How can you sit there and come out with that tired, threadbare argument?"

He got to his feet, throwing the *Herald* onto the table. "I'm simply telling you the way things are! That is what the majority of men in our movement *believe!*"

It was Dorothy who now stood up. That would have been bad enough, but then she thrust her face towards his and that was far worse, completing her transformation into the person he had first seen almost three years earlier at the Hackney Empire.

"Yes, that's what the *men* believe! Are you totally incapable of putting yourself in a woman's shoes and seeing how the situation might appear to her? Are you? *Well are you?*"

By now, her face was contorted into a mask—at least he hoped it was no more than a mask—of fury at the reality to which Mickey had pointed and contempt for his failure to challenge it. He reached out to calm her; to try to reclaim her would be reaching too high.

"Don't touch me!" She almost spat the words.

He said nothing, could say nothing. Instead, his eyes said it all: "Touching you, Dorothy, is the one thing I cannot live without, so please, please, please never forbid me to do it."

Seeming to read his eyes, she gasped and added, "Not now." But would this be enough? His eyes continued to tell her what was at stake, and she knew she had a decision to make. Why didn't he say something to help?

He reached for the *Herald* and briefly reread the concluding paragraphs. "She says here that the *employers* will see to it that women will always compete with men."

"Give that to me!" She snatched the newspaper from Mickey's hand, reread the passage to which he had referred and then laughed in his face. "Is this how you argue your case—by distorting her argument? She says the employers will do that *'if the men Trade Unionists are misguided enough to force the women into the enemy's camp.'* She threw the newspaper from her. "I'm surprised you didn't quote her when she says that this will be the case as long as capitalism lasts..."

"Well, she does say that..."

Her face came closer once more. "And she *also* says that Congress gave no indication of capitalism ending! What do you think she meant by that? *Eh? Tell me!*"

Mickey arrived at two destinations simultaneously: he saw his way out of this conflict, and he grasped the argument. He pushed Dorothy away—not violently, but firmly enough to move her back a pace or two—and delivered his riposte with a raised voice. "She meant that we will never have socialism until men see that women have a greater role than staying at home so that the wages of their husbands and fathers will continue to be sufficient to keep them there. And she's right! But that can change. It wasn't until 1889 that the movement began to organise the unskilled. If that had never happened, imagine where the trade union movement would be now! But *how* did it happen? It happened because the unskilled—with, yes, some help from activists—began to organise *themselves*! And that will have to happen with women too, so that the whole movement, just as it was forced to accept the inclusion of the unskilled in its ranks, accepts the presence of women—in both the workplace and the movement—in the same way!"

Dorothy stood before him, blinking, her mask gradually dissolving. She prepared to speak.

"I haven't finished!" he cried, forestalling her. "So, women have to organise! But you, Dorothy, need to change your ways if you hope to be part of that. I told you something like this outside the Hackney Empire, and I'm telling you again now. Because you know what you've been doing in the past ten or fifteen minutes? *You were in danger of driving me into the enemy's camp!* If you talk to people as if they are enemies, the chances are that they will *become* enemies. Do you understand that?"

She reached out to touch him, suddenly tearful and vulnerable. "Oh, Michael..."

"Not now," said Mickey. He turned and walked away.

37

"What the fuck," asked Eric Rice, "is a Special General Meeting? I've looked for it in the rule book and I can't find it."

"Me neither, mate," said George Sanders. "What are they up to, Barney?"

They were sitting with Dennis Davies in the Italian café in Gerrard Street, attempting to decipher the latest move of the Executive Council.

"I told you back in the summer, George," said Barney Macauley, "that the cab section wants Tich back. This is how they're planning to do it."

"At a meeting that has no constitutional standing?"

Barney gave an abrupt nod. "12 November, Euston Theatre. And that, of course, is nine days before our Special Delegate Meeting where we're going to roast my colleagues on the EC over their recent shenanigans. They want to present the SDM with a *fait accompli*."

"So what should we do about it?" asked Sanders.

"Boycott the bugger," suggested Dennis Davies. "I'll have to be there, because it sounds as if it's pretty much a cab section thing, but I would suggest that the bus and tram boys give it a wide berth. We've got a meeting of the Vigilance Committee in a few days, so we can put out the word there."

"And what will that achieve, apart from ensuring that Tich is returned as president with no opposition?"

"It will weaken even further the legitimacy of any decision they make," said Davies. "So let's assume they get back Tich as president..."

"Not as general secretary?"

"No, my understanding is that he wants to come back as president, and the cab boys—the Owner-Drivers Branch, anyway—are quite happy with that. So let's say they vote for his reinstatement. After that, it's up to us: we can stand on the constitution and get it ruled out of order, or, if it was part of a broader package, we might accept it."

"And part of this broader package would be?" This from Eric Rice.

"The resignation of the EC."

Sanders whistled through his teeth. "As a member of the current EC, Barney, what do you think of that?"

Barney pointed to Davies. "Listen to the constitutionalist. Dennis has been around longer than any of us."

Sanders grinned. "Oh, alright. If you have to resign, I daresay you'll get re-elected easily enough. But how confident are we that this unconstitutional meeting will vote for the resignation of the EC?"

"You shouldn't forget," said Davies, "that it's not just that *I've* been around longer than most of you: the cab section *was* the union at one time, and while it was willing to go along with the resignation game, the way that turned out, and the more recent manoeuvres of the EC, have been plain embarrassing." He nodded. "Yes, they'll vote for the resignation of the EC."

"And who will move it?" asked Sanders.

Davies shrugged. "Me, of course."

The other three laughed, exultant.

"And if they refuse to resign?"

Macauley chuckled. "And they will, of course. I can see them now, arguing that the meeting was unconstitutional, with no power to demand their resignations. Well, if it's gonna be constitutional enough to decide on Tich's reinstatement..."

"Barney's right," said Davies. "They *will* refuse to resign, so we'll get 'em nine days later at the SDM; and until that time, I suggest we delay a final position on Tich's reinstatement."

*

"How effective was the boycott?" asked Sanders. It was 13 November and Dennis Davies was reporting back to Sanders, Archie Henderson and Eric Rice. Barney Macauley was driving a bus.

"Very. More so because someone telephoned the theatre just before the kick-off to say that the meeting had been cancelled, so the first bunch that arrived were turned away." He looked to first Sanders, Archie, then Eric. "Any idea who did that?"

Eric Rice rattled a tattoo on the table with his fingers, whistling tunelessly as he gazed at the ceiling, while the others laughed.

"Anyway, there were only about four hundred there, with few bus and tram members in sight. Most of them were from the Owner-Drivers Branch, and George Blundy was obviously calling the tune. And because they were in such a majority, there was a fair bit of criticism, lads, about how this has become a busmen's union."

"Well," said Eric, "as we decided to organise busmen, that shouldn't have come as a surprise."

"No, but it's just as well you know how they're feeling."

"But apart from that..." ventured Archie Henderson.

"Apart from that, it all went like clockwork. Blundy moved that the EC rescind its motion to accept Tich's resignation and request that he reoccupy the position of president. I then moved an addendum calling on the EC to resign. Both sailed through with only one vote against."

Sanders whistled; Archie brought his palms together; Eric asked, "Who the bloody hell was that?"

"It's not important," said Davies. "There was then another motion condemning the Vigilance Committee, so we need to be on our guard."

"Did it pass?" asked Eric.

"It did."

"With one vote against?"

Davies grinned. "No, there were a few more than that, but it had a sizeable majority."

"Well, I think we can safely ignore that," said Archie. "The Vigilance Committee may be *non*-constitutional, but this Special General Meeting was *un*constitutional."

Davies levelled a finger at him. "Excellent point, Archie."

"And did the EC resign?" asked Sanders.

"Not yet." Davies winked. "So you may have to give them a nudge at the SDM."

"Jesus," said Sanders, blowing a cloud of cigarette smoke over the table, "if they can see that even the Owner-Drivers' Branch is against them, how do they hope to survive the SDM?"

Davies shrugged. "Hope," he said, "springs eternal."

*

But hope alone was not enough, and the Special Delegate Meeting on 21 November at the Club and Institute Hall, Clerkenwell Road, administered one defeat after another to the recalcitrant Executive Council.

The first test came when, the union still having no president, the EC put up Godfrey Moorhouse, one of their own, to chair the conference. Moorhouse was a cabdriver and a Bywater-Russell partisan, and as he stepped towards the chair, a good half of the conference rose and voiced its objection: "No! No! No!" Moorhouse stood there for a good ten seconds, blinking in shock and apprehension, before resuming his seat among the other EC members.

A plainly uncomfortable Ben Smith stood up and the conference

415

fell silent. "Then who will you have to chair this conference?" he asked.

"I nominate George Blundy," came a voice from the Cab Section.

When this met with a muted response, Dick Mortlake stood and cried, "I nominate George Sanders!"

When a clear majority roared its approval, Ben Smith asked, "Do we need to put this to the vote?"

Practically the whole conference now cried "NOOOOOO!!!!" and even Blundy was waving his arms to indicate that he would not stand.

As Sanders strode to the rostrum amid a chorus of cheers, he knew that the whole conference was won: if the delegates would not trust a member of the EC to chair the proceedings, what possible chance was there of them accepting a single proposal emanating from that body? None. This EC was finished. At the same time, he noted that even some who did not usually support him had acclaimed his election to the chair. Possibly, he thought, they took the view that, as chairman, with an obligation to be even-handed, he would be constrained from voicing an opinion; well, there was something in that, but he was confident that this conference would need no persuasion from him; that job had been done by the Vigilance Committee over the preceding months. Still, he would leave no doubt as to where his sympathies lay.

"Brothers," he said, addressing the conference from the chair, "before we proceed, it might be useful to remind ourselves why this Special Delegate Meeting has been called. Over the last eighteen months, the branches have practically been in open revolt over the actions of the Executive Council: its refusal to issue nomination papers for the positions of general secretary and organising secretary, despite the fact that this was a decision of the Annual Delegate Meeting in April 1915; this was followed by the inordinate delay in calling the Special Delegate Meeting at which this was put right; the nomination papers were then issued, but the EC then decided to allow the nominations of Brothers Bywater and Russell to stand, even though the issue of nomination papers was occasioned by their enlistment in the Army; this was followed by the decision to grant Brothers Bywater and Russell leave of absence, although this was later rescinded; then, in the summer, there was the acceptance of the charter negotiated with the London General without putting it to a vote of the members concerned.

"Regardless of where we might stand on any of these questions, I think we will all agree"—here his right arm swept the whole of the conference, then the EC seated behind him—"that these are the reasons we are assembled here today in yet another Special Delegate Meeting." He picked up the agenda paper from the table before him and held it up. "Now, it is interesting to note that the EC has, in its wisdom, decided that today's agenda should consist largely of motions which it has itself put forward, most of which seek to gain conference's acceptance of the very practices which I have just outlined. Some delegates may find this rather curious. Some may find it objectionable and seek to have the agenda rewritten on the hoof."

A rumble of agreement came from the conference, with some delegates clearly believing that Sanders was issuing an invitation, but he then surprised them.

"However, brothers, I intend to chair this meeting in a manner which is completely fair and objective. I therefore put it to you that we should allow the EC to have its way in this matter." He smiled as the conference sat in a stunned silence. "If you doubt the wisdom of this, I ask you to just ponder the matter for a while. Does it really matter whether we debate a motion from the floor declaring the nominations of Brothers Bywater and Russell invalid, or an EC motion declaring them valid? Should we debate an EC motion seeking to justify the practice of accepting agreements without a vote of the membership, or a motion from the Branches condemning this practice?" He threw out his arms. "What difference will it make? The discussion in each case will be the same, as will be the vote at the conclusion of the debate. So should we not let the EC have its way on this matter, or must we waste precious time by debating a rewriting of the agenda?"

Heads were nodded; chuckles were heard. Those who before the meeting, outraged to see that their Branch motions had been ignored by the EC, had discussed the overturning of the agenda, now accepted that the debates and the votes would be all.

"There is, however, a problem," stated Davey Hall, a delegate from the Islington tram branch. "My branch submitted a motion calling for the abolition of the post of president, and there is no mention of that in the EC motion."

"I must confess to some confusion," said Sanders. He turned to the EC. "Is it really the case that a Branch motion has been ignored? Perhaps the acting general secretary can throw some light on this. Was such a motion received from the Islington tram branch, Brother Smith?"

Ben Smith, looking somewhat relieved at this opportunity to clear himself of suspicion, stood and nodded. "It was indeed, Chairman. I took the view that it must be included in the agenda, but by a majority the EC overruled me."

Sanders had, in fact, been advised by Barney Macauley that this had been the case, and he had already worked out how this might be rectified. "Brothers," he addressed the meeting, "it now seems to me that the agenda does, after all, require amendment. Would you find it acceptable that the Islington motion be debated in the event that the EC motion on the nominations is defeated?"

At the rear of the hall, Eric Rice and Archie Henderson sat alone, as observers. With a frown, Archie turned to whisper to Eric, "What's the point of the Islington motion? Am I missing something?"

Eric grinned. "You must be, mate. Listen, if the EC motion is defeated, Bywater and Russell are out. The cab boys want Tich back. If the post of president is abolished, he can only come back as general secretary, and can no longer threaten to resign every five minutes, as that would mean he's completely out."

"And so poor old Ben will be organising secretary again?"

Eric shrugged. "He'll be okay with that; he never expected to be acting general secretary in the first place."

The conference accepted Sanders' proposal. "Now, can we proceed to the first item on the agenda?"

Several delegates now stood. "Afraid not, Chairman." "No, Chairman." "What about my branch's resolution?" And more of the same.

Sanders made a good job of feigning astonishment, passing a hand over his brow and turning to glance at the EC. "Alright, let's hear from Brother Mortlake first."

"The Middle Row bus branch," said Dick Mortlake, "sent in a motion condemning the EC for accepting the London General agreement without putting it to the vote and demanding that the whole Council resign."

"And the other delegates who indicated? Your branches submitted similar motions? Alright, let's see how many branches submitted motions calling for the resignation of the EC. Let's see your hands...Eight, nine." He turned to the EC, hands held out, seeking an explanation. When none was offered, he turned to Ben Smith. "I call the acting general secretary."

"Those motions were received," explained Ben Smith, "but the EC took the view that if its motion on the acceptance of agreements were to be passed, they would be redundant, and therefore should not appear on the agenda."

"Oh, really?" He chuckled. "There's confidence for you! Well, conference, is it your desire that those motions now make their appearance on the agenda?"

A roar of affirmation came in reply. Sanders turned to gauge the reaction of the EC to this, and saw them as men who, awaiting their turn at the guillotine, were beginning to doubt the possibility of rescue.

"It is entirely possible, brothers, that the EC motion will be accepted"—a pause to allow the guffaws, oaths and imprecations to die—"and so I would propose that one of those nine motions be debated only in the event that the EC proposal fails to gain your support. I would suggest that the nine delegates confer together to decide which of their motions will go forward. Is that acceptable?"

It was.

First on the agenda was the EC motion to declare that the nominations of Bywater and Russell had been valid. This proved to be the most closely-argued motion of the day, with many of the cab section delegates supporting the EC. It had been Sanders' intention that the back-door dealings between Harry Bywater and Albert Stanley should be revealed during this debate, but Sanders himself was constrained by the fact that he was chairing the meeting, and Ben Smith was obliged, even if by his silence, to support the position of the EC. Having foreseen the possibility of such a problem arising, however, Sanders had taken steps to overcome it. Thus, at one point during the debate, he surveyed the raised hands and called upon Dave Marston to speak.

"Chairman," said the south London bus driver, "I have listened with interest to those speakers, mainly from the cab section, who have described Brothers Bywater and Russell as 'comrades,' arguing that to turn our backs on such comrades would amount to treachery. Possibly, the speakers I refer to have known them and have fond memories of the old days, before busmen were organised and the LPU was formed. From the point of view of the bus section, I think we need to ask ourselves just how good these comrades were. Now, I know very little about Brother Russell, but I have certain information concerning Brother Bywater that leads me to believe that he was not a very good comrade at all!"

One part of the conference fell silent, while another erupted in protest. "This is slander, Mr Chairman!" "If Bro Marston has information, he should lay it before us!" "This is a disgrace!" And even, "What do you expect from a busmen's union?"

Sanders raised the gavel and let it fall. "Let us get one thing clear, brothers. This is *not* a busmen's union, neither is it a cabdrivers' union; it is a *vehicle workers* union! Let's have no more divisive talk like that." He paused. "Now, I did not get the impression that Brother Marston had finished." He extended a hand towards Marston, who had remained standing through the brief tumult, patiently waiting for it to die. "Continue, Brother Marston."

"Even before this union was recognised by the London General, Brother Bywater was meeting that company's managing director, Albert Stanley, without the knowledge of the officers or the EC, let alone the members. Then, when the recognition dispute broke out, he met Albert Stanley and agreed to go to arbitration—again, without the knowledge of the EC."

Once again, uproar threatened, but this was forestalled by George Blundy, who got to his feet and, waving his agenda paper, roared, "Point of order, Chairman, point of order!"

"Yes, Brother Blundy, and what might that be?"

"This conference cannot accept—*cannot* accept—such allegations without a shred of evidence or corroboration. I therefore move, Chairman, that you rule Brother Marston's contribution out of order and that it be omitted from the minutes."

Sanders nodded calmly. "Thank you, Brother Blundy. You are quite right: I will recognise your intervention as a point of order...*if* Brother Marston is unable to offer either proof or corroboration. Brother Marston?"

"Chairman, I can offer corroboration. You were the one who imparted this information to me. I also understand that the acting general secretary has knowledge of these incidents."

Conference was in turmoil, some delegates out for blood and demanding that the matter now be put to the vote, while some in the Cab Section found the whole matter suspicious, given the involvement of George Sanders. Sanders used his gavel to quell the uproar and then leaned forward.

"Yes, conference, I was advised of both of these incidents, by an impeccable source, shortly after they occurred. On the first occasion, I was advised by word of mouth, and on the second by telegram. On each occasion, I advised Brother Ben Smith. Brother Smith?"

Ben Smith got to his feet, seemingly glad that a way had been found to release him from his silence. "It's all perfectly true, conference. Regarding the first incident, Brother Sanders advised me that the then general secretary had been at Electric Railway House, in the office of Albert Stanley. On a later occasion, Brother Bywater admitted as much when we confronted him with this information. On the second incident, Brother Sanders showed me the telegram he had received, advising him that HB had met AS that very morning, and that arbitration had been agreed. At the meeting in the afternoon, however, Brother Bywater denied that he had been to Stanley's office, claiming that he had only spoken to him on the telephone."

The doubters were now silenced. A chastened George Blundy raised his hand. "But why, Chairman, has this information not been placed before us before? If Brother Bywater had been meeting an employer without the knowledge of the EC, we should have been told."

"I'll take that one if you don't mind, Chairman," said an affable Ben Smith. He looked around the hall and shrugged. "Why didn't we spill the beans before? To be honest, conference, we didn't think it was necessary. We—and in particular George—gave him such a roasting that we thought he had learned his lesson."

Several delegates now moved progress, and so Sanders put the EC motion to the vote. Each delegate voted by holding aloft a card inscribed with the number of members he represented. After the tellers had finished their task, with each double-checking the work of another, Sanders announced that the EC motion had been lost by 5,000 to 13,000. The Islington motion, calling for the abolition of the post of president, and installing Tich Smith as general secretary and Ben Smith as organising secretary, was then debated and carried.

*

"Let me see if I've got this right," said Ernie Fairbrother, the delegate from the Stockwell Branch. "This EC has ignored one decision after another by the members, so it obviously thinks that the members are not fit to take decisions. Oh, it thinks democracy is a fine thing, but it's not for us. We don't deserve it; we're not *fit* for it! So they'll keep all the democracy to themselves, thank you very much. Now they're taking this a step further: if the members are not fit to take decisions, why should they be allowed to elect the full-time organisers? No, says the EC, they should leave that to us; we know the kind of organisers this union needs."

The SDM was debating the second motion of the day: that organisers should be appointed rather than elected. This had been moved by a very nervous EC member from the Cab Section, who had stuttered and stammered his way through a speech in which he had pointed out that unless organisers were fully accountable to the leadership, the union would continue to see attacks on the EC in the union journal, attempts to mobilise the membership against unpopular decisions, and the growth of unofficial organisations. He had been barracked and heckled throughout his brief speech, tasting the venom of delegates who were convinced that their union was being stolen from them. Sanders, who had introduced the item by saying that he obviously had a vested interest in the outcome, had allowed the debate to take its own course, only intervening when a delegate resorted to the coarsest of language or threatened to physically attack EC members.

"Well, brothers," continued Fairbrother, "I think the EC probably knows what kind of union organisers the employers would like to see, but that's not the kind *my* members are prepared to tolerate!"

A wave of cheers greeted this assertion.

"Just imagine, brothers, the kind of organisers that would be appointed by this shower of bastards!"

"Language, Brother Fairbrother!"

"We want organisers that will stand up to the employers and fight our corner. We want organisers that will be there when they're needed. And, yes, *we want organisers who will stand with us when they see injustice in our own union!* And what kind of organisers are they? They're *elected* organisers, brothers, accountable to the members!"

"And where will it end, brothers?" asked Stan Morrison from Bow. "If this year they get the power to appoint organisers, next year they'll have the general secretary appointing the EC."

"Is there a doctor in the house?" asked one delegate. "No, I'm serious, Chairman, deadly serious. How is it possible that an EC that has earned the contempt of practically the whole union come here and seriously think they're going to get away with a proposal like this? And they must have believed they *could* get away with it, or they wouldn't have put it forward, would they? They must be out of their minds, Chairman, and that's why I call for a doctor: they need to be put away!"

"Don't worry," someone called from the floor, "they will be."

Delegate after delegate went to the rostrum to attack the EC motion, and this continued long after it was perfectly obvious that it would be defeated, Sanders recognising that they were using this opportunity—although another would come later—to give vent to their outrage at the conduct of an EC which had been, until now, out of control. He sat in a cloud of tobacco smoke, thoroughly enjoying the debate until he judged the time was ripe to terminate it.

"Time to put this one to bed, I think brothers," he announced. "You ready to vote on it? Alright, let's see all those in favour."

The EC motion met with a crushing defeat: 300 to 17,400.

"What can the EC possibly say when they move this next one?" asked Archie Henderson.

Eric Rice shrugged. "Your guess is as good as mine, mate. It'll be a brave man that stands up to argue for it."

There was no such brave man. As George Sanders called upon a mover for the motion to empower the EC, whenever it deemed it appropriate and prudent, to accept agreements without reference to the membership, an ashen Martin Summers stood up and issued a terse "Formally moved, Chairman."

The conference erupted in a chorus of laughter and catcalls.

Having secured a formal seconder, a grinning George Sanders shrugged. "Alright, brothers, it's open for discussion. Who's going first? Brother Fairbrother."

Ernie Fairbrother strode to the rostrum.

"Comrades," he said, speaking without notes, "this motion has no more chance of being passed than I have of being appointed to the board of the London General Omnibus Company. The action of the EC—and maybe, anticipating the result of the next debate, I should say the *outgoing* EC—was..." He paused as the delegates cheered. "The action of the EC in accepting this year's Charter was damnable, deceitful and dishonest! But in condemning that action, let's not lose sight of the effects of that Charter. Do I have to tell you about the strain on the men—and the women, now—in consequence of the intensification of their labour as a result of the darkened streets— and they're even darker now, since the latest order issued last month—and the overloading of buses, alongside the great increase in money taken per bus, and at a time when there was, and still is to a certain extent, a shortage of labour? No, of course I don't. And what did the EC get in the way of concessions? An increase out of all proportion to the increased takings and the rise in the cost of living! And the three months' notice to terminate the agreement is a distinct advantage to the masters, enabling them to defeat us in a dispute by giving them more time to prepare.

"Now, brothers, there's not a doubt in my mind that we're all wondering what the EC would have had to say about this motion if it had not been formally moved." He paused to let the laughter die. "Oh, they might have said, we were confident that it was a decent result and it never crossed our minds that the membership might reject it, so why bother with the time and expense of a ballot? I think they would have *said* something like that. What they were *thinking*, however, was another thing entirely. They signed this Charter behind the backs of the membership, brothers, because they *knew* it would be rejected if put to a ballot! I recall how Harry Bywater reacted two years ago when the 1914 agreement was rejected: he was embarrassed; he hardly knew what he would say to Albert Stanley; he was angry not with the employers but with his own members! And do you know what?" He turned to gesture to the EC members with a wave of his hand. "The majority of the members of this EC seem to have drunk long and deep of the Bywater formula. I'll now tell you something you may not know: it was Harry Bywater who, when that 1914 Charter was finally accepted, suggested that it would be a good idea if after future negotiations the members were denied the opportunity of a ballot; and it was Harry Bywater who first suggested that the oganisers be appointed rather than elected! And what do we have today? The ideas of Harry Bywater presented to this Special Delegate Meeting as if they had just sprung new-born from the mighty brains of the geniuses sitting on that platform! It seems to me, then, comrades, that while we have shown the door to Brother Bywater, we now need, in the debate that will surely follow this one, to escort his disciples to the same exit!"

The response of the delegates was both raucous and prolonged, and Fairbrother waited patiently before continuing.

"It is my earnest hope, comrades," he resumed, "that the directors of the London General Omnibus Company receive a full report of our deliberations today, because what is in store for them is very similar to the fate suffered by the EC today! After this war is over, when there are no more excuses, no more sob stories about the need to keep London moving at this time of crisis for the British Empire, when the company is once more fully staffed,"—his voice, which had been gradually rising, now reached its crescendo—"and this red-button union is once again led by men who fully respect the members and their demands, *we will be back to Electric Railway House to take what is rightfully ours!*"

Throughout the meeting, Sanders had been jotting down notes in preparation for the report he would have to write for the *Licensed Vehicle Trades Record*. "EC absolutely overwhelmed by the flood of antagonism towards them," he had just written when Fairbrother's speech came to an end. As the roar of applause commenced, he lit a cigarette and calmly smoked as it continued, deciding to use this as a timing device. As it died, he got to his feet.

"Let the minutes show," he boomed, "that the applause for Brother Fairbrother's speech was one-third of a cigarette in duration!" He paused to allow space for the laughter. "And that the laughter following the Chairman's joke lasted for two puffs."

From the rear of the hall, Eric Rice scrutinised Sanders closely. He had never seen him so happy. Look at him there, bathing in the day's victories; and they were to a very large extent *his* victories, for George Sanders had kept the red flag flying through thick and thin, keeping the troops together, never allowing setbacks to sap his confidence, always ready to point the way forward. George Sanders, smartly dressed as ever, a little grey in the moustache now, the hair a bit farther back from the broad forehead, the lights of the hall falling onto his smiling face as he threw open his arms and asked, "Comrades, if the reception you have just given Brother Fairbrother is a true indication of your sentiment, do we need to continue this debate?"

"No!" came the reply. "Let's have the vote!"

Sanders called for those in favour of the EC motion to show, and one hand—that of the Putney delegate—was raised.

"Against?"

All hands but one went up.

*

Given all that had gone before, the *coup de grace* came as something of an anti-climax. The nine delegates whose branches had submitted motions calling upon the EC to resign had agreed that the Middle Row motion should go forward, and so after Sanders had read the motion aloud it was Dick Mortlake who walked to the rostrum. He stood silently for several seconds, gazing at the delegates.

"I don't really need to do this, do I?" he asked the meeting.

"No!"

"Call the vote!"

"Vote!"

Dick turned to Sanders. "I formally move, Chairman."

"Vote!"

"Call it, George!"

"Brothers, brothers, brothers. Calm down. Have a little patience. Do you really want to go to the vote and then have a judge rule the thing out of order? No? In that case, give me a seconder!"

"Formally seconded!" cried Ernie Fairbrother.

"All those in favour, please show!"

A forest of arms was raised in response, and Sanders was interested to see that that of Eamonn Quinlan, who had been silent throughout the meeting, was among them.

"Against!"

A few hands went up.

"Does anyone demand a card vote?"

Silence.

Then I declare the motion carried overwhelmingly."

This entirely predictable result was greeted by polite applause, following which Sanders, preparing to close the meeting, thanked the delegates for their attendance.

"Point of order, Chairman!" Dick Mortlake was on his feet.

"At this late stage, Brother Mortlake?"

"Yes, Chairman. We have seen in the past that this EC has ignored constitutional decisions by this body. It is for this reason that the resolution we have just adopted calls for its *immediate* resignation. This surely means, Chairman, that they should leave the platform now, indicating that they have, indeed, resigned."

From their reaction, it seemed that the delegates agreed with this.

Smiling wryly, Sanders nodded. "A very fair point, I believe." He looked over his shoulder at the EC members. "Boys?"

Barney Macauley sprang to his feet and, followed by his fellow progressives, descended the steps at the side of the stage and, applauded by delegates, walked to a row of vacant seats on the left side of the hall.

The remaining EC members stayed in their seats, looking anywhere but at the delegates, some with arms folded, others with heads in hands, gazing at the floor, all looking like condemned men.

"Brothers," counselled Sanders in a level tone, "you have heard the decision of this SDM. I must ask that you leave the platform to indicate your resignations."

No one moved.

No one on the platform, anyway. On the floor, where many delegates had stood in expectation of the meeting's close, some now strode towards the platform.

"Get off that platform before I come up there and throw you off!" cried one delegate.

"Get off the platform!"

"Come on, boys, let's sort 'em out!"

Finally, one EC member got to his feet and walked by the steps, followed by first one, then another, eventually the rest.

Breathing a sigh of relief, Sanders turned to his notes for the *Record* and jotted: "Euston Theatre resolution called on EC to resign, then SDM. It was not, I regret to state, until violence had been threatened that they agreed to clear out."

38

In November, there were signs of a new Walter Runciman when he announced the creation of the post of Food Controller, which would usher in government control of the food supply, fixing the prices of milk, potatoes and other domestic products, the standardisation of bread, and possibly the introduction of food tickets, which sounded as if Runciman had changed his mind on rationing. Merchants and warehousemen would be required to produce returns regarding stocks held, contracts entered into, the prices of sale and purchase and the costs of production. There would be no new legislation, as these new powers would be assumed under the Defence of the Realm Act.

Some newspapers swiftly dubbed the controller of food supplies a "food dictator," but the only real criticism in the country was that the measures were not drastic enough and could have been taken long ago. Soon after this announcement, Runciman met hotel managers to discuss effective ways to eliminate "luxurious dining," as five- and six-course meals were still being served in top hotels and restaurants for up to a guinea a head. The menus he had seen, he told the managers, were evidence of "senseless, wasteful extravagance," and deserving of censure. In particular, he drew attention to an event advertised for New Year's Eve at the Savoy; the advertisement was promptly withdrawn, the event cancelled. The hotels, he said, should be able to come up with something in a week, and if they were unable to make up their minds the Government would do it for them.

In the office, Dorothy asked Runciman if he had seen that some newspapers were suggesting that he would be the best candidate to occupy the post of Food Controller.

He laughed at this. "My dear Miss Bridgeman," he replied jovially, "why do these people think that I created the position in the first place, if not to escape weeks and weeks of debate about food prices?" Earlier in the year, such a comment would have been uttered in desperation, accompanied by nervous hand movements and a facial tic. Not so now: this was, indeed, a new Walter Runciman.

This same Walter Runciman in October told a delegation from the Scottish TUC that the Government was considering the introduction of a minimum wage, and in November announced that all ships being constructed for neutral owners would be either sold to British owners or chartered by the Government at around half the market rate until the end of the war or shortly thereafter.

When the South Wales Coal Conciliation Board met on November 10, the union demanded a fifteen-percent increase in wages, while the employers sought a ten-percent reduction. The miners' representatives said that they would report the proceedings to Runciman and that, in fact, they wished to place the whole matter before him. At the end of the month, he issued new regulations under the Defence of the Realm Act empowering the Board of Trade to take over coal mines, those in South Wales and Monmouthshire being the first to fall into the net.

*

"Your boss is acting like a socialist, Dorothy!" Mickey exclaimed one evening.

Dorothy smiled. "You're absolutely right, Mickey: he's acting *like* a socialist, not *as* one."

Mickey suppressed a groan. Was this Dorothy being clever again? Since returning from Italy, she would now and again come out with something she obviously considered *witty*; he often tried to visualise how it might have been in Pallanza, Dorothy soaking up the repartee of Runciman and Rennell Rodd over the after-dinner mints. "Do you don't think he's serious?"

"Oh, he's *serious*, alright, but these measures are not intended to be socialist. You need to consider the state interventionist measures alongside the other things he's said and done since he returned to work. For example, last month he and Arthur Henderson met trade union leaders and employers to discuss the extension of dilution to firms engaged in private work. A few weeks later, he was saying that although the railway companies have released 140,000 men, they would have to release more. Now this is the man who opposed conscription on the grounds that industry would be depleted and yet here he is, calling for it to be *further* depleted. It goes against his true sentiments. And so why is he doing it? I get the impression that Mr Runciman is not alone in this; I think the whole Government has suddenly realised that unless they pull their socks up they will never win this dreadful war. It's as if the Government's report-card for warfare has been marked 'Must Try Harder!'"

"And yet he seems to be enjoying himself."

"Oh, yes, without a doubt! On a personal level, this new decisiveness has done him the world of good. In part, his breakdown

428

was caused by excessive caution, which meant that he would be attacked both by those who disagreed with what he was doing and those who thought he should go further. Now he realises that it's perfectly alright to upset people—particularly if they own coalfields or posh hotels. But that doesn't mean he's a socialist."

Mickey smiled. "No, of course not. And, Dorothy, I must apologise to you."

She looked genuinely surprised. "Whatever for?"

"I doubted you for a moment. I thought you were trying to be clever."

"But I *am* clever, darling."

"Yes, I know, but...you know what I mean." He sighed. "You know, once or twice since you've been back from Italy, I've wondered whether you might be finding me...inadequate."

"In which department, darling?"

"Not that one, maybe. But come on, I'm being serious now. You were rubbing shoulders with ministers, ambassadors and at least one prime minister, and yet all you had to come home to was a bus driver."

"Don't be ridiculous, Mickey. They're just...men."

He smiled. "Funny you should say that. That's what I said to Stanley back in August when he asked me whether I'd had any qualms about assaulting a government minister."

"There you are, then!"

"There is a difference, though. Your background allows you to look upon the high and mighty like that, and they accept it—if they even think about it. But when people like me do it, we usually end up in prison or on the gallows."

"That's stretching it a bit, Mickey,"

"Not so many years ago, that's what happened, Dorothy. When *you* assume equality, you're just saying that *they* are the same as *you*. When people like me do it, we're claiming that *we* are equal to *them*. And usually they don't like that; they find it threatening. People like me are expected to know our place, or the next thing you know, we'll be demanding the vote."

"Well, there's the flaw in your argument, Mickey, because that puts us in the same boat. It turns out that I'm not the equal of these people after all."

He laughed. "You're only partly right, sweetheart: you're their *social* equal, and so your demand for the vote is the *only* thing they fear; because people like me are their social inferiors, they're afraid that, given the chance, we'll take everything."

"In which case, Mickey, *they* are only partly right. All they have to

429

do is look at the calibre of the average Labour MP to see that that is not the case—necessarily."

"Ah, I grant you that." He frowned. "But I thought I was a cut above the average Labour MP."

"Oh, you are, sweetheart, you are. That's why I added that 'necessarily.'"

"I also got the impression from your letter that you missed southern skies and, maybe, that you wished you were could be back in Portugal rather than stuck in gloomy London."

"But Mickey, I've never actually lived in Portugal. I visited several times as a girl, but..."

"Even so."

She smiled and touched his face. "Well, yes, I would like to visit again, but with you alongside me, Mickey."

"I don't see how that could happen, Dorothy," he said softly.

She shrugged. "Then maybe it won't. But that's alright, as long as you're with me here. Don't you see?" She looked at him with a tiny frown of concern. "Mickey, you seem to be imagining reasons why I might leave you. Why is that, my love?"

He shook his head. "No, it's not as bad as that, sweetheart. Maybe it's because we don't see as much of each other now, what with your hours and my hours. I must admit, though, that I have wondered whether this job of yours is taking you away from us."

"Us?"

"Yes. Me, and the movement. Us."

She laughed, took his face between her hands and kissed him lightly on the lips. "You know, you're right, Mickey: not seeing so much of each other, it seems we no longer have the time to talk, and that allows misunderstandings to arise. So let me take this opportunity to explain." She withdrew her arms and placed her clasped hands in her lap. "There's no doubt that my job is *interesting*, Mickey; sometimes it's absolutely *fascinating*. But I sometimes ask myself what I'm doing. Not only do the hours prevent me from playing any significant role in the movement, but my working day is spent basically aiding the war effort, because that's what the role of the Board of Trade has come to be. So, to be honest, just lately I've been thinking that I might look for another job. I might have to in any case."

The last sentence seemed to have been unheard. "Dorothy, how wrong can a man be? For months now, I've had one view of you, and in five minutes of discussion you've painted a completely different picture."

"Well, it's partly my fault; I should have discussed my thoughts with you previously." She grimaced. "That's one of the effects that long hours have: I merely assumed that you knew what my thoughts and misgivings were, but I was usually too fatigued to make sure you did. I'm sorry, Mickey."

He sighed. "As we're still on the subject of apologies, it's about time that I apologised for turning away from you when we had that argument back in September, my love."

"But surely we made up the following day."

That was true: they had made up physically, each knowing that they must if the gulf between them was not to widen. He had chanced to brush against her while entering the living room; she had turned to him, wondering whether the contact had been deliberate, hoping that it had been, and he, although knowing that it had been accidental, wanted only to make her think otherwise. The result had been intense and unforgettable.

Mickey smiled in recollection. "We certainly did. But we didn't talk about it."

"No, we didn't." She paused. "If you're saying that we need to talk about it in order to make sure we both understand it in the same way, I think you're right."

"That's exactly what I mean, sweetheart."

She nodded, then cautiously asked, "So do you want to tell me why you turned away from me when I tried to touch you?"

He nodded. "I've thought about it ever since, and I'm still not sure I can make sense of it. When you told me not to touch you, it was as if you had slammed a door in my face. I thought you knew how I loved touching you, and I thought that you loved me to touch you." As he spoke these words, his hands roamed over her as if to demonstrate his meaning, touching her hand, her face, her breasts. He watched as she became aroused. "I just didn't understand how you could say that. It hurt me, sweetheart, but for a little while it also changed me, because after I'd lost my temper with you and you reached out your hand, that door was still there." He shook his head. "And I suppose I wanted to hurt you the way you had hurt me. That was dangerous, my love, and we must make sure we never get into that situation again."

"I agree, Michael. But I started it. I had one of my tantrums, and I'm so, so sorry, my love." She held her hand over his, pressing it to her breast. "Now, Michael, I want you to put this hand"—she guided it onto her knee, while with her free hand drawing up her skirt—"under here like this. Michael, touch my quim. Yes, I love you touching me, I love it, I love it, I love it!"

He stroked her labia until he felt the moisture come and then slid two fingers into her. "Take off your blouse, Dorothea."

"Yes!"

"By the way, my love, what did you mean—ah!—when you said that you might have to look for another job?"

"Because—deeper, my love—one's ear is to the ground—mmm—and it seems—ah!—that Mr Asquith cannot survive much—ohhh!—longer!"

*

In early December, it was clear that there was an impending Cabinet crisis brought about by the conduct of the war. Lloyd George, now Secretary of War, argued that the War Council should be smaller and more decisive, its decisions final. Asquith agreed to a membership of five but Lloyd George, knowing who the five would be, argued for three. Most members of the Cabinet seemed to think that Asquith should remain as Prime Minister but that he should not sit on the War Council, as he was seen as the main cause of the indecision. Asquith now suggested that after the conclusion of business on Monday, 4 December, the House should adjourn until Thursday. That evening, Runciman, Chancellor of the Exchequer Reginald McKenna, Foreign Secretary Viscount Grey, and the Leader of the House of Lords the Marquess of Crewe, told Asquith that they would resign if Lloyd George's plan for the War Council was adopted; Runciman and McKenna also objected to Ulsterman Edward Carson's membership of the Cabinet.

But events moved faster than Asquith had anticipated. Lloyd George was now saying that he had no objection to Asquith sitting on the War Council, but that he could not be Prime Minister as well. Faced with the option of forming a Cabinet without Lloyd George or resigning, on 5 December Asquith tendered his resignation to the King, who summoned Bonar Law, leader of the Conservative Party. At this point, breaths were held at the Board of Trade, as Walter Runciman was willing to serve in a Bonar Law government, but would not work under Lloyd George. Bonar Law, however, declined, giving his support to Lloyd George, who was summoned by the King on 6 December.

*

"So Lloyd George is now Prime Minister," Mickey remarked, passing the 8 December edition of *The Times* to Dorothy.

They were at home, Dorothy reading J.A. Hobson's *Imperialism* while Mickey, exhausted after a day on route 7, had just finished skimming the newspaper Dorothy had bought earlier.

"Yes," replied Dorothy. "I suppose Asquith's resignation confirmed Sylvia's worst fears."

"Why do you say that, sweetheart?"

"Well, he had as good as promised that he would introduce legislation for women's suffrage after the war—not that Sylvia's trust in his word was particularly strong."

"Mm. I don't suppose Lloyd George is that way inclined, after your mother's lot blew up that house he was having built."

"Oh, but that was over two years ago, Mickey. A lot of water had flowed under the bridge since then. In fact, when George Lansbury took Sylvia to a breakfast meeting with the Welsh wizard..."

"Recently?"

"No, no: before the war broke out, when he was Chancellor. He told her then that he would support legislation if Christabel could be persuaded to discontinue her terror campaign. At the time, Sylvia saw no possibility of that, but since then, of course, Christabel has turned patriot, so I don't see why Lloyd George should not introduce legislation if he is still in Downing Street when the war ends."

"And so why do you say that her fears have been confirmed?"

"Because I think she trusts Lloyd George even less than she did Asquith."

There was a knock of the door.

"Must be Dick," said Mickey, stepping towards the door.

It was—and Gladys, who had moved in a fortnight previously. This meant that Mickey and Gladys, as they worked on the same bus, often found themselves walking to and from the garage together—something which, Mickey suspected, gave rise to speculation in the neighbourhood, although not at the garage as it was well-known that Gladys was Dick Mortlake's girlfriend. Some nights, she visited her mother's in order to spend an hour or two with her boy, and on her rest days she brought him to the flat. Despite Mickey's high regard for Gladys's skills as a conductor, he had offered to do a swap with Dick, but the latter had declined, saying that spending twenty-four hours together, day after day, would probably not be healthy.

"Come in, Dick. We were just discussing Asquith's resignation."

Dick waved at Dorothy and threw himself onto the sofa, patting the place at his side for Gladys. "You'd think he owned the place, wouldn't you, the way he's behaving?" Gladys tut-tutted to Dorothy. Dick glanced sharply at Mickey, who now wondered whether Gladys was aware that he *did* own the place.

"Yes," Dick said, "I don't think we can expect a negotiated peace with Lloyd George in the driving seat, particularly as Asquith was forced out not just because of the Gallipoli mess, but because of the earlier munitions shortage and his dithering over conscription."

"I make you right there, Dick."

"And, of course, the bloody Labour Party will join his coalition."

"I'd put money on it."

"Anyway, Gladys and I have been talking about having a bit of a party around here at Christmas—the day before Christmas Eve, say, because most people will want to be with their families that night. We were wondering how you two would feel about making it a two-flat party, to give us a bit more space."

"*Christmas?*" queried Dorothy. "Are you seriously thinking of celebrating *Christmas*?"

"Not at all, old thing," Dick drawled, adopting the pose he often donned when talking socially to Dorothy, speaking as if he were dressed in a smoking jacket and pushing his words around the stem of a pipe, one former member of the wealth-appropriating class to another. "Actually, before these Christian chaps came along, the pagans of northern Europe held a winter festival to celebrate the winter solstice. And, let's face it, in these climes you need something to cheer yourself up at this time of year. So that's what we're proposing, old stick, and it's entirely up to these other chaps if they want to call it Christmas. So how about it: bit of a pagan knees-up at both our flats?"

Dorothy played along. "Well, I'm sure we would be absolutely delaighted," she said, fluttering her eyelashes and turning to Mickey, "wouldn't we, dahling?"

Mickey tugged his forelock. "If it pleases you, mum, sir. An' it'll be me 'n' Gladys wot serves the vittals."

Still in character, Dick brought his hands together. "Oh, splendid!" He turned to Dorothy. "What an absolutely spiffing chap! Wherever did you find him, Lady Bridgeman?"

"Pretty much the same place, I fancy, as you found your gal Gladys, Sir Richard: in the proletariat!"

Everyone laughed except Gladys, who now called the meeting to order. "Alright, enough of this nonsense. Talking of vittals, who's gonna provide 'em? And the drink? Are we asking people to bring their own, or what? And how many are we inviting? *Who* are we inviting, come to that?"

"That-that-that's a damn good question, Gladys," said Dick who, although no longer in character, appeared to have taken a drink or two during the two hours since he had finished work.

"Who are we thinking of? People from the garage?" asked Mickey.

"Well, primarily, yes..."

"Then I would suggest we keep it to the committee. Throw it open any wider and people will complain if they aren't invited. This way, there's a simple answer: 'Sorry, mate, we had to confine it to the committee.'"

"Eminently sensible, old bean." Dick was drifting back into character.

"But that means no women," Gladys pointed out.

Dick's face fell. "Ah."

"Committee members *and* their wives or girlfriends?" suggested Mickey.

"And who will look after their children, if they have any?" That was Dorothy.

Dick held up a finger. "Their older siblings, if they have any. If they don't, then the nippers can come as well." He looked around at the others.

Gladys pondered for a moment. "Sounds alright to me. Dorothy?"

Dorothy nodded.

"So that's the invitation list, then," concluded Gladys. She nudged Dick with her elbow. "But by this time next year we need some women on that committee."

"Yes, dear," replied Dick. "In fact, I have one in mind."

"How about my brother Eric?" asked Mickey. "Should I invite him?"

"Don't see why not."

Mickey bit his lip. "Second thoughts: how about the reps from the garages in the area?"

"Getting a bit crowded by the sound of it, old boy."

"Not spread over the two flats." He chuckled. "And the staircase, if necessary."

"Job done, then."

"Not quite," said Gladys. "Food and drink."

"It would be sensible to tell them that it starts at eight." suggested Dorothy. "That way, they will have eaten already. Between us, we could provide a few snacks for later on, but nothing like a meal. We could also suggest that they bring a drink or two. Wouldn't that make it more affordable for everyone?"

"Good thinking, sweetheart. Talking of drinks," said Mickey with a grin, "how many have you had this evening, Dick?"

435

"Talking of drinks," Dick shot back, "did you see that Jack London died a fortnight ago?"

"Ah, *shit!*" Mickey looked as if his face had been slapped.

Dorothy glanced at Gladys and raised her eyebrows.

"It's alright, Dorothy," Gladys assured her. "I studied language at school."

"Are you saying he died of drink, Dick?"

"Complications arising therefrom, probably, although there's some speculation that he might have taken his own life."

"And him not even fifty."

"In fact, Mickey, he was only forty."

"Shit!"

"Dick, you described this event as a pagan knees-up," recalled Dorothy. "What exactly do you mean by a 'knees-up?'"

"It's a proletarian term, old stick..."

"Yes, I *know* that, but what are we all going to dance *to*?"

"Well,"—Dick waved in the direction of the gramophone—"you have the music box..."

"But hardly the kind of music one can dance to, Dick."

"Yes, yes, I realise that, and so we can ask our guests to bring not only some drinks, but also a record or two, if they have any."

"Is that likely?"

Dick shrugged. "We'll see."

*

On 23 December, the pagan knees-up began just after 8.30, with the arrival of several members of the Branch Committee, three of whom brought their wives; four reps from local garages drifted in before 9 o'clock; at just after nine, Eric arrived with Elsie and Jacko, who was now almost six years old. A week earlier, the Committee had had a whip-round, allowing Mickey to order a pin of beer and hire twenty pint glasses from the Artesian on the corner of Chepstow Road. Equivalent to half a firkin, the pin contained around 43 pints and now sat, newly tapped, on a rough table in Dick's flat that Andy Dixon had borrowed from his father's second-hand shop. The other reps brought bottles of India Pale Ale and brown ale, while Eric contributed half a bottle of whisky.

The party began in Dick's flat, but as the numbers swelled some poured themselves a drink and followed Mickey and Dorothy upstairs. Some of the men poured half a pint from the pin into their glasses and then topped it up with light ale from a bottle, a practice that had grown increasingly popular during the war, as some cask beer, weakened anyway by government regulation, was found to lose its liveliness rather quickly. From that point, guests circulated freely between the two flats, maybe joining a discussion in Mickey's flat until, finding their glass empty, they would wander downstairs for a refill and find themselves drawn into a new discussion. Most of the guests were meeting Dorothy for the first time, and some seemed to consider her a novelty, hanging about in her vicinity just to hear her speak. Mickey was unable to suppress a smile as he overheard Dave Springer's wife Betty chatting to Dorothy, inserting aitches where they didn't belong and dropping them where they did. Dave glanced across at him and rolled his eyes.

Eric came and touched his glass to Mickey's. "Merry Christmas, bruv."

Mickey grinned. "Merry Christmas, Eric."

"You going to make your announcement at this party?"

"About standing for the EC?"

"What else? Unless Dorothy's pregnant, of course."

Mickey nodded and looked into his glass. "Yeah, a bit later."

Dorothy looked over Betty Springer's shoulders at the two brothers. How different they looked, Eric so tall and lean, Mickey compact and muscular.

After an hour or so, someone downstairs began to sing.

"Mickey!" Dorothy called across to him. "We've forgotten the music!"

The same thing had obviously occurred to Dick, for he now came up with an armful of records. "I underestimated the lads: some of them *do* have records, although I think one or two of these are borrowed. I've also brought a few of my own."

Mickey frowned at him. "But you don't have a gramophone."

Dick grinned wryly. "Not currently, no. But I *did* have one. Casualty of a previous relationship, I'm afraid; had to leave it with her, but I kept most of the records."

First on the turntable was Al Jolson's "Down Where the Swanee River Flows," and people began to drift up from Dick's flat. John McCormack's "The Sunshine of Your Smile," the words so clearly enunciated, was greeted warmly, although when this was followed by the same tenor's version of "The Wearing of the Green," there were one or two frowns.

"You're taking a bit of a chance playing that, Dick, so soon after the Rising," murmured Eric. "Who brought that one?"

"It's actually one of mine," said Dick. "And you'd be surprised at the amount of sympathy there is for the Irish now, after the way the government carried out the executions."

When Billy Murray's "Pretty Baby" was played, Mickey's living room became a music hall, with almost everyone singing along and swaying. The children squeezed through the tightly-pressed bodies to stand near the gramophone, gazing around the room at the singing adults.

"They'll have a bit of trouble singing along with this one," said Dick, winking at Mickey. "O Sole Mio" may have been one of the year's hits for Caruso, but none of this audience knew Italian.

"Oohh," said Muriel Franklin, "I likes a bit of opera."

"Well, of course," Dick began, "it's not actually..." but he caught Mickey's subtle shake of the head and desisted.

Gladys had come up from the flat below and stood silently at the door until the record finished. "Now, brothers and sisters," she announced, "there's sandwiches ready downstairs, but if you think I'm traipsin' up and down these stairs to serve you, you'd better think again. I do enough of that six days a week, thank you. So if you're peckish, come and help yourselves."

Biting into a cheese and pickle sandwich, Mickey found himself standing next to Steve Mason, the rep from Dollis Hill. The word was that a few months earlier Mason had tried for a point inspector's job but had been turned down; then, when the rep's position had fallen vacant due to the conscription of Brian Elliot, he had stood and been elected. To Mickey's mind, this made Mason a careerist, keen to advance himself and not too particular about which side of the industry it was on. To an extent, it was curious that the Dollis Hill members had not seen through him, but it had to be admitted that Mason had a way about him. In his early thirties, stocky, dark-haired and good-looking in a rough-hewn way, he had a forceful manner, and you could imagine him leading a strike—if such a thing had ever occurred to him—or putting a driver on report—which obviously *had* occurred to him.

"Nice little party, Mickey," he said, peeling off the top slice of a sandwich before grimacing and moving on to inspect one on an adjacent plate. "How are things with you?"

"No worse than with most, I suppose," said Mickey, noting that Mason seemed determined not to look at him. "You?"

Mason nodded and, having found an acceptable sandwich, took a bite. "Think I've got my garage super just where I want him." He chuckled. "It's a bad week when I have to drive a bus more than three days."

"Is that so?" Mickey was of course aware that there were such reps, but he had never sought to emulate them, taking the view that it was important that his members saw him working just as hard as them.

"Yeah. You going for the EC?"

"I might, if I'm nominated."

"Yeah," said Mason, finally turning to look at Mickey, "me too."

*

"I'm not so sure about making an announcement this evening," Mickey told Eric when they were both upstairs again.

"Why's that, bruv?"

"Mason's just told me that he'll be running as well."

Eric thought for a moment, then shrugged. "So?"

"It wouldn't seem right, me using a party at my own place to make the announcement, with another candidate present."

"In that case, make the announcement for both of you. Be interesting to see how he takes it."

Mickey grinned. "That's an idea."

At that point, Harry Dawlish, having been unable to get a duty exchange, arrived in his uniform. Tall, with a salt-and-pepper moustache, Harry had been co-opted onto the Branch Committee to replace one of the conscripts. He lifted a newspaper from his jacket pocket. "Got this evening's *Globe* here if anyone's interested," he announced.

"May I?" asked Dorothy, stepping forward to reach for the newspaper.

"Of course you can, dear." Then to Mickey: "And I nipped home on the way here to collect a record."

"Dick's in charge of the music tonight, Harry."

Harry turned to Dick and handed him the record. "Nice drop of ragtime, Dick."

"Ah, splendid!"

The record turned out to be Arthur Collins's version of "Alexander's Ragtime Band" which, having been released five years earlier, giving the public ample time to memorise the lyrics, now generated even more audience participation than the earlier "Pretty Baby."

"*Very* popular," Dick said, winking at Harry as the record came to an end. He looked around and saw that Mickey was in no position to intervene. "But, of course, it's not *really* ragtime."

Harry's face dropped. "No?"

"No. It's by Irving Berlin, after all." Dick leaned forward conspiratorially. "Have you ever heard any real ragtime, Harry?"

"Well, I *thought* I had, but you've just told me I haven't."

"Oh, don't get me wrong, Harry. 'Alexander's Ragtime Band' is a nice little piece, alright. It's just not ragtime. *Now*, if you've really not heard any of the real stuff, you're in for a treat, because I have here"—he picked up a record from the pile and slid it from its paper sleeve—"a composition from the master himself, Scott Joplin."

"Maple Leaf Rag" seemed to meet the approval of almost everyone, with plenty of feet tapping.

Steve Mason, though, seemed determined to piss on the chips. "I suppose you realise he's a coon," he said to Dick.

"I realise that he's a very talented musician," Dick responded. "And, by the way, we don't tolerate that sort of language in our branch."

"More to the point," said Mickey, who had, overhearing Mason's remark, taken a step forward, "we don't allow it in this house."

Unperturbed, Mason turned towards Mickey. "That sort of surprises me, seeing as how your mates George Sanders and Ben Smith were at the London District meeting of the Transport Workers' Federation the other week, looking for support in their campaign against women drivers and coloured labour."

Eric now came across and entered the argument. "And you know damn well," he told Mason, "that they were more concerned with the bosses' driving down wages than with the colour of anyone's skin!"

"What I'm concerned with is hearing some more music," insisted Harry Dawlish. "You can play that last one again, Dick. If that's what real ragtime is like, I have to say I'm partial to it."

Dick did as he was asked, and the tension was defused, Mason retreating downstairs for a refill.

The party rolled on, the sandwiches disappeared, the pin of beer was still about a third full, but there being no new music after Dick had played Joplin's "Cascades" and "Elite Syncopations," they listened again to Billy Murray and Caruso, but people soon began to call for something new.

"Alright, brothers and sisters," Mickey announced, "this isn't really new, but I think you'll find it different. Dick, put on the last movement of the Organ Symphony."

The powerful C Major chord caused the hubbub to die as eyes were raised to the gramophone. The few hardened drinkers downstairs came up and shouldered their way into the room, pint glasses soon forgotten in their hands. In those spots where the organ rested and, say, the woodwind took the lead, conversation was

440

resumed, only to die again as the organ returned. Here and there, a head was shaken in disbelief; expressions came, dissolved and were transformed as the audience of busworkers and their wives followed the music from passage to passage, each considering what it meant to him or her. As the climax came, a quite audible moan arose in the room. And then silence.

Mickey, who seemed to be on the verge of tears, cleared his throat. "I said it was different, didn't I?"

"Well," said Harry Dawlish, "it may not be ragtime, but bloody 'ell it's good."

Thankful that someone else had been the first to speak, the others cheered and—if they were not holding a drink—applauded.

"You should play that at a branch meeting, Mickey!" called Billy Franklin.

Mickey stood beaming, his gaze sweeping the room, profoundly gratified that the music meant as much to these men and women as it did to him. As he turned towards the gramophone, he saw that Dorothy, in her usual chair, newspaper folded on her lap, had buried her face in her hands, and it was only with an effort that he did not burst into tears himself. Steve Mason was standing quite close to the gramophone, a piece of white notepaper in his hands.

"Alright, brothers and sisters," said Mickey, raising his voice, "before we return to something lighter, and while I'm in the mood, let me make an announcement. As you all know, the elections for the Executive Council are just around the corner, and I can tell you now that Steve Mason, the Dollis Hill rep, will be in the running." In the stunned silence, broken by the slightest patter of hand against hand, Mickey took a long pause, then drew in a deep breath, before continuing, "But he'll have stiff competition, because if my Branch will nominate me, I'll be running against him."

This was followed by a roar of approval, but Mason merely grinned.

"And may the best man win!" called someone at the back.

"Oh, I certainly hope he does," said Dick, glowering at Mason.

Mason stepped forward and clasped Mickey's hand. "Good luck, Mickey. Oh, and by the way..." He handed Mickey the folded notepaper he had been holding. "I think this slipped out of the sleeve of that last record," he murmured. He winked. "*Very* interesting reading, Mickey."

Dorothy, who had not witnessed this exchange, now stood up. "Before we get back to the enjoyment, brothers and sisters, there is one final announcement." She held up the *Globe*. "I have just read that your managing director has been declared elected unopposed for the parliamentary seat of Ashton-under-Lyne."

This caused some confusion. "Albert Stanley is now an MP?" asked Mickey. "But why?"

"So, Mickey, he can sit in Lloyd George's Cabinet."

"As what, for Christ's sake?"

"As President of the Board of Trade."

"So you'll be working for your old boss again?"

She pursed her lips. "Yes, but not at the Board of Trade. And this, brothers and sisters, is the *real* announcement: I've handed in my notice, and on Tuesday, 2 January I start training as a conductor at Shepherd's Bush."

PART FIVE

1917

39

After completing all the necessary forms on the first day of training, Dorothy and six other women were led to a small room where the garage superintendent delivered a brief lecture concerning the glorious traditions of the company they were seeking to join before entrusting them to the care of an instructor called Mr Fellows, a pipe-smoking veteran of the horse-bus days, who began to familiarise them with the waybill and the method of issuing tickets. Like so many on first acquaintance, Mr Fellows found Dorothy to be a fascinating novelty. Although she appeared proficient enough he, misled by her accent and demure demeanour, at one point made the mistake of expressing doubts concerning her durability.

"Are you quite sure that you'll be able to cope with the public, dearie?" he asked, regarding her not unkindly from beneath his bushy eyebrows. "They can be a rough lot, you know."

"Mr Fellows, I have survived an argument with my boyfriend in order to be here today, so I rather doubt that the public will prove to be too much of a problem."

The other women tittered. Mr Fellows grinned at them, seeing them as potential allies in what might develop into a joust with this strange trainee, the first toff he had encountered in this line of work, although it was reported that several middle-class women had come forward in various parts of London. "Ah, your boyfriend. Titled gent is he, dearie?"

"Yes. His title is Mister, or more usually Brother."

The other trainees were now silent, interested to see how this would play out. Fellows was on his guard as, inclining his head, he asked, "And would I know this boyfriend of yours?"

"You might. His name is Mickey Rice."

"Ah, yes. Mickey Rice of Middle Row. In fact, I trained him four years ago. Come a long way since then, hasn't he?" He nodded judiciously. "Well, yes, if you've survived an argument with Mickey Rice, you may indeed be equipped to deal with the public."

"Thank you. Now tell me, Mr Fellows, would you mind terribly if I called you 'Pop?'"

Fellows was momentarily at a loss, his mouth working silently as it sought a reply. Eventually, he said, "No, I don't think that would be right. You should call me 'Mr Fellows.'"

Dorothy smiled. "Of course. And I would thank you, Mr Fellows, to stop calling me 'dearie.'"

Her six colleagues now straightened their backs and tried to suppress their smiles. Thinking about it afterwards, Dorothy realised that she had, without really intending it, demonstrated leadership.

Her argument with Mickey had not been particularly bitter, and in fact it had not really been an argument, but it had extended over two days.

"Why the buses, Dorothy?" he had asked on Christmas Eve, the morning after the party.

"Because I will be part of the movement—an *active* part of it."

"Why does that sound like a challenge?"

"It's certainly not intended as such. Unless, of course, you *feel* challenged. *Do* you feel challenged, Mickey?"

He managed a smile. "Why should I feel challenged, Dorothy?"

"Well, you might be fearful that I'll campaign for the retention of women conductors after the war—go against the party line, so to speak. I'd imagine you'd feel quite challenged by *that*."

He regarded her closely and, although seeing that she was not on the verge of an eruption, decided that it would be foolish to run the risk of provoking one. "Not necessarily; circumstances change, after all."

They left it at that for a while, although Mickey knew that, on the domestic front at least, the women's question would have to be negotiated very skilfully in the months ahead.

"So why Shepherd's Bush?" he asked her later.

"Why do you think, Mickey?"

"Because you want to be thought of as being more than Mickey Rice's girlfriend?"

She actually laughed at the notion. "Actually, that had not occurred to me." She gave it some thought. "No, I don't think I would have much trouble moving out of your shadow and demonstrating that I'm my own person..."

Mickey took no offence at this, knowing only too well that none was intended. Dorothy was simply stating what they both knew: that she was sufficiently forthright to be able to make her own mark.

"Now, that being the case, I daresay that I'll get into a number of scrapes, and what I would *not* want would be for you, as rep, to be constantly having to rush to my defence; that *would* attract comment, and would do neither of us any good."

"But I would treat you the same as any other member, Dorothy."

She sighed patiently. "Yes, that might be the way it looked to us, but the rest of the garage would see it rather differently. And then, of course, the garage officials would probably treat me leniently, not wanting to upset Mickey Rice, overlooking little infringements that would find other people put on report."

He nodded. "Yes, I can see that, sweetheart."

On Christmas Day, Mickey shifted the discussion into territory similar to that which Mr Fellows would enter the following week. "I hope you realise, love," he said, "that it's hard work."

"But I'm a hard worker, Mickey."

"I mean physically hard, Dorothy. You'll suffer from aches and pains in muscles you never knew you had. Have you discussed it with Gladys?"

"Of course I have; she says I'll get used to it after a couple of weeks."

"Well. *She* did, but look at the size of her!"

"Oh, I see! You think the little lady will be unable to cope with physical labour. Mickey, you really are scraping the bottom of the barrel now."

Actually, it was more than *just* that: he also knew that her hands would be roughened and blackened by the coppers that passed through them, but he didn't know how to tell her this without inviting her scorn. Similarly, he feared that some men would mock her accent, while others would try to feel her up, although he suspected that she would be better able to cope with these possibilities than with the physical demands of the job.

"Well, listen, sweetheart," he said, placing a hand on her arm, "if you find it too much, just jack it in. No one will think any less of you, least of all me."

She grinned and patted his arm. "Don't worry. Although there may be some nights when I ask you to massage me—and I'm sure you won't mind that—I will be equal to the job."

In fact, of the objections raised by Mickey, this last proved to be the most well-grounded.

*

Once they left the classroom and got onto the road, Dorothy soon learned that route 11 started from the same point, Wormwood Scrubs, and ended at the same destination, Liverpool Street station, as Mickey's route 7, and so once in service, if indeed she ended up on route 11, there was a chance that they would often see each other on the road. Route 11, however, parted company with route 7 shortly after leaving the Scrubs, following a southerly path, down Wood

Lane to Hammersmith, then Fulham Palace Road, Danes Road, Kings Road, Pimlico Road, Buckingham Palace Road, Victoria Street, Charing Cross, the Strand, Fleet Street, Cannon Street and finally into Liverpool Street. Both there and back, Mr Fellows instructed them in the mysteries of fare stages, showing them, for example, just where the ticket should be punched if a passenger boarded at Charing Cross.

"Would you know if there is a newsagent's shop in the station, Mr Fellows?" she asked when they arrived at Liverpool Street.

"There is indeed, Miss Bridgeman: W.H. Smith. You want to buy a newspaper?" He handed her a penny. "Very well, please be so good as to bring me a *Daily Mirror* while you're about it. You'll find us in the canteen."

She handed him back the penny. "In that case, I'd be grateful if you would order me a cup of tea."

He touched the peak of his cap. "Right you are, madam," causing the other women to laugh. Since their minor confrontation on the first day, he and Dorothy had arrived at a permanent ceasefire peppered with good-natured jokes and mild teasing.

When she found them in the canteen, she handed Fellows his *Daily Mirror* and sat down to drink her lukewarm tea.

"What's that you've got there, Miss Bridgeman?" Fellows asked, nodding to the newspaper folded at her side.

"*The Times*, Mr Fellows."

"*The Times!* But you're surely not a Tory, Miss Bridgeman."

"Of course not. I read *The Times* for its news, not for the politics of its editorials. It's known as a newspaper of record, Mr Fellows. And besides, they didn't have a copy of this week's *Herald*." Since the outbreak of hostilities, the daily had become a weekly.

Fellows nodded. That made a kind of sense.

"The weather is very mild for the time of year," Dorothy remarked as, riding back west, they stood on the top deck passing through Trafalgar Square.

Fellows grimaced. "For now, yes, but it won't last." He regarded her with a rheumy eye. "Be prepared, Miss Bridgeman, be prepared."

By the time she completed her training, Dorothy was fully kitted out with uniform jacket and skirt, hat and overcoat, to which she added a black chiffon scarf and a pair—several pairs, in fact, as they were of limited longevity—of thin, black cotton gloves. The first few days brought mixed fortunes, for although the weather was fair, she soon found that the weight of her coin bag was almost intolerable, and her leg muscles were a misery. She tried to hide her physical discomfort from Mickey, although her drawn features and unconvincing smile told him all he needed to know. On the evening of her third day in service, he entered the bedroom and instructed her to take off her nightdress and lie face down.

"I'm alright, Mickey. Just let me sleep."

"Do as I say."

She did as he said and he massaged her slender back and shoulders with Tiger Balm. Her right shoulder, he noted, bore a red welt from the strap of her cash bag. "Tell me where, sweetheart."

"This is quite unnecessary, you know. Oh yes! There!"

After five minutes, he halted, panting a little. "Is that better?"

She murmured something into her pillow.

"What was that, sweetheart?"

"Can you please do my legs?" she asked shyly.

Swallowing a wave of affection, he did her legs without a word, covering her when he had finished and leaving her to sleep.

After the first week, it was not so difficult, although the weight of the coin bag was still a problem. She partially solved this by, when the weight became unbearable, transferring coins into the pockets of her coat.

Overloading passengers were also a problem, but one she quickly overcame, and in the process she made a dispiriting discovery. On the western section of the route, the overloaders tended to be working-class, and after some experimentation she found that they were best controlled if she emphasised, rather than attempted to disguise, her ruling-class origins. Early one evening, just as she was about to give her driver the double bell at Hammersmith Broadway, having advised those still waiting that the vehicle was full, a tall man of around twenty, dressed in overalls, on the left strap of which was pinned a war service badge, insisted on boarding, casting her a defiant glance. Clutching the handrail to prevent his further progress, she addressed him sternly.

"No, no, young man, you will *not* ride on this omnibus. It is *quite* contrary to the regulations, in addition to which you will imperil your own life and those of the other passengers. Alight now. Off you go...That's right...Thank you."

Mickey, when she told him, laughed at Dorothy's self-impersonation. "And so he just got off again?"

"Like a lamb!" She shook her head. "I found it quite worrying, really."

He frowned. "Worrying?"

"Yes, worrying. I mean, if that's all it takes to force the working class to retreat, our movement is in trouble, Mickey."

"Ah, yes. Good point."

If this tactic caused working-class overloaders to shrink in the face of her social superiority, she also found that it worked well with the middle-class variety, most frequently encountered at Charing Cross and Liverpool Street, who tended to comply due to their recognition of her as a social equal.

The weather broke on 11 January with a downpour that lasted all day. This was not so bad, as the top deck was empty and Dorothy was able to shelter on the platform or inside the saloon, but this was followed by a very cold spell, sometimes with snow showers, that lasted into February. It was hell. The main problem was her fingers. She had not bought the gloves to protect her from the cold, and they did not. Digging into her bag to find the correct change, she often found that her fingers had no feeling, and the gloves simply made the transaction all the more cumbersome, so she took them off. Her fingers were still without feeling, and as she grasped at the coppers in the bag she was unable to gauge how many she had in her hand, meaning that she had to place them on the palm of her left hand and count them out with her right. Once, as she drew her right hand from the bag, unable to feel the coins between her fingers, she watched in despair as they fell and scattered on the deck. She fell to her knees and attempted to gather them, in the process contacting some of the detritus that lay there—cigarette ends, loose ash, sputum. Regaining her feet, she hurriedly gave the passenger his change and, not bothering to collect the remaining fares, stumbled downstairs, where she stood on the platform and, unashamed, wept. Jack it in if it's too much for you, Mickey had said. Surely that would be a reasonable thing to do in these deplorable conditions. How can I possibly continue to do this, hour after hour, day after day? I won't think any less of you, he said. No, but I would, so bugger it. She wiped her eyes on the back of her hand and clambered back up the stairs.

*

In early January, as soon as the Middle Row branch nominated Mickey for an EC position, word began to circulate that he had received the gift of a gramophone from Sir Albert Stanley. He expected his members to confront him, but the only one who did was Dick Mortlake.

"Is it true?" Dick asked as he opened his front door and saw Mickey standing there, eyes evasive.

"Yes." He stepped into Dick's flat and made for the sofa.

"But why? You of all people!" Dick had taken the armchair opposite the sofa, the better to observe him.

"It wasn't *like* that, Dick. He had the gramophone delivered after he saw us at the Albert Hall. Here, read this." He took Stanley's note from his shirt pocket and handed it over. "Mason read this when it fell out of the record sleeve at our party."

Dick spent a moment to scan the note. "Well, yes, I can see that this puts a different complexion on the matter." He drew his lips together. "The problem, however, is not that Stanley gave you the gramophone but that you accepted it. You even lied to me, saying it came from Dorothy's father, so you must have felt it was wrong."

"It wasn't that *I* thought it was wrong but that *other people* would think it was wrong. And, yes, I'm sorry I lied to you. Dick, all I wanted was to listen to the music, and I couldn't do that unless I had the gramophone."

Dick smiled. "Well, many of us want to listen to the music, Mickey…You should have told the Branch Committee and asked for their opinion. If you'd done that, none of this would be happening."

For the first time in a very long while, Mickey's self-assurance had deserted him; he knew himself to be in error, and at the moment he was nobody's equal, least of all Dick's. If he hoped to regain his self-respect and the respect of others, he knew he must rectify his error, and he had already spent many hours considering how this might be done. For the first time since entering the room, Mickey looked at Dick squarely. "I intend to make it right," he said.

"How?"

"You'll see." With only partial success, he tried a smile. "Now, I have a favour to ask you as a cricketing man."

"As a cricketing man?"

"Yes, I'll need your bat tomorrow night."

*

The Vigilance Committee was, despite its name, not really a committee: although it strived to secure representation from every branch, anyone who agreed with the purposes of the organisation was free to attend its meetings. Thus, on the following evening, the attendance from Middle Row was larger than usual: not just Mickey and Dick, but also Dave Springer, Harry Dawlish and Billy Franklin; and there, sat at the back, was the new clippie from Shepherd's Bush, Dorothy Bridgeman.

The main business of the meeting concerned the forthcoming EC elections, as the Vigilance Committee was anxious to ensure that in each division there was a progressive candidate with a chance of winning. This being the case, the full-time organisers were not present, and the meeting was in the capable hands of Dennis Davies, who was looking forward to regaining his EC seat.

At one point in the evening, Davies scratched his face and frowned at the meeting. "Now, comrades," he said, "it seems that we're somewhat over-represented in one division, as we have two candidates present—Mickey Rice from Middle Row and Steve Marston from Dollis Hill..."

"The name is Mason, Chairman," came Mason's voice.

"Oh is it? You'll have to forgive me, Brother, if I'm not familiar with your name. Mind you, that's not surprising, as I believe this is the first time we've seen you at one of our meetings."

"I stand," said Mason—and he did, indeed, stand, gripping his lapels like a market-square orator—"for the interests of the membership and have never taken a bribe."

"Apart from the three or four days a week he spends off the road," murmured a Rice partisan.

"Now that is something that my opponent in this election cannot say," bellowed Mason. "Can you, Brother Rice?"

Sitting in the front row, arms crossed, Mickey did not turn his head. Others, however, especially those who had not heard the rumour, began to mutter.

"What's he on about, Mickey?"

"Mickey Rice take a bribe? Never!"

"Well, let's hear it from the 'orse's mouth!"

"Blimey, you can't trust anyone these days, can you?"

"Brother Marston," warned Dennis Davies, "I have to tell you that you're on dangerous ground. Are you prepared to prove this allegation?"

"Of course I am! Do I strike you as an inventor of fairy tales?" Mason let go of his lapels and threw out his arms, turning from side to side until he had scanned the whole of the meeting. "And the name by the way is *Mason*. M-A-S-O-N: that's how it'll be spelt on the ballot paper."

"Out with it, then," said Dennis Davies. And it was difficult to tell whether his scowl was directed at Mason or Mickey.

"Sir Albert Stanley, managing director of the Traffic Combine, gave Driver Mickey Rice a gramophone and a set of records. I've seen the gramophone and records in his flat, and the letter that came with 'em! Let's see if he'll deny it!"

Mickey stood up. "Chairman, with your permission, I'd like to

452

address the meeting from the table, as I'll need some space."

Receiving Davies's nod, he picked up a hessian sack which lay at his feet and walked to the top table, placing the sack on the floor.

"That's not a weapon in there, is it?" asked Davies.

"Sort of," replied Mickey, "but it's not meant for anyone in this room." He looked towards the back of the room. "Dorothy?"

Dorothy walked down the aisle, carrying something covered with what looked like a table cloth. Reaching Mickey, she handed over her cargo and he placed it, still covered, on the table.

"Comrades, for those who haven't met her, this is Dorothy Bridgeman, the love of my life, and now a conductor at the Bush."

They were a few catcalls and rather more cheers and sighs of appreciation. Dorothy glared at Mickey before returning to her seat.

"Chairman, comrades," Mickey now began, "it is true that some fourteen months ago I received a gift from Albert Stanley." He paused. The room was silent. "Was it a bribe? No, of course it wasn't! But I was wrong to keep it to myself, not telling anyone." He turned to the chairman. "Dennis, I hope that you and our comrades here will be patient enough and allow me to tell the whole story."

With a slim agenda, Davies, perhaps grateful that the time would be filled, and probably entertainingly at that, waved a hand: no problem.

"For the past few years, comrades, thanks largely to Dorothy and my friend Dick Mortlake, I have become a lover of music, and when I say music I mean the serious stuff, what most call classical. Yes, Mozart, Beethoven, but also more recent stuff. Why? That was the question I asked myself, and so I kept thinking about it until I found the answer. Some of this music, comrades, is... up*lifting*, by which I mean that it hits me here." He struck his heart with the flat of his hand. "Or seems to. Really, of course, it's the mind that it gets to. But in what way is it uplifting?" He screwed his eyes shut as if not so much to find the right words but to recapture that feeling of upliftment so that he could verbalise it. He spoke slowly and softly, with no need to raise his voice because the room was silent. "It makes me feel that I'm part of something that's bigger than just me. I feel as if I'm growing inside, and that I can reach out and touch this thing that's bigger than me. And do you know what it is, this huge thing?"

"God?" It was Dave Springer who broke the silence.

Mickey grinned and shook his head. "I don't believe in such a thing. No, not God, although this thing would be a good substitute." He sighed. "It's other people, comrades. *Our* people. Workers. The whole working class, in fact." Looking around the room, he could see

453

that not many could grasp his point, but he had not expected them to at this stage. "Let me come back to that.

"Now, some of you might think that Mickey Rice has gone all airy-fairy, or is pretentious, having ideas beyond his station." He paused to allow some in the audience to chuckle, seemingly relieved that Mickey seemed to be saying that it was alright, or at least understandable, to think such things. "I probably would have agreed with you a few years ago, because we were all taught pretty much the same thing: classical music is for toffs, for men in top hats and dinner jackets and women with jewels on their fingers and around their necks. And it's true, in a way; it *is* for them and them alone while the rest of us think that way and can't, anyway, afford to listen to it.

"Anyway, let me give you an example of what I mean." He drew the cloth away from the item on the table, revealing the gramophone. "With your permission, Dennis..."

A bemused Dennis Davies nodded, then glanced at the meeting with raised eyebrows.

Mickey bent over the machine and wound it up as Dorothy strode to the table and placed a single record on it. Having placed the record on the turntable, Mickey again addressed his audience.

"I'm just going to play you a part of the final movement of the symphony that the three of us—me, Dorothy and Dick Mortlake—heard at the Albert Hall in November 1915. This gramophone, by the way, is the gift from Albert Stanley."

He raised the arm and eased the needle gently onto the record. There was not sufficient space on one side to contain the whole movement, and so when the side was finished, he eased the record from the turntable and was about to return it to its sleeve, assuming that a tolerance level was in danger of being breached.

"Play the other side," said Dennis Davies.

Mickey looked from Davies to the audience with a questioning shrug.

"Yes," came the answering rumble from the audience.

And so he played the second side, watching the audience closely. The music had captured them—even the two supporters that Mason had brought with him, although Mason himself, having heard the piece at the party, managed to maintain an attitude of indifference. The climax was greeted with a spontaneous burst of applause.

"Well," said Mickey, nodding, "perhaps now you can understand a little better what I was saying earlier. When we heard it at the Albert Hall, it affected all three of us in the same way, and we were on our feet, cheering, clapping and hugging each other. Why?" He looked around at the meeting, pausing for dramatic effect. Knowing his propensity for tears, he had rehearsed this section of his speech at home several times, playing the climax and silently mouthing his lines over and over again until he was confident that he could get through it with a dry eye. "When I hear that music, it puts me in mind of the eventual victory of our class; I imagine it playing in celebration when we finally conquer power, when exploitation and poverty will be banished forever.

"Does everyone feel that way when they hear it? No, of course not! Did the Frenchman who wrote it in 1886 have that in mind? Of course he didn't! In fact, as we were leaving the Albert Hall, Dick and Dorothy said that the people who arranged the concert probably thought that the audience would take it as a prediction of the Allies' eventual victory in this war which most of us oppose. Albert Stanley and his party were in a box opposite us, and that was probably the way it affected him. It probably affects different people—or different classes of people—in different ways.

"Now we come to the point. As we left the Albert Hall, Albert Stanley called to me and the four of us—five, actually, as the President of the Board of Trade was there as well—had a brief chat. A few days later, this gramophone arrived at our flat, along with this." He took Stanley's note from his pocket and held it aloft. "This is the note that Brother Mason saw fall out of the record's sleeve when it was played at the Christmas party we had at our flat, the note which he opened and read before handing it back. I'll read it to you."

He did so. Most people in the meeting leaned forward, frowning in concentration.

"And who," asked Barney Macauley at the back when Mickey had finished reading, "is this Polonius? What garage is he out of?"

Mickey laughed along with the rest. "Well, that's another confession I have to make, comrades: the managing director and I sometimes quote Shakespeare at each other. I suppose that's something else that Brother Mason will hold against me.

"But now that you've heard what was said in Stanley's note, you should be in a position to judge. Was the gramophone a bribe? When he says 'to thine own self be true,' does he mean 'take this gramophone and I'll be back for my pound of flesh when it suits me?' Sorry, Shakespeare again. No, he doesn't. He tells me I don't even need to reply to the note. Are those the words of a man who intends to corrupt me? 'You and I will disagree on many things,' he says. Could anything be clearer than that?

"Mind you, if he knew that this music inspired thoughts of

working-class victory in me, he probably would never have thought of sending this gramophone. And let me talk about that just a little bit more. I can see that most of you were affected by this music. You can now see what music can do. But we have to realise that it didn't simply emerge from the mind of an individual genius. That Frenchman could never have written a note of this music if there hadn't been people like us to create the wealth—the surplus value—that allowed him and others like him to produce culture rather than manufactures or food—or transport. So why should things like classical music be looked upon as the property of the rich and the middle class? It should surely be the property of *our* class as well. And when I say, comrades, that I imagine this particular piece of music playing as our class finally defeats capitalism, I don't see that as a time when *only* the means of production—including Albert Stanley's buses, trams and tube trains—will be taken into collective ownership, but when our class also appropriates the very best of bourgeois culture and makes it available to all!"

The applause which this earned should have cheered Mickey, but he now looked quite sober.

"Having said a-a-a-a-all"—a sweep of the arm—"of that, comrades, the fact remains that I made a mistake. I accepted this gift for myself and I told no one about it. Dorothy told me it was wrong to accept it and that it could only lead to trouble, as it has done. I persuaded her by reminding her that over the previous few years I had created a considerable amount of surplus value for Albert Stanley, and I looked upon the gramophone as a part-repayment. Well, that was wrong too, because of course all of *you* have created plenty of surplus value as well. So, if this gramophone is going to come between me and the movement..."

He bent down to retrieve the sack at his feet, from which he took a cricket bat.

"Bloody hell," muttered Dennis Davies, as the rest of the meeting uttered a collective gasp of dismay.

"...then it should be destroyed." Gripping the bat with both hands, he raised it above his head.

"NO!" This was cried in unison by Harry Dawlish and Dick Mortlake, both on their feet, while more muted protests issued from other members.

"Hang on, hang on, hang on," insisted Dennis Davies. "*Mickey!* I believe the brother there has a point of order, so lower the bat."

"Mickey," said Harry Dawlish, "for the life of me, I can't follow your logic. First you say that this kind of music should be the property of our class, but now you're proposing to destroy the thing that might give some of us the opportunity to enjoy it while we wait for that great day. You're looking at this thing far too personally, son. You're right when you say that we've all produced our share of surplus value, and so why not donate the gramophone to the union, so we'll *all* have a part-repayment?"

"That's a grand idea, comrade," said Dennis Davies. "Is it not, Mickey? But it would be pretty meaningless to donate it to the union as a whole, so I suggest you donate it to your branch, perhaps on the understanding that other branches or union bodies can borrow it when they need to put on a bit of music."

The meeting agreed.

"But where can the branch keep it?" asked Mickey. "It's not as if we have premises..."

"I'll suggest to the Branch Committee," said Harry Dawlish, "that you look after it for us, Mickey. I think we can trust you to do that."

"Alright, comrades, that's branch business. I think, however, that this Vigilance Committee has a question to answer: did Mickey Rice accept a bribe?"

"NO!" came the resounding reply, whereupon Steve Mason, but not his two supporters, stood up and made for the door.

"And I daresay," muttered Dennis Davies, "that we won't be seeing *him* again." He pushed his notepad and pencil towards Mickey. "Hey, Mickey, write down the name of that music and the composer for me, will you?" Suddenly, he clapped a palm to his forehead. "I'm sorry, Brother Mortlake, did you have a point to make?"

"It's alright, Chairman," Dick drawled. "I was just a little concerned that Mickey was going to damage my cricket bat."

40

"I've had," said George Sanders, "a bit of a tiff with Mickey Rice."

"Oh?" Ben Smith's eyebrows shot up. "Nothing serious, surely?"

They sat in Ben's office after Sanders had come in after a morning touring the garages.

"Not sure. He had a go at me because of that motion we pushed at the Federation meeting last month."

"On black and female labour?"

"Yes. He asked me what I had against Joe Clough."

"Joe Clough?"

"Yeah, the Jamaican bloke at the Bush."

"Oh, yes, I remember now."

"I told him I had nothing against Joe Clough, apart from the fact that he'd volunteered in 1915 and has been driving an ambulance in Belgium for the best part of two years."

"Hah! I bet that took the wind out of his sails."

"You'd have thought so, wouldn't you? But not a bit of it. No, he said, so it was okay for black labour to serve in the Army—telling me how many thousands of colonial troops are doing precisely that—but not to drive buses in London. Look, I said, this isn't about colour: if there were hundreds of black drivers brought over here the employers would use 'em to reduce wages, simple as that."

"What did he say to that?"

"Told me there's hundreds of women conducting buses in London, and they would be as firm as the men if there was any suggestion of a wage-cut. It would, he said, be the same with black drivers as long as we organised them."

Ben grinned. "Sounds like you had a hard time of it, George."

Sanders nodded. "Damn right, Ben, and it got to the point where I started wondering whether he might be right, that it might be about colour rather than wages."

"Tell me now, did this Joe Clough ever join the union?"

"I put that to Mickey. 'Yes,' he said, 'and I was the one who gave him the application!'"

"Oh, well…"

"And you know what set this off, don't you?"

"Tell me, George."

"That idiot at the London Trades Council meeting last weekend! One of our delegates decided to put forward a motion calling on the government to urge the government to enter peace negotiations because of the danger of black labour being introduced into the country." He passed a hand over his face. "That tells you something about the level of understanding of even some of our *active* members! Is that why we call for peace negotiations—in order to prevent black labour from entering the country?"

"So what happened to the motion?"

"Ruled out on procedural grounds, as the delegate had taken it upon himself to move it as an individual." He sighed. "But the whole discussion with Mickey made me uncomfortable, Ben—more the way he looked at me than anything else, almost as if he was disappointed in me."

"Well, you'll be seeing a lot more of him in the future, because he romped home in the EC ballot."

Sanders brightened. "Ah, the results are out?"

"Yes, George, and they should make you happy. Barney's back in, along with Dennis..."

Sanders rubbed his hands, as much from the biting cold from which he had just emerged as in relish at this news. "Do we have a progressive majority?"

"We do," Ben nodded, "although of course Blundy walked it."

"Oh, of course." He nodded at the newspaper on Ben's desk. "What do you think?"

"The *Record*? Oh, a good issue, George, no doubt about it." He grinned. "A bit bold printing that report from the German transport workers, weren't you? You'll have Auntie DORA knocking on the door if you're not careful."

He was referring to a piece from the German Union of Transport Workers which reported that after an 18-month "severe time of trial" the unions had "splendidly proved their power of resistance" and that the transport union in particular had "endeavored to steer clear of all chauvinism and bellicose machinations, to which, unfortunately, so many sister unions appear to have fallen victim."

"I can't see that Auntie DORA would have much of a case," Sanders replied. "It's hardly giving succour and comfort to the enemy, is it?"

"No, you're right. You had any backlash from the members?"

"Nothing to speak of, Ben. To tell you the truth, I've had more complaints for printing that letter from Larry Russell." The former organising secretary had written to complain that the journal was "being used for the purpose of most grossly insulting employers of labour with whom we have agreements."

Ben Smith laughed. "Circulation holding up?"

"Oh, it's doing more than that, Ben. Battersea is selling 250 copies a fortnight and Merton has doubled its sales—and that's *after* we doubled the price to tuppence."

"Must be doing something right, George," Ben said with a wink.

*

The severe weather, with the exception of a mild spell in the final ten days of February, continued—and, with it, Dorothy's misery. Even in March, there was occasional snow and hard frosts, and the temperature on the night of 9 March fell to minus 6 degrees

Centigrade. The deception of February was then repeated, with milder weather in the middle of the month, only to be followed by a return of the cold days and colder nights. Somehow, Dorothy struggled on, wearing her gloves when she could and laying them aside when it became impossible, so that her hands became blackened from the coins she handled, and her fingers cracked and bleeding, necessitating the wearing of bandages instead of gloves. Her morale was at its lowest, and the agony of the cold, along with the fatigue caused by the job itself, meant that she gave no thought to attending a branch meeting, and the Vigilance Committee meeting in early January was the last one she was at until the weather turned warmer. Arriving at Liverpool Street station, she often neglected to purchase a newspaper at W.H. Smith, hurrying instead to the canteen and ordering a tea so that she might warm her fingers on the cup.

It was during this time that the union was confronted with the issue of women drivers. In February, the *Record* reported that the Home Secretary had agreed to issue licences, and the journal pointed to the strenuousness of the job and to the fact that the darkened streets had contributed to 700 deaths and 35,000 injuries in 1916. The union had agreed to the employment of women conductors, who now constituted 75 percent of the total, but the line must be drawn when it came to driving. So far, Dorothy, struggling as a conductor, could not disagree with the union's position, and at the one gathering she did attend during this period, a mass meeting at the Euston Theatre on 8 February, she and 2,000 others voted for the resolution, moved by Ben Smith, pledging resistance to the employment of women drivers "at all costs." Curiously, Archie Henderson, although seconding the resolution, was of the view that the men would not resist "at all costs." His speech was subject to frequent interruptions. Dorothy craned her neck in an attempt to gauge the reaction of Mickey, who sat on the platform as a member of the new EC, but he was expressionless. Finally, Dennis Davies, restored to the EC, successfully moved that a ballot be called on the question, and that all work should cease as soon as the first woman driver appeared. During the proceedings, Dorothy found herself wondering whether her own view might be overly influenced by the difficulties she was experiencing as a conductor. While she had no doubt whatsoever that she was not driver material, could the same be said of all women? Would Gladys be suitable as a driver?

On 13 February, Tich Smith wrote to the Home Secretary to ask that he receive a six-strong deputation to discuss the matter, warning that the EC predicted "serious consequences" if the matter was not resolved. It was not until almost a month later, however, that Sir George Cave condescended to receive the deputation. In the meantime, the ballot called for at the Euston Theatre mass meeting had resulted in a large majority for strike action. According to Tich Smith, the Home Secretary's response to the demand that he revoke the order permitting women to be licensed to drive cabs, trams and buses was "not entirely" satisfactory, as he had conceded on trams and buses, but stood firm on cabs. Cave told the Commons that the licensing of women cab drivers would be reconsidered after the war, but this was insufficient for the union, and thus mass meetings of the whole membership were arranged for Sunday, 18 March.

In February, when women had been allowed to study for the Knowledge, the cab section had threatened to call out ten men for every woman employed, and Dorothy thought then that there might be a case for such action, for if the authorities succeeded in putting women cab drivers on the street, they would be more likely to press the case for women on the buses and trams. But that argument no longer held, as Cave had already given an assurance on buses and trams, and Dorothy now began to question the union's position.

"Do you *really* believe that a woman would be unfit to drive a cab?" she asked Mickey.

Mickey had anticipated such a question, and was surprised that it had been so long in coming, something he put down to Dorothy's frequent exhaustion. In the meantime, he had rehearsed the replies he might give her. The ill-lit streets contributed to the high accident rate. But why would a woman be more affected by this than a man? There was the risk of assault. But the driver was separated from the passengers. And so now he surprised her. "No, I don't Dorothy," he said, "and maybe this was what Archie was thinking of when he questioned the commitment of the men at the Euston Theatre."

"Well." Dorothy sat back, pleased but, for a few seconds, speechless.

Mickey knew what was coming next, and had realised long before that Dorothy would award him few points for admitting the weakness of the cab section's case unless he was prepared to take the logical—to her—next step.

"And so how will you argue on the EC, Mickey?"

He shook his head. "I don't know, Dorothy."

She frowned. "How can you possibly say that?"

"It will depend on the balance of forces. Above all else, we have to maintain the unity of the union."

"Above all else?"

He looked at her and nodded. "Yes, Dorothy, above all else."

461

She held his gaze, but it was impossible to gauge her thought. It was possible that this moment would, maybe days or weeks later, prove the starting point for a furious argument between them, although it was equally possible that it would be forgotten, as it was doubtful whether she had yet given much thought to the question of red-button unity.

*

To begin with, the atmosphere at the EC meeting on the Saturday was tense.

"There are reports," said Tich Smith, "that feeling for a strike has become lukewarm." He looked around the room. "We need an honest appraisal of the situation, because if we're going to have a scrap over this question, we must all be in it together."

"Alright, brothers," said Dennis Davies from the chair, "who'll be first, and let's have some honesty."

"The cab section," declared George Blundy, "is as firm as it ever was. When the time comes, we'll be out to a man."

"Well," mused Dennis Davies, "that's only to be expected, George, as the cabs are now the only section directly affected by this issue, but I think Tich was referring more to the trams and buses. Are they still as firm?"

This was greeted with an uneasy silence. Mickey, who had hoped to come in later, having first heard the views of other EC members, now sighed, attracting the chairman's attention. He glanced at Barney Macauley across the table, who warned him with an almost imperceptible shake of the head, but it was too late.

"Brother Rice," announced Davies.

"If the mass meetings decide on a strike, I think the majority will come out, but I doubt whether it will be solid—in my division, anyway. It's only beginning to sink in that the dispute is now confined to the cabs, and people are beginning to question the wisdom..."

"Ha!" exclaimed Blundy. "Wet behind the ears, been on the EC five minutes, and already the young so-called militant is trying to undermine the unity of the union!"

"George..." Davies warned.

"That's alright, Chairman," said Mickey. "I'm capable of defending myself. Unity of the union, Chairman, is precisely what I'm anxious to preserve, if Brother Blundy will do me the courtesy of listening. As the general secretary says, if we're going to fight, we must do it together. Now, we've been asked to give honest opinions, and that's what I'm trying to do. In my division, there a few people in virtually every garage, and a lot of people in one garage in particular—Dollis Hill—who are pointing to the fact that the Home Secretary has retreated as far as we're concerned. Some of them—those who read the papers—are saying that he has also said he'll review the question of women cab drivers when the war is over. These people are a minority, but they're making their views heard and their voices are getting louder every day.

"Now, whether this is the pattern in the other divisions, I don't know. That's what we're here to find out, surely. When the other comrades have reported, we'll be in a position to see whether we have sufficient strength to go ahead, and *that* will be the time to discuss unity. And it's not just the unity of the union as a whole we'll be discussing, but unity of the bus section, and unity of the tram section. We've still got our own battles to fight, and the last thing we want is to have differences and disunity in our own sections.

"And finally, Chairman, if the intervention of Brother Blundy is an example of the comradeship we can expect on the EC, I'm beginning to understand how some of the women feel!"

This went down well with most members of the Council, although Blundy spluttered and indicated an intention to reply to Mickey's last barb, but Davies cut him short.

"No, George, you've dished it out, so you must learn to take it. Besides, we're discussing the strength of feeling in the other two sections. I asked for honesty, and Brother Rice has given it, so let's see who's next."

This part of the debate was interrupted by the ringing of the telephone in reception. Eric Rice, present as an observer along with the other organisers, got to his feet and jerked his thumb towards reception. "Do you want me to...?"

"No, that's alright, Eric," said Tich Smith. "I think Frank is using his broom out there. He'll get it."

A few moments after the ringing stopped, Frank put his head around the door.

"It's John Hodge, the Minister of Labour," he announced with a grin. "Do you want to speak to him, Tich, or shall I tell him to leave a message?"

This caused a ripple of laughter. Playing along, Barney Macauley leaned back in his chair and called out, "That's alright, Frankie, you handle it. We have complete confidence in you."

Amid more laughter, Tich stood and, giving Macauley something between a grin and a scowl, hurried out to the reception area.

Dennis Davies gave half a shrug, palms upward. "Any predictions, brothers?"

"Hodge is at least a trade unionist," said Mark Burton from south London, a neophyte like Mickey.

"From my neck of the woods," said Archie Henderson, "born in Ayrshire. Founded the British Smelters' Association when he was thirty."

"But one of the super-patriots," said Macauley. "Claims that every strike during this war is treasonous, so don't expect too much from him."

When Tich Smith returned, he was almost smiling. Walking slowly to his seat next to Dennis Davies, he eased himself down and folded his hands on the table, clearly enjoying the suspense he was creating.

"Well?" prompted Dennis Davies.

"He says that the Home Secretary is almost persuaded. He's confident that he'll revoke the Order regarding women cab drivers."

"But this is a man," said George Sanders, "who'll do anything to prevent a strike."

Tich nodded. "True, and for that reason, I pressed him as hard as I could, telling him that if we call off the meetings and this turns out to be a fairy tale, he'll have more strikes than ever."

"Call off the mass meetings?" echoed Blundy. "Where did that idea come from?"

"Hodge, of course," said Sanders.

Tich Smith nodded again. "Yes, that's what he's asking. My own view is that we should give him a chance to work on the Home Secretary."

"And call off tomorrow's mass meetings?" This was Blundy.

"That's right."

Sanders sighed. "Here we go, lads. Hold tight."

The debate was furious and at times acerbic, with threats of resignation from a couple of cab members and a new representative from the Bus Section out to demonstrate his militancy, and once again there were allegations that the LPU was becoming a "busmen's union." But by a sizeable majority the Council decided to call off the mass meetings.

"Seems we've upset the cab section," Mickey said as he left the building with Eric.

"They'll get over it soon enough. They're about to enter a dispute with the railway companies, who want to change cabs a penny a time for ranking up on their property, so that'll take their minds off

464

this vote."

"Can Hodge be trusted?"

"Probably not, but the main question is whether the Home Secretary wants a scrap with us."

The following Tuesday, Minister of Labour John Hodge was forced to admit that he may have taken liberties in interpreting a comment by the Home Secretary. But Sir George Cave took no action, and the issue of the licensing of women drivers in London, whether for cabs, buses or trams, died for want of oxygen, even though the blue-button union had permitted the introduction of women tram drivers in Cardiff, Blackburn and other towns—for which its Executive would be criticised at the AAT annual conference in May. The cab section withdrew its members from London's railway stations until December, when the railway companies dropped their demand for payment.

*

On that Saturday evening, Mickey returned home with a light heart, confident that Dorothy would be pleased with the EC decision. But when she came in two hours after him, shivering and wet, he could see from her face that nothing would please her. He removed her raincoat and held her to him for a few moments, then told her to undress while he ran a bath for her; there was a plate of warm food in the kitchen, he said.

Food was becoming a problem. The bread was now grey, costing eleven pence for a four-pound loaf, double the pre-war price, as were most other foodstuffs. This month, potatoes were almost impossible to find, and the first food queues had appeared. In order to supplement the produce of the farms and imports, the London County Council had begun to provide small plots of land for use as allotments. Unless they were to go hungry, thought Mickey, either he or Dorothy would have to take time off work to queue. Coal was also scarce, although Mickey had noted with some satisfaction that the Board of Trade's Coal Controller had advised wholesalers that if they found their depots besieged by threatening crowds, they should halt deliveries to the well-off, and he wondered to what extent the recent revolution in Russia had influenced this decision. Albert Stanley was, in fact, proving as decisive as his predecessor at the Board of Trade, and within days of his appointment the government had taken control of the Irish railways, granting the workers a was bonus of seven shillings. Not that Mickey was fooled by this, knowing that while John Hodge was intent on preventing strikes, Stanley had probably set himself the larger—although not, in British conditions, necessarily more difficult—task of preventing a revolution.

They both had rest-days on the Sunday and so stayed in bed until late, although at seven Mickey had dashed to the window and, noting the frosted pane as he drew back the curtain, returned to Dorothy's side to lay his head against her warm back and slide his left arm about her waist.

When he awoke again at eight-thirty, they were still in the same positions; for some time now, ever since the job had begun to beat her down, Dorothy had slept with her back to him. It was not often, however, that their rest-days coincided, and for Mickey, as he pulled her closer to him, this was a luxury. He placed a hand on her breast and gently squeezed, moving his groin against her buttocks.

"Mmm, just a few more minutes, Mickey."

Mickey. Not Michael, or darling or sweetheart.

"Alright, sweetheart, but not too long."

"Why? Do you have an appointment?"

"Yes, sweetheart, with you."

After five or six minutes, his hand resumed its gentle pressure on her breast. He slipped his right arm underneath her side and cupped the right breast as well, moving his thickening penis against her back.

"I've missed you, my love."

"So it seems, but it's nice just to lie here and doze."

"You haven't missed me too?"

"Of course I have, darling."

He wondered, not particularly seriously, if she had met someone else.

"Do the men at the Bush every bother you, sweetheart?

"Oh, God, why won't you let me sleep? Bother me? In what way?"

"Well…do they ever try to chat you up? Are they attracted to you?"

She sighed and, raising her voice, asked, "Have you really looked at me lately? *Have* you?" Now she was up on her elbow and, turning to him, jabbed a finger at her face. "*Look* at me." Her teeth were bared, her eyes blazing. "What man could possibly be attracted to *this*?"

Mickey decided that he would not be intimidated by any of this. "This one could be and is," he replied, replacing his right hand on her breast.

She drew her hair back from her face. "Are you sure? Look closer! Look, damn you, and wipe that silly grin off your face!"

He looked. The lines had deepened, the weather had coarsened the skin somewhat, and the grey hairs, although still a small minority, had grown more numerous. And yet he found her beautiful still. At least, he usually did so, but he found this display of vanity— the first one he could recall— very unattractive, and he knew he must hold his temper and continue his soft words if he were not to allow her to push him into a harsh judgement of what might be no more than a passing mood, an uncharacteristic display of self-pity.

"Look at me: thirty-four years old and already a hag!" she urged him on.

With both hands now, he fondled her breasts, loose beneath her nightdress, willing the silly grin into a warm smile. He tried to recall the words of Shakespeare he had quoted when, two years earlier, she had bewailed her appearance at thirty-two. "Love," he said, "is not love that changes…"

"You see!" she charged. "You can't even remember the words!" But she had softened, and her breasts were being pushed into his hands.

"That's the problem," he said, "when you search Shakespeare for words to please your lover rather than learning the thing for its own sake. But try this: Love is not love that alters when it alteration finds."

"Better."

His thumbs found her nipples and rubbed them until they stood erect.

"Ohhh, *much* better, Michael." She released her hair and her harsh expression dissolved into an almost forgotten softness. Her hand went to his pyjama trousers. "Give me this, Michael."

"This what?"

"This cock."

"Ah, there she is: my Dorothea. Welcome home, my love."

*

Afterwards, she lay across him, breathing gently. He reached for the blankets and drew them over her back.

"Shouldn't we think about getting up, Michael?"

He stroked her head. "Not while you call me Michael."

She raised herself and crossed her hands on his chest, her face close to his. "I suppose we *could* stay here all day."

"We could—with a meal-break now and then."

She placed a finger on his lower lip. "Are you hungry, my darling?"

"Yes—for you."

She smiled. "Eat me, then, whichever part you like."

"I will, my Dorothea, when I've recuperated." He hesitated until, having assured himself that there were no danger signals, he asked, "Can we talk for a bit?"

"Of course we can, although I assume that you're going to attempt to persuade me to find another job."

He sighed. "No, not persuade, although you should think about it. The job is not good for you, sweetheart."

"You see, you *do* think it's turning me into a hag!"

"No I don't, my love, but I *can* see that it's making you unhappy. You surely can't deny that. Eh? Come on, it's just you and me here, Michael and Dorothea."

She nodded without breaking eye contact. "Of course it's making me unhappy. But it's not really the job itself. I can *do* the job."

"Agreed."

"But in this weather it's so absolutely, unremittingly *awful*."

"As I recall it, sweetheart, it wasn't really the job itself that attracted you, but the thought of being active in the movement again—or, at least, the union—but you..."

"Yes, I know, my love. The hours and the weather have so disabled me that I haven't been up to it. But that will change. The weather will change and I will be in the swing of things again. Really, trust me."

"But later this year there will be another winter..."

"Yes there will, but hopefully it will be nothing like this one. So let's just see how I fare over the summer—assuming we'll have one."

He nodded. "Alright, we'll see how you go. But it'll be your decision. It always has been."

Dorothy leaned forward and kissed him on the chin. She pushed herself up and knelt, gripping her naked breasts in her hands. "And in the meantime, there's every reason to be happy."

"Because you want me to bite your nipples?"

"No. Yes. But I was referring to Russia."

"Glad you reminded me. Theo Rothstein is giving a talk at Gerrard Street on Tuesday night. All welcome. Will you come?"

She grimaced. "I'm on late."

"Ask for a duty exchange."

The grimace became a smile. "I will. And I promise to be nice to Theo. Now bite them, Michael."

41

"In the Russian Empire, and in Russia itself," commenced Theo Rothstein as he addressed the crowded hall at 39, Gerrard Street on 20 March, "the working class is still relatively small. However, there are some very large industrial workplaces in the major centres, and therefore the working class was able to play a major role in the revolution that has just taken place. Indeed, it is not going too far to say that without the working class, the revolution would not have happened."

He looked about the hall, his short beard jutting upwards. "I see that tonight we have some women comrades in the meeting, and so before I go any further I must, if only for my own protection,"—having sought out Dorothy, he smiled broadly—"mention at the outset that the participation of the women of Petrograd was also crucial.

"The women joined the uprising twelve days ago, on 8 March...Wait, wait, wait. I also must point out that a different calendar is used in Russia. Perhaps it is a sign of our backwardness, but we are twelve days behind you. So, your 8 March was our 23 February."

This was the occasion of some comment in the audience, most of its members having had no idea that one sixth of the world's surface was twelve days out of date.

"Yes, yes, all very fascinating, comrades. Now you know why you have never received a New Year's greeting from me! But forget this, please, because throughout my speech I will use the western calendar." He gave his waistcoat a tug. "So, the women joined the uprising on 8 March, and it is possible that future historians will use this date as the beginning of the revolution. But in fact there was a very big event six days earlier, on 2 March. This was when the workers of the Putilov factory in Petrograd—a machine-building plant—protested against the rejection of their demand for higher wages in order to cope with the rapidly increased food prices. As a result, the company locked out 20,000 workers. Yes, 20,000! Petrograd was outraged, and by 7 March 100,000 were on strike. The Tsar thought it best to leave town..."

"Where did he go?" asked Barney Macauley, who probably knew the answer and what a joke Theo would make of it.

"He went to the front." Rothstein shrugged. "Maybe he was less afraid of the Central Powers than he was of the workers of Petrograd."

Allowing the laughter to die, Rothstein raised a finger. "And then, comrades, on the next day, 8 March…" He dropped his finger. "What is the significance of 8 March? Come on, who can tell me? You think you can invite me along here and have me do all the work? No, you must do some work also. And you get extra points if a man can give me the answer."

"It's International Women's Day," called Dick Mortlake.

"Excellent!" Rothstein was beaming. "But that's the easy part. Can anyone tell me the origin of International Women's Day? Ah, that's a tricky one! Very well, I will tell you, and you will be surprised. It started in America! In 1909, the Socialist Party of America organised a Women's Day in New York. In New *York*, the financial centre of the USA! Then an international socialist conference decided that this should be an annual event—everywhere." He spread his hands. "So you see, comrades, this movement of ours is truly international. Now, where was I?" He looked at the table behind him in mock confusion. It was Mickey who obliged him: "Petrograd!"

Rothstein joined in the laughter, wagging his finger at Mickey. "Oh, I remember you, young Rice, the sharp one. I see you're on the top table now." He pointed at his feet. "Maybe you should be here, telling the jokes.

"Yes, in Petrograd!" His finger came up again, wagging now. "In Petrograd on 8 March, it being International Women's Day, thousands of women were on the streets, and they were using this occasion to protest against the way in which the government was rationing the food supplies. And what else did they do?" He threw out his arms. "Well, of course, they joined with the strikers and what began as a strike was now becoming a revolution! All over the city there were bread riots, and the women marched to factory after factory, calling out more strikers. By 9 March, there were 200,000 on the streets, and their demands became clearer: no more food shortages, away with the Tsar, and an end to the war.

"The following day, the Tsar cabled the garrison commander to use force against the rioters, dispersing them with rifle fire. On 11 March, troops began to mutiny and join the strikers, and by now virtually all the factories in Petrograd were closed. Not only that, but police stations, the premises of the secret police, and the district court were seized and burned. Prisoners were released. The arsenal was seized.

"Meanwhile, the Tsar's political power crumbled. The Duma,

which was his parliament, was ordered suspended, but it continued to meet, if unofficially, and out of this came a provisional committee supported by major capitalists and bankers who wanted to see order restored, regardless of the fate of the Tsar. At the same time, the workers and soldiers formed their own committee, or soviet, to which they elected representatives. The leadership of the Petrograd Soviet appears to be in Menshevik, that is to say moderate, hands, although this may change. The Tsar finally abdicated five days ago, on 15 March, and a provisional government led by Prince Georgi Lvov assumed office. Don't be misled by his title, comrades, because there are many princes in Russia. This does not mean that he is related to the Romanovs of the Tsar. No, this one is descended from the Viking princes of Yaroslavl.

"Does this mean that Tsarism is finished, once and for all?" He raised a warning finger. "Not necessarily, comrades, not necessarily. Nicholas II abdicated in favour of his brother, the Grand Duke Michael, who has said that before he accepts he will await the decision of the Constituent Assembly which will be convened by the provisional government to agree a new constitution." He looked up sharply. "Now, I don't want to burden you with too much detail, because to the unpractised eye the situation in Russia is very confusing. So any questions so far?"

"Yes, comrade." Ron Vickers, the Shepherd's Bush rep, stood up. "Just now, you mentioned the three main demands of the people on the streets, but it seems that they've won only one of these, and that only partly. True, the Tsar has gone, but you may soon have a new one. And the other two—ending the food shortages and withdrawing from the war—have still not been won. Does that mean that we have nothing to celebrate?"

Rothstein chuckled. "Good question, comrade, good question. But yes, there is much to celebrate. Given its composition, I do not have *too* much faith in the provisional government, but I am confident that there will be some reforms. And look at what is happening *outside* the Duma. There is an outpouring of ideas, opinions, speeches, newspapers and pamphlets. This is democracy. Look at the Petrograd Soviet, where the workers and soldiers themselves have come together to elect their representatives in order to govern the city. That also is democracy, and democracy of a completely new kind. The Tsarist regime of oppression and terror has been swept away, and I don't think it can ever come back, regardless of what the Constituent Assembly may come up with.

"But yes, you're right, we still have to end the food shortages and withdraw Russia from this inter-imperialist war. And these two things go hand in hand, of course: the food shortages will continue *unless* Russia withdraws from the war."

"But doesn't Russia risk losing the democracy it's just won if it withdraws from the war? A ceasefire by Russia won't guarantee that the Central Powers will walk away from their eastern front." This came from a thoughtful fellow from one of the East End garages, an infrequent attender of the meetings of the Vigilance Committee, but a staunch trade unionist.

Rothstein spent a moment in thought, having once again enlisted the support of his index finger. Then his head snapped up. "Another good question. I think you are wrong, comrade, but it is a good question. And, funnily enough, a Russian friend of mine, until now an internationalist as opposed to a 'patriotic'"—both index fingers this time, describing the quotation marks—"socialist, recently made exactly the same point to me. 'The Russian Revolution,' he said, 'though effected mainly by the efforts of the socialist proletariat, is not a socialist revolution. It is a middle-class revolution which will establish in the country the rule of democracy. Of course, middle-class democracy is not everything, but it is a sufficiently precious acquisition to be defended against Germany. I am, therefore, for national defence.' Those were his words."

The corners of his mouth drawn down, Rothstein looked around the audience, nodding. "That sounds sensible, does it not?" He leaned forward and, lowering his voice, as if he were imparting a secret, breathed, "But it is *wrong*, comrades, it is *wrong*. It is the same argument that the French socialists have advanced since 1914, claiming that it is both their right and their duty to defend the work of the great French Revolution and the existence of the Republic against the absolutist monarchy of Prusso-Germany. The Russian internationalists, therefore, who now argue in favour of national defence by Russian socialists, are only repeating the words of the French patriotic socialists, which they themselves opposed in the past. Either the French patriotic socialists have been right all along, and in that case we internationalists were wrong; or the French patriotic socialists have been wrong, and then the Russian internationalists, now turned patriotic, are also wrong. There is, and can be, no third view."

His hands, held with fingers splayed towards the audience, sought forgiveness, although the eyes behind the glasses twinkled. "I regret, comrades, that I must now embark on a short history lesson.

"The French socialists have all through their career lived much too exclusively in the traditions of the first French Revolution. That

472

was always their misfortune, but it became a positive disaster during this war. They still picture to themselves the condition of things which prevailed in 1793, when continental absolutism mobilised its forces with a view to crushing the French Revolution and effecting a restoration of the old regime.

"Deeply influenced by that history, the French socialists, in my view, fail to understand the character of the present war, which originated, and is being fought out, in a totally different place. It is an *imperialist* war, which has for its source the rivalry of the various capitalist powers in the financial and colonial markets of the world, and has to settle how the world is to be divided among these rivals.

"What has the political form of the state to do with it? Russia started it when she was still an autocracy. France supported though she is a republic, Rumania was drawn into it, though she was an abominable oligarchy, and America now joins in under a Democratic administration. And, on the other side, we see semi-absolutist Germany fighting shoulder to shoulder with democratic Bulgaria and a nondescript, bureaucratic, non-national monarchy—Austria-Hungary. The political forms of these states are as varied as the colours of the rainbow, and the only thing they have in common is a capitalist class in power or emerging to power. *It is between these capitalist classes* that the fight is proceeding, and not between the political forms of the state.

"But we should also ask if the patriotic socialists have thought out the meaning of the word 'defence' in its military application. Defence, in this application, does not mean the same as 'defence' in a political sense. It means not only repelling the attacks of the enemy, but also their anticipation, their frustration in advance by means of a preventive offensive, the pursuit of the enemy beyond his own lines, the invasion, if needs be, of his own territory, and ultimately the breaking of his will.

"But when it comes to this game of attack and counter-attack, of offensive and counter-offensive,"—Rothstein's arms, held parallel, swayed now one way, now the other—"does not the word 'defence' also become applicable to the position of the enemy? Or has the enemy, if he has not a republic, nothing to 'defend?' The patriotic socialists of Germany also declare that they have something important to defend against all comers: their social legislation, their trade union and socialist movement, their splendid municipal organisation, their schools, their industry, in all of which Germany is far in advance of all other countries, and all of which Germany would lose in case of defeat, dismemberment and liability to a large indemnity."

473

Rothstein's chin sank to his chest, and he spent a moment contemplating the floor in front of him. He looked up and smiled. "Dear friends and comrades," he said, "I fear that I have gone too fast for some of you, and I may have left you with an imperfect understanding of the situation. If so, please forgive me. My main point is this: it is perfectly futile for workers to talk of 'national defence' in an era of capitalist imperialist rivalries, when one's country, whether it be a republic or an autocracy, is threatened and threatens other countries in turn, or even at the same time, just on account of those rivalries. A Russian or French or American republic is still a republic of the bourgeois classes, and its conflicts with other states are conflicts of the ruling capitalist interests." Rothstein's audience applauded him warmly, and if there were some who had, as he feared, been left behind by his remarks, even they seemed to appreciate that the argument had been profound.

The speaker turned to the table behind him. "I wonder, comrades, would one of you pass me a glass of water?"

"You're not finished, Theo?" Sanders asked.

Rothstein shrugged. "Not necessarily. If there are more questions, I will do my best to reply."

"That last reply was longer than your opening remarks, Theo," Sanders joked.

"Yes, yes, I know. But I'm grateful for having had the opportunity of giving it. It's helped me to clarify my own thinking, and I'm pretty sure I now have an article for the next issue of *The Call*."

Replacing the glass on the table, he turned once more to his audience. "After that long reply, comrades, I suspect many of you will be a little cautious about asking this longwinded Russian, actually Lithuanian, journalist more questions, but if you have any…"

"Yes, comrade," came a voice from behind him.

Rothstein turned. "Ah, Comrade Rice!"

"I think many in this country, and even in our own movement, are still confused about Russia. Yes, there has been a revolution, but what kind of revolution? This evening, however, you have made it very clear: although socialists were the driving force of the revolution, the revolution is not socialist, and the most we can expect, unless it develops further, is a capitalist democracy. How do the Russian comrades hope to move towards socialism? Is that a possibility?"

"Is a turn towards socialism possible?" He threw this out at the audience and then turned back to Mickey. "You couldn't find an easier question?"

His audience laughed. They couldn't help liking this Russian, actually Lithuanian, bloke, but what only a few among them realised was that Theo Rothstein used humour to relax his audience, usually as a prelude to presenting them with something they were forced to think hard about.

"Of course socialism is possible, but whether it will be achieved depends upon a number of factors. And listen, Mickey Rice has said that many people in this country find the situation in Russia confusing. Hah!" He threw out his arms and leaned forward, mouth agape, eyebrows raised. "You think it is any different for the comrades in Russia? If anything, it's probably *more* confusing for them, because you at least have the advantage of distance. If you view a situation from a distance you are able, if you are sufficiently observant, to view the *whole* of that situation. But imagine now if you're a politically active worker in Petrograd. What must it be like for him?" He threw a grin at Dorothy. "Or her? On the one hand, he—she—*they!*—must keep an eye on the provisional government, working out which personalities predominate and which class forces they represent. On the other hand, they must constantly press the Petrograd Soviet...The problem with the Petrograd Soviet, as I mentioned earlier, is that it is largely led by Mensheviks and Socialist Revolutionaries, while we Bolsheviks are in the minority."

He paused and looked about the audience. "Ah, I see too many frowns, so I must explain. The second congress of the Russian Social Democratic Labour Party opened in Brussels in July 1903, but the Belgian police were too active, so the delegates came to London." Rothstein's face came alight. "Ah, I see that surprises many of you! Yes comrades, this very important congress was held right here, in your own city!"

"Well I'll be buggered," commented Lenny Hawkins, amid chuckles.

"Anyway, there was a big disagreement at this congress. To cut a very long story short, it boiled down to what type of party the RSDLP should be. One group, led by Lenin, took the view that it should be tightly disciplined, a party of professional revolutionaries. This group emerged victorious, and so became known as the Bolshevik faction—meaning the majority faction, comrades. The second group, led by Martov, which had unsuccessfully argued for a looser form of organisation, took the name Menshevik, meaning minority.

"So, as I was saying, the Petrograd Soviet is led by Mensheviks and Socialist Revolutionaries, the SRs. About the SRs, I will offer just one piece of advice: do not be fooled into thinking that a Socialist Revolutionary is a revolutionary socialist! I might also add that many of their leaders believe in—and practice—terrorist methods. Their organisation, although very large, is even looser than that of the Mensheviks, and I believe that this will tell against them in the months ahead.

"So, as I was saying, another task for our comrades in Russia is to push the Petrograd Soviet in a more progressive direction, ensuring, for example, that it does not waver over the demands for food and peace. And one of the ways we do that, of course, is to ensure that the strength of the Bolsheviks in the Soviet grows and, at the same time, that we win over those of the Mensheviks and the SRs who are willing to fall in behind our programme.

"But this is just Petrograd, comrades. Beyond Petrograd lies this vast land of Russia and its Empire, and in much of this there is, since the departure of the Tsar, a political vacuum which we must seek to fill. How? Wherever we can, by the formation of soviets on the Petrograd model! Much of this land is populated, of course, by the peasantry and here we have a powerful potential ally. But why would the peasantry join us? Because the land will be theirs! So, in addition to our current demands of food and peace will be added land." He held up a finger. "Wait, comrades, wait. Food, Peace and Land! No!" He gave it another try, emphasising each noun with a punch of his fist. "Bread, Peace and Land!"

"Can you get bread before you have peace?" asked a member of the audience.

"Excellent point, comrade! So it's...Peace! Bread! Land!" Satisfied, he nodded, then looked up at his audience. "It has a certain ring to it. You agree?" They agreed. The index finger wagged. "That slogan may be useful in the near future."

"But why, comrade," asked Dick Mortlake, "aren't the Bolsheviks stronger in the Petrograd Soviet?"

"One reason," said Rothstein, "is that some of the Bolsheviks are wrongheadedly supporting the provisional government. Another reason is that so many of our leaders have been forced into exile. Once they are back home—and efforts are underway to ensure that this happens soon—the first problem will be rectified." He grinned. "And this brings us back to what I was saying earlier: Russia is in chaos and confusion, and what is desperately required is the presence of a leadership with the ability to view the whole situation, to analyse it carefully, put all the pieces together, and come up with the correct strategy to carry us forward. Given that, socialism will indeed be possible."

"And do you have anyone particular in mind?" asked Dick.

Theo Rothstein shrugged. "Lenin, of course."

*

Unwinding after an early April EC meeting with a pot of tea, Sanders, Archie Henderson, the Rice brothers and Barney Macauley sat around the table in the meeting hall in 39, Gerrard Street. Sanders was frowning at a single sheet of paper he held before him.

"What's eating you, George?" asked Macauley.

"This." Sanders held up the sheet of paper. "It seems Theo struck a chord with some members when he spoke here a couple of weeks ago. This is from someone calling himself 'Hendonian,' obviously intended for the *Record*. I've a pretty good idea who the author is, and if I'm right he was at the Rothstein meeting." He bit his bottom lip. "Not sure whether to use it or not."

Archie Henderson cleared his throat. "Let's hear it, then."

"But make sure you spell our names right when you announce the formation of an editorial committee," Macauley joked.

"Alright, here goes," Sanders complied.

> "We are being enslaved by bureaucracy; we are daily being crushed by the heel of a vile tyranny that has wiped out nations and peoples, and has stifled the word liberty in their mouths...Our brothers in Ireland have for years been awake to the ever-growing tentacles of this vile octopus, whose birthplace is London, and they have kept his tentacles well cut so that he may not suck their blood. Well done the Irish! Our Russian brothers have found their strength, and what strength it is! How glorious their victory! The tyrant rulers pulled from their pedestals, and the people's own elect established thereon in a few days.
>
> "I put it to you, what Ireland and Russia can do, are we not also capable of doing?
>
> "...There is one answer, Revolution, and then lasting peace...
>
> "As a final word, brothers, I would say that I am a man who has seen active service in France, and therefore no milk and water pacifist. I appeal to those of my brothers who possess time, money and influence to organise themselves for the coming war, which must be soon and short.
>
> "Like Russia, like Britain. Stand firm, we cannot fail!"

"Well, if he was at the meeting with Theo," commented Eric Rice, "he can't have been paying attention, because I don't remember hearing that 'the people's elect' had replaced the Romanovs."

"And to listen to him," contributed Macauley, "you'd think the Easter Rising had been a success."

"Ah, come on," said Mickey, "don't be too hard on the man. He's probably never given a thought to revolution before. Maybe his mind could do with a bit of fine tuning, but his heart's in the right place."

"Maybe that's right, Mickey, and I'll probably find space for it in a future issue," said Sanders. He let out a cloud of cigarette smoke. "But there's some awful nonsense been spoken in recent days."

"What do you have in mind, George?" asked Macauley.

"Well, the Russia Free meeting at the Albert Hall last Saturday night, for one thing. Organised by Lansbury's Herald League."

"Packed out, according to the papers," said Archie. "Twelve thousand in the hall and another five turned away. Is that right, George?"

"If twelve thousand is what the Albert Hall holds, then yes. There were a lot turned away, but whether it was five thousand is anybody's guess. No, all that enthusiasm is obviously a positive thing, and I'd be the last person to denigrate it. But you have to question what's in the minds of some of these people."

"Which people, George?" asked Eric.

"The organisers of the meeting, for one thing. Did you see the resolution they put forward?" His hand dipped into the inside pocket of his jacket, drawing out the programme for the meeting. He threw it on the table. "Here, pass it round."

Each in turn read the resolution's single paragraph:

> This Meeting sends joyful congratulations to the Democrats of Russia, and calls upon the Governments of Great Britain and of every country, neutral and belligerent alike, to follow the Russian example by establishing Industrial Freedom, Freedom of Speech and the Press, the Abolition of Social, Religious and National inequalities, an immediate Amnesty for Political and Religious offences, and Universal Suffrage.

Macauley shook his head. "What an awful load of bollocks!"
The others nodded, tutting.

"You see what I mean? In Russia, you had people shot down in the street, but *here*? Oh, all we have to do is call upon the government to follow the Russian example! For Christ's sake!"

"Mind you, if you look at the speakers, it's maybe no surprise," said Macauley. "Lansbury in the chair, then Henry Woodd Nevinson, a middle-class liberal, Colonel Josiah Wedgwood, a pro-war, pro-conscription Liberal MP, the Irish MP Arthur Lynch, another pro-war man. Who's this Israel Zangwill?"

"Jewish writer," replied Sanders. "Wrote a number of novels set in the ghetto. Anti-war. He's a Zionist, but opposes a Jewish settlement in Palestine."

"Why's that?" asked Macauley.

"Because," said Archie Henderson, "he says that instead of being empty, as the leading Zionists claim, there are 600,000 Arabs there."

"So what was he doing at the Russia Free meeting?" asked Eric. "What's the connection?"

"His parents both came here from the Russian Empire," said Sanders.

"Ah."

"Then there's Maude Royden," Macauley continued.

"Suffragist, anti-war, so she's basically okay."

"In other words, she should have known better than to support that stupid resolution," Macauley concluded, "and that goes for the rest of the speakers: our own Bob Williams, secretary of the Transport Workers' Federation, Albert Bellamy, president of the NUR, Bob Smillie of the miners, and William Crawford Anderson, the anti-war Labour MP."

"It's fair to say, though," said Sanders, "that some of the speeches were a lot more sensible than the resolution."

Mickey cleared his throat. "So what do you think the resolution should have said, George?" He had been sitting silently, listening as the Albert Hall resolution was criticised, and scrutinising each of his comrades in turn, casting his mind back to the meeting in this very hall two weeks earlier, waiting for someone to do what Theo Rothstein had appeared to do so effortlessly, to cut to the heart of the matter, put forward a penetrating analysis and, on its basis, come up with something resembling a policy. Hence his question to Sanders, whom he now watched carefully.

But Sanders failed to rise to the occasion, seeming to dismiss the question with a wave of the hand before venturing, "Of course it was right to have welcomed the revolution in Russia—although it should have avoided giving the impression that the matter was now settled. And of course the one thing it *didn't* call for was peace; that should have been the main thrust of the thing."

This wasn't enough for Mickey. "But if there were pro-war people on the platform, how would that have been possible? Maybe the resolution was a result of compromise, because, after all, its demands could *only* be realised with the end of the war. Perhaps the pro-war people weren't prepared to go along with a clear-cut *call* for peace, but were willing to accept an implication of it."

"But what good is that to us?" Sanders demanded, somewhat irritated that he was in danger of being upstaged.

"None at all," Mickey replied equably, "but we have to realise that this was not a meeting of Marxists. Then it makes sense that the resolution didn't go beyond celebrating the bourgeois freedoms that will now be introduced in Russia: it's probably all those people want, with the exception of Bob Williams, I suppose."

"Never mind the people on the platform," said Sanders, "the fact is that many of the people in the audience could have been won for a firmer policy."

"Yes, they probably could have been, had there been some preparation for the meeting. But we don't have a Bolshevik party. The BSP has got rid of the pro-war faction, but it's still not a tightly-disciplined party. That sort of party would have sat down its activists two days before the meeting and planned: how to intervene from the floor, the contents of the leaflets to be handed out at the door, and so on."

"Jesus," said Eric, "what's happened to you, Mickey?"

Mickey grinned. "That Hendonian bloke wasn't the only one fired up by Theo Rothstein the other week, you know."

"You know our problem?" asked Sanders, determined to make up some ground. "And I'm talking of our union now, not the party." He looked around the small group and sighed. "Our problem is that our EC decides to run candidates under the auspices of the so-called Labour Party. These men we have showered money on in the past have aped the master class's habits, have got bestial and luxurious. They have fallen so low that what little energy they possess they use in kidding the flower of the manhood of the country to go and be slaughtered."

As he reached for his Gold Flake packet, Sanders glanced quickly at Mickey, as if hoping that he was now satisfied, little realising that he had revealed more of himself than he had intended. For this pithy little speech, while superficially eloquent, struck Mickey as being completely irrelevant to the current discussion, and he suspected that it was something that Sanders had written for, but not yet published in, the *Record*. He suspected Archie of a similar practice, for ever since he had written it in the journal last October, he would take every opportunity to tell an audience that, "We hope, some day, when strong enough, to be able to manage our own trade without the assistance of the profiteer." True, the Labour Party *was* a problem, but so were those Marxists who tended to think that capitalism would collapse due to its own internal contradictions, and the syndicalists like Archie and George, who in their advocacy of workers' control seemed to lose sight of the state. He wondered how much of this he should put on the table now, but looking at Sanders he saw that he looked tired—fatigued was a better word. Well, maybe that was all it was, and he had been judging him too harshly.

"Yes," he agreed with a smile, "you're right there, George."

42

Superintendent Patrick Quinn stood at his office window, gazing dejectedly down at the Embankment. Flurries of snow in April! Who would have thought it?

"Are you ready for me, Super?"

Quinn turned as Ralph Kitchener's head came around the door. "I am indeed. Come and sit yourself down." He slid his large body behind his desk and watched as Kitchener eased himself into the chair on the opposite side of it, then shot a quick glance back to the window, as if fearing that in the short time since he had turned away from it a spy might have abseiled into hearing distance. No, nothing. He patted his blotter. "Well, now, Kitchener, do we have anything to be worried about?"

Kitchener pursed his lips. "We should be concerned, sir—but worried?" He shook his head. "No, I think not. Not yet, anyway."

Quinn pretended to mop his brow. "Well, that's a weight off me mind. And there was me, thinking that the Empire was imperilled." He bared his teeth in what might have been intended as a smile. "Tell me, Kitchener, how have you managed to quell the turbulence fomented by the pacifists and the socialists?"

Not for the first time, Kitchener wished that Quinn would stop taking the piss. Apart from anything else, it was often, as now, impossible to tell whether he intended a rebuke or simply to have a bit of fun with whoever was sitting—or, as was usually the case, standing—in front of him.

"Hardly any need for action at all at the moment, sir. After the Albert Hall meeting on the 31st, the pacifists have become more active, but it's nothing we can't handle."

"And how would you suggest that we do so?"

"I was anticipating, sir, that you would be issuing an instruction under DORA that we raid the peace organisations."

"Has the list been updated lately, Kitchener?"

"The list is up to date, sir."

"Good. I shall call a meeting for three this afternoon in order to timetable the raids and assign targets, so be sure you bring it with you. Twenty copies."

"All the subversive organisations, sir, or just the peace groups?"

Quinn frowned in thought for a moment. "Just the peace groups. For now."

"Right, sir." Kitchener drew his chair closer to the desk and eased a black notebook from the inside pocket of his jacket.

Quinn lifted his chin. "Got something for me there, Kitchener?"

"Yes, sir. I think that you may be interested in the Victoria Park peace rally at the weekend."

Quinn raised an eyebrow. "All ears, Kitchener, all ears. Good news or bad?"

"Bit of both, I think, sir. The march was organised, you will not be surprised to hear, by Sylvia Pankhurst and Charlotte Despard..."

Quinn chuckled.

"I'm sorry, sir?"

The superintendent waved a hand. "It's nothing, Kitchener, nothing."

"Well, sir..."

"It's just," Quinn interrupted once more, genuinely amused, "that whenever I hear that woman's name I think she should be a character in *A Tale of Two Cities*, sitting over her knitting as the heads fall into the basket. You know, Dickens."

"Quite, sir. The slogan of the march, displayed on the banner at the head of the procession was 'Spring and Peace Must Come Together.'"

"In which case, Kitchener," Quinn intervened, glancing again at the window, "they may have a while to wait."

"Yes, sir. Bitterly cold, still. Now, the bad news is that when the march passed Poplar Hospital, it was cheered by staff and wounded soldiers who were standing outside."

"Soldiers? That's a bad sign, Kitchener." He grimaced. "Very bad."

"Exactly, sir. However, this was followed by a rather more positive development in that inside the park the proceedings were violently attacked and broken up by more patriotic citizens."

"A spontaneous outburst of patriotism?"

Kitchener inclined his head to the left, narrowing his eyes. "Ah no, sir, definitely organised. Quite hefty chaps, under the control of a clearly identifiable leader."

"You took, I trust, no steps to apprehend this leader?"

"Of course not, sir."

Quinn nodded in satisfaction, gestured for Kitchener to continue, and then for some reason seemed to lose interest, picking up a pencil to doodle on a pad which lay on his blotter.

"On the contrary, sir, I took it upon myself—in order to blend in, as it were, and establish the appearance of kinship with the attackers—to land a few kicks myself. After the pacifists had been dispersed, I walked alongside one of the attackers and struck up a conversation with him, telling him that I had just happened to be out on a bit of a stroll when I came across the inspiring action of him and his comrades. Oh, what a fine body of men they were, I told him, and asked where I might sign up to become one of their number." He leaned forward. "You'll find this hard to believe, Super, but they're all bloody trade unionists."

Quinn gave him the merest glance and the lift of an eyebrow before returning to his pad. "Is that so?" He held up a palm. "Just give me a moment, Kitchener." He scribbled rapidly on his pad, turned it face-down and then, folding his hands before him, nodded for Kitchener to continue.

"Yes, Super. All of them seamen, apparently, led by a certain Edward Tupper. Now he seems to be an interesting character. Sometimes claims to be a captain, but no one can name a vessel he's captained. Works hand in hand with Havelock Wilson, the general secretary of the seamen's union, the same Wilson who leads the Patriotic Crusade we know a bit about." He looked up from his notebook and frowned, as Quinn appeared to be paying little attention. "I'm sorry, sir, but you don't seem to find this information of interest."

"Oh, it's interesting, alright; it's just that I have it already." He turned over his pad and slapped it before Kitchener.

Kitchener narrowed his eyes and discerned, just below the passable sketches of trees, a horse and a rifle, the scrawled words "TUPPER/SEAMEN/WILSON."

Deflated, Kitchener sank back into his chair. "But I don't understand, chief. If you already knew...? Why haven't we been...?"

"You haven't been told, Kitchener, because the powers that be have only recently seen fit to advise *me!*" Such a situation was obviously not to Superintendent Quinn's liking, and his cheeks had reddened.

"The powers that be, sir? The Home Office?"

"No, Kitchener, the bloody War Office!" He nodded vigorously. "Our instructions are to look the other way. The uniformed branch has been told the same thing, apparently."

"Well, sir. I don't think I've ever..."

"No, Kitchener, I daresay you haven't!" Quinn was about to thump his desk when, visited by a stray thought, he brought his hand to a halt in mid-air, let it hang there for just a second and then had it re-join its fellow on the blotter. Narrowing his eyes, he asked in lowered tones. "Tell me, Kitchener, how long were you chatting to this chap?"

"Oh, a good ten minutes, I would think, sir, while we walked back to the road."

"And what impression did you form, lad, of his attitude—of his *sincerity*, shall we say?"

"His sincerity, sir?"

"Yes, Kitchener, his sincerity. Did he, for example, give vent to any expression of his own patriotism, or anger at the marchers' lack of it?"

"Funnily enough, Super, he did not."

"Did he make any mention at all of the activity in which he had been engaged?"

Kitchener thought for a moment and then shrugged. "He just seemed to think that it was a job well done."

Quinn nodded. "A job well done," he repeated. "Yes, that would fit, that would fit."

Kitchener looked at him expectantly, obviously hoping that Quinn would explain this last observation, but the older man merely grinned and shook his head. If, as one of his own sources within the War Office claimed, Tupper's men were being paid for their activity, it was hardly surprising that they would look upon it as a job to be done rather than, as Havelock Wilson pretentiously termed it, a "patriotic crusade." It might be a mistake, however, to impart this information to Kitchener.

43

It was Mickey Rice's first ADM, even though he sat on the platform alongside his colleagues on the EC and the leading officers. Like the rest of the neophyte members of the Council, he had been excessively keen, arriving in the hall and stepping onto the platform while less than half the delegates were in their seats, the more seasoned EC members having remained in the café for a second cup. The two Smiths, Tich and Ben, were at the top table already, though,

Tich looking through his copy of the agenda and making a note here and there with his pencil, while Ben leafed through a typed document, scratching his right sideboard and giving this page or that a nod. Having completed his reading, he looked around the hall, as if seeking a kindred spirit and, finding none, turned in his chair and spotted Mickey behind him.

"Ah, Mickey," he said, proffering the document. "A few weekends ago I attended the second annual meeting of the National Guilds League. Just got the draft minutes. Would you like a glance at them?"

"I would, Ben, thank you," Mickey replied with less than total sincerity. He stood and leaned across the row of chairs separating them.

"Make sure I have it back though," said Ben as he passed the document. "You know about the League, I suppose?"

Mickey nodded. "They have a spot in the *Record*."

"We do, indeed."

Mickey resumed his seat and scanned the document. That "we" was soon explained: the second annual conference of the League, formed in 1915, was chaired by Fred Button of the Engineers on the Saturday and by Ben Smith on the Sunday. A few big names had been present—G.D.H. Cole, for example, one of the League's founders. Guild Socialism. Each industry should be controlled by the workers employed in it, with the state owning the means of production. This was the kind of thing Archie Henderson was always talking about. It was never quite explained, thought Mickey, how the workers as a whole would get control of the state, enabling it to come into ownership of all the major industries in the country, although it seemed to be assumed that the ballot box would play a major role here. That would explain why the Fabians thought Guild Socialism was such a great thing. He remembered that evening in 1913 after the agreement with the LGOC and Tilling's had been negotiated, when he was about to shoot off to meet Dorothy at the St. James's Theatre to see *Androcles and the Lion*. "Be careful of that Shaw: he's a Fabian," Sanders had warned. And here was the funny thing: Guild Socialism seemed to be attempting to take men like Sanders and Archie Henderson, industrial militants who had no time at all for professional politicians, and marry them up with the milk-and-water socialism of the Fabian Society. He called Ben's name, standing to hand the document back to him.

And then they all flooded in: the rest of the delegates, Archie, Eric and George, and the EC veterans like Dennis Davies and Barney Macauley. The three officers took chairs from the back row and placed them against the wall: the observers' gallery. Dick, who had been walking with the EC men, peeled off and took a seat in the middle of the hall, while Macauley and Davies strode to the platform. As chairman, Davies went to the seat between the two Smiths. Demonstratively, Tich took out his pocket watch.

"What time do you call this, Dennis? We should have started ten minutes ago."

"No point in me coming over with a good third of the delegates were still in the café," Davies responded.

"They were only there because they could see that you weren't ready to make a move!" Tich protested.

Davies, having pulled his chair back, paused in thought. "Well, I never thought of that! Yes, you might be right, Tich." He broke into a smile. "Go on, we've plenty of time. We'll have you home before midnight, no problem."

From Macauley there was a different performance. Seeing Mickey, his mouth opened in surprise. "You're in my seat, Brother Rice."

Without thinking, Mickey rose.

"Sit down, Mickey," Macauley chuckled, beaming at him. "I'm surprised, by the way, that you didn't come to the café. Your man Dick Mortlake was with us."

"Us?"

"Archie, George, Eric, Dennis, one or two others." He nudged Mickey's arm and lowered his voice. "For future reference: the café's the place to get business done before the start of any meeting or conference."

"Anything I should know about?"

Macauley laughed and called to Davies just as he was about to open the proceedings. "Hey, Dennis, young Mickey here wants to know if he should know about any of the business we did in the café."

"You mean the business about Eamonn Quinlan moving a vote of no confidence in him? Oh, don't tell him about that, for God's sake!"

Mickey laughed at the banter and felt glad to be there, confident that he would enjoy his first ADM.

He was wrong, though.

*

After Dennis Davies belatedly opened the meeting, Tich Smith gave the EC report on the year just past, treating the internal controversies as lightly as possible, while painting a picture of barely relieved gloom on the industrial and political fronts. And had things improved recently? They had not. In fact, they had worsened, with hundreds of drivers departing for the Army Service Corps, and the tightening of the petrol supply meaning that many buses never left their garages, leaving the crews that did to suffer the overloading, the abuse and the utter, utter exhaustion. On the taxi front, things were just as bad, due to a shortage of spare parts and skilled mechanics. And prices continued to rise; that, at least, could be addressed and this ADM *would* address it.

There followed some business which was not particularly controversial, as when the ADM instructed the EC "to utilise the Political Levy for the purpose of educating the members up to their class position."

"I wonder," Macauley mused as he surveyed the sea of arms voting for this proposition, "how many of them understand what it means."

"That's why," Mickey shot back, somewhat irritated by Macauley's cynicism, "they need to be educated."

Macauley raised a finger, acknowledging that Mickey had scored a point.

The ADM pledged to take action in support of six men and four women at Palmers Green garage who had been sacked by the LGOC after they had run their buses in protest at the company's refusal to pay them for the 104 minutes they had spent on the stand, the maximum period of non-paid stand-time being 15 minutes.

On wages, it was agreed that a war bonus of ten shillings per week for drivers and conductors and five shillings for Inside Staff should be demanded.

Macauley leaned towards Mickey and murmured, "That means we'll settle for five bob all round."

And then the decision which would lead to the strike.

"Last year," said Dick Mortlake in moving, "the employers refused to allow a representative of the National Transport Workers' Federation to be present at our negotiations. Why did we affiliate to the Federation? So that we could call upon its members for assistance whenever we were in difficulties, and they, in turn, could call upon us whenever we were needed. It's called solidarity, comrades. That's the glue that binds the trade union movement together. And why did the employers now tell us that the Federation could play no part in our negotiations? They pointed, comrades, to Clause 3 of the 1913 recognition agreement, which reads:"—he held a copy of the agreement before him—"The companies are not to be affected by disputes with companies with whom they have no direct concern.'

"Well, comrades, if Clause 3 is what is preventing us from involving the Transport Federation in our negotiations, the way forward is, I think, crystal clear: our union must terminate Clause 3, and that is what this motion calls upon the EC to do. I so move, Chairman."

This had been George's brainwave. Peering around the heads on the top table, Mickey could see him at the back of the hall, a smile on his face as he applauded Dick, then turning to Archie as the latter spoke, paying no attention as a delegate got to his feet and formally seconded the motion. But now, as the chairman called Dave Marston to the rostrum, George held up a restraining hand. Later, Archie; I need to listen to this.

"Chairman, this motion needs amendment," Marston began, and the hall fell silent, perhaps suspecting that the Tilling's man was about to attempt to water down the motion. "On 5 January, there was apparently a meeting at the Ministry of Labour where an undertaking was given that this union would not use its machinery to defend members who had broken the agreement with the employers. This undertaking was minuted, and the minute was signed by our organising secretary, Brother Ben Smith. If Clause 3 is to go, Chairman, then this undertaking must also be repudiated, and I therefore move that the motion be amended accordingly."

The hall was now in uproar. Ben did that? Surely not! Let him explain himself! Can we trust none of these officers? Resign! But Sanders, Mickey noted, was as calm as could be, resting his head back against the wall and following the proceedings as he stroked his chin with an index finger. So, wondered Mickey, was this the "business" conducted in the café this morning? He turned to Macauley, who put a finger to his lips and nodded in the direction of Ben Smith, just a few feet away.

Dennis Davies used his gavel. "Brothers," he shouted above the din, "an amendment has been moved. Is there no seconder?"

There was, and a hand went up; formally seconded.

"In that case, brothers, I think you will agree that it's only fair that the organising secretary be given the opportunity to respond to the allegation. Brother Smith."

Ben Smith, who had stiffened upon hearing Dave Marston's contribution, straightening his arms and placing them on the table, now stood, ashen-faced, and faced the ADM. It was difficult to discern his emotion until he spoke, but it soon became clear that he was an angry man.   "Chairman," he declared in a voice loud and clear, "it is true that I gave the undertaking that has been mentioned. Oh, come on, brothers, there's no need for you to gasp and shake your heads as if this is something unheard of. A full-time officer often has to do things that he doesn't necessarily like or, deep down, even agree with. This was one of them. When an officer of the union meets an employer, they confront each other as guardians of the agreement signed by the two parties. When the employer breaks the agreement, we pounce on him, don't we? Of course we do!" He narrowed his eyes, lowering his voice. "But what does that officer do when the employer asks him for an assurance that the union will abide by that agreement? Does he have any alternative but to give that assurance?" He shook his head. "It always depends on the circumstances, but in nine times out of ten he does not."

His voice rose again. "Now, what was the precise nature of the assurance I was asked to give? That the union would not come to the defence of a member who himself acted contrary to the agreement. Why did I agree to that?" He banged the table with his fist. "Because it was meaningless, brothers, *meaningless*, and if the employer had an ounce of sense he would *know* that it was meaningless. Didn't the employer know full well that this union is led by its lay members? Didn't he know that when an officer gives an assurance of this nature it will mean nothing if the lay members take another view and come to the defence of a man who has cut corners regarding the agreement?

"And you, brothers, have proven my point this very day! Take the ten members at Palmers Green. Didn't they break the agreement by running their buses in before going through the grievance procedure? Of course they did. But today you have agreed that you will come to their defence—regardless of any assurance Ben Smith may have given on 5 January!" He shrugged and turned to Dennis Davies. "Chairman, I rest my case."

This received some applause, although its modesty indicated that Ben Smith was still in trouble. At the back, George Sanders seemed to admire the spirited nature of Ben's defence, grinning wryly and bringing his hands together twice.

The next few speakers, perhaps not realising what the consequences might be, favoured the amendment, and so Tich Smith then got to his feet and reminded the delegates that he had himself, on several occasions, sent out circulars instructing the membership to abide by the agreement. Did they not remember that he had warned that, having received an imperfect set of schedules, the members must follow the procedure rather than going on strike prematurely? Ben Smith had merely agreed something similar, the importance of which should not be exaggerated. Some cab delegates then came to Ben's defence, he being a veteran cab-man, despite his relative youth, but it was not enough to save him. When Dennis Davies called the vote on the amendment, the majority was around two to one. Further discussion on the original motion being unnecessary, the amended version was then put to the vote and carried by an even greater majority.

Perhaps the amendment could have been worded more kindly, but the ADM had been called upon to "repudiate the organising secretary's signature," and it had now done so. Ben Smith stood and turned to Dennis Davies. "Under the circumstances," he said with great dignity, "I cannot remain as organising secretary. Therefore, Chairman, I tender my resignation." And with that, he left the top table, descended the steps at the side of the platform and strode down the central aisle. Mickey watched as George Sanders followed him to the door and out into the street.

"Was this meant to happen?" Mickey asked Barney Macauley.

"Ah, he'll be back," said Macauley without answering the question. He waved his hand dismissively. "The man's still only 38. Do you think he wants to be conscripted? He'll be back within a week, take my word for it."

After he closed the ADM, Davies huddled briefly with Tich Smith and then, turning to the rest of the EC, announced that they would meet at Gerrard Street on the evening of 10 May, by which time the employers should have responded to their demands. Sanders returned, his left hand in his trouser pocket and holding a cigarette in his right, and walked to the platform. He looked up at the top table and shrugged. "Couldn't talk him out of it," he said. He contemplated the red tip of his cigarette. "Give it a day or two and he may come round, though."

*

And so to the pub on Clerkenwell Green. Mickey was invited by Dick and, having missed the discussion in the café that morning, he thought it might be unwise to refuse. There was quite a crowd: Dennis Davies, Dave Marston, Ron Vickers, Barney Macauley, Archie and Eric, one or two tram delegates and, of course, George Sanders at the centre of it all. Service was slow as the landlord, claiming that he had been threatened with the loss of his licence, was insisting on a strict observance of the "no treating" rule.

"Ah, Mickey!" Sanders greeted him. "How did you like your first ADM?"

Mickey studied Sanders for a moment. His moustache and hair were flecked with more grey and he looked tired. His confidence, once unshakeable, seemed to have ebbed, and Mickey suspected that he either realised that he had made a wrong move—or two—or he had simply lost it.

"I was enjoying it," he replied, having decided to pull no punches this time, "until the amendment—or, rather, until Ben's resignation."

Silence fell, and Dave Marston, who had moved the amendment, bristled, protesting, "There was no intention to force Ben's resignation."

"That's right," Sanders said in support, blinking nervously. "And don't worry, we'll get him to withdraw it."

"Ben over-reacted," said Macauley. "There was no need for that. He's probably over-worked. That would explain the resignation *and* the undertaking he gave in January."

"That's possible," said Eric. "You know sometimes, when you're meeting an employer over one issue, and there are a hundred others buzzing in your mind, you don't always have either the time or the energy to think things through. That could be what happened in January."

"It seems to me that, with due respect to the mover," Mickey said in reference to Marston, but with his eyes on Sanders, "that the amendment was the over-reaction. Why was it necessary? Didn't Ben give an acceptable explanation?"

Sanders chuckled. "Oh, he gave a *fine* explanation! But his undertaking was minuted, and he signed the minute." He shrugged. "We felt that he needed to be taught a lesson. But resignation? No."

So there it was. "*We* felt he needed to be taught a lesson." And maybe that was right. Maybe Ben *did* need a rap over the knuckles, because an officer who one day gave an employer an undertaking he had no intention of keeping might give another to his members the next. Yes, Mickey could see that. But plotted in a café, and then administered before representatives of the whole union? Why not at an EC meeting? All this passed through his mind, but he said none of it, having no wish at the moment to be isolated as the moral purist within the left.

"If over-work *was* behind Ben's actions," said Dennis Davies, "maybe we should give him some help and appoint an assistant organising secretary."

Ah, now it all made sense!

"Yes, I might run for that job myself," Mickey joked, and they all laughed, dispersing the tension.

Sanders now smiled around at the gathering. "You'll remember, some of you, that when we visited this pub after an earlier ADM, we were in the company of Reuben Topping, since conscripted." He drew a sheet of paper from his jacket pocket. "Private Topping now sends greetings to his comrades—both men and women, he underlines—in the union. He's in the guard-rooms at Warminster awaiting his trial, 'charged with being a deserter from something which I refused to join.' Whatever his sentence, he says, 'I will never become a soldier for capitalism.'"

This brought cheers and applause, causing the intervention of the landlord. "Come on, lads, we'll have none of that..."

Mickey took a step back to give himself a clear view of the bar and fixed a hard stare on the landlord who, perhaps realising that he, while he might get away with implementing the "no treating" rule, would have some difficulty in enforcing patriotism on this crowd, swallowed the end of his sentence and waved a hand in dismissal.

"That's what our military friends would call a tactical withdrawal," murmured Davies.

"So will you be printing Reuben's letter in the *Record*, George?" asked Macauley.

"Be in the next issue, Barney."

"I can't help thinking," Mickey now said, "that while Ben's drama has our attention, we're taking our eye off of the more important issue."

"And what would that be, Mickey?" asked Sanders just a little patronisingly.

"Clause 3, of course. What do you think the companies will do?"

Sanders threw out his arms. "Do? Why, what *can* they do?"

*

On 4 May, Mr H.E. Blain, Operating Manager for the London General Omnibus Company, telephoned the President of the Board of Trade.

"Stanley."

"It's Blain, Sir Albert. There have been some developments in the company with which I think you should be acquainted."

"Admirable grammar, Blain. Alright, go ahead."

"We've had two letters from the union, Sir Albert, one dated yesterday and one dated this morning."

"Well, look, you know that in my current position I cannot become involved in matters that may in due course come across my desk at the Board."

"I realise that, Sir Albert, but this is rather important...I merely seek your consent to a certain course of action."

A sigh. "What is the union demanding, Blain?"

"They say that their Annual Delegate Meeting has decided that the union should withdraw from Clause 3 of the 1913 agreement, and they have repudiated an agreement made by Mr Ben Smith in January, i.e. that the union would not support any of its members who act in contravention of the agreement."

"Anything else?"

"Yes, they are seeking a war bonus of ten shillings for operating staff and five shillings for Inside Staff. And they demand the reinstatement of ten members dismissed for running their buses in after a disagreement about payment."

"You'll have to explain that last one, Blain."

Blain duly gave an account of events at Palmers Green.

"And should they have been paid?"

"Well, on the face of it, yes, but they ran their buses in."

"Who was the fool who dismissed them? No, don't answer that! It doesn't matter. Whoever he is, he may have done you a favour. What do you propose, Blain?"

"We surely cannot accept their withdrawal from Clause 3, Sir Albert. If Clause 3 is null and void, so is the whole agreement of which it is part."

"So you propose to derecognise the union?"

"In a nutshell, Sir Albert, yes. And, consequently, to deny the application for the war bonus."

"Then why don't you do it?"

"That's what I wanted to hear, Sir Albert."

"You realise that they will strike?"

"Yes, of course, but we surely cannot let them walk away from Clause 3. If we do, they'll be on strike every time the cabbies have a disagreement with the Police Commissioner or, as is the case at the moment, the railway companies."

"Oh. I quite agree. But you'll need to give them at least a small victory. I therefore suggest that you adamantly refuse to reinstate the Palmers Green people until this becomes part of an overall settlement. Do you understand?"

"I do, Sir Albert. And the war bonus?"

"Once they return to work after their inevitable strike, this can be submitted to arbitration by the Committee on Production. I'll make sure I have nothing to do with it, of course. Askwith will deal with it in the normal way."

*

The first item on the agenda of the EC meeting on 10 May was the resignation of Ben Smith.

"I have met with Ben," announced Tich Smith, "and he has said that he regrets his impulsive action in tendering his resignation, and he is willing to withdraw it. I took the opportunity to ask him what led him to give that undertaking at the Ministry of Labour in January, and he gave me much the same answer as he gave the ADM last week. I then told him that it had been suggested to me that overwork might have been a factor. He tended to dismiss this— partly from pride, I think, not wanting to admit that any workload could be too much for him. So I then asked him to give me details of his commitments: the number of statutory meetings per month, the members he services, the average number of disciplinary appeals where he represents the members, etc." He looked around the table. "I have to tell you, brothers, that *I* could not manage such a workload, and, I suspect, neither can Ben Smith."

Macauley then moved that Ben Smith's resignation not be accepted, that he be asked to resume his post with no loss of wages, and that George Sanders be appointed as assistant organising secretary.

This was duly seconded. And then Malcolm Purvis, a new EC member from East London, raised his hand.

"Surely, Chairman, this should be amended to read 'until the requisite election can be held.'"

Mickey felt relieved that it had not been left to him to raise this prickly point.

"No, that won't be necessary," said Dennis Davies. "The only full-time officers that are elected are those listed in the Rule Book." A copy lay on the table before him, which he now held up. "You will find no mention of the post of assistant organising secretary in this Rule Book, brothers. Thus, Brother Sanders will remain in his current post, at his current salary, and his new designation will merely mean that certain of the organising secretary's duties will be transferred to him."

Sanders cleared his throat. "Now let's be clear about this..."

"Is it the money, George?" asked Tich Smith.

"No, of course it's not the money!" responded Sanders, genuinely affronted until he looked up and saw the mischievous grin on Tich's face.

Well, thought Mickey, whatever else I might be feeling about

George at the moment, it has to be admitted that he's as straight as they come regarding such matters.

"If it's purely a matter of relieving Ben of some of his servicing burden," Sanders continued, "I, along with Eric and Archie, could take a bit each, and you wouldn't need to bother with changing anyone's title. But if I'm to be assistant organising secretary it can only be on the basis of me taking over some of Ben's *non*-servicing duties."

"So, for example, Chairman," said Mickey, "can we assume that this would mean that some meetings, such as the one at the Ministry of Labour in January, could well be taken by George rather than Ben?"

Davies turned to Tich. "General secretary?"

Tich nodded. "Yes, that is certainly what is in my mind, although it must be understood that Ben will still be the senior of the two." He turned to Macauley. "Barney, perhaps you could rewrite your motion to reflect this. Clear enough, George?"

Sanders nodded. "Crystal clear."

Yes, thought Mickey, and the situation is not as murky as I feared: George is simply being assigned to keep an eye on Ben, and maybe take a firmer line with some employers.

Next, somewhat surprisingly, came amalgamation, with Tich announcing that talks with the AAT were ongoing; the AAT's annual conference would take place next week, and possibly news of its views would be forthcoming.

"Are you confident that amalgamation is realistic?" asked Sanders. "After the tram strike two years ago, our members are still smarting at the behaviour of the AAT. Then again, we couldn't even get the two-thirds majority to amalgamate with the National Union of Vehicle Workers, so it would take a miracle to get the members to agree to join with a union based in Manchester, with few of our democratic credentials."

Tich smiled. "Things are changing. First of all, Bob Williams of the National Federation of Transport Workers has been playing a big role in encouraging the transport unions to amalgamate. He's been joined recently by Ernie Bevin, of the Dockers' Union, who sits with him on the National Federation. Bevin is making a name for himself, and is asked by union after union to put forward their cases for wage increases at the Committee on Production. That's the first thing. The second is that we're hopeful that there will soon be new legislation allowing amalgamations to go ahead on the basis of a simple majority." He turned his hands palms-upward. "So we'll wait and see."

Sanders nodded. "We will indeed."

Dennis Davies tapped the table. "Now to the main business."

"Arising from our ADM, brothers, we have a number of issues before us: our withdrawal from Clause 3 of the 1913 agreement and repudiation of Ben's signature on the 9 January minute, our demand for a war bonus, and the sacking of the ten members at Palmers Green. In the days following our ADM, I communicated all of this to the LGOC as the lead company on the employers' side. Two days ago, I received their response: derecognition."

Had this been news, there would have been uproar at this point, but word had got around during the past two days, and those still in the dark had had it whispered in their ears as they arrived for the meeting; Mickey had heard it from Eric on the day the response was received. He and Sanders now exchanged glances, and Mickey was unable to resist a taunt, raising his eyebrows and gesturing with his palms. Yes, what *can* they do, Brother Sanders? Well, now we know. Sanders slowly closed his eyes and looked away.

"This being the case," Tich continued, "it goes without saying that our demand for a war bonus has been refused."

Despite the fact that the situation had the makings of the greatest crisis yet faced by the red-button union, discussion was brief. All the EC members being of the same mind, it was rapidly agreed that the bus membership would be balloted for strike action on the following day, with the result announced at a mass meeting at the Euston Theatre of Varieties on the evening of Sunday, 13 May.

"Do we know whether it's available?" asked Eric.

"I've already made a provisional booking," replied Tich.

"But what about the ballot papers?"

"Had them run off this morning, but some of you lads will have to get 'em round the garages tonight."

*

"What a bloody cock-up!" Mickey oathed as he and Eric, each laden with a parcel of ballot papers, walked up Gerrard Street towards Oxford Street.

Eric, taken aback by this outburst, halted. "What the 'ell do you mean by that?"

"Why are we going on strike?"

"Because the bastards have derecognised us, of course."

"And why have they derecognised us?"

"Because we've told 'em to stick Clause 3."

"And how do you think the strike will end? Do you reckon we'll force them to accept that Clause 3 is as dead as a doornail?"

Eric Rice looked at his brother, who had been as green as grass when he came to London four years ago. Now, he had to admit, Mickey was fast leaving him behind. "So you think we should have left it alone?"

"That's what I think now, yes. If the time ever comes when we need to strike in support of another union, we'll do it, won't we, Clause 3 or no Clause 3?"

"Well, yeah, we will. But look, Mickey, we can hardly go cap in hand to the employers and say we've had second thoughts, can we?"

"No, we can't, because that would make us look weak. That's why it was a mistake to withdraw in the first place. Had it not been for that, it's possible we wouldn't be dragging the members out on strike, because the war-bonus claim would be going to arbitration and the Palmers Green issue, from what I've heard of it, could probably have been resolved within the procedure."

"So why didn't you say any of this at the time, Mickey, when the EC was agreeing the ADM agenda?"

"Because I hadn't worked it out back then. I'm still learning, for fuck's sake."

He strode ahead, leaving Eric to catch up with him.

*

Warmer weather had come towards the end of April, and now May had made the bus conductor's job almost tolerable—apart, of course, from the hours, the overloading, the constant climbing and descending of stairs and the weight of the money-bag on Dorothy's slender shoulder. But during these warmer days a smile came often to her lips, her face was less drawn, and her fingers mercifully healed. By the time of the strike ballot, she had even attended two branch meetings. At the close of the first of these, Ron Vickers had sidled up to her.

"Dorothy, could you do me a favour, love?"

"I might, Ron."

He looked about him as the room cleared and, lowering his voice, winked and said, "Would you have a word with some of the other girls and encourage 'em to attend our meetings? I know it might be 'ard for some of 'em, with families at home, but I want to stop the mutterin' and complainin' by the blokes who don't think women should be on the job. It'll be easier to do that if they see that you

497

and the others are as good trade unionists as they are. Know what I mean?"

She nodded. "I do, Ron, and, yes, I'll do what I can."

"Good girl." He smiled. "So what did you think of your first meeting?"

"Well, to be honest, Ron, I found the level of discussion to be appallingly low."

*

And now a strike was in the offing. "At *last!*" she joked in the canteen. "I can't believe that I've been here for four months and there hasn't been a *single* strike."

When Dorothy entered the output early in the morning of 11 May, she found herself facing Ron. "Ah, Dorothy! Can you run the ballot with Reggie? By rights, we have to have two on the ballot box."

"Well I could, but what about my duty?"

Ron winked. "I've squared it with the allocation official; he'll get it covered by a spare. And don't worry—the Branch will cover your wages."

And so instead of a day on route 11, Dorothy spent twelve hours, less two meal breaks, sat next to Reggie Pearson, the Branch Secretary, a man of some sixty years, conducting the ballot and reminding voters that the result would be announced on Sunday evening and that, if they were scheduled to work, they should run their buses in and be at the Euston Theatre of Varieties by seven. It was easier work than conducting, but dreadfully boring.

"Will you be at the meeting, Dorothy?" asked one driver.

"Wouldn't miss it for the world," she replied.

"In that case, I'll be there too. I'll keep an eye out for you."

On the Sunday, according to Monday's newspapers, there were by late afternoon only twenty buses on the streets of London, as members prepared for the mass meeting. Dorothy had rarely seen such a gathering: not only was the theatre packed, but there was one overflow on the road in front of the theatre and another beneath the St. Pancras arches. The atmosphere was electric, but good-humoured.

Tich Smith read out the results: for the strike, 5,152; against, 699; spoilt papers, 69. Although fully expected, this was greeted by a huge roar of approval. A motion for an immediate strike was moved by Bill Gladley and seconded by Ernie Fairbrother, names made familiar to Dorothy by Mickey. Support came from George Sanders and Ben Smith, back in harness after his recent holiday. The business did not take long to complete, although the meeting was prolonged as several members insisted on making their feelings about the company known, even though their points may have been made several times previously. Dennis Davies was tolerant, giving the members the opportunity to get it all off their collective chest. As the meeting came to an end, Dorothy stood at the side and waited until the EC members and officers came down from the stage. Mickey, when she caught sight of him, was despite the reservations he had made known to her obviously excited by the meeting.

"Look at you, Mickey!" she cried in delight. "Your eyes are alight!"

He threw an arm around her and bent to her ear. "That's because they've seen you, sweetheart."

The next day, the streets were bereft of omnibuses. As Mickey joined the picket line at Middle Row, Dorothy attended hers at Shepherds Bush, one of several women to do so. Ron Vickers was pleased. But she soon discovered that being on strike was rarely exciting, and when not chatting to the other pickets Dorothy often spent her time daydreaming. On one such occasion, Ron asked her why she was smiling, and she was at a loss to explain herself without telling a very long story. As she had left home that morning, Mickey had called after her: "Don't go throwing any rocks!" How to explain that?

The company and the authorities exerted pressure on the strikers whenever they could. The LGOC announced its refusal to entertain any notion of an arbitration hearing regarding the war-bonus claim if the London and Provincial Union of Licensed Vehicle Workers' Union would be in attendance; instead, it would leave its staff to arrange representation. On the second day of the strike, Police Commissioner Henry issued a notice, with instructions that this be posted in all London bus garages, in which he declared that to "wilfully cause or bring about a cessation of tram and omnibus services used by munitions workers would necessarily constitute a breach" of Regulation 42 of the Defence of the Realm Act. The strikers read this and laughed. Possibly irked by the ineffectiveness of this order, one munitions worker, George Lee by name, on 16 May appeared at Bow Magistrates' Court charged with breaking two windows valued at £4 15s at 39, Gerrard Street. LGOC Operating Manager H.E. Blain told the press that one of the Palmers Green men had requested an appeal hearing and that this would be granted, although there would be no question of representation by the union. Tilling's, perhaps seeking to take a leaf out of the book of Aubrey Llewellyn Coventry Fell, called upon its striking staff to return their uniforms.

There was some talk of solidarity action. There were claims that Tube staff were ready to come out, but this claim was denied by Blain, who assured the public that the rail staff had no sympathy for the strike. The EC of the Transport Workers' Federation, meanwhile, protested that the LGOC had refused "the elementary right of trade union recognition" and that "organised labour in the Metropolis and throughout the country will resist by every possible means in its power any and every effort to repudiate trade unionism."

"Big talk," Mickey remarked to Dorothy that evening, "but nothing of the sort is happening, despite the fact that the right to take solidarity action is the fundamental issue in the strike. Hah! There's not even been a suggestion that our own tram and cab members be brought out!"

"Blain says that 110 buses were running today," she said. "Will the strike hold?"

"There was virtually nothing on the main routes, sweetheart. Will it hold? Not for longer than a few more days, once the members begin to think about how the dispute started."

It was at this point that the government, in the form of Labour leader Arthur Henderson, Minister without Portfolio in the War Cabinet, intervened.

*

May had been a rainless month, but on the 17th around 20 millimetres fell and the temperature fell back to not much more than 10°C. To the superstitious, this may have seemed an inauspicious day for the red-button union to meet the LGOC at the Board of Trade, but in fact, a settlement was found. If anyone had challenged Mickey Rice to put money on the detail of that settlement, he would have made a fortune.

The union side consisted of the Smiths, George Sanders, due to his new status as assistant organising secretary, the thirteen members of the Executive Council and Bob Williams of the National Transport Workers' Federation. Williams, 36, was a former coal trimmer from South Wales. Stocky and clean-shaven, with a widow's peak, he had been secretary of the Federation since 1912. Staunchly anti-war, Williams was a keen advocate of the amalgamation of the transport unions.

Prior to meeting the company, they had a pre-meeting with

Henderson. Now 53, smart and a little chubby, with a well-tended moustache, Henderson was born in Glasgow and brought up in Newcastle. Throughout the brief discussion. Mickey watched him closely.

"I've already spoken to the company, and it seems they're willing to settle." Henderson had been the first Labour politician to hold a Cabinet position. Asquith had given him Education, which was somewhat ironic as he had left school at twelve to work in a foundry, where he soon became an active trade unionist. Now a member of Lloyd George's War Cabinet, he seemed confident enough, with hardly a trace of his background showing. "It'll need a bit of give and take on both sides, though."

"What are we expected to give?" asked Tich Smith.

"Withdraw the letters of 3 and 4 May, and an immediate return to work."

Despite his industrial background, Henderson was opposed to strikes, something he had in common with the Minister of Labour. A Methodist lay preacher. He looked around the table, his gaze unflinching, sure enough of his ground and yet far from overbearing. But Mickey saw no sign of any quality to set him apart from his fellows, raising him above them. Just another man.

"And in return?" asked Tich.

"The situation reverts to that which existed before your ADM, with recognition reinstated."

At this point, there was a rap on the door and a Board of Trade junior official presented his head. "We have a telephone call for Mr Smith."

"Alfred or Benjamin?" asked Tich.

The official looked lost. "I'm afraid, I don't..."

"Well, who is calling?"

"Mr Hirst of the Amalgamated Association..."

"Then it's for me." Tich got to his feet and turned to Henderson. "You'll have to excuse me for just a few minutes, Minister. This may be important."

"I have to say, Arthur," said Bob Williams as the door closed, "that in view of the fact that this whole dispute is really about Clause 3 of the agreement, I'm surprised that the company has agreed to my attendance at this conference."

Henderson smiled. "They wouldn't have it at first, Bob. 'We don't recognise the National Transport Workers' Federation,' they said. 'I realise that,' I said, 'but we do, and as the LPU's affiliation to the TWF is really at the heart of this dispute, it's surely sensible to have a representative present.'"

Mickey could see that Henderson welcomed the question, for it gave him the opportunity to demonstrate that he was not taking the company's side in this matter. Equally welcome was Williams' familiarity, for it allowed him to reciprocate, marking him as a friend.

"When they refused to have the TWF present at our negotiations," said Sanders, "we pointed out that this would in no way bring Clause 3 into question, because in the event of a dispute it would mean other groups coming out in support of us rather than the reverse."

"You know, that struck me as well when I read it," said Henderson. "When Tich returns, I'll suggest a way out on this."

Tich came back into the room with a smile on his face.

"You look as if you've received good news, Brother Smith," said Henderson. "Should I give you a few minutes with the lads?"

"No, no, it'll keep until we've heard your proposals, Minister. Sorry for the interruption. Now, where were we?"

"They'll reinstate recognition if you withdraw the two letters," Henderson recapped.

"But that leaves Clause 3," said Tich.

"It does, and while you were out I mentioned to the lads that I have a suggestion regarding that: what if I put it to them that Clause 3 should be the subject of a separate conference here between the union and the company, chaired by Sir George Askwith?"

"When?"

"As soon as possible."

"Alright, we'll take a look at that when we adjourn. What have they said about our claim for a war bonus?"

"Arbitration by the Committee on Production, with any award implemented from the date of the decision."

"We'll consider it in the adjournment."

"So that leaves the Palmers Green issue."

"Yes, we might have trouble on that one, because they claim that our members ignored the procedure when they ran their buses in, and they point to the January minute where an undertaking was given that we wouldn't defend such actions."

Henderson nodded. "Exactly. On the other hand, they know they have to give you something to take away, so it's really just a question of how we make it easy for them to agree to reinstatement." He patted the table in front of him and grinned. "I have an idea on how to achieve that. Are you prepared to trust me to put it to them? If it doesn't work, we can always go back to the drawing board."

"Well, I think we'd need to hear what your suggestion is first, Minister."

"Very well, it's simply this: I'll tell them that the request for the reinstatement of the ten Palmers Green members comes not from the union but from me."

Mickey caught Henderson's eye at this point, and they exchanged grins. Yes, just another man, maybe, but a clever one.

During the adjournment there was some opposition to Henderson's proposal, although this was easily dissipated "If the company agrees to it," objected Bill Gladley, "it'll be a victory for Arthur bloody Henderson, not for the union."

"But would a member of the War Cabinet be asking the company to reinstate our members if we weren't on strike?" asked Mickey. "Of course it'll be a victory for the union!"

"Out of the mouths of babes and sucklings," observed Macauley, to a certain amount of laughter.

"And how do we feel about his suggestion regarding Clause 3?" asked Dennis Davies.

We need to be clear," said Sanders, "about what he *is* suggesting. He's suggested a *conference*. The word 'arbitration' has not been used. That means that the company can just sit there and say no, no, no, and we'll be back where we started."

"Unless," said Bob Williams, "Askwith is impressed by your argument and, despite the fact that he won't be arbitrating, brings his influence to bear on the company."

"When you were out taking the telephone call, Brother Smith," said Mickey, who did not yet call the general secretary 'Tich,' "he described his suggestion as 'a way out.' Isn't that what we need? If we're honest with ourselves, haven't we got ourselves into a pickle over Clause 3? The company is saying that we have a choice: recognition *with* Clause 3, or *no* Clause 3 and *no* recognition. Well, obviously most of us would choose the first of those two, but we should never have got ourselves into the situation where we're faced with that choice."

Sanders was almost glaring across the table at Mickey, but Mickey chose not to notice this.

"It seems to me," he continued, "that we're not even arguing about the same thing as the company. When we suggested that a TWF representative join our negotiations, the company saw the name TWF and immediately thought: *sympathy strikes!* Their next thought? *Clause 3!* And because *they* linked our request to Clause 3, *we*, in turn, decided to withdraw from that clause. Brothers, if our *real* aim is to have a TWF representative at our negotiations, surely what we need to do is convince the *company* that this is the case. Let's tell them: yes, you can *have* Clause 3, but give us TWF representation, because the two are not contradictory. In fact, when

503

we get to that conference with Sir George Askew, we should perhaps suggest that Clause 3 remains, but with an amendment reading something like 'The union, however, is free to call upon the assistance of the TWF, to which it is affiliated, in negotiations with the company.' So, yes, the conference is a way out, but might *just* be a way to solve the problem for good."

Sanders' features had softened, and he was now nodding.

"If there's one thing I appreciate," said Dennis Davies from the chair, "it's clarity, and I believe that is what Brother Rice has just given us. Pity he didn't speak up earlier, though."

"Oh, that's right," Mickey conceded. "I'm as much at fault as anyone else. However, as I told someone a few days ago, I have an excuse: I'm still bloody learning."

That brought a burst of laughter, and the atmosphere immediately became more relaxed.

"Now, then," said Dennis Davies, "the war bonus."

"Can't see a problem," said Macauley. "We'd have been going to the Committee on Production anyway."

"But," Sanders interjected, "we should insist that the award is paid from the date of resumption—which is going to be tomorrow by the look of it."

Agreed.

*

"Now, Tich," said Dennis Davies, "are you going to let us in on what Stan Hirst had to say?"

"Well," replied Tich with a smile, "it's welcome, but nothing to get excited about. It might have been, had it come a few days ago, but now? No. As you know, the AAT has some 200 or so members involved in this dispute, employed by British Automobile Traction, which is partly owned by Tilling's. When I was in contact with Stan earlier in the week, urging him to declare the strike official, he said that, with their annual conference coming up, his executive were wary about going out on a limb. Let's wait for the conference, he said.

"Well, that conference has today declared the strike official, and has also said that the AAT will take part in joint action to achieve a settlement."

Those who remembered the 1915 tram strike laughed.

"Late to the party as usual!" declared Ben Smith.

"Well, it *does* mean that their members will receive strike pay, so it's not completely without value," said Tich. "They have also offered to place their London District Secretary at our disposal, should the need arise."

"Just as well we're settling now, then," said Barney Macauley to a knowing rumble.

"And, finally, the conference agreed that amalgamation talks should continue," Tich concluded.

"Ah," said Dennis Davies, "now it makes a bit of sense."

Ben Smith, sitting sideways with his back to Tich, looked at Sanders and mouthed "Be warned."

*

Having called Arthur Henderson back in, Tich Smith advised him that the formula was acceptable, subject to the war bonus being paid from the date of resumption, adding that he and Bob Williams wished to say something regarding Clause 3. Henderson suggested that, rather than wasting time, he would convene the plenary session, where the union could make its points across the table. The company had agreed to his suggestion of a conference to review Clause 3.

Mr H.E. Blain, a short man with a tidy dark beard, was accompanied by George Shave, formerly manager of the Walthamstow works where the "B" type was constructed, who had transferred to the operating side of the company three years earlier. A burly man with a thin moustache, Shave also commanded the LGOC's special constabulary division; he looked the part, thought Mickey.

"My goodness!" Blain exclaimed in mock alarm as, surveying the numbers on the union side, he took his seat. "It seems that we are surrounded, Mr Shave!"

Sir George Askwith, who sat next to Henderson at the head of the table, smiled. "You need not concern yourself with numbers, Mr Blain," he said. "In my experience, a trade union side will speak with one voice, so in fact you are evenly matched." He cleared his throat. "Now, I understand, Mr Smith, that with one or two qualifications you are prepared to accept the formula put forward by Mr Henderson and agreed by the company. Is that correct?"

"Yes, Sir George, we are willing to withdraw the two letters and resume work from tomorrow. We also agree that our application for a war bonus should go to the Committee on Production. However, we believe that any award should apply from the date of resumption."

Askwith turned to the Operating Manager. "Mr Blain?"

Blain conferred briefly with Shave. "Agreed."

They were prepared to concede that all along, thought Mickey.

"And now, as to Clause 3 of the 1913 agreement: we are prepared to go along with the suggestion of a conference between the two parties to review the clause, but we feel that there has been a great deal of confusion concerning this matter, which we wish to immediately clear away. To be honest, the responsibility for this confusion lies with both sides. All we initially wanted was to have a representative of the Transport Workers' Federation at our negotiations with the company. In response, the company pointed to Clause 3, presumably in the belief that participation by the TWF would mean that we would be drawn into disputes with other companies. This, of course, would not be the case. Now, the fact of the matter is that, Clause 3 or no Clause 3, this union remains affiliated to the TWF, and so the company's reservations make no sense. *Our* error, on the other hand, lay in our withdrawal from Clause 3—merely because the company had cited this as the basis for its refusal to allow TWF representation—whereas we should have done more to clarify the nature of our request.

"Now Mr Williams, secretary of the TWF, is with us today, and he will also address this question. You, Sir George, need no introduction to Mr Williams, as your paths have crossed on several occasions."

Askwith smiled and nodded. "Indeed, Mr Smith. Good afternoon, Mr Williams."

Williams leaned forward, hands clasped before him. "Good afternoon, Sir George.

"The company appears to be under the impression that any involvement with the TWF automatically brings with it the threat of industrial action. Perhaps you more than anyone, Sir George, will know that this is not true. Our Federation covers a wide range of trade unions in the transport sector. To each of those unions, affiliation to the Federation means that, should the need arise, it can call upon the Federation for assistance. In theory, of course, that assistance *could* take the form of industrial action." He unclasped his hands and held up his palms. "But how often *has* it? Indeed, here we are, discussing a derecognition dispute. There is, in truth, no issue more likely to lead the TWF to take action in support of an affiliate. But has it? Why, no, because we are here today to discuss a *settlement* of that dispute.

"And you are aware from personal experience, Sir George, that this is the form our assistance takes in the overwhelming majority of cases. How many times have I or Mr Bevin been called upon to represent an affiliate at the Committee on Production? I don't know whether you have kept a tally, Sir George, but I have certainly lost count. And in each case, what has been our aim?" Not at all violently but in emphasis nevertheless, he brought a palm down onto the table. "To seek a settlement. So, gentlemen," he said, turning to Blain and Shave, "you may rest easy."

Askwith frowned and glanced at the two company representatives. "Well, Mr Blain, it is, in fact, impossible for me to disagree with anything Mr Williams has said..."

"But we must have Clause 3," Blain interjected.

"You can have it!" Tich Smith responded. "All you need do is add an amendment or addendum to the effect that this undertaking does not rule out the attendance of a TWF representative at negotiations with the union."

Askwith moved closer to Blain and there was a whispered conversation between the two. Askwith, thought Mickey, is asking why, given what the union is offering, there is a need for a separate conference. But Blain is not having it, is he? Blain, in fact, is not the brightest light in the harbour, unable to think on his feet. Mickey began to dash off a note on his pad.

"We hear what you say, gentlemen," said Blain, "and it has given us a degree of reassurance, but we really need to sound out the opinion of others on this matter and return to the subject as suggested by Mr Henderson."

Mickey ripped the page from his pad, folded it and passed it down to Tich Smith who, having opened it, smiled at Mickey in amusement and shook his head.

"Well," Arthur Henderson was saying, "I will await the outcome of that conference with great interest, although it seems to me that, given the comments by the general secretary and Mr Williams, it promises to be a very short meeting."

"Possibly so," Askwith agreed. "Now I believe that leaves us with the Palmers Green situation which, as you know, is a somewhat ticklish one as far as the company goes, involving as it does observance of the agreed procedures. I think you were saying that you have a suggestion regarding this, Minister."

"I do, Sir George. Today, gentlemen, the request for the reinstatement of the Palmers Green people comes from me, not the union. I'm not concerned about whether or not the procedure was broken. As a member of the War Cabinet, my only concern is to get London moving again, and if the reinstatement of these people will achieve that, it's my duty to request that you do it."

For the first time, Blain's face showed signs of animation, as he looked at Henderson and smiled at his ingenuity. He nodded. "Agreed."

Askwith spread his hands. "Gentlemen, I believe that concludes out business. Thank you for your attendance and civility. We will meet again as soon as we can arrange a date for the Clause 3 conference."

As the meeting broke up, Henderson paused at Tich's seat to pick up Mickey's note, read it—"Ask him whether he'd like an adjournment, so he can nip upstairs to see if it's agreeable to Sir Albert"—and, waving a finger at Mickey, laughed. "You must have read my mind, son."

44

"Take a good look at this bloke," Sanders murmured to Mickey, gesturing through the window of the railway carriage at the platform of Leeds Central Station, where a burly man in his mid-forties, with a thick, dark moustache, forced his way forward, holding a travelling bag before him.

"Who is he?"

Sanders cast a look at the other occupants of the compartment: Dennis Davies and several BSP delegates. "Edward Tupper, Havelock Wilson's right-hand man in the National Sailors' and Firemen's Union. You've heard about the thugs that go around attacking peace meetings? Well, he's their leader." He leaned closer. "A little bird recently told me that they're being paid by the government. Pound a day per man, plus expenses."

"The bastards. Do you think they'll try something at the conference?"

It was Dennis who answered. "No chance. There'll be too much press around."

*

After the British Socialist Party was accepted into the Labour Party in 1916, a United Socialist Council, consisting of the BSP and the Independent Labour Party, had been formed. Until now, it had been inactive, largely due to differences over the war, but in the wake of the Russian Revolution in March, it had convened a broad conference in Leeds, at which four resolutions would be adopted. Sanders, Dennis Davies and Mickey were attending as delegates of the red-button union, Tich Smith having suggested to the EC that Sanders—"our leading revolutionary," as Tich had called him with gentle mockery—be accompanied by representatives of both maturity and youth.

On the morning of Sunday, 3 June, after a night spent in one of Leeds's more modest hotels, the three men made their way to the Coliseum in Cookridge Street, where they joined the throng lining up to register. The white-stone façade of the theatre resembled that of a church, thought Mickey, which some might find appropriate, this being a Sunday, although he hoped that there would be a minimum of high-minded moralising at the conference. At the table in the large vestibule, having signed the attendance sheet, they collected copies of the resolutions and began to make their way to the hall.

"Hey, lads," Sanders cried suddenly, as he made his way to an elderly man at the entrance to the hall, "let me introduce you to a legend."

The man turned at Sanders' approach and broke into a smile. "Well, bless my soul if it isn't George Sanders! I might have known I'd see you here."

At 61, Tom Mann was of distinguished appearance, a bow tie at his throat and the tips of his moustache waxed. Like so many of his contemporaries in the movement, Mann was self-educated, a Christian as well as a socialist. Active in a host of trade unions and political organisations, he was basically an engineer. After his role in the London Dock Strike of 1889, he had become the first president of the Dock, Wharf, Riverside and General Workers' Union, with Ben Tillett as general secretary. Eight years later, he had helped form the Workers' Union. He had played leading roles in the Fabian Society and the Independent Labour Party, and had recently joined the BSP. He was the first president of the International Transport Workers' Federation, and several European countries had deported him because of his union activities. During a decade in Australia, he had founded the Socialist Party of Victoria. Returning to England in 1910, he went to work as an organiser for Tillett, helping to form the National Transport Workers' Federation and leading the victorious Liverpool transport strike in 1911, as a result of which Havelock Wilson's National Sailors' and Firemen's Union was recognised by the ship-owners. The following year, he had been jailed after his paper, *The Syndicalist*, published an article calling upon soldiers not to fire upon strikers, although public pressure had secured his release after less than two months of the six to which he had been sentenced. So, yes, a legend.

"Ah, it gladdens my heart to see you here, Tom," Sanders greeted him enthusiastically. "I think you might know Dennis Davies here, a veteran from the old Cabdrivers' Union."

Mann nodded, narrowing his eyes. "Why, yes, our paths have crossed once or twice, haven't they, Dennis? Nice to see you again."

"And this young man," Sanders continued, "is Mickey Rice, a rising star of the red-button union."

Mickey shook Tom Mann's hand. "An honour to meet you, Brother Mann. You know, when I came to London four years ago, the first thing George gave me to read was your pamphlet *Socialism.*"

"Get away! You know, I wrote that in Australia..." He said this in the tones of a man, advanced in years, who is about to embark upon a reminiscence.

"And, of course," Sanders intervened, "you and Mickey have a mutual acquaintance: Dorothy Bridgeman."

"Really? The last time I saw Dorothy was after she had defended herself against that policeman..."

"So tell me, Tom, are you here as a BSP delegate?"

Mann hesitated. "Ah, no, George. National Sailors' and Firemen's Union. You know I've been their organiser in Liverpool since 1914."

"But Tom..."

Possibly, the disappointment in Sanders' eyes was painful to behold, but Mann nevertheless gave him a frank look in return. "Yes, George, I know. There are certain...ah...contradictions between myself and Brother Wilson which will have to be resolved sooner rather than later."

"Not to mention Edward Tupper."

Again, that frank look. "Indeed, George, indeed."

"Morning, Tom!"

Mann turned to see Philip Snowden, a Methodist and teetotaller with a face like the blade of an axe, striding by, a hand raised in greeting. "Good morning to you, Comrade Snowden," he responded, and then to Sanders, once the Labour MP had passed out of hearing, "Snowden has little time for me, I fear. Says I have an inability to stay with an organisation for more than a few years." He shrugged. "Maybe he has a point, although it's far too late to do anything about it now. Anyway, George, I must spend a few minutes rereading the resolutions. Please excuse me, lads."

And off he went.

"There goes the past," said Dennis Davies. "And here comes the future."

They were approached by a thickset man of medium height and a rolling gait. In his mid-thirties, he wore a pugnacious expression that softened into a smile as he recognised Sanders.

"Hello, George. I expect you're surprised to find me in this nest of revolutionaries, aren't you?"

"Revolutionaries, Ernie? MacDonald? Snowden?"

Ernie laughed. "Well, now you mention it...Here, Bob Williams told me about your meeting at the Board of Trade and that lad of yours..."

Dennis Davies pointed to Mickey. "Mickey Rice is his name."

Ernie thrust out his hand. "Well, Mickey Rice, my name's Ernie Bevin, and I hope we'll be seeing more of each other in the future."

*

They walked into the hall, with its panelled walls and high ceiling of dark pine, to find that sufficient light fell through the large windows to enable the delegates to do their work without recourse to electricity. Although 1,150 delegates were in attendance, there was space to spare, as the amphitheatre-shaped hall was able to hold 4,000. There were four resolutions to be discussed: a welcome for the Russian Revolution; a call for a negotiated peace, with no annexations or indemnities; on the broadening of democracy in Britain, with the expansion of civil liberties; and on the establishment of Workmen's and Soldiers' Councils throughout Britain. Although there was no doubt that this was—or could be— an historic gathering, and there was considerable excitement in the hall as delegates congratulated each other on the mere achievement of coming together, Mickey did not really know what would come of it. The fourth resolution was daring at first sight. Just imagine the audacity of calling for the formation of Workmen's and Soldiers' Councils across the country, just as the Russians were working on covering their vast land with Soviets! But wasn't this a mere attempt at emulation, at slavishly adopting tactics employed elsewhere in the hope that a similar result might be achieved? Would soldiers in this country really stand up alongside trade unionists to fight for the demands contained in the second and third resolutions? Sanders surely had a point: people like Snowden and Ramsay MacDonald, even though they had opposed the war and conscription, were not revolutionaries. Many of the delegates were, although undoubtedly sincere, of the same stripe. Well, he would wait to hear what the platform had to say.

The convention was chaired by the Scot Bob Smillie, 60, vice-president of the Miners' Federation of Great Britain and a founder-member of the Independent Labour Party. He began by reading messages: from the Russian Soldiers' and Workers' Deputies, who hoped to meet representatives of today's initiative at the forthcoming peace conference in Stockholm in July; from George Lansbury, unable to attend as "I am on my back—a crock," who hoped that Smillie and Bob Williams would be sent to Stockholm; a unit of the Royal Army Medical Corps sent cordial support; and an imprisoned conscientious objector wrote that this event gave him great hope that his sacrifice had not been in vain.

In his opening remarks, Smillie claimed that "we have not come here to talk treason. We have come here to talk reason." That got a cheer, alerting Mickey to the true feeling of the convention. And what was the purpose of the fourth resolution? Why, said Smillie, the soldiers were without a voice. Has the treatment of their relatives and dependents been satisfactory? The treatment of themselves at the Front? When wounded or retired? He seemed to see the proposed councils, thought Mickey, as nothing more than pressure groups for the soldiers. And, he went on, he did not support a separate peace for Russia.

"Well," said Sanders, turning to Mickey, "you can read that in two ways, can't you?"

"He should try telling it to the Russian comrades," said Mickey.

The first resolution congratulated the Russian Revolution for liberating the people for "the great work of establishing their own political and economic freedom on a firm foundation and of taking a foremost part in the international movement for working-class emancipation from all forms of political, economic and imperialist oppression and exploitation."

In moving the resolution, James Ramsay MacDonald, who had relinquished the leadership of the Parliamentary Labour Party because of his anti-war stance, was not bad—in parts. "When this war broke out," he said as he approached his conclusion, "organised labour in this country lost the initiative. It became a mere echo of the old governing classes' opinions. Now the Russian Revolution has once again given you the chance to take the initiative yourselves. Let us lay down our terms, make our own proclamations, establish our own diplomacy, see to it that we have our own international meetings."

Mickey turned to Sanders. "That's not so bad."

Sanders winked. "Wait for it; he won't leave it at that."

"Let us say to the Russian democracy," continued MacDonald, "'In the name of everything you hold sacred in politics, in morality, in good government, and in progress, restrain the anarchy in your midst, find a cause for unity, maintain your Revolution, stand by your liberties, put yourselves at the head of the peoples of Europe."

"In other words," said Mickey, "settle for a bourgeois democracy."

"You've got it," agreed Sanders.

Dora Montefiore, a suffragist and BSP member in her sixties, seconded. Carried.

Moving the second resolution, Snowden was both effective and, surprisingly, amusing. "For three years, we have been appealing to the Government to tell us their peace terms. The time has now come for us to tell the Government what *our* peace terms are." This was greeted with cheers. The resolution had adopted the same wording as that of the first declaration of the Russian Workmen's and Soldiers Council. The war "must be brought to an end as soon as possible by an international understanding between the democracies...The basis of peace should be no annexation and no indemnity, and the right of every nation to dispose of its own destiny."

Snowden mercilessly mocked the stance of the political establishment towards such demands. In the House of Commons, Lord Robert Cecil, Undersecretary of State for Foreign Affairs, accepted the formula and "repudiated all imperialist aims and ambitions on behalf of the British Government,"—the Leeds delegates laughed at this—"but he then refused to concede one single word of alteration in the Allied Note to President Wilson" in response to the latter's call for a League of Nations. This Note had called for "reparation, restitution and such guarantees to which they are entitled." Asquith, leader of the opposition, had also concurred with the formula, but went on to identify four conditions in which annexation would be justified, one of which concerned strategic security and purposes, and another "the liberation of subject peoples groaning under the tyranny of an alien oppressor." This was greeted with even greater gales of laughter, and one delegate cried "Ireland!" Snowden responded: "Yes, and I might add India and Egypt!"

In seconding, Edwin Fairchild, a member of the same Hackney branch of the BSP as Theo Rothstein, pointed out that indemnities would increase the burden on the working class of the other side and were "a device of imperialist capitalism in order to further its own process of exploitation."

Bearded and bespectacled, William O'Brien, the MP for Cork, was shown respect by the delegates, despite his support for the war on the misguided basis that it might lead to Home Rule for Ireland, as he called for the release of the Irish political prisoners.

Charles Roden Buxton, a former Liberal now with the ILP, made Mickey smile as he, like many before him, quoted Shakespeare without regard to context: "There is a tide in the affairs of men..."

As Smillie was about to call the midday break, Edward Tupper strode to the rostrum and Mickey, feeling his hackles rise, prepared to get to his feet. Sanders placed a restraining hand on his arm, murmuring, "Careful, lad, careful."

"Mr Chairman and comrades," Tupper began.

Ignoring Sanders' hand, Mickey got up. "Withdraw the 'comrades!' We're not your comrades! How can a man who leads a band of thugs to attack peace campaigners be allowed to address this conference?"

The convention was in tumult as those who were aware of Tupper's reputation added their voices to Mickey's, and Smillie struggled to restore order. Through it all, Mickey was aware that Tupper's eyes were on him. Eventually, Tupper was allowed to proceed, arguing that there must be indemnities, for without them who would provide for the widows and orphans of merchant seamen?

"The ship-owners!" cried several delegates.

His reply to this belied his reputation for toughness: "They will not do so!"

"Then make them!"

As Tupper left the rostrum and marched down the aisle, his eyes were once more upon Mickey, and to Mickey it seemed that, rather than seeking to intimidate him, he was memorising every detail of his appearance, marking him.

"You've done it now, Mickey," said Sanders with a rueful shake of the head.

"Fuck him," said Mickey.

"Come on, I'll buy you a drink across the road."

"Thanks, George, but I'll get a sandwich somewhere."

"On a Sunday?"

"If I have a drink now, I'll be nodding off to sleep this afternoon."

"Alright, but keep an eye out for Tupper."

*

After lunch, the discussion of the second resolution was resumed by Ernie Bevin, the self-educated Somerset man who, having become branch secretary of the dockers' union in Bristol in 1910, when he was twenty-one, was its national organiser four years later. He was a firm advocate of amalgamations, and was becoming known in the wider movement through his work with the National Transport Workers' Federation. As he now demonstrated, he had little time for intellectuals or professional politicians, but it was not easy to know where in the political spectrum he might be located.

If this policy was forced upon the government, asked Bevin, where "do our fatuous friends in the ILP stand with their Bermondsey resolution?" At this, Mickey threw a quizzical look at Sanders, who shrugged: he didn't know what it meant, either.

If there was no response from Germany, Bevin continued, would these fatuous friends join in a vigorous prosecution of the war until it *did* respond? Where was the evidence that the German Social Democrats, whom Bevin seemed to hold in low esteem, were prepared to reverse their policy? Bevin declared that he was not a pacifist—and neither did he look like one, speaking with his right fist held before him and his lower lip pushed into a belligerent pose. He believed that "even in our country there will have to be the shedding of blood to attain the freedom we require."

His remarks seemed to be without structure, and Mickey thought that he had either entered the debate determined to point to the several contradictions and omissions in the proposals, but without telling his audience that this was what he was doing, or he was simply making it up as he went along.

Next, he waxed—or seemed to—progressive. Why was there no mention of a plebiscite by which Africans might decide their own futures? Why no mention of whether the Crown Colonies were to be given a vote to decide on their form of government?

"The platform says," he remarked in a further change of direction, "that 'the tide is on the rise for us.' For whom? The professional politicians of the Labour Party!"

This led to some disorder in the hall—although not totally in protest: Sanders, for example, had thrown back his head in laughter, sharing Bevin's opinion of the politicians—and Smillie now told Bevin that his time was up.

Next came Tom Mann, but this was a shadow of the Tom Mann of earlier years. He agreed with the proposals. He had always agreed with them. The opinion of organised labour had changed.

"And so, Tom," Sanders muttered sadly, "you feel that it's now safe to come out and say what you really think. Then why, oh why are you still with Havelock Wilson?"

The resolution was overwhelming approved.

The third resolution called on the government to place itself in accord with Russian democracy and introduce "a charter of liberties establishing complete political rights for all men and women, unrestricted freedom of the press, a general amnesty for all political and religious prisoners, full rights and independence of political association, and the release of labour from all forms of compulsion and restraint."

This was moved by Charles Ammon, a conscientious objector and member of the ILP. "In this war for freedom," he declared, "freedom is a memory and Labour is enchained." Nearly a thousand conscientious objectors were in prison, some beginning their third or fourth terms. "They will be kept in prison unless we do what Russia has done."

Bertrand Russell also spoke about those prisoners of conscience. "It is by their refusal to serve that they have shown the world that it is possible for the individual to stand in this matter of military service against the whole power of the organised State. This is a very great discovery. It is something which enhances the dignity of men, something which makes every one of us feel freer as we look out upon the world."

Fine words, noble sentiments, thought Mickey, but the confusion was readily apparent, because while the mover had suggested that "we do what Russia has done," the resolution itself called for the introduction of "a charter or liberties"—by the existing government.

After a minute's silence to honour the late Keir Hardy, the final resolution was moved by William Anderson, MP, a former chairman of the ILP. This called upon the bodies represented at the convention to establish "in every town, urban and rural district, Councils of Workmen's and Soldiers' Delegates for initiating and coordinating working-class activity in support of the policy set out in the foregoing resolution," to work for a people's peace and for the complete political and economic emancipation of international labour, and to take up the concerns of wounded and disabled soldiers. The mover, however, viewed these Councils in much the same way as had Bob Smillie at the beginning of the meeting, saying that the resolution was not meant to be subversive of the military responsibilities; but workers and soldiers were men and had the rights of men, and for this reason "we set up an organisation, not subversive, not unconstitutional unless the authorities care to make it so."

Seconding the motion, Bob Williams put forward his own interpretation. "I want," said the dark Welshman, "to accept the resolution in its very fullest implication. The resolution, if it means anything at all, means that which is contained in the oft-used phrase from Socialist platforms: *the dictatorship of the proletariat!*" This brought a round of cheers. Bob Smillie had said "that we have come here to talk not treason but reason; but I would remind Smillie, if he needs it, that under the Defence of the Realm Regulations reason has become treason."

Convince the governing classes that you are serious about this resolution, he thundered, and they will implement the other three. "They will make every sacrifice and concession short of getting off your backs." He turned his sights on Tupper. "If you want restitution, reparation, and guarantees, in God's name get it from the profiteers of your own country!"

"We want to break the influence of the industrial and political labour 'machine'"—cheers, although presumably not from those who were components of that machine—"and this Convention is our attempt to do so!" Representatives of the thousands of workers here should go back to their members and convince them to use the power which lay in their hands. "Parliament will do nothing for you. Parliament has done nothing for you for the whole period of the war...We want to assert our right to the ownership and control of the country...We are competent to speak in the name of our class, and damn the Constitution! Had the Russian revolutionaries been disposed to be concerned with the Constitution of Holy Russia, the Romanoffs would still be on the throne today, and I say to you: Have as little concern for the British Constitution as the Russians you are praising had for the Romanoffs. You have a greater right to speak in the name of our people—civilians and soldiers—than have the gang who are in charge of our political destinies at the moment...The workpeople have assumed the directorate of matters in Russia!

"Workers of the world unite! You have nothing to lose but your chains, and you have a world to win!"

"Well," said Sanders as he added to the applause, "that was worth coming for!"

Yes, pondered Mickey, if this Convention had been a speech competition, Bob Williams would undoubtedly have been awarded first prize, but would anything come of it?

Williams was followed by more moderate voices. Speaking for the

517

second time, Snowden urged the involvement of women in the councils and coined what proved to be, for Mickey at least, a memorable phrase: "Keep up your hearts when this conference is over and you have to meet the dismal people who can see no light ahead."

Sylvia Pankhurst, who had given Mickey a curt nod of recognition as the conference had broken for lunch, saw the Provisional Committee becoming the Provisional Government, and called for the inclusion of working women in "your Committee and your Central Government."

Next came engineer Fred Shaw, a member of the executive committee of the BSP, and the ILP's R.C. Wallhead, soon to be detained under DORA. And then George Sanders walked to the rostrum.

"I represent a union who have just come through a strike and are never happy unless we are on strike."

The grammar was certainly curious, and Mickey wondered whether Sanders was affected by his lunchtime drink. But the fatuousness of the remark! What strike? A dispute, which Sanders was instrumental in bringing about, which left the members no better off than they would otherwise have been. Never happy unless we're on strike? Are the causes and the results of no importance? And this is the man who asked me if I had familiarised myself with dialectics! The rest of Sanders' brief contribution consisted merely of a request that those in the body of the hall also be allowed to participate in the proposed councils. No mention of the sacrifices of London's transport workers since 1914. Mickey caught the eye of Dennis Davies, and it was clear that the other man was also disappointed. It now struck Mickey that the disillusionment he had recently been feeling in Sanders might be very similar to that which Sanders felt in Tom Mann. Perhaps his political understanding had always been limited, a fact unrevealed when the issues had been relatively minor, but now, when the question was whether to prepare for revolution or simply to continue the industrial struggle, he seemed to be at a loss regarding the way forward. When, a little later, the organisers of the convention published a verbatim report, Mickey would note that they even got Sanders' name wrong, printing his contribution under "J. Sanders."

Joe Toole apologised to the conference, as he had been mandated to vote for the first three resolutions and against the fourth. The councils were, in his view, not required, as the movement already had sufficient organisations to work for the first three. And then, a telling point: conditions in Russia were very different to those in this country; in Russia, the Soviet had been formed *after* the overthrow of the monarchy and the autocracy. Yes, agreed Mickey, *that's* dialectical thinking!

Willie Gallacher, chairman of the Clyde Workers' Shop Stewards' Committee, made a point entirely neglected by the other delegates: the Russian Revolution was not yet settled, but the capitalists of this and other countries had already decided that the Russian socialists must be beaten back. The task of the proposed councils, as he saw it, was simple: "Give your own capitalist class so much to do that it will not have time to attend to it!"

Finally, Noah Ablett, author of "The Miners' Next Step," the syndicalist pamphlet published by the South Wales Miners' Federation five years earlier, made the practical suggestion that rather than simply call for the establishment of Workers' and Soldiers' Councils, a guide or programme should be produced.

The Convention sent a telegram to the Russian Workmen's and Soldiers' Council, advising it of the momentous events of the day, following which it was agreed that Britain should be divided into thirteen districts, each of which would elect a representative to the central Council.

*

The next day, on the train back to Euston, the red-button trio happened to share a compartment with Bob Williams.

"So what do you think, Bob?" asked Dennis Davies.

"About the Convention?"

"Yeah. Will anything come of it?"

"After that telegram, the comrades in Petrograd won't be very pleased if nothing does," Mickey threw in while Williams was still chewing his lip.

"And, to be honest, I think they *will* be disappointed," said Williams. "But you comrades are just as able to judge as me. You were there yesterday." He shook his head in disbelief. "Virtually every one of those resolutions meant different things to different people, so it's difficult to see how these local councils are going to work. Then again, a lot more thought should have been put into the Convention before we called it. Ablett was right: how can you call upon eleven hundred people to go away and form local soviets— which is basically what we were calling for—without a single guideline as to how they should go about it? Joe Toole also made a crucial point: the Russians overthrew the Tsar first and *then* formed the Petrograd Soviet, with the idea that the workers should rule the country through such organisations, whereas our convention proposed that its own councils be established while the traditional constitutional machinery stands unscathed."

"But your own speech talked about the dictatorship of the proletariat, Bob," Sanders reminded him.

Williams shook his head. "Wishful thinking, George, wishful thinking. With the benefit of hindsight, I can see the mistake we made."

"In calling the Convention in the first place?" queried Mickey.

"In calling it prematurely, taking Joe Toole's point. Either that, or in calling it in the *way* we did. Instead of becoming carried away by the romance of the Russian Revolution—still only a bourgeois revolution, mind—maybe we should have simply called for the organisation of local campaigns to mobilise support for our concrete demands, leaving out all talk of Workers' and Soldiers' Councils until later."

"Maybe Gallacher had a point, too," said Dennis Davies.

"I think he did," nodded Williams. "The Bolsheviks are gaining strength all the time, and we can expect our leaders to try to snuff them out at some point. So yes, use our councils to put so much on our authorities' plate that they don't have time to interfere in Russia." He grinned ruefully. "And maybe that's as much as the councils will be able to manage."

"I got the impression," said Mickey, "that that was also Gallacher's view."

"Maybe," said Williams, "maybe."

"Bob," Mickey began after a brief lull in the discussion, "you're from the Dockers' Union..."

Williams smiled. "And you want to know what I think of Ernie Bevin."

Mickey laughed. "I do, comrade."

Williams leaned back onto the headrest and folded his arms. "Well," he began slowly, "I'll be as honest as I can, Mickey. For a start, you didn't see him at his best yesterday. Politics is not his forte, and as you might have gathered he has contempt for professional politicians, even in the Labour Party—*particularly* in the Labour Party, in fact, because he doesn't think that many of them really represent the working class, or that they *can* represent the working class if they come from the intellectual elite, or if they put forward ideas that the average worker doesn't understand or isn't ready for."

"What does he read?" asked Sanders.

"He doesn't read."

"Ah, well…"

"What he *does* do is listen. He is one of the most intelligent men I've ever known. He soaks up knowledge—not through the eye but through the ear. If someone says something to him that he considers significant, he won't forget it; he'll store that away until he needs to use it sometime in the future. He is the most formidable negotiator I've ever come across. Usually, he'll come to a meeting with a full knowledge of the industry or trade in question. If for some reason he lacks that knowledge, he'll put forward question after question until he understands it. He'll listen very carefully to the employers, putting what they say into his knowledge bank. If they're talking nonsense, mind you, or are trying to pull the wool over his eyes, he'll know it, and he'll come down on them like a ton of bricks. Once he understands the trade, he'll start putting forward his own arguments to justify the demands of his members, often using the very facts the employers have put forward. Oh, I've never seen anything like it, comrades!

"Industry is where he's comfortable, where he feels he belongs, where he can excel. Never underestimate his loyalty to his members and his class, because he is *fiercely* loyal to them. And from what I can see he's not out for money or privilege. That's the positive. The problem, as I see it, is that his loyalty to the workers seems to go no further than the workers as they are now. D'you know what I mean? Yes, he wants to see them living lives that are more comfortable and secure, and he looks forward to a time when the trade unions will be taken seriously by both employers and government—treated as equals. But that's as far as it goes. He doesn't necessarily see them as one day running their own industries, or the country as a whole."

"But didn't he say yesterday," said Dennis Davies, "something about blood needing to be shed if we're to get the kind of freedom we need in this country?"

Williams nodded firmly. "He did, and it's something he often says when he's in front of an audience that might be a bit to the left of him. But what he means by that—if he really believes it—is that the employers and the state will force the bloodshed on us before they treat us as equals. I think he'd already left the conference yesterday when I mentioned the dictatorship of the proletariat, but if he'd been there you would only have to look at his face to know what he thought about it."

"We know what we are," Mickey intoned, "but know not what we may be."

"Bloody hell, lad," said Williams, "that's a good line. Where did you pick it up from? It's probably too late now, but that's the sort of thing Bevin should read!"

"It's Shakespeare," Mickey confessed.

"Ophelia," said Sanders with a smile, "in *Hamlet*."

Mickey glanced at Sanders, who met his gaze. Maybe, thought the younger man, he's due more credit than I've been giving him of late.

"In that case," chuckled Williams, "maybe not. Anyway, the other thing about Ernie is that once he gets an idea in his head, he won't let go of it, even if it takes him months or years to put it into practice. Amalgamation is one such idea, and he should be a valuable ally for your union when the TWF meets in Bristol next week. Will you be moving it, George?"

Williams was referring to the motion submitted by the red-button union, calling on the WTF to work for the amalgamation of all unions in the transport sector, on the basis of industrial unionism.

"No, that's a job for Tich," Sanders replied with a marked lack of enthusiasm.

"You still not keen on the idea, George?"

"In theory, I don't have a problem with it, but you don't need me to tell you that we're the most militant union in the sector, and you know damn well what will happen if we get in bed with the AAT."

Williams nodded soberly. "Yes, I can see that's a risk, George. Well, we'll see what happens."

"By the way, Bob," said Sanders, not keen to discuss amalgamations, "Ernie told us that you've been singing the praises of our Mickey to him. He told the lad yesterday that he hopes to see more of him."

"Something tells me," said Mickey, "that I won't have much choice in the matter."

45

Dorothy had arranged to have her rest-day on Monday so that she would be at home when Mickey arrived back from Leeds. As the day passed, however, she wished that she had merely exchanged her duty for an early finish, as she found herself with little to do after she had dropped off their wash at the laundry, bought a newspaper, queued for meat at the butcher's shop on Westbourne Grove and taken her purchase back home to marinate it. They had been together for almost four years now, but except for her brief visit to Holloway Prison and her trip to Italy this had been the first time they had spent a night apart. And not just one night, but two! It was not just that she missed him; for some reason she was worried about him. But what could possibly have happened to him in Leeds? Well, the patriotic populace of the city might have rallied against the peace advocates. True, there was no word of such an incident in today's report in *The Times*, but it did mention the bridled hostility of local hoteliers, and there might well have been an isolated occurrence or two, possibly at night. But he was with comrades, after all, and locals were hardly likely to choose someone of Mickey's build and bearing as the target of their outraged patriotism. Despite her concern, she giggled at the thought. There was always, though, the possibility of a train accident; over 200 had died in the Quintinshill crash two years ago. As the hours passed, she had to wrestle down the urge to go out and buy a copy of the early edition of the *Globe* or the *Evening News*. Oh, stop this foolishness, Dorothy!

When he arrived, she was in her usual chair, dozing over *The Times*.

"Oh!" She started awake as he placed his bag on the floor and lifted the newspaper from her lap. "Oh, sweetheart, I wanted to be awake for you."

He watched as her eyes fluttered open and her mouth assumed that smile, the smile he had loved for four years. "You are now, my love."

He leaned forward to kiss her brow but she, wanting more, placed a hand on his neck and pulled his mouth to hers. As they often did, they watched each other, as if marvelling that they could ever be together.

"I was so worried," Dorothy confessed, a palm on his cheek. "I was sure that something had happened to you."

"But nothing did, and nothing will." He eased her up and put his arms around her, feeling her warmth against him. "Nothing will, Dorothea."

That proved to be a little optimistic.

*

Later that week, Mickey attended the EC meeting to discuss a number of items of business, including the war bonus award.

Tich looked around the table. "You ready for this?"

"Let's have it, Tich," said Dennis Davies.

"Five shillings a week for drivers and conductors, four shillings for Inside Staff."

Barney Macauley caught Mickey's eye and winked. Mickey grinned and nodded.

"Are we accepting it?" asked Davies.

"Can I suggest, Dennis," said Tich, "that the Council authorises me to tell the press that while we're of the view that it's insufficient, we accept it for now but we hope to have the matter reopened."

"Agreed?"

Agreed.

"At the same time, the London County Council has awarded the tram-workers sixpence a day." He shook his head. "Why they can't say three bob a week is beyond me, but that's Aubrey Llewellyn Coventry Fell for you. Anyway, it's obviously inadequate, and so I propose to write to the Committee on Production, asking them to consider it."

"Agreed?"

Agreed.

Dennis Davies led the way down the agenda, which included a report by Sanders of the Leeds Convention. He gave this a positive slant, although agreeing with the reservations made by Bob Williams.

"There have, however, already been consequences, and not particularly helpful ones. A day later, Havelock Wilson called a national meeting of the Sailors' and Firemen's Union—in fact, he must have arranged it even before the Convention took place—which condemned the Convention and agreed that its members will not work on ships transporting the peace delegates to Stockholm."

This news triggered a wave of pejorative utterances from around the table, causing Davies to issue a cautionary, "Careful, brothers, careful now; let's watch our language."

"Then," continued Sanders, "their conference went one step further and agreed to send a delegation to Petrograd to inform the workers that British merchant seamen are opposed to any peace without indemnities."

The protests now were louder and more vehement, but this time Davies made no attempt to stem them.

"They'll probably sail on the same ship as Mrs Pankhurst," said Mickey.

The noise subsided. "Mrs Pankhurst?" said Davies. "What's she got to do with it?"

"You obviously haven't heard, have you?" said Mickey. "Emmeline Pankhurst, with the blessing of our Prime Minister, is going to Petrograd to try to persuade the Provisional Government to remain in the war."

This was greeted with scorn by some EC members, laughter by others.

Sanders greeted these interruptions with a smile on his face. "You think that's funny?" he asked. "Wait till I give you the jewel in the crown: one of the delegates elected by Wilson's conference was Tom Mann!"

A shocked silence. Davies leaned forward. "*Surely* not, George, *surely* not! Are you sure you've got that right?"

"Absolutely sure, Chairman. And this, of course, is an indication of the contempt in which Wilson holds anyone who disagrees with his so-called Patriotic Crusade. How do you punish Tom Mann when he turns up at the Leeds Convention and agrees with the platform? Well, you send him to Petrograd under instruction to agree with Mrs Pankhurst and Edward Tupper, don't you?"

It was now an incredulous Tich who leaned forward. "But he's not going is he? Tom, I mean."

Sanders was grinning broadly. "No, of course he's not! And he's not doing any more organising work for that union in Liverpool, either. He's told Wilson where to stuff it!"

Cheers and applause.

"Finally, Chairman, the North London Herald League advises me that they have challenged Havelock Wilson to a debate in Finsbury Park next Sunday afternoon, and they ask that we help to swell the attendance."

"Presumably Tupper and his thugs will be in attendance," said Dennis Davies.

Sanders nodded. "I expect so."

*

The North London Herald League was one of several established to support the *Daily Herald*, the labour-friendly newspaper, from late 1912, and these were needed more than ever when, with the outbreak of war, the *Herald* was forced to go to weekly publication. The fortunes of the North London group grew as it took to holding public meetings in Finsbury Park, often attracting large crowds; not all of those in attendance were supporters because, as when the subject was peace or opposition to conscription, opponents turned up to heckle. Hitherto, however, their meetings had not seen violence on the scale that would visit the debate between the League and Havelock Wilson and his aide Edward Tupper.

The pressure of work would probably have kept most busworkers away anyway, but the possibility of violence also had its effect, and Mickey found himself accompanied by just two: Lenny Hawkins and Andy Dixon.

As they arrived at the edges of the crowd, Edward Tupper was getting into his stride, bending to his audience, swinging his fist in time with his voice as he bellowed his contempt for the pacifists who were betraying our brave soldiers and seamen—yes, the seamen, who when they were torpedoed lost either their lives or all their worldly possessions; and, their wages stopped the moment the waves closed over their vessels, they were left to make their way home by their own devices and at their own expense. Mickey wondered why a man like Tupper could support a war being fought in the interests of those who, like the ship-owners, were making piles of cash and yet treated their employees as mere units of labour, unlamented and forgotten as soon as they were no longer in a position to continue creating those profits. He watched this man who, stripped to his shirt, sweat beading on his brow, now urged patriots to oppose those who, following Ramsay MacDonald and Snowden, favoured a peace without indemnities, in much the same way as in 1911 he had harangued the seamen in Cardiff to strike against the shipping companies until they agreed to recognise the union and cough up £5 a month instead of the £3 they were paying. Now he boasted of how he would prevent Ramsay MacDonald from travelling to Stockholm. Couldn't Tupper see that the employers of Germany and Austria were in all likelihood no different from the shipping magnates he claimed to hold in contempt, and that the workers in those countries had common interests with those in Britain? And why did he and his ilk insist on calling those who were opposed to the war "pacifists," whereas in fact many were simply against *this* war, as it was waged on behalf of the imperialists of both camps? Tupper now gave him an answer to this as he claimed that the British Empire owed its very existence to the merchant seaman, and that if this war was lost so too would the Empire be lost. The Briton, he claimed, was a special breed. No matter how bad things may have been in the past, improvements had been made, and would continue to be made—and all without the need for bloodshed or revolution. Had the fool never heard of Peterloo? Had he lost sight of the fact that millions of British workers were now wearing khaki and shedding more blood than would be lost in any revolution? At least Mickey now understood him. Reading was a town from which many wished to escape, and in earlier years he had known a number of men who had joined the merchant marine for this very purpose.

He recalled now how some of them had described their lives ashore in distant lands above which the Union Jack fluttered, how they were treated as kings—or, Mickey suspected, tried to act like them. Those who made such boasts tended to be the lowest of the low, men who had made no attempt to better life either for themselves or others before they went to sea; failures at home, they strode like giants in lands where skins were darker. If Tupper could rightfully claim to serve the interests of workers, it was this degenerate type for which he catered: men who cloaked the poverty of their lives and spirits with the Union Jack. Yes, in Snowden's words, "dismal people who can see no light ahead."

Mickey surveyed the crowd. Among the anti-war forces, there appeared to be few enough workers. Gathered around the rostrum from which Tupper spoke were a handful of busmen from the North London garages, sprinkled throughout the crowd a few from the East End. There were men who might be engineers or railwaymen, but they were vastly outnumbered by middle-class types, men who had been drawn to some form of socialism by intellectual conviction or moral revulsion rather than driven to it by the daily struggle for existence. Mickey listened as Tupper claimed that the vast majority of those in attendance at Leeds had been of this stripe. This was not true, as 371 of the delegates had come from trade union organisations, with a further 209 from trades councils and local Labour Parties. Nevertheless, workers were in the minority in Finsbury Park today—unless one included the Tupper supporters who had accompanied their "captain," some 200 seamen he claimed had been torpedoed; they were clearly identifiable by the way they stood in groups, apart from the anti-war people, as if on the alert for trouble.

As his eye moved around the crowd, he spotted a group of men clad in khaki: Australians, and with them the large sergeant whose nose he had broken at the Hackney meeting the previous year. Either this was a coincidence, or the sergeant had been permanently assigned to duties such as those he would be performing today. As Mickey turned to advise Andy and Lenny of the sergeant's presence, the man looked in his direction, paused and nodded. Seems I have a date for later on, thought Mickey. During this time, Tupper was constantly dealing with interruptions and heckling and now, as one of the busmen near the rostrum shouted something at him, he happened to look towards the furthest edge of the crowd and, like the sergeant, he spotted Mickey. Allowing the busman to continue, he waved the nearest group of supporters to his side and, nodding in Mickey's direction, appeared to give them instructions.

Mickey scanned the park and realised that there was not a single policeman present. The men Tupper had spoken to walked around the outskirts of the crowd, obviously working their way to a spot behind Mickey.

"Lads," he said to Andy and Lenny, "don't go any closer to the rostrum. No one will think badly of you if you decide to scarper now. I think I'm in for a beating."

*

It came to him that he was going to die. For a while, everything was silent, and in slow motion. The members of the crowd were moving, heads raised, mouths open, here and there an arm waving, but oh so slowly, as if under water, and in complete silence. Over their heads, he could see trams and buses on Green Lanes, and turning his head ninety degrees also over to the right on Seven Sisters Road, a tram, a bus, and through the railings tiny pedestrians: all reminders of a normality which was suddenly and dreadfully absent from this park. Gazing over at the rostrum he caught sight, sat beside Tupper, of the figure of Havelock Wilson, handsome with his greying moustache, crippled by arthritis although not yet sixty. The mayhem about to commence was a component of this man's Patriotic Crusade; it was he as much as Tupper who was sending death to claim Mickey Rice.

How often since meeting Dorothy had he tried to peer into the future and, despite his best efforts, been unable to visualise their life together in years to come? Time and again, he had been unable to picture Mickey and Dorothy as middle-aged, as parents, as an old married couple; even an attempt to imagine them in the Alexander Street flat in five years' time had failed. And now he knew why. Previously, these had been fleeting thoughts, barely registering consciously, but today in Finsbury Park they had an appalling resonance.

Visions now succeeded each other rapidly, although they were themselves slow-moving and silent: things he regretted having done, things he was glad to have done, and a love now lost forever. Standing in the gallery at the EC meeting to discuss the first wage award; fencing with James Shilling at their first meeting; not having stood for election to the EC sooner; raising his voice to Dorothy when there would have been another way; not marrying Dorothy; their first meeting on the Paddington train; listening to the Organ Symphony at the Albert Hall; and, of course, the vision of Dorothea

528

as she stood on the upper deck of a bus on the other side of Oxford Street, waving, waving, waving, although it was clear now that she was waving goodbye. That was the last of the visions, after which the sound returned and movements were no longer slowed.

Edward Tupper brought a white handkerchief from his trouser pocket and wiped his mouth, and at this signal the frenzy began. The colours were sharp now, the movement swift. The seamen, roughly clothed in drab colours, began to move through the crowd, pushing, punching, kicking, and many of the anti-war men either went down or ran; those who resisted found themselves dealing with two, three, even four of the patriots.

"Behind you, lads!" Mickey cried to Lenny and Andy.

As Mickey turned, a seaman was almost upon him, arms outstretched to push him to the ground, and so he leaned to the right and the man, with an unshaven face and bad teeth, lurched past him. Lenny and Andy were engaged, each fighting off two attackers. Mickey stepped forward to assist but was suddenly stunned as a heavy object came down on the back of his head and he dropped to his knees. A boot to his back sent him sprawling, and as he rolled over he caught sight of a large figure in khaki drawing back his boot for a second kick. The sergeant was grinning.

*

He was dimly aware of a conversation somewhere above him.

"Federation meeting in Bristol bit...mixed bag...Williams under attack...anti-war activity...And Bevin defended...called on...withdraw their censure motion..."

Sounded like Sanders but his voice was distorted. Like the gramophone when it needed winding up. He must have grinned at the thought, because a pain shot through his right cheek and up to his eye.

"Motion Tich moved on amalgamation heavily defeated."

"Bad news for us?" Was that Dick?

"So-so. Won't stop the talks with blue-button..."

Wind up the gramophone, for Christ's sake. Did he say that, or just think it?

"He's trying to speak!" That was Dorothy!

He forced his eyelids open and there she was, looking as if she had been crying, and behind her Dick, Sanders and Lenny Hawkins. Lenny had a shiner.

"What did you say, sweetheart?"

"Bind it up." There was something wrong with his lip.

"Bind what up, Mickey?"

"The phona...Phonagram?" What was it called? "The bruddy gramophone!"

Dorothy had bent over him, her face close, frowning, confused.

"Voices like...like under water." His lower lip definitely felt sore.

A slow, deep laugh. Sanders. "He's coming round."

"Yeah," Mickey agreed. "I'm alive."

"Glad to hear it, mate," said Lenny Hawkins.

"What's wrong with me? How long have I been here?"

"Me and Andy dragged you to a cab this afternoon," said Lenny. "When I told him you was on the EC, he didn't even charge me. You're in 'Ackney 'Ospital, mate."

He straightened up and looked beyond them. Sure enough, there was two lines of beds on the left-hand side, just a wall and a window on the right. "How bad am I?"

Dorothy sighed. "Cuts, bruises—quite a lot of them—a fat lip and concussion. And a huge lump on your head."

"Nothing broken?"

"You mean apart from my heart?"

He extended his hand and Dorothy gripped it. "I thought it was the end, Dorothy, I really did. I've always worried about losing you, but today I was sure that I was going to be the one to go." He looked at the others. "So how did you all know where I was?"

"I got the 'ospital to telephone Dick," explained Lenny. "He called George, and then him and Dorothy come here together."

"So how come I'm *not* dead, mate? That fat sergeant was gonna give me at *least* as much as I gave him last year."

"Well, to be honest, I thought he 'ad, Mickey: he was the one what belted you on the napper. Used a cosh. Then he put the boot in."

Mickey extended an exploratory finger to his head, only to find a dressing there.

"And so they just left us after I was down and out?"

"Pretty much," said Lenny. "Mind you, the seamen probably thought they wouldn't find much on us an' that there was richer pickin's elsewhere."

"What d'you mean, Lenny?"

Lenny leaned forward. "They was *thievin'*, wasn't they? Or some of 'em was. I saw one bloke lose his wallet, another one lost his pocket watch...They call 'emselves patriots? Bloody pirates, more like it!"

"What a bunch of bastards Wilson and his crusade are!" oathed Dick.

"Well blow me down. *Here!* What happened to Andy?"

"Oh, he's alright," said Lenny. "After we got you into the cab, he shot off, didn't he?"

"So what do I look like?"

As no one seemed inclined to answer him, Dorothy took a mirror from her shoulder bag and handed it to him.

Actually, it was not as bad as he had feared: a large bruise on his right cheek and a swollen lower lip.

"I would suggest you lay off the flute for a day or two," quipped Dick.

"Yeah, very amusing, Dick. Next question: how do I get out of this place?"

46

Getting out of the hospital was easier than getting out of the flat. On the Monday morning, he swung his legs out of bed as the alarm sounded and made the effort to walk to the bathroom without stumbling. Having brushed his teeth and gingerly splashed his face with cold water, he returned to the bedroom to find Dorothy standing with arms crossed, a disapproving frown on her face.

"No, Mickey," she said. "No. The alarm was for me, not you. Now get back into bed before you make me really angry."

"But I'm ok, Dorothy. Really."

"Your headache has gone?"

"Well, not totally, but it's a damn sight better than it was."

"Bed."

He obeyed, half-glad that she was taking a firm line with him. "Are Dick and Gladys still downstairs?"

"I think so. I haven't heard the front door slam, anyway."

"Alright. On your way out, could you ask one of them to tell Shilling I'll be in tomorrow?"

"I'll ask them to tell Mr Shilling that you *may* be in tomorrow. Do you want me to boil you a couple of eggs before I leave? I've got time. And for lunch, there's some ham in the pantry."

"Thank you, sweetheart, that's very kind of you."

She stood looking at him for a moment longer, then shook her head. "My wounded soldier."

*

At midday Dick, on his break halfway through a spreadover, came up to see him.

"Did you tell Shilling that I'll be back tomorrow?"

"I did, but he asked me what your injuries were, and when I mentioned mild concussion he said you should see the company quack first, so he's made an appointment for you: ten o'clock tomorrow morning at Electric Railway House."

*

On Tuesday, just as she had the previous day, Dorothy spent every idle minute worrying about Mickey. Yes, he had looked better this morning, but who could tell with a head injury? As much as she wanted to be with him, she dreaded the thought of returning home to be told that the company doctor had discovered some awful complication. At one point, she was visited by a vision of a brain-damaged Mickey, sitting in the Alexander Street flat, drooling and making inarticulate noises, but rather than horrifying her this caused her to burst into laughter, as much at the foolishness of the thought as at the vision.

And yet.

Yes, she was now forced to admit to herself that whenever during the past four years she had attempted to picture her and Mickey together in some far-off future, the picture had not come. She had never mentioned this to Mickey; had she done so, of course, she would have found that he had shared this experience.

At first, she had taken it as a premonition that their relationship would not survive—maybe because Mickey, as he rose in the movement, would be seduced by a younger woman not prone to irrational outbreaks. Then had come the Leeds Convention and her concern that he would come to physical harm, swiftly followed by the attack in Finsbury Park. Just as, on 4 June, she had felt the urge to rush out and buy an evening newspaper in order to see if there had been a rail disaster, she now, during the second half of her duty, considered walking off the job to rush home and reassure herself that Mickey Rice was alive and well. But she brought herself under control and continued working.

*

"Were you in a brawl at the weekend, Driver Rice?"

"You might call it that, Doctor Bushaway."

"Had you been *drinking?*" The voice was now raised, the face, contorted with some private disgust at the thought of alcohol and contempt for those of the lower orders who consumed it, just inches from Mickey's. The doctor's grey hair, tangled and apparently uncombed, radiated wildly about his head. In the few years since he had joined the company, Bushaway had gained a certain notoriety for intimidating the hapless workers who came before him, men easily overawed by someone claiming to be a man of science.

"No, I had not." Mickey sighed. "Look, just do what you have to do and let me get back to work."

Doctor Bushaway, tall, thin and in his late forties, straightened suddenly, as if repelled by this outburst of incivility. "It seems, Mr Rice," he said, narrowing his eyes, "that you have come down with a dose of insolence. There is a cure for that, you know."

Mickey surveyed the physician, taking in his grubby white coat and scuffed brown shoes. "No cure has been found for the strain that I have," he said. "I'm pretty sure, anyway, that *you* don't have a cure for it—or for much else, come to that."

At first, Bushaway was outraged, and his impulse was to find him permanently unfit, and thus unemployable. But as he saw that Mickey calmly held his gaze, he realised that this man had somehow, after an acquaintance of merely minutes, read his character so accurately that his inadequacies and insecurities were revealed. He coughed. "Well, let's take a look at that head," he said.

Dr Bushaway pronounced him fit to resume work the next day; he would telephone the garage to confirm this. And as Mickey left Electric Railway House, he fully understood for the first time why, when negotiating the 1916 agreement, the union had insisted on a clause providing for an appeal to its own doctor.

*

That evening, Dorothy was relieved to find that Mickey had passed his medical examination and seemed cockily self-assured. Carefully, avoiding the bruises, she kissed him and held him to her, hoping desperately that her fears were now at an end. She called him Michael and he responded by referring to her as Dorothea.

The next morning, Wednesday, 13 June, she left home somewhat earlier than him in order to reach the Bush in time for her duty. As she would be on route 11, he told her that he would probably see her on the road. As he left the house with Gladys, they flagged down a passing 31 bus and rode it to Westbourne Park, from where they walked down to the garage in the early morning sunshine. In the output, there was a certain amount of good-natured ribbing as some of the other crews remarked on Mickey's temporarily altered appearance, but he gave as good as he got.

On the first journey, as Mickey turned into Du Cane Road from Scrubs Lane, he saw another bus approaching, and there she was on the top deck! He sounded his klaxon to attract her attention, waving wildly and she, leaning on the rail, waved back. Although they had done this frequently since Dorothy had become a regular on route 11, it always took him back to that glorious evening, almost exactly four years ago in Oxford Street. Ah, what a morning, the air warm, the trees in full leaf, and Mickey as deeply in love as ever!

*

On that same bright morning, Hauptmann Ernst Brandenburg watched as the twenty Gotha G.IV bombers lined up for take-off on the airfield of the Kampfgeschwader der Obersten Heeresleitung 3— Kagol 3—in Sint-Denijs-Westrem just outside Ghent in occupied Belgium. Commanded by Brandenburg, the Kagol, consisting of six flights, was a specialised bombing unit directly controlled by the Army high command, and this was its third mission using the new Gotha aircraft. There had been high-altitude Zeppelin raids in March and May, but these had been dismal failures. Operation *Turkenkreuz*, as the London bombing campaign was known, had opened in earnest with the first raid using the G.IV on 25 May; this, however, had, bedevilled by cloud, been diverted from London to Folkestone and an Army camp in the same vicinity, although the British press had reported 95 dead and double that in injuries; the second raid, eight days ago, had been diverted to Sheerness. Given the warm spell which had started a few days earlier, today's raid had every chance of reaching London.

The plywood G. IV biplane, with its impressive wingspan of almost 78 feet, certainly looked as if it could deliver a blow; and if the defending British aircraft managed to gain sufficient height, which was doubtful, each bomber was armed with three machine guns. Hopefully, thought Brandenburg, after today the British public would be begin to reconsider its support of the war.

Despite the unevenness of the grass runway, there was no tendency to bounce as the huge aircraft, each laden with its defensive armaments and just over 1,000 pounds of bombs, was carried to take-off speed by their two 260-horsepower Mercedes D.IVa engines before being lifted into the air, white against the clear blue sky.

*

Approaching Liverpool Street on that first trip, Mickey spotted Dorothy's bus as, heavily-laden, it passed them on its way back to the Scrubs, but Dorothy was too busy to notice him, although he heard both Gladys's call to her and Dorothy's hurried reply. On his own return journey, he almost missed her again, as her vehicle had already turned south down Scrubs Lane as he approached Du Cane Road from the north, but he sounded his klaxon furiously and was rewarded by the sight of a tiny figure waving back at him as it receded into the distance.

*

The flight crossed the Suffolk coastline above Felixstowe, with the clear weather still holding. A few miles inland, they were joined by enemy fighters, possibly from the Royal Flying Corps camp at Martlesham Heath; later still, British fighters could also be seen approaching from the opposite direction, sent up from one of the fighter stations in Essex. But the tiny fighters, lacking the ability to match the G.IV's 16,000-feet flight ceiling, remained far below, and were not even an irritant. The flight continued its journey to London.

*

They had just passed Bank, Mickey pushing the X-type towards Liverpool Street, when he noticed people in the street gazing up at the sky. First of all, they were doing so individually, some shading their eyes with their hands as they peered upwards, and then they began to gather in knots, little groups, huddling together as if for safety. He pulled in to pick up a knot of passengers and the people in the queue, rather than boarding the bus, stared at the sky.

"Hey, mate!" he called to a fat man in the queue. "What's going on?"

The fat man, in a white linen jacket, with florid cheeks and a

535

bristling ginger moustache, turned to him, his face a mask of disbelief and horror. "Can't you 'ear 'em? Can't you 'ear 'em?" he cried in a high-pitched singsong voice.

Mickey turned off his engine. He thought he heard a distant popping sound. This was followed by a furious flapping, and briefly the street was full of pigeons fleeing to the west. Then he heard them: a low drone, almost a buzz, like a swarm of angry bees. Leaning out of the cab, he craned his neck and narrowed his eyes, looking upward. There they were, high in the sky, maybe ten of them, flying in rough formation, and as these disappeared from view, suddenly obscured by the financial houses of the area, there came another three. And then an almighty bang, the loudest sound Mickey had ever heard, and behind him the windows of the bus shattered. In the street, several people were prone, obviously alive but felled by the shock wave. When he looked at the kerb, he saw that the shoulder of the fat man's linen jacket was speckled with red: his ears were bleeding. Women were screaming and running.

"Mickey. *Mickey.* MICK!"

Suddenly, he was aware that someone was calling his name, and he realised that he had been slightly—if temporarily—deafened by the blast. Turning, he saw Gladys on the kerb, cool as you please. She lifted her shoulders in a shrug. "What we gonna do, Mick?"

"Did your training prepare you for this, Glad?" It was a stupid thing to say, but for the moment he could think of nothing else.

"Of course it bloody didn't."

"Nor did mine." He looked down the street, but any real damage was obscured by the curve to the left just ahead of him. The only clue as to what might be there lay in the column of smoke rising steadily over the roofs. "Listen, Glad. Give the passengers the choice: they can either stay with us and come to Liverpool Street or they can get off. Come to think of it, Glad, that goes for you too."

"What passengers would that be, Mick?" she asked, frowning at him.

He glanced over his shoulder and saw that the saloon was empty, the passengers having run off. "Oh, okay. What about you, then?"

"I'll come with you, but why don't you just swing around and shoot back to the garage?"

"Because I have to get to Liverpool Street."

"Why, Mick?"

"Because Dorothy might be there!" This came out as a choking sob. "Did you see her pass us?"

A suddenly ashen Gladys swallowed. She nodded. "Okay, darlin'. Let me climb aboard and we'll go to Liverpool Street."

They did not quite get to Liverpool Street station, of course, because the traffic soon came to a halt. Mickey switched off the engine, left the cab and hurried to the back of the bus where, followed by Gladys, he climbed the outside staircase. At the front of the bus, he gripped the rail and peered over the traffic ahead—cabs, private cars, delivery vans, a few more buses, a horse-drawn dray— and saw that the smoke seemed to be coming from the station.

"We gonna leg it, Mick?"

"Yeah, come on."

As they walked away from the bus, a policeman stepped forward and held up a hand. "You can't leave that there, you know."

Mickey slapped away the hand and charged forward. As the policeman opened his mouth, Gladys raised a finger to his face and issued a single-word command: "*Don't.*" She strode after her driver, cursing the heavy money-bag on her shoulder.

Most people they passed were either in panic or in shock. With few exceptions, they were running westward. None seemed to be injured. They had to fight their way forward against the flow and Gladys had difficulty keeping up with Mickey. Once, she lost sight of him completely, but rounding a bend she saw him standing as if mesmerised outside a shop window. It was a women's outfitter's, its plate-glass window shattered. At first, she could not fathom why this detained him, but as she stood next to him and looked into the window, she understood. The window had contained several plaster mannequins modelling the latest summer wear; presumably, before the blast they had exhibited poise and sophistication, but now they lay in disarray, some with an arm or leg detached, others with the limbs grotesquely contorted. Here and there, a head lay alone, its wig awry. And while the faces had never been alive, there could be no doubt now that they were dead.

*

Feeling Gladys touch his arm, Mickey tore himself away and, his heart pounding, began to trot towards the station. She was probably nowhere near Liverpool Street, he told himself. Why, then, was his mind shrouded by this dark fear? Why did he suddenly see their whole relationship in a perspective he had never viewed before? Why was he now realising that it had, from the very outset, been impossible, and that its termination—whether by this means or some other—had been inevitable? Even though he found it difficult to breathe, he forced himself to imagine how it would be if she were still alive, how he would exult that she still walked the earth, how she would smile at him when they met, how he would crush her to him and never let her go, but these images were fleeting, impossible to sustain, telling him that this day would have a darker outcome.

Already, the police, many of them members of the special constabulary recruited from the LGOC, the mainline railway companies and the Underground, had sealed off the entrances to the station, preventing traffic from entering, although the exits were open and buses were still being instructed to leave. Mickey pushed through a detachment of special constables, at least one of whom seemed to know him, possibly thinking that he was there to help, and entered the station, making his way to the bay where route 11 buses were usually to be found. There were no vehicles there, and he felt a wave of relief and optimism break over him. A panting Gladys came to his side.

"She not here, Glad!" he cried. "She's alive! She's alive!"

Instead of replying, Gladys tugged at his sleeve and pointed to the wall just beyond the head of the bay, where a lone B-type stood. Immediately, he knew how it had got there: for some reason unable to leave, the driver had been instructed to pull forward and park it by the wall, thus allowing the buses behind him to evacuate the station. The signboard running along the side identified it: Wormwood Scrubs—11—Liverpool Street. Almost blinded by misery, Mickey staggered towards the bus. He glimpsed a figure moving through the saloon towards the platform, and allowed himself to hope once more: the conductor was on board! But it was the driver who, having been relaxing inside, now stepped down from the platform and walked towards him.

"Mickey Rice!" He had seen the man at a few meetings, although the name didn't come to him.

"Where's your conductor?" Mickey was breathing hard, almost panting.

The driver removed his cap and ran his hand over his close-cropped head. "If I knew that, Mickey, I would be long gone. I don't know where she went. When those bombs hit, I was in the canteen..."

"There was more than one bomb?"

"Two, Mickey—both through the roof of the station, so they tell me. So I ran out to the bus and she was nowhere to be seen. I just hope she ran away."

"And this is Dorothy? Your conductor is Dorothy?"

The driver nodded. "That's her. They call her Bolshevik."

"Yes, yes, yes, yes!" Mickey affirmed without bothering to explain.

"That's her, that's my Dorothy. How come you're not looking for her?"

"The officials told me to stay with the bus and they went off to find her."

"Found her."

Mickey turned and saw an inspector, a cocky-looking young man with his peaked cap at a jaunty angle, approaching.

"Where?"

Instead of replying, the inspector gave Mickey the once-over.

"*Where?*"

Seeing the state Mickey was in, the inspector relented, jerking his head towards the station entrance. "Over there, just outside the main doors. She's leaning against a pillar. We're getting a stretcher for her."

Mickey was gone. "Here, don't you..." the inspector began, raising his arm but then, realising the futility of his gesture, letting it fall to his side.

Leaning against a pillar! She was injured, but alive! Dodging officials and special constables, Mickey ran to the station entrance, soon encountering broken glass and other debris. And there, against a fluted iron stanchion, was Dorothy. She sat with her back to the pillar, one hand, palm upwards, at her side, while the other clutched a copy of *The Times*. Her cap lay on the ground, a few feet away. Her head was tilted a little to the left, as if she had stopped there to rest, and her eyes were closed. She was obviously unconscious. Then he saw the matted blood in her hair. Mickey fell to his knees beside her, and, gently lifting back the hair over her right eye, saw the terrible wound to her temple.

By now, he was surrounded by uniformed men, one of whom dropped a stretcher on the flags and extended a hand to Dorothy's shoulder.

"Get away from her! Don't touch her! Leave us alone!"

At Mickey's cry, Gladys silently pushed the men back, creating a space around the two people, one dead and one alive.

Mickey picked up Dorothy's right hand and raised it to his lips. He saw that her face seemed relaxed, as if she had felt no pain when the missile had struck her temple. But she was dead, and Mickey lifted his head and began to howl like a child. At first, he cursed, and those watching were unable to determine whether his words were directed at a god in whom he did not believe or at the Germans who had killed his lover. But when this phase had passed, he addressed his desperate entreaties to Dorothy.

"Why did you have to do this?" he wailed. "Why couldn't you have got another office job? Why did you always feel that you had to prove yourself? Wasn't it enough that I loved you? Loved you? Dorothy, I *worshipped* you, and now I'll never be able to tell you that! Why, *why*, WHY did you have to go?"

And then it came to him that this was not Dorothy. This was just her corpse, the shell which had once housed the woman he had called Dorothy. But Dorothy herself was gone. Forever. Once more there came to his mind that early evening almost exactly four years ago when they had passed each other in Oxford Street, happily waving from their respective buses. He saw that image very clearly and, yes, they were now waving not in greeting but in farewell.

*

For some time he was dazed, a crazy man. He didn't go to the garage and made no effort to contact the garage superintendent. Some things, he forced himself to do: he arranged for Dorothy's burial with a funeral home, then searched through her belongings for her father's address and sent him a telegram with both the news and the details of the burial. Other than that, for most of the first day he sat in the Alexander Street flat, not eating, ignoring Dick or Eric when they rapped on the door. Glancing at the copy of The Times which Gladys had taken from Dorothy's hand, he saw that at the time of her death she seemed to have been reading the report of the previous day's Commons debate on the Representation of the People Bill, which would give the vote to all women over 30 and all men over 21.

On the morning of the second day, he went to Paddington and caught a train for Reading. He would remember nothing of the journey, but when he walked from Reading General Station he noted that the statue of Edward VII was still there. The only things that had changed were those that had changed in London: less men on the street, and some of those that were wore bandages or had an arm in a sling, or were supported by crutches. He walked to Broad Street and boarded a tram on which neither the motorman nor the conductor were known to him; nor, for that matter, were the passengers. The tram crossed into Oxford Road and he watched as the sadly familiar, totally meaningless buildings passed by. Why had he come here? He had not realised until now how much his life in London had been anchored upon Dorothy. They had begun their relationship within days of him starting work on the buses, and while he might have thought—not that he did give the matter much thought—that his union work was what gave meaning to his life in London, it now seemed that this might not have been the whole case. Only now did he see to what an extent his life had revolved around Dorothy, and now she was not there he appeared to have been cast adrift. And so he supposed he was in Reading because he had nowhere else to go—or so it seemed. He was not entirely sure how unbalanced he had become as a result of Dorothy's death, or to what extent his mind was clouded and confused by the hunger that gnawed at his stomach. Oh, Christ, he was so hungry. If this was what Sylvia Pankhurst went through, he was not sure whether he could ever be as brave as her.

He stepped off the tram and crossed the road, walking past the Pond House pub before turning right into Tidmarsh Street. As if in a dream, he passed down the short street until, halfway down, he turned into the "garden"—the wooden gate, reduced by weather, had long ago fallen from its hinges—of one of these rented dwellings. Two paces took him to the front door, upon which he knocked just once. No one came, and he realised that it was 2 o'clock on a Friday afternoon; the old man would be at work. He knocked again, twice this time, and now he heard a shuffling movement inside. The door opened a crack and a man's bleary blue eye appeared. As the eye opened wider, so did the door, and now John Rice stood before him, seemingly much smaller than he used to be, his back no longer straight, a history of dissipation recorded on his thin, lined face.

"It's air nipper!" he cried, and it was not clear whether this was intended as a greeting to Mickey or an announcement to someone in the house.

For some moments, Mickey stood before John Rice, not speaking, not sure whether he should enter the house or return to the station. From the smell coming from inside the house, someone had been frying with lard. "Can you give me something to eat?" he asked finally, in a monotone. "I really need something to eat."

At this, John Rice studied Mickey more closely, his eyes wandering from his unshaven, bruised face to his dirty blue work shirt and creased London General Uniform. "'Ere, you alright, boy?" he asked with a frown.

"'E looks all done in," said a voice behind John Rice, and by shifting his gaze Mickey could make out the form of a portly woman in the passageway. "Move out the way an' let 'im in the house, John."

The Reading accent, once Mickey's own, grated: "eht" for "out," "ehse" for "house." Why had he come here? But he allowed himself to be led down the passageway and into the living room. As he sank onto the sofa, he noticed that the furniture was the same as it had always been since the death of his mother, only now even more scratched, torn and worn. He laid his head back and spotted a cobweb in the corner of the ceiling.

"I need something to eat," he repeated. "If I don't eat something soon I'll pass out."

John Rice turned to the woman. "We got anything in the larder, Doris? Oh, Mickey, you remember Doris, don't you? Used to live three doors dehn."

Mickey looked from the cobweb to the face of John Rice, who was leaning over him. He noticed that the old man's lower lip was heavy and dry, desiccated. "No work today, then?"

This took the old man aback somewhat. The boy looked as if he was at death's door and yet here he was, coming out with the old criticisms. But he let it pass, sighing, "Bit of a back problem."

"There's a slice or two of cold pork, a tomato and what's left of yesterday's bread," said Doris as she returned from the larder. She was around fifty, maybe five years younger than Rice, and she may have been attractive once, but sharing a life with John Rice—which is what she appeared to be doing—had left its mark.

"Any butter?"

"You kiddin'?" This was the elder Rice. "Nah. If you don't want drippin', you'll have to 'ave it dry. You can 'ave a drop of brehn ale to wash it dehn, though."

"No dripping, and no brown ale. Just some water from the tap."

"So what's 'appened to you, Mickey? By the looks of it, you ent washed or shaved in a week an' you're wearing your work clothes."

Mickey hauled himself to his feet and stumbled to the table, where Doris was placing his plate and cutlery. "Later, after I eat."

Taking a cigarette from a Woodbine packet, the old man joined him at the table, and as Mickey ate, bowed over the plate, he was conscious of his scrutiny, and he knew that, having sensed some unreleased violence in Mickey, John Rice was trying to estimate whether the younger man would have sufficient strength to resist him if they came to blows. Biting into the cold, stringy pork, Mickey recalled how, as a youngster, he had dreaded the sound of the old man's nightly return from the Pond House, as often arguments and blows would follow. He took a mouthful of the grey, wartime bread and swiftly followed it with a swig of water. The only thing he really enjoyed about the meal was the tomato, but nevertheless he felt his strength beginning to return. Perhaps, he thought, the meagre meal would also help clear his mind.

Having cleared his plate, Mickey sat back in his chair and uttered a sigh.

The old man managed a smile. "Feelin' better, boy?" He looked across the table where Doris sat, chin in hand as she tried to work out what was happening, and gave her a wink.

Mickey nodded. "Yes. Thank you." Politeness cost nothing.

"Neh, then, tell us all abeht it, Mickey. What the devil 'as 'appened?"

It suddenly came home to Mickey that he would now have to explain Dorothy—her former existence, her beauty, her intelligence, and now her cruel demise—to this bibulous cretin. Unsure that he would be equal to the task, he sensed the onset of tears, which surprised him; but John Rice would come to his rescue.

"It's my Dorothy," he began, the words coming out almost as a sob.

"That the posh tart that Eric told me abeht when he came dehn last year? Hah! Left you for a toff, eh?"

Stunned, Mickey sat for a moment, his mouth half-open. Then his right hand snaked out, knocking the cigarette from between the old man's lips. Mickey stood, gripping the older man by the collar, but the only words that would come from between his gritted teeth were "Don't, don't, don't, don't..."

Across the table, Doris gasped but did not scream, and it would have been difficult for an objective observer to determine whose side she was taking.

At last, Mickey's mind seemed to clear, releasing him from his inarticulacy, and he let go of John Rice, allowing him to drop back into the chair from which he had been effortlessly lifted, and then the words poured out.

"I loved her, and she was killed by a German bomb! Do you hear me? She's dead, and so am I! She was my life, and now she's gone!" He threw open his arms in a gesture of confusion and hopelessness. "So what was I to do? All of a sudden, I no longer knew where I belonged, so you know what I did? *I came here!* Can you believe that?" He sneered at the old man. "What a stupid bastard I was to think that I might belong here."

John Rice seemed to see this an opportunity to bring to a close a matter that had long troubled him, and he gathered his courage and spoke. "Don't know where you belongs? You belongs in France, that's where you belongs, foightin' for your country. But no, you and that brother o' yorn think you're too good for that, don't you? Most of the boys you grew up with are eht there, an' some of 'em won't be comin' back. But you? You an' that useless brother o' yorn want to act the big I am in London, pullin' men eht on stroike when they've

543

families to feed and a war to foight."

Narrowing his eyes, Mickey looked at the old man as if seeing him for the first time. Here was the voice of the jingoes. This decrepit man who, having never read a book, having been miseducated in public bars all over Reading, was one of those foolish enough to think that King George, Kitchener and Lloyd George were thinking of people like him when they talked of the national interest and the need to defend the Empire. It now occurred to Mickey that four years ago he had fled Reading in order to escape this failed human being and all those like him, and that his memory of them would have played a part in his decision to adopt an anti-war position.

John Rice, misinterpreting the silence of the younger man, now made the greater error of pressing his attack, striking at the source of a torment that had been with him for more than a quarter of a century. "But you're roight abeht a couple o' things: you *are* a bastard, and you've never belonged in any ehse o' moin."

"John, no!" cried Doris.

Mickey, still distracted by his consideration of the person before him, had not really been listening as the old man had uttered these words, and it was Doris's admonition that drew his attention to them. He tilted his head and engaged the old man's gaze. "What do you mean by that?"

Ignoring Doris's obvious agitation, John Rice lifted his gangly frame from his chair, leaned forward and almost spat the words into Mickey's face. "What do Oi mean? Oi'll *tell* you what Oi means! Your slut of a mother opened her legs for that foreman at Huntley and Palmers. *That's* what Oi means! Oi wasn't good enough for 'er, Oi suppose. Your mother was a *whore*, Mickey, just loik that fancy tart o' yorn!"

Mickey's fist caught him on the side of the face, sending him backwards, first onto his chair and then the floor. Doris looked at Mickey and almost shrugged, as if indicating that this was the outcome she had expected.

*

"You're Mickey Rice, yeah?"

Mickey nodded. The tram conductor, several years Mickey's junior, looked vaguely familiar.

"You won't remember me. I'd just started on the job when you left."

"They didn't call you up, then?"

544

The conductor tapped his thin chest. "Something wrong in 'ere."

"You can be thankful for that, mate."

The conductor considered him for a moment, then nodded. "What's that uniform, Mickey—London General?"

Mickey nodded again.

"What's that like?"

"Hard. But the men—and the women now—make it worthwhile."

"And you're wearin' the red button."

Despite himself, Mickey smiled. "Yeah, I'm wearing the red button."

The conductor frowned. "But—hope you don't mind me sayin', Mickey—you're lookin' a bit rough."

"It's a long story. But I'm feeling better now."

"So you been visitin' your family?"

Mickey grunted. "Apparently not." He grinned at the young conductor. "But that's another long story."

*

It was mid-evening when, having stopped at a restaurant on the way from Paddington, he arrived back at the Alexander Street flat. He let himself in and switched on a light, and there she was, sitting in the same armchair she had occupied when, having been released from Holloway two years earlier, she had waited for him to come in from his late turn. This time, however, she was not asleep, and she was looking at him as he came through the door.

He crossed the room and perched on the sofa, next to her armchair.

"I thought you might be here, Dorothy," he said calmly, conversationally. "No, as I walked down Alexander Street I *knew* you would be here. Do you remember the time, just after we'd seen each other in Oxford Street, when I had to collect some mail from Electric Railway House? You said you knew it would be me who came to collect it, and I said that I had had the same feeling: I knew it would be you who brought the envelope down to me. I had that feeling just now as I walked down the street."

She smiled. "Not quite the *same* feeling, Mickey. Similar, but not the same."

"Why not the same, my love?"

"This time, you really *did* know that you would *see* me," she explained, "but not that I would really *be* here. Because I'm *not* really here. You know that, don't you?"

He nodded. "Yes, I suppose I do. I'm not stupid."

She smiled again. "No, you never were, Mickey."

"So you're really just in my mind."

Dorothy's eyes closed once and reopened. "Of course, Mickey."

"Because I miss you more than I thought it was possible to miss anyone. I suppose that's why I'm seeing you, Dorothy."

"Yes, Mickey. But you also want my advice, don't you?" Her smile was almost teasing.

He sighed and looked away from her for the first time. "Yes, that too."

"And you know what that advice is likely to be, don't you?"

"So you know what I'm thinking of doing?"

She chuckled. "Well, of course I do, Mickey. If I'm in your head along with your other thoughts, how could I not know?"

"I've been thinking of enlisting," he confessed, returning his gaze to her.

"You may not be stupid, Mickey, but you can at times be rather foolish. What good would it do if you enlisted?"

He clenched his teeth. "You were killed by a German bomb, Dorothy. Isn't it natural that I should want to avenge your death?"

"I would say conventional rather than natural, Mickey, but I ask again: what good would it do?"

His sigh this time was one of exasperation. "It would make me *feel* better!"

She gave him a penetrating sideways glance. "Would it, Mickey?" A shake of the head. "I doubt it." She placed her elbows on her knees and leaned forward, lowering her voice. "German civilians are killed too, you know. Some die of starvation, due to the blockade. Do you believe that all the Germans opposed to the war who have lost loved ones should now enlist? Some of them must surely feel the same as you."

He shook his head emphatically. "No, of course I don't believe that!"

"Then why should *you* enlist?"

"Because I want to die!" He slumped back onto the sofa, holding her gaze.

"Why do you want to die, Mickey?" Her tone was soft and solicitous, like that of a nurse comforting a sick child.

"So that I can be with you!" he blurted, his eyes wide with illogical desperation.

Her softness receded and her expression was now serious. "Mickey, you must stop this foolishness. Do you hear me? I am *dead*, Mickey. There is no afterlife, and so we can never be together again except this way. I can live in your mind, but nowhere else. Do you accept that?"

He nodded almost feverishly, as if fearing that a refusal to comply would lead to the withdrawal of even this form of communication.

She held out a hand demonstratively. "I must tell you, Mickey, that this is not the Mickey Rice I knew and loved so dearly. Are you prepared to forsake all you believe to be true and right because this system has robbed you of the person you loved? How can you be so subjective?"

He looked at her sharply, fearful that she was about to become the hectoring Dorothy who had attacked Theo Rothstein at the Hackney Empire; but, no, she was merely being logical, genuinely desiring to make him see sense.

"What do you think I would want you to do, Mickey? I *certainly* don't want you to die! Surely your only course is to continue to fight against the system that caused this war, the war that led to my death and the deaths of countless others. You *know* that is what I would want you to do, Mickey."

He had recovered himself. He was calm now. His dilemma was over. He would do as she wished.

"Yes, Dorothy, and that is what I will do. Thank you, my love." He frowned. "But tell me, Dorothy, if that is what you want me to do, why do you say it is what you *would* have wanted me to do?"

She smiled. "You know very well that it is what I *would* have wanted you to do if I were really here, Mickey."

An almost imperceptible nod. "But how is it that you even *sound* as if you were really here, Dorothy? Not just the sound of your voice but the arguments you use."

"You not only loved me deeply, Mickey: you also *knew* me as much as anyone has ever known me. The image you see before you is in your mind, my sweet, but so also are the words I use. You *know* the words I would use, the arguments I would employ in these matters. In fact, when you walked into this room tonight, you already knew the answers to the questions you wanted to ask, and you were already aware of how the dilemma you faced should be resolved." Her smile was deeply sympathetic. "It's just that you wanted me to be the one to tell you. If I were alive, I would be so very flattered, Mickey."

"And will we always be able to meet like this, my sweetheart?"

"As long as you wish it, Mickey," she said. "But it's entirely up to you. I'm not a ghost, so I cannot simply appear. You must summon me, and whenever you do, I will come."

AUTHOR'S NOTE

Although much of my previous writing has been in the field of history (see "About the Author"), it never occurred to me to write an historical novel until the TV series *Peaky Blinders* irritated me into it. If you've seen the series, you'll know that the production values are very high and the acting passable, although now and then a Brummy accent will slide into Scouse. Much of the history, however, is just plain wrong. Characters join the Communist Party of Great Britain before there was such a party; funds are provided by the "Russian embassy" at a time when Britain had no diplomatic relations with the new Soviet Russia; Winston Churchill (who uses his office to paint nudes during his lunch break) is given a role which might be appropriate for a Home Secretary but not for a Minister of War, which, inconveniently, is what he was at the time. And so on.

Surely it is possible, I thought, to write an historical drama without doing quite so much violence to history itself. And that, hopefully, is what I have done.

My starting point was my own *Radical Aristocrats*, a labour history of London busworkers published in 1985 by Lawrence and Wishart. What if I took the early chapters dealing with the London and Provincial Union of Licensed Vehicle Workers (1913-1919), known as the "red-button union," and fictionalised this material? I did not have to look far for a title, as *Red-Button Years* was an obvious candidate. This proved untenable when I realised that a novel covering the whole red-button period would be far too long. Thus, the title became *Love and Labour*, the first volume in the *Red-Button Years* series. Obviously, this first novel could not be allowed to end at some arbitrary point but must terminate with a significant event, like the death of a major character. Poor Dorothy.

A fictional couple, Mickey Rice and Dorothy Bridgeman, are inserted into the history of the red-button union, the British Socialist Party and the East End suffrage movement. Several of the minor characters—Mickey's workmates, some of the people Dorothy comes across—are also fictional. The major characters in the union—George Sanders, Bywater, Russell, Archie Henderson, the Smiths—lived and breathed, as did, of course, the major political figures. Some of the members of the union's Executive Council have been invented, although sometimes, usually when I could be reasonably sure of their personalities and outlooks, I have used their real names. Even in such cases, however, names are sometimes half-invented (I do not know that D.J. Davies was a Dennis or H.A. Bywater a Harry).

Continually reminding myself of my original mission, I have scrupulously avoided falsifying historical events, although on one occasion this was unavoidable: if Mickey Rice was to have his brush with death before the German air raid of June 13, 1917, the violence conducted by the thugs of Edward Tupper in Finsbury Park had to be brought forward by a couple of weeks.

That said, I have probably done violence to the *personal* histories of some of the characters. Did H.A. Bywater meet secretly with Albert Stanley before the union was recognised by the LGOC? I don't know, but he strikes me as the kind of union leader who might have done so. Did Lloyd George, upon learning that he was to be Minister of Munitions, pick up the telephone and suggest that London County Council Tramways pressure strikers of military age to enlist in the Army? Possibly not, but the LCC certainly did follow that advice, wherever it came from. Lewis Harcourt did not assault Dorothy Bridgeman, but he *was* a sexual predator: in 1922, he would commit suicide after the mother of a young Etonian he had assaulted decided she would not be silenced.

The major source for *Love and Labour* was my own *Radical Aristocrats*. Much period flavour and detail was gleaned from Jerry White's *Zeppelin Nights* (London: The Bodley Head, 2014), *The Times* Archive and the British Newspaper Archive. Readers may be surprised to learn the identity of Jack London's UK publisher, as was at least one agent; the quotation from "Revolution" in Chapter 1 is taken from his *Revolution and Other Essays* (London: Mills & Boon, c. 1910). Details of developments in the trade union movement were provided by A.L. Morton and George Tate, *The British Labour Movement* (London: Lawrence and Wishart, 1979). For knowledge of Sylvia Pankhurst, I turned to Mary Davis, *Sylvia Pankhurst: A Life in Radical Politics* (London: Pluto Press, 1999), Shirley Harrison, *Sylvia Pankhurst: Rebellious Suffragette* (London: Sapere Books, 2012), Sarah Jackson, "East London Suffragettes vs the Prime Minister" (https://www.eastlondonsuffragettes.com/blog/east-london-suffragettes-vs-the-prime-minister) and the *Women's Dreadnought*, the newspaper Sylvia edited.

Ralph Kitchener's account of the re-arrest of Sylvia Pankhurst in Victoria Park is taken from Ralph Kitchener, *The Memoirs of an Old*

Detective (edited by Ian Adams, publisher and place of publication unknown, 2010). The story of Special Branch can be found in Ray Wilson and Ian Adams, *Special Branch: A History, 1883-2006* (London: Biteback Publishing, 2015).

Details of Holloway Prison were provided by June Purvis, "The Prison Experiences of the Suffragettes in Edwardian Britain," (*Women's History Review*, Volume 4, Number 1, 1995) and John Camp, *Holloway Prison: The Place and the People* (Newton Abbot: David & Charles, 1974).

Albert Stanley, who in 1920 would be ennobled as Lord Ashfield, has somewhat surprisingly attracted no biographer, and it was from Christian Wolmar's *The Subterranean Railway* (London: Atlantic Books, 2012) that I learned that he was "dapper, a ladies' man." That was enough.

In Chapter 11, Dorothy Bridgeman tells Theodore Rothstein that his speech "appeared to be cobbled together from the articles you wrote for *Justice* in 1911." She is correct, although it was cobbled together by me rather than Rothstein. Henry Hyndman's speech in the same chapter is also based on a piece he wrote for *Justice*. In Chapter 41, Rothstein, having given a lengthy reply to a question from his audience, tells George Sanders that this has "helped me to clarify my own thinking, and I'm pretty sure I now have an article for the next issue of *The Call*." In fact, I based his reply on a piece he wrote at a later date for *The Call*. The writings of both Rothstein and Hyndman in *Justice* and *The Call* are available at www.marxists.org.

After reading Sir James Rennell Rodd's *Social and Diplomatic Memories, Volume III, 1902-1919* (Pickle Partners Publishing, 2013; original publication 1925), I felt sufficiently equipped to compose Dorothy's letter from Italy.

The proceedings at the Leeds Convention are taken from *What Happened at Leeds: Report Published by the Council of Workers' & Soldiers' Delegates* (1917). See https://wdc.contentdm.oclc.org/digital/collection/russian/id/169 3. Edward Tupper's confessions can be found in his *Seamen's Torch: The Life Story of Captain Edward Tupper* (London, Hutchinson & Co., 1938). My brief portrait of Ernest Bevin, along with Bob Williams's estimate of his strengths and weaknesses, is based on the account given by Alan Bullock in *The Life and Times of Ernest Bevin, Volume One: Trade Union Leader, 1881-1940* (London: Heinemann, 1960).

Thanks are due to the staff of the London Transport Museum, who replied swiftly and helpfully to an author inconsiderate enough to email his queries from the Philippines.

ABOUT THE AUTHOR

In the first ten years of his working life, Ken Fuller was an office boy, a baker, and a merchant seaman. He then drove a London bus for eleven years, followed by twenty years as a full-time official in the Transport & General Workers' Union. His first published book was *Radical Aristocrats: London Busworkers from the 1880s to the 1980s* (London: Lawrence and Wishart, 1985), upon which some events in *Love and Labour* are based.

His other published work is as follows:

- *Forcing the Pace: The Partido Komunista ng Pilipinas, From Foundation to Armed Struggle* (University of the Philippines Press, 2007). This was a finalist for a National Book Award (Manila Critics Circle), 2008.
- *A Movement Divided: Philippine Communism, 1957-1986* (University of the Philippines Press, 2011).
- *The Lost Vision: The Philippine Left, 1986-2010* (University of the Philippines Press, 2015). This was a finalist for a National Book Award (Manila Critics Circle), 2016.
- *The Long Crisis: Gloria Macapagal Arroyo and Philippine Underdevelopment* (commercially published as an e-book by Flipside, Quezon City, in 2013, and in 2019 republished as a paperback via Kindle Direct Publishing).
- *Hardboiled Activist: The Work and Politics of Dashiell Hammett* (Glasgow: Praxis Press, 2017).
- *Foreigners: A Philippine Satire* (paperback and e-book via Kindle Direct Publishing, 2019).

Since 2003, Ken Fuller has lived in the Philippines.

Printed in Great Britain
by Amazon

66226921R00319